ROBERT E. HOWARD
WESTERN TALES

Introduction by James Reasoner
Edited by Rob Roehm and Paul Herman

THE

Robert E. Howard

FOUNDATION PRESS

For Glenn Lord (1931-2011), preserver of Howard's typescripts and manuscripts, godfather of Howard studies, and the greatest fan that ever lived.

The photographs on pages 482-485 were taken by Robert E. Howard himself, and a photographer currently unknown.

ISBN: 978-1-955446-43-3 (Paperback)
ISBN: 978-1-955446-42-6 (Hardcover)
ISBN: 978-1-955446-44-0 (eBook)

Published by the REH Foundation Press, LLC by arrangement with Robert E. Howard Properties Inc.

https://rehfoundation.org
https://rehfpress.com

Cover illustration copyright © 2025, Mark Wheatley.

https://markwheatleygallery.com

Book prepared for publication by Ståle Gismervik, Savage Studios.

Version 2.0 - Ultimate Edition.

Acknowledgments

Most of the Howard stories, poems and portions thereof contained in *Western Tales* come from Howard's original typescripts, manuscripts, and carbons, when possible. Virtually all of the typescripts were scanned from the Glenn Lord collection, now at the University of Texas, Austin; the Robert E. Howard collection at Texas A&M University; or the typescript collection at Cross Plains Library.

Other sources for texts herein include: "The Man on the Ground," from first publication in *Weird Tales*, July 1933; "Old Garfield's Heart," from first publication in *Weird Tales*, December 1933; "The Thunder-Rider" is a combination of two separate drafts to make a complete story; "The Ghost of Camp Colorado," from first publication in *The Texaco Star*, April 1931; "'Golden Hope' Christmas," from a partial draft along with text from first publication in *The Tattler*, December 22, 1922.

CHANGES FROM THE FIRST EDITION: "Vultures' Sanctuary," synopsis, is new to this edition; "The Dead Remember" is now using the final draft; "Gunman's Debt," synopses, 1st edition had three of these, we have now added a fourth; poetry from the 1st Edition has been updated to the versions in *Collected Poetry*; poetry added for this edition includes "The Lost San Saba Mine," "Modest Bill," "The End of the Glory Trail," "The Alamo," "San Jacinto," both (1) and (2); "Ghost Dancers," "The Bandit," "Farewell, Proud Munster," and "The Trail of Gold"; and, a short introduction has been added to a set of four poems regarding characters going to Mexico.

Contents

Western Tales

The Weird West

Essays

Miscellanea

Juvenilia

Robert E. Howard: Western Pulp Pioneer

introduction by James Reasoner

By the latter stages of his career, Robert E. Howard was moving away from the genres which had formed the main building blocks of his success. Some of this was due to the ever-evolving pulp markets and Howard's dedication to doing whatever it took to remain a working freelance writer; some may well have resulted from a natural inclination to move on once he felt that he was close to exhausting the potential in a particular genre.

Regardless of the reason, in 1935 he would remark in a letter to H. P. Lovecraft that he was seriously contemplating devoting his efforts almost totally to Western fiction. In May 1936, only weeks before his death, Howard mentioned to August Derleth that it had been more than a year since he'd written a weird story. That same month he wrote to Lovecraft, "I find it more and more difficult to write anything but Western yarns."

Of course, the Western story had been part of Howard's repertoire for a long time, almost from the very beginning. Two of his earliest stories, "A Faithful Servant" and "'Golden Hope' Christmas" (both included in this collection) are Westerns. "A Faithful Servant," the story of a rancher and his dog who venture into the desert in search of a lost horse, and the dangers they find there, was written as a school assignment when Howard was only 15 years old and has some vivid descriptive writing in it, as well as a real sense of urgency. It's no surprise that Howard received a grade of "A" for his work. "'Golden Hope' Christmas" was published in *The Tattler*, the student newspaper of Brownwood High School, and it marked one of the first occasions when Howard's work went out to a broader audience.

Around the same time, he was creating his first Western series hero in the character of Steve Allison, also known as the Sonora Kid.

There are a number of false starts and unfinished stories featuring Allison, and Howard seems undecided whether to make him a cowboy, an outlaw, or a globe-trotting jewel thief. There are even several Allison stories in which he serves as the lead in domestic comedies featuring his sisters.

It's the cowboy/gunman version that Howard comes back to most of the time, though, including several later, fully developed stories. In these early tales, Steve often is accompanied by another young cowboy, Bill "Drag" Buckner. Although we have no way of knowing for sure, it seems likely to me that that name comes from the hero of Charles Alden Seltzer's popular Western novel *"Drag" Harlan*, which was serialized in *Argosy* in 1919 and published in hardback in 1921. There's no record of Howard having read this novel or anything else by Seltzer, for that matter, but given his fondness for *Argosy* I think there's a good chance he read it and appropriated the nickname for Steve Allison's sidekick.

Gold is the lure in "Drums of the Sunset," Howard's first commercially published piece of Western fiction, a novelette that ran as a nine-part serial in the *Cross Plains Review*, his hometown newspaper, from November 2, 1928 to January 4, 1929. He had already sold several stories to *Weird Tales*, but the $20 he received from the *Cross Plains Review* for "Drums of the Sunset" matched or even bettered some of his payments from "The Unique Magazine."

The story is a good one, solidly in the tradition of Western fiction at the time, with a stalwart hero from Texas, Steve Harmer; a feisty old-timer with a colorful name (Hard Luck Harper) as his sidekick; and a beautiful girl, a trio of despicable villains, a fabulously valuable lost vein of gold, and a tribe of Indians on the warpath. Howard throws in the slightly unusual angle of a crime more associated with modern times, counterfeiting, demonstrating his tendency to stray from the standard tropes of whatever genre was coming from his typewriter.

"The Extermination of Yellow Donory" was submitted to *Argosy*, *Adventure*, and *Western Story* but failed to sell at any of those markets, possibly because it's not an action-packed "gun dummy" story of the sort that was dominant in the Western pulps of the time. Instead it's a character story with a nice twist in which a showdown with a deadly gunman takes an unexpected turn. Even this early in his career, Howard had to put his own spin on what could have been a standard tale. His next few Westerns were more traditional.

As in "Drums of the Sunset," the search for gold also figures in "The Judgment of the Desert." In this tale, the golden lure is a fortune in Spanish coins hidden somewhere in the Infernos Mountains. We don't have any submission records for this one, but I'm a little surprised it didn't sell to one of the Western pulps. It has a hidden treasure map, a gang of outlaws, a beautiful girl, and a mysterious gunman, a mixture of ingredients almost guaranteed to produce a rousing Western yarn. If the plot twists it contains don't exactly surprise, the breakneck pace of Howard's prose carries the reader along anyway, and the character of the guilt-haunted gunman "Spike" is a foreshadowing of the noir elements that would figure prominently in some of Howard's later Westerns, starting with the next tale.

In "Gunman's Debt" Howard begins a series of stories set in Kansas cowtowns that center around Texas cowboys and gunmen who have come up the Chisholm Trail on cattle drives. It's also a feud story, as its hero John Kirby runs up against an old enemy from Texas who he thought was dead.

Even though it went unpublished in his lifetime, "Gunman's Debt" is an important story in the development of Howard's Western fiction. In it we see the first real flowering of one of the sub-genres which he was to pioneer, the Western noir. The term "noir fiction" didn't exist in 1933 when this story was written, since it came out of post-war film criticism (and there are some who say that prose can't be noir at all, since the term was coined in relation to film, but I don't agree with that stance). "Gunman's Debt" certainly borders on noir in the way we use the word now.

Consider this passage:

> He hesitated, with a feeling of being caught in a web of fantasy and illusion. This part of it was like a dream; the rest, the violence of men, the trickery, the murder, he could understand; but this strange, beautiful evil woman moved through the skeins of the pattern like a cryptic phantom, inscrutable, inexplicable. He realized that he was in her power; a scream would fetch a horde of armed men. He must trust her or pretend to trust her; she spoke of a debt; perhaps she really sought to pay the grisly debt she seemed to consider she owed him. He looked at her as at a being more and yet less than human; he was repelled by her strange, bloody nature, yet drawn powerfully by her beauty. Like a rabbit hypnotized by a snake, he followed her.

Other than the abundance of semi-colons, common in fiction from the pulp era, this paragraph could be right out of a 1950s Gold Medal crime novel by Gil Brewer or Charles Williams or Harry Whittington. You've got the feeling of being trapped, the feverish desperation, the femme fatale, all of it leading up to a bleak, apocalyptic ending. This is noir, pure and simple, and it's something no one else was doing in Westerns in 1933. Just as Howard married the hardboiled with the weird to create sword and sorcery, he's merged two other genres here to come up with something powerful, and he did it before anyone else. It's just that no one knew it at the time since the story went unsold.

One other note about "Gunman's Debt": it features as a supporting character a buffalo hunter named Grizzly Elkins, surely a relative of our old friend Breckinridge.

Steve Allison, the Sonora Kid, returns in "The Devil's Joker," but the days of writing Allison fragments are over for Howard. This is a fully developed story with a lot of surprisingly graphic violence, which may be why it didn't sell in Howard's lifetime. It may have been too gritty for the Western pulps (although by now Eugene Cunningham was turning out stories with an abundance of gunplay and plenty of dead bodies littering the pages).

There's an alternate version of "The Devil's Joker," also included in this collection, which features Steve Allison and the same basic plot, but the other characters are different and the storyline, which is never really fully developed, goes in a different direction in some respects. It has some nice action and vivid descriptive writing, and a setting that I wish Howard had returned to, the Mountains of the Dead in northern Mexico.

Steve is also the protagonist in "Knife, Bullet and Noose," an excellent story that features a mystery angle as well as plenty of action. As the trail boss for a Texas rancher, Steve collects a big payday for his employer after delivering a herd, but getting out of town alive and unscathed with the money turns out to be quite a problem.

"Lawshooters of Cowtown" features as its hero Grizzly Elkins, who first appeared in "Gunman's Debt," and like Steve Allison in the previous story he finds himself needing to get out of a town where nearly every hand is turned against him. Steve is a gunman, though, while Grizzly is a brawler, so the Elkins approach to this dilemma is somewhat different, though no less entertaining.

Which brings us to "Wild Water," my favorite Howard short story and one of my favorite short stories, period. It's a contemporary story, set in 1932, but its protagonist Jim Reynolds is a throwback to the Old West who prefers to settle things with a Colt .45. That contrast between modern times and an earlier era dominates the story, and the dam that's going to impound the newly built Lake Bisley is a striking physical symbol of that contrast. Its fate parallels that of Reynolds, who is one of Howard's most compelling characters. Some of Howard's best writing is to be found in this story, including a closing paragraph that's still tremendously effective, even after numerous rereadings.

On a personal note, "Wild Water" is special to me because the apocalyptic rain storm that takes place in it is based on a real storm that occurred on July 3, 1932 and filled up Lake Brownwood overnight, just as the storm in the story fills Lake Bisley. My father, who grew up in Brown County, had vivid memories of that storm and talked about it the rest of his life. I'd heard about it many times before I ever read Howard's story, so that makes "Wild Water" resonate even more with me.

"The Last Ride," published in the October 1935 issue of *Western Aces* under the title "Boot-Hill Payoff," was Howard's longest Western to date, but it wasn't his alone. This novella is a rewrite of an unsold story written by Chandler Whipple (a.k.a. Robert Enders Allen), a New York-based writer and editor who didn't know Howard but was aware of his reputation. The rewrite deal was put together by Otis Adelbert Kline, Howard's agent at the time, who was acquainted with Whipple and suggested that Howard rewrite the manuscript.

It's the fast-paced story of Buck Laramie, the only survivor of an outlaw family who returns to his hometown to try to make recompense for his brothers' past crimes, only to run smack-dab into trouble as another gang of desperadoes is pretending to be Buck's dead brothers. Naturally he has to set this right, which involves plenty of gunplay.

We don't know how much of "The Last Ride" is Howard's work and how much is Whipple's, but my hunch is that most of the writing is Howard's. The action has the same flow as his other work. I suspect that most of the characters, the plot, and the basic structure of the story came from Whipple. "Buck Laramie" just doesn't sound like a Howardian name to me. Regardless of who was responsible for what, "The Last Ride" is a very traditional but entertaining yarn that's really not indicative of the other Western work Howard was doing at the time, a professional job that he did at the urging of his agent in an attempt to make a sale, but one that he probably enjoyed to a certain extent as well, judging by the vigor of the story.

"The Vultures of Wahpeton" is Howard's longest, most ambitious, and in my opinion best Western. Everything comes together perfectly in this tale about Texas gunman Steve Corcoran, who becomes a deputy marshal in the mining boomtown of Wahpeton. There are plenty of dark forces at work in Wahpeton, and Corcoran soon realizes that no one can be trusted, not even the forces of law and order. The only spot of light in this noirish maze is the beautiful young soiled dove Glory Bland.

This story contains some of Howard's finest writing. The action scenes are crisp and vividly described, and he steadily ratchets up the plot twists and the resulting tension. The two main characters, Steve Corcoran and John Middleton, are each based on different aspects of a real-life Old West gunman, Hendry Brown, and that dual nature and the resulting deceptions form the theme that runs throughout the story, culminating in one of the bleakest, most effective endings I've ever read in a Western.

Howard doesn't just base his characters and plot on history in this one. The setting, too, is drawn from life, as Wahpeton is clearly modeled after the infamous Deadwood, Dakota Territory. Having been to Deadwood and written quite a bit about it myself, reading this story is almost like going back there for me.

"The Vultures of Wahpeton" was one of Howard's last sales while he was alive. The story was accepted by the pulp magazine *Smashing Novels* on June 5, 1936, less than a week before Howard's suicide. Another thing that makes it stand out is that Howard wrote two different endings for it, one relatively happy, one definitely not, and both of them were printed in its appearance in *Smashing Novels*. Both are included in this collection as well. I prefer the darker ending and think of it as the "real" one, but I suppose that decision is up to the reader.

While I haven't read every story in every Western pulp, of course, I feel confident in saying that nothing quite like "The Vultures of Wahpeton" would appear elsewhere for several more years. So, while the noir elements in Howard's earlier tale "Gunman's Debt" were unknown to the public at large, the publication of "Vultures" in 1936 made Howard a pioneer in the Western noir genre.

"Vultures' Sanctuary" appeared in *Argosy* following Howard's death, in the November 28, 1936 issue of that venerable pulp. The sanctuary of the title is the Guadalupe Mountains, an actual mountain range along the border of Texas and New Mexico, and Howard does a fine job describing the region.

"Vultures," in this case, refers to the outlaw gang led by El Bravo (who despite his name is rumored to be a white man), who make their headquarters in the mountains and murder anyone who ventures into their stronghold. Texas cowboy Bill McClanahan, known as Big Mac, dares to do so in order to rescue a kidnapped girl and settle an old score.

"Vultures' Sanctuary" shows Howard at the top of his game as a traditional Western writer. While it lacks the overtly noir elements of "The Vultures of Wahpeton" and "Gunman's Debt"—in fact, the ending is somewhat sentimental—it definitely has a hardboiled feel to it, and Howard's prose is as smooth and effective as it's ever been. Big Mac McClanahan is a good hero, and I wish we'd seen more of him. This is also the last of Howard's purely traditional Westerns.

* * * * *

The Western noir was not the only sub-genre Howard introduced to the world. He's also widely acknowledged as the creator of the Weird Western, a type of tale currently enjoying a resurgence in popularity. The first example of this is "The Horror from the Mound," and right out of the gate, Howard came up with a perfect example of this sort of story. Texas cowboy Steve Brill dares to dig into what he thinks is an old Indian burial mound, only to discover that something even older and more sinister is buried there. It's a gruesome, atmospheric story that despite its Western setting was right at home in *Weird Tales*, where, in fact, it was published.

I'm not sure that this fusing of genres is deliberately here. It seems that Howard is just writing what he likes, and the gradual blending of weird fiction with the Western was a natural development.

He continues that development in "The Valley of the Lost," which was accepted by one of *Weird Tales'* rivals, *Strange Tales*, only to be returned to Howard when the magazine suspended publication before the story could appear. It went unpublished in his lifetime, which is a shame because it's an excellent yarn.

In this story, Howard introduces the supernatural into the classic plot of a Western feud and brings back the concept of an evil hidden under the ground, although in "The Valley of the Lost" that evil is to be found not in a grave but in a sealedup cave. That cave winds up being opened in the course of the Reynolds-McCrill feud, and John Reynolds discovers an ancient, sinister civilization that allows him to emerge triumphant in his battle, but only at great cost. Howard would explore this same theme in several of his heroic fantasy stories.

A feud also figures prominently in "The Man on the Ground," although the scope of this story is much smaller: two men filled with hate, each of them desperately driven to kill the other, no matter what the cost. This is a short, grim, and very effective tale.

"Old Garfield's Heart" also appeared in *Weird Tales* and is more of a contemporary story, but its origins are in frontier Texas, where a battle with Indians and some sorcery from the dawn of time result in immortality of sorts for one of its characters. This one is set in the town of Lost Knob, which is Howard's fictional version of Cross Plains, and to me there's always something special about these stories, an air of authenticity that makes them resonate despite the sometimes fantastic elements of their plots.

Finally, we come to "The Dead Remember," Howard's last foray in a genre he created, the Weird Western, and one of his best stories. Otto Binder, working for Otis Kline's agency, sold it to Jack Byrne following Howard's death, and it appeared fairly quickly in the August 15, 1936 issue of *Argosy*. Is it a ghost story, a tale of vengeance from beyond the grave, or simply the story of a man going mad and sealing his own fate? Howard leaves that up to the reader to determine.

What's clear, though, is that Howard takes a risk in this story, telling it not in the form of straight narrative but rather by means of a letter, official statements from several witnesses, and a coroner's report. He pulls off this trick quite effectively, delivering a story that flows well and packs a stinger of a punch in its last line.

Looking back on Howard's attempts at writing traditional Westerns, it's not really surprising that he wasn't all that successful at the time. The Western pulps of the Twenties and early Thirties relied heavily on the so-called "gun dummy" stories, with an abundance of simplistic, "save the ranch" plots. There were exceptions, of course, but Howard's stories were simply too offbeat and often too violent for a magazine like *Western Story*, which on the cover of every issue boasted of featuring "Big, Clean Stories of Outdoor Life." In the early Thirties, Popular Publications editor Rogers Terrill began attempting to bring a new realism and maturity to the Western pulps with his magazines *Dime Western* in 1932 and *Star Western* in 1933. But even here, most of Howard's Westerns were probably too far off the trail and too gritty for the editor's tastes. The only Western pulp Howard cracked in his lifetime was *Western Aces*, published by A. A. Wyn's notoriously low-paying Ace Publications. *Western Aces* and its companion magazine *Western Trails* were considered salvage markets where an author could send a manuscript that had been rejected by Street & Smith, Popular, and all the other higher-paying pulps. Despite that, I've always considered the Ace Western pulps to be pretty entertaining, because in addition to getting the stories that truly weren't very good, they also provided a home for those yarns that were just too unusual for the other Western pulps.

Which brings us to the eternal, unanswerable question: what would Howard have done if he'd lived? Considering that by his own comments to Lovecraft and others he wanted to concentrate on writing Westerns, I think there's a good chance he would have done just that. And within a few years, I think he would have found the markets much more receptive to his work. Authors such as Luke Short (Frederick Glidden), T. T. Flynn, and H. A. DeRosso were starting to contribute darker, more nihilistic yarns to the Western pulps and having some success with them. Jack Byrne at *Argosy* surely would have been willing to buy more Western stories from Howard. *Star Western* and *Big-Book Western* both featured novella-length stories, a length at which Howard excelled. He could have become a regular contributor to those and other Western pulps, and then when the paperback revolution of the Fifties came along, moved right over to Gold Medal along with other hardboiled Western pulpsters such as Lewis B. Patten, Gordon D. Shirreffs, William Heuman, Joseph Chadwick, Giles Lutz, and Dan Cushman.

But that's all speculation, of course, based on the stories Howard has left us. Those stories, many of them somewhat ahead of their time, form a collection of solidly entertaining Western fiction, written by a man who loved what he was doing.

You can tell. Just read the stories.

Western Tales

Drums of the Sunset

A Tales of the West of Twenty Years Ago

Chapter .1.
The Wanderer

"Now, come all you punchers, and listen to my tale,
When I tell you of troubles on the Chisholm Trail!"

Steve Harmer was riding Texas-fashion, slow and easy, one knee hooked over the saddle horn, hat pulled over his brows to shade his face. His lean body swayed rhythmically to the easy gait of his horse.

The trail he was following sloped gradually upward, growing steeper as he continued. Cedars flanked the narrow path, with occasional pinions and junipers. Higher up, these gave place to pines.

Looking back, Steve could see the broad level country he had left, deeply grassed and sparsely treed. Beyond and above, the timbered slopes of the mountains frowned. Peak beyond peak, pinnacle beyond pinnacle they rose, with great undulating slopes between, as if piled by giants.

Suddenly, behind the lone rider came the clatter of hoofs. Steve pulled aside to let the horsemen by, but they came to a halt beside him. Steve swept off his broad-brimmed hat.

There were two of the strangers, and one was a girl. To Steve she seemed strangely out of place, somehow, in this primitive setting. She sat her horse in an unfamiliar manner and her whole air was not of the West. She wore an Eastern riding habit—and then Steve forgot her clothes as he looked at her face. A vagrant curl, glinting gold in the sun, fell over her white forehead, and from beneath this two soft, grey eyes looked at him. Her full lips were half parted—

"Say, you!" a rough voice jarred Steve out of his daydreams.

The girl's companion was as characteristically Western as she was not. He was a heavily built man of middle life, thickly bearded and roughly clad. His features were dark and coarse, and Steve noted the heavy revolver which hung at his hip.

This man spoke in a harsh, abrupt manner.

"Who're you and where do you reckon you're goin'?"

Steve stiffened at the tone. He shot a glance at the girl, who seemed rather pale and frightened.

"My name's Harmer," said he, shortly. "I'm just passin' through."

"Yeah?" the bearded lips parted in a wolfish grin. "I reckon, stranger, you done lost your way—you shoulda took that trail back yonder a ways that branched off to the south."

"I ain't said where I was goin'," Steve responded, nettled. "Maybe I have reason for goin' this way."

"That's what I'm thinkin'," the bearded man answered, and Steve sensed the menacing note in his voice. "But you may have reason for takin' the other trail yet. Nobody lives in these hills, and they don't like strangers! Be warned, young feller, and don't git into somethin' you don't know nothin' about."

And while Steve gaped at him, not understanding, the man flung a curt order to the girl, and they both sped off up the trail, their horses laboring under the stress of quirt and spur. Steve watched in amazement.

"By golly, they don't care how they run their broncs uphill. What do you reckon all that rigmarole meant? Maybe I oughta taken the other trail, at that—golly, that was a pretty girl!"

The riders disappeared on the thickly timbered slope, and Steve, after some musing, nudged his steed with his knee and started on.

"I'm a goin' West and punch Texas cattle!
Ten dollar horse and forty dollar saddle."

Crack! A sharp report cut through the melody of his lazy song. A flash of fire stabbed from among the trees further up the slope.

Steve's hat flew from his head, his horse snorted and reared, nearly unseating his rider.

Steve whirled his steed, dropping off on the far side. His gun was in his hand as he peered cautiously across his saddle in the direction from which the shot had come. Silence hovered over the tree-masked mountainside and no motion among the intertwining branches betrayed the presence of the hidden foe.

At last Steve cautiously stepped from behind his horse. Nothing happened. He sheathed his gun, stepped forward and recovered his hat, swearing as he noted the neat hole through the crown.

"How did that whiskered galoot stop up there some place and sneak back for a crack at me?" he wondered. "Or did he tell somebody else to—or did that somebody else do it on their own idea? And what is the idea? What's up in them hills that they don't want seen? And was this sharpshooter tryin' to kill me or just warn me?"

He shook his head and shrugged his shoulders.

"Anyway," he meditated as he mounted, "I reckon that south trail is the best road, after all."

The south branch, he found, led down instead of up, skirting the base of the incline. He sighted several droves of sheep, and as the sun sank westward, he came upon a small cabin built near a running stream of clear water.

"Hi yah! Git down and set!" greeted the man who came to the door.

He was a small, wizened old fellow, remarkably bald, and he seemed delighted at the opportunity for conversation which Steve's coming afforded. But Steve eyed him with a suspicious glance before he dismounted.

"My name is Steve Harmer," said Steve abruptly. "I'm from Texas and I'm just passin' through. If you hone for me to ride on, just say so and they won't be no need for slingin' lead at me."

"Heh, heh!" laughed the old fellow. "Son, I kin read yore brand! You done fell in with my neighbors of the Sunset Mountains!"

"A tough lookin' *hombre* and a nice-lookin' girl," admitted Steve. "And some fellow who didn't give his name, but just ruined my best hat."

"Light!" commanded the old man. "Light and hobble yore bronc. This ain't no hotel, but maybe you can struggle along with the accommodations. My name is 'Hard Luck' Harper, and I aim to live up to that handle. You ain't by no chance got no corn juice in them saddle bags?"

"No, I ain't," answered Steve, dismounting.

"I was afeard not," sighed the old man. "Hard Luck I be to the end—come in—I smell that deer meat a-burnin'."

After a supper of venison, sourdough bread and coffee, the two sat on the cabin stoop and watched the stars blink out as they talked. The sound of Steve's horse cropping the luxuriant grass came to them, and a night breeze wafted the spicy scents of the forest.

"This country is sure different from Texas," said Steve. "I kinda like these mountains, though. I was figurin' on campin' up among 'em tonight; that's why I took that west trail. She goes on to Rifle Pass, don't she?"

"She don't," replied the old man. "Rifle Pass is some south of here and *this* is the trail to that small but thrivin' metropolis. That trail you was followin' meanders up in them hills and where she goes, nobody knows."

"Why don't they?"

"Fer two reasons. The first is, they's no earthly reason for a man in his right mind to go up there; and I'll refer you to yore hat for the second."

"What right has this bird got to bar people from these mountains?"

"I think it must be a thirty-thirty caliber," grinned the old man. "That feller you met was Gila Murken who lays out to own them mountains, like, and the gal was his niece, I reckon, what come from New York.

"I dunno what Gila's up to. I've knowed him, off and on, fer twenty years, and never knowed nothin' good. I'm his nearest neighbor, now, but I ain't got the slightest idee where his cabin is—up there somewhere." He indicated the gigantic brooding bulk of the Sunset Mountains, black in the starlight.

"Gila's got a couple fellers with him, and now this gal. Nobody else ever goes up that hill trail. The men come up here a year ago."

Steve mused.

"An' what do you reckon is his idee for discouragin' visitors?"

The old man shrugged his shoulders and shook his head. "Son, I've wondered myself. He and his pards lives up in them mountains, and regular once a week one of 'em rides to Rifle Pass or maybe clean to Stirrup, east. They have nothin' to do with me or anybody else. I've wondered, but, gosh, they ain't a chance!"

"Ain't a chance of what?"

"Steve," said Hard Luck, his lean hand indicating the black vastness of the hills, "somewhere up there amongst them canyons and gorges and cliffs is a fortune! And sometimes I wonder if Gila Murlon ain't found it.

"It's forty year ago that me and Bill Hansen come through this country—first white men in it, so far as I know. I was nothin' but a kid then, an' we was buffalo hunters, kinda strayed from the regular course.

"We went up into them hills—Sunset Mountains, the Indians call 'em—and away back somewheres we come into a range of cliffs. Now, it don't look like it'd be that way, lookin' from here, but in among the mountains they's long chains of cliffs, straight up and down, maybe four hundred feet high, clay and rock—mighty treacherous stuff. They's maybe seventeen sets of these cliffs, Ramparts we call 'em, and they look just alike. Trees along the edge, thick timber at the base. The edges is always crumblin' and startin' landslides and avalanches.

"Me and Bill Hansen come to the front of one of these Ramparts, and Bill was lookin' at where the earth of the cliff had kinda shelved away, when he let out a whoop!

"Gold! Reef gold—the blamedest vein I ever see, just lying there right at the surface, ready for somebody to work out the ore and cart it off! We dropped our guns and laid into the cliff with our finger-nails, diggin' the dirt away. And the vein looked like she went clear to China! Get that, son, reef gold and quartz in the open cliff face.

"'Bill,' says I, 'we're milyunaires!'

"And just as I said it, somethin' came whistlin' by my cheek, and Bill give one yell and went down on his face with a steel-pointed arrow through him. And before I could move, a rifle cracked and somethin' that felt like a red-hot hammer hit me in the chest and knocked me flat.

"A war party—they'd stole up on us while we was diggin'. Cheyennes they was, from the north, and they come out and chanted their scalp songs over us. Bill was dead and I lay still, all bloody but conscious, purtendin' I was a stiff, too.

"They scalped Bill and they scalped me—"

Steve gave an exclamation of horror.

"Oh, yes," said Hard Luck tranquilly. "It hurt considerable fact is, I don't know many things that hurt wuss. But somehow I managed to lie still and not let on like I was alive, though a couple of times I thought I was goin' to let out a whoop in spite of myself."

"Did they scalp you plumb down to the temples?" asked Steve, morbidly.

"Naw—the Cheyennes never scalped that way." Hard Luck ran his hand contemplatively over his glistening skull. "They just cut a piece out of the top—purty good sized piece, though—and the rest of the ha'r kinda got discouraged and faded away, after a few years.

"Anyway, they danced and yelled fer awhile, an' then they left an' I began to take invoice to see if I was still livin'. I was shot through the chest but by some miracle the ball had gone on through without hittin' anything important. I thought, though, I was goin' to bleed to death. But I stuffed the wound with leaves and the webs these large white spiders spin on the low branches of trees. I crawled to a spring which wasn't far away and lay there like a dead man till night, when I came to and lay there thinkin' about my dead friend, and my wounds and the gold I'd never enjoy.

"Then, I got out of my right mind and went crawlin' away through the forest, not knowin' why I did it. I was just like a man that's drunk; I knowed what I was doin' but I didn't know why I was doin' it. I crawled and I crawled, and how long I kept on crawlin' I don't know, for I passed clean out, finally, and some buffalo hunters found me out in the level country, miles and miles from where I was wounded. I was ravin' and gibberin' and nearly dead.

"They tended to me and after a long time my wounds healed and I come back to my right mind. And when I did, I thought about the gold and got up a prospectin' party and went back. But seems like I couldn't remember what all happened just before I got laid out. Everything was vague and I couldn't remember what way Bill and me had taken to get to the cliff, and I couldn't remember how it looked. They'd been a lot of landslides, too, and likely everything was changed in looks.

"Anyway, I couldn't find the lost mine of the Sunset Mountains, and though I been comin' every so often and explorin' again, for forty years, me nor no other livin' man has ever laid eyes on that gold ledge. Some landslide done covered it up, I reckon. Or maybe I just ain't never found the right cliff. I don't know.

"I done give it up. I'm gettin' old. Now I'm runnin' a few sheep and am purty contented. But you know now why they call me Hard Luck."

"And you think that maybe this Murken has found your mine and is workin' it on the sly?"

"Naw, really I don't. 'Twouldn't be like Gila Murken to try to conceal the fact—he'd just come out and claim it and dare me to take it away from him. Anyway," the old man continued with a touch of vanity, "no dub like Gila Murken could find somethin' that a old prospector like me has looked fer, fer forty years without findin', nohow."

Silence fell. Steve was aware that the night wind, whispering down from the mountains, carried a strange dim throbbing—a measured, even cadence, haunting and illusive.

"Drums," said Hard Luck, as if divining his thought. "Indian drums; tribe's away back up in the mountains. Nothin' like them that took my scalp. Navajoes, these is, a low-class gang that wandered up from the south. The government give 'em a kind of reservation back in the Sunset Mountains. Friendly, I reckon—trade with the whites a little.

"Them drums is been goin' a heap the last few weeks. Still nights you can hear 'em easy; sound travels a long way in this land."

His voice trailed off into silence. Steve gazed westward where the monstrous shadowy peaks rose black against the stars. The night breeze whispered a lonely melody through the cedars and pines. The scent of fresh grass and forest trees was in his nostrils. While stars twinkled above the dark mountains and the memory of a pretty, wistful face floated across Steve's vision. As he grew drowsy, the face seemed nearer and clearer, and always through the mists of his dreams throbbed faintly the Sunset drums.

Chapter .2.
Mystery

Steve drained his coffee cup and set it down on the rough-hewn table.

"I reckon," said he, "for a young fellow you're a pretty good cook—Hard Luck, I been thinkin'."

"Don't strain yoreself, son. It ain't a good idee startin' in on new things, at this time of yore life—what you been thinkin' about?"

"That mine of yours. I believe, instead of goin' on to Rifle Pass like I was thinkin' of doin', I'll lay over a few days and look for that lost gold ledge."

"Considerin' as I spent the best part of my life huntin' it," said Hard Luck testily, "it's very likely you'll stub yore toe on it the first thing. The Lord knows, I'd like to have you stay here as long as you want to. I don't see many people. But they ain't one chance in a hundred of you findin' that mine, and I'm tellin' you, it ain't healthy to ramble around in the Sunsets now, with Gila Murken hatchin' out the Devil only knows what, up there."

"Murken owes me a new hat," said Steve moodily. "And furthermore and besides, it's time somebody showed him he ain't runnin' this country. I crave to hunt for that mine. I dreamed about it last night."

"You better forgit that mountain business and work with me here on my ranch," advised Hard Luck. "I'll give you a job of herdin' sheep."

"Don't get insultin'," said Steve reprovingly. "How far up in them hills can a horse go?"

"You can navigate most of 'em on yore bronc if you take yore time an' let him pick his way. But you better not."

In spite of Hard Luck's warning, Steve rode up the first of the great slopes before the sun had risen high enough for him to feel its heat. It was a beautiful morning; the early sunlight glistened on the leaves of the trees and on the dew of the grass. Above and beyond him rose the slopes, dark green, deepening into purple in the distance. Snow glimmered on some of the higher peaks.

Steve felt a warmth of comfort and good cheer. The fragrance of Hard Luck's coffee and flapjacks was still on his palate, and the resilience of youth sang through his veins. Somewhere up there in the mysterious tree-clad valleys and ridges, adventure awaited him, and as Steve rode, the lost mine of the Sunsets was least in his thoughts.

No trail led up the way he took, but his horse picked his route between boulders and cedars, climbing steep slopes as nimbly as a mountain goat. The cedars gave way to pines and occasionally Steve looked down into some small valley, heavily grassed and thickly wooded. The sun was slanting toward the west when he finally pulled up his horse on the crest of a steep incline and looked down.

A wilder and more broken country he had never seen. From his feet the earth sloped steeply down, covered with pines which seemed to cling precariously, to debauch into a sort of plateau. On three sides of this plateau rose the slanting sides of the mountains. The fourth, or east side, fell away abruptly into cliffs which seemed hundreds of feet high. But what drew Steve's gaze was the plateau itself.

Near the eastern cliffs stood two log cabins. Smoke curled from one, and as Steve watched, a man came out of the door. Even at that distance Steve recognized the fellow whom Hard Luck had designated as Gila Murken.

Steve slipped from the saddle, led his horse back into the pines a short distance and flung the reins over a tree limb. Then he stole back to the crest of the slope. He did not think Murken could see him, hidden as he was among the trees, but he did not care to take any chances. Another man had joined Murken, and the two seemed to be engaged in conversation. After awhile they turned and went into the second cabin.

Time passed, but they did not emerge. Suddenly Steve's heart leaped strangely. A slim girlish form had come from the cabin out of which the men had come, and the sunshine glinted on golden hair. Steve leaned forward eagerly, wondering why the mere sight of a girl should cause his breath to come quicker.

She walked slowly toward the cliffs, and Steve perceived that there was what seemed to be a deep gorge, presumably leading downward. Into this the girl disappeared. Steve now found that the mysterious cabins had lost much of their interest, and presently he went back to his horse, mounted and rode southward, keeping close to the crest of the slopes. At last he attained a position where he could look back at the plateau and get a partial view of the cliffs. He decided that they were some of the Ramparts, spoken of by Hard Luck. They rose steep and bare for four hundred feet, deeply weathered and serrated. Gorges cut deep into them and promontories stood out over the abysses beneath. Great boulders lined the edge of the precipices and the whole face of the cliffs looked unstable and treacherous.

At the foot, tall forest trees masked a rough and broken country. And as he looked, Steve saw the girl, a tiny figure in the distance, come out into a clearing. He watched her until she vanished among the trees, and then turned his steed and rode back in the direction from which he had come, though not following the same route. He took his time, riding leisurely.

The sun slanted westward as he came to the lower slopes and looked back to see the rim of the Ramparts jutting below the heights he had left. He had made a vast semicircle and now the cliffs were behind and above him, instead of in front and below.

He went his leisurely way and suddenly he was aware of voices among the cedars in front of him. He slipped from his saddle, dropped the reins to the horse's feet, and stole forward. Hidden among the undergrowth, he looked into a small glade where stood two figures—the girl of the cliffs and a tall lanky man.

"No! No!" the girl was saying. "I don't want to have anything to do with you. Go away and let me alone or I'll tell my uncle."

"Haw! Haw!" the man's laugh was loud but mirthless. "Yore uncle and me is too close connected in a business way for him to rile me! I'm tellin' you, this ain't no place for you, and you better let me take you away to whar there's people and towns and the like."

"I don't trust you," she answered sullenly.

"Aw, now don't you? Come on—admit you done come down here just to meet me!"

"That's a lie!" the girl cried, stung. "You know I just went for a stroll; I didn't know you were here."

"These mountains ain't no place for a stroll."

"My uncle won't let me have a horse and ride, unless he's with me. He's afraid I'll run away."

"And wouldn't you?"

"I don't know. I haven't anywhere to go. But I'd about as soon die as stay here much longer."

"Then let me take you away! I'll marry you, if you say so. They's many a gal would jump to take Mark Edwards up on that deal."

"Oh, let me alone! I don't want to marry you, I don't want to go away with you, I don't even want to look at you! If you really want to make a hit with me, go somewhere and shoot yourself!"

Edwards' brow darkened.

"Oh ho, so I ain't good enough for you, my fine lady. Reckon I'll just take a kiss anyhow."

His grimed hands shot out and closed on her shoulders. Instantly she clenched a small fist and struck him in the mouth, so that blood trickled from his lips. The blow roused all the slumbering demon in the man.

"Yore a spitfire," he grunted. "But I 'low I'll tame you."

He pinioned her arms, cursed soulfully as she kicked him on the shins, and crushed her slim form to him. His unshaven lips were seeking hers when Steve impulsively went into action.

He bounded from his covert, gripped the man's shoulder with steely fingers and swung him around, smashing him in the face with his left hand as he did so. Edwards gaped in astonishment, then roared and rushed in blindly, fingers spread to gouge and tear. Steve was not inclined to clinch rough-and-tumble fashion. He dropped his right fist nearly to his ankle and then brought it up in a long sweeping arc which stopped at Edwards' chin. That worthy's head went back as if it were hinged, and his body, following the motion, crashed to the leaf-covered earth. He lay as if in slumber, his limbs tossed about in a careless and nonchalant manner. Steve caressed his sore knuckles and glanced at the girl.

"Is—is—is he dead?" she gasped, wide eyed.

"Naw, miss, I'm afraid he ain't," Steve answered regretfully. "He's just listenin' to the cuckoo birds. Shall I tie him up?"

"What for?" she asked reasonably enough. "No, let's go before he comes to."

And she started away hurriedly. Steve got his horse and followed her, overtaking her within a few rods. He walked beside her, leading his steed, his eyes admiringly taking in the proud erect carriage of her slim figure, and the faint delicate rose-leaf tint of her complexion.

"I hope you won't think I'm intrudin' where I got no business," said the Texan apologetically, "but I'm a-seein' you to wherever you're goin'. That bird might follow you, or you might meet another one like him."

"Thank you," she answered in a rather subdued voice. "You were very kind to help me, Mr. Harmer."

"How'd you know my name?"

"You told my uncle who you were yesterday, don't you remember?"

"Seems like I recollect, now," replied Steve, experiencing a foolish warm thrill that she should remember his name. "But I don't recall you saying what your name was."

"My name is Joan Farrel. I'm staying here with my uncle, Mr. Murken, the man with whom you saw me yesterday."

"And was it him," asked Steve bluntly, "that shot a hole in my hat?"

Her eyes widened; a frightened look was evident in her face.

"No! No!" she whispered. "It couldn't have been him! He and I rode right up on to the cabin after we passed you. I heard the shot, but I had no idea anyone was shooting at you."

Steve laughed, rather ashamed of having mentioned it to the girl.

"Aw, it wasn't nothin'. Likely somebody done it for a joke. But right after you-all went on, somebody cracked down on me from the trees up the trail a ways and plumb ruint my hat."

"It must have been Edwards," she said in a frightened voice. "We met him coming down the trail on foot after we'd gotten out of sight of you, and Uncle stopped and said something to him I couldn't hear, before we went on."

"And who is Edwards?"

"He's connected with my uncle's business in some way; I don't know just how. He and a man named Allison camp up there close to our cabin."

"What is your uncle's business?" asked Steve with cool assumption.

She did not seem offended at the question.

"I don't know. He never tells me anything. I'm afraid of him, and he doesn't love me."

Her face was shadowed as if by worry or secret fear. Something was haunting her, Steve thought. Nothing more was said until they had reached the base of the cliffs. Steve glanced up, awed. The great walls hung threateningly over them, starkly and somberly. To his eye, the cliffs seemed unstable, ready to crash down upon the forest below at the slightest jar. Great boulders jutted out, half embedded in the clay. The brow of the cliff, fringed with trees, hung out over the concave walls.

From where he stood, Steve could see a deep gorge, cut far into the face of the precipice and leading steeply upward. He caught his breath. He had never imagined such a natural stairway. The incline was so precipitous that it seemed it would tax the most sure-footed horse. Boulders rested along the trail that led through it, as if hovering there temporarily, and the high walls on each side darkened the way, looming like a sinister threat.

"My gosh!" said he sincerely. "Do you have to go down that gulch every time you leave your cabin?"

"Yes—or else climb the slopes back of the plateau and make a wide circle, leaving the plateau to the north and coming down the southern ridges. We always go this way. I'm used to climbing it now."

"Must have took a long time for the water to wash that out," said Steve. "I'm new to this mountain country, but it looks to me like if somebody stubbed their toe on a rock, it would start a landslide that would bring the whole thing down in that canyon."

"I think of that, too," she answered with a slight shudder. "I thank you for what you've done for me. But you mustn't go any further. My uncle is always furious if anyone comes into these mountains."

"What about Edwards?"

"I'll tell my uncle and he'll make him leave me alone." She started to go, then hesitated.

"Listen," said Steve, his heart beating wildly. "I'd like to know you better—will—will you meet me tomorrow somewhere?"

"Yes!" she spoke low and swiftly, then turned and ran lightly up the slope. Steve stood, looking after her, hat in hand.

Night had fallen as Steve Harmer rode back to the ranch of Hard Luck Harper.

"Clouds in the west and a-lookin' like rain,
And my blamed old slicker's in the wagon again!"

He declaimed to the dark blue bowl of the star-flecked sky.

The crisp, sharp scent of cedar was in the air and the wind fanned his cheek. He felt his soul grow and expand in the silence and the majesty of the night.

"Woke up one mornin' on the Chisholm Trail—
Rope in my hand and a cow by the tail!"

He drew rein at the cabin stoop and hailed his host hilariously. Old Hard Luck stood in the door, and the starlight glinted on the steel in his hand.

"Huh," grunted he suspiciously. "You done finally come back, ain't you? I'd 'bout decided you done met up with Gila Murken and was layin' in a draw somewheres with a thirty-thirty slug through yore innards. Come in and git yore hoofs under the table—I done cooked a couple of steers in hopes of stayin' yore appetite a little."

Steve tended to his horse and then entered the cabin, glancing at the long rifle which the old man had stood up against the cabin wall.

"That was a antique when they fought the Revolution," said Steve. "What's the idea? Are you afraid of Murken?"

"Afeared of Murken? That dub? I got no call to be afeared of him. And don't go slingin' mud at a gun that's dropped more Indians than you ever see. That's a Sharp .50 caliber, and when I was younger I could shave a mosquito at two hundred yards with it."

"Naw, it ain't Murken I'm studyin'. Listen!"

Again Steve caught the faint pulsing of the mountain drums.

"Every night they get louder," said Hard Luck. "They said them redskins is plumb peaceful, but you can't tell me—the only peaceful Indian I ever see had at least two bullets through his skull. Them drums talks and whispers, and they ain't no white man knows what's hatchin' back in them hills where nobody seldom ever goes. Indian magic! That what's goin' on, and red magic means red doin's.

I've fought 'em from Sonora to the Bad Lands and I know what I'm talkin' about."

"Your nerves is gettin' all euchered up," said Steve, diving into the food set before him. "I kinda like to listen to them drums."

"Maybe you'd like to hear 'em when they was dancin' yore scalp," answered Hard Luck gloomily. "Thar's a town about forty mile northwest of here whar them red devils come to trade sometimes, 'steader goin' to Rifle Pass, and a feller come through today from thar and says they must be some strange goin's on up in the Sunsets.

"'How come?' says I.

"'Why,' says he, 'them reservation Navajoes has been cartin' down greenbacks to buy their tobaccer and calico and the other day the storekeepers done found the stuff is all counterfeit. They done stopped sellin' to the Indians and sent for a Indian agent to come and investigate. Moreover,' says he, 'somebody is sellin' them redskins liquor, too.'"

Hard Luck devoted his attention to eating for a few moments and then began again.

"How come them Indians gets any kind of money up in the mountains, much less counterfeit? Reckon they're makin' it their-selves? And who's slippin' them booze? One thing's shore, Hell's to pay when redskins git drunk, and the first scalp they'll likely take is the feller's who sold them the booze."

"Yeah?" returned Steve absentmindedly. His thoughts were elsewhere.

"Did you find the mine?" asked Hard Luck sarcastically.

"What mine?" the Texan stared at his host blankly.

Hard Luck grunted scornfully and pushed back his chair. After awhile silence fell over the cabin, to be broken presently by Steve's voice rising with dolorous enjoyment in the darkness.

"And he thought of his home, and his loved ones nigh,
And the cowboys gathered to see him die!"

Hard Luck sat up in his bunk and cursed, and hurled a boot.

"For the love of mud, let a old man sleep willya?"

As Steve drifted off into dreamland, his last thoughts were of gold, but it was not the gold ore of the Sunsets; it was the soft curly gold that framed the charming oval of a soft face. And still through the shimmery hazes of his dreams beat the sinister muttering of the Sunset drums.

Chapter .3.
The Girl's Story

The dew was still on the mountain grass when Steve rode up the long dim slopes to the glade where he had fought Edwards the day before. He sat down on a log and waited, doubting if she whom he sought would really come.

He sat motionless for nearly an hour, and then he heard a light sure step and she stood before him, framed in the young glow of the morning sun. The beauty of her took Steve's breath, and he could only stand, hat in hand, and gape, seeking feebly for words. She came straight to him, smiling, and held out her hand. The touch of her slim firm fingers reassured him, and he found his voice.

"Miss Farrel, I plumb forgot yesterday to ask you where you'd rather meet me at, or what time. I come here because I figured you'd remember—I mean, you'd think—aw heck!" he stumbled.

"Yes, that was forgetful of us. I decided that you'd naturally come to the place where you found me yesterday, and I came early because—because, I was afraid you'd come and not find me here and think I wasn't coming," she finished rather confusedly.

As she spoke, her eyes ran approvingly over Steve, noting his six-foot build of lithe manhood and the deep tan of his whimsical face.

"I promised to tell you all I know," said she abruptly, twisting her fingers. She seemed paler and more worried than ever. Steve decided that she had reached the point where she was ready to turn to any man for help, stranger or not. Certainly some deep fear was preying on her.

"You know my name," she said, seating herself on the log and motioning him to sit beside her. "Mr. Murken is my mother's brother. My parents separated when I was very young, and I've been living with an aunt in New York State. I'd never been west before, until my aunt died not long ago. Before she died, she told me to go to her brother at Rifle Pass and, not having anywhere else to go, I did so.

"I'd never seen my uncle, and I found him very different from what I had expected. He didn't live at Rifle Pass then, but had moved up in these mountains. I came on up here with a guide, and my uncle seemed very much enraged because I had come. He let me stay, but I'm very unhappy because I know he don't want me. Yet, when I ask him to let me go, he refuses. He won't even let me go to Rifle Pass unless he is with me, and he won't let me go riding unless he's with me. He says he's afraid I'll run away, yet I know he doesn't love me or really want me here. He's not exactly unkind to me, but he isn't kind either.

"There are two men who stay up there most of the time: Edwards, the man you saw yesterday, and a large black-bearded man named Allison. That one, Allison, looks like a bandit or something, but he is very courteous to me. But Edwards—you saw what he did yesterday, and he's forever trying to make love to me when my uncle isn't around. I'm afraid to tell uncle about it, and I don't know whether he'd do anything, if I did tell him.

"The other two men stay in a smaller cabin a little distance from the one occupied by my uncle and myself, and they won't let me come anywhere near it. My uncle even threatened to whip me if I looked in the windows. I think they must have something hidden there. My uncle locks me in my cabin when they are all at work in the other cabin—whatever they're doing there.

"Sometimes some Indians come down the western slopes from somewhere away back up in the hills, and sometimes my uncle rides away with them. Once a week, one of the men loads his saddlebags full of something and rides away to be gone two or three days.

"I don't understand it," she added almost tearfully. "I can't help but believe that there's something crooked about it. I'm afraid of Edwards, and only a little less afraid of my uncle. I want to get away."

Suddenly she seized his hands impulsively.

"You seem good and kind," she exclaimed. "Won't you help me? I'll pay you—"

"You'll what?" he said explosively.

She flushed.

"I beg your pardon. I should have known better than to make that remark. I know you'll help me just from the goodness of your heart."

Steve's face burned crimson. He fumbled with his hat.

"Sure, I'll help you. If you want I'll ride up and git your things—"

She stared at him in amazement.

"I don't want you committing suicide on my account," said she. "You'd get shot if you went within sight of my uncle. No, this is what I want you to do. I've told you my uncle won't let me have a horse, and I certainly can't walk out of these mountains. Can you meet me here early tomorrow morning with an extra horse?"

"Sure I can. But how are you goin' to get your baggage away? Girls is usually got a lot of frills, and things—"

"I haven't. But anyway, I want to get out of this place, if I have to leave my clothes, even, and ride out in a bathing suit. I'll stroll out of the cabin in the morning, casually, come down the gulch and meet you here."

"And then where will you want to go?"

"Any place is as good as the next," she answered rather hopelessly. "I'll have to find some town where I can make my own living. I guess I can teach school or work in an office."

"I wish—" said he impulsively, and then stopped short.

"You wish what?" she asked curiously.

"That them drums would quit whoopin' it up at night," he added desperately, flushing as he realized how closely he had been to proposing to a girl he had known only two days. He was surprized at himself; he had spoken on impulse, and he wondered at the emotion which had prompted him.

She shivered slightly.

"They frighten me, sometimes. Every night they keep booming, and last night I was restless and every time I awoke I could hear them. They didn't stop until dawn. This was the first time they've kept up all night."

She rose.

"I've stayed as long as I dare. My uncle will get suspicious of me and come looking for me if I'm gone too long."

Steve rose. "I'll go with you as far as the gorge."

Again Steve stood among the thick trees at the foot of the Ramparts and watched the girl go up the gorge, her slim form receding and growing smaller in his sight as she ascended. The gulch lay in everlasting shadow, and Steve unconsciously held his breath, as if expecting those grim, towering walls to come crashing down on that slender figure.

Nearly at the upper mouth, she turned and waved at him, and he waved back, then turned and made his way back to his horse. He rode carelessly, and with a slack rein, seeming to move in a land of rose-tinted clouds. His heart beat swiftly and his blood sang through his veins.

"I'm in love! I'm in love!" he warbled, wild-eyed, to the indifferent trees. "Oh heck! Oh golly! Oh gosh!"

Suddenly he stopped short. From somewhere further back and high above him came a quick rattle of rifle fire. As he listened, another volley cracked out. A vague feeling of apprehension clutched at him. He glanced at the distant rim of the Ramparts. The sounds had seemed to come from that direction. A few straggling shots sounded faintly, then silence fell. What was going on up above those grim cliffs?

"Reckon I ought to go back and see?" he wondered. "Reckon if Murken and his bold boys is slaughterin' each other? Or is it some wanderin' traveler they're greetin'? Aw, likely they're after deer or maybe a mountain lion."

He rode on slowly, but his conscience troubled him. Suddenly a familiar voice hailed him, and from the trees in front of him a horseman rode.

"Hi yah!" The rider was Hard Luck Harper. He carried the long Sharp's rifle across his saddlebow and his face was set in gloomy lines.

"I done got to worryin' about a brainless maverick like you a-wanderin' around these hills by yoreself with Gila Murken runnin' wild thataway, and I come to see if you was still in the land of the livin'!"

"And I reckon you're plumb disappointed not to run into a murder or two."

"I don't know so much about them murders," said the old man testily. "Didn't I hear guns a-talkin' up on the Ramparts a while ago?"

"Likely you did, if you was listenin'."

"Yeah—and people don't go wastin' ammunition fer nothin' up here—look there!"

Hard Luck's finger stabbed upward, and Steve, a numbing sense of foreboding gripping his soul, whirled to look. Up over the tree-lined rim of the Ramparts drifted a thin spiral of smoke.

"My Lord, Hard Luck!" gasped Steve. "What's goin' on up there?"

"Shet up!" snarled the old man, raising his rifle. "I hear a horse runnin' hard!"

The wild tattoo of hoofs crashed through the silence and a steed burst through the trees of the upper slope and came plunging down toward them, wild-eyed, nostrils flaring. On its back a crimsoned figure reeled and flopped grotesquely. Steve spurred in front of the frantic flying animal and caught the hanging rein, bringing the bronco to a rearing, plunging halt. The rider slumped forward and pitched to the earth.

"Edwards!" gasped Steve.

The man lay, staring up with blank wide eyes. Blood trickled from his lips and the front of his shirt was soaked in red. Hard Luck and Steve bent over him. At the first glance, it was evident that he was dying.

"Edwards!" exclaimed Hard Luck. "What's happened? Who shot you? And whar's yore pards and the gal?"

"Dead!" Edwards' unshaven lips writhed redly and his voice was a croak.

"Daid!" Hard Luck's voice broke shrilly. "Who done it?"

"Them Navajoes!" the voice sank to a ghastly whisper as blood rose to the pallid lips.

"I told you!" gibbered Hard Luck. "I knowed them drums meant deviltry! I knowed—"

"Shut up, can't you?" snarled Steve, torn by his emotions. He gripped the dying man's shoulder with unconsciously brutal force and shook him desperately.

"Edwards," he begged, "you're goin' over the ridge—can't you tell us how it was before you go? Did you see Murken and his niece die?"

"Yes—it—was—like—this," the man began laboriously. "I was—all set to go—to Rifle Pass—had my bronc loaded—Murken and Allison was out near—the corral—the gal was—in the cabin. All to once—the west slopes began to shower lead. Murken went down—at the first fire. Allison was hit—and I got a slug through me. Then a gang of—Navajoes come ridin' down—the slopes—drunk and blood crazy.

"I got to my bronc—and started ridin' and—they drilled me—a couple of times from behind. Lookin' back I saw—Allison standin' in the cabin door with—both guns goin' and the gal—crouchin' behind him. Then the whole mob—of red devils—rushed in and I saw—the knives flashin' and drippin' as—I come into—the gulch."

Steve crouched, frozen and horrorstruck. It seemed that his heart had crumbled to ashes. The taste of dust was in his mouth.

"Any of 'em chasin' you, Edwards?" asked Hard Luck. The old Indian fighter was in his element now; he had sloughed off his attitude of lazy good nature and his eyes were hard and cold as steel.

"Maybe—don't know," the wounded man muttered. "All our fault—Murken would give 'em whiskey. Warned him. They found out—the money—he was givin' 'em—was no good."

The voice broke suddenly as a red tide gushed to Edwards' lips. He lurched up on his elbows, then toppled back and lay still.

Hard Luck grunted. He stepped over to Edwards' horse which stood trembling, and cut open the saddlebags. He nodded.

"No more'n I expected."

Steve was rising slowly, mechanically wiping his hands on a wisp of grass. His face was white, his eyes staring.

"She's dead!" he whispered. "She's dead!"

Hard Luck, gazing at him, felt a pang in his heart. The scene brought back so poignantly the old bloody days of Indian warfare when men had seen their loved ones struck down by knife and arrow.

"Son," said he, solemnly, "I never expected to see such a sight as this again."

The Texan gave him a glance of agony, then his eyes blazed with a wild and terrible light.

"They killed her!" he screamed, beating his forehead with his clenched fists. "And by God, I'll kill 'em all! I'll kill—kill—"

His gun was swinging in his hand as he plunged toward his horse. Hard Luck sprang forward and caught him, holding him with a wiry strength that was astounding for his age. He ignored the savage protests and curses, dodged a blow of the gun barrel which the half-crazed Texan aimed at his face, and pinioned Steve's arms. The youth's frenzied passion went as suddenly as it had come, leaving him sobbing and shaken.

"Son," said Hard Luck calmly, "cool down. I reckon you don't want to lift them Navajo scalps any more'n I do, and before this game's done, we're goin' to send more'n one of 'em over the ridge. But if you go gallopin' up after 'em wide open thataway, you'll never git the chancet to even the score, fer they'll drill you before you even see 'em. Listen to me, I've fought 'em from Sonora to the Bad Lands and I know what I'm talkin' about. Git on yore bronc. We can't do nothin' more fer Edwards, and we got work to do elsewhar. He said Allison and Murken and the gal was dead. I reckon Murken and Allison is gone over the ridge alright, but he didn't rightly see 'em bump off the gal, and I'll bet my hat she's alive right now."

Steve nodded shortly. He seemed to have aged years in the last few minutes. The easygoing young cowpuncher was gone, and in his place stood a cold steel fighting man of the old Texas blood. His hand was as steady as a rock, as he sheathed his pistol and swung into the saddle.

"I'm followin' your lead, Hard Luck," said he briefly. "All I ask is for you to get me within shootin' and stabbin' distance of them devils."

The old man grinned wolfishly.

"Son, yore wants is simple and soon satisfied; follow me."

Chapter .4.
A Trail of Blood

Steve and Hard Luck rode slowly and warily up the tree-covered slopes which led to the foot of the Ramparts. Silence hung over the mountain forest like a deathly fog. Hard Luck's keen old eyes roved incessantly, ferreting out of the shadows, seeking for sign of something unnatural, something which was not as it should be, to betray the hidden assassins. He talked in a low, guarded tone. It was dangerous, but he wished to divert Steve's mind as much as possible.

"Steve, I done looked in Edwards' saddlebags, and what you reckon I found? A whole stack of greenbacks, tens, twenties, fifties and hundreds, done up in bundles! It's money he's been packin' out to Rifle Pass. Whar you reckon he got it?"

Steve did not reply nor did the old man expect an answer. The Texan's eyes were riveted on the frowning buttresses of the Ramparts, which now loomed over them. As they came under the brow of the cliffs, the smoke they had seen further away was no longer visible.

"Reckon they didn't chase Edwards none," muttered Hard Luck. "Leastways they ain't no sign of any horses followin' his. There's his tracks, alone. These Navajoes is naturally desert Indians, anyhow, and they're 'bout as much outa place in the mountains as a white man from the plains. They can't hold a candle to me, anyhow."

They had halted in a thick clump of trees at the foot of the Ramparts and the mouth of the steep defile was visible in front of them.

"That's a bad place," muttered Hard Luck. "I been up that gulch before Gila built his cabins up on the plateau. Steve, we kin came at them Navajoes, supposin' they're still up on there, by two ways. We kin circle to the south, climb up the mountainsides and come down the west slopes, or we kin take a chance an' ride up the gulch. That's a lot quicker, of course, pervidin' we ain't shot or mashed by fallin' rocks afore we git to the top."

"Let's take it on the run," urged Steve, quivering with impatience. "It'll take more'n bullets and rocks to stop me now."

"Alright," said Hard Luck, reining his horse out of the trees, "here goes!"

Of that wild ride up the gorge Steve never remembered very much. The memory was always like a nightmare, in which he saw dark walls flash past, heard the endless clatter of hoofs and the rattle of dislodged stones. Nothing seemed real except the pistol he clutched in his right hand and the laboring steed that plunged and reeled beneath him, driven headlong up the slope, with spurs that raked the panting sides.

Then they burst into the open and saw the plateau spread wide and silent before them, with smoldering masses of coals where the cabins and corral should have stood. They rode up slowly. The tracks of horses led away up into the hills to the west and there was no sign of life. Dreading what he might see, Steve looked. Down close to where the corral had been laid the body of Gila Murken. Lying partly in the coals that marked the remnants of the larger cabin, was the corpse of a large dark-faced man, who had worn a heavy beard, though now beard and hair were mostly scorched off. There was no sign of the girl.

"Do you—do you think she burned in the cabin, Hard Luck?"

"Naw, I know she didn't fer the reason that if she hada, they'd be some charred bones. They done rode off with her."

Steve felt a curious all-gone feeling, as if the realization that Joan was alive was too great a joy for the human brain to stand.

Even though he knew that she must be in a fearful plight, at least she was living.

"Lookit the stiffs," said Hard Luck admiringly. "There's whar Allison made his last stand—at the cabin door, protectin' the gal, I reckon. This Allison seemed to be a mighty hard *hombre*, but I reckon he had a streak of the man in him. Stranger in these parts to all but Murken."

Four Navajoes lay face down in front of the white man's body. They were clad only in dirty trousers and blankets flung about their shoulders. They were stone dead.

"Trail of blood from whar the corral was," said Hard Luck. "They caught him in the open and shot him up afore he could git to the cabin, I figure. Down there at the corral, Murken died. The way I read it, Allison made a break and got to the cabin whar the gal was. Then they surged in on him and he killed these four devils and went over the ridge hisself."

Steve bent over the grim spectacle and then straightened.

"Thought I knowed him. Allison—Texas man he was. A real bad *hombre* down on the border. Got run outa El Paso for gunrunnin' into Mexico."

"He shore made a game stand fer his last fight."

"Texas breed," said Steve grimly.

"I reckon all the good battlers ain't in Texas," said Hard Luck testily. "Not denyin' he put up a man-sized fight. Now then, look. Trails of fourteen horses goin' west—five carryin' weight, the rest bare—tell by the way the hoofs sink in, of course. All the horses missin' out of the corral, four dead Indians here. That means they warn't but a small party of 'em. Figurin' one of the horses is bein' rid by the gal, I guess we got only four redskins to deal with. Small war party scoutin' in front of the tribe, I imagine, if the whole tribe's on the warpath. Now they're lightin' back into the hills with the gal, the broncs they took from the corral, and the horses of their dead tribesmen—which stopped Allison's bullets. Best thing fer us to do is follow and try to catch up with 'em afore they git back to the rest of their gang."

"Then let's go," exclaimed Steve, trembling with impatience. "I'm nearly crazy standin' here doin' nothin'."

Hard Luck glanced at the steeds, saw that they had recovered from the terrific strain of that flying climb, and nodded. As they rode past the embers of the smaller cabin, he drew rein for an instant.

"Steve, what's them things?"

Steve looked somberly at the charred and burnt machines which lay among the smoking ruins.

"Stamps and presses and steel dies," said he. "Counterfeit machines. And look at the greenbacks."

Fragments of green paper littered the earth as if they had been torn and flung about in anger or mockery.

"Murken and Edwards and Allison was counterfeiters, then. Huh! No wonder they didn't want anybody snoopin' around. That's why Murken wouldn't let the gal go—afeard she knew too much."

They started on again at a brisk trot and Hard Luck ruminated.

"Mighta known it when they come up here a year ago. Reckon Edwards went to Rifle Pass every week, or some other nearby place, and put the false bills in circulation. Musta had an agent. And they give money to the Indians, too, to keep their mouths shet, and give 'em whiskey. And the Indians found they'd been given money which was no good, and bein' all fired up with Murken's bad whiskey, they just bust loose."

"If so be we find Joan," said Steve somberly, "say nothin' about her uncle bein' a crook."

"Sure."

Their steeds were mounting the western slopes, up which went the trail of the marauders. They crossed the ridge, went down the western incline and struck a short expanse of comparatively level country.

"Listen at the drums!" muttered Hard Luck. "Gettin' nearer. The whole tribe must be on the march."

The drums were talking loud and clear from somewhere in the vastness in front of them, and Steve seemed to catch in their rumble an evil note of sinister triumph.

Then the two riders were electrified by a burst of wild and ferocious yells from the heavily timbered levels to the west, in the direction they were going. Flying hoofs beat out a thundering tattoo and a horse raced into sight running hard and low, with a slim white figure lying close along his neck. Behind came four hideous painted demons, spurring and yelling.

"Joan!" the word burst from Steve's lips in a great shout and he spurred forward. Simultaneously he heard the crash of Hard Luck's buffalo gun and saw the foremost redskin topple earthward, his steed sweeping past with an empty saddle. The girl whirled up beside him, her arms reaching for him.

"Steve!" Her cry was like the wail of a lost child.

"Ride for the plateau and make it down through the gulch!" he shouted, wheeling aside to let her pass. "Go!"

Then he swung back to meet the oncoming attackers. The surprize had been as much theirs as the white men's. They had not expected to be followed so soon, and when they had burst through the trees, the sight of the two white men had momentarily stunned them with the unexpectedness of it. However, the remaining three came on with desperate courage and the white men closed in to meet them.

Hard Luck's single-shot rifle was empty, but he held it in his left hand, guiding his steed with his knees, while he drew a long knife with his free hand. Steve spurred in, silent and grim, holding his fire until the first of the attackers was almost breast to breast with him. Then, as the rifle stock in the red hands went up, Steve shot him twice through his painted face and saw the fierce eyes go blank before the body slumped from the saddle. At the same instant Hard Luck's horse crashed against the bronc of another Indian and the lighter mustang reeled to the shock. The redskin's thrusting blade glanced from the empty rifle barrel and the knife in Hard Luck's right hand whipped in, just under the heart.

The lone survivor wheeled his mustang as if to flee, then pivoted back with an inhuman scream and fired pointblank into Steve's face, so closely that the powder burned his cheek. Without stopping to marvel at the miracle by which the lead had missed, Steve gripped the rifle barrel and wrenched.

White man and Indian tumbled from the saddles, close-locked, and there, writhing and struggling in the dust, the Texan killed his man, beating out his brains with the pistol barrel.

"Hustle!" yelled Hard Luck. "The whole blame tribe is just over that rise not a half a mile away, if I'm to jedge by the sounds of them riding drums!"

Steve mounted without a backward glance at the losers of that grim red game who lay so stark and motionless. Then he saw the girl, sitting her horse not a hundred yards away, and he cursed in fright. He and Hard Luck swept up beside her and he exclaimed:

"Joan, why didn't you ride on, like I told you?"

"I couldn't run away and leave you!" she sobbed; her face was deathly white, her eyes wide with horror.

"Hustle, blast it!" yelled Hard Luck, kicking her horse. "Git movin'! Do you love birds wanta git all our scalps lifted?"

Over the thundering of the flying hoofs, as they raced eastward, she cried:

"They were taking me somewhere—back to their tribe, maybe—but I worked my hands loose and dashed away on the horse I was riding. Oh, oh, the horrors I've seen today! I'll die, I know I will."

"Not so long as me and brainless here has a drop of blood to let out," grunted Hard Luck, misunderstanding her.

They topped the crest which sloped down to the plateau, and Joan averted her face.

"Good thing scalpin's gone outa fashion with the Navajoes," grunted Hard Luck under his breath, "or she'd see wuss than she's already saw."

They raced across the plateau and swung up to the upper mouth of the gulch.

There Hard Luck halted.

"Take a little rest and let the horses git their wind. The Indians ain't in sight yit, and we kin see 'em clean across the plateau. With this start and our horses rested, we shore ought to make a clean gitaway. Now, Miss Joan, don't you look at—at them cabins what's burned. What's done is done and can't be undid. This game ain't over by a long shot and what we want to do, is to think how to save us what's alive. Them that's dead is past hurtin'."

"But it is all so horrible," she sobbed, drooping forward in her saddle. Steve drew up beside her and put a supporting arm about her slim waist. He was heart torn with pity for her, and the realization that he loved her so deeply and so terribly.

"Shots!" she whimpered. "All at once—like an earthquake! The air seemed full of flying lead! I ran to the cabin door just as Allison came reeling up all bloody and terrible. He pushed me back in the cabin and stood in the door with a pistol in each hand. They came sweeping up, like painted fiends, yelling and chanting.

"Allison gave a great laugh and shot one of them out of his saddle and roared: 'Texas breed, curse you!' And he stood up straight in the doorway with his long guns blazing until they had shot him through and through, again and again, and he died on his feet." She sobbed on Steve's shoulder.

"Sho, Miss," said Hard Luck huskily. "Don't you worry none about Allison; I don't reckon he woulda wanted to go out any other way. All any of us kin ask is to go out with our boots on and empty guns smokin' in our hands."

"Then they dragged me out and bound my wrists," she continued listlessly, "and set me on a horse. They turned the mustangs out of the corral and then set the corral on fire, and the cabins too, dancing and yelling like fiends. I don't remember just what all did happen. It seems like a terrible dream."

She passed a slim hand wearily across her eyes.

"I must have fainted, then. I came to myself and the horse I was on was being led through the forest together with the horses from the corral and the mustangs whose riders Allison had killed. Somehow I managed to work my hands loose, then I kicked the horse with my heels and he bolted back the way we had come."

"Look sharp!" said Hard Luck suddenly, rising in his saddle. "There they come!"

The crest of the western slopes was fringed with war-bonnets. Across the plateau came the discordant rattle of the drums.

Chapter .5.
Thundering Cliffs

"Easy all!" said Hard Luck. "We got plenty start and we got to pick our way, goin' down here. A stumble might start a regular avalanche. I've seen such things happen in the Sunsets. Easy all!"

They were riding down the boulder-strewn trail which led through the defile. It was hard to ride with a tight rein and at a slow gait with the noise of those red drums growing louder every moment, and the knowledge that the red killers were even now racing down the western slopes.

The going was hard and tricky. Sometimes the loose shale gave way under the hoofs, and sometimes the slope was so steep that the horses reared back on their haunches and slid and scrambled. Again Steve found time to wonder how Joan found courage to go up and down this gorge almost every day. Back on the plateau, now, he could hear the yells of the pursuers and the echoes shuddered eerily down the gorge. Joan was white, but she handled her mount coolly.

"Nearly at the bottom," said Hard Luck, after what seemed an age. "Risk a little sprint, now."

The horses leaped out at the loosening of the reins and crashed out onto the slopes in a shower of flying shale and loose dirt. "Good business—" said Hard Luck—and then his horse stumbled and went to its knees, throwing him heavily.

Steve and the girl halted their mounts, sprang from the saddle. Hard Luck was up in an instant, cursing.

"My horse is lame—go on and leave me!"

"No!" snarled Steve. "We can both ride on mine."

He whirled to his steed; up on the plateau crashed an aimless volley as if fired into the air. Steve's horse snorted and reared—the Texan's clutching hand missed the rein and the bronco wheeled and galloped away into the forest. Steve stood aghast, frozen at this disaster.

"Go on!" yelled Hard Luck. "Blast you, git on with the gal and dust it outta here!"

"Get on your horse!" Steve whirled to the girl. "Get on and go!"

"I won't!" she cried. "I won't ride off and leave you two here to die! I'll stay and die with you!"

"Oh, my Lord!" said Steve, cursing feminine stubbornness and lack of logic. "Grab her horse, Hard Luck, I'll put her on by main force and—"

"Too late!" said Hard Luck with a bitter laugh. "There they come!"

Far up at the upper end of the defile a horseman was silhouetted against the sky like a bronze statue. A moment he sat his horse motionless and in that moment Hard Luck threw the old buffalo gun to his shoulder. At the reverberating crash the Indian flung his arms wildly and toppled headlong, to tumble down the gorge with a loose flinging of his limbs. Hard Luck laughed as a wolf snarls and then the riderless horse was jostled aside by flying steeds as the upper mouth of the defile filled with wild riders.

"Git back to the trees," yelled Hard Luck, leading the race from the cliff's base, reloading as he ran. "Guess we kin make a last stand, anyway!"

Steve, sighting over his pistol barrel as he crouched over the girl, gasped as he saw the Navajoes come plunging down the long gulch. They were racing downslope with such speed that their horses reeled to their knees again and again, recovering balance in a flying cloud of shale and sand. Rocks dislodged by the flashing hoofs rattled down in a rain. The whole gorge was crowded with racing horsemen. Then—

"I knowed it!" yelled Hard Luck, smiting his thigh with a clenched fist.

High up the gulch a horse had stumbled, hurtling against a great boulder. The concussion had jarred the huge rock loose from its precarious base and now it came rumbling down the slope, sweeping horses and men before it. It struck other boulders and tore them loose; the gorge was full of frantic plunging steeds whose riders sought vainly to escape the avalanche they had started. Horses went down screaming as only dying horses can scream, a wild babble of yells arose, and then the whole earth seemed to rock.

Jarred by the landslide, the overhanging walls reeled and shattered and came thundering down into the gorge, wiping out the insects which struggled there, blocking and closing the defile forever. Boulders and pieces of cliff weighing countless tons shelved off and came sliding down. The awed watchers among the trees rose silently, unspeaking. The air seemed full of flying stones, hurled out by the shattering fall of the great rocks. And one of these stones through some whim of chance came curving down through the trees and stuck Hard Luck Harper just over the eye. He dropped like a log.

Steve, still feeling stunned, as if his brain had been numbed by the crash and the roar of the falling cliffs, knelt beside him. Hard Luck's eyes flickered open and he sat up.

"Kids," said he solemnly, "that was a terrible and awesome sight! I've seen a lot of hard things in my day and I ain't no Indian lover, but it got me to see a whole tribe of fighting men git wiped out that way. But I knowed as shore as they started racing down that gulch, it'd happen."

He glanced down idly at the stone which had struck him, started, stooped and took it up in his hand. Steve had turned to the girl, who, the reaction having set in, was sobbing weakly, her face hidden in her hands. The Texan put his arms about her hesitantly.

"Joan," said he, "you ain't never said nothin' and I ain't never said nothin', but I reckon it hasn't took words to show how I love you."

"Steve—" broke in Hard Luck excitedly.

"Shut up!" roared Steve, glaring at him. "Can't you see I'm busy?"

Hard Luck shrugged his shoulders and approached the great heap of broken stone and earth, from which loose shale was still spilling in a wide stream down the slight incline at the foot of the cliffs.

"Joan," went on Steve, "as I was sayin' when that old buzzard interrupted, I love you, and—and—and if you feel just a little that way towards me, let me take care of you!"

For answer she stretched out her arms to him.

"Joan, kid," he murmured, drawing her cheek down on his bosom and stroking her hair with an awkward, gentle hand, "reckon I can't offer you much. I'm just a wanderin' cowhand—"

"You ain't!" an arrogant voice broke in. Steve looked up to see Hard Luck standing over them. The old man held the stone which had knocked him down, while with the other hand he twirled his long drooping mustache. A strange air was evident about him—he seemed struggling to maintain an urbane and casual manner, yet he was apparently about to burst with pride and self-importance.

"You ain't no wanderin' cowboy," he repeated. "You'll never punch another cow as long as you live. Yore one fourth owner of the Sunset Lode Mine, the blamedest vein of ore ever discovered!"

The two stared at him.

"Gaze on this, yer dornick!" said Hard Luck. "Note the sparkles in it and the general appearance which sets it plumb apart from the ordinary rock! And now look yonder!"

He pointed dramatically at a portion of the cliff face which had been uncovered by the slide.

"Quartz!" he exulted. "The wildest, deepest quartz vein I ever seen! Gold you can mighta near work out with yore fingers, by golly! I done figured it out—after I wandered away and got found by them buffalo hunters, a slide come and covered the lode up. That's why I couldn't never find it again. Now this slide comes along, forty year later, and uncovers it, slick as you please!

"Very just and proper, too. Indians euchred me outa my mine the first time and now Indians has give it back to me. I guess I cancel the debt of that lifted ha'r.

"Now listen to me and don't talk back. One fourth of this mine belongs to me by right of discovery. One fourth goes to any relatives of Bill Hansen's which might be living. For the other two fourths, I'm makin' you two equal partners. How's that?"

Steve silently gripped the old man's hand, too full for speech. Hard Luck took the young Texan's arm and laid it about Joan's shoulders.

"Git to yore lovemakin' and don't interrupt a man what's tryin' to figure out how to spend a million!" said he loftily.

"Joan, girl," said Steve softly, "what are you cryin' about? It's easy to forget horrors when you're young. You're wealthy now, we're goin' to be married just as soon as we can—and the drums of Sunset Mountains will never beat again."

"I guess I'm just happy," she answered lifting her lips to his.

"He first come in the money, and he spent it just as free!
He always drank good liquor wherever he might be!"

Sang Hard Luck Harper from the depths of his satisfaction.

The Lost San Saba Mine

Under the grim San Saba hills
It sleeps the years away:
The gold that Don Miranda found
When unnamed woods and nameless ground
First heard the Spanish trumpets sound
Like doom on Judgment Day.

But waving plumes and flying flame
On shrieking winds were brought;
Over the hills war-bonnets streamed,
The lances flashed and the horses screamed;
On Lipan arms the bracelets gleamed
That Spanish hands had wrought.

Cordovan boot and tinkling spur
The hill-paths knew no more;
Till Bowie reeled before the flame
That put the bursting sun to shame,
When to the hidden cave he came,
And stood before the door.

A grimmer sun, a redder flame
In billowing death clouds rolled
On Bowie and the Alamo.
And from the north as sandstorms blow
Burst a feathered and painted foe
On the guardians of the gold.

Scalps with their braids in crimson dyed
Trailed from Comanche spears.
The hills forgot the Lipan tongue,
But not the songs the ancients sung,
And out of the hills the conquerors wrung
Spoils of the vanished years.

White men and red men, breast to breast,
In the birth throes of a state,
Blind in the gun smoke, slashed and thrust,
Screaming mad with the slaughter lust,
Grappled and died in the bloody dust,
With a frozen grin of hate.
The moccasin left a bloody track
From shore to mountain crest;
From roof and beam the red sparks rained;
But the plow bit deep and the oxen strained,
And the red war-bonnets dimmed and waned
Into the lurid West.

Like dim and ghostly caravan
Of painted shapes astride
Phantasmal mustangs, pass the years.
A crest of plumes each rider rears.
With sinking reins and drooping spears
The phantom horsemen ride.

Scant are the relics Time has left
To set men wondering.
A flint by careless boot heel spurned.
A skull by straining plow upturned.
A shattered kiln where once was burned
The ransom of a king.

And men forget the maddening lure
Which cast men's lives away;
Gaunt specters guard the gleaming tills,
The gold which seven caverns fills,
And under blue San Saba hills
It sleeps till Judgment Day.

John Ringold

There was a land of which he never spoke.
    A girl, perhaps, but no one knew her name,
    And few there were who knew from whence he came
For from his past he never raised the cloak.
No word he spake except to sneer or joke,
    Or, deep in drink, to curse men, life and Fate;
    Often his fierce black eyes, Hell-hot with hate,
Gleamed wolf-like through the shifting powder smoke.
His trail lay through saloon and gambling hall,
    Lone, sombre devil in a barren land.
    Perhaps, when drunk, he dreamed of mansions old,
    Ballrooms and women, proud and fair as gold —
Trail's-end, upon the strangest stage of all,
    The sun, a lone mesquite tree and the sand.

The Extermination of Yellow Donory

Fate works in a manner unreasonable and paradoxical; men are driven by desperation to plunge headlong into the depths they have spent their lives trying to avoid or escape. There is on record the suicide of a man who, rather than fight a duel in which he had an even chance of surviving, chose the certain path and shot himself the night before . . .

"All my life," wailed Joey Donory, "I been a scringin', scrawlin', whimperin' gutless *yellow coward!*"

He paused as if for response, but none was forthcoming. The wind sighed mournfully and monotonously outside his shack; except for this noise there was silence. Which is not surprizing considering that Joey was entirely alone. Nor was his aloneness surprising, for Joey was raving in his way, and he raved only in solitude. Never had he been known to express a deep emotion in public, or lift his voice with undue feeling. In the presence of strangers or unfriendly acquaintances he maintained a dumb and prayerful silence; even among his few friends he was not garrulous. And the reason thereof cut him to the marrow. Even now he raised his voice and spoke bitterly on the subject.

"Yah! I ain't even got the guts to *talk* back at 'em. They kick me around and make wisecracks and razz me till the world turns blue, an' never a come back I got. An it gets worse, the older I get, 'cause a grown man ain't 'sposed to take things like a kid does. Whata break I get!"

Maudlin tears gathered in his bleared and reddened eyes as he reached uncertainly for the ominously dark bottle which stood at his elbow. This he shook anxiously, showing some slight relief when a sensuous and throaty gurgle came from within. The relief was brief, however. He drank long and sadly, then began his rambling monologue again, which monologue was becoming rather incoherent.

Joey Donory was not an imposing man. He was young, but he did not look it, nor did his manner suggest it. He was short and wiry with a slight stoop, a long neck and a sun-wrinkled melancholy face set off by long drooping whiskers. Those whiskers were his solitary pride. All else was bitterness. Born and bred in an environment where most men were large and imposing, his lack of size was bad enough, but his handicaps were more than physical.

"An' it ain't so much me bein' that a way. Most of the real bad *hombres* wasn't so big. Lookit Billy the Kid; no bigger'n what I be. 'Tain't tallness an' 'tain't beef. It's what ya got in ya, an' I just ain't got it. Why'nt I? How'n thunder'd I know? Lackin' the necessary heft fur fist fightin' I oughter be a wildcat with knives and guns, but knives gimme the creeps an' the feel of a gat upsets my belly. I should oughta stayed on th' ole man's ranch up on the Sour Water Range where folks knowed me an' where I coulda kept outa their way.

"An' lookit me, too," his voice rose, embittered, for just as many lonely men do, Joey was in the habit of talking aloud to himself. "Look here at me, top hand and first-class miner, 'spite uh my size! How many these big hams can make that brag? How many fellers runnin' loose, cow punch' an miner too?

"An' kin I keep a job anywheres? Like 'ell I kin! Some big ham starts bullyraggin' me till I up and clear, or else I lose my nerve so bad and fall down on the work so bad, I get th' ole can. Me, what oughta be drawin' 's good wages 's any man in th' Copper Basin country. N' now what'm I goin' do? Broke—no way uh getting' any money—outa grub—an' that dam' Bull Groker riden me till th' worl' turns blue n' I can't even keep a job dishwashin' f' fear he'll come in n' poke me in th' jaw just to be comic. Wish I had th' guts to give 'm the works—'f I's a man, I'd shoot 'm s' fulla holes he'd look lika open windy.

"Today he slaps me on th' back s' hard I spill my liquor all over m' shirt front n' 'en, 'Haw! Haw!' he laughs. 'Haw! Haw! Haw!' th' big ham!"

Again the bottle for which Joey had spent his last dollar was tilted upward and Joey's mumbling profanity and self-pity merged with sounds indicative of liquid refreshments.

The bottle bumped on the table. Joey, prone though he was to exaggerate his troubles, a failing characteristic of those to whom life has been over rough, was really in desperate circumstances. He was, as he had said, broke, and though there were plenty of jobs for such as he, a barrier stood in the way. Any job he took would entail coming into daily contact with large, rough and ready men. He shuddered and became nauseated. Physical fear was more than a fault of his; it was a black incubus, a monstrous cancer, born in him and nurtured by fear and a realization and contempt of himself. And it was growing with the years. He knew unreasoning fear of arrogant men and bullies, and always among any gang of men, there is a bully—maybe a nasty-minded tyrant, maybe a blatant jackass who is at heart good-natured—but a bully just the same. From job to job had Joey flitted until he was broken—a mass of quivering nerves—about ready for the psychopathic ward.

"Never, in all m' fool life, have I did one blame thing which could possibly be called courageous! All m' life. When I was a kid, I didn't mind—never kept no job over four months—when they started ridin' me I started ridin' for new ranges. Good thing I learned up to bein' top hand on m' ole man's ranch 'fore I started driftin'. Minin', that come natural. I picked her up easy, workin' in short snatches. 'F I'd had eddication I'd a been uh minin' engineer. Used to when I'd quit uh job, I'd not worry—go get 'nother 'un. Stummick's turned on that. Los' what little nerve I ever did have."

Joey laid his head on his arms and wept. What seemed trivial to others is the pure essence of Hell to the sufferer, and the incubus of realized cowardice is the worst that haunts manhood. From that orgy of weakness and tears, Joey Donory rose with an iron resolve crystallizing in his liquor-muddled brain. He had reached the state in which even the most trivial discomforts loom monstrously and with deathly portent. And Joey's troubles were not trivial.

"Better t' be dead than t' be yellow!" he muttered, a light of almost feral desperation growing in his weak, reddened eyes. "F' thought it'd get better—but I've been thinkin' that fur twenty-five years an' it gets worse. T'morrow I won't have the nerve—got to decide tonight. Already decided—goin' kill m' fool self!"

He paused and looked around with a sort of dreary triumph, aware that he had made a statement dramatic and fraught with dire portent.

"Goin' kill m' self," he repeated. "Then they'll see!"

He felt suddenly invested with a deep, dark significance. Somberly, and with a brooding majesty slightly affected by a wabbling walk, he crossed the room and, after some uncertain fumbling, jerked open a drawer. A cold blue glitter of steel winked up at him. Joey Donory's soul shriveled within him. He covered his face with his hands and reeled away.

"Oh, m'Gawd," he groaned, tears of humiliation and helpless fury flooding his eyes. "I ain't even got th' guts ta bump m'self off!"

He raised his head, hopelessly. The night wind blew drearily, and faint on its whisper came the far-off blare of a tinny talking machine. The noise conjured up a mental picture of the Elite Saloon, that dive of iniquity where men talked loud, drank hard and died suddenly. Out of the depths of self-abasement and alcohol, an idea fantastic and paradoxical was born. Joey Donory turned cold at the mere conception of that idea, but he was past the borderline of desperation.

"They say Demon Darts hit town today," he whispered to himself, cold sweat beading his brow.

The merriment in the Elite was in full swing. Men reeled, shouted and swung the shrill-voiced ladies of the resort, but man or woman, drunk or sober, they were all careful to leave clear a generous space near the end of the bar. In the center of this forbidden spot, throned in somber regality and crowned with a brooding and sinister aloofness, stood Demon Darts in all his glory. Your true killer is ever the actor, the perfect showman.

This particular gunman was almost a legend in the Copper Basin country, though he had never before honored the locality with his presence. For that matter, he was almost traditional all over the West. Lurid and terrible were the tales of his deeds, and no one, looking at the great dark bulk of him, and at the sinister, lined face with the narrow cold merciless eyes glittering beneath the heavy black brows, could doubt that there was a large measure of truth in most of those tales.

All the local bad *hombres* were silent and subdued. Even—nay, and especially—Bull Groker, the burly miner who ruled supreme over the Copper Basin fighting men, had seen fit to make an early and unobtrusive exit. He breathed a frank sigh as the saloon doors swung shut behind him, guided by his careful hand; and at that moment a smaller figure heaved up suddenly in the gloom and a set of thin steely fingers clutched his arm with a nervous grip.

"Donory!" said Groker with disapproval, "ain't I tell you early in th' evenin' not to come foolin' 'round where they's men?"

"Is Demon Darts in there?" hissed Joey unheeding.

The unexpectedness of the question almost rendered Groker speechless and he could only find words as follows: "Uh, yeah, why, uh, yeah, he is, but whata *you* want—"

Joey had already pushed past him, and Groker, burned up with curiosity to know what the most arrant coward in the country wanted with the most notorious killer, followed him. Joey had not been in the Copper Basin many months, but even so he had endured enough at the hands of Bull to assure that worthy of the smaller man's lack of courage. Now he noted that Joey was white-faced and was shaking as if in the grip of a chill.

In an element rude and elemental, where human passions are frank and blatant, shocks and surprises may be expected. Jars unexpected and sudden had come to the hardened sinners who frequented the Elite, but it is safe to say that never were they so jolted out of their cynic callousness than that night. The unexpected frightens, and it was with a sudden icy chill of real horror that the drinkers, dancers and gamblers heard a sudden voice blatt: "*Demon Darts! He's th' shrinkin' vi'let I'm lookin' fur!*"

Dancing, drinking, gambling stopped as if the participants had all been struck dead. A cocktail shaker slipped from a nerveless hand and crashed on the floor like the crack of Doom. There in the doorway, with his arms still widespread, holding apart the swinging doors, and with his mouth still gaping from yelling those frightful words, stood Joey Donory.

Joey Donory had yelled at Demon Darts. Strong men held their breaths and waited for the skies to fall. The watchers blanched, fearful lest the insulted gunman include all present in the sweeping doom which must inevitably mow down the lunatic at the door.

As for Darts, he had jerked about at the sound of the voice, his hand shooting to the big black gun at his hip; but he had not drawn, and now he stood eyeing the intruder somberly. To the horrified watchers that stare was an assurance of sudden death in its most grisly form, but a close observer would have noted not a little amazement and bewilderment in the killer's icy eyes. Not in years had any man addressed Demon Darts thus. The not inconsiderable few who had called with the intention of giving him a one-way ticket to the next world had been either wary and subtle or blazing and passionate, but one and all had accorded him the respect due him. Yet here this shrimp—that made it more sinister. Darts did not know Joey. Had the maniac been a giant it would have been easier to understand, for notwithstanding the time-honored adage that Colonel Colt makes all men equal, few people really believe it, and still are prone to think that a blazing gun is more effective in the hand of a big powerful man than in the hand of, say, one of Joey's proportions.

Now Donory strode forward and the people gave back as if he were a leper. He saw all eyes were turned from him to the man who stood alone at the bar, and with a sinking feeling he knew it was the killer. The sight chilled him to the marrow, but he was wild with drink, with desperation engendered by a lifetime of humiliation, and to a lesser extent, by the dramatics of the moment. Even in this deadly hour he was aware of the intense stares and they went to his head. Always Joey Donory had craved to be the center of attraction. Now he was *it* with a vengeance, and as he had burned all his bridges, he would make the most of the moment.

He walked up to the silent and somber Darts and eyed him insolently.

"D-Demon Da-arts!" he sneered, unable to keep his voice from shaking a little or the cold sweat from beading his brow. "A Hell of gunman *you* are, you lousy tramp!"

A sudden and really painful gurgling gasp escaped the onlookers. Joey instinctively shut his eyes and waited for the end. But in a couple of seconds he realized that he was still alive and his eyes jerked open—wide. Darts had not even drawn; he was eyeing the smaller man with a strange expression growing in his eyes. Darts moved quickly but he did not think quickly. However, an idea was fermenting in his skull.

He spoke for the first time: "Ya tired uh livin', feller? Don't ya know I'm just as liable to plug ya as look at ya?"

The audience shivered in an ecstasy of anticipatory fright.

Joey was getting shaky. It was not courage but a sort of insanity that was keeping him up, and his knees began to rattle. He wanted to get this over with before he lost all his nerve and broke down. Of course, suicide was his object. Badgering Darts to make the gunman kill him. A quick ending ("They don't have time ta suffer when they stop my lead" the killer had boasted), a way out without using his own hand, courage for which he lacked—moreover the empty honor of leaving a certain glamour about his taking off, as the man who had baited the terrible Demon Darts. And now Darts seemed inclined to prolong the agony and Joey went wild. Maybe the Demon thought so little of him that he would not even waste powder on him!

"Go on!" he shouted, "shoot me, why don't ya?" He tore open his shirt and crowded forward almost against the staring gunman; his voice broke in a great sob which sounded like fury to the crowd.

"Ya always bragged yore victims didn't kick after ya pulled the trigger! Go on, if ya got the guts of a louse!"

"Listen here!" said Darts in a strange, strangled voice, "you got no call to be pickin' a fight with me. I ain't never even seen you before!"

The feeling was growing. This fellow was some terrible gunfighter, so terrible that even Demon Darts would be no match for him. Else how would he dare the Demon? He must know he had a cinch, to thus face Darts' empty hands and goad him to wrath. What was that cinch? Gunmen planted in the crowd? T.N.T. under the floor? Derringers up his sleeves and inhuman skill at using them? Cold sweat began to appear on the brow of Demon Darts. He was far from being a coward, but this was ghastly! This fellow knew he had him—Darts—in a triple cinch, somehow! There is nothing so numbing as the experience of a man who has for years been used to frightened respect, and is suddenly confronted with someone who not only seems to hold no fear of him, but to actually be contemptuous of him. The higher a man values his own prowess, the higher he is likely to value the untested prowess of a scornful foe. Most gunmen are high strung—human panthers—a panther is a terrible fighter, but the flutter of a girl's handkerchief will sometimes stampede him. Demon Darts began to shake like a leaf. His hand fell limply from his belt.

"Don't you go pickin' no fight wi' me," he said thickly and with some difficulty. "I got no quarrel wi' you. Less—less have a drink an' forget it."

Joey scarcely knew what the man was saying. All he knew was that this nightmare was being prolonged. He went temporarily crazy.

"You ain't nothin' but a big false alarm!" he screamed, seeking wildly for insults which would sting this man out of what Joey thought to be a contemptuous indifference. "You big tramp. I ain't even got a pocketknife and you got on two guns! Yore yellow! Yore a lousy, yellow, lowdown, thievin' coyote that ain't got the guts to drill a man only in the back—"

He stopped for breath, perceiving as though through a fog that Demon Darts, blue about the lips and ghastly as to eye, said nothing. Entirely distraught, Joey slapped his face with resounding force. At that, Darts ducked wildly and gave a strangled cry.

"Ya ain't goin' to force me into no one-sided slaughter-fight, ya cold-blooded murderer!" he screamed. "If ya kill me, ya gotta do it—*now!*"

And reeling like a man blind drunk, he crowded past Joey and ran blunderingly to the doors, plunging through them into the night—to be seen no more in the Copper Basin country.

Silence lay like a black pall over the Elite Saloon. Joey, dazed, entirely incapable of coherent thought, moved mechanically and without his conscious volition, toward the door. He could not yet realize what had happened. Men and women cowered back from him, horror mirrored in their eyes.

At the side of the door stood Bull Groker, and this worthy croaked hoarsely like a frog as Joey neared him. The dreary portent of the noise drew Joey's lackluster gaze and Groker made infantile and futile motions with his feet as though he would flee but could not. Then with a heroic effort he said, after several gagging false starts:

"M-m-m-mister D-D-Donory, b-be ya goin' to drill me?"

"Me?" said Joey in a mechanical but ghostly whisper. "Naw—I come here to see Demon Darts—it's him I wants."

"He's in Californy by this time," said Groker with a vast whimpering sigh of prayerful relief. "Mister Donory, I wanta thank ya for not havin' killed me. I know I been kinda offensive at times, but ya knowed it was just my friendly hearty way. I'll take care not to do it no more. Will ya not be sore at me, Mister Donory?"

"No!" whispered Joey, still in a daze.

"L-l-lemme shake yore hand, please sir, Mister Donory," gulped Groker, almost weeping with relief; he shook Joey's limp hand with awe, but his instincts were all for kissing it. Then he moved away to the bar, looking back over his shoulder and walking with stiff automaton-like steps. The other men in the place stood staring spellbound. As yet they were mostly incapable of thought.

As Joey opened the doors to depart, someone touched him respectfully on the shoulder. He turned to meet the admiring gaze of one of the wealthiest mine owners in the Copper Basin country.

"Mister Donory, I've been wanting to meet a man like you for a long time; a man all fire and steel, but of perfect control of himself! You're just the man to handle some big deals I'm planning. I've had a lot of trouble with the men lately, but under you, they'll be lambs. You'll pardon me if I say this was a big surprise. I should have known though, that you have too much self-control, that you're too big to fool with such small calibers as Bull Groker and the like. Like all real gunmen, you were just waiting for a fellow who was more on your level, weren't you?"

"Er-ya-ump—" gurgled Donory, staring wildly.

"Sure, you were. And Mr. Donory," the last in a low confidential voice, "don't think I'm intruding, but why do you have it in for Darts?"

"I ain't—I don't—" began Joey finding partially coherent speech.

"The true old type of Western gunfighter," said the mining magnate admiringly. "You fellows don't have to have a grudge—it's just to see who is the best man!" he slapped Joey rather timidly on the shoulder, evidently much awed at the new-risen celebrity. "You come around—No, *I'll* come around to your shack tomorrow and we'll talk business."

"Ahh-uh-ayeah—" garbled Joey. "Uh-uh –goo-goo-night—"

"Goodnight, Mister Donory!" came the respectful chorus from the entire crowd.

Donory drifted out into the darkness, walking like a man in a trance.

"Strange nuts, these real gunfighters," said the magnate to the wan and pallid crowd, "cold as ice—yet he was a flaming firebrand when he was calling Darts."

"Gimme a drink," said a cowboy suddenly. "By Judas, I kin hardly believe it yet. Say, fellers, this here is somethin' ya kin tell yore grandchillern. That ya saw Demon Darts take water an' back down—take a cussin' an' a rap in th' pan, an' *run* like a jackrabbit.

Bullieve me, it's *Mister* Donory from now on out with me! Who ya reckon he is, anyhow?"

"Lord knows—" "Tex Slade, maybe—" "Gotta string uh killin's nine mile long, I bet!—" "Anyway, Darts shore knowed him—" "Yeah, he plumb turned blue when Donory come in—" "An' who'da thought it, him being so mild like—" "Them mild ones is the real bad 'uns—" Thus the saloon buzzed with semi-hysterical conversation.

Back at his shack the situation was beginning to dawn on Joey.

"By golly!" yammered that hero wildly, "I plumb bluffed the liver outa Darts, not intendin' to, an' he took it on the lam!"

Joey was shaking as from an ague.

"Musta been clean outa my head! Thank th' Lord I'm still alive. And now, by golly, I got a reputation that I'll never have to defend an' which nobody'll question 'cause Darts is such a bloody devil. I went out to get exterminated—" a slow grin overspread his homely countenance which of late years had known few grins—"By golly, they was a killin' 'cause right there Yellow Donory was exterminated and in his place now is *Mister* Donory, with a man's job I kin keep at last, an' a man's rightful respect!"

Old Faro Bill

Old Faro Bill was a man of might
In the days when the West was young,
He drank a gallon of booze each night —
The toughest galoot unhung!
Oh, some men shrink at the sight of blood!
Bill roomed in a cougar's lair
And for tobacco he carried a cud
Of Mexican prickly pear!
Old Faro came of a wolfish breed,
When he was a suckling child
He laughed at the marijuana weed
For he said that it was too mild.
Old Faro he was a buffalo
When it came to rough-and-tumble,
He laid the toughest battlers low
With never a miss or fumble.
Some men stammer and halt and pause
At the sight of lover's moons,
But Faro married a hundred squaws,
And a couple of octaroons.

Modest Bill

Back in the summer of '69
'Way out west on the frontier line,
There was a guy who was a fightin' fool,
He could hit a blow like the kick of a mule,
He'd been a'fightin' all o' his life,
With fists or a gun or a club or a knife.
His name was Bill Bender, (fit name as you'll see)
And he was a bear-cat, a bear on a spree.
Six foot tall and lean and spare,
Quick as a cougar and strong as a bear,
He packed two guns and a Bowie knife,
An' he was forever seeking strife.
He'd jump in the air and let out a roar,
And wave his guns and stomp on the floor,
Twirl a rope and jump through the loop,
Twist his whiskers and snort and whoop,
"I'm a shootin', hootin', rootin', scootin' coot from Arkansaw,
"I'm quick as a cat, smart as a rat, and tough as a grizzly's claw!
"Whoopee! Whoopee! Yuh listen to me,
"And see what I got to say,
"I can lick any man in the whole darn land
"Both now or any day!
"I'm a hummin', zummin' terror with a knife
"Back away, guys, er I'll hev yer life!
"Never wuz a guy as quick on the draw
"Ever come out of Arkansaw!"

Ten guys piled on him one day,
When he was a-chantin' of his lay,
Shore they expected him to run,
But instead of his feet he used his gun.
When that was empty he used his knife
And when that broke he kept up the strife,
For he never did know when he was beat,
So he fought on with his fists and feet.
And when it was over they was all on the floor,
What hadn't gone out by the winder or door,
And Bender with torn and tattered clothes,
Was dancin' and yellin' among his foes.
"I'm a knifin', strifin', lifin', riflin' guy from Arkansaw
"And they ain't no man in the whole darn land
"Can beat me on the draw!
"I'm a whole blamed army by myself alone,
"I'm a straight hurricane and a twistin' cyclone!
"I can lick any guy from the Gulf to Powder River,
"Look a grizzly in the eye and make him shiver!
"I'm a river in flood and a avalanche,
"If nerve was money I'd own a ranch."

Out in the middle of the Utah plain,
The Mormons surrounded a wagon train.
Fifty Mormons and twenty white,
All they could do was put up a fight,
The Mormon was worse than the blame red-skin,
And it was a cinch they'd scoop 'em in,
Kill every man and steal every girl.
When out of the desert there came with a whirl,
A long-whiskered guy a whoopin' and braggin',
He jumped his horse right over a wagon.
Gave a yell like a hungry wolf,
"Come on, guys! We'll run 'em to the Gulf!"
Then the rifle flashed and the bullets hummed

And the pistols cracked and the slugs zummed.
And above the crackle and the roar of the shooting,
They could hear the voice of Bender hooting,
"I'm a ramblin', gamblin', shamblin', scramblin' guy from Arkansaw,
"The toughest, roughest gay galoot that ever broke the law!
"I'm a rarin', tearin' son uh strife,
"I cut my teeth on a Bowie knife!
"I'm tougher than any other man alive,
"I trim my beard with a .45!
"I comb my hair with a circle saw
"And pick my teeth with a grizzly's claw!
"I'm a bald he-eagle from a mountain peak
"Just yuh hark to the snappin' uh my beak!
"I hate all Mormons like I hate a snake,
"I can lick the whole tribe with a picket stake!
"I'm a panther and a bear and a long gray wolf
"And I'll chase these Mormons into the Gulf!"
Then the few Mormons that was left, they run,
And Bill said, "H — l, I never have no fun!"

The Wells Fargo stage was shooting down the line
Loaded with passengers and gold from the mine,
When down from the hills with yells and hoots,
Came a big war-party of red-skinned Utes.
They circle the stage at a flyin' run,
Slingin' arrows and bullets like fun.
There was a roar inside the stage,
And Bender jumped out in a regular rage,
Both of his gun's a blazin' of course,
He knocked a Ute over and straddled his horse.
Tore into them Utes with his guns a-crashing.
Whiskers flyin' and knife a-flashing.
He landed on the Utes like a eagle's swoop,
Yellin' louder than they could whoop:
"I'm a rarin', tearin', barin', scarin' guy from Arkansaw,

"If there's a guy that I can't lick, that guy I never saw.
"Never saw a tree I couldn't climb, never saw a river I couldn't swim.
"Never saw a horse I couldn't ride, never saw a trader I couldn't skin.
"I'm bad on all Injuns, worse on a Ute,
"For the whole darn tribe I don't give a hoot.
"I'm as hard and tough as a hick'ry nut's hull,
"I'm a rompin', stompin' buffalo bull!
"My horns are long and sharp and keen,
"My claws are strong and powerful mean!
"I'm the guy that can make a panther shiver,
"And I'll chase these Utes across the Platte River!"
Well, the folks still say that was some battle,
But the Utes broke at last and run like cattle,
And old Bill Bender wiped his knife,
"Never had sich fun in all muh life."

Bender was in a saloon one time,
Didn't have a dollar, not even a dime.
The guys they said, "He's never been on the floor,
"Never drunk enough that he couldn't drink more.
"Now, by golly, we'll all stand treat,
"And we'll drink Bill Bender off his feet."
So they bought whiskey and beer and rum,
Bill emptied the glasses fast as they come,
One by one, the guys fell on the floor,
But Bill stood up and shouted for more,
He drank ten glasses of whiskey straight,
Gulped down beer at a wonderful rate,
Of brandy he drank not less than a quart,
Tossed off a gallon of rum at a snort.
The price of licker began to mount,
At last the bartender, he lost count,
The others emptied their glasses as fast as he could fill
But, gosh, they couldn't keep up with Bill!
That Bill Bender was still on his shoes,

When the saloon ran out of booze.
And Bill was drunk, no doubt of that,
He couldn't hit the floor with his hat,
"I thank you kind, my friends," says he.

[. . .]

[Missing last page]

The Judgment of the Desert

Chapter .1.
"The left barrel—"

Somewhere a Mexican was singing to the drowsy accompaniment of a guitar. The sound came clearly to Stan Brannigan as he picked his way along the narrow, unpaved and unlighted street, and the unfamiliar words reminded him forcibly that he was a long way from home and in a foreign land, where no one either knew or cared that he was alive.

It was late; late even for this wild Border village where revelry and debauchery lasted until the stars began to pale, as a general rule. Most of the 'dobe houses along the one street were dark and silent, and only from one, a more pretentious frame building, light streamed and voices mingled with the click of roulette wheels. Stan paused a moment in front of the doors, which were closed, hesitated, then started on. As he did so, voices were raised in fierce altercation inside the saloon; there sounded a rush of feet and the sudden crack of a pistol.

Stan whirled as the doors crashed open; etched in the flood of lamplight from the bar, a figure reeled across the sill and pitched headlong out into the street. Stan sprang forward, knelt and lifted the man's head, noting that the victim was a white-bearded old man.

"Any way I can help you?"

The old man's breath was coming in terrible rattling gasps; his withered fingers gripped Stan's wrist like claws. He opened his mouth and a trickle of blood stained his beard.

"My hut—" he gasped, fighting hard for a moment's life. "—My—gun—the—left—barrel—"

The form went limp in Stan's arms, then stiffened. The young man eased the corpse to the earth and rose, mechanically cleansing his bloodstained hands. He was then aware that quite a crowd had gathered; they had evidently come out of the saloon, and now they stood back and whispered among themselves.

Standing above the dead man was a huge, powerfully built man, and to him Stan's gaze was drawn as by a magnet. This man was tall and broad, with broad stooping shoulders and gnarly arms, but it was his face which drew Stan's attention. If ever a face was stamped with evil and hate, it was this man's. His thick lips writhed in a snarl and from under heavy black brows, his eyes blazed, gleaming with a sort of magnetic savagery. Stan's gaze travelled down to the smoking pistol in the fellow's right hand.

"Dead?" the word was jerked out, more an assertion than a question.

"Yes," Stan nodded.

"Tried to hold up my joint," the other said slowly, his ferocious eyes glaring into Stan's as though in challenge. "I plugged him."

Stan made no reply, but from somewhere among the knot of Mexicans and white men who looked on, there came a short sardonic laugh. The head of the killer came up with a jerk and his eyes flamed with a new and sinister light as they roved vainly for the laughter. Then those eyes came back to Stan.

"He say anything before he croaked?" the killer asked harshly.

Stan hesitated. He could not have told just what instinct prompted him to lie, but under the burning intensity of those savage eyes, he felt somehow that the truth had better be withheld.

"No," he answered briefly. "He didn't say anything."

The killer scanned his face with an almost painful intensity, then grudgingly holstered his gun, and said a few abrupt words in Spanish. A couple of Mexicans lifted the body of the old man and carried it back into the saloon. Stan hesitated, and then turned away. He had not taken four steps when he was aware that he was being accompanied. His sudden companion was a man of medium height, wiry and incredibly broad shouldered and long armed. In the light which streamed from the open saloon door, Stan saw that he was clad in worn cowboy garb, with two guns hung low at his hips. His face was hard and brown as an Indian, his eyes narrow and piercing. Then the doors slammed and the man was only a shadowy figure at his side, indistinct in the pale starlight.

Stan, undecided, said nothing, and the pair strode along for awhile in silence; then—

"That old boy, pard," said the stranger softly, "shore got a rough deal."

"Yeah?" Stan's voice was noncommittal.

"Yeah, he did. He wasn't tryin' to hold up no joint. That fellow, Hansen, and him had a row; Hansen started for him, he started for the door, and Hansen shot him in the back."

Stan gave an involuntary exclamation of horror and anger.

"Easy!" whispered the other. "They may be somebody within hearin'."

"But how can a thing like that happen, with all those fellows lookin' on?" asked Stan angrily.

His companion laughed shortly. "You ain't in the U.S.A. now. You're in Old Mexico, and a particular tough part of Mexico at that. Right here in Sangre Del Diablo anything can happen—and quite often does. The old idee of 'might's right' goes over great here, and that fellow Hansen just now happens to be the might. He owns that saloon and is the real ruler of the whole village. As for the onlookers, the only onlooker a while ago in the saloon that wasn't Hansen's man, hand and heart, was me. What's your name and what you doin' across the Border?"

"In the first place," said Stan, nettled, "it ain't any of your business."

"Shore," the other returned amiably, "that's always understood. You say it's none uh my business and I agrees. Now, that bein' settled, who are you and what you doin' here?"

Stan laughed, half irritated, half amused.

"I haven't anything to hide," he said. "My name's Stan Brannigan and I've been punchin' cows across the line in Arizona. I come across the Border just to see what I could find, for fun and adventure, like, but so far I've found nothin' but chile con carne, tortillas and lukewarm beer."

"You ain't been goin' to the right joints—most of these fellows keeps ice for the beer—but as for findin' nothin'—Hell! You've busted right into the middle of the wildest and most dangerous adventure you ever heard of. My name is—er, that is, you can call me Spike. I'm Texas born, original, and I'm in Sangre Del Diablo on business. And that business concerns the old codger that just stopped Hansen's lead.

"Wait!" As they had walked, Spike had casually steered Stan toward the edge of the tiny village, and now they stood on the edge of the desert, dotted darkly in the starlight by cactus and a few straggling mesquites. Behind them loomed the black bulks of the 'dobe houses.

"Let's set down a minute," suggested Spike. "This is a lot better'n talkin' in a house where fellers can git behind doors and listen to yore secrets. Now, then, pard, me and you are due for a great break! Luck's flyin' our way, with all wings spread—but it all rests with you."

"What rests with me?"

"Whether the good luck keeps flyin' or settles on our shoulder."

"I don't get you at all," said Stan, bewildered. "What you mean?"

"It hinges," said Spike mysteriously, "on what old Sour Sanson said before he died, to you."

"Didn't you hear me tell Hansen he didn't say nothin'?"

"Be reasonable," said Spike imperturbably, lighting a cigarette. "You'd naturally lie to Hansen; somethin' about him what inspires falsehood in anybody. The average bird not only feels inclined to lie to Hansen instinctively, but also to steal from him, slander him—if it could be did—and poke him in the jaw. Hansen's that kind of a bird. Shootin' him oughta come under the head uh public improvements. But anyway, let's git down to facts. I don't know no more'n Hansen does, what old Sour said when he was dyin', but I do know that a feller like Sour will say somethin' before he dies, no matter how much lead he's got in him. With all the mystery that they was hangin' over him, it ain't right or decent to suppose that he kicked out without saying *nothin'*."

Stan remained silent.

"I'll give you the lowdown," said Spike, puffing at his cigarette, "and then it'll be up to you whether you talk or not.

"Back several years ago when old Pancho Villa was raisin' Cain in these parts, they was a very wealthy old Mexican which lived in Spain. This Mex had been run outa the country by the Federal government, but had managed to take mosta his private fortune along. He went into business in Spain, so I been told, and the more he thought about the deal he'd got, the worse it burned him up. He musta gone clean coo-koo. Anyway, he finally got together a terrible lot of money and sent it from Spain to Mexico. It was intended for Pancho Villa. 'Take this gold,' the old Mex wrote, 'and fight the Federals till Hades freezes,' or somethin' like that.

"But the gold never got to Villa—who coulda sure used it about that time. Some say his own men to whom it was delivered double-crossed him, some say a passel uh Yaquis hopped 'em and scuppered the lot; anyway, the gold disappeared and no man's ever seen or heard of it since, unless—"

"Unless what?"

"Unless it's old Sour Sanson! Now wait; this old galoot's a old-time prospector. Been roamin' the deserts uh Texas, Arizona, California and Mexico for gosh knows how long. Never made a real strike yet. But wait! A few weeks ago, old Sour blows into Sangre Del Diablo with gold—plenty of it. He says he's struck it back in the hills, but won't say where, not even when he's drunk. But it don't sound right, nor look right. The gold's all in one hunk, and a lot of fellers, who knows gold too, decides that it's been melted down. See? Right away they remember Villa's gold, lost or stolen somewhere in these parts. This is what Hansen and several others thinks, includin' me: that the gold was hid long ago and the hiders was killed and never come back to git it. Then old Sour stumbles onto the hidin' place, but is afeard to pack it all out at once. So he melts some of the coins down, see, and pretends it's virgin lode.

Heck—he couldn'ta got away with that with anybody—anybody could see the stuff had been melted.

"Hansen and his gang gits after the old boy and after tryin' kindness and coaxin' and gittin' him drunk—all of which fails—they git rough. Tonight Hansen grabs the old man and tries to *make* him talk, and you know what happened. Sanson broke away and run, but Hansen, crazy with rage, got him.

"I happened to be there—drifted up from Sonora a few days ago, havin' had wind uh this 'gold strike.' Now you know all I know. If you know any more, I'd be glad to hear from yuh. Yuh know, we'd make a fine pair to go after that gold—yuh couldn't hope to git it by yourself."

"Alright," said Stan thoughtfully, "I'll tell you—the old man said: 'My hut—my gun—the left barrel.' Maybe you can make somethin' out of that. I can't see no reason to it."

"Me neither," confessed Spike, "but we 'ull investigate. 'My hut.' That's old Sour's hut across on the other side of town. 'My gun.' He usually packs a queer old muzzle loadin' pistol, but he wasn't wearin' it tonight. 'The left barrel.' Maybe he's got the gold hid in a barrel uh flour! Let's go."

Chapter .2.
The Face at the Window

"Light that candle," said Spike. "Maybe Hansen set spies to foller you and maybe people might git suspicious if they see a dead man's hut all lit up. But the village as a whole is asleep and don't know old Sour's dead, and anyway we got to have a light to work by."

Stan complied, glancing curiously about him at the squalid 'dobe hut which had housed the murdered Sour Sanson. A bunk, a rude chair and table, an open fireplace, a pack saddle, and a few mining tools met his gaze. The candle guttered on the table and dripped hot tallow ceaselessly.

"Understand Hansen had the hut searched before now, while Sour was drunk," said Spike. "Anyhow, we 'ull do a better job. Tear it apart if necessary."

"What are you expectin' to find?"

"I dunno. But I bet my hand that Sour's last words referred to the gold, somehow."

Stan looked intently at his companion, taking in again the low hung gun, the quick nervous motions of the hands, and above all the cold steel intensity of the narrow eyes.

"Say, who are you anyhow?" Stan asked bluntly. "And what are you?"

"As for who I am," said Spike stolidly, bending down to examine the bunk, "one name's as good as another, South of the Border. As for what I am, I'm just only merely nothin' but a wanderin' cowpuncher, mild and peaceful, with the hankerin's and instincks of a prospector."

Stan stood idly in the center of the room while Spike prowled about, gouging into holes and breaking furniture. His eyes roaming about, centered on a belt hanging from a nail driven into the wall. From this belt hung a long black holster holding a pistol of antique and curious design.

The old prospector's last words in his mind, Stan crossed the room and lifted the gun from its scabbard. It was an old muzzle loader of European manufacture, ornately carved and scrolled as to stock, lock and barrel—Stan started, remembering. The gun was double-barreled, and the percussion cap was missing on the nipple of the left barrel.

He drew forth the tiny ramrod from its groove beneath the twin barrels, and turning the screw on the end, inserted it into the muzzle. He felt something which might or might not be a charge, twisted carefully, felt the screw catch, and withdrew the rod.

Transfixed by the screw was a wadded up piece of very thin leather. He unfolded it; drawn in faint red lines was a map of some sort, with words laboriously scrawled beneath.

"Spike!" he exclaimed, but Spike was already at his side, his eyes blazing.

"A map!" the other exclaimed. "A map where the gold's hid! I knowed it! And look! The old man writ it out plain—the Canon Los Infernos in the mountains of—"

Looking over Spike's shoulder, Stan cried out sharply and suddenly. Framed in the one window there was a face, swarthy and evil—a Mexican whose eyes gleamed with hate and avarice as he glared at the map in Spike's hand. Only for an instant did Stan see the face before it vanished—only the merest fraction of a second, but in that instant Spike whirled, drew and fired. It seemed he did it all in one motion, with a volcanic quickness which stunned and bewildered his companion.

While Stan still stood in amazement, Spike leaped to the door and slid through. Stan came to himself and leaped after him, but at the threshold he met Spike returning.

"Got away," snarled the Texan. "Missed him. Not far though." And he tossed a tall sombrero on the floor. Stan noted the hole in the crown.

"For a peaceful cowpuncher," said Stan slowly, "you sure unleathered your gun in a hurry. I just caught a glance of him as he ducked, yet you managed to draw and shoot at him so quick he didn't have time to get his hat out of the way."

"Oh, I been practisin' with guns a good deal," said Spike, a slight shadow of seeming annoyance crossing his dark features. "Forgit it; here's the map. It says plain that the gold's hid in Hell's Canyon up in the mountains south of here. The hardest part is before us. That Mex was bound to been one uh Hansen's men. We got to git outa here before the whole gang descends on us. They's miles uh bare desert, and a lot uh terrible rough mountains between here and the canyon we wants. Right now we 'ull beat it out to my camp at the edge uh town. 'Tain't so long till daylight and they's no time to sleep now. We gotta be away out on the desert by sunup. Come on."

"Still and all," persisted Stan as they left the hut, "that speed of yours is sure a revelation. Nobody could have done it no quicker, not even that famous border bad man, Mike O'Mara."

"Don't mention that bloody devil to me," snarled Spike. "Less git goin'."

Chapter .3.
Fruit of the Desert

The swiftly mounting sun blinded Stan Brannigan as its blazing rays beat back from the alkali sand. He hitched at his belt and cursed softly. He was inured to desert travel, but this beat any desert he had ever seen for heat and drought; besides, he was feeling the effect of last night's loss of sleep.

He glanced at Spike, slumped in his saddle and swaying easily with the motion of his plodding mount. A slouchy but effective rider Spike was. The heat beat down on Stan and he cursed himself for allowing a stranger to inveigle him into a wild goose chase. He fumed at the time they were making, though he realized that it would be suicide to attempt any faster pace, considering the distance they must traverse.

They had left the little village of Sangre Del Diablo just before the utter blackness which precedes dawn. Four horses made up their string—their mounts, one pack horse loaded with as much economy as was possible, and a spare mount. They had one pick, one shovel, their weapons, canteens, and a supply of food, which, with proper use, would last them until their return.

Now the sun was high in the heavens and Stan continually looked back, always expecting to sight the cloud of dust which would announce a band of pursuers.

"I ain't expectin' a fight yet," said Spike, as Stan spoke to him. "Hansen knows we got the map now, and if I'm any judge, he'd rather wait till we get the gold and then try to take it away from us. Anyway, I figure he'll let us lead him to the gold—if he can—before he looms on the scene. Still, he's got no idea which way we went. We sneaked out so cautious like, I don't think no one saw us. Maybe he can track us, and maybe he can't. This sand shifts pretty fast. Anyhow, I ain't worryin' about him till I see him—and maybe not then. Only one uh that gang that's really dangerous. That's Yaqui Slade; not a Injun, a bad white man. Real gunfighter. Hansen? Bah. Harder to whip than a buffalo in rough-and-tumble, but slow as mud with a gun."

"Then he ought to be easy for you," said Stan slowly.

Spike spat in the sand and did not reply. Stan gazed at the great bulk of mountains looming far away in the heat-laden sky. Heat waves shimmered between, making them seem vague and illusive. But even at that distance, Stan could tell that those craggy heights were barren and terrible. They seemed fraught with menace, brooding there like prehistoric monsters, evil things of another age.

"One mountain spring I know," said Spike, following his companion's gaze; "It's kind of a freak. You don't find much water in them hills. Right in the mouth uh Canon Los Infernos, too. Blame lucky and convenient for us."

A long silence followed, broken only by the creak of sweaty leather and the scruff of the horses' feet through the sand. Stan wiped the sweat from his brow. Spike slumped further into his saddle, swaying with such perfect rhythm in accord to his mount's motions that he seemed part of the animal.

They did not stop for a midday meal. The grip of the gold lust had its talons on Spike, and the spirit had entered Stan's blood to a certain extent.

"How much money did that old Mex send Villa?" asked Stan.

"A million dollars, they say."

"Applesauce. In gold? It'd take a train to carry that much gold."

"I ain't sayin' how it was packed," answered Spike. "But the story has it a million dollars. If we find it, we'ull pack out what we can and hide the rest in a different place."

The sun passed the zenith and slanted westward, but with scant abatement of the heat which curled the leather of the saddles.

"We been easy on the horses," said Spike, as the sun began to set, "but they got to rest and have a little water. We 'ull unsaddle 'em and wait till the moon sets. That ain't so terrible long, but long enough for 'em to rest and us to eat a little. Then we 'ull move on and rest again about daylight."

"Alright," Stan answered. Again a silence fell as the stars blinked out. The two men rode on through the pallid light of the young moon like phantoms—like the last men alive in a dead world. The sands glinted silver, shading into blackness. The cactus reared up like stunted giants, silent and brooding.

They halted, threw off packs and saddles, watered the horses from the canteens and sat down to eat, rest and smoke. They said little. Stan was weary and not inclined to conversation. His mind dallied with the thought of the treasure, but he was unable to become enthusiastic. It seemed too much like a dream, too unreal. Real life consisted, to Stan Brannigan, of hard, heart-breaking toil—riding through all kinds of weather, hot and cold, sweating in the dust and fury of the round up—branding, roping—he sighed. No, a million dollars in gold was too good to be true. He glanced at his companion.

Spike's eyes gleamed in the glow of his cigarette. He seemed darkly brooding, drawn apart from human fellowship. Something about him set him apart; even though he was friendly and jovial, Stan sensed that there was a barrier of reserve between them. Again the younger man wondered—who was this steely-eyed man who called himself Spike?

Stan yawned and stretched, humming to keep himself awake. An old Border ballad came to his lips:

> *"Mike O'Mara rode up from Sonora,*
> *Packin' a forty-five gun;*
> *He met a Texas ranger,*
> *And says, 'Good mornin' stranger,*
> *Yore work on earth is done."*

Spike made a fierce, passionate gesture, as if stung out of his calm.

"Can't ya lay off that bird?" His tone was vibrant with a strange passion. "What you wanta keep draggin' up the name uh—uh O'Mara?"

"Why," said Stan, puzzled, "anybody's likely to sing that song; it ain't been but a few years since O'Mara was raisin' Cain on the Border down around Tijuana, and further down in Sonora."

"Let him rest," said Spike harshly. "Mike O'Mara's dead and gone; he'll never come back. Forgit him. Let the world forgit him."

"What you got against him?" asked Stan curiously.

"That's neither here nor there. Lay down and git some sleep. I'll wake you when the moon sets."

"Ain't you sleepy?"

"Naw—git to sleep. As for O'Mara, I'll just say this, and I don't want to ever hear the swine mentioned again—he killed one man too many—the last man he shot down in cold blood. Git to sleep now."

Stan spread his blanket and dropped into a dreamless sleep, from which it seemed he was awakened in a few minutes by a hand on his shoulder.

"Le's git on the move," Spike was saying. "Moon's down and it's time we was travelin'."

A few minutes of fumbling at cinches and bridles and then they moved out across a darkened desert which pulsed blackly beneath the stars. Stan, rubbing the clinging sleep out of his eyes, stared ahead at the vague black bulk of the mountains. They seemed no nearer.

At the first tint of dawn they again halted for awhile, then moved on again. The sun was coming up over the desert like a red shield of flame. The sands throbbed crimson, like a shallow sea of blood, and through those red shadows, Stan saw a figure stumbling.

"Look, Spike!"

"I see him," rapped the other, quickening his mount's pace. "Some feller that's lost his bronc and got lost. Hey!"

Stan added his voice to Spike's stentorian shout, and at the sound the distant figure wavered about uncertainly, started toward them at a weak stumbling gait.

"A boy," said Spike, reaching for his canteen. "Just a kid—no, by Judas, it's a *girl!*"

Stan cried out; the slim figure had pitched headlong in the sand and lay still. They hastened forward, dismounted beside the still form. Stan lifted her gently in his arms and, tilting his canteen, let a thin stream of water trickle through the parched and blistered lips. Spike fanned the fainting girl with his hat, and presently she opened her eyes, stared wildly about her, then clutched at the canteen with the piteous cry of a famished animal.

"Easy, sister, easy," cautioned Stan gently. "Don't drink too fast; it ain't good for you."

The girl looked up at him uncertainly, and Stan squirmed uneasily from the glance of her deep large eyes. She was a slim little figure, dressed in a khaki shirt and riding breeches, and the slouch hat had fallen from her head, revealing a mass of unruly golden curls. Her eyes were a soft grey, shaded by long dark lashes, and though her full red lips were blistered and her delicate cheeks burned brown by the sun, Stan realized in a panic that this was the most beautiful girl he had ever met.

"Class, here," he thought dazedly. "Looks and blood, too. High class family, I betcha a nickel. What's she doin' wanderin' around here?"

"Let me have some more water, please," she begged, and Stan put the canteen to her lips, again cautioning her to drink slowly.

At last she sat up, replaced her hat and drew her hand dazedly across her brow.

"Where am I?" she asked like a lost child.

"In the desert between Sangre Del Diablo and the Infernos Mountains."

She shook her head wearily.

"That doesn't mean anything to me. I rode and rode and rode, till my horse gave out almost. Then when I dismounted to rest him, he got away from me. I've been wandering—all night, it seems."

"Lucky we found you when we did. A few hours of this sun would have about finished you. We 'ull take you back to—"

"Stan!" Spike broke in harshly, speaking for the first time; he was standing beside his horse and a black look was on his face—a worried, angry expression.

"Stan, we can't take her back! We got to go on!"

"But we can't leave her here, Spike!"

"She can go with us. Anyway—we can't go back till we've done what we started to do. I tell yuh, this is our only chance." His hands clinched hard.

"But Spike," began Stan uncertainly and somewhat angered.

"Oh, don't send me back!" The girl's cry was as sharp as a wounded bird's. "No, no!" She caught Stan's arm and clung desperately to him. "Take me with you—or leave me here where you found me—anything, but don't, please don't take me back! I'd rather die here!"

"Alright," Stan was rather appalled at the desperation in her tone and her face. "We got a long dangerous journey in front of us, but if you won't go back—it's a cinch you can't stay here."

"Get her on the spare bronc," Spike said shortly. "Let's git movin'. We got no time to waste. Hansen's on our track right now, like as not, and we can't fight his gang out in the open. We *got* to git in the mountains before they catch up with us."

Stan helped the girl on the horse, but his heart smote him as he thought of the perils which faced them, and to which she would necessarily be exposed if she accompanied them. But evidently from her manner a worse peril lay behind her, and letting her go seemed the only way out.

They took up their journey again in silence. Spike's manner had changed. His air of lazy good nature had dropped from him. Stan heard him curse beneath his breath as he glanced at the girl, and several times he shook his head, either in pity or anger.

As for the girl, she said nothing, neither asked their names nor, when Stan introduced himself and Spike, did she volunteer her own, except to say briefly: "You may call me Joan." She was evidently at the point of nervous collapse from fatigue and mental strain of some sort, but she bore up bravely and uttered no word of complaint, even when the increasing heat made her sway in her saddle. Stan watched and pitied her suffering from the depths of his heart, but he realized their desperate need of covering miles. There was no time to stop—and in this blazing wilderness, no refuge from the merciless sun if they should stop. Somehow the fearful day wore on, and as the sun rocked down the West, the first cactus-covered slopes of the foothills rose in front of them.

As darkness fell, Spike drew rein.

"Here we camp," he said harshly. "Horses had a hard day—we all got to be fresh when we tackle them mountains tomorrer. We 'ull rest here all night and start out early in the mornin'. I think we've got enough start on Hansen for that. Anyway, we 'ull keep a look out all night."

Stan realized that Spike, with his burning urge for the gold, would have gladly pushed on through the night, and he felt more warmly toward the strange man as he knew that it was because of the girl that Spike had decided to wait until morning.

Joan was so exhausted that she had to be lifted from her saddle, and she crumpled in Stan's arms in a state of collapse. He made a pillow for her with his blankets and bathed her forehead and face, using as much water for the purpose as he dared. Their canteens were getting low and they might not find the spring of which Spike had spoken. Joan submitted meekly and silently to his care, and Stan experienced a foolish protective glow in his bosom. He was glad to care for her, and he began to feel a tingling about his heart which, he decided with a sigh, must be the beginnings of this love stuff he had heard and read so much about.

They supped sparingly on water and the cooked food which they had brought along, not daring to light a fire lest the light betray them to possible pursuers. Afterward, the men smoked cigarettes and the girl sat in silence, watching the stars. Suddenly she spoke, and her voice was hard and bitter.

"I suppose you wonder why I ran away from somewhere?"

"Miss, it ain't any of our business," answered Stan.

"But I'll tell you," she cried with a swift passionate gesture. "I'm a member of a party of tourists who are camped back there across the border. There's a man there whom I hate—yesterday my father told me that I had to marry this man. My family were going to make me—you don't know my family. They've been making me do things

I didn't want to do, all my life. That night I saddled a horse and ran away. I rode straight across the Border, and kept riding.

"Oh, I know it was the act of a fool. I didn't stop to think. I *couldn't* think. I was nearly crazy. I knew if I stayed my family would force me into marrying him—and I hate him! I hate him!"

Stan did not doubt this statement. Her beautiful eyes blazed and her small hands clinched into tiny fists.

"I guess you think I'm a fool, and bad, too," she said savagely.

"I reckon we don't," said Stan, but she gave no heed.

"I'll never go back and marry a man I hate," she said slowly. "I don't know who you men are and I don't care. I don't know where you're going or what you intend to do about me. And I don't care. I've always done what the family wanted me to do—now the family can go to Hell!"

"You're workin' yourself into a unnecessary passion," said Stan calmly. "We're just a couple of hard-workin' decent cow punchers, and you're as safe with us as you'd be anywhere, as far as we're concerned. After we finish our job, we got to take you back to your family, but if I'm any judge of parents, they'll be so blame glad to get you back, they won't want you to do nothin' you don't want to do. Now you better git some sleep so as to be fresh in the mornin'."

Chapter .4.
Hell's Canyon

Sunrise found the wanderers toiling up the cactus-grown slopes that marked the lower reaches of the Infernos Mountains. As they mounted, the way grew rougher and more barren. The soil grew thinner, less sandy, even more arid, and the cactus thinned out. The sun beat back insufferably from the bare rocks which pulsed in the heat. Stan wondered if this illusive treasure were worth all this trouble, but the light in Spike's cold eyes grew in ferocious intensity. The horses suffered, and the humans suffered more. No word of complaint came from any of them, but even Spike snarled beneath his breath as the mounting sun hurled all his power upon their unprotected heads.

The higher they climbed, the wilder and more rugged grew the hills.

"The hills of Hell!" thought Stan dizzily—an appropriate name. Not men, but demons surely flung up this waste of waterless Purgatory, this range of burning soil and baked rock where even cactus would not grow. The Hills of Hell—again and again this phrase beat on Stan's brain, keeping time with the stumbling clink of the horses' hoofs.

Midafternoon found them riding through a terrific maze of plateaus and gorges, overshadowed by great black crags and over-hanging ledges. Here there was no breath of air and even in the shadow of the crags the heat was terrible.

"Spike," said Stan, "they better be a million in gold—after all we've went through."

Spike nodded shortly. He had scarcely spoken since the girl joined them, and Stan sensed that he bitterly resented her presence, though his attitude toward her was impersonally polite. If Joan felt this, she gave no sign of it.

At nightfall they pushed on through a nightmarish chaos of ghostly crags and distorted cliffs, which, silvered by the moon, took on goblin shapes and fantastic designs.

The moon had not yet set, but it hovered on the western rim when Spike drew rein at the broad mouth of a canyon and pointed.

"Here's Canon Los Infernos—and there's the spring."

"You're all wet," Stan was weary and skeptical. "There's no water in these hills."

"Yes, they is. I told you it was a freak. Right over yonder under them overhangin' rocks. It bubbles outa the earth right by the side of a boulder that yuh could build a hotel on. Just a small spring. But now we can drink all we want to."

They could and did. Even Spike, burning with impatience, realized the futility of a treasure hunt by starlight, and they ate, fed and watered the horses, and sank down beside the spring, thankful for the opportunity of rest and drink.

Stan lighted a cigarette and puffed with deep satisfaction.

"Nothin' to it," said he. "Takes a heap of discomfort to make a man appreciate a few hours of ease. And believe me, this country's plumb full of discomforts."

"I've seen worse," muttered Spike.

"Maybe I have too, but I don't remember where—how do you like the Border, Miss Joan?"

"I hate it," her eyes flashed in the gloom. "My only brother—the only one of my family who ever showed any consideration for me—died in one of these vile Border towns, years ago when I was just a child. Killed in a gambling hall in Tijuana."

"What was his name?" Spike's voice rasped the stillness.

"Tom Kirby; he was murdered by a desperado named Mike O'Mara."

Stan shot a swift glance at Spike. The man sat as if frozen; the cigarette had fallen from his lips, the color had drained from his face, and his hands clinched until the nails sank into the palms. Then, muttering something about seeing to the horses, he rose and lurched away into the gloom, moving like a drunken man. Stan shook his head in puzzlement. What connection was there between his strange friend and the desperado who, some years since, had blazed meteor-like along the wild Border, leaving a name that had become almost a myth, surrounded by bloody legends?

Suddenly Spike appeared again, looming up like a carven image, indistinct in the shadows.

"You all better git to sleep," he said. "I'll watch awhile, then wake yuh up, Stan, and we 'ull take time about. Miss Joan—I—uh—you—yore brother was the last man Mike O'Mara killed, and he regretted it all uh his life. It was right after that that O'Mara died, and he suffered plenty, if it'll help you to know that."

Then before the girl could speak, he had faded into the shadows again.

The night passed uneventfully. At dawn, Spike and Stan were poring over the map.

Stan read aloud the scrawling characters of old Sour Sanson: "This here is the map of the gold I found. Twenty paces from the boulder marked on the map, in the face of the cliff."

Spike bent over the faint tracery on the leather. "Here's the boulder he marked. Must be away up the canyon. Let's fill the canteens, saddle up and be gittin' along. When—or if—we find the mazuma we 'ull leave the canyon by another route; longer way, but more apt to dodge Hansen and his men. By golly, I can't understand why they ain't hove in sight. We musta slipped clean away from 'em. I hope so."

"I thought you was kinda honin' for a tussle with 'em."

"I was, till the girl joined us. That makes things different."

Stan nodded. Spike's attitude had changed strangely toward Joan. There was a gentle, almost tender note in his voice when he spoke to her, and he was careful to see that she got various small considerations, which before he had neglected.

The sun was high in the heavens when they reached the place marked on the dead prospector's map. It was a wild rugged region, boulder strewn and overhung by threatening crags.

"This here must be the boulder," said Spike, indicating a huge rock which rose not far from the face of the cliff that towered above the floor of the canyon. Stan felt his pulse quicken. Maybe there was something to the tale of the gold! Spike, on the other hand, seemed to have lost much of his fire. He was cold and calculating, and Stan felt that this change was largely a result of the girl—why, he could not say.

"Before we start huntin'," said Spike, "we 'ull let Miss Joan sit in the shadow of this rock where it's not so hot, while we climb that bluff there and take a look around. We can see a long way from there."

Joan sat patiently watching, while her two protectors struggled up the steep slope in the glare of the pitiless sun. Stan was sweat soaked and sun blinded long before they reached the top; his chest heaved with the exertion and his knees trembled, but Spike showed no particular distress.

"You must be made outa iron," said Stan, half in envy, half in irritation.

"I been livin' in this country a long time," Spike answered absently, drawing a pair of binoculars from a case.

"Look here; we're a long ways above the canyon wall proper, and most uh the crags; we can see clean back to the mouth of it where the spring is, and a lot further—say!" his body stiffened as he glared through the lens, then he handed them to Stan.

"Focus back beyond the canyon mouth some ways."

Stan gazed and presently he saw six tiny figures swim into view. He caught only a glimpse, then they vanished into a deep defile.

"Six men on horseback!"

"Yeah!" Spike rapped. "We gotta work fast. Hansen and his bullies, uh course. Blame good thing we clumb up here. They're away back there where the goin's terrible hard. I reckon they're trailin' us, but I believe we got time to git the gold—if it's there—and git out before they arrive. Take 'em hours to git here at the rate they're goin'."

They hastened down the slope recklessly, tearing clothing and risking broken bones. Saying nothing to Joan about what they had seen, they went to work.

"Twenty paces to the face of the cliff." Spike stepped them off and attacked the cliff with a kind of fierce savagery. A few blows of his pick and a crumbling of loose rocks revealed one large rock, apparently blocking some sort of an aperture. Stan stepped forward, but Spike shoved him away and, digging his fingers into the dirt beside the rock, gripped the edge and exerted all his terrific strength. The sweat flowed from his bronzed features, blood trickled from under his fingernails, but he still jerked and heaved. Then suddenly the stone gave way, precipitating him to the earth in a tiny avalanche of dirt and pebbles. Stan gave an exclamation. A small cave was revealed, and in this cave stood a rotting sack through whose crumbling sides bulged a stream of glinting gold!

Stan gaped in bewilderment. His brain reeled. After all, he had never really expected to find the treasure.

"Holy jumpin' Jerusalem!" he gasped, finding his voice. "It's true! Great Moses, Spike, it's true!"

Spike scrambled up, his eyes blazing.

"True!" he snorted. "You ack like you didn't believe! Git the slack outa yore jaw and bring me them saddlebags. We got no time to waste."

Joan had left her shade and was standing there, her eyes wide as she gazed upon the crumbling sack with its shimmering treasure.

"Spanish coins!" she exclaimed. "There must be thousands of dollars! Now I understand why you men came here!"

"Hustle with them bags," snarled Spike. "Yeah, this is why, Miss, and what's more, you're goin' to share in it. Naw, shut up; we ain't got time to talk."

"No million here by a long shot," said Stan as they scooped the coins into the bag.

"Lucky for us," rapped Spike. "We couldn't carry out a million in gold and we likely wouldn't want to leave it. No time to count it—but they's thousands of dollars here. We can pack it all by throwin' away everything but just what we need. I can walk, if necessary."

"Wonder how old Sour found it?" Stan was working fast and talking faster.

"No tellin'. Them old prospectors is always slammin' a pick into the cliff or somewhere. S'a cinch he took some uh the gold, and fixed the place back like it was. Come on, the bags is full. Throw away everything but the water and enough food for one meal. We gotta starve if necessary, but we gotta git out! By golly, with the gold and the girl too, we 'ull be lucky if we ever see the Border!"

Chapter .5.
The Coming of Hansen

Loose shale shifted and clinked beneath the hoofs of the horses. Stan gazed up at the narrow walls of the defile down which they were riding and strove to correlate his thoughts. Within the last two hours things had happened with such amazing quickness that he was almost dizzy. The sight of their pursuers, the finding of the gold—the flight. Above all, the gold! The sudden transition from poverty to wealth is enough to stun any man. Stan could scarcely believe, but the bulging saddlebags which swung on each side of the pack horse and at his own saddle were proof indisputable.

They were traversing a narrow gorge which led away from Hell's Canyon at right angles.

"Got only about a half hour start of Hansen now," Spike had said. "Chances are that our horses are fresher though, and our only chance is to dodge in and out among all these canyons and gorges, and try to lose 'em. They don't know the country like I do."

So they rode, and when Stan glanced at the trim little figure ahead of him, riding between himself and Spike, he felt a gnawing apprehension that drowned all thought of the gold. Hansen would stop at nothing, he knew. Still, Hansen had yet to catch them, and even if he did, the matter was not decided—though Stan realized that six to two was terrific odds.

They rode and the sun slanted westward. They had made so many turns and twists that Stan was already lost. He could not have retraced his steps to the canyon where they found the gold, without Spike's guidance, though he felt that he could, if necessary, find a way through the mountains to the desert.

"We gotta make all the time we can," said Spike, "so we 'ull have a good start when we hit the desert. On the straightaway run, that's when we 'ull catch Hell. Once Hansen sees us, he'll kill every horse they got to catch us. We can't kill our horses and we can't let him git in sight of us. So you see what we're up against. And, Stan," his voice dropped low and became a trifle diffident, "if I don't make it through, see that the kid gits my share, will yuh?"

"You mean Joan?"

"Yeah."

"Sure. But we 'ull make it alright."

"I dunno," muttered the Texan. "Somehow I feel like I'll never see the line; last night I dreamed about Tom Kirby."

"Joan's brother that got killed? Was he a friend of yours?"

"He musta been," Spike said with a bitterness that startled Stan, and the subject was dropped.

The sun sank westward, but still the heat waves shimmered and danced with mocking life.

"I been thinkin'," suddenly Stan began, "this money now, have we got any real right to it, Spike?"

"Why not?" Spike exclaimed passionately. "Ain't we gone through Hell to get it? It's ours by right uh discovery. The old Mex sent it to Villa; old Sour found it—Sour's dead and so is Villa, and none of 'em left any heirs, so far as I know. Likely the old Mex is dead, too. No, sir! This here money is ours!"

Stan subsided. The sun was beginning to set and they were riding through a broad, low-walled defile. Spike drew rein.

"We got to stop awhile. Another hour's ride will git us out onto the desert where we can't stop. This is risky, but the best chance we got. We ain't heard or seen a thing of Hansen. We got to rest and water the horses for the long pull tonight. We 'ull rest here awhile."

They unsaddled and placed the packs, saddlebags and saddles close to the canyon wall.

"I'll go back a ways and watch," said Spike. "I'll go back past that bend in the canyon; from there I can see 'em comin' a long way. If you hear shots, mount and ride!"

Stan cried out in protest. "And leave you there to fight Hansen by yourself? A great chance! If they heave in sight, you flag it back to camp, and we 'ull all take it on the run."

Spike merely nodded and strode away up the canyon.

"Who is he?" asked Joan curiously, as she stretched out on the blanket Stan spread for her, grateful for the chance to rest.

"You know as much as I do," answered Stan. "He's a fine fellow, but I don't know what his real name is."

Joan sighed in pure weariness. Stan's heart smote him as he looked at her, as if he were responsible for her exhaustion. Her pretty face was drawn and haggard, her skin dark and sunburned, her eyes burned darkly, as if they had sunk into their sockets.

"This has been a terrible trip for you, kid," he said gently. "And I'm afraid the worst ain't over yet."

"I'm not worrying," she answered. "It's not the suffering of the journey—I can stand that. It's what is waiting for me back north of the Border."

"Don't let that worry you," Stan said. "I dunno how old yuh are; you're mighty young but I know you're past eighteen. Nobody can make you marry somebody when you're of age, that way. And now you ain't dependent on nobody because you're wealthy, same as us."

"You don't mean you're going to share your gold with me?" she cried.

"Sure I do; ain't you gone through as much as we have? And didn't you hear Spike say you was to share equal? Sure."

To his utter horror, tears gathered in the deep grey eyes and her lip trembled.

"Oh, for gosh sakes!" he wailed contritely. "What I done now?"

"N-nothing," she gulped. "You're so good to me, I can't help crying. Since my brother Tom was killed, I haven't been used to much kindness. You two men have treated me just as if I were a queen; you've been so courteous and kind to me—I can't help crying because I'm happy."

Stan sighed in relief, though his bewilderment was not abated.

"Dames is sure queer critters," he thought. "They squall when they're sad and squall when they're glad. But this girl is a mighty nice little kid."

The sun was setting in a wallow of red behind the canyon wall. The last rays emblazoned the red clay bluffs and the barren rocks, lending illusion and enchantment. The cliffs seemed banded with bloody fire, and the deepening sky above was a great copper bowl.

"You know," said Stan, "I was just thinking—what a lucky chance it was we come on to you. If Spike and me hadn't been gold huntin' and if we hadn't found you right early in the mornin'—"

His full attention was fastened on his listener; simultaneously he heard a foot crunch in the shale, and the girl's eyes flared wide with terror. Stan whirled and came up with a bound, cursing himself for his negligence. As in a dream he saw, with one fleeting glance, the heavy bestial features of Hansen, the dark somber face of Slade— even as he turned, he drew and fired full at Hansen. But the man was slightly behind the others. A stocky fellow between them reeled and fell, and before Stan could pull the trigger again, Slade's pistol spat. Stan felt a terrible blow on the side of his head; there was a blinding blaze of fire, then the light went out and he knew no more.

Chapter .6.
"O'Mara Pays His Debts!"

Slowly Stan drifted back to life. His head throbbed unbearably and when he sought to lift his hands to his wound, he was unable to do so. He realized then that he was bound hand and foot, so closely that the circulation of his blood was almost cut off, and his limbs were numb. There was a great deal of dried blood on his head and face, but the wound seemed to have ceased bleeding.

A strange radiance leaped and flickered in front of him, and he saw that this was a campfire. About this fire sat several figures. He saw the huge bulk of Hansen, the lean, Indian-like figure of Yaqui Slade, La Costa, the Frenchman—all bad men whom he recognized from Spike's former descriptions. Then there was a Mexican and a tall man in riding clothes. This man was a stranger to Stan and evidently to the rest. There was an air of wealth about him; the manner of one to whom life has been good. He was handsome in an arrogant sort of way and, gazing at him, Stan hated him more than Hansen, somehow. Across from this man, white under tan and staring eyed, sat Joan Kirby.

She cried out when she saw Stan's eyes were open, and tried to rise to come to him, but Hansen reached out a restraining hand.

"No you don't, sister, you stay where you're at."

"But he needs attention," she begged. "He needs water—and you wouldn't let me bandage his wound, you beast!"

"You'll git nowhere callin' me names," said Hansen stolidly. "As for attention, he'll git that quicker'n he wants it, I reckon."

"Say listen," broke in Slade, "here's us sittin' around this fire like a passel uh fools with this bird's pard runnin' loose. What's to prevent him pickin' us off at a distance?"

"He ain't got no rifle. We're here in the angle uh the canyon wall and the only way he can get to us is to show hisself right in front of us. I hope he does do that. But he won't. I betcha that bird's on his way to the Border right now."

"I dunno," muttered Slade. "He looks like a bad *hombre* to me. Some place I've seen him, but I can't remember where."

"Keep an eye out for him, anyhow. And now," turning toward Stan, "maybe our little friend here would like to know how come us to git the drop on him—before he kicks out.

"I'll tell you, feller, and when I git through tellin', yuh'll see Bad Hansen ain't to be fooled with. My Mex come back on the run after your pard had shot at him and missed, and told me you birds had found a map in old Sour's hut.

"You stole a march on me, I admit. When I finally found where Spike had been camped, you was already a long time gone. But some Mexes had seen you leave, and they said you'd headed for the mountains. Knowin' old Sour had been up in the Hell Mountains before he come back with that gold, I put two and two together and we sot out after you.

"Alright. After coverin' considerable many miles, we run onto this feller," indicating the stranger, "Mr. Harmer. Lookin' for a runaway girl, he was."

Stan saw Joan shudder, and he cursed.

"You're the swine they was goin' to make her marry, huh? If I could get my hands free, I'd teach you to persecute a helpless girl, you—"

"No use ravin', Brannigan," said Hansen, with a grin. "I'd be glad to untie you just to see the fight, if I could afford to. But they's too much at stake. We got the gold now and I ain't goin' to risk it.

"Alright; Mr. Harmer's Mexican guide—this spig here—had found by the tracks that a girl had joined the party we was trackin'. So I give Mr. Harmer the lay uh the land and he agreed to throw in with us. We pushed our horses hard and made for Hell's Canyon. The Mex figured that you birds would head there first, no matter where else you was goin', because the only spring in these mountains is there.

"Maybe you thought we didn't know about the spring. We didn't, but the Mex did. We wasn't many hours behind you when you found the gold, and you hadn't more'n got outa sight when we rode up to where you found it. We didn't waste no time there. The Mex, he knows these hills better'n your pard knows 'em, and we ain't had no trouble at all in follerin' you. We been keepin' just behind you all the way, stayin' outa sight and lettin' you wear your broncs down. We figured it'd be better to let you pack the gold as far as possible 'cause the load is so hard on the horses.

"The Mex knew just about which way you'd take leavin' Hell's Canyon and gittin' outa the mountains, so we didn't have to stay in sight of you to keep track of you. Then we was watchin' when you stopped, with a high-power telescope from back yonder. We saw your pard go up to the bend uh the canyon to watch, and so we took a easier way around and come in from another side. Right down yonder a ways is a gorge comin' into this canyon that I bet even your pard don't know about. And you was so interested in the girl, you didn't hear us comin'.

"Oh, we've took you good and plenty all the way," Hansen concluded with a hard, satisfied laugh.

"Anyway," Stan snarled, "I settled one of you."

"Yep," agreed Hansen, "you shore wound Shorty's clock. But it saved my life, so I ain't kickin'. Somebody's always got to die in the gettin' of a treasure like this, and I'd rather it'd been Shorty than me.

"And a treasure that don't cost some lives ain't no good," he continued, more to himself than to his listeners. "This 'un's shore been baptized in blood. I don't know how many men got kilt in the gettin' and hidin' of it, but old Sour Sanson died for it, Shorty died for it, you're goin' to die for it, and yore pard, too, if he's got the guts to come and fight for it.

"A kind of a pity Slade's lead didn't kill you right off the bat. But he had to shoot over La Costa's shoulder, and shoot quick, so the bullet just grazed yore skull and knocked you out for a while. I ain't decided just how we 'ull finish you."

"Shoot and be damned," Stan snarled, though his flesh crawled. "You ain't got the guts to kill a man les'n you shoot him in the back."

"Hard words, Brannigan," said Hansen imperturbably. "But I understand how you feel. I'd like feel the same way if I was in yore place. But I don't hold no grudge. We got the gold and the girl—"

"I beg your pardon, Mr. Hansen," broke in Harmer with the crisp accent of the Easterner. "I have the girl."

"My mistake, Mr. Harmer," Hansen bowed politely, but Stan sensed a ponderous mockery in the man's courtesy.

"Eenough of theese talk," broke in the Frenchman, La Costa. "Let us devide the gold, like you said, Hansen."

"No hurry," said Hansen. "I'm kind of hopin' Spike will show up and git bumped off. And I'm inclined to rest. Ain't we done agreed to wait till mornin' to start back to Sangre Del Diablo? Then what's the hurry? We can divide the gold any time."

A silence fell. Hansen gazed into the fire, his huge hairy hands on his knees; there was a bestial light in his eyes. The keen eyes of Slade roved the shadows outside the circle of firelight. The Mexican shifted and muttered, uneasily. The glance of the Easterner, Harmer, roved between Hansen and the girl. As for Joan, she sat with her hands clasped, and never lifted her eyes except to look at Stan. Beneath her sun-browned skin, her face was white, and her eyes were filled with a horror which made Stan writhe. A wave of insane fury and desperation rose redly in his brain, and he strove vainly against his bonds. Where in God's name was Spike?

As if divining his thought, Hansen spoke:

"Guess yore pard feels plenty like a fool, Brannigan. While he was settin' there by the bend, we come down on you from the other way. We'd a gone after him, too, only we figured when he heered the shots, he'd come runnin'. But he didn't; too slick, I guess."

Another silence fell. The moon was obscured by clouds, a rare thing. The firelight made the further gloom seem deeper. Somewhere out there Spike was lurking; what did he mean to do? Had he deserted his friends? Stan dismissed the thought.

A tension was in the air. Stan knew that some sort of a climax was approaching; he read it in the fright of the girl, in the dark somberness of Slade's face, in the meaningful glances Hansen stole at Joan.

Harmer evidently sensed this also, for suddenly he rose abruptly.

"I think that Joan and I will move on," he said, and spoke to the Mexican.

Hansen shot a few terse words to the guide and he sank back again.

"No hurry," said Hansen, his gleaming eyes belying his lazy tone. "The girl's worn out; you'd be a fool to start this time of night."

"I'm beginning to think I'd be a fool to stay here," said Harmer bluntly. "There's no reason why we should continue in each other's company. We each have what we were looking for. I have the girl who is engaged to marry me; you have the gold. That's fair enough."

"Maybe, maybe," said Hansen. "I know yore a wealthy man, Harmer, and the money's nothin' to you. Alright," the giant seemed to tense, and his air of good nature fell from him, "you want the girl—*have you thought that maybe I want her too?*"

Harmer stood stock still for a moment as these words penetrated his consciousness; then, with an oath, he jerked open his coat and tore out a revolver.

And even as he did so, Hansen shot him—once through the head and twice through the body as he fell. The Easterner crumpled, spinning clear around as he toppled in a sort of staggering arc that carried him outside the circle of firelight. He never moved after he struck the earth. The thundering reverberations of the shots roared through the canyon, echoing and re-echoing. Joan cried in nauseated horror and covered her eyes.

"'Nother one marked up agin the gold," said Hansen with a brutal laugh. "Though yuh might say as how this bird died for a dame instead of money. Mighty cheap thing to die for, says I. I've killed men before over women, but I'd a sight rather git killed over gold than over a girl. There, there, kid, don't look so frightened; I know from the things you said to Harmer when we first caught you that you hadn't no love for him. I've saved you from marryin' him, and, after all, I'm the better man—you'll git used to me—or maybe it's Brannigan you love."

"It is!" she retorted, lifting her head defiantly.

"Say, listen," broke in Slade harshly. "Enough uh this stuff. We got to do somethin' about this feller Spike—"

Even as he spoke—as if his words had materialized the man—Spike stood before them. There had been no sound, or else no one had heard his stealthy approach. One moment there was no one there, the next instant Spike was crouching in the fire-lit shadows, both guns roaring death at the three men about the fire.

At the first crackle of the volley Hansen went to his knees, spurting blood but clawing for his gun; La Costa toppled over and lay without moving; Slade, hard hit, staggered, but even in that split second, drew and began firing pointblank, his shots mingling with the booming of Spike's guns. At that range neither of them could miss; Stan plainly heard the smack of the bullets. Spike's knees were buckling, his shirt front was a crimson stain. The gun slid from Slade's nerveless hand and he crumpled, dying on his feet.

Spike dropped an empty, smoking gun and groped blindly for the angle of the canyon wall, for support. Hansen, on his knees, had found his gun at last and now, gripping it with both hands, he shot Spike through the chest as Slade fell. Spike reeled, then leaning against the wall at his back, steadied himself and sent his last bullet through Hansen's brain.

A deathly silence followed the inferno of battle; a silence that stunned. Joan had fainted. Spike, dripping blood at every step, lurched over to where Stan lay bound; he moved slowly, uncertainly, like a man in a dream, and his breath came in rattling gasps.

He dropped to his knees beside Stan and cut him loose, then, as Stan worked his numb arms, Spike slipped to the earth and lay prostrate. Stan lifted his head.

"Spike, old boy," he almost sobbed, "are yuh hurt bad?"

"Shot all to pieces, Stan," the voice came almost in a whisper. "That Slade, I knowed he was bad; the others woulda been easy. I'd a come—before—but—I—wanted—to take—'em off guard. Slipped up—while—Hansen—was—killin'—Harmer.

"Joan—see—she—gits—my share. I'm glad—in a way—that this happened. I feel better—dyin'—now. I partly paid my debt—to her. Years ago—I killed her brother—Tom Kirby. I'm Mike O'Mara—the killer. Found after—Tom Kirby—died—I'd killed—an innocent man. Broke me—up. They thought—O'Mara wandered away—and died—in the desert. I didn't. I—changed—my name—left—that part of—the country. Kirby's face—haunted me. Couldn't stand—the thought—or the name—of Mike O'Mara. Glad I can—die—in some peace now. Tell 'em—O'Mara—always—paid—his—debts!—"

His laboring voice trailed away into silence. Stan felt the body go limp in his arms. He lifted his face to the stars which were blinking through the clouds.

"Gunman or not, Mike O'Mara," he said huskily, "you were a man! If your heart was black, your soul was white, and if you can hear me, up among them stars where you've gone, know, Mike O'Mara, that you've more'n made up for your sins."

The Sand-Hills' Crest

Here where the post-oaks crown the ridge,
   and the dreary sand drifts lie,
I'll sit in the tangle of chaparral till my enemy passes by —
Till the shotgun speaks beneath my hand to my
   enemy passing by.

(My grandfather came from Tennessee,
And a fine blue broadcloth coat wore he —
In a ragged, torn shirt I wait
For my enemy passing by.)

The drouth burned up the wheat I sowed,
   my gaunt scrub-cattle died,
Because the winter pasture failed,
   and the last branch-water dried.
The young corn withered where it stood in the field
   on the bare hill-side.

I had one horse to work my land —
   one horse, and he was lame;
I hid my still in the shinnery where no one ever came.
I hid it deep in the thickets; the corn was from my own bin,
The laws would never have found it, but my neighbor
   turned me in.
For an old spite I'd clean forgot, my neighbor turned me in.

(When my grandfather was a lad,
A hundred slaves his father had;

He clothed them better than I am clad.
They were sleek and fat and prime,
I've been hungry many a time.
They fed full, child, man and wife;
I've been hungry most of my life.)

I found a man to go my bond — he knows that I won't run;
I've never been forty miles from home;
   the drouth starved all my steers.
The sinking sun is shining on the barrel of my gun.
They'd try me in the county court and give me seven years.

Seven years behind the bars because they found my still;
He showed it to the snooping laws, the man I'm going to kill.
Then they'll give me Life or the Chair,
   according to the judge's will,
Death's not so damned hard to a man that's lived all his
   life on a post-oak hill.

(When my grandfather first came West
Was never a fence on the prairie's breast,
There was land to choose, and he chose the best,
But it slipped through his fingers, like the rest,
Driving his sons to the sand-hills' crest.)

The post-oaks stand up dull and brown against the tawny sky;
I hate them like I hate the man who'll soon be passing by;
At fifty feet I cannot miss, I'm going to watch him die.
Die like the dirty dog he is, where the drifted sand-beds lie.

Gunman's Debt

John Kirby suddenly straightened in his saddle, and his whole body went taut as he stared after the figure which had just vanished around the corner of a horse pen. There was a tantalizing familiarity about that figure, but his glimpse had been so brief he was unable to place it. He turned his glance away to the cluster of houses that marked San Juan, a huddle of raw-board houses breaking the monotony of the prairie. Crude, primitive in its newness, it was a smaller counterpart of other prairie towns he had seen. But the rails had not yet reached it, nor the trail herds that came up the long road men called the Chisholm.

Three saloons, one of which included a dance hall and another a gambling dive, stables, a jail, a store or so, a double row of unpainted board houses, a livery stable, corrals, that made up the village men now called San Juan.

Kirby turned into the stable. He was a hard-bodied man, somewhat above medium height, darkened by the sun and winds of many dim trails. The scabbard at his right hip hung low, and the butt that jutted from it was worn smooth from much handling. Something in the man's steely gaze set him apart from the general run of the cowboys who rode up the trail yearly in increasing hordes.

Kirby left his horse at the stable, and emerging, halted in response to a gesture from a thick-bodied man, dark faced, who wore a silver-plated star on his dingy shirt.

"I'm Bill Rogers, the marshal of San Juan," said he. "This is my deputy, Jackson," jerking a thumb at a nondescript-looking individual who accompanied him. "Just hit town?"

"Yeah; my name's Kirby; I was ridin' with a trail herd headin' for Ellsworth, and turned off this way, havin' business in San Juan."

"You'll have to hand over that gun to me," said Rogers, apologetically. "We got a law against wearin' guns in town. When you start to leave, come around to my office and I'll give it back to you. That's it, down there in the front part of the jail."

Kirby hesitated instinctively. It was no light matter to ask a man of his caliber to disarm himself. Then he shrugged his shoulders. This was not the Texas border country, where each clump of chaparral might conceal a feudist enemy. He had no enemies in Kansas, to the best of his knowledge. One man had come up the trail whom he would have to kill if he met, but that man was dead. Unbuckling his gun-belt, he handed it to the marshal. Rogers grunted what might have been thanks or an expression of relief, and hurried away, the scabbarded six-shooter swinging from his hand, trailed by his silent deputy.

Kirby felt his empty thigh curiously, aware of a strange unrest at the absence of the familiar weight there. Then with a shrug, he strode up the dusty street toward a saloon, in which a light had just sprung up against the gathering darkness. The town seemed quiet, in contrast with those towns which had already received the rails and become shipping centers for the Texas herds. Only a few figures passed along the street, vague in the deepening dusk.

Kirby entered the saloon, which was really a dance hall, provided with a bar. It was the biggest building in town, and really elaborate for a village of that size. It boasted two stories, the second floor being occupied by the girls who worked in the establishment. San Juan expected an eventual boom.

Voices rose in altercation from within: a feminine voice, strident with anger, holding a hint of hysteria, and a deeper voice, masculine, and slightly alcoholic.

"Aw, leave me alone, Joan. I told you I was through. Get away from me."

"You can't throw me down like this!" the voice broke in a sob that sounded more like rage than grief. "You can't! I won't—"

There was the sound of an open-handed blow, and a shriek.

"Now will you lemme 'lone?"

"You filthy breed!" the woman was screaming like a virago. "Throw me over and knock me around, will you? Damn you, Jack Corlan, you won't live to see the sun come up again!"

"Aw, shut up!" The swinging doors opened as Kirby reached a hand for them, and a lithe figure lurched through, brushing against the cowboy; a slender, darkly handsome youngster, whose aquiline features bore more than a suggestion of Indian blood. Beyond him, in the saloon, Kirby saw the woman, a supple, black-haired girl in the costume of the dancing halls. Abruptly she ceased her shrill tirade, turned and fled up the stair, sobbing. Kirby's eyes narrowed; not at the violence of the scene, but at the holstered gun he had noted swinging at the man's hip. Why had he not been disarmed, if the law required it?

The dance hall was empty, save for one bartender, and the slender figure mounting the stair. The night rush had not begun—if there ever was one in San Juan. Kirby leaned on the bar and ordered whiskey; the barkeep began polishing the bar with a cloth. He worked with a preoccupied air, but Kirby, who missed little of what went on about him, noted that the man was watching him sidewise, and was moving further away from him all the time, toward the other end of the bar.

Booted feet stamped on the threshold, and the door was flung open. Natural alertness made Kirby turn; and he froze, his whiskey glass half-lifted. A dozen steps away stood a big, black-bearded man, leering at him. This man stood on wide-braced legs, his thumbs hooked into his sagging belt, just above the jutting butts of his pistols.

"Jim Garfield!" Kirby hissed the name, in a voice so low as to be scarcely audible.

"Yeah, Jim Garfield!" jeered the bearded man, his whiskers bristling in a savage grin. "Your old friend! Ain'tcha glad to see me, Kirby?"

"I thought you was dead," growled Kirby. "Your old man said you were."

"That was the idee!" Garfield showed yellowed teeth as his grin broadened, grew more venomous. "I wanted you damned Kirbys to think that. I come up here on business that concerned you all, and I didn't want nothin' known about it. I thought you was trailin' me when Red Donaldson here brought me word you had rode into town; but I reckon it's just one of them there coincidences!" He guffawed loudly.

Kirby looked beyond him at a tall lean man whose cold eyes contrasted with his flaming mop of hair.

"So it was you I saw duck behind that corral. I thought I knew you."

"So we arranged a welcome committee," Garfield spread his legs wider and seemed to hug himself with glee. "Before we give you the keys to the city, though, I want to tell you why I come up here. See them boys there?" He indicated half a dozen men clustering behind him—men whose sinister profession was stamped on their features. "Them boys work for me now, Kirby. I've done hired 'em. They're ridin' back to Texas with me when I go, them and maybe a dozen more. When they get through with the Kirbys—" again he guffawed, but there was no mirth in the laughter, only a saw-edged threat.

Kirby said nothing, but he was white under his bronze. For a dozen years merciless feud had waged between the Kirbys and the Garfields, down there on the lower reaches of the Rio Grande. Ambushes in the brush had followed on the heels of terrible gun-battles in the streets of little border towns. The original reason for the feud was immaterial. At last the Kirbys had seemed to triumph. But now John Kirby stood face to face with a threat that bade fair to wipe his very name off the earth in blood. He knew the type of the men who stood behind Jim Garfield: barroom gladiators, two-gun men, cow-town killers, who slew for pay, and sold their guns to the highest bidder. It was these that Jim Garfield planned to loose on Kirby's unsuspecting kin. John Kirby felt suddenly sick, and his skin was beaded with cold sweat.

Garfield perceived this. "Hey, John, what you sweatin' about? Don't you like your licker?" He guffawed at his own humor, then suddenly went hard and grim as steel. "I got somethin' that'll fix it," he muttered, his eyes beginning to burn like coals of blue fire. He drew his gun and cocked it, and took deliberate aim at Kirby's breast. Behind him his henchmen likewise drew. Kirby stood frozen with fury, helplessness, and the horror of dying like a sheep. His hand twitched at his empty hip. Where in God's name was the marshal? Why had he, John Kirby, been disarmed, when every outlaw that rode up the trail was allowed to swagger through the streets armed to the teeth? In unnatural clarity he saw the whole scene: the booted figures, guns in hand, the dark faces leering at him, the girl at the head of the stair above, leaning over the railing, frozen with dreadful fascination. The one lamp that lighted the place hung just above her, and bathed her features in its light. All this John Kirby saw without exactly realizing that he saw it. His whole consciousness was focused on that burly, menacing figure that half-crouched before him, head bent down, squinting along the dull blue barrel.

"Just takin' toll now, John," mumbled Garfield. "You remember my brother Joe you killed in Zapata? You're goin' to meet him right away—"

Crash! The lamp splintered; Garfield, startled, yelped and fired blindly. Kirby heard the bullet smash into the bar close by. But he was already moving. Galvanized into frantic action, he raced down along the bar, wheeled and dived headfirst through a window, limned faintly in the blackness. Behind him guns banged wildly in the dark, men yelled, and the bull-like voice of Jim Garfield dominated the clamor, intolerable with bloodlust and primitive disappointment.

Scrambling up, Kirby ran around the corner of the building. Just as he did, he caromed into a dark figure which was emerging from a back door. He caught at it savagely, checked his grip as his fingers encountered flesh too soft for a man.

"Don't!" a voice gurgled. "It's only me—Joan!"

"Who the devil's Joan?" he demanded.

"Joan Laree!" There was haste and urgency in the tone. "I smashed the lamp—saved your life!"

"Oh, you're the girl that was on the stair!" muttered Kirby.

"Yes—but don't stop. Come on!"

She seized his hand and pulled him away from the building. He followed. He was bewildered, and a stranger in the town. She had aided him already; there was no reason to distrust her.

She led him out on the bald prairie that ran up the very back stoops of San Juan. Behind them the clamor increased as a light was lit. Doors crashed as vengeful men ran out into the street. Kirby cursed his lack of weapons beneath his breath. He was not used to flight. The girl panted, urged him to increased efforts. He saw her goal—a shack a short distance from any other house. They reached it, and she fumbled at the door, opened it, and beckoned him in. He stepped into the darkness and she followed and threw something—a cloak perhaps, over the one window. She pushed the door shut, which creaked on thick leather hinges. There was the scratch of a match, and her face was limned in its yellow glow as she lighted a coal oil lamp. Kirby gazed at her, fascinated. She reminded him of a young panther—slim, supple, youthful. Her black hair caught burnished glints in the lamplight. Her dark eyes glowed. She raked back her locks with a nervous hand as she faced him.

"Why did you do this? He demanded. "They'll skin you for breakin' that lamp."

"They weren't noticin' me," she answered scornfully. "They don't know I did it. Why did Jim Garfield want to kill you? Why did you come here?"

"I came here to see a friend of mine I heard was tendin' bar," he answered. "Bill Donnelly; know him?"

"I did know him," she answered. "He's dead."

"Somebody shoot him?" Kirby's grey eyes narrowed.

"No," she laughed hardly. "He shot himself—in the back. Quite a few men have committed suicide that way. Those that wouldn't take orders from Captain Blanton."

"Who's he?"

"He owns this town. Never mind. It isn't a good idea to talk about Blanton, even when nobody's listening. Sit down. Don't worry. Nobody'll think of you coming here. This is my shack. I sleep here when I get fed up with the racket at the Silver Boot."

"If I could get hold of a gun I wouldn't need to bother you," he muttered, seating himself on a rawhide bottomed chair.

"I'll get you a gun," she promised, seating herself on the opposite side of the rough-hewn table. She cupped her chin in her hands, rested her elbows on the table, and stared closely at him.

"There's a feud between you and Jim Garfield?"

"You heard what he said."

"I can't understand where Garfield got the money to hire all them gunmen," said Kirby.

She shook her head. "I don't know. He didn't seem to have any money when he blew in with Red Donaldson. I think he and Captain Blanton were old friends. They seem to be working in partnership. Those men are Blanton's men; he pays them, but Garfield has the use of them whenever he wants.

"Blanton has plenty of money, and he makes more. He owns all the saloons, dance halls and gambling joints in town. Garfield hasn't been here long. Blanton's a bad man to fool with. He deals in cattle, and he stakes buffalo hunters; he furnishes the supplies and goes in partnership with them.

"Rogers and Jackson are his tools; he told Rogers to disarm you so Garfield could murder you without any risk. Everybody packs guns in San Juan."

"He'd have killed you if it hadn't been for me."

He assented, but stirred restlessly; he had learned that such a remark from a woman generally preceded a demand for services of some kind.

"Would you do something for me?" she asked bluntly.

"Anything in reason," he answered warily.

"I want a man killed!"

His head snapped up angrily; just that blunt, naked statement, as if he were a hired gunman, a thug ready to do murder for a price.

"What man?" he asked, controlling his resentment.

"Jack Corlan. He passed you as you came into the Silver Boot. The dirty half-breed—" Her white hands clenched convulsively.

"Didn't look like he had that much Indian in him to me," said Kirby.

"Well, he's got Cheyenne blood, anyway," she said sullenly; "his father was white, and he's been raised white, but—well, that's got nothing to do with it. He's done me dirt. I was fool enough to think I loved him. He threw me over for another woman. Then he cursed me and hit me. You saw him hit me. I want you to kill him."

Revulsion swept over John Kirby and he rose, picking up his hat.

"I shore appreciate what all you've done for me, Miss," he drawled. "I wish I could do somethin' for you some time."

She sprang up, white.

"You mean you won't help me?"

"I mean I'll catch this fellow and beat him to a pulp," said Kirby. "But I'm not killin' a man that never harmed me, just because a jealous woman wants me to. I'm not that low."

"Low!" she sneered. "Who are you to talk of being low? I know you. I've heard of you. You're a gunman, a killer! You've killed half a dozen men in your life."

"I live in a land where men have to fight," he answered somberly. "If I wasn't quick with a gun, I wouldn't have lived to get grown. But I never killed a man that wasn't threatenin' my life, or the lives of my kin. If I saw you bein' threatened by a man, I'd blow his light out. But I don't consider that there's sufficient cause to kill the man you mentioned."

She was livid and shaking with fury; she gasped and panted.

"You fool! I'll tell Garfield where you're hiding!"

"Surely you didn't think I'd stay here?" he retorted. "I'm leavin'; I thank you for what you did tonight, and I aim to repay you some time, but in a decent way."

He turned away; and with a cry of ungovernable fury, she caught up a pistol from the table, threw it down with both hands. He whirled just in time to hear the crack of the shot, and to get the lead on the side of the head instead of the back. He did not feel the impact, but the light went out like the snuffing of a candle.

John Kirby regained consciousness slowly, but with perfect realization of where he was and what had occurred. The oil lamp still burned on the table. The shack was empty except for himself; the door stood open a crack. He gripped the table and reeled up, sick, weak and dizzy. He lifted a hand to his scalp, discovered a ragged tear. The bullet had grazed him. He cursed, holding on to the table. His head throbbed, and his movements had started the wound bleeding afresh. The heat of the oil lamp nauseated him. He reeled to the door, threw it open and passed out into the star-lighted night. Walking sent waves of agony through his bruised brain. He weaved around the corner of the house, blind and dizzy. Suddenly his stumbling feet met empty air and he plunged downward to strike the earth with sickening force.

The jolt brought the blood down his face in streams, but cleared his head. He shook himself and sat up, seeing more clearly. He realized that he had fallen into a ravine at the back of the house. That ravine, he believed, was the same one that meandered around one end of the town, skirting the back of the building which served as a jail. He started to pull himself up, then halted as voices reached him. Somebody was approaching the shack. He recognized a clear feminine voice.

"I tell you, I don't know how he got in my shack! He was there when I opened the door. He jumped for me, and I screamed and shot him. I lit the lamp and saw he was the fellow that was in the Silver Boot."

"Blast it, gal," that was Jim Garfield's plaint, "if you've robbed me of the pleasure of killin' John Kirby—"

"I don't know whether he's dead or not! I shot him in the head. He was still breathing when I left. I ran to the Silver Boot as fast as I could—"

"Alright, alright," that was a deeper, unfamiliar voice which carried a tone of command. "Here's the shack; get your guns ready; if he isn't dead he might be laying for us—here, McVey, open the door."

Almost instantly followed a yelp of animal disappointment.

"He ain't here!"

The deep voice broke in: "Joan, are you lying to us?"

Red Donaldson cut in: "You drop that tone, Captain Blanton. I don't like it. No, she ain't lyin'. See that blood on the floor? And there's the mark of bloody fingers on that table. He was here alright, but I reckon he come to and left."

Garfield broke into violent profanity.

"Well, we'll find him," assured Blanton. "Get out of here, you fellows, and scatter through town. He can't have gone far, if he's wounded. Go to the stable first, and see if his horse is still there. Joan, go with them; get back to the Silver Boot and tend to the customers. That's where you belong, anyway."

"Captain Blanton," it was Red Donaldson's voice, dangerously silky, "if I was you, I'd be more polite to a lady. Come on, Miss Laree, I'll see you back safe."

Boots clumped away, and Kirby, momentarily expecting a search of the ravine, heard Blanton, still in the shack, say: "Corlan, what are you doing here? I thought I told you fellows—"

"I don't care what you told them fools!" the voice rose with the petulancy of intoxication. "I ain't your dog to order around. I do more work than any of your men, and you treat me like a dog. I rode fifty miles between midnight last night and this noon, and you know what I did before I made that ride!"

"Shut up, you fool!" exclaimed Blanton.

"I won't shut up unless you give me some more money!" shouted Corlan. "I'm the only man that can do your dirty work in that direction, because any other man of yours would lose his scalp if he tried it! You can't treat me like you treat the rest! I want more money!"

"I'd have given you more if you'd asked for it with some decency," snapped Blanton. "But you can't bulldoze me, Corlan. Not another cent tonight."

"No?" mouthed the inebriated one. "Suppose I tell what I know? Oh, I ain't talkin' about Bill Donnelly. Everybody knows I killed him for you, and nobody cares. I'm talkin' about Grizzly Elkins. What do you think them buffalo hunters would do if—"

"You cursed fool!" There was fear, and bloodlust, too, in Blanton's voice, and then came the sound of a heavy blow, the stumbling fall of a heavy body. Corlan mouthed a shrieking curse: "I'll kill you!" Then there was the reverberating report of a .45. Kirby glared at the tiny square of light that was the window, wishing he could see through the solid walls.

Then came Blanton's voice: "You've killed him!"

"Well," it was Garfield speaking, "if I hadn't drilled him, he'd have got you. You know how them Indians and breeds is when they're drunk. Come on; leave him lay; we'll send some of the boys after him. Let's get out and look in that gully."

Electrified, Kirby began to grope his way along the winding bank. The floor of the ravine was narrow, but fairly even, and he made good time. Evidently Garfield and Blanton had halted to indulge in some other discussion or argument. He heard Blanton say: "Garfield, I don't like the idea of your taking so many of my men down into Texas to fight out your feud. We have too good a thing of it here."

"Well," answered Garfield, "I like your idee of rakin' in the trail herds and controllin' the buffalo hide trade, and all, but money ain't everything. We've went over that before."

"And another thing," grated Blanton; "that fellow Donaldson is too brash. I don't like him."

"Oh, he's stuck on the Laree gal," replied Garfield. "Red's a good sort."

"He'll be a dead man if he don't watch his step," ground Blanton. "I don't have to endure the insolence of your companions, just because I have to put up with your society—"

"You bet you have to put up with me!" exclaimed Garfield. "You needn't to be so high and mighty. I know you was with the Cullen Baker gang in Arkansas—"

"Shut up, curse you!" exclaimed Blanton.

"Well," said Garfield, "the Federal Government paid ten thousand dollars for Baker's body at Little Rock, in '69, and it's my understandin' that there's a equal sum on *your* head, provided they ever catch you. You're safe, after all these years, that is if somebody—

like me, for instance—don't bring up the matter to the government. Or if somethin' was to happen to me, my brother Bill's got a letter down in Texas I writ him, tellin' him what to do."

"You've got me in a cleft stick," muttered Blanton. "Say no more about it. You have no cause to complain; you'll be rich as I am, if you'll deal square with me." Then they left the shack.

Stumbling and groping along the ravine, Kirby suddenly realized that the building that loomed up against the stars was the jail. A light was burning there, and Kirby crawled out of the ravine, stole around the corner and looked in through the window. In the small room which was separated from the cells—now empty—by iron bars, and which served as marshal's office, the deputy Jackson was sprawled in a chair, reading what looked like a paperback novel. Kirby's eager gaze rested on a familiar object glinting dully on a table. His gun!

He slipped around the corner of the house, then crying out incoherently, he threw open the door and staggered in. Jackson bounced out of his chair like a jumping jack, a gun flashing into his hand. Then he gaped stupidly, evidently not recognizing Kirby; the cowboy's features were masked with half-dried blood, he was dusty and disheveled.

"What in hell—"

"I've been robbed!" gasped Kirby. "Somebody slugged me back of a saloon and robbed me—call the marshal—"

He reeled and fell against the table. Jackson glared at him, his six-shooter hanging limp.

"Robbed?" he mouthed. "Slugged? Who done it?"

"I dunno; I couldn't see him," mumbled Kirby, slumping further over the table.

"Well what do you want me to do?"

"I want you to drop that gun and reach high!" snapped Kirby coming up with his gun cocked in his hand. Jackson's mouth flew open; his pistol thumped on the floor; his hands went up like a puppet's on a string.

Kirby caught up a bunch of keys from the table.

"Into that cell! Hustle!"

"You can't do this!" mouthed Jackson, obeying with automaton-like steps. "I'm a law—you can't do this!"

Kirby grunted and snapped the lock. Jackson grabbed the bars and glared wildly through them; his, "You can't do this!" came faintly to Kirby's ears as he hurried out on the street.

The cowboy glided into the shadows of the houses. It was later than he had supposed. All lights were out in the dwellings; only the saloons were illuminated. Staying in the shadows, he approached the stable, when he heard the pounding of hoofs down the road. The rider came into sight, in the light streaming across the street from the saloons—a big man on a reeling horse. He pulled up before the Buffalo Horn, and fell, rather than descended from his saddle. He was surrounded by a crowd which streamed out of the bars. Excited voices rose in a babble, over which the stranger's voice dominated—a bull's bellow, gasping and panting.

"Plumb wiped out," Kirby heard him say. "Old Yeller Tail's braves—dunno hardly how I got clear—been ridin' and hidin' for a night and a day, and this night—gimme a drink, dammit!"

He was half-carried, half-guided into the bar; as he passed through the door, Kirby got a glimpse of him—a burly giant clad in buckskins; somebody addressed him as Elkins.

The cowboy turned away and hurried to the stable. His instinct caused him to glide around behind and peek through a knothole. Three men, with Winchesters across their knees, squatted in the stall where his horse was confined. They chewed tobacco, spat and conversed in low monotones.

"I don't believe that puncher's goin' to show up," quoth one. "I bet he's stole a horse and lit a shuck."

"Well, we stay here till mornin', anyhow," answered another. "Say, didn't Joan Laree carry on when she saw Jack Corlan?"

"Yeah," said the other, "she was plenty sweet on him. Doggone, that was a dirty trick—shootin' a man through the winder that way. He must have been aimin' at Garfield, don't you reckon?"

"Well," opined the first speaker, "he'll be aimin' for Glory at the end of a rope if the boys catch him. Bringin' his Texas feuds up here and killin' Jack Corlan just for nothin'. Dern him!"

"I liked Jack," said another. "He was all white, even if he did have Injun blood in him."

"Yes, he was!" snorted another in disgust. "You mutts make me sick; just because a man's croaked, you got to make him out a saint. Corlan was a yellow dog and you know it; he'd sell his soul for a drink to the highest bidder."

Voices rose in fresh squabbling as Kirby turned and moved silently away, bewildered. It became evident to him that Garfield and Blanton had accused *him* of Corlan's murder. After all, they were the only witnesses.

He stood, hesitant. They were taking no chances of his escaping. Doubtless every horse in town would be well guarded. And if he did not get away at once, it would be too late. When daylight came, they would find him, wherever he hid. The bare prairie offered no hiding place. If he started on foot, it would be suicide. And it was imperative that he ride south, to warn his kin of the impending doom. But was it? He was galvanized by a sudden realization. If Jim Garfield died, the gunmen would never ride south. Better that he finished Garfield here and now. If he died in the attempt—well, his was the fanatical clan spirit of the Scotch-Irish Southwesterner. He was willing to sacrifice his life for the good of his family, if need be.

He took half a dozen steps, then a dim form rose in the shadow. Instantly he covered it, his finger quivering on the trigger; then he saw it was a woman; dark eyes, reflecting the starlight, looked levelly at him.

"Joan Laree!" he hissed. "What are you doin' here?"

"I've been waiting here," she answered in a low voice. "I thought you would come for your horse. I wanted to tell you he was being guarded, but you came from the other end of the stables."

"But why—?" he was uneasy and suspicious.

"I wanted to thank you!" she whispered. "You—you killed him, after all!"

"No, I didn't!" he protested. "I—"

"Oh, they told me!" she exclaimed. "I saw him—and the broken window through which your bullet came. Garfield said you were aiming at him—but I don't care. I'm sorry I shot you. I owe you a debt."

"My God, this is awful," he shuddered slightly in revulsion. "What kind of a woman are you, anyhow? I tell you, though, I didn't—"

"Don't talk," she murmured. "We'll be overheard; men are looking for you everywhere. Come with me; trust me once more."

He hesitated, with a feeling of being caught in a web of fantasy and illusion. This part of it was like a dream; the rest, the violence of men, the trickery, the murder, he could understand; but this strange, beautiful, evil woman moved through the skeins of the pattern like a cryptic phantom, inscrutable, inexplicable. He realized that he was in her power; a scream would fetch a horde of armed men. He must trust her, or pretend to trust her; she spoke of a debt; perhaps she really sought to pay the grisly debt she seemed to consider she owed him. He looked at her as at a being more and yet less than human; he was repelled by her strange, bloody nature, yet drawn powerfully by her beauty. Like a rabbit hypnotized by a snake, he followed her.

There was a hint of dawn in the air. It was the darkness that precedes dawn. Not a light burned in San Juan. Even the saloons were dark. She led him behind the houses, and as they went, he was impelled to ask: "Who was that fellow who rode into town an hour or so ago, yellin'?"

"Grizzly Elkins, the buffalo hunter," she answered. "His outfit was one that Captain Blanton grub staked. They'd gotten a load of hides, and sent them on into San Juan with Blanton's drivers. The wagons got here yesterday morning. Elkins and his men stayed in camp to get another load; the wagons were to return with supplies, and get the other hides. But after the wagons left, a band of Comanches swooped down on the hunters and killed them all except Elkins. They couldn't kill him. He's a brute of a man. Here's the place."

She fumbled at a door, opened it, and stepped inside into total darkness. With her lips close to his ear, she whispered: "I'll hide you here until I can steal you a horse."

"Alright," he grunted. "A fast horse for a getaway—but I'm goin' to kill Jim Garfield before I leave here, whether I get away or not."

She led him across a room, groping in the dark, to another door.

"In here," she whispered. He entered, and she shut the door. He stood for a few moments in the dark, thinking she had entered with him. He spoke to her. There was no answer. Somewhere he heard an outside door close softly. In a panic he turned to the door. His hands slid over it, he thrust strongly against it. It was solid oak that might balk a bull; and it was bolted on the other side. There was no lock to blow off. Turning, he stumbled about the room, groping for other doors. He found neither doors nor windows. But he discovered one thing; the room was built of square-cut logs; the only log hut in San Juan; doubtless it had been at one time used for a jail. There was no bursting out of it. He was trapped. A wave of frantic fury swept over him. Trapped, after all the warnings he had had! Dawn begin to steal through the cracks between the logs.

He stood upright, in the middle of the floor, waiting. Nor did he have long to wait. A door was thrown up, boots stamped on the dirt floor, and voices he knew and hated boomed.

"In that room," said Joan, her voice cold and deadly as steel.

"You was mistook once tonight," rumbled Jim Garfield. "You sure he's in there?"

"Sure, he's in there." She lifted her voice and it was like the slash of a keen knife edge. "Open the door, Kirby! Here are friends of yours!"

The cowboy made no reply.

"What's this all about, anyway?" complained a bull-like voice that Kirby recognized as that of Grizzly Elkins.

"We have a criminal trapped in that room, Elkins," answered Blanton; "that is, if this girl isn't lying."

"I'm not lying," she answered. "He's in there. I led him here, telling him I was going to help him. He killed the man I loved."

And inside the silent room, John Kirby shook his head in bewilderment at the everlasting paradox that was woman; she had tried to kill him because he refused to kill the man who had jilted her; now she trapped him to his doom, because she thought he had killed that man. It was fantastic, impossible, yet it was the truth.

"Yes, he killed Jack Corlan," said Blanton. "Killed your friend, Bill Donnelly, too."

"He did?" It was a roar of wrath. "Why, the low-down hound! I'll go in and drag him out myself!"

"No, wait!" Blanton lifted his voice. "Kirby, are you coming out and surrender?"

Kirby made no reply.

"Aw, hell!" snorted McVey; "le's bust it down." He threw the bolt, hurled his shoulder against the door. Kirby shot at the sound. The heavy bullet splintered through the oak, and McVey cried out and fell heavily. An answering volley sent lead ripping through the panels, but Kirby was flattened out against the wall, out of range.

"Get back there, you dern fools!" bellowed Jim Garfield. "You don't know that *hombre* like I do. Aw, shut up!" This last to the groaning McVey; "man with no more sense'n what you got oughta be shot."

"Well, what are we goin' to do?" demanded another voice—that of Hopkins. "He can't get out without runnin' into our lead—but no more can we get in at him. Le's burn him out."

"No, you won't," exclaimed Blanton. "This cabin is my property, and it's too close to the saloons. Start a fire here and the whole town might go."

"Water, for God's sake, Captain, get me some water!" moaned McVey.

"Shut up," snarled Blanton; "we can't help you, laying right in front of that door; want to get us killed? Crawl out of range if you want help."

"I can't crawl!" sobbed McVey. "My back's broke. For God's sake, somebody, get me some water!"

"You don't need water," snapped Blanton. "Go ahead and die, can't you?"

"That ain't no way to talk to a dyin' man, Cap'n," protested Grizzly Elkins. He raised his voice: "Hey, Kirby, I'm goin' to haul McVey away from that door! I ain't got no gun, and I ain't makin' no move at you till I get McVey out of the way. If you want to shoot me through the door, shoot and be damned!"

With which defiance the burly buffalo hunter rolled forward on his moccasined feet, grasped the dying man and lugged him over by the wall. Kirby did not fire. Elkins laid McVey down, and drawing a whiskey flask from his pocket, put it to the man's lips.

"You're crazy, risking your life for a fool like that," sneered Blanton.

McVey's glazing eyes flamed with a brief fire and he hitched himself painfully on his elbow. "Fool?" he cried, his voice breaking in a sob of pain and hysteria. "That's the thanks a man gets for doin' your dirty work! You wouldn't give me a drink of water when I'm dyin'! You damn' bloodsucker, you take everything a man's got, and give him nothin'. I hope Kirby kills you, too, just like you killed Jack Corlan!"

"*What!*" It was a scream from Joan Laree. She sprang forward, caught the dying man in a frantic grasp. "What are you talking about? Kirby killed Jack Corlan!"

"He didn't, neither!" The gasp was growing fainter. "Corlan owed me money and was goin' to get it from Blanton and pay me; when Blanton sent us off, I sneaked back. I heered 'em arguing, and a shot. It came from inside the shack, not from the outside. Either Blanton or Garfield killed Corlan."

Blood welled from his lips, his head sank back. Joan Laree started up, a mad woman. She rushed at Blanton, beating frantically on his breast with her clenched fist, screaming: "You lied! You killed Jack! You killed him! You devil! You killed him!"

Garfield squirmed guiltily and said nothing. Blanton, face contorted with anger, caught her wrist and slung her away from him.

"Well, what of it?" he snarled. "What does it matter who sent the dirty breed to hell? What are you going to do about it?"

"I'll show you!" she screamed, whirling on the gaping Grizzly Elkins. "You want to know why Yellow Tail knew where to find your camp?" she shrieked.

"Shut up!" roared Blanton. "Don't listen to her, Elkins; she's mad as a hare!"

"I'm not!" she screamed, terrifying in her frenzy. "Corlan talked to me before he left San Juan the other day! He talked after he came back, yesterday. He'd been to the Cheyenne camp! He was a friend with old Yellow Tail, because he was kin to the chief, on the Indian side! He betrayed you, Elkins, and set the Indians on to you—"

"What?" roared the giant hunter, electrified.

"She lies!" screamed Blanton, livid.

"I don't lie!" she cried. "Blanton did this so he'd own all the hides you'd shipped into San Juan! They amount to a small fortune, and they're his if you were all blotted out! It's part of his plan—cows, hides, land—he means to steal all—"

There was a crashing report, a burst of flame and smoke. Joan staggered, catching at her breast. Blanton ran out of the door, the gun smoking in his hand. The girl slid to her knees, holding out one hand toward the petrified hunter in agonized appeal.

"Believe me!" she gasped. "Blanton betrayed you—had your friends murdered—"

She sank sidewise and lay still. And suddenly the buckskin-clad giant exploded into a deafening roar. His hand swept to his hip and up, with a broad glimmer of steel. Garfield yelped and fired point-blank, but the great body was in motion with a blur of quickness, induced by coiled steel muscles. Garfield missed as Elkins bounded into the air and the hunter's butcher knife was sheathed to the hilt in Hopkins' breast. Ashley plunged frantically away from the threat of that dripping blade, and caromed into Garfield, staggering him, and making his second bullet fly wild. And then a new factor entered the brawl.

The door flew open and framed in the opening stood John Kirby, his gun burning red. Ashley dropped; Sterling shot once, missed, and sank to his knees, shot through the belly and breast, vainly groping for his left-hand gun. Garfield yelled and fired, and Kirby's hat leaped from his head. The next instant Garfield howled as a bullet ripped along his ribs, and turning, fled from the cabin. As he went through the door, Elkins' knife, hurled with vengeful force, flashed by his head and sank deep into the log jamb. Spouting blood, Garfield ran across the street into the Silver Boot.

Kirby came out into the room, reloading his empty gun. The place was like a shambles. Elkins, snorting like a buffalo, blood trickling from a nicked ear, tugged his knife out of the wood, and turned to Kirby: "No use in us scrappin'. Come on; out this way!"

Kirby made no reply; chance had made allies of them, and it was useless to waste words. They ran out a side door, darted across the space that lay between the cabin and the next house. From across the street Winchesters cracked and bullets whined past. Then they reached the house and flung themselves inside. They were met by a frightened woman who sobbed: "Oh my God, what kind of goin's on is these: We'll all be murdered! Here I am, tryin' to run a respectable boardin' house—"

"You better pike it out the back door, Mizz Richards," boomed Elkins. "We got to use your house for a spell, and they's liable to be some lead floatin' around in the air. Gwan, beat it, before they start shootin' into here. I'll pay you for whatever damage is done."

A .45-90 slug, ripping its way through the thin wall, was more convincing than the buffalo hunter's eloquence. Mrs. Richards gave vent to shrill lamentations and scurried out the back door and across the prairie as if the Sioux were on her trail.

"This here's my room," grunted Elkins, kicking open a door; "here, grab this!" He thrust a Winchester repeater into Kirby's willing hands, and himself picked up a Sharpe .50—one of the single shot buffalo guns used by the hunters. "Now we'll fix 'em. These walls won't stop bullets, but neither'll theirs."

Crouching each at a separate window, the fighters gazed slit-eyed across the street. No one was in sight; the town might have been deserted; but every now and then, belying the thought, there sounded the vicious crack of a rifle, a wisp of smoke curled upward, and there was the splintering impact of lead on wood.

"Garfield's in the Silver Boot," muttered Kirby, squinting along the Winchester barrel. Don't know how many men there are in there with him. I just caught a glimpse of Blanton. He's in the Big Chief bar; seems to be just one gun speakin' there."

"Nobody in there but the bartender," said Elkins, "and I know him; he'd high tail it the minute the shootin' started." He pressed the trigger and the thundering crash of the heavy gun was answered by an angry yelp from the Silver Boot.

A puff of smoke jetted from a window in the Big Chief, and a bullet ploughed across the sill, showering Elkins with splinters. Kirby answered the shot, but without success. Blanton was alone in the saloon. Four rifles were cracking over in the Silver Boot, and feminine shrieks of protest from the second floor told that the dancing girls had awakened and were not enjoying the sport.

"Wish these walls was logs," grumbled Elkins. "Damn this high falutin' style of board houses. Wouldn't stop bird shot. Le's make a break back to the cabin."

"Wait!" exclaimed Kirby. "Who's that ridin' down the street? By God, it's Red Donaldson!"

He threw up his rifle and fired, and with the crack of the shot, the red-haired gunman shot from the saddle, and ran into the cabin. Kirby cursed.

Then there sounded a cry from inside the cabin so poignant that the gunfire stopped. Donaldson ran madly into the open, and something about him halted Kirby's finger.

"Who killed her?" Red was shrieking. "Joan Laree! She's shot! Who did it? Who did it?"

A disheveled head stuck out of an upstairs window of the Silver Boot, and the owner shrilled: "Blanton did it! I heard the shot and saw him run out with a gun in his hand, just before all the shooting started—"

She yelped and vanished as a bullet from the Big Chief smashed the window above her head.

Red Donaldson yelled bloodthirstily, whipped out his gun and charged recklessly across the street, eyes glaring. Even as he mounted the low porch in front of the saloon, a shotgun thundered inside and the blast knocked him down, to lie writhing in the dirt. At that Jim Garfield yelled vengefully.

"By God, Blanton!" he howled. "You can't kill my friends that way!"

As reckless as Donaldson had been, he charged out of the Silver Boot, shotgun in hand. He yelped in exultation as he got a view of his former companion through a window, dropped to one knee and threw the shotgun to his shoulder—and at that instant a six-shooter cracked in the doorway behind him and the bullet smashed between his shoulders. He bellowed like a wounded bull, his shotgun futilely blasting the air. He fell writhing, half-raised himself and sent the contents of the second barrel roaring through the doorway out of which he had just come. A howl told that some of the pellets were fleshed.

Kirby fired at the glimpse through a window, and a man crashed down heavily across the sill and lay there twitching. He missed Elkins, then saw him. The buffalo hunter, while the attention of the fighters was held by the killing of Garfield, had slipped out of the boarding house, run down the street, dashed recklessly across, and gained the back of the Silver Boot. Kirby got a glimpse of him, running, stooped, like a great bear, grotesque in his swiftness, a flaming mass of rubbish in his hands.

Soon smoke began to rise. Elkins yelled in primitive exultation, ran hither and yon, ducking the slugs, firing the buildings. First the girls, then the men ran from the Silver Boot. Kirby let them go. The fight was taken out of them. They forked their mustangs and headed out of town on the run. The Big Chief began to blaze, and Blanton charged out. Kirby fired and saw him stagger, but he came on, a shotgun in his hands. Elkins was before him, charging him recklessly with his knife. The shotgun went up, covered the hairy giant. Behind Blanton the tattered shape that was Red Donaldson moved, life still in it. A gun came up, wavered, exploded. Blanton staggered to the impact of the lead in his back, and his charge went wild. Elkins covered the distance between them in one long bound and drove his knife to the hilt in Blanton's breast.

San Juan was burning; smoke mounted in the morning sky; together Elkins and Kirby rode southward.

The Devil's Joker

The Sonora Kid hated snakes with an obsessional hatred that embraced all species, venomous or harmless. Big Bill Harrigan was a practical joker whose sense of humor sometimes ran away with his judgment. Otherwise he would never have played the joke he did on the Sonora Kid in the Antelope Saloon. He could not have realized the full extent of the Kid's fear and loathing for reptiles. At any rate, he approached the lean young cowpuncher, with a wink at the crowd, accosted him jovially—and tossed a chicken-snake over his arm. The Kid, at the sight and touch of that wriggling horror, recoiled with a frantic yell that set the crowd off in a thunder of riotous mirth. And the Kid went temporarily crazy. White and blazing with unreasoning, instinctive mad fury, he drew and shot Big Bill Harrigan in the belly. Big Bill's roar of laughter broke short in a grunt of agony and he crashed to the floor.

The general mirth was cut off just as suddenly. The Kid, almost as stunned by his action as were the rest, was the first to recover himself. His other gun flashed from its scabbard, and both muzzles trained on the numbed crowd, as the killer backed to the door, face white and eyes blazing.

"Keep back!" he snarled. "Don't move, none of you! Keep your hands up!"

"You can't get away with this, Kid!" it was Sheriff John Mac-Farlane, a tall, stalwart man, and utterly fearless. "It's cold-blooded murder, and you know it! Harrigan ain't even got a gun—"

"Shut up!" snarled the Kid. "Right or wrong, the noose ain't wove for me, yet. Don't none of you move, if you don't wanta get your guts blown out!"

"I'll get you!" raved MacFarlane. "I'll follow you clean to Hell—"

With a snarl, the Kid bounded through the door, out of the square of light and into the darkness by the hitching racks. So quickly he moved that he was in the saddle and wheeling his tall bay away, even as the first figures framed themselves in the doorway, baffled by the darkness, and wary of a shot from it. As the Kid whirled away, he crashed a volley into the earth among the hoofs of the horses at the rack that sent them plunging and screaming and breaking loose in frantic terror.

Shots spat red in the dark behind him as he fled, and the night crackled with shouts and curses as the vengeful men sought to catch and quell frantic steeds. By the time the first pursuers were spurring on the trail of the fugitive, the drum of his horse's hoofs had vanished in the night.

They did not catch the Sonora Kid that night, or the next, nor for the many days and nights that he kept the trail, putting much country between him and the memory and friends of Big Bill Harrigan. He knew John MacFarlane's threat had been no idle one. The sheriff had his own ideas of justice, and he had never failed to make good his promise to any man, lawbreaker or not. The Kid knew Mac-Farlane would follow him; would follow him across state lines, even into Mexico, if necessary. And the Kid did not want to meet him. He was not afraid of MacFarlane; young as the Kid was, his name was mentioned with respect in that wild hill country southwest of the Pecos, from which he had come to MacFarlane's country. But the Kid did not wish to kill the sheriff; he knew MacFarlane was a good man. He knew his own action had seemed the act of a cold-blooded murderer. MacFarlane had never objected to a fair fight. But this, the Kid admitted, had been murder. Harrigan had been wearing no gun; he had stood empty-handed and laughing when the Kid's .45 knocked him down. The Kid swore with sick regret and fury. He knew how he must appear in the sight of those who saw it. They could not understand that shock and fright of a fear that had haunted him since babyhood had made him momentarily loco. They would not—they could not—believe him if he said that he did not realize what he was doing when he shot jovial, good-natured Harrigan.

And because, rightly or wrongly, the Kid was human enough to desire not to decorate the end of a rope, he put days and nights of hard riding between him and the scene of the shooting.

It was not by chance that he rode into the camp of Black Jim Buckley, dusty and worn from sleeplessness and the grind of that long trek.

Buckley greeted him without any appearance of surprize.

"Glad to see you, Kid. I been wonderin' how long it'd be before you started ridin' outlaw trails. Man of your talents got no business herdin' cows for a dollar a day. We can use you."

Frank Reynolds and Dick Brill were with Buckley—veteran outlaws, gunfighters with an awesome list of dead, men hard and tough and dangerous as the mountain land that bred them. They readily welcomed the Kid on Buckley's say-so; there was no question of friendship or trust. They were a wolf pack, banded together for mutual protection, wary of each other as of the rest of the world. These men were untamed, not amenable to the rules governing the mass of humanity. While they lived, they lived hard, violently, ruthlessly taking what they wished; when they died it would be in their boots, with their guns blazing, no more asking quarter than they had given it.

"I knew the Kid on the Pecos," said Buckley easily. "Call him his regular name of Steve Allison back there. Never heard of him pullin' no rustlin' or stickup jobs, but he was almighty quick with his shootin' irons. You-all have heard of him."

His companions nodded without changing expression. The Kid's reputation was a dangerous thing to him, making it hard for him to live an ordinary life. Already famed as a gunfighter, with several killings behind him, the natural thing was for him to either turn law enforcer or law breaker. Circumstances had forced him into the latter course. It was impossible for a gunman to live the life of an ordinary cowhand.

"Got a job in mind down Rio Juan way," said Buckley. "Been kinda waitin', hopin' another good man would ride in. You couldn't come at a better time."

"Cattle or railroad?" demanded the Kid.

"Mine payroll. Hard for three men to work it. Need a man that ain't known so well. You was made for the part. Look here—"

On the hard earth, with the point of his stockman's knife, Buckley scratched a map, pointing out salient details as he unfolded his plan with a clarity and logic that showed why he was famed as the greatest of his profession. The three faces bent over his work, keen, alert, with an almost wolflike keenness that set them apart from other men. This keenness was no less apparent in the Kid's features than in the grimmer, more hardened faces of his companions.

"Tomorrow we ride down to meet Shorty and get the rest of the details," said Buckley. "You stay here and watch the cabin. Don't want nobody to get a peek at you till we spring the trick. Anybody see you with us, it'd spoil the whole deal."

After his companions had fallen asleep in their bunks, the Kid sat silent and immobile before the dying fire, his chin propped on his bronzed fist. He seemed to glimpse the implacable hand of Fate driving him inexorably on to a life of crime. All his killings except the last had seemed necessary to him; at least they had been in fair fights. But because of them he had moved on continually, always restless and turbulent, yet always avoiding the actual state of outlawry by narrow margins. Now this latest twist of Fate had plunged him into it, and in a paroxysm of reasonless rage against the whims of Chance, he determined to play out the hand Life had dealt him to its red finish. If he were destined to ride the outlaw trail, then he would be no half-hearted weakling, but would carry himself in such a way that men would remember him longer for his crimes than they had remembered him for an honorable life. It was with a sort of bitter satisfaction that the Kid at last sought his bunk.

At dawn, Buckley and the others rode away to their meeting with the mysterious Shorty—probably a treacherous employee of the mining company they intended looting. The Kid believed he knew why Buckley took both the others; the bandit chief was afraid to leave one of them alone with him. Reynolds and Brill were jealous of their lethal fame. The Kid was quick-tempered. Without the modifying presence of Buckley, a quarrel between Allison and either of the others was too likely a prospect to risk. Buckley wanted his full force for the job in hand. Afterwards—well, that was another matter. The Kid realized that sooner or later he would be drawn in a quarrel, to test his nerve, or because of some gunman's quick-triggered vanity.

Alone, the time dragged slowly. The Kid's restless nature abhorred idleness. His thoughts stung him. If he had any liquor he would have gotten blind drunk. He kept thinking of Big Bill Harrigan slumping to the floor. None of his other killings had ever worried him; but those men had died with their guns in their hands. Big Bill's belt had been empty. The Kid swore sickly and resumed his panther-like pacing of the cabin.

Toward sundown he heard the noise of approaching hoofs. Quick suspicion flashed across his mind, as he recognized it as the sound of a single horse. He went quickly to the leather-hinged door and threw it open, just in time to see a tall horseman on a tired black stallion ride into the clearing. It was Sheriff John MacFarlane.

At the sight, all other emotions were swept from the Kid's brain by a surge of red fury, the rage of a cornered thing.

"So you've hunted me down, you damned bloodhound!" he yelled, seeing red.

"Wait, Kid—" shouted MacFarlane, then reading the unreasoning killer's lust in the Kid's glaring eyes, he snatched at his gun. Even as it cleared the leather, the Kid's .45 roared. MacFarlane's hat flew from his head and he pitched from the saddle and lay still in an oozing pool of blood, and his horse reared and bolted.

The Kid came forward, cursing, his pistol smoking in his hand. He kicked the prostrate form in a paroxysm of resentment, then bent closer to examine his enemy. MacFarlane was still living. The Kid discovered that his bullet had ploughed through the Sheriff's scalp, instead of going through the skull. He could not tell if the skull were fractured. He stood above the senseless man, an image of bewilderment.

If he had killed his enemy, the matter would have been at an end. But he could not put his muzzle to the senseless man's head and finish him. The Kid did not reach this conclusion by any elaborate method of reasoning on morals and ethics. It was a part of him, just as his blinding speed with a gun was part of him. He could not murder in cold blood like that; nor could he leave the man there to die without attention.

At last, swearing heartily, he lifted the limp form and lugged it into the cabin. MacFarlane was taller and heavier than the wiry Kid, but the task was accomplished, and the sheriff laid on a bunk in the back room of the cabin. The Kid set to work cleansing and dressing the wound, with skill acquired in many such tasks. MacFarlane began to show some signs of returning consciousness, and the bandaging was just about completed when the Kid heard horses outside, and the sound of familiar voices. Recognizing them, he did not leave his work, and had just completed the bandages when Buckley stalked in, followed by his companions. They halted short at the sight of the man in the bunk.

"What the hell, Kid," said Buckley softly. "What's the deal?"

"Fellow followed me from the Antelope," Allison answered briefly. "Said he would. Reckon he came alone. I creased him."

"Reckon that's middlin' pore shootin', Kid," murmured Frank Reynolds.

The Kid took no notice of the remark. MacFarlane groaned and stirred, and Buckley leaned forward to peer into the wounded man's face.

"Well, I'll be damned," he murmured. "This here's a visitor I shore never expected to receive like this. Reckon you know who this is, Kid?"

"Reckon I do," returned the other.

"Then why'n Hell are you so polite with him?" demanded Brill. "If you know him, why didn't you put another bullet in him, and finish him?"

Icy lights flickered in the Kid's steely grey eyes.

"Reckon that's my business, Brill," he returned slowly. No need to try to tell them that he couldn't leave even a wounded enemy to die; needless as to tell the crowd in the Antelope that the touch of a fangless snake could drive a man momentarily loco.

"Drop it boys," requested Buckley. "No use in wranglin' amongst ourselves. The Kid done a good job when he dropped this coyote. Everybody makes a mistake now and then. I savvy how you feel, Kid. You ain't been in the business long enough to realize that a fellow like this is just pizen to us, and don't deserve mercy no more'n a copperhead snake. You reckon this sheriff would tend to you and bandage you up after he shot you, les'n it was to save you for the gallows or the pen?"

"Don't make no difference whether he would or not, Buckley," the Kid answered. "That ain't the point at all. If I'd killed him the first crack, it'd been alright. But I wouldn't let an egg-suckin' hound lay and die without doin' somethin' for him."

"That's alright, Kid," answered Buckley soothingly. "You don't have to. You done what you felt like was your duty. Now you just leave the rest to me. You don't even have to watch, if you don't wanta. Just go out and turn our hosses into the corral, and when you get back, everthing'll be o.k."

The Kid scowled.

"What you mean, Buckley?"

"Why, Hell!" broke in Dick Brill. "Are you so damned innocent, Kid? This here's John MacFarlane; you think we're goin' to let him live?"

"You mean you're goin' to murder him?" ejaculated the Kid, aghast.

"That's a hard way of puttin' it, Kid," protested Buckley. "We just aim to see that he don't get in our way no more. I got my personal reasons, outside of the matter of ordinary precautions of safety."

"He's comin' to," said Reynolds.

The Kid turned to see the sheriff's eyes flicker open. They were dazed. He muttered incoherently. The Kid bent and put a canteen of water to his lips. The wounded man drank mechanically.

"Kid," said Buckley, "come out into the cabin and we'll get all this straight."

The Kid was the last to leave the back room. He closed the door after him.

"What you figgerin' on doin' with this rat, Kid?" asked Buckley.

"Why, tend to him till he's dead or well," answered Allison.

Brill swore beneath his breath. Buckley shook his head.

"Are you crazy, Kid? We got to dust outa here pronto. Everything's set down at Rio Juan. We won't be ridin' back this way."

"Then you'll ride without me," the Kid answered doggedly.

"You mean you'll throw us over, pass up the job?" Buckley's voice was soft. "You mean you'll let us down, for this bloodhound that's been trailin' you?"

"I mean I ain't no murderer!" exclaimed the goaded Kid. "I can't kill a man after I've knocked him out. I can't leave him to die. I can't let him be murdered. Any of them things would be just like blowin' his brains out after I shot him down. I got no love for this *hombre*. But it ain't a matter of like or dislike."

"This fellow killed my brother," Buckley's voice was softer yet, but red lights were beginning to glimmer in his eyes.

"And you can look him up and kill him after he gets on his feet. It ain't nothin' to me. But you ain't massacrein' him like a sheep."

"Kid," breathed Buckley, "you've showed your hand; now I'm showin' mine. You can't let us down and get away with it. This coyote of the law don't leave this shack alive. Take or leave it; if you leave it, you got to say your say with gun smoke."

There was an instant of tense silence, like a tick of Eternity in which Time seemed to stand still, and the night held its breath. In that brief space the Kid knew that he faced his supreme test. He saw the faces of his former companions, frozen into hard masks, in which their eyes burned with a wolfish light. Like a flicker of lightning his hand snapped to his gun.

Buckley moved with equal speed. Their guns crashed together. The Kid reeled back against the wall, his six-shooter falling from his numb fingers. Buckley dropped, the whole top of his head torn off. On the heels of the double report came the thunder of the guns of Brill and Reynolds. Even as he reeled, the Kid's left-hand gun was spurting smoke and flame. He rocked and jerked to the impact of lead, but he kept his feet. Reynolds was down, shot through the neck and belly. Brill, roaring like a bull and spouting blood, charged with a staggering rush, shooting as he came. He tripped over Buckley's prostrate form, and as he fell, the Kid shot him straight through the heart.

The silence that followed the brief deadly thunder was appalling. The Kid lurched away from the wall. The cabin with its staring dead men and shreds of drifting smoke swam before his blurred sight. His whole right side seemed dead, and his left leg refused to balance his weight. Suddenly the floor seemed to rush up and strike him heavily. In the confused mist which engulfed him, he seemed to hear John MacFarlane calling to him, as if from a vast distance.

A little later he looked dizzily into MacFarlane's face. The big sheriff was pale and his words seemed strange.

"Hang on, Kid; I ain't much of a sawbones, but I'm goin' to do the best I can."

"Lay off me, or I'll blow your head off," snarled the Kid groggily. "I ain't askin' no favors from you. I thought you was about dead."

"Just knocked out," answered MacFarlane. "I came to and heard everything that went on out here. My God, Kid, you're shot to pieces—broken shoulder bone, bullets in your thigh, breast, right arm—you realize you've just killed the three worst gunfighters in the State? And you done it for me. You got to get well, Kid—you got to."

"So you can see me kick in a noose?" snarled the Kid. "Don't you put no bandages on me. If I got to cash, I'll cash like a gent. I wasn't born to be hanged."

"You got it all wrong, Kid," answered MacFarlane. "Get this straight—I wasn't trailin' you to arrest you. I was huntin' you to put you right. The law ain't lookin' for you. Harrigan ain't dead. He ain't even hurt."

The Kid laughed unpleasantly.

"No? Don't lie, MacFarlane. I shot him plumb in the belly."

"I know you did, but listen: Big Bill wasn't wearin' no gunbelt, you remember. Well, he had his six-shooter stuck under his shirt, inside his waistband. Your bullet just flattened out against the cylinder of his gun. It knocked him down and took all the wind outa him and bruised his belly somethin' fierce, but otherwise it didn't hurt him none. He don't hold no grudge. I got to thinkin' about it, and decided you just didn't think what you was doin'. Now I know it. Now get your mind to thinkin' about getting over these wounds."

"I'll do it, alright," grunted the Kid, concealing his joy with the instinct of his breed. "Gottta redeem myself—I shoot Harrigan and I shoot you, and you both live to tell about it. Got to do somethin' to persuade people I ain't such a poor shot as all that."

McFarlane, knowing the Kid's kind, laughed.

The Feud

He did not glance above the trail to the laurel where I lay
As he rode down to Lincoln town to swear my life away.
He did not look till my rifle cracked as the deathly ball I sped.
Then he clutched his beard as the mustang reared
   and fell from the saddle dead.
I cursed and spat at his silent form and left it on the trail
And climbed my way up the slopes of clay and the stones
   and sliding shale.
And as I went a strange thought grew, a queer and
   curious one:
I'd killed the man whose brother I slew because he
   killed my son.

High on a rock above the vale I sat till the sun went down
And thought of the corpse on the mountain trail that leads
   to Lincoln town.
The stars blinked out and the night wind blew and
   I thought how fine and fair;
Yet over the hills like a crimson fog,
   feud's shadow hovered there.

Knife, Bullet and Noose

Steve Allison, also known as the Sonora Kid, was standing alone at the Gold Dust Bar when Johnny Elkins entered, glanced furtively at the bartender, and leaned close to Allison's elbow. Out of the corner of his mouth he muttered: "Steve, they're out to get you."

The Kid showed no sign that he had heard. He was a wiry young man, slightly above medium height, slim, but strong as a cougar. His skin was burned dark by the sun and winds of many dim trails, and from under the broad rim of his hat, his eyes glinted grey as chilled steel. Except for those eyes he might have been but one more of the army of cowpunchers that rode up the Chisholm yearly; but low on his hips hung two ivory-butted guns, and the worn leather of their scabbards proclaimed that their presence was no mere matter of display.

The Kid emptied his glass before he answered, softly.

"Who's out to get me?"

"Grizzly Gullin!" Elkins shot an uneasy glance toward the door as he whispered the formidable name. "The town's full of buffalo hunters, and they're on the prod. They ain't talkin' much, but I got wind of who they're stalkin', and it's you!"

The Kid rang a coin on the bar, scooped up his change and turned away. Elkins rolled after him, trying to match his friend's long stride. Elkins was freckled, bow-legged, and of negligible stature. They emerged from the saloon and tramped along the dusty street for some yards before either spoke.

"Dawggone you, Kid," panted Elkins. "You make me plumb mad. I tell you, somebody in this cow town is primin' them shaggy-hided hunters with bad licker and devilishness."

"Who?"

"How'm I goin' to know? But that blame' Mike Connolly ain't got no love for you, since you took some of the boys away from him that he was goin' to lock up when we was up here last year. You know he was a buffalo hunter too, once. Them fellows stand in together. They can pot you cold, and he won't turn a finger."

"Nobody asks him to turn a finger," retorted Allison with the quick flash of vanity that characterized the gunfighter. "I don't need no buffalo-skinnin' cow town marshal to shoo a gang of bushy-headed hunters off of me."

"Le's ride," urged Elkins. "What are you waitin' on? The boys pulled out yesterday."

"Well," answered Allison, "you know we brought in the biggest herd that's come to this town this year. We sold to R. J. Blaine, the new cattle-buyer, and we kind of caught him flatfooted. He didn't have enough ready cash to pay for the herd in full. He give me enough to pay off the boys, though, and sent to Abilene for more. It may get here today. Yesterday I sent the boys down the trail. They'd blowed in most of their money, and with all these buffalo hunters that's swarmin' into town, I was afraid they'd get into a ruckus. So I told 'em to head south, and I'd wait for the money and catch up with 'em by the time they hit the Arkansas."

"Old man Donnelly is so blame sot in his ways he's a plumb pest sometimes," grumbled Elkins. "Why couldn't Blaine send him a draft or somethin'?"

"Donnelly don't trust banks," answered the Kid. "You know that. He keeps his money in a big safe in the ranch house, and he always wants his trail boss to bring the money for the cows in big bills."

"Which is plumb nice for the trail boss," snarled Elkins. "It ain't enough to haze four thousand mossy horns from the lower Rio Grande clean to Kansas; his pore damn' sucker of a trail boss has got to risk his life totin' the cash money all the way back. Why, Hell, Steve, at twenty dollars a head, that wad'll make a roll that'd choke a mule. Every outlaw between here and Laredo will be gunnin' for yore hide."

"I'm goin' to see Blaine now," answered the Kid abruptly. "But money or not, I ain't dustin' out till I've had a showdown with Gullin. He can't say he run me out of town."

He turned aside into the unpainted board building which served as dwelling place and office for the town's leading businessman.

Blaine greeted him cordially as he entered. The cattle buyer was a big man, well fed and well dressed. If not typical, he was a good representation of one of the many types following the steel ribbons westward across the Kansas plains, where, at the magic touch of the steel, new towns blossomed overnight, creating fresh markets for the cattle that rolled up in endless waves from the south. Shrewd, ambitious, and with a better education than most, the man was the dominating factor in this new-grown town, which hoped to rival and eclipse the older cow towns of Abilene, Newton and Wichita. Blaine had been a gambler in Nevada mining camps before the westward drive of the rails had started the big cattle boom. Though he wore no weapon openly, men said that in his gambling days no faro dealer in the west was his equal in gun-skill.

"I guess I know what you're after, Allison," Blaine laughed. "Well, it's here. Came in this morning." Reaching into his ponderous safe he laid a bulky roll of bills on the table. "Count 'em," he requested. The Kid shook his head.

"I'll take your word for it." He drew a black leather bag from his pocket, stuffed the bills into it, and made the drawstring fast. The whole made a package of no small bulk.

"You mean to tote all that money down the trail with you?" Blaine demanded.

"Clean to the Tomahawk ranch house," grinned the Kid. "Old man Donnelly won't have it no other way."

"You're taking a big risk," said Blaine bluntly. "Why don't you let me give you a draft for the amount on the First National Bank of Kansas City?"

"The old man don't do business with no banks," replied the Kid. "He likes his money where he can lay hands on it all the time."

"Well, that's his business and yours," answered the cattle buyer. "The tally record and the bill of sale we fixed up the other day, but suppose you sign this receipt, just as a matter of form. It shows I've paid you the money in due form and proper amount."

The Kid signed the receipt, and Blaine, as he folded the paper for placing it in safekeeping, remarked: "I understand your *vaqueros* pulled out yesterday."

"Yeah, that's right."

"That means you'll be riding alone part of the way," protested Blaine. "And with all that money—"

"Aw, I'll be all right, I reckon," answered the Kid. Because he was naturally reticent, he did not add that he would be accompanied by Johnny Elkins, a former Tomahawk hand who had remained in Kansas since the drive of the last year, and now, wearied of the northern range, was riding south with his old friend.

"I reckon the trail will be a lot safer than town, maybe," said Allison; "so I'm goin' to leave this money with you for safekeepin' for awhile. I got some business to 'tend to. I'll call for it sudden-like, maybe, late tonight, or early in the mornin'. If I don't call at all— well, I can trust you to see it gets to old man Donnelly eventually."

As he strode from Blaine's office, his spurs jingling in the dust, a ragged individual sidled up to him and said: "Grizzly Gullin and the boys want to know if you got guts enough to come down to the Buffalo Hump."

"Go back and tell 'em I'll be there," as softly answered the Kid.

The fellow hurried away in the deepening dusk, and the Kid went swiftly to his hotel, thence to a livery stable. Presently he again came up the street, but this time astride a wiry mustang. The cow town was awake and going full blast. Tinny pianos blared from dance halls, boot heels stamped on the boardwalks, saloon doors swung violently, and the yipping of hilarious revelers was punctuated by the shrill laughter of women, and the occasional crack of pistols. The trail riders were celebrating, releasing the nervous energy stored up on that grinding thousand-mile trek.

There was nothing restrained, softened or refined about the scene. All was primitive, wild, raw as the naked boards of the houses that stood up gaunt and unadorned against the prairie stars.

Mike Connolly and his deputies stalked from dance hall to dance hall, glared into every saloon, into every gambling dive. They maintained order at pistol point, and they had no love for the lean bronzed riders who hazed the herds up the trail men called the Chisholm.

There were, indeed, hard characters among these riders. It was a hard life that bred hard men. At first the trail drivers came seeking only a peaceful market. Fighting their way through hostile lands swarming with Indians and white outlaws, they expected to find rest, safety and the means of enjoyment in the Kansas towns. But the cow towns soon swarmed with gamblers, crooks, professional killers, parasites that follow every boom, whether of gold, silver, oil or cattle. An unsophisticated cowboy found the dangers of the trail less than the dangers of the boomtowns.

They began to ride up the trails with their guns strapped down, ready for trouble, ready to fight Indians and outlaws on the trail, gamblers and marshals in the towns. Gunfighters, formerly limited mainly to officers and gamblers, began to be found in the ranks of the cowboys. Of this breed was Steve Allison, and it was because of this that old John Donnelly had chosen him for his trail boss.

The Kid tied his horse to the hitching rack by the Buffalo Hump, and strode lightly toward the square of golden light that marked the doorway. Inside, glasses crashed, oaths and boisterous laughter crackled, and a voice roared:

> *"It wuz on a starry night, in the month of July,*
> *They robbed the Danville train;*
> *It wuz two of the Younger boys what opened the safe,*
> *And toted the gold away!"*

A shadowy form bulked up before the Kid, and even as his right-hand gun slid silently from its scabbard, Johnny Elkins' voice hissed: "Steve, are you locoed?"

Johnny's fingers gripped the Kid's arm, and Allison felt the youngster trembling in his excitement. His face was a pale blur in the dim light.

"Don't go in there, Steve!" his voice thrummed with urgency.

"Who-all's in there?" the Kid asked softly.

"Every damn' buff-hunter in town! Grizzly Gullin's been ravin' and swearin' he'll cut out yore heart and eat it raw. I tell you, Steve, they know it 'uz you that killed Bill Galt, and they craves yore scalp."

"Well, they can have it if they got the guts to take it," said the Kid without passion.

"But you know their way," protested Johnny. "If you go in there and get into a fight with Gullin, they'll shoot you in the back. Somebody'll shoot out the light, and in the scramble nobody'll know who done it—or give a damn."

"I know." None knew the tricks of the cow town ruffians better than the Kid. "That's the way some of these tinhorns got Joe Ord, trail boss for the Triple L, last month. Robbed him, too, I reckon. Leastways, he'd been paid for the cows he brung up the trail, and they never found the money. But that was gamblers, not hunters."

"What's the difference?"

"None, as far as stoppin' a bullet goes," grinned the Kid. "But listen here, Johnny—" His voice sank lower, and Elkins listened intently. He shook his head and swore dubiously, but when the Kid turned and strode toward the lamp-lit doorway, the bowlegged puncher rolled after him.

As the Kid framed himself in the door, the clamor within ceased suddenly. The fellow who had been singing, or rather bellowing, broke short his lament for Jesse James, and wheeled like a great bear toward the doorway.

Allison's quick gaze swept over the saloon. It was thronged with buffalo hunters, to which the establishment catered. Besides the bartenders, there was but one man there not a hunter—the marshal, Mike Connolly, a broad-built man, with a hard immobile face, and a heavy gun strapped low on either hip.

The hunters were all big men, many of them clad in buckskin and Indian moccasins. All were burned dark as Indians, and they wore their hair long. Living an incredibly primitive life, they were hard and ferocious as red savages, and infinitely more dangerous. Hairy, burly, fierce, their eyes gleamed in the lamplight; their hands hovered near the great butcher knives in their belts.

In the midst of the room stood one who loomed above the rest—a great shaggy brute who looked more like a bear than a man: Grizzly Guilin. This man gave a roar as Allison entered, and rolled toward him, small eyes blazing, thick hairy hands working as if to tear out his enemy's throat.

"What you doin' here, Allison?" His voice filled the saloon, and almost seemed to make the one kerosene lamp flicker.

"Heard you all craved to meet me, Gullin," the Kid answered tranquilly. His eyes never exactly left Gullin's hairy face, but they darted sidelong glances that took in all the room.

Gullin rumbled like an enraged bull. His shaggy head wagged from side to side, his hairy hands moved back and forth, without actually reaching toward a weapon. Like most of the other hunters he wore a gun, but it was with the long broad-bladed butcher knife strapped high on his left side, hilt forward, that he was deadly.

"You killed Bill Galt!" he roared, and the crowd behind him rumbled menacingly.

"Yeah, I did," admitted the Kid.

Gullin's face grew black; his veins swelled; he teetered forward on his moccasined feet as if about to hurl himself bodily at his enemy.

"You admit it!" he yelled. "You killed him in cold blood—"

"I shot him in a fair fight," snarled the Kid, his eyes suddenly icy. "Last year he stampeded a herd of Tomahawk cattle just out of pure cussedness—run a herd of buffalo into 'em. They went over a bluff by the hundreds, and took one of the hands with 'em. He was smashed to a pulp. When we come up the trail this year, I met

Bill Galt on the Canadian, and I blew his light out. But he had an even break."

"You're a liar!" bellowed Gullin. "You shot him in the back. A man heard you braggin' about it, and told us. You murdered Bill and let him lay there like he was a dog."

"I wouldn't have let a dog lay," answered the Kid with bitter scorn. "When I rode off Galt was buzzard meat and I didn't feel no call to cover him up. But I didn't shoot him in the back."

"You can't lie out of it!" howled Gullin, brandishing his huge fists.

The Kid cast a quick look at the hemming faces, dark with passion, the straining bodies. It was something more than the old feud of cowpuncher and buffalo hunter. Mike Connolly stood back, aloof, silent.

"Well, why don't you start the ball rollin'?" demanded the Kid, half crouching, hands hovering above his gun butts.

"'Cause we ain't murderers like you," sneered Gullin. "Connolly there is goin' to see fair play. You're a gunman; you got guts enough to fight with a man's weapons?"

"Meanin' a butcher knife? Gullin, there ain't no weapon I'm afraid to meet you with!"

"All right!" yelled the hunter, tearing off his gun belt and tossing it to Mike Connolly. "You ain't wearin' no knife; git him one, Joe."

The bartender ducked down into an assortment of lethal weapons pawned to him at various times, in return for drinks, by impecunious customers, and laid half a dozen knives on the plank bar.

The Kid, drawing both his guns, handed them to Johnny Elkins, who casually backed toward the door. Allison, after a brief inspection, took up a knife with a heavy hilt and a narrow, comparatively short blade—a weapon of unmistakable Spanish make.

The hunters had drawn back around the walls, leaving a space clear. The Kid had no illusions about what was to follow. He knew his own reputation; knew that the whole affair was a trap, planned to get his deadly guns out of his hands. If Gullin's knife failed, it would be a bullet in the cowboy's back. The Kid stamped in the sawdust as if trying the footing, moving near an open window as he did so. Then he turned and indicated that he was ready. Gullin ripped out his knife and charged like the bear for which he was named. For all his bulk he was quick as a cat. His moccasin-shod feet were adapted to the work at hand. Opposing was the Kid, much inferior in bulk, wearing high-heeled boots unfitted for quick work on the sawdust-strewn floor. The knife in his hand looked small compared to the great scimitar-curved blade of Gullin. What the hunters overlooked, or did not know, was that Allison was raised in a land swarming with Mexican knife-fighters.

The Kid, facing that roaring, hurtling bulk, knew that if they came to handgrips, he was lost. He had seen Gullin, his shoulder broken by a cowboy's bullet, leap like a huge cat through the air and drive the knife, with his left hand, through his enemy's heart.

Gullin roared and charged; the Kid's hand went back and snapped out. The Spanish knife flashed through the lamplight like a beam of blue lightning, and thudded against Gullin's breast the hilt quivered under his heart. The giant stopped short, staggered. His mouth gaped and blood gushed from it. He pitched headlong—

As Gullin fell, the Kid's hand whipped inside his shirt and out again, gripping a double-barreled derringer. Even as it caught the lamplight, it cracked twice. A hunter lifting a cocked six-shooter crumpled, and the lamp shattered, casting a shower of blazing oil.

In the darkness bedlam burst loose. There were wild shots, stampeding of feet, splintering of chairs and tables, curses, yells, and Mike Connolly's stentorian voice demanding a light.

The Kid had wheeled, even as the room was plunged in darkness, and dived headlong through the nearby window. He hit on his feet, catlike, and raced toward the hitching rack. A form loomed up before him, and even as he instinctively menaced it with the empty derringer, he recognized it.

"Johnny! Got my guns?"

Two familiar smooth butts were shoved into his eager hands.

"I beat it as soon as everybody was watchin' you all," Johnny spluttered with excitement. "You nailed him, Steve? By the good golly—"

"Get your cayuse and hit the trail, Johnny," ordered Allison, swinging up on his horse. "Dust it out of town and wait for me at that creek crossin' three miles south of town. I'm goin' after the money Blaine's holdin' for me. Vamoose!"

A few minutes later the Kid dropped reins over his horse's head and slid up to the lighted window inside which he saw Richard J. Blaine busily engaged in writing. At the Kid's hiss he looked up, gaped, and started violently. The Kid pushed the partly open window up the rest of the way, and climbed in.

"I ain't hardly got no time to go around to the door," he apologized. "If you'll give me the money, I'll be makin' tracks."

Blaine rose, still confused, hastily crumpling up the sheet on which he had been writing, and thrusting it into his pocket. He turned toward his safe which stood open, and inside which Allison could see the black leather bag, then turned back, as if struck by a sudden thought.

"Any trouble?"

"No trouble; just a bunch of fool buffalo hunters."

"Oh!" The cattle buyer seemed to be regaining some of his composure. The color came back to his face.

"You startled the devil out of me, coming through that window. What about those hunters?"

"They took it ill because I killed that stampedin' sidewinder Bill Galt," answered the Kid. "I don't know how they found out. I ain't told nobody in this town except you and Johnny Elkins. Reckon some of my outfit must have talked. Not that I give a damn. But I don't go around braggin' about the coyotes I have to shoot. They sure planned to get me cold—" in a few words he related what happened at the Buffalo Hump. "Now I reckon they'll try lynch law," he concluded. "They'll swear I murdered somebody."

"Oh, I guess not," laughed Blaine. "Bed down here till mornin'."

"Not a chance; I'm dustin' now."

"Well, have a drink before you go," urged Blaine.

"I ain't hardly got time." The Kid was listening for sounds of pursuit. It was quite possible the maddened hunters might trail him. And he knew that Mike Connolly would give him no protection against the mob.

"Oh, a few minutes won't make any difference," laughed Blaine. "Wait, I'll get the liquor."

Frontier courtesy precluded a refusal. Blaine passed into an adjoining room, and the Kid heard him fumbling about. The Kid stood in the center of the office room, nervous, alert, and because it was his nature to observe everything, he noticed a ball of paper crumpled on the floor, ink stained—evidently part of a letter Blaine had spoiled and discarded. He would have paid no attention to it, but suddenly he saw his own name scrawled upon it.

Quickly he bent and secured it. Smoothing out the crumpled sheet, he read. It was a letter addressed to John Donnelly, and it said: "Your trail boss Allison was killed in a barroom brawl. I had paid him for the cows, and have a receipt, signed by him. However, the money was not found on his body. Marshal Connolly verifies that fact. He had been gambling heavily, I understand, and he must have used your money after he ran out of his own. It's too bad, but—"

The door opened and Blaine stood framed in it, whiskey bottle and glasses in hand. He saw the paper in the Kid's fingers, and he went livid.

The bottle and glasses fell to the floor with a shattering crash. Blaine's hand darted under his coat and out, just as the Texan's .45 cleared leather. The shots crashed like a double reverberation—but it was the .45 which thundered first. The window behind Allison shattered, and Blaine tumbled to the floor, to lie in a widening pool of dark crimson.

The Kid snatched the bulky black leather pouch from the open safe, and stuffed it into his shirt as he ran from the room. He forked his mustang and headed south at a run. Behind him sounded the mingled clamor of cow-town nightlife, mixed now with an increasing, ominous roar—the bellow of the manhunt. The Kid grinned hardly—knife, bullet, noose—all had failed that night; as well as the sinister plotting of the last man in Kansas Allison would have dreamed of suspecting.

Johnny Elkins was waiting for him at the appointed place, and together they took the trail that ran southward for a thousand miles.

"Well?" Johnny wriggled impatiently. Allison explained in a few words.

"I see it all now. Blaine figgered on gettin' cows and money too. He held up the pay for the herd, so as to get me in town alone, so he thought. He worked them hunters up to get me. He had the receipt to prove that he'd paid me the dough. Then if I got killed, and the money not on me—. Right at the last he tried to keep me there, till the mob found me, I reckon."

"But he couldn't know you'd leave the dough with him for safekeepin'," objected Johnny.

"Well, it was a natural thing to do. And if I hadn't, I reckon Connolly would have took it off me, after I was killed in the Buffalo Hump. He was Blaine's man. That must have been how and why Joe Ord got his."

"And everybody figgered Blaine was such a big man," meditated Johnny.

"Well," answered Allison, "a few more big herds grabbed for nothin', and I reckon he would have been a big man; but big or little, it's all the same to a .45."

Which comment embraced the full philosophy of the gunfighter.

Law-Shooters of Cowtown

Clamor of cowtown nights . . . boot-heels stamping on sawdust-strewn floors . . . thunder of flying hoofs down the dusty street . . . yipping of the lean trail drivers, reeling in the saddle, hilarious after the thousand-mile trek . . . cracking of pistols, smash of glasses, flutter of cards on the tables . . . oaths, songs, laughter in all the teeming saloons and dance halls, louder yet in the plank-barred Silver Boot.

Grizzly Elkins slapped a twenty-dollar gold piece down on the Monte game. Elkins stood out, even in that throng of tall men. He was hairy as a bear, burly and powerful as a bear. Burned dark as an Indian, he wore the buckskins and moccasins of an earlier day. His shoulders were broad and thick as those of an ox. One of the army of buffalo hunters wandering between the Pecos and the upper Missouri, he was as much a part of that wild land as one of the beasts he hunted.

He leaned over the table with the men about him, watching the play of the cards. He grunted explosively as he saw the winning card come up.

The dealer's narrow white hand raked up the coins.

"Wait there, you!" Grizzly Elkins' voice was a roar that filled the saloon. "Gimme my change. I bet just five outer that twenty piece."

The dealer looked up with a sneer on his thin lips. He was Jim Kirby, gambler and gunman, his metal proven in many a game of chance—both with cards and with six-shooters.

"I never give change," he retorted. "If you don't want to bet your wad, don't lay it on my board. I've got no time for pikers."

Elkins' small eyes blazed.

"Why, you dirty thief—!" His bellow brought the men at the bar around as on a pivot.

Kirby's hand darted like the head of a snake to his scabbard; but Elkins, for all his bulk, moved quick as a great cat. With a berserk bellow he ripped out his butcher knife and hurled himself recklessly across the table. The great blade flashed blue in the lamplight and plunged to the hilt in the gambler's breast, as the table tilted and buckled beneath the headlong impact. The explosion of Kirby's gun nearly deafened the hunter, the flash of powder stinging and blackening his neck and beard. Out of the tangle of chairs, limbs, and broken wood, Elkins heaved up like a bear out of a trap, roaring and brandishing his knife, red to the hilt. Under his feet Kirby lay still and white in a broadening pool of crimson.

For an instant Elkins rocked on his straddling legs, glaring about him, shaggy head jutting truculently, knife lifted. Then with a yell he turned and ran for the door. A clamor broke out about and behind him, as a pack bays the fleeing wolf. Jim Kirby had been popular with the scum of the cowtowns.

"Stop him!" "Grab him!" "Shoot him!" "He murdered Kirby, the son of a—"

Another stride would carry the fugitive through the door and into the night, but in the square of light outside, a tall, lean figure loomed suddenly—Buck Chisom, the marshal's gunfighting deputy. He heard the yells and acted with the steel-trap comprehension of his breed.

Elkins halted short; his thick arm shot back—but before it could snap forward in the motion that could nail a man to a tree with the thrown knife, Chisom's hand, moving too quick for the sight to follow, came up with a gleam of blue steel. A jet of flame ripped the night. Elkins jerked spasmodically; he swayed backward, then pitched on his face, his fingers relaxing about the bloody hilt of his butcher knife.

When the buffalo hunter regained consciousness, his first sensation was a dizzy pain in his head. His next was an astonishment that he was alive, after having been shot by Buck Chisom at such deadly close range. He lifted his hand tentatively to his scalp, and discovered it was crusted with dried blood, with which his bushy hair was likewise clotted. He swore. The bullet had merely creased his scalp, knocking him senseless. Evidently the light directly behind his target had dazzled Chisom. That his captor had not bothered to bandage his wound, Elkins did not resent, or even think about. Born and bred on the frontier, living a life incredibly primitive, the buffalo hunter had all the tough stoicism of the wild, and its contempt for pain and injury.

He was lying on a rude wooden bunk, which was scantily covered with a ragged blanket. He sat up, swearing, and instinctively reaching for the butcher knife he always wore strapped high on his left side, hilt forward. The sheath was empty, as he might have known it would be.

As he glared about him, a mocking laugh caused him to bristle truculently. He was where he would have expected to be—in the jail. It was a one-room building, made of undressed logs, with one door and one window. The window was barred, but even without the bars, it was too small to have accommodated Elkins' bull shoulders. There were two bunks, and on the other sat the man who had laughed.

Elkins glared at him with scant favor. He knew him; a fellow named Richards, a lean, black-haired, shifty-eyed cowboy.

"Well, how you like it, fellow?" this customer greeted the discomfited plainsman.

"How would I like it, you bowlegged hedgehog?" roared Elkins. Attuned to the wide spaces and the winds of the great plains, the buffalo hunter's voice was always a roar. "Just wait'll I get my hands on that blamed marshal and his gun-throwin' deperty! I'll scour the street with their blasted carcasses!"

"Talk's cheap," sneered Richards.

"What you doin', takin' up for them rats?" demanded Elkins. "Didn't they throw you in?"

"For drunk and disorderly conduck, yes," admitted the other. "But I ain't no derned murderer."

"Who is?" rumbled Elkins, bristling instantly.

"You murdered Jim Kirby."

"You're a liar. I killed him like I would any other varmint. And when I get out of this den, I'm a-goin' to commit some more necessary homicides."

"When you git out," predicted Richards vindictively, "you're goin' to be decoratin' a tree limb at the end of a rope. Listen!"

Elkins stiffened abruptly. The night wind carried the various sounds of the cowtown—but it carried another sound: the swelling, awesome roar of maddened men. The hunter knew what it meant.

"They's enough rats in this town to hang me if they could get me," he snarled; "but I reckon the marshal will handle 'em."

"Well," Richards leered as if at a secret jest, "I wouldn't rely too much on Joel Rogers if I was you—nor Buck Chisom neither."

Elkins wheeled suddenly. He seemed to fill the place, not only with his great bulk, but with his somber and ferocious personality.

"What you mean?" he demanded.

"That's all right," grinned Richards. "What I know, well, I know it; and what you don't know won't hurt you none—not after tonight!"

"You damned rat!" roared Elkins, eyes a-flame, beard a-bristle; "you'll tell me right now what you're a-hintin' at!"

As he rushed like a maddened bull at the cowboy, the latter leaped from his bunk and met the hurtling giant with a smash that spattered blood from his mouth. Elkins replied with a bloodthirsty yell, and bent the lanky puncher double with a mallet-like blow to the belly, and then they grappled and went to the floor together.

Richards lacked the buffalo hunter's bulk, but he was equally tall, and as hard and rangy as a timber wolf. Neither knew anything about scientific wrestling or boxing, but both were products of the frontier, and their style of fighting was as primitive and instinctive as that of a pair of grizzlies.

Kicking, biting, tearing, gouging, mauling, they rolled back and forth across the floor, smashing into the bunks and caroming against the walls. Rearing upright again, they slugged with primordial abandon, oblivious to the growing roar of the mob, to everything but the lust to obliterate each other. There was no attempt at defense; each blow was driven with the power and will to destroy.

Reeling back from a bearlike smash that tore his ear from his head and left it hanging by a shred of flesh, Richards kicked savagely at Elkins' groin. The plainsman caught his ankle and wrenched sideways. Richards went down with a crash, and Elkins's moccasin heel caught him squarely in the mouth, splintering his teeth.

With an inhuman yell the hunter leaped on the fallen man, driving his knee into Richards's midriff; then seizing the man's throat, he began to hammer his head against the log wall with a fury that would quickly have put the cowboy beyond human aid.

"Wait!" gasped the victim. He was a sorry sight, with one eye closed, an ear mangled, face skinned, blood streaming from smashed nose and torn lips. "I'll tell you—"

"Then hustle!" panted Elkins, spitting out the fragments of a broken tooth. Blood trickled down the hunter's beard, and his buckskin shirt was ripped open, revealing his great hairy chest which heaved from his exertions. "Hustle! I hear that derned mob." His big hands maintained their viselike grip on his victim's neck.

"I had a bottle about a quarter full of whiskey on me when I come in here," mumbled Richards. "I drunk it and laid down on the bunk to sleep, and whilst I was layin' there, I woke up and heered Rogers and Chisom talkin'. They seen the empty bottle and thought I was dead drunk. They throwed you in here, and Rogers said tonight was as good a night as any to pull what they aimed to pull. He said he'd planned to set a house on fire, and do it whilst everybody was at the fire, but he said he knowed a mob was gatherin' on account of Jim Kirby, he had so many friends, and people would turn out to a lynchin' even better'n they would to a fire, so tonight was the night. And Chisom said yes."

"But what they plannin' to do?" roared Elkins bewilderedly.

"Rob the bank!" answered Richards. "I heered 'em talk about it."

"But they're laws!" protested Elkins.

"I don't care. I knowed Chisom in Nevada. Regular outlaw then, and I guess he ain't changed none. Who knows anything about Rogers? Ain't no tellin' what he was before he come here."

Elkins realized the truth of this statement. In the cowtowns officers were likely to be chosen for their gun skill, and no questions asked about their previous life. Hendry Brown came straight from Billy the Kid's gang to the office of marshal of Caldwell; John Wesley Hardin, with a price on his head in Texas, was deputy sheriff in Abilene.

The buffalo hunter sprang up, brought back to a realization of his own predicament by a clamor that surged up and around the jail. He heard the sound of many feet running up the hard-packed road, a mingled thunder of shouts and oaths. There is no sound on earth so terrifying as the roar of a mob bent on the destruction of a fellow man. Richards, though he was not the one menaced, turned white and cowered back on one of the bunks.

Elkins snorted, much as a wicked old bull might snort in defiance. His beard bristled, his eyes flamed. A stride took him to the window and he gripped one of the long, thick bars in both his hands. Outside, men surged around the building, gun butts hammered on the door. Strident yells cut the night. Pistols cracked, and lead thudded into the door, bringing a yell of agonized protest from Richards, who was trying to compress himself into as small a space as possible. Elkins yelled back in wordless defiance. He braced his feet; his muscles cracked and bulged; the veins in his temples swelled. An explosive grunt burst from him, as the bar gave way at one end, and was torn out bodily. Another heave, and it was free in his hands.

He wheeled to the door, now groaning and bending inward beneath a terrific assault—he knew the mobsters had a log that they were using as a battering ram.

The door splintered inward, and for an instant he glared into the convulsed faces of the lynchers that ringed the doorway in the light of flickering torches—gamblers, barmen, gunmen—tinhorns, thieves, criminals—not an honest cowboy or hunter among them.

An instant all stood frozen as he faced them, an awesome figure, tousled, bloodstained, gigantic, with his blazing eyes and iron bludgeon—then with a roar he hurtled through the broken door and crashed into the thick of them.

Yells of fury rose deafeningly, mingled with howls of pain and fear. Torches waved wildly and went out. Guns cracked futilely. In that melee, no man could use a pistol effectively. And in the midst of them Grizzly Elkins ravened like a blood-mad bear among sheep. Swinging the heavy bar like a club, he felt skulls cave in and bones snap beneath its impact. Blood and brains spattered in his face; the taste of blood was in his mouth. Men swarmed and eddied about him in the darkness; bodies caromed against him, wild blows fanned him, or glanced from his arms and shoulders. A better aimed or more lucky stroke crashed full on his head, filling his eyes with sparks of fire, and his brain with momentary numbness. A blindly driven knife broke its point on his broad belt buckle, and the jagged shard tore his buckskin and gashed his side raggedly.

Hands clawed at him, booted feet stamped about him. He tore, slugged, and ripped his way through a seething, surging sea of gasping, screaming, cursing humanity, ruthlessly smashing out right and left. Driving like a crazed bull, he plunged through the bewildered throng, leaving a wake of writhing, bloody figures to mark his progress. A dimly seen hand jammed a gun-muzzle full into his belly, but even as he caught his breath, the hammer snapped on an empty chamber, and the next instant the iron bludgeon fell and the unknown gunman crumpled.

Over his fallen form Elkins leaped, stampeding for the darkness. Behind him the crowd surged and eddied, screaming, cursing, not yet aware that their prey had escaped them. Blows were still struck blindly, pistols banged in the dark.

Reaching the first of the houses that lined the straggling street, a short distance from the isolated jail, Elkins darted behind them, and keeping to the darkness, gained the hitching rack of the Silver Boot. No one was in sight; even the barmen and the loafers had gone to watch the lynching. His bay horse stood as he had left it.

"Blast 'em!" swore Elkins, swinging into the saddle, "reckon they'd of left my hoss here to starve, dern 'em!"

He wheeled his mount, then hesitated, remembering what Richards had said of Joel Rogers and his gun-fanning deputy. He did not doubt its truth. The time could not be riper for a bank robbery. In it reposed thousands of dollars, belonging to the cattle buyers, ready for the herds that would soon be drifting up the Chisholm Trail. Elkins had no love for the buyers or the trail drivers; the animosity between the buffalo hunters and the cattle men was a living issue. But the marshal and his deputy had done him an injury, left him as a bait to the raving mob; and in Elkins' primitive code, a wrong unavenged was an unpaid debt. He reined his bay around and rode swiftly toward the bank.

He approached the building from the back. Like all things in that rude town on the western prairies, which had never seen steel rails until the past few months, it was crude—merely a plank structure, unpainted. Inside a wooden grille cut the building in half, and near the back wall stood a heavy iron safe which served as vault. No regular watchman was hired; guarding the bank was part of the duties of the marshal and his deputies.

Elkins halted behind the bank, threw the reins over his horse's head, and drew from its saddle-scabbard the heavy single shot Sharps .50 caliber buffalo rifle. He had no six-shooter, and his knife was gone. Silently as a panther he approached the back door, ordinarily kept bolted. Now it stood partly open, and nearby Elkins saw a couple of horses standing in the deep shadow of the building. The thieves intended a quick getaway. A light showed through the crack of the door. A small candle on the floor lighted the figures of Joel Rogers and Buck Chisom. They were bending over the safe, and as Elkins looked, he saw Rogers strike a match and put it to the end of a fuse.

"We got to jump quick now, Buck," the marshal hissed. "They's enough of that stuff to blow us clean out—"

At that instant Elkins plunged through the door, threw down his big rifle and roared, "Han's up, you all!"

Both men cursed, wheeled and came erect simultaneously. Rogers' hand lurched to his scabbard. The roar of the big Sharps was deafening; a gush of smoke filled the place, through which Elkins saw Rogers sway and fall, his head a gory travesty. At that range the heavy slug had torn off the whole top of his skull.

Through the swirling smoke Elkins saw Buck Chisom's hand dip like a flash and come up with a long six-shooter. Helplessly he stood, the empty rifle in his hands for the flashing second it took to transpire—then, even as the gunman's blue barrel leveled—behind Chisom belched a cataclysmic detonation; the whole building rocked drunkenly; there was a terrible, blinding flash, the rending crash of tortured metal, the air was full of singing fragments, and something hit Elkins with a paralyzing impact.

Half-conscious, he found himself lying out in the dust behind the bank, with a heavy weight pinning him down. This weight was Buck Chisom, whether dead or unconscious, the buffalo hunter did not stop to determine. Groggily he realized that the fuse lit by Rogers just before he ordered the men to surrender had exploded the charge meant to blow the safe. And he realized that an explosion terrific enough to catapult Chisom against him and hurl them both through the door would have been heard for miles. People would be coming on the run to investigate, and he did not care to be found there.

Thrusting aside the limp figure of the gunfighting deputy, the hunter staggered up and whistled shrilly. His horse had bolted with the others, but obedient to its long training, it came galloping back, its reins streaming. On the great plains of the buffalo, a man's life depended on his horse. Elkins swung into the saddle and headed south.

"Get along, Andrew Jackson; I don't crave no words with the people of this here town. I've saved their dern' bank, or anyways, the money in it, and I've done rid 'em of a couple of law-shootin' thieves, but I don't reckon I'll try to explain. Things moves too fast for me in town, anyway. It's us for the Nations, where nobody but Comanches yearns for our scalps."

Wild Water

Saul Hopkins was king of Locust Valley, but kingship never turned hot lead. In the wild old days, not so long distant, another man was king of the Valley, and his methods were different and direct. He ruled by the guns, wire clippers and branding irons of his wiry, hard-handed, hard-eyed riders. But those days were past and gone, and Saul Hopkins sat in his office in Bisley and pulled strings to which were tied loans and mortgages and the subtle tricks of finance.

Times have changed since Locust Valley reverberated to the guns of rival cattlemen, and Saul Hopkins, by all modern standards, should have lived and died king of the Valley by virtue of his gold and lands; but he met a man in whom the old ways still lived.

It began when John Brill's farm was sold under the hammer. Saul Hopkins' representative was there to bid. But three hundred hard-eyed ranchers and farmers were there, too. They rode in from the river bottoms and the hill country to the west and north, in ramshackle flivvers, in hacks, and on horseback. Some of them came on foot. They had a keg of tar, and half a dozen old feather pillows. The representative of big business understood. He stood aside and made no attempt to bid. The auction took place, and the farmers and ranchers were the only bidders. Land, implements and stock sold for exactly $7.55; and the whole was handed back to John Brill.

When Saul Hopkins heard of it, he turned white with fury. It was the first time his kingship had ever been flouted. He set the wheels of the law to grinding, and before another day passed, John Brill and nine of his friends were locked in the old stone jail at Bisley. Up along the bare oak ridges and down along the winding creeks where poverty-stricken farmers labored under the shadow of Saul Hopkins' mortgages, went the word that the scene at Brill's farm would not be duplicated. The next foreclosure would be attended by enough armed deputies to see that the law was upheld. And the men of the creeks and the hills knew that the promise was no idle one. Meanwhile, Saul Hopkins prepared to have John Brill prosecuted with all the power of his wealth and prestige. And Jim Reynolds came to Bisley to see the king.

Reynolds was John Brill's brother-in-law. He lived in the high post oak country north of Bisley. Bisley lay on the southern slope of that land of long ridges and oak thickets. To the south the slopes broke into fan-shaped valleys, traversed by broad streams. The people in those fat valleys were prosperous; farmers who had come late into the country, and pushed out the cattlemen who had once owned it all.

Up on the high ridges of the Lost Knob country, it was different. The land was rocky and sterile, the grass thin. The ridges were occupied by the descendants of old pioneers, nesters, tenant farmers, and broken cattlemen. They were poor, and there was an old feud between them and the people of the southern valleys. Money had to be borrowed from somebody of the latter clan, and that intensified the bitterness.

Jim Reynolds was an atavism, the personification of anachronism. He had lived a comparatively law-abiding life, working on farms, ranches, and in the oil fields that lay to the east, but in him always smoldered an unrest and a resentment against conditions that restricted and repressed him. Recent events had fanned these embers into flame. His mind leaped as naturally toward personal violence as that of the average modern man turns to processes of law. He was literally born out of his time. He should have lived his life a generation before, when men threw a wide loop and rode long trails.

He drove into Bisley in his Ford roadster at nine o'clock one night. He stopped his car on French Street, parked, and turned into an alley that led into Hopkins Street—named for the man who owned most of the property on it. It was a quirk in the man's nature that he should cling to the dingy little back street office in which he first got his start.

Hopkins Street was narrow, lined mainly with small offices, warehouses, and the backs of buildings that faced on more pretentious streets. By night it was practically deserted. Bisley was not a large town, and except on Saturday night, even her main streets were not thronged after dark. Reynolds saw no one as he walked swiftly down the narrow sidewalk toward a light which streamed through a door and a plate glass window.

There the king of Locust Valley worked all day and late into the night, establishing and strengthening his kingship.

The grim old warrior who had kinged it in the Valley in an earlier generation knew the men he had to deal with. He wore two guns in loose scabbards, and cold-eyed gunmen rode with him, night or day. Saul Hopkins had dealt in paper and figures so long he had forgotten the human equation. He understood a menace only as a threat against his money—not against himself.

He bent over his desk, a tall, gaunt, stooped man, with a mop of straggly grey hair and the hooked nose of a vulture. He looked up irritably as someone bulked in the door that opened directly on the street. Jim Reynolds stood there—broad, dark as an Indian, one hand under his coat. His eyes burned like coals. Saul Hopkins went cold, as he sensed, for the first time in his life, a menace that was not directed against his gold and his lands, but against his body and his life. No word was passed between them, but an electric spark of understanding jumped across the intervening space.

With a strangled cry old Hopkins sprang up, knocking his swivel chair backward, stumbling against his desk. Jim Reynolds' hand came from beneath his coat gripping a Colt .45. The report thundered deafeningly in the small office. Old Saul cried out chokingly and rocked backward, clutching at his breast. Another slug caught him in the groin, crumpling him down across the desk, and as he fell, he jerked sidewise to the smash of a third bullet in his belly. He sprawled over the desk, spouting blood, and clawing blindly at nothing, slid off and blundered to the floor, his convulsive fingers full of torn papers which fell on him in a white, fluttering shower from the blood splashed desk.

Jim Reynolds eyed him unemotionally, the smoking gun in his hand. Acrid powder fumes filled the office, and the echoes seemed to be still reverberating. Whistling gasps slobbered through Saul Hopkins' grey lips and he jerked spasmodically. He was not yet dead, but Reynolds knew he was dying. And galvanized into sudden action, Reynolds turned and went out on the street. Less than a minute had passed since the first shot crashed, but a man was running up the street, gun in hand, shouting loudly. It was Mike Daley, a policeman. Reynolds knew that it would be several minutes, at least, before the rest of the small force could reach the scene. He stood motionless, his gun hanging at his side.

Daley rushed up, panting, poking his pistol at the silent killer.

"Hands up, Reynolds!" he gasped. "What the hell have you done? My God, have you shot Mr. Hopkins? Give me that gun—give it to me!"

Reynolds reversed his .45, dangling it by his index finger through the trigger guard, the butt toward Daley. The policeman grabbed for it, lowering his own gun unconsciously as he reached. The big Colt spun on Reynolds' finger, the butt slapped into his palm, and Daley glared wild eyed into the black muzzle. He was paralyzed by the trick—a trick which in itself showed Reynolds' anachronism. That roll, reliance of the old time gunman, had not been used in that region for a generation.

"Drop your gun!" snapped Reynolds. Daley dumbly opened his fingers and, as his gun slammed on the sidewalk, the long barrel of Reynolds' Colt lifted, described an arc and smashed down on the policeman's head. Daley fell beside his fallen gun, and Reynolds ran down the narrow street, cut through an alley and came out on French Street a few steps from where his car was parked.

Behind him he heard men shouting and running. A few loiterers on French Street gaped at him, shrank back at the sight of the gun in his hand. He sprang to the wheel and roared down French Street, shot across the bridge that spanned Locust Creek, and raced up the road. There were few residences in that end of town, where the business section abutted on the very bank of the creek. Within a few minutes he was in open country, with only scattered farmhouses here and there.

He had not even glanced toward the rock jail where his friends lay. He knew the uselessness of an attempt to free them, even were it successful. He had only followed his instinct when he killed Saul Hopkins. He felt neither remorse nor exultation, only the grim satisfaction of a necessary job well done. His nature was exactly that of the old-time feudist, who, when pushed beyond endurance, killed his man, took to the hills and fought it out with all who came against him. Eventual escape did not enter his calculations. His was the grim fatalism of the old-time gun fighter. He merely sought a lair where he could turn at bay. Otherwise he would have stayed and shot it out with the Bisley police.

A mile beyond the bridge the road split into three forks. One led due north to Sturling, whence it swung westward to Lost Knob; he had followed that road, coming into Bisley. One led to the northwest, and was the old Lost Knob road, discontinued since the creation of Bisley Lake. The other turned westward and led to other settlements in the hills.

He took the old northwest road. He had met no one. There was little travel in the hills at night. And this road was particularly lonely. There were long stretches where not even a farmhouse stood, and now the road was cut off from the northern settlements by the great empty basin of the newly created Bisley Lake, which lay waiting for rains and head rises to fill it.

The pitch was steadily upward. Mesquites gave way to dense post oak thickets. Rocks jutted out of the ground, making the road uneven and bumpy. The hills loomed darkly around him.

Ten miles out of Bisley and five miles from the Lake, he turned from the road and entered a wire gate. Closing it behind him, he drove along a dim path which wound crookedly up a hill side, flanked thickly with post oaks. Looking back, he saw no headlights cutting the sky. He must have been seen driving out of town, but no one saw him take the northwest road. Pursuers would naturally suppose he had taken one of the other roads. He could not reach

Lost Knob by the northwest road, because, although the lake basin was still dry, what of the recent drought, the bridges had been torn down over Locust Creek, which he must cross again before coming to Lost Knob, and over Mesquital.

He followed a curve in the path, with a steep bluff to his right, and coming onto a level space strewn with broken boulders, saw a low-roofed house looming darkly ahead of him. Behind it and off to one side stood barns, sheds and corrals, all bulked against a background of post oak woods. No lights showed.

He halted in front of the sagging porch—there was no yard fence—and sprang up on the porch, hammering on the door. Inside a sleepy voice demanded his business.

"Are you by yourself?" demanded Reynolds. The voice assured him profanely that such was the case. "Then get up and open the door; it's me—Jim Reynolds."

There was a stirring in the house, creak of bed springs, prodigious yawns, and a shuffling step. A light flared as a match was struck. The door opened, revealing a gaunt figure in a dingy union suit, holding an oil lamp in one hand.

"What's up, Jim?" demanded the figure, yawning and blinking. "Come in. Hell of a time of night to wake a man up—"

"It ain't ten o'clock yet," answered Reynolds. "Joel, I've just come from Bisley. I killed Saul Hopkins."

The gaping mouth, in the middle of a yawn, clapped shut with a strangling sound. The lamp rocked wildly in Joel Jackson's hand, and Reynolds caught it to steady it.

"Saul Hopkins?" In the flickering light Jackson's face was the hue of ashes. "My God, they'll hang you! Are they after you? What—"

"They won't hang me," answered Reynolds grimly. "Only reason I run was there's some things I want to do before they catch me. Joel, you've got reasons for befriendin' me. I can't hide out in the hills all the time, because there's nothin' to eat. You live here alone, and don't have many visitors. I'm goin' to stay here a few days till the search moves into another part of the country, then I'm goin' back into Bisley and do the rest of my job. If I can kill that lawyer of Hopkins' and Judge Blaine and Billy Leary, the chief of police, I'll die happy."

"But they'll comb these hills!" exclaimed Jackson wildly. "They can't keep from findin' you—"

"Hang on to your nerve," grunted Reynolds. "We'll run my car into that ravine back of this hill and cover it up with brush. Take a regular bloodhound to find it. I'll stay in the house here, or in the barn, and when we see anybody comin', I'll duck out into the brush. Only way they can get here in a car is to climb that foot path like I did. Besides, they won't waste much time huntin' this close to Bisley. They'll take a sweep through the country, and if they don't find me right easy, they'll figger I've made for Lost Knob. They'll question you, of course, but if you'll keep your backbone stiff and look 'em in the eye when you lie about it, I don't think they'll bother to search your farm."

"Alright," shivered Jackson, "but it'll go hard with me if they find out." He was numbed by the thought of Reynolds' deed. It had never occurred to him that a man as "big" as Saul Hopkins could be shot down like an ordinary human.

Little was said between the men as they drove the car down the rocky hillside and into the ravine; wedged into the dense shinnery, they skillfully masked its presence.

"A blind man could tell a car's been driv down that hill," complained Jackson.

"Not after tonight," answered Reynolds, with a glance at the sky. "I believe it's goin' to rain like hell in a few hours."

"It is mighty hot and still," agreed Jackson. "I hope it does rain. We're needin' it. We didn't get no winter seasonin'—"

"What the hell do you care for your crops?" growled Reynolds. "You don't own 'em; nobody in these hills owns anything. Everything you all got is mortgaged to the hilt—some of it more'n once. You, personally, been lucky to keep up the interest; you sag once, and see what happens to you. You'll be just like my brother-in-law John, and a lot of others. You all are a pack of fools, just like I told him. To hell with strugglin' along and slavin' just to put fine clothes on somebody else's backs, and good grub into their bellies. You ain't workin' for yourselves; you're workin' for them you owe money to."

"Well, what can we do?" protested Jackson. Reynolds grinned wolfishly.

"You know what I done tonight. Saul Hopkins won't never throw no other man out of his house and home to starve. But there's plenty like him. If you farmers would listen to me, you'd throw down your rakes and pick up your guns. Up here in these hills we'd make a war out of it that'd make the Bloody Lincoln County War look plumb tame."

Jackson's teeth chattered as with an ague. "We couldn't do it, Jim. Times is changed, can't you understand? You talk just like them old-time outlaws my dad used to tell me about. We can't fight with guns like our fathers used to do. The governor'd send soldiers to hunt us down. Keepin' a man from biddin' at a auction is one thing; fightin' state soldiers is another. We're just licked and got to know it."

"You're talkin' just like John and all the others," sneered Reynolds. "Well, John's in jail and they say he's goin' to the pen; but I'm free and Saul Hopkins is in hell. What you say to that?"

"I'm afeared it'll be the ruin of us all," moaned Jackson.

"You and your fears," snarled Reynolds. "Men ain't got the guts of lice no more. I thought, when the farmers took over that auction, they was gettin' their bristles up. But they ain't. Your old man wouldn't have knuckled down like you're doin'. Well, I know what I'm goin' to do, if I have to go it alone. I'll get plenty of them before they get me, damn 'em. Come on in the house and fix me up somethin' to eat."

Much had been crowded into a short time. It was only eleven o'clock. Stillness held the land in its grip. The stars had been blotted out by a grey haze-like veil which, rising in the northwest, had spread over the sky with surprizing speed. Far away on the horizon lightning flickered redly. There was a breathless tenseness in the air. Breezes sprang up, blew fitfully from the southeast, and as quickly died down. Somewhere off in the wooded hills a night bird called uneasily. A cow bawled anxiously in the corral. The beasts sensed an impending something in the atmosphere, and the men, raised in the hills, were no less responsive to the portents of the night.

"Been a kind of haze in the sky all day," muttered Jackson, glancing out the window as he fumbled about, setting cold fried bacon, corn bread, and a pot of red beans on the rough-hewn table before his guest. "Been lightnin' in the northwest since sundown. Wouldn't be surprized if we had a regular storm. 'Bout that time of the year."

"Likely," grunted Reynolds, his mouth full of pork and corn bread. "Joel, dern you, ain't you got nothin' to drink better'n buttermilk?"

Jackson reached up into the tin-doored cupboard and brought down a jug. He pulled out the corn-cob stopper and tilted the mouth into a tin cup. The reek of white corn juice filled the room, and Reynolds smacked his lips appreciatively.

"Hell, Joel, you ought not to be scared of hidin' me, long as you've kept that still of your'n hid."

"That's different," muttered Jackson uneasily. "You know, though, I'll do all I can to help you out."

He watched his friend in morbid fascination as Reynolds wolfed down the food and gulped the fiery liquor with keen relish.

"I don't see how you can set there and eat like that. Don't it make you kind of sick—thinkin' about Hopkins?"

"Why should it?" Reynolds' eyes became grim as he set down the cup and stared at his host. "Throwed John out of his home, and him with a wife and kids, and then was goin' to send him to the pen—how much you think a man ought to take off a skunk like that?"

Jackson avoided his gaze and looked out the window. Away off in the distance came the first low grumble of thunder. The lightning played constantly along the northwestern horizon, splaying out to east and west.

"Comin' up sure," mumbled Jackson. "Reckon they'll get some water in Bisley Lake. Engineers said it'd take three years to fill it, at the rate of rainfall in this country. I say one big rain like some

I've seen, would do the job. An awful lot of water can come down Locust and Mesquital."

He opened the door and went out. Reynolds followed. The breathlessness of the atmosphere was even more intense. The haze-like veil had thickened; not a star was visible. The crowding hills with their black thickets rendered the darkness even more dense; but it was cut by the incessant glare of the lightning—distant, but growing more vivid. In the flashes a long low-lying bank of inky blackness could be seen hugging the northwestern horizon.

"Funny the laws ain't been up the road," muttered Jackson. "I been listenin' for cars."

"Reckon they're searchin' the other roads," answered Reynolds. "Take some time to get up a posse after night, anyway. They'll be burnin' up the telephone wires. I reckon you got the only phone there is on this road, ain't you, Joel?"

"Yeah; folks couldn't keep up the rent on 'em. By gosh, that cloud's comin' up slow, but it sure is black. I bet it's been rainin' pitchforks on the head of Locust for hours."

"I'm goin' to walk down towards the road," said Reynolds. "I can see a headlight a lot quicker down there than I can up here, for all these post oaks. I've got an idea they'll be up here askin' questions before mornin'. But if you lie like I've seen you, they won't suspect enough to go prowlin' around."

Jackson shuddered at the prospect. Reynolds walked down the winding path, and disappeared among the flanking oaks. But he did not go far. He suddenly remembered that the dishes out of which he had eaten were still on the kitchen table. That might cause suspicion if the law dropped in suddenly. He turned and headed swiftly back toward the house. And as he went, he heard a peculiar tingling noise he was at first unable to identify. Then he was electrified by sudden suspicion. It was such a sound as a telephone would make, if rung while a quilt or cloak was held over it to muzzle the sound from someone near at hand.

Crouching like a panther, he stole up, and looking through a crack in the door, saw Jackson standing at the phone. The man shook like a leaf and great beads of sweat stood out on his grey face. His voice was strangled and unnatural.

"Yes, yes!" he was mouthing. "I tell you, he's here now! He's gone down to the road, to watch for the cops. Come here as quick as you can, Leary—and come yourself. He's bad! I'll try to get him drunk, or asleep, or somethin'. Anyway, hurry, and for God's sake, don't let on I told you, even after you got him corralled."

Reynolds threw back the door and stepped in, his face a death-mask. Jackson wheeled, saw him, and gave a choked croak. His face turned hideous; the receiver fell from his fingers and dangled at the end of its cord.

"My God, Reynolds!" he screamed. "Don't—don't—"

Reynolds took a single step; his gun went up and smashed down; the heavy barrel crunched against Jackson's skull. The man went down like a slaughtered ox and lay twitching, his eyes closed, and blood oozing from a deep gash in his scalp, and from his nose and ears as well.

Reynolds stood over him an instant, snarling silently. Then he stepped to the phone and lifted the receiver. No sound came over the wire. He wondered if the man at the other end had hung up before Jackson screamed. He hung the receiver back on its hook, and strode out of the house.

A savage resentment made thinking a confused and muddled process. Jackson, the one man south of Lost Knob he had thought he could trust, had betrayed him—not for gain, not for revenge, but simply because of his cowardice. Reynolds snarled wordlessly. He was trapped; he could not reach Lost Knob in his car, and he would not have time to drive back down the Bisley road, and find another road, before the police would be racing up it. Suddenly he laughed, and it was not a good laugh to hear.

A fierce excitement galvanized him. By God, Fate had worked into his hands, after all! He did not wish to escape, only to slay before he died. Leary was one of the men he had marked for death. And Leary was coming to the Jackson farmhouse.

He took a step toward the corral, glanced at the sky, turned, ran back into the house, found and donned a slicker. By that time the lightning was a constant glare overhead. It was astounding—incredible. A man could almost have read a book by it. The whole northern and western sky was veined with irregular cords of blinding crimson which ran back and forth, leaping to the earth, flickering back into the heavens, crisscrossing and interlacing. Thunder rumbled, growing louder. The bank in the northwest had grown appallingly. From the east around to the middle of the west it loomed, black as doom. Hills, thickets, road and buildings were bathed weirdly in the red glare as Reynolds ran to the corral where the horses whimpered fearfully. Still there was no sound in the elements but the thunder. Somewhere off in the hills a wind howled shudderingly, then ceased abruptly.

Reynolds found bridle, blanket and saddle, threw them on a restive and uneasy horse, and led it out of the corral and down behind the cliff which flanked the path that led up to the house. He tied the animal behind a thicket where it could not be seen from the path. Up in the house the oil lamp still burned. Reynolds did not bother to look to Joel Jackson. If the man ever regained consciousness at all, it would not be for many hours. Reynolds knew the effect of such a blow as he had dealt.

Minutes passed, ten—fifteen. Now he heard a sound that was not of the thunder—a distant purring that swiftly grew louder. A shaft that was not lightning stabbed the sky to the southeast. It was lost, then appeared again. Reynolds knew it was an automobile topping the rises. He crouched behind a rock in a shinnery thicket close to the path, just above the point where it swung close to the rim of the low bluff.

Now he could see the headlights glinting through the trees like a pair of angry eyes. The eyes of the Law! he thought sardonically, and hugged himself with venomous glee. The car halted, then came on, marking the entering of the gate. They had not bothered to close the gate, he knew, and felt an instinctive twinge of resentment. That was typical of those Bisley laws—leave a man's gate open, and let all his stock get out.

Now the automobile was mounting the hill, and he grew tense. Either Leary had not heard Jackson's scream shudder over the wires, or else he was reckless. Reynolds nestled further down behind his rock. The lights swept over his head as the car came around the cliff-flanked turn. Lightning conspired to dazzle him, but as the headlights completed their arc and turned away from him, he made out the bulk of men in the car, and the glint of guns. Directly overhead thunder bellowed and a freak of lightning played full on the climbing automobile. In its brief flame he saw the car was crowded—five men, at least, and the chances were that it was Chief Leary at the wheel, though he could not be sure, in that illusive illumination.

The car picked up speed, skirting the cliff—and now Jim Reynolds thrust his .45 through the stems of the shinnery, and fired by the flare of the lightning. His shot merged with a rolling clap of thunder. The car lurched wildly as its driver, shot through the head, slumped over the wheel. Yells of terror rose as it swerved toward the cliff edge. But the man on the seat with the driver dropped his shotgun and caught frantically at the wheel.

Reynolds was standing now, firing again and again, but he could not duplicate the amazing luck of that first shot. Lead raked the car and a man yelped, but the policeman at the wheel hung on tenaciously, hindered by the corpse which slumped over it, and the car, swinging away from the bluff, roared erratically across the path, crashed through bushes and shinnery, and caromed with terrific impact against a boulder, buckling the radiator and hurling men out like tenpins.

Reynolds yelled his savage disappointment, and sent the last bullet in his gun whining viciously among the figures stirring dazedly on the ground about the smashed car. At that, their stunned minds went to work. They rolled into the brush and behind rocks. Tongues of flame began to spit at him, as they gave back his fire. He ducked down into the shinnery again. Bullets hummed over his head, or smashed against the rock in front of him, and on the heels of a belching blast there came a myriad venomous whirrings through the brush as of many bees. Somebody had salvaged a shotgun.

The wildness of the shooting told of unmanned nerves and shattered morale, but Reynolds, crouching low as he reloaded, swore at the fewness of his cartridges.

He had failed in the great coup he had planned. The car had not gone over the bluff. Four policemen still lived, and now, hiding in the thickets, they had the advantage. They could circle back and gain the house without showing themselves to his fire; they could phone for reinforcements. But he grinned fiercely as the flickering lightning showed him the body that sagged over the broken door where the impact of the collision had tossed it like a rag doll. He had not made a mistake; it was chief of police Leary who had stopped his first bullet.

The world was a hell of sound and flame; the cracking of pistols and shotguns was almost drowned in the terrific cannonade of the skies. The whole sky, when not lit by flame, was pitch black. Great sheets and ropes and chains of fire leaped terribly across the dusky vault, and the reverberations of the thunder made the earth tremble. Between the bellowings came sharp claps that almost split the eardrums. Yet not a drop of rain had fallen.

The continual glare was more confusing than utter darkness. Men shot wildly and blindly. And Reynolds began backing cautiously through the shinnery. Behind it, the ground sloped quickly, breaking off into the cliff that skirted the path further down. Down the incline Reynolds slid recklessly, and ran for his horse, half frantic on its tether. The men in the brush above yelled and blazed away vainly as they got a fleeting glimpse of him.

He ducked behind the thicket that masked the horse, tore the animal free, leaped into the saddle—and then the rain came. It did not come as it comes in less violent lands. It was as if a floodgate had been opened on high—as if the bottom had been jerked out of a celestial rain barrel. A gulf of water descended in one appalling roar.

The wind was blowing now, roaring through the fire-torn night, bending the trees, but its fury was less than the rain. Reynolds, clinging to his maddened horse, felt the beast stagger to the buffeting. Despite his slicker, the man was soaked in an instant. It was not raining in drops, but in driving sheets, in thundering cascades. His horse reeled and floundered in the torrents which were already swirling down the gulches and draws. The lightning had not ceased; it played all around him, veiled in the falling flood like fire shining through frosted glass, turning the world to frosty silver.

For a few moments he saw the light in the farmhouse behind him, and he tried to use it as his compass, riding directly away from it. Then it was blotted out by the shoulder of a hill, and he rode in fire-lit darkness, his sense of direction muddled and confused. He did not try to find a path, or to get back to the road, but headed straight out across the hills.

It was bitter hard going. His horse staggered in rushing rivelets, slipped on muddy slopes, blundered into trees, scratching his rider's face and hands. In the driving rain there was no seeing any distance; the blinding lightning was a hindrance rather than a help. And the bombardment of the heavens did not cease. Reynolds rode through a hell of fire and fury, blinded, stunned and dazed by the cataclysmic war of the elements. It was nature gone mad—a saturnalia of the elements in which all sense of place and time was dimmed.

Nearby a dazzling white jet forked from the black sky with a stunning crack, and a knotted oak flew into splinters. With a shrill neigh, Reynolds' mount bolted, blundering over rocks and through bushes. A tree limb struck Reynolds' head, and the man fell forward over the saddle horn, dazed, keeping his seat by instinct.

It was the rain, slashing savagely in his face, that brought him to his full senses. He did not know how long he had clung to his saddle in a dazed condition, while the horse wandered at will. He wondered dully at the violence of the rain. It had not abated, though the wind was not blowing now, and the lightning had decreased much in intensity.

Grimly he gathered up the hanging reins and headed in the direction he believed was north. God, would the rain never cease? It had become a monster—an ogreish perversion of nature. It had been thundering down for hours, and still it threshed and beat, as if it poured from an inexhaustible reservoir.

He felt his horse jolt against something and stop, head drooping to the blast. The blazing sky showed him that the animal was breasting a barbed wire fence. He dismounted, fumbled for the wire clippers in the saddle pocket, cut the strands, mounted, and rode wearily on.

He topped a rise, emerged from the screening oaks and stared, blinking. At first he could not realize what he saw, it was so incongruous and alien. But he had to believe his senses. He looked on a gigantic body of water, rolling as far as he could see, lashed into foaming frenzy, under the play of the lightning.

Then the truth rushed upon him. He was looking at Bisley Lake! Bisley Lake, which that morning had been an empty basin, with its only water that which flowed along the rocky beds of Locust Creek and Mesquital, reduced by a six months' drought to a trickle. There in the hills, just east of where the streams merged, a dam had been built by the people of Bisley with intent to irrigate. But money had run short. The ditches had not been dug, though the dam had been completed. There lay the lake basin, ready for use, but, so far, useless. Three years would be required to fill it, the engineers said, considering average rainfall. But they were Easterners. With all their technical education they had not counted on the terrific volume of water which could rush down those post oak ridges during such a rain as had been falling. Because it was ordinarily a dry country, they had not realized that such floods could fall. From Lost Knob to Bisley the land fell at the rate of a hundred and fifty feet to every ten miles; Locust Creek and Mesquital drained a watershed of immense expanse, and were fed by myriad branches winding down from the higher ridges. Now, halted in its rush to the Gulf, this water was piling up in Bisley Lake.

Three years? It had filled in a matter of *hours!* Reynolds looked dazedly on the biggest body of water he had ever seen—seventy miles of waterfront, and God only knew how deep in the channels of the rivers! The rain must have assumed the proportions of a waterspout higher up on the heads of the creeks.

The rain was slackening. He knew it must be nearly dawn. Glints of daylight would be showing, but for the clouds and rain. He had been toiling through the storm for hours.

In the flare of the lightning he saw huge logs and trees whirling in the foaming wash; he saw broken buildings, and the bodies of cows, hogs, sheep, and horses, and sodden shocks of grain. He cursed to think of the havoc wrought. Fresh fury rose in him against the people of Bisley. Them and their cursed dam! Any fool ought to know it would back the water up the creeks for twenty miles and force it out of banks and over into fields and pastures. As usual, it was the hill dwellers who suffered.

He looked uneasily at the dark line of the dam. It didn't look so big and solid as it did when the lake basin was empty, but he knew it would resist any strain. And it afforded him a bridge. The rain would cover his tracks. Wires would be down—though doubtless by this time news of his killings had been spread all over the country. Anyway, the storm would have paralyzed pursuit for a few hours. He could get back to the Lost Knob country, and into hiding.

He dismounted and led the horse out on the dam. It snorted and trembled, in fear of the water churned into foam by the drumming rain, so close beneath its feet, but he soothed it and led it on.

If God had made that gorge especially for a lake, He could not have planned it better. It was the southeastern outlet of a great basin, walled with steep hills. The gorge itself was in the shape of a gigantic V, with the narrow bottom turned toward the east, and the legs or sides of rocky cliffs, towering ninety to a hundred and fifty feet high. From the west, Mesquital meandered across the broad basin, and from the north, Locust Creek came down between rock ledge banks and merged with Mesquital in the wide mouth of the V. Then the river thus formed flowed through the narrow gap in the hills to the east. Across the gap the dam had been built.

Once the road to Lost Knob, climbing up from the south, had descended into that basin, crossed Mesquital and led on up into the hills to the northwest. But now that road was submerged by foaming water. Directly north of the dam was no road, only a wild expanse of hills and post oak groves. But Reynolds knew he could skirt the edge of the lake and reach the old road on the other side, or better still, strike straight out through the hills, ignoring all roads and using his wire clippers to let him through fences.

His horse snorted and shied violently. Reynolds cursed and clawed at his gun, tucked under his dripping raincoat. He had just reached the other end of the dam, and something was moving in the darkness.

"Stop right where you are!" Someone was splashing toward him. The lightning revealed a man without coat or hat. His hair was plastered to his skull, and water streamed down his sodden garments. His eyes gleamed in the lightning glare.

"Bill Emmett!" exclaimed Reynolds, raising his voice above the thunder of the waters below. "What the devil you doin' here?"

"I'm here on the devil's business!" shouted the other. "What *you* doin' here? Been to Bisley to get bail for John?"

"Bail, hell," answered Reynolds grimly, close to the man. "I killed Saul Hopkins!"

The answer was a shriek that disconcerted him. Emmett gripped his hand and wrung it fiercely. The man seemed strung to an unnatural pitch.

"Good!" he yelled. "But they's more in Bisley than Saul Hopkins."

"I know," replied Reynolds. "I aim to get some of them before I die."

Another shriek of passionate exultation cut weirdly through the lash of the wind and the rain.

"You're the man for me!" Emmett was fumbling with cold fingers over Reynolds' lapels and arms. "I knowed you was the right stuff! Now you listen to me. See that water?" He pointed at the deafening torrent surging and thundering almost under their feet. "Look at it!" he screamed. "Look at it surge and foam and eddy under the lightnin'! See them whirlpools in it! Look at them dead cows and horses whirlin' and bangin' against the dam! Well, I'm goin' to let that through the streets of Bisley! They'll wake up to find the black water foamin' through their windows! It won't be just dead cattle floatin' in the water! It'll be dead men and dead women! I can see 'em now, whirlin' down, down to the Gulf!"

Reynolds gripped the man by the shoulders and shook him savagely. "What you talkin' about?" he roared.

A peal of wild laughter mingled with a crash of thunder. "I mean I got enough dynamite planted under this dam to split it wide open!" Emmett yelled. "I'm goin' to send everybody in Bisley to hell before daylight!"

"You're crazy!" snarled Reynolds, an icy hand clutching his heart.

"Crazy?" screamed the other; and the mad glare in his eyes, limned by the lightning, told Reynolds that he had spoken the grisly truth. "Crazy? You just come from killin' that devil Hopkins, and you turn pale? You're small stuff; you killed one enemy. I aim to kill thousands!

"Look out there where the black water is rollin' and tumblin'. I owned that, once; leastways, I owned land the water has taken now, away over yonder. My father and grandfather owned it before me. And they condemned it and took it away from me, just because Bisley wanted a lake, damn their yellow souls!"

"The county paid you three times what the land was worth," protested Reynolds, his peculiar sense of justice forcing him into defending an enemy.

"Yes!" Again that awful peal of laughter turned Reynolds cold. "Yes! And I put it in a Bisley bank, and the bank went broke! I lost every cent I had in the world. I'm down and out; I got no land and no money. Damn 'em, oh, damn 'em! Bisley's goin' to pay! I'm goin' to wipe her out! There's enough water out there to fill Locust Valley from ridge to ridge across Bisley. I've waited for this; I've planned for it. Tonight when I seen the lightnin' flickerin' over the ridges, I knew the time was come.

"I ain't hung around here and fed the watchman corn juice for months, just for fun. He's drunk up in his shack now, and the flood-gate's closed! I seen to that! My charge is planted—enough to crack the dam—the water'll do the rest. I've stood here all night, watchin'

Locust and Mesquital rollin' down like the rivers of Judgment, and now it's time, and I'm goin' to set off the charge!"

"Emmett!" protested Reynolds, shaking with horror. "My God, you can't do this! Think of the women and children—"

"Who thought of mine?" yelled Emmett, his voice cracking in a sob. "My wife had to live like a dog after we lost our home and money; that's why she died. I didn't have enough money to have her took care of. Get out of my way, Reynolds; you're small stuff. You killed one man; I aim to kill thousands."

"Wait!" urged Reynolds desperately. "I hate Bisley as much as anybody—but my God, man, the women and kids ain't got nothin' to do with it! You ain't goin' to do this—you *can't*—" His brain reeled at the picture it evoked. Bisley lay directly in the path of the flood; its business houses stood almost on the banks of Locust Creek. The whole town was built in the bottoms; hundreds would find it impossible to escape in time to the hills, should this awful mountain of black water come roaring down the valley. Reynolds was only an anachronism, not a homicidal maniac.

In the urgency of his determination he dropped the reins of his horse and caught at Emmett. The horse snorted and galloped up the slope and away.

"Let go me, Reynolds!" howled Emmett. "I'll kill you!"

"You'll have to before you set off that charge!" gritted Reynolds.

Emmett screamed like a tree cat. He tore away, came on again, something glinting in his uplifted hand. Swearing, Reynolds fumbled for his gun. The hammer caught in the oilcloth. Emmett caromed against him, screaming and striking. An agonizing pain went through Reynolds' lifted left arm, another and another; he felt the keen blade rip along his ribs, sink into his shoulder. Emmett was snarling like a wild beast, hacking blindly and madly.

They were down on the brink of the dam, clawing and smiting in the mud and water. Dimly Reynolds realized that he was being stabbed to pieces. He was a powerful man, but he was hampered by his long slicker, exhausted by his ride through the storm, and Emmett was a thing of wires of rawhide, fired by the frenzy of madness.

Reynolds abandoned his attempts to imprison Emmett's knife wrist, and tugged again at his imprisoned gun. It came clear, just as Emmett, with a mad howl, drove his knife full into Reynolds' breast. The madman screamed again as he felt the muzzle jam against him; then the gun thundered, so close between them it burnt the clothing of both. Reynolds was almost deafened by the report. Emmett was thrown clear of him and lay at the rim of the dam, his back broken by the tearing impact of the heavy bullet. His head hung over the edge, his arms trailed down toward the foaming black water which seemed to surge upward for him.

Reynolds essayed to rise, then sank back dizzily. Lightning played before his eyes, thunder rumbled. Beneath him the tumultuous water roared. Somewhere in the blackness there grew a hint of light. Belated dawn was stealing over the post oak hills, bent beneath a cloak of rain.

"Damn!" choked Reynolds, clawing at the mud. Incoherently he cursed; not because death was upon him, but because of the manner of his dying.

"Why couldn't I gone out like I wanted to?—fightin' them I hate—not a friend who'd gone bughouse. Curse the luck! And for them Bisley swine! Anyway—" the wandering voice trailed away— "died with my boots on—like a man ought to die—damn them—"

The bloodstained hands ceased to grope; the figure in the tattered slicker lay still; parting a curtain of falling rain, dawn broke grey and haggard over the post oak country.

Cowboy

Poets and novelists have sung of me;
Made me a bronzed-faced Centaur, leather-girt.
The real man they all have failed to see;
A weary, ignorant man in an unwashed shirt.

The Last Ride

with Robert Enders Allen

Chapter .1.
The Laramies Move On

Five men were riding down the winding road that led to San Leon, and one was singing, in a flat, toneless monotone:

"Early in the mornin', in the month of May,
Brady came down on the mornin' train—
Brady came down on the Shinin' Star,
And he shot Mr. Duncan in behind the bar!"

"Shut up! Shut up! *Shut up!*" It was the youngest of the riders who ripped out like that, with a note of hysteria in his voice. A lanky, tow-headed kid, with a touch of pallor under his tan, and a rebellious smolder in his hot eyes.

The biggest man of the five grinned and spat.

"Bucky's nervous," he jeered genially. "You don't want to be no derned bandit, do you, Bucky?"

The youngest glowered at him.

"That welt on yore jaw ought to answer that, Jim," he growled.

"You fit like a catamount," agreed Big Jim placidly. "I thought we'd never git you on yore cayuse and started for San Leon, without knockin' you in the head. 'Bout the only way you show yo're a Laramie, Bucky, is in the handlin' of yore fists."

"'Tain't no honor to be a Laramie," flared Bucky. "You and Luke and Tom and Hank has dragged the name through slime. For the last three years you been worse'n a pack of starvin' lobos—stealin' cattle and horses; robbin' folks—why, the country's blame near ruint just on account of you-all. And now yo're headin' to San Leon to put on the final touch—robbin' the Cattlemen's Bank, when you know dern well the help the ranchmen got from that bank's been all that kept 'em on their feet. Old man Brown's stretched hisself nigh to the bustin' p'int to help folks. And you-all flap around like a passel of blasted buzzards gorgin' on what belongs to honest men. And now you got *me* dragged into it." He gulped and fought back tears that betrayed his extreme youth. His brothers grinned tolerantly.

"It's the last time," he informed them bitterly. "You won't git me into no raid again!"

"It's the last time for all of us," said Big Jim, biting off a cud of tobacco. "You know that, Bucky. We're through after this job. We'll live like honest men in Mexico."

"Serve you right if a posse caught us and hanged us all," said Bucky viciously.

"Not a chance." Big Jim's placidity was unruffled. "Nobody but us knows the trail that follows the secret waterholes acrost the desert. No posse'd dare to foller us. Once out of town and headed south for the Border, and the devil hisself couldn't catch us."

"I wonder if anybody'll ever stumble onto our secret hideout up in the Los Diablos Mountains," mused Hank.

"I doubt it. Too well hid. Like the desert trail, nobody but us knows them mountain trails. It shore served us well. Think of all the steers and horses we've hid there, and drove through the mountains to Mexico! And the times we've laid up there laughin' in our sleeves whilst the posse chased around a circle like a pup chasin' its own tail."

Bucky muttered something under his breath; he retained no fond memories of that hidden lair high up in the barren Diablos. He had hated the sight of it from the first, when, three years before, he had reluctantly followed his brothers into it, with their scrub cattle and meager household furnishings, from the little ranch in the foothills where Old Man Laramie and his wife had worn away their lives in hard work and futile efforts. The old life, when their parents lived and had held their wild sons in check, had been drab and hard, but had lacked the bitterness he had known when cooking and tending house for his brothers in that hidden den from which they had ravaged the countryside. Four good men gone bad—mighty bad.

San Leon lay as if slumbering in the desert heat as the five brothers rode up to the doors of the Cattlemen's Bank. None noted their coming; the Red Lode saloon, favorite rendezvous for the masculine element of San Leon, stood at the other end of the town, and out of sight around a slight bend in the street.

No words were passed; each man knew his part beforehand. The three elder Laramies slid lithely out of their saddles, throwing their reins to Bucky and Luke, the second youngest. They strode into the bank with a soft jingle of spurs and creak of leather, closing the door behind them.

Luke's face was impassive as an image's, as he dragged leisurely on a cigarette, though his eyes gleamed between slitted lids. But Bucky sweated and shivered, twisting nervously in his saddle, he cursed the fate that had brought him here, fighting a tendency toward nausea. By some twist of destiny, one son had inherited all the honesty that was his parents' to transmit, and one son only. Regardless of what his brothers did, he had kept his hands clean. But now, in spite of himself, he was scarred with their brand, an outlaw, against his will.

He started convulsively as a gun crashed inside the bank; like an echo came another reverberation.

Luke's Colt was in his hand, and he snatched one foot clear of the stirrup, then feet pounded toward the street and the door burst open to emit the three outlaws. They carried bulging canvas sacks, and Hank's sleeve was crimson.

"Ride like hell!" grunted Big Jim, forking his roan. "Old Brown throwed down on Hank. Old fool! I had to salivate him permanent."

And like hell it was they rode, straight down the street toward the desert, yelling and firing as they went. They thundered past houses from which startled individuals peered bewilderedly, past stores where leathery-faced storekeepers were dragging forth blue-barreled scatter-guns, swept through the futile rain of lead that poured from the excited and befuddled crowd in front of the Red Lode, and whirled on toward the desert that stretched south of San Leon.

But not quite to the desert . . . For as they rounded the last bend in the twisting street and came abreast of the last house in the village, they were confronted by the grey-bearded figure of old "Pop" Anders, sheriff of San Leon County. The old man's gnarled right hand rested on the ancient single-action Colt on his thigh, his left was lifted in a seemingly futile command to halt.

Big Jim cursed and sawed back on the reins, and the big roan slid to a halt within half a dozen feet of the old lawman.

"Git outa the way, Pop!" roared Big Jim. "We don't want to hurt you."

The old warrior's eyes blazed with righteous wrath.

"Robbed the bank this time, eh?" he said in cold fury, his eyes on the canvas sacks. "Likely spilt blood, too. Good thing Frank Laramie died before he could know what skunks his boys turned out to be. You ain't content to steal our stock till we're nigh bankrupt; you got to rob our bank and take what little money we got left for a new start. Why, you damned human sidewinders!" the old man shrieked, his control snapping suddenly. "Ain't there *nothin'* in God's world that's too dirty lowdown for you to do?"

Behind them sounded the pound of running feet and a scattering banging of guns. The crowd from the Red Lode was closing in.

"You've wasted our time long enough, old man!" roared Luke, jabbing in the spurs and sending his horse rearing and plunging toward the indomitable figure. "Git outa the way, or by God—"

The old single action jumped free in the gnarled hand . . . Two shots roared together, and Luke's sombrero went skyrocketing from his head. But the old sheriff fell face forward in the dust with a bullet through his heart, and the Laramie gang swept on into the desert, feeding their dust to their hurriedly mounted and disheartened pursuers.

Only young Buck Laramie looked back, to see the door of the last house fly open, and a pig-tailed girl run out to the still figure in the street. It was the sheriff's daughter, Judy. She and Buck had gone to the same school in the old days before the Laramies hit the wolf trail. Down on her knees she went, in the dust beside her father's body, seeking frantically for a spark of life where there was none.

A red film blazed before Buck Laramie's eyes as he turned his livid face toward his brothers.

"Hell," Luke was fretting, "I didn't aim to salivate him permanent. The old lobo woulda hung every one of us if he could of—but just the same I didn't aim to kill him."

Something snapped in Bucky's brain.

"You didn't aim to kill him!" he shrieked. "No, but you did! Yo're all a pack of lowdown sidewinders just like he said! They ain't nothin' too dirty for you!" He brandished his clenched fists in the extremity of his passion. "You filthy scum!" he sobbed. "When I'm growed up I'm comin' back here and make up for ever' dollar you've stole, ever' life you've took. I'll do it if they hang me for tryin', s'help me God!"

His brothers did not reply. They did not look at him. Big Jim hummed flatly and absently:

"Some say he shot him with a thirty-eight,
Some say he shot him with a forty-one—
But I say he shot him with a forty-four,
For I saw him as he lay on the barroom floor."

Bucky subsided, slumped in his saddle and rode dismally on. San Leon and the old life lay behind them all. Somewhere south of the hazy horizon the desert stretched into Mexico where lay their future destiny. And his destiny was inextricably interwoven with that of his brothers. He was an outlaw too, now, and he must stay with the clan to the end of their last ride.

Some guiding angel must have caused Buck Laramie to lean forward to pat the head of his tired sorrel, for at that instant a bullet ripped through his hat brim, instead of his head.

It came as a startling surprize, but his reaction was instant. Almost before the sound of the shot had died away, he was off his horse and diving for the protection of a sand bank. A second bullet spurted dust at his heels as he leaped, and then he was under cover, and peering warily out, Colt in hand.

The tip of a white sombrero showed above a rim of sand, some two hundred yards in front of him. Laramie blazed away at it, though knowing as he pulled the trigger that the range was too long and the target too small for six-gun accuracy. Nevertheless, the hat top vanished.

"Takin' no chances," muttered Laramie. "Now who in hell is *he*? Here I am a good hour's ride from San Leon, and folks pottin' at me already. Looks bad for what I'm aimin' to do. Reckon it's somebody that knows me, after all these years?"

He could not believe it possible that anyone would recognize the lanky, half-grown boy of six years ago in the bronzed, range-hardened man who was returning to San Leon to keep the vow he had made as his clan rode southward with two dead men and a looted bank behind them.

Peering cautiously over the crest of his sandbank, he caught the sun gleaming on a blue circle, and ducked just as the shot cracked, and the slug knocked dust where his head had been. He shoved his Colt over the rim and fired back, but the rifle-muzzle had already vanished. It cracked again, presently, from another point, but the slug was wild, the shot apparently unhurried. Evidently the unknown attacker was not disposed to take any chances with his hide.

But Laramie knew this could not go on forever. The sun was burning hot, and the sand felt like an oven beneath him. His canteen was slung to his saddle, and his horse was out of his reach, drooping under a scrubby mesquite. The other fellow would eventually work around to a point where his rifle would outrange Laramie's six-gun—or he might shoot the horse and leave Buck afoot in the desert.

It was the realization of this possibility which sent Laramie into aggressive action. The instant his attacker's next shot sang past his refuge, he was up and away in a stooping, weaving run to the next sand hill, to the right and slightly forward of his original position. Bullets bit at his heels, but he reached his goal safely and grunted with satisfaction as he noted the broken and uneven quality of the ground from that point on. He began a slow, crawling circuit that he hoped would bring him to close quarters with his unknown enemy.

He wriggled from cover to cover, and sprinted in short dashes over narrow strips of open ground, taking advantage of every rock, cactus bed and sandbank, with lead hissing and spitting at him all the way. The hidden gunman had guessed his purpose, and obviously had no desire for a close-range fight. He was slinging lead every time Laramie showed an inch of flesh, cloth or leather, and Buck counted the shots. He was within striking distance of the sand rim when he believed the fellow's rifle was empty.

Springing recklessly to his feet, he charged straight at his hidden enemy, his six-gun blazing. That he had miscalculated about the rifle was shown by a bullet tearing through the slack of his shirt. But then the Winchester was silent, and Laramie was raking the rim with such a barrage of lead that the gunman evidently dared not lift himself high enough to line the sights of a six-gun.

But a pistol was something that must be reckoned with, and as he spent his last bullet, Laramie dived behind a rise of sand and began desperately to jam cartridges into his empty gun. He had failed to cross the sand rim in that rush, but another try would gain it—unless hot lead cut him down on the way. Drum of hoofs reached his ears suddenly, and glaring over his shelter he saw a pinto pony beyond the sand rim heading in the direction of San Leon, and its rider wore a white sombrero.

"Damn!" Laramie slammed the cylinder in place and sent a slug winging after the rapidly receding horseman. But he did not repeat the shot. The fellow was already out of range.

"Reckon the work was gettin' too close for him," he ruminated as he trudged back to his horse. "Wish he'd stayed till I could line him proper. Them that fights and runs away—hell, maybe he didn't want me to get a good look at him; maybe he knew I'd know him;

but why? Nobody in these parts would be shy about shootin' at a Laramie, if they knew him as such. But who'd know I *was* a Laramie?"

He swung up into the saddle.

"Get along, cayuse. Somebody don't want us to go to San Leon, but they got to do better'n that if they want to stop us. I got big business there."

He absently slapped his saddlebags and the faint clinking that resulted soothed him. Those bags were loaded with fifty thousand dollars in gold eagles, and every penny was meant for the people of San Leon.

"It'll help pay the debt the Laramies owe for the money the boys stole," he confided to the uninterested sorrel. "But how I'm goin' to pay back for the men they killed is more'n I can figure out. But I'll try."

The money represented all he had accumulated from the sale of the Laramie stock and holdings in Mexico—holdings bought with money stolen from San Leon. It was his by right of inheritance, for he was the last of the Laramies. Big Jim, Tom, Hank, Luke, all had found trail's end in that lawless country south of the Border. As they had lived, so had they died, facing their killers, with smoking guns in their hands. Buck, dispassionately reviewing their ends, realized it could not have been otherwise. Men who have once followed the wolf trail are not destined to die in bed. They had tried to live straight in Mexico, but the wild blood was still there. Fate had dealt their hands, and Buck looked upon it all as a slate wiped clean, a record closed—with the exception of Luke's fate.

That memory vaguely troubled him now, as he rode toward San Leon to pay the debts his brothers contracted.

"Folks said Luke drew first," he muttered. "But it wasn't like him to pick a barroom fight. Funny the fellow that killed him cleared out so quick, if it was a fair fight. Maybe I'll meet him this side of the Border—and if I do—"

He dismissed the old problem and reviewed the recent attack upon himself.

"If he knowed I was a Laramie, it might have been anybody. But how could he know? Joel Waters wouldn't talk."

No, Joel Waters wouldn't talk; and Joel Waters, old time friend of Laramie's father, long ago, and owner of the Boxed W Ranch, was the only man who knew Buck Laramie was returning to San Leon.

So Laramie dismissed the unknown gunman as a mystery for the present unsolvable, and rode on, engrossed in speculations as to what lay before him, in the town to which he was bringing every cent he owned in the world, but in which the hand of every man would be raised against him, were his identity suspected.

"San Leon at last, cayuse," he murmured as he topped the last desert sand hill that sloped down to the town. "Last time I seen it was under circumstances most—what the devil!"

He started and stiffened as a rattle of gunfire burst on his ears. Battle in San Leon? He urged his weary steed down the hill. Two minutes later, history was repeating itself.

Chapter .2.
Beside the Law

As Buck Laramie galloped into San Leon, a sight met his eyes which jerked him back to a day six years gone. For tearing down the street in full career came six wild riders, yelling and shooting. In the lead rode one, who, with his huge frame and careless ease, might have been Big Jim Laramie come back to life again. Behind them the crowd at the Red Lode, roused to befuddled life, was shooting just as wildly and ineffectively as on that other day when hot lead raked San Leon.

And confronting the onrushing horsemen, there was but one man to bar their path—one man who stood, legs braced wide, guns drawn, in the roadway before the last house in San Leon. So old Pop Anders had stood, that other day—and there was something about this man to remind Laramie of the old sheriff, though he was much younger. In a flash of recognition Laramie knew him—Bob Anders, son of Luke's victim.

He, too, wore a silver star . . . And this time Laramie did not stand helplessly by to see a sheriff slaughtered. With the swiftness born of six hard years below the Border, he made his decision and acted. Gravel spurted as the sorrel threw back his head against the sawing bit and came to a sliding stop, and all in one motion Laramie was out of the saddle and on his feet beside the sheriff—half-crouching, and his six-gun cocked and pointed. This time two would meet the charge, not one.

The sight of the unexpected reinforcements caused a slight wavering in the oncoming ranks. For an instant they seemed about to swerve for cover, then they came on again, burning powder, narrowing the space between them and the two men on foot—now it was a hundred yards, now fifty—

Laramie saw that masks hid the faces of the riders as they swept down, and contempt stabbed through him. No Laramie ever wore a mask . . . His Colt vibrated as he thumbed the hammer. Beside him the young sheriff's guns were spitting smoke and lead.

The clumped group split apart at that blast. One man, who wore a Mexican sash instead of a belt, slumped in his saddle, clawing for the horn. Another with his right arm flopping broken at his side was fighting his pain-maddened beast which had stopped a slug intended for its rider.

The big man who had led the charge grabbed the fellow with the sash as he started to slide limply from his saddle, and dragged him across his own bow. He bolted across the roadside and plunged into a dry wash. The others followed him; the man with the broken arm abandoning his own crazed mount and grabbing the reins of the riderless horse. Beasts and men, they slid over the rim and out of sight in a cloud of dust.

Anders yelled and started across the road on the run, but Laramie jerked him back.

"They're covered," he grunted, sending his sorrel galloping to a safe place with a slap on the rump. "We got to get out of sight, *pronto!*"

The sheriff's good judgment overcame his excitement then, and he wheeled and darted for the house, yelping: "Follow me, stranger!"

Bullets whined after them from the gulch as the outlaws began their stand. The door opened inward before Anders' outstretched hand touched it, and he plunged through without checking his stride. Lead smacked the jambs and splinters flew as Laramie ducked after Anders. He collided with something soft and yielding that gasped and tumbled to the floor under the impact. Glaring wildly down Laramie found himself face to face with a vision of feminine loveliness that took his breath away, even in that instant. With a horrified gasp he plunged to his feet and lifted the girl after him, his all-embracing gaze taking her in from tousled blond hair to whipcord breeches and high-heeled riding boots. She seemed too bewildered to speak.

"Sorry, Miss," he stuttered. "I hope y'ain't hurt. I was—I was—"
The smash of a windowpane and the whine of a bullet cut short his floundering apologies. He snatched the girl out of line of the window and in an instant was crouching beside it himself, throwing lead across the road toward the smoke wisps that curled up from the rim of the dry wash.

Anders had barred the door and grabbed a Winchester from a rack on the wall.

"Duck into a back room, Judy," he ordered, kneeling at the window on the other side of the door. "Partner, I don't know you—" he punctuated his remarks with rapid shots, "—but I'm plenty grateful."

"Hilton's the name," mumbled Laramie, squinting along his six-gun barrel. "Friends call me Buck—damn!"

His bullet had harmlessly knocked dust on the gulch rim, and his pistol was empty. As he groped for cartridges he felt a Winchester pushed into his hand, and, startled, turned his head to stare full into the disturbingly beautiful face of Judy Anders. She had not obeyed her brother's order, but had taken a loaded rifle from the rack and brought it to Laramie, crossing the room on hands and knees to keep below the line of fire. Laramie almost forgot the men across the road as he stared into her deep clear eyes, now glowing with excitement. In dizzy fascination he admired the peach-bloom of her cheeks, her red, parted lips.

"Th-thank you, Miss!" he stammered. "I needed that smoke-wagon a right smart. And excuse my language. I didn't know you was still in the room—"

He ducked convulsively as a bullet ripped across the sill, throwing splinters like a buzzsaw. Shoving the Winchester out of the window he set to work. But his mind was still addled. And he was remembering a pitifully still figure sprawled in the dust of that very road, and a pig-tailed child on her knees beside it—but the child was no longer a child, but a beautiful woman; and he—he was still a Laramie, and the brother of the man who killed her father.

"*Judy!*" There was passion in Bob Anders' voice. "*Will* you get out of here? There! Somebody's callin' at the back door. Go let 'em in. And stay back there, will you?"

This time she obeyed, and a few seconds later half a dozen pairs of boots clomped into the room, as some men from the Red Lode who had slipped around through a back route to the besieged cabin, entered profanely and vociferously.

"They was after the bank, of course," announced one of them. "They didn't git nothin' though, dern 'em. Old Ely Harrison started slingin' lead the minute he seen them masks comin' in the door. He didn't hit nobody, and by good luck the lead they throwed at him didn't connect, but they pulled out in a hurry. Old Harrison shore s'prized me. I never thought much of him before now, but he showed he was ready to fight for his money, and our'n."

"Same outfit, of course," grunted the sheriff, peering warily through the jagged shards of the splintered windowpane.

"Sure. The damn' Laramies again. Big Jim leadin', as usual."

Buck Laramie jumped convulsively, doubting the evidence of his ears. He twisted his head to stare at the men in the room.

"Big Jim? The *Laramies?*"

"Yeah. The Laramie gang," responded Bob Anders, cocking his rifle. "Bandits and killers." His face grew hard and old. "If yo're a stranger to these parts likely you ain't heard of 'em. They raised hell all over this country six years ago."

"Killed his old man right out there in front of his house," grunted one of the men, selecting a rifle from the rack. The others were firing carefully through the windows, and the men in the gulch were replying in kind. The room was full of drifting smoke.

"And you think it's the Laramies out there?" Buck's brain felt a bit numb. These mental jolts were coming too fast for him.

"Sure," grunted Anders. "Couldn't be nobody else. They was gone for six years—where, nobody knowed. But a few weeks back they showed up again and started their old deviltry, worse than ever."

"But I've heard of 'em," Laramie protested. "They was all killed down in Old Mexico."

"Couldn't be," declared the sheriff, lining his sights. "These are the old gang alright. They've put up warnin's signed with the Laramie name. Even been heard singin' that old song they used to always sing about King Brady. Got a hideout up in the Los Diablos, too, just like they did before. Same one, of course. I ain't managed to find it yet, but—" His voice was drowned in the roar of his .45-70.

"Well, I'll be a hammer-headed jackass!" muttered Laramie under his breath. "Of all the—"

His profane meditations were broken into suddenly as one of the men bawled: "Shootin's slowed down over there! What you reckon it means?"

"Means they're aimin' to sneak out of that wash at the other end and high tail it into the desert," snapped Anders. "I ought to have thought about that before, but things has been happenin' so fast—you *hombres* stay here and keep smokin' the wash so they can't bolt out on this side. I'm goin' to circle around and block 'em from the desert."

"I'm with you," growled Laramie. "I want to see what's behind them masks."

They ducked out the back way and began to cut a wide circle which should bring them to the outer edge of the wash. It was difficult going and frequently they had to crawl on their hands and knees to take advantage of every clump of cactus and greasewood.

"Gettin' purty close," muttered Laramie, lifting his head. "What I'm wonderin' is, why ain't they already bolted for the desert? Nothin' to stop 'em."

"I figger they wanted to get me if they could, before they lit out," answered Anders. "I believe I been snoopin' around in the Diablos too close to suit 'em. Reinforcements from the Red Lode likely discouraged 'em; but one of 'em's hurt, and—look out! They've seen us!"

Both men ducked as a steady line of flame spurts rimmed the edge of the wash. They flattened down behind their scanty cover and bullets cut up puffs of sand within inches of them.

"This is a pickle!" gritted Anders, vainly trying to locate a human head to shoot at. "If we back up, we back into sight, and if we go forward we'll get perforated."

"And if we stay here the result's the same," returned Laramie. "Greasewood don't stop lead. We got to summon reinforcements." And lifting his voice in a stentorian yell that carried far, he whooped: "Come on, boys! Rush 'em from that side! They can't shoot two ways at once!"

They could not see the cabin from where they lay, but a burst of shouts and shots told them his yell had been heard. Guns began to bang up the wash and Laramie and Anders recklessly leaped to their feet and rushed down the slight slope that led to the edge of the gulch, shooting as they came.

Under ordinary conditions they would have been riddled before they had gone a dozen steps, but the outlaws had recognized the truth of Laramie's statement. They couldn't shoot two ways at once, and they feared to be trapped in the gulch with attackers on each side. A few hurried shots buzzed about the ears of the charging men, and then outlaws burst into view at the end of the wash farthest from town, mounted and spurring hard, the big leader still carrying a limp figure across his saddle.

Cursing fervently, the sheriff ran after them, blazing away with both six-shooters, and Laramie followed him. The fleeing men were shooting backward as they rode, and the roar of six-guns and Winchesters was deafening. One of the men reeled in his saddle and caught at his shoulder, dyed suddenly red.

Laramie's longer legs carried him past the sheriff, but he did not run far. As the outlaws pulled out of range, he slowed to a walk and began reloading his gun. The fight was won, but the race was lost. The outlaws were heading out across the desert that had so often furnished sanctuary for the real Laramie gang. He did not doubt that once out of sight, they would swing around and head for the Diablos, along the old, secret trail he knew so well.

"Let's round up the men, Bob," he called. "We'll follow 'em. I know the waterholes—"

He stopped short, with a gasp. Ten yards behind him Bob Anders, a crimson stream dyeing the side of his head, was sinking to the desert floor.

Laramie started back on a run just as the men from the cabin burst into view. In their lead rode a man on a pinto—and Buck Laramie knew that pinto.

"Git him!" howled the white-hatted rider. "He shot Bob Anders in the back! I seen him! *He's a Laramie!"*

Laramie stopped dead in his tracks. The accusation was like a bombshell exploding in his face. That was the man who had tried to dry-gulch him an hour or so before—same pinto, same white sombrero—but he was a total stranger to Laramie. How in the devil did *he* know of Buck's identity, and what was the reason for his enmity?

Laramie had no time to try to figure it out now. For the excited townsmen, too crazy with excitement to stop and think, seeing only their young sheriff stretched in his blood, and hearing the frantic accusation of one of their fellows, set up a roar and started blazing away at the man they believed was a murderer.

Out of the frying pan into the fire—the naked desert was behind him, and his horse was still standing behind the Anders' cabin—with that mob between him and that cabin.

But any attempt at reasoning or explanation would be fatal. Nobody would listen. Laramie saw a break for him in the fact that only his accuser was mounted, and probably didn't know he had a horse behind the cabin, and would try to reach it. The others were too excited to think anything. They were simply slinging lead, so befuddled with the mob impulse they were not even aiming—which is all that saved Laramie in the few seconds in which he stood bewildered and uncertain.

He ducked for the dry wash, running almost at a right angle with his attackers. The only man capable of intercepting him was White-Hat, who was bearing down on him, shooting from the saddle with a Winchester.

Laramie wheeled, and as he wheeled a bullet ripped through his Stetson and stirred his hair in passing. White-Hat was determined to have his life, he thought, as his own six-gun spat flame. White-Hat flinched sidewise and dropped his rifle. Laramie took the last few yards in his stride and dived out of sight in the wash.

He saw White-Hat spurring out of range too energetically to be badly wounded, and he believed his bullet had merely knocked the gun out of the fellow's hands. The others had spread out and were coming down the slope at a run, burning powder as they came.

Laramie did not want to kill any of those men. They were law-abiding citizens acting under a misapprehension. So he emptied his gun over their heads and was gratified to see them precipitately take to cover. Then without pausing to reload, he ducked low and ran for the opposite end of the wash, which ran on an angle that would bring him near the cabin.

The men who had halted their charge broke cover and came on again, unaware of his flight, and hoping to get him while his gun was empty. They supposed he intended making a stand at their end of the wash.

By the time they had discovered their mistake and were pumping lead down the gully, Laramie was out at the other end and racing across the road toward the cabin. He ducked around the corner with lead nipping at his ears and vaulted into the saddle of the sorrel—and cursed his luck as Judy Anders ran out the rear door, her eyes wide with fright.

"What's happened?" she cried. "Where's Bob?"

"No time to pow-wow," panted Laramie. "Bob's been hurt. Don't know how bad. I got to ride, because—"

He was interrupted by shouts from the other side of the cabin.

"Look out, Judy!" one man yelled. "Stay under cover! He shot Bob in the back!"

Reacting to the shout without conscious thought, Judy sprang to seize his reins.

Laramie jerked the sorrel aside and evaded her grasp. "It's a lie!" he yelled with heat. "I ain't got time to explain. Hope Bob ain't hurt bad."

Then he was away, crouching low in his saddle with bullets pinging past him; it seemed he'd been hearing lead whistle all day; he was getting sick of that particular noise. He looked back once. Behind the cabin Judy Anders was bending over a limp form that the men had carried in from the desert. Now she was down on her knees in the dust beside that limp body, searching for a spark of life . . .

Laramie cursed sickly. History was indeed repeating itself that day in San Leon.

Chapter .3.
Old Trails

For a time Laramie rode eastward, skirting the desert, and glad of a breathing spell. The sorrel had profited by its rest behind the Anders' cabin, and was fairly fresh. Laramie had a good lead on the pursuers he knew would be hot on his trail as soon as they could get to their horses, but he headed east instead of north, the direction in which lay his real goal—the Boxed W Ranch. He did not expect to be able to throw them off his scent entirely, but he did hope to confuse them and gain a little time.

It was imperative that he see his one friend in San Leon County. When he had written Joel Waters, telling him his plan of restoring the money stolen from San Leon, he had anticipated trouble, and the need of a staunch friend to help him. But he had never anticipated anything like this; he had looked for distrust and hostility, which Waters could dispel, but he had run into a situation beyond his grasp.

As he rode he brooded over the tangled maze. He had come to San Leon to pay a debt of conscience; and already he was a hunted man. If Bob Anders died without speaking, how could he, Laramie, ever prove his innocence? Who were those masked bandits who called themselves Laramies? Why had they adopted that name? And the fellow on the pinto, where did he fit into the jigsaw puzzle?

"To hell with it!" quoth Laramie with passion. "None of it don't make no sense. Maybe Joel Waters can un-riddle some of it. Git along, cayuse."

He had been forging eastward for perhaps an hour when, looking backward from a steep rise, he saw a column of riders approaching some two miles away through a cloud of dust that meant haste. That would be the posse following his trail—and that meant that the sheriff was dead or still senseless.

Laramie wheeled down the slope on the other side and headed north, hunting hard ground that would not betray a pony's hoofprint.

Dusk was fast settling when he rode into the yard of the Boxed W. He was glad of the darkness, for he had feared that some of Waters' punchers might have been in San Leon that day, and seen him. But he rode up to the porch without having encountered anyone, and saw the man he was hunting sitting there, pulling at a corncob pipe.

Waters rose and came forward with his hand outstretched as Laramie swung from the saddle.

"You've growed," said the old man. "I'd never knowed you if I hadn't been expectin' you. You don't favor yore brothers none. Look a lot like yore dad did at yore age, though. You've pushed yore cayuse hard," he added, with a piercing glance at the sweat-plastered flanks of the sorrel.

"Yeah . . ." There was bitter humor in Laramie's reply. "I just got through shootin' me a sheriff."

Waters jerked the pipe from his mouth. He looked stunned. *"What?"*

"All you got to do is ask the upright citizens of San Leon that's trailin' me like a lobo wolf," returned Laramie with a mirthless grin. And tersely and concisely he told the old rancher what had happened in San Leon and on the desert.

Waters listened in silence, puffing smoke slowly.

"It's bad," he muttered, when Laramie had finished. "Damned bad—well, about all I can do right now is to feed you. Put yore cayuse in the corral."

"Rather hide him near the house, if I could," said Laramie. "That posse is liable to hit my sign and trail me here any time. I want to be ready to ride."

"Blacksmith shop behind the house," grunted Waters. "Come on."

Laramie followed the old man to the shop, leading the sorrel. While he was removing the bridle and loosening the cinch, Waters brought hay and filled an old log trough. When Laramie followed him back to the house, the younger man carried the saddlebags over his arm. Their gentle clink no longer soothed him; too many obstacles to distributing them were rising in his path.

"I just finished eatin' before you come," grunted Waters. "Plenty left."

"Hop Sing still cookin' for you?"

"Yeah."

"Ain't you ever goin' to get married?" chaffed Laramie.

"Shore," grunted the old man, chewing his pipe stem. "I just got to have time to decide what type of woman'd make me the best wife."

Laramie grinned. Waters was well past sixty, and had been giving that reply to chaffing about his matrimonial prospects as far back as Buck could remember.

Hop Sing remembered Laramie and greeted him warmly. The old Chinaman had cooked for Waters for many years. Laramie could trust him as far as he could trust Waters himself.

The old man sat gripping his cold pipe between his teeth as Laramie disposed of a steak, eggs, beans and potatoes and tamped it down with a man-sized chunk of apple pie.

"Yo're follerin' blind trails," he said slowly. "Mebbe I can help you."

"Maybe. Do you have any idea who the gent on the showy pinto might be?"

"Not many such paints in these parts. What'd the man look like?"

"Well, I didn't get a close range look at him, of course. From what I saw he looked to be short, thick-set, and he wore a short beard and a mustache so big it plumb ambushed the rest of his pan."

"Why, hell!" snorted Waters. "That's bound to be Mart Rawley! He rides a flashy pinto, and he's got the biggest set of whiskers in San Leon."

"Who's he?"

"Owns the Red Lode. Come here about six months ago and bought it off of old Charlie Ross, who'd been runnin' the dump for thirty years and 'lowed it was time he retired. Ever since then poor old Charlie's wanderin' around like a locoed stray. Reckon he was too danged old to retire."

"Well, that don't help none," growled Laramie, finishing his coffee and reaching for the makings. He paused suddenly, lighted match lifted. "Say, did this *hombre* ride up from Mexico?"

"He come in from the east. Of course, he could have come from Mexico, at that; he'd have circled the desert. Nobody but you Laramies ever hit straight across it. He ain't said he come from Mexico original, and he ain't said he ain't."

Laramie meditated in silence, and then asked: "What about this new gang that calls theirselves Laramies?"

"Plain coyotes," snarled the old man. "Us San Leon folks was just gittin' on our feet again after the wreck yore brothers made out of us, when this outfit hit the country. They've robbed and stole and looted till most of us are right back where we was six years ago. They've done more damage in a few weeks than yore brothers did in three years. I ain't been so bad hit as some, because I've got the toughest, straightest-shootin' crew of punchers in the county, but most of the cowmen around San Leon are mortgaged to the hilt, and stand to lose their outfits if they git looted any more. Old Ely Harrison—he's president of the bank now, since yore brothers killed old man Brown—old Ely's been good about takin' mortgages and handin' out money, but he cain't go on doin' it forever."

"Does everybody figure they're the Laramies?"

"Why not? They send letters to the cowmen sayin' they'll wipe out their whole outfit if they don't deliver 'em so many hundred head of beef stock, and they sign them letters with the Laramie name. They're hidin' out in the Diablos like you all did; they's always the same number in the gang, and they can make a getaway through the desert, which nobody but the Laramies ever did. Of course, they wear masks, which the Laramies never did, but that's a minor item; customs change, so to speak. I'd have believed they was the genuine Laramies myself, only for a couple of reasons—one bein' you'd wrote me in your letter that you was the only Laramie left—you didn't give no details." The old man's voice was questioning.

"Man's reputation always follows him," grunted Buck. "A barroom gladiator got Jim, aimin' to raise his own rep a notch. Hank got that gunfighter the next week, but was shot up so hisself he died. Tom joined the revolutionaries and the *rurales* cornered him in a dry wash. Took 'em ten hours and three dead men to get him. Luke—" He hesitated and scowled slightly.

"Luke was killed in a barroom brawl in Santa Maria, by a two-gunfighter called Killer Rawlins. They said Luke reached first, but Rawlins beat him to it. I don't know. Rawlins skipped that night. I've always believed Luke got a dirty deal, some way. He was the best one of the boys. If I ever meet Rawlins—" Involuntarily his hand moved toward the worn butt of his Colt. Then he shrugged his shoulders, and said: "You said there was two reasons why you knowed these coyotes wasn't Laramies; what's t'other'n?"

"They work different," growled the old man. "Yore brothers was bad, but white men, just the same. They killed prompt, but they killed clean. These rats ain't content with just stealin' our stock. They burn down ranch houses and pizen waterholes like a tribe of cussed Apaches. Jim Bannerman of the Lazy B didn't leave 'em two hundred of steers in a draw like they demanded in one of them letters I told you about. A couple of days later we found nothin' but smokin' ruins at the Lazy B, with Jim's body burned up inside and all his punchers dead or bad shot up.

"Then they was an old prospector over in the foothills of the Diablos who wouldn't tell 'em where he'd hid a little sack of gold. They burnt the soles nearly off his feet with a red-hot iron, and branded him with the old Laramie brand, and then they staked him out on an ant hill in the sun. A puncher happened along right after they left, and cut him loose. He lived, but he's crazy as a locoed mustang. Such things as that—and the other things they've did— showed me they warn't Laramies."

Buck's face was grey beneath its tan. His fist knotted on the gun butt.

"*God!*" he choked, in a voice little above a whisper. "And the Laramies are gettin' the blame! I thought my brothers dragged the name low—but these devils are haulin' it right down into hell. Joel Waters, listen to me! I come back here to pay back money my brothers stole from San Leon; I'm stayin' to pay a bigger debt. The desert's big, but it ain't big enough for a Laramie and the rats that wears his name. If I don't wipe that gang of rattlers off the earth they can have my name, because I won't need it no more."

"The Laramies owe a debt to San Leon," agreed old Joel, filling his pipe. "Cleanin' out that snake-den is the best way I know of payin' it."

*   *   *   *   *

Some time later Laramie rose at last and ground his cigarette butt under his heel.

"We've about talked out our wampum. From all I can see, everything points to this Mart Rawley bein' connected with the gang, somehow. I can't see why he'd want to kill me, unless these fake Laramies wanted me out of the way—which it's easy to see they would. I dunno how he come to know I was comin' along that trail; I dunno how he knowed me. I don't remember ever seein' him before. But he must have been the one that shot Bob Anders. He was ahead of the other fellows; they couldn't see him for a rise in the ground. They was just comin' over that rise when I turned and saw 'em, and he was well on the other side. They wouldn't have seen him shoot Anders. He might have been aimin' at me; or he might have just wanted Anders out of the way.

"Anyway, I'm headin' for the Diablos tonight. I know yo're willin' to hide me here, but you can help me more if nobody suspects yo're helpin' me, yet. If it was just the matter of givin' back the money, I'd stay here till you could explain to the folks, like we planned in our letters to each other. But it's more complicated than that now. And I believe I'll find the key to this here riddle in the Diablos.

"I'm leavin' these saddlebags with you. If I don't come back out of the Diablos, you'll know what to do with the money. So long."

They shook hands.

"So long, Buck. I'll take care of the money. If they git to crowdin' you too close, duck back here. And if you need help in the hills, try to git word back to me. I can still draw a bead with a Winchester, and I've got a gang of hard-ridin' waddies to back my play."

"I ain't forgettin', Joel."

Laramie turned toward the door. Absorbed in his thoughts, he forgot for an instant that he was a hunted man, and relaxed his vigilance. As he stepped out onto the veranda he did not stop to think that he was thrown into bold relief by the light behind him.

As his boot heel hit the porch yellow flame lanced the darkness and he heard the whine of a bullet that fanned him as it passed. He leapt back, slamming the door, wheeled, and halted in dismay to see Joel Waters sinking to the door. The old man, standing directly behind Laramie, had stopped the slug meant for his guest.

With his heart in his mouth Laramie dropped beside his friend.

"Where'd it get you, Joel?" he choked.

"Low down, through the leg," grunted Waters, already sitting up and whipping his bandanna around his leg for a tourniquet; he came of a rawhide breed. "Nothin' to worry about. You better git goin'."

Laramie took the bandanna and began knotting it tightly, ignoring a hail from without.

"Come out with yore hands up, Laramie!" a rough voice shouted. "You can't fight a whole posse. We got you cornered!"

"Beat it, Buck!" snapped Waters, pulling away his friend's hands. "They must have left their horses and sneaked up on foot. I ain't heard no horse hoofs. Sneak out the back way before they surround the house, fork yore cayuse and burn the breeze. That's Mart Rawley talkin', and I reckon it was him that shot. He aims to git you before you have time to ask questions or answer any. Even if you went out there with yore hands up, he'd kill you. Git goin', dern you!"

"All right!" Laramie jumped up as Hop Sing came out of the kitchen, almond eyes wide and a cleaver in his hand. "Tell 'em I held a gun on you and made you feed me. 'Tain't time for 'em to know we're friends, not yet."

The next instant he was gliding into the back part of the house and slipping through a window into the outer darkness. He heard somebody swearing at Rawley for firing before the rest had taken up their positions, and he heard other voices and noises that indicated the posse was scattering out to surround the house. He ran for the blacksmith shop and, groping in the dark, tightened the cinch on the sorrel and slipped on the bridle. He worked fast because he was sure that when the ring of men was completed about the house, somebody would take cover in or behind the shop. And such a move was intended, for before Laramie could lead the horse outside he heard a jingle of spurs and the sound of footsteps. One of the posse was approaching the shop.

Laramie swung into the saddle, ducked his head low to avoid the lintel of the door, and struck in the spurs. The sorrel hurtled through the door like a thunderbolt. A startled yell rang out, a man jumped frantically out of the way, tripped over his spurs and fell flat on his back, discharging his Winchester in the general direction of the Big Dipper, and the sorrel and its rider went past him like a thundering shadow to be swallowed in the darkness. Wild yells answered the passionate blasphemy of the fallen man, and guns spurted red as their owners fired blindly after the receding hoofbeats. But before the posse men could untangle themselves from their bewilderment and find their mounts, left some distance down the road in the interests of stealth, the echoes of flying hoofs had died away and night hid the fugitive's trail. Buck Laramie was far away, riding to the Diablos to find an answer to the riddle in whose meshes he was snarled.

Chapter .4.
The Man Behind the Scenes

Midnight found Laramie deep in the Diabios. He halted, tethered the sorrel, and spread his blankets at the foot of a low cliff. Night was not the time to venture further along the rock-strewn paths and treacherous precipices of the Diablos. He slept, pursued in uneasy dreams by a bewhiskered man on a pinto, a man about whom there was an illusive familiarity, a fleeting something that he was always just on the point of remembering.

Before the first grey of dawn he was up and breakfasted on the grub Hop Sing had packed for him the night before. When a faint light showed over the tips of the mountains to the east he was riding familiar trails, trails that would lead him to the cabin in the hidden canyon that he knew so well—a canyon bitter with old, aching memories. He was heading for the old hideout of his gang, where he believed he would find the new band which was terrorizing the country.

This was a logical supposition. True, none but the Laramies had known of the place. It had but one entrance, a rock-walled tunnel that, in some prehistoric time, must have been the subterranean bed of a river that fed the lake, the dry bed of which was now the flat-bottomed canyon where the Laramies had built their cabin. How the fake gang could have learned of the place Laramie could not know—but it was no more of a mystery than the fact that they knew the only watered route across the desert, and were familiar with the winding mountain trails as no others but the real Laramies had been before them.

The hideout was in a great bowl, on all sides of which rose walls of jumbled rock, impassable to a horseman. It was possible to climb the cliffs near the entrance of the tunnel, which, if the fake gang were following the customs of the real Laramies, would be guarded.

Half an hour after sunrise found him making his way on foot toward the canyon entrance. His horse he had left concealed among the rocks at a safe distance, and lariat in hand he crept along behind rocks and scrub growth toward the old riverbed. Presently, gazing through the underbrush that masked his approach, he found that his suspicions had been well founded. Half hidden by a rock, a man in a tattered brown shirt sat at the mouth of the canyon entrance, his hat pulled low over his eyes, and a Winchester across his knees.

Evidently a belief in the security of the hideout made the sentry careless. Laramie had the drop on him; but to use his advantage incurred the possibility of a shot that would warn those inside the canyon and spoil his plans. So he retreated to a point where he would not be directly in the line of the guard's vision, if the man roused, and began working his way to a spot a few hundred yards to the left, where, as he knew of old, he could climb to the rim of the canyon.

Looping his rope over his shoulder, he started the climb carefully, working his way up over boulders and crags. In a few moments he had clambered up to a point from which he could glimpse the booted feet of the guard sticking from behind the rock, and he renewed his caution, trying to keep shale and pebbles from rattling down. If the sluggish guard happened to look in that direction, he could see the man toiling up the pitch. Laramie's flesh crawled at the thought of being picked off with a rifle bullet, like a fly off a wall.

But the boots did not move, he dislodged no stones large enough to make an alarming noise, and presently, panting and sweating, he heaved himself over the crest of the rim and lay on his belly gazing down into the canyon below him.

A surge of mixed emotions swept over him as he looked down into the bowl which had once been like a prison to him, yet had housed the only men in whose veins ran the same blood that filled his own. Bitterness of memory was mingled with a brief, sick longing for his dead brothers; after all, they *were* his brothers, and had been kind to him in their rough way.

The cabin below him had in no wise changed in the passing of the years. Smoke was pouring out of the chimney, and in the corral at the back, horses were milling about in an attempt to escape the ropes of two men who were seeking saddle mounts for the day.

Laramie lay motionless, his brain busy. He had found the headquarters of the outlaws who were terrorizing the country under the Laramie name; but what was his next move? The identity of the men was still a mystery. He could not ride back to San Leon and tell his tale with any expectation of being believed. The men of San Leon might come and wipe out this nest of rattlers, but his innocence in the shooting of Bob Anders would be still unproven, Mart Rawley's connection with the gang unproven. And it was doubtful if the men of San Leon would believe him if he told them of the hideout, and offered to guide them there. They would think a trap; suspect him of being a decoy; and probably hang him out of hand. He must have proof more convincing than his unsupported word.

There remained one desperate alternative, and Laramie took it without hesitation. Shaking out his lariat, he crept along the canyon rim until he reached a spot where a stunted tree clung to the very edge. To this tree he made fast the rope, knotted it at intervals for handholds, and threw the other end over the cliff. It hung twenty feet short of the bottom, but that was near enough.

As he went down it, with a knee hooked about the thin strand to take some of the strain off his hands, he grinned thinly as he remembered how he had discovered the possibility of this means of descent, long ago; returning from some forbidden excursion in the hills, and wanting to dodge Big Jim who was waiting at the entrance to give him a licking. His face hardened.

"Wish he was here with me now. We'd mop up these rats by ourselves. Tough job, playin' a lone hand. Maybe I'll be able to bring Joel and his rowdies in on the deal, later. But just now I've got to find out who's behind them masks."

Dangling at the end of the rope at arm's length he dropped, narrowly missing a heap of jagged rocks, and lit in the sand on his feet, going to his all-fours from the impact. He did not hesitate now. He was in the bowl, with many chances against his ever getting out alive, and every second counted.

Bending low, sometimes on hands and knees, he headed circuitously for the cabin, keeping it between himself and the men in the corral, and taking advantage of what little undergrowth and trees there were, even wriggling along in the tall, lush grass that carpeted the canyon floor.

To his own wonderment he reached the cabin without hearing any alarm sounded. Maybe the occupants, if there were any in the canyon beside the men he had seen, had gone out the back way to the corral. He hoped so.

Cautiously he raised his head over a windowsill and peered inside. He could see no one in the big room that constituted the front part of the cabin, and he could see most of it from where he crouched. Behind this room, he knew, were a bunkroom and kitchen, and the back door was in the kitchen. There might be men in those backrooms; but he was willing to take the chance. He wanted to get in there and find a place where he could hide and spy; and he was afire with curiosity now that he had penetrated into the heart of the hideout.

The door was not locked; he pushed it open gently and stepped inside with a cat-like tread, Colt poked ahead of him.

"Stick 'em up!" Before he could complete the convulsive movement prompted by these unexpected words, he felt the barrel of a six-gun jammed hard against his backbone. He froze—opened his fingers and let his gun crash to the floor. There was nothing else for it.

The door to the bunkroom swung open and two men came out with drawn guns and triumphant leers on their unshaven faces. A third emerged from the kitchen. All were strangers to Laramie. He ventured to twist his head to look at his captor, and saw a big-boned, powerful man with a scarred face, grinning exultantly.

"That was easy," rumbled one of the others, a tall, heavily built ruffian whose figure looked somehow familiar. Laramie eyed him closely.

"So yo're 'Jim'," quoth he.

The big man scowled, but Scarface laughed.

"Yeah! With a mask on nobody can tell the difference. You ain't so slick, for a Laramie. I seen you sneakin' through the bresh ten minutes ago, and we been watchin' you ever since. I seen you aimed to come in and make yoreself to home, so I app'inted myself a welcome committee of one—behind the door. You couldn't see me from the winder. Hey, you Joe!" he raised his voice pompously. "Gimme a piece of rope. Mister Laramie's goin' to stay with us for a spell."

Laramie was inwardly seething with chagrin and rage, but outwardly he was imperturbable.

"Easy on that rope, you flea-backed coyote," he advised as Scarface looped his wrists together behind him. "No use tryin' to cut my hands off."

"You ain't goin' to have no need for 'em much longer," Scarface consoled him. "We just cain't have a real honest-to-God Laramie runnin' 'round loose. It'd spile our plans. Jim, go tell Mister Harrison we done got this critter corralled, and's waitin' for further orders."

The tall outlaw strode out through the bunkroom door, and Scarface shoved Laramie into an old Morris chair that stood near the kitchen door. Laramie remembered that chair well; the brothers had brought it with them when they left their ranch home in the foothills.

He was trying to catch a nebulous memory that had something to do with that chair, when steps sounded in the bunkroom and "Jim" entered, accompanied by two others, who had evidently been waiting there. One was an ordinary sort of criminal, slouchy, brutal faced and unshaven. The other was of an entirely different type. He was elderly and pale faced, but that face was bleak and flinty. He did not seem range-bred like the others. Save for his high-heeled riding boots, he was dressed in town clothes, though the well-worn butt of a .45 jutted from a holster at his thigh.

Scarface hooked thumbs in belt and rocked back on his heels with an air of huge satisfaction. His big voice boomed in the cabin.

"Mister Harrison, I takes pleasure in makin' you acquainted with Mister Buck Laramie, the last of a family of honest horse-thieves, what's rode all the way from Mexico just to horn in on our play. He's follerin' in his late lamented brothers' footprints, because we just catched him red-handed in the act of bustin' and enterin', which is a plumb violation of the law. Reckon we'll have to make a example of him, in the interests of law and order. And Mister Laramie, since you ain't long for this weary world, I'm likewise honored to interjuice you to Mister Ely Harrison, high man of our outfit and President of the Cattlemen's Bank of San Leon!"

Scarface had an eye for dramatics in his crude way. He bowed grotesquely, sweeping the floor with his Stetson and grinning gleefully at the astounded glare with which his prisoner greeted his introduction.

Harrison was less pleased.

"That tongue of yours wags too loose, Braxton," he snarled.

Scarface lapsed into injured silence, and Laramie found his tongue.

"Ely Harrison!" he said slowly. "Head of the gang—the pieces of this puzzle's beginnin' to fit. So you generously helps out the ranchers yore coyotes ruins—not forgettin' to grab a healthy mortgage while doin' it. And you was a hero and shot it out with the terrible bandits when they come for yore bank; only nobody gets hurt on either side. I get you, alright. Nothin' would make you more solid with honest people than fightin' off the gang to pertect *their* money. Nobody'd ever think of suspectin' such a noble hero. Mister Harrison, stand still a bit, I want to get a good, close-range look at a human rattlesnake."

"Look well," growled Harrison. "It's about the last thing you'll do."

Laramie was inclined to agree with that statement; the cold eyes of the banker glittered murderously. Harrison would never dare to let him live after this. He had found what he had come to find—the identity of the gang's chief, but it seemed that barring a miracle he would take that discovery into Eternity with him. His mind was desperately and futilely revolving, seeking some loophole out of this deadly mess. Unconsciously he leaned further back in the Morris chair—and a lightning jolt of memory hit him just behind the ear. He stifled an involuntary grunt, and his fingers, hidden by his body from the eyes of his captors, began fumbling between the cushions of the chair.

He had remembered his jackknife, a beautiful implement, and the pride of his boyhood, stolen from him and hidden by his brother Tom, for a joke, a few days before they started for Mexico. Tom had forgotten all about it, and Buck had been too proud to beg him for it. But Tom had remembered, months later, in Mexico, had bought Buck a duplicate of the first knife, and told him that he had hidden the original between the cushions of the old Morris chair . . .

Laramie's heart almost choked him. It seemed too good to be true, this ace in the hole, yet obviously the cabin had not been used from that time until the present, and there was no reason to suppose anybody had found and removed the knife—his doubts were set at rest as his fingers encountered a smooth, hard object. It was not until that moment that he realized that Ely Harrison was speaking to him. He gathered his wits and concentrated on the man's rasping voice, while his hidden fingers fumbled with the knife, trying to open it.

"—damned unhealthy for a man to try to block *my* game," Harrison was saying harshly. "Why didn't you mind your own business?"

"How do you know I come here just to spoil yore game?" murmured Laramie absently.

"Then why *did* you come here?" Harrison's gaze was clouded with a sort of ferocious uncertainty. "Just how much did you know about our outfit before today? Did you know I was the leader of the gang?"

"Guess," suggested Laramie.

Sudden death leaped at him from Harrison's cold eyes.

"I know you Laramies are poison," he rasped. "But you'd better sing small. You'll find me no lamb."

"Reckon nobody'd accuse you of that," retorted Laramie. The knife was open at last. He jammed the handle deep between the cushions and the chairback, wedging it securely. The tendons along his wrists ached. It had been hard work, manipulating the knife with his cramped fingers which could move just so far. His steady voice did not change in tone as he worked. "As for my name, I was kind of ashamed of it till I seen how much lower a man could go than my brothers ever went. They was hard men, but they was white, at least. Usin' my name to torture and murder behind my back plumb upsets me. Maybe I didn't come to San Leon just to spoil yore game; but maybe I decided to spoil it after I seen some of the hands you dealt."

Harrison's snarl of cold laughter was echoed by the derision of the others. Laramie eyed them quizzically as he began to move the cords back and forth along the keen blade with a sawing motion of his bound wrists. There was bound to be some motion of his arms that could not be concealed from the outlaws, but he moved restlessly, as if nervous.

Harrison saw this and laughed.

"Nerves jumpy, eh?" he sneered. "You'll spoil our game! Fat chance you've got of spoiling anybody's game. But you've got only yourself to blame. Nobody asked you to butt in. You've done damage enough, as it is. In another month I'd have owned every ranch within thirty miles of San Leon."

"So that's the idea, huh?" murmured Laramie, leaning forward to expectorate, and dragging his wrists hard across the knife-edge.

He felt one strand part, and as he leaned back and repeated the movement, another gave way and the edge bit into his flesh. If he could sever one more strand, he would make his break.

"Just how much did you know about our outfit before you came here?" demanded Harrison again, his persistence betraying his apprehension on that point. "How much did you tell Joel Waters?"

"None of yore derned business," Laramie snapped. His nervousness was real enough now, his nerves getting on edge with the approach of the crisis.

"You'd better talk," snarled Harrison. "I've got men here who'd think nothing of shoving your feet in the fire to roast. Not that it matters. We're all set anyway. Got ready when we heard you'd ridden in. It just means we move tonight instead of a month later. But if you can prove to me that you haven't told anybody that I'm the real leader of the gang—well, we can carry out our original plans, and you'll save your life. We might even let you join the outfit."

"Join the—do you see any snake-scales on me?" flared Laramie, fiercely expanding his arm muscles. Another strand parted and the cords fell away from his wrists.

"Why you—!" Murderous passion burst all bounds as Harrison lurched forward, his fist lifted. And Laramie shot from the chair like a steel spring released, catching them all flatfooted, paralyzed by the unexpectedness of the move.

One hand ripped Harrison's Colt from its scabbard. The other knotted into a fist that smashed hard in the banker's face and knocked him headlong into the midst of the men who stood behind him.

"Reach for the ceilin', you yellow-bellied polecats!" snarled Laramie, livid with fury and savage purpose; his cocked .45 menaced them all. "*Reach!* I'm dealin' this hand!"

Chapter .5.
First Blood

For an instant the scene held—then Scarface made a convulsive movement to duck behind the chair.

"Back up!" yelped Laramie, swinging his gun directly on him, and backing toward the door. But the tall outlaw who had impersonated Big Jim had recovered from the daze of his surprise. Even as Laramie's pistol muzzle moved in its short arc toward Braxton, the tall one's hand flashed like the stroke of a snake's head to his gun. It cleared leather just as Laramie's .45 banged.

Laramie felt hot wind fan his cheek, but the tall outlaw was sagging back and down, dying on his feet and grimly pulling trigger as he went. A hot welt burned across Laramie's left thigh, and another slug ripped up splinters near his feet. Harrison had dived behind the Morris chair and Laramie's vengeful bullet smashed into the wall behind him. It all happened so quickly—the ticks of time between Laramie's shout at Braxton and his leap through the door—that the others had barely unleathered their irons as he reached the threshold. He fired at Braxton, saw the scar-faced one drop his gun with a howl, wringing a numbed hand—saw the tall man sprawl on the floor, done with impersonation and outlawry forever—and then he was slamming the door from the outside, wincing involuntarily as bullets smashed through the panels and whined about him.

His long legs flung him across the kitchen at a stride and he catapulted through the outer door and collided head-on with the two men he had seen in the corral, who were returning to the house, with drawn guns, to see what the shooting was about. All three went into the dust in a heap and one, even in falling, jammed his six-gun into Buck's belly and pulled trigger without stopping to see who it was. The hammer clicked on an empty chamber and Laramie, flesh crawling with the narrowness of his escape, crashed his gun barrel down on the other's head and sprang up, kicking free of the second man—and that man he recognized as Mart Rawley, he of the white sombrero and flashy pinto.

Rawley's gun had been knocked out of his hand in the collision, and with a yelp the dry gulcher scuttled around the corner of the cabin on hands and knees, without waiting to rise. Laramie did not stop for him. He had seen the one thing that might save him—a horse, saddled and bridled, and tied to the corral fence.

He heard the furious stamp of boots behind him, Harrison's voice screaming commands, and then the thunder of guns as his enemies streamed out of the house and started pouring lead after him. But a dozen long leaps carried him spraddle-legged to the startled mustang and with one movement he had ripped loose the tether and swung aboard. Over his shoulder he saw his enemies spreading out to head him off in the dash they expected him to make toward the head of the canyon—and then he wrenched the cayuse around and spurred through the corral gate which the outlaws had left half-open, when interrupted in their purpose of taking another saddle mount.

In an instant Laramie was the center of a milling whirlpool of maddened horses as he yelled, fired in the air, and lashed them with the quirt hanging from the horn.

"Close the gate!" shrieked Harrison, sensing his intention, as the outlaws hesitated, bewildered by Laramie's action. One of the men ran to obey the command—but as he did, the snorting beasts came thundering through, and only a frantic leap backward saved him from being trampled.

His companions yelped and ran for the protection of the cabin, firing blindly into the dust cloud that rose as the herd pounded past, giving them only a fleeting glimpse of the rider who rode like a madman in the midst of the stampede. Then he was dashing through the scattering horde and drawing out of six-gun range, while his enemies howled like wolves behind him.

"Git along, cayuse!" yelled Laramie, drunk with the exhilaration of the hazard. "We done better'n I hoped. They got to round up their broncs before they hit my trail, and that's goin' to take time! Hi yi yippee ki yi! You sand-foggin' snake-hunters! Roll yore tails and burn the breeze! I hope yore bosses have to chase you a hundred miles before they sling saddle leather astraddle of yore mangy backbones!"

Thought of the guard waiting at the canyon entrance did not sober him. His wild blood was seething in his veins and he was primed for any sort of recklessness.

"Only way out is through the tunnel. Maybe he thinks the shootin' was just a family affair, and hesitates to drill a gent ridin' from *inside* the canyon. Anyway, cayuse, we takes it on the run, and may the best man win! Yippee! The ball's openin'!"

A Winchester banged from the mouth of the tunnel and the bullet cut the air past his ear.

"Pull up!" yelled a voice, but there was hesitancy in the tone. Doubtless the first shot had been a warning, and the sentry was puzzled and uncertain. Laramie gave no heed; he ducked low and jammed in the spurs. He could see the rifle now, the blue muzzle resting on a boulder, and the ragged crown of a hat behind it. Even as he saw it, flame spurted from the blue ring and Laramie's horse stumbled in its headlong stride to the bite of lead ploughing through the fleshy part of its shoulder. That stumble saved Laramie's life for it lurched him out of the path of the next slug, and then his own six-gun roared.

The bullet smashed on the rock beside the rifle muzzle, knocking splinters of stone into the outlaw's face. Dazed and half-blinded he reeled back, into the open, and fired pointblank and without aim. The Winchester flamed almost in Laramie's face, and the rider's answering slug knocked the guard down as if he had been hit with a hammer. The Winchester flew out of his hands as he rolled on the ground, and Laramie jerked the half-frantic mustang back on its haunches and dived out of the saddle, grabbing for the rifle.

"Damn!" It had struck the sharp edge of a rock as it fell, bending the lock and rendering the weapon useless. He cast it aside disgustedly, wheeled toward his horse, and then halted, staring down at the man he had shot. The fellow had hauled himself to a half-sitting position against a rock. His face was pallid, and blood oozed from a round hole in his shirt bosom. He was not dead, but he was dying. Sudden revulsion shook Laramie as he saw his victim was hardly more than a boy. His berserk excitement faded, leaving him sick.

"Laramie!" gasped the youth. "You must be Buck Laramie!"

"Yeah," admitted Laramie. "Anything—anything I can do?" Even as he spoke he realized the uselessness of the question. He knelt helplessly beside the youth.

The boy grinned in spite of his pain.

"Thought so. Nobody but a Laramie could ride so reckless and shoot so straight. Seems funny—bein' plugged by a Laramie after worshippin' 'em most of my life."

"What?" ejaculated Laramie.

"I always wanted to be like 'em," gasped the youth. "Every since I was a little kid and they was hellin' around here, I wanted to. Nobody could ride and shoot and fight like them. That's why I j'ined up with these polecats. They said they was startin' up a gang that was to be just like the Laramies. But they ain't; they're a passel of dirty coyotes. Once I started in with 'em, though, I had to stick."

Laramie said nothing, he was sicker than ever. He knew the unreasoning hero-worship which some youngsters feel for the more romantic type of outlaws. But it was appalling to think that a young life had been so warped, and at last destroyed, by the evil example of his brothers.

"Heard the shootin' and run back through the tunnel," muttered the youth. "Wouldn't of shot at you if I'd knowed who it was. Might have knowed, though. You better hustle. Them skunks'll be on yore neck in no time."

"They'll have to walk down their saddle horses first," said Laramie. "I stampeded 'em all out of the corral."

The youth grinned with boyish adoration.

"Just like a Laramie!" he praised; there is no loyalty like youthful idealization. "But you better go, and raise a posse if yo're aimin' to git them rats. They's goin' to be hell to pay tonight."

"How's that?" questioned Laramie, remembering Harrison's remarks about something planned for the night.

"You got 'em scared," murmured the boy. "They're afeared you know too much about 'em. Harrison's scared you might have told Joel Waters he was boss-man of the gang. That's why he come here last night. They'd aimed to keep stealin' for another month. Old Harrison woulda had most all the ranches around here by then, foreclosin' mortgages. When Mart Rawley failed to git you, old Harrison sent out word for the boys to git together here today. They figgered on huntin' you down, if the posse from San Leon hadn't already got you. If they found out you didn't know nothin' and hadn't told nobody nothin', they just aimed to kill you and go on like they'd planned from the first. But if they didn't git you, or found you'd talked, they aimed to make their big cleanup tonight."

"What's that?" asked Laramie.

"They're goin' down tonight and burn Joel Waters' ranch buildings, and the sheriff's, and some of the other big ones, and drive all the cattle off to Mexico over the old Laramie trail. Then old Harrison'll divide the loot and the gang will scatter. If he finds you ain't spilled the works about him bein' the top man, he'll stay on in San Leon. That was his idee from the start—ruin the ranchers, buy up their outfits cheap and be king of San Leon."

"How many men's he got?"

"'Tween twenty-five and thirty," panted the youth. He was going fast. He choked, and a trickle of blood began at the corner of his mouth. "I ought not to be squealin', maybe; 'tain't the Laramie way. But I wouldn't to nobody but a Laramie. You didn't see near all of 'em. Two died on the way back from San Leon, yesterday. They left 'em out in the desert. The rest ain't got back from drivin' cattle to Mexico, but they'll be on hand by noon today."

Laramie was silent, reckoning on the force he could put in the field. Waters' punchers were all he could be sure of: six or seven men at the most, not counting the wounded Waters. The odds were stacking up.

"Got a smoke?" the youth asked weakly. Laramie rolled a cigarette, placed it between the blue lips and held a match. Looking back down the canyon, Laramie saw men saddling mounts. Precious time was passing, but he was loath to leave the dying lad.

"Get goin'," muttered the boy uneasily. "You got a tough job ahead of you—honest men and thieves both agen you—but I'm bettin' on the Laramies—the real ones—" He seemed wandering in his mind. He began to sing in a ghastly whisper the song that Laramie could never hear without a shudder.

"When Brady died they planted him deep,
Put a bottle of whisky at his head and feet,
Folded his arms across his breast,
And said: 'King Brady's gone to his rest!'"

The crimson trickle became a sudden spurt; the youth's voice trailed into silence, and the cigarette slipped from his lips; he went limp and lay still, through forever with the wolf trail.

Laramie rose heavily and groped for his horse, trembling in the shade of the rock. He tore the blanket rolled behind the saddle and covered the still figure. Another debt to be marked up against the Laramies. A youth gone bad from boyhood worship of outlaw men, and struck down at last by a Laramie bullet. But the devil was driving and there was no time to be spent in bitter meditations.

He swung aboard and galloped through the tunnel to where his own horse was waiting—a faster mount than the cayuse he was riding. As he shifted mounts he heard shouts behind him, knew that his pursuers had halted at the body, knew the halt would be brief.

Without looking back, he hit the straightest trail he knew that led toward the ranch of Joel Waters.

Chapter .6.
"String Him Up!"

It was nearly noon when Laramie pulled up his sweating bronc at the porch of the Boxed W ranch house. There were no punchers in sight. Hop Sing opened the door.

"Where's Waters?" rapped out Laramie.

"Solly!" Hop Sing beamed on the younger man. "He gone to town to see doctluh and get leg fixed. Slim Jones dlive him in in buckbload. He be back tonight."

"Damn!" groaned Laramie. He saw his plan being knocked into a cocked hat by this circumstance. That plan had been to lead a band of men straight to the outlaws' hideout and bottle them up in their stronghold before they could scatter out over the range in their planned raid. He had counted on Waters' punchers as the nucleus of his fighting force, with Waters acting as recruiting officer to round up a crowd of townsmen and ranchers. Contact with Waters was absolutely necessary. The Boxed W punchers would not follow a stranger without their boss's orders, and only Waters could convince the bellicose citizens of San Leon that Laramie was on the level. Time was flying, and every minute counted.

There was only one course left open, and it was full of risk for himself, but it had to be taken. He swung on his tiring horse and reined away on the road for San Leon.

He met no one on the road, for which he was thankful. When he drew up on the outskirts of the town his horse was drawing laboring breaths. He knew the animal was at the limits of its endurance, and would be useless in case he had to dust out of town with a posse on his heels. He cursed himself for not having procured a fresh mount at the Boxed W. But he had come to bring a peace pipe, not to play tag with posses.

It was bright afternoon, and there would be people on the streets, but Laramie knew of a back alley that led to the doctor's office, and by which he hoped to make it unseen. He dismounted and headed down the alley, leading the gelding by the reins. It was touch and go now, with his plan, and life itself, hinging on the chance of reaching Joel Waters without being seen by the townsfolk.

Ahead of him he sighted the little adobe shack where the town's one physician lived and worked, when a jingle of spurs behind him caused him to jerk his head in time to see a man passing the end of the alley. It was Mart Rawley, and Laramie ducked behind his horse, cursing his luck. That was no trick of chance. Rawley must have been prowling around the town, expecting him, and watching for him. His yell instantly split the lazy silence.

"Laramie!" howled Rawley. "Laramie's back! Hey, Bill! Lon! Joe! Everybody! Laramie's in town again! This way!"

Laramie forked his mustang and spurred it into a lumbering run for the main street, just ahead. Fate's wheel again was weighted against him. Rawley must have headed straight for San Leon while Laramie was riding for the Boxed W. Harrison must have counted on Laramie's making for the town.

Lead was singing down the alley as Laramie burst into Main Street, and saw Joel Waters sitting in a chair on the porch of the doctor's shack.

"Get all the men you can rustle and head for the Diablos!" he yelled at the astonished ranchman. "I'll leave a trail for you to follow. I found the gang at the old hideout—and they're comin' out tonight for a big cleanup!"

Then he was off again, his clattering hoofs drowning Waters' voice as he shouted after the rider. Men were yelling and .45s banging. For as he reached Main Street, the town had come alive. Men were vomited from doorways and swept around corners. Ahorse and afoot they came at him, shooting as they ran. The dull, terrifying mob-roar rose, pierced with yells of: "String him up!" "He shot Bob Anders in the back!" "String up the Laramie whelp!" Rawley had done his work well. This was no time to depend on Joel Waters reasoning with them. They were too blood-crazy to listen. Words, explanations now would be worse than useless.

But his way to open country was blocked, and his horse was exhausted. Like a trapped rat Laramie looked desperately for a place to hide, or to make a last stand. For if he must go out, he preferred to go out on the end of a bullet rather than a rope. The mob's unreasoning rage roused a kindred emotion in his own breast.

With a snarl he wheeled and rode for a narrow alley on his right that did not seem to be blocked. It led between two buildings to a side street, and was not wide enough for a horse to pass through. Maybe that was the reason it had been left unguarded. Laramie reached it, threw himself from his saddle and dived into the narrow mouth.

For an instant his mount, standing with drooping head in the opening, masked his master from bullets, though Laramie had not intended sacrificing his horse for his own hide. Wearily it stood, motionless, and Laramie had run half the length of the alley before someone reached out gingerly, grasped the reins and jerked the horse away. Laramie half-turned, without pausing in his run, and fired back down the alley, high and harmlessly; the whistle of lead kept the alley clear until he bolted out the other end.

There, blocking his way in the side street, stood a figure beside a black racing horse. Laramie's gun came up—then he stopped short, mouth open, in glaring amazement. It was Judy Anders who stood beside the black horse.

Before he could speak she sprang forward and thrust the reins in his hand.

"Take him and go! He's fast!"

"Why—what—?" Laramie sputtered, his thinking processes in a muddle. The mere sight of Judy Anders seemed to have that effect upon him. Then reason returned and he took the gift the gods had given him without stopping for question. As he grabbed the horn and swung up he managed: "I sure thank you kindly, Miss—"

"Don't thank me," Judy Anders retorted curtly; her color was high, but her red lips were sulky. "You're a Laramie and ought to be hung, but you fought beside Bob yesterday when he needed help. The Anderses pay their debts. Will you go?"

A nervous stamp of her little foot emphasized the request. The advice was good. Three of the townsmen appeared with lifted guns around a corner of a nearby building, having circled about through another alley. They hesitated as they saw the girl near him, but began maneuvering for a clear shot at him without endangering her.

"See Joel Waters, at the doctor's office!" he yelled to her, and was off for the open country, riding like an Apache, and not at all sure that she understood him. Men howled and guns crashed behind him, and maddened citizens ran cursing for their mounts, too crazy-mad to notice the girl who shrieked vainly at them.

"Stop! Stop! Wait! Listen to me!—" Deaf to her cries they streamed past her, ahorse and afoot, and burst out into the open, the mounted men spurring their horses savagely after the figure that was swiftly dwindling in the distance.

Judy stamped her foot in passionate chagrin, dashed aside an angry tear and declaimed her opinion of men in general, and the citizens of San Leon in particular, in terms more expressive than ladylike.

"What's the matter?" It was Joel Waters, limping out of the alley, supported by the doctor. The old man seemed stunned by the rapidity of events. "What in the devil's all this mean? Where's Buck?"

She pointed. "There he goes, with all the idiots in San Leon after him."

"Not all the idiots," Waters corrected. "*I'm* still here. Dern it, the boy must be crazy, comin' here. I yelled myself deef at them fools, but they wouldn't listen—"

"They wouldn't listen to me, either!" cried Judy despairingly. "But they won't catch him—never, on that black of mine. And maybe when they come limping back, they'll be cooled down enough to hear the truth. If they won't listen to me, they will to Bob!"

"To Bob?" exclaimed the doctor. "Has he come out of his daze? I was just getting ready to come over and see him again, when Joel came in for his leg to be dressed."

"Bob came out of it just a little while ago. He told me it wasn't Laramie who shot him. He's still groggy and uncertain as to just what happened, and he doesn't know who it was who shot him, but he knows it wasn't Buck Laramie. The last thing he remembers was Laramie running some little distance *ahead* of him. The bullet came from behind. He thinks a stray slug from the men behind them hit him."

"I don't believe it was a stray," grunted Waters, his eyes beginning to glitter. "I got a dern good idee who shot Bob. I'm goin' to talk—"

"Better not bother Bob too much right now," interrupted the doctor. "Give him time to regain his strength. He's had a bad shock, though the wound itself isn't serious. I'll go over there—"

"Better go in a hurry if you want to catch Bob at home," the girl said grimly. "He was pulling on his boots and yelling for our cook to bring him his gun-belt when I left!"

"What? Why, he musn't get up yet!" The doctor transferred Waters' arm from his shoulder to that of the girl, and hurried away toward the house where Bob Anders was supposed to be convalescing.

"You give Buck a horse?" asked the old man, as she helped him along the street.

"My fast black. They can't catch him. When I heard the shooting and yelling, and heard them shouting, 'Hang the Laramie!' I knew what was up, so I grabbed the black and rode into the streets to try and tell the men that Laramie didn't shoot Bob. When I saw him afoot, I did the only thing I could think of to save him. They were all like crazy men, they wouldn't listen to me."

"Me neither," grunted the old man angrily. "Mobs is all like that, though."

"But why did he come back here?" she wailed.

"From what he hollered at me as he lighted past, I reckon he's found somethin' up in the Diablos. Somethin' too big for him to handle alone. He come for help. Probably went to my ranch first, and findin' me not there, risked his neck comin' on here. Said send men after him, to foller signs he'd leave. I relayed that there information on to Slim Jones, my foreman. Doc lent Slim a horse, and Slim's high tailin' it for the Boxed W right now to round up my waddies and hit the trail. As soon as these San Leon snake-hunters has ruint their cayuses chasin' that black streak of light you give Buck, they'll be pullin' back into town, and this time, I bet they'll listen to folks that knows the truth."

"I'm glad he didn't shoot Bob," she murmured. "But why—why did he come back here in the first place?"

"He come to pay a debt he figgered he owed on behalf of his no-account brothers. His saddlebags is full of gold he aims to give back to the citizens of this here ongrateful town. What's the matter?"

For his fair companion had uttered a startled exclamation.

"N-nothing, only—only I didn't know it was that way! Then Buck never robbed or stole, like his brothers?"

"Course he didn't!" snapped the old man irascibly. "Think I'd kept on bein' his friend all his life, if he had? Buck ain't to blame for what his brothers did. He's straight and he's always been straight."

"But he was with them, when—when—"

"I know." Waters' voice was gentler. "But he didn't shoot yore dad. That was Luke. And Buck was with 'em only because they made him. He wasn't nothin' but a kid."

She did not reply and old Waters, noting the soft, new light glowing in her eyes, the faint, wistful smile that curved her red lips, wisely said nothing.

And in the meantime the subject of their discussion was proving the worth of the sleek piece of horseflesh under him. He had laughed grimly at the sight of the maddened citizens pouring out of the town behind him, as he felt the velvet smooth play of the animal's running stride. Like a startled streak of light he swept over a ridge that sheltered him from long-range rifle fire, and by the time they topped the rise he was far ahead of them and increasing the lead with every stride. He grinned as he saw the distance between him and his pursuers widen, thrilled to the marvel of the horse between his knees as any good horseman would. In half an hour he could no longer see the men who hunted him. He was free to do the task he had set for himself.

He pulled the black to an easier, swinging gait that would eat up the miles for long hours on end, and headed for the Diablos. But the desperate move he was making was not dominating his thoughts. He was mulling over a new puzzle: the problem of why Judy Anders had come to his aid. If Bob had survived his wound, and asserted

Laramie's innocence, why were the citizens so hot for his blood? If not—would Judy Anders willingly aid a man she thought shot her brother? Laramie had heard something about feminine intuition and he wondered hazily if this mysterious power had caused the girl to decide that he was an honest man, despite appearances. Yet her words to him had been harsh, even while making him the gift that saved his life.

"I give it up, bronc," he sighed. "But she sure saved one Laramie neck, that pass. Gosh, I hope Anders has come to hisself and told them ragin' feather-heads I didn't shoot him. Waters will send his boys after me, I know derned well. But they ain't enough. And who in San Leon would risk his neck comin' to the aid of Buck Laramie? How'd Joel be sure to convince 'em a Laramie was anything but a lobo wolf?

"Oh, to hell with it. Harrison's gang's got to be stopped before they get out of that hideout. I got to make a trap out of their fort, and if I got no aid, I got to do it by myself. Git along, cayuse; I got a date with Mr. Ely Harrison, esquire and what not."

And he rode toward his desperate venture as recklessly and unerringly as men of his breed have ridden to die for lost causes the world over, through all the ages.

Chapter .7.
The Blocked Way

A good three hours before sundown Laramie was in the foothills of the Diablos. In another hour, by dint of reckless riding over trails that were inches in width, and which he ordinarily would have shunned, he came in sight of the entrance to the hideout. He had not failed to leave signs farther down the trail to indicate, not the ways he had come, but the best way for Waters' punchers to follow him.

Once more he dismounted some distance from the tunnel and stole cautiously forward. There would be a new sentry at the entrance, and Laramie's first job must be to dispose of him silently. A six-gun barrel is as good as a black jack in the hands of an expert.

He was halfway to the tunnel when he glimpsed the guard, sitting several yards from the mouth, near a clump of bushes. It was the scar-faced fellow Harrison had called Braxton, and he seemed wide awake.

Falling back on Indian tactics, acquired from the Yaquis in Mexico, Laramie began a stealthy, and necessarily slow, advance on the guard, swinging in a circle that would bring him behind the man.

After what seemed centuries of noiseless creeping and egging forward, Laramie reached a point within a dozen feet of Braxton—and there the cover dwindled out entirely. Laramie considered the possibility of covering the man and ordering him to drop his gun. But Scarface had already demonstrated his readiness to take desperate chances, and Laramie believed he would whirl and fire, even with the drop on him. A gunshot would warn the men in the canyon and ruin his plan completely.

Braxton was getting restless. He shifted his position, craning his neck as he stared suspiciously about him. Laramie believed he had heard, but not yet located, faint sounds made in Laramie's progress. In another instant he would turn his head and stare full at the bushes which afforded the attacker scanty cover.

Gathering a handful of pebbles, Laramie rose stealthily to his knees and threw them over the guard's head. They hit with a loud clatter some yards beyond the man, and Braxton started to his feet with an oath, glaring in the direction of the sound with his Winchester half-lifted, neck craning. At the same instant Laramie leaped for him with his six-gun raised like a club.

Scarface wheeled, and his eyes flared in amazement. He jerked the rifle around, but Laramie struck it aside with his left hand, and brought down his pistol barrel crushingly on the man's head. Braxton went to his knees like a felled ox, slumped full-length and lay still.

Working fast Laramie ripped off belts and neckerchief from the senseless figure, bound and gagged his captive securely. He appropriated his pistol, rifle, and spare cartridges, and dragged him away from the tunnel mouth, shoving him in among a cluster of rocks and bushes, effectually concealing him from the casual glance.

"Won the first trick, by thunder!" grunted Laramie. "And now for the next deal!"

The success of that deal depended on whether or not all the outlaws of Harrison's band were in the hideout. Braxton was unconscious and could be expected to lie about anything he was asked, anyway. But the boy Laramie had shot had said all the absent members of the band would be in the hideout by noon. Mart Rawley was probably outside, yet, maybe still back in San Leon. But Laramie knew he must take the chance that all the other outlaws *were* inside.

He glanced up to a ledge overhanging the tunnel mouth, where stood precariously balanced the huge boulder which had given him his idea for bottling up the canyon.

"Cork for my bottle!" muttered Laramie. "All I need now's a lever."

A broken tree limb sufficed for that, and a few moments later he had climbed to the ledge and was at work on the boulder. He drove his pry pole deep and heaved with all his shoulders and sinewy back, grunting profanely. A moment's panic assailed him as he feared its base was too deeply imbedded for him to move it. But under his fierce efforts he felt the great mass give at last, a few minutes more of back-breaking effort, another heave that made the veins bulge on his temples—and the boulder started toppling, crashed over the ledge and thundered down into the tunnel entrance. It jammed there, almost filling the space.

He swarmed down the wall and began wedging smaller rocks and brush in the apertures between the boulder and the tunnel sides. Nobody could crawl under or over or around the big rock, or lever the boulder away from the inside, when he got through. The fortress of his enemies had become a prison. The only way they could get out was by climbing the canyon walls, a feat he considered practically impossible, or by laboriously picking out the stones he had jammed in place, and squeezing a way through a hole between the boulder and the tunnel wall. And neither method would be a cinch, with a resolute gent slinging lead at everything that moved.

Laramie estimated that his whole task had taken about half an hour. Fate could not be expected to allow him much more time to get ready for the grand bust. Slinging Braxton's rifle over his shoulder he clambered up the cliffs, and having reached the spot on the canyon rim where he had spied upon the hideout that morning, he forted himself by the simple procedure of crouching behind a fair-sized rock, with the Winchester and pistols handy at his elbows. He had scarcely taken his position when he saw a mob of riders breaking away from the corral behind the cabin. As he had figured, the gang was getting away to an early start for its activities of the night.

He counted twenty-five of them; and the very sun that glinted on polished gun hammers and silver conchas seemed to reflect violence and evil deeds. This was outlawry on a wholesale scale.

"Four hundred yards," muttered Laramie, squinting along the blue rifle barrel. "Three fifty—three hundred—now I opens the ball!"

At the ping of the shot dust spurted in front of the horses' hoofs, and the riders scattered like quail, with startled yells.

"Drop them shootin' irons and hi'st yore hands!" roared Laramie. "Tunnel's corked up and you can't get out!"

His answer came in a vengeful hail of bullets, spattering along the canyon rim for yards in either direction. He had not expected any other reply. His shout had been more for rhetorical effect than anything else; but there was nothing theatrical about his second shot, which knocked a man out of his saddle. The fellow never moved after he hit the ground.

The outlaws converged toward the tunnel entrance, firing as they rode, aiming at Laramie's aerie, which they had finally located. Laramie replied in kind. A mustang smitten by a slug meant for his rider rolled to the ground and broke his rider's leg under him. A squat raider howled blasphemously as a slug ploughed through his breast muscles.

Then half a dozen men in the lead jammed into the tunnel and found that Laramie had informed them truthfully. Their yells reached a crescendo of fury, and the others, interpreting them, slid from their horses and took cover behind the rocks that littered the edges of the canyon, dragging the wounded men with them.

From a rush and a dash the fight settled to a slow, deadly grind, with nobody taking any rash chances. Having located his tiny fort, they concentrated their fire on the spot of the rim he occupied. A storm of bullets drove him to cover behind his breastworks, and became exceedingly irksome. He fervently yearned for the blood of his foes, but to expose himself long enough to pick out a protruding arm or head in the rocks below, meant that he would probably be riddled in return. He had not seen either Rawley or Harrison. Rawley, he hoped, was still in San Leon, but the absence of Harrison worried him. Had he, too, gone to San Leon? If so, there was every chance that he might get clean away, even if his band was wiped out. There was another chance, that he or Rawley, or both of them, might return to the hideout and attack him from the rear. He cursed himself for not having divulged the true identity of the gang's leader to Judy Anders; but he always seemed addled when talking to her.

The ammunition supply of the outlaws seemed inexhaustible. He knew at least six men were in the tunnel, and he heard them cursing and shouting, their voices muffled. He found himself confronted by a quandary that seemed to admit of no solution. If he did not discourage them, they would be breaking through the blocked tunnel and potting him from the rear. But to affect this discouragement meant leaving his point of vantage, and giving the men below a chance to climb the canyon wall. He did not believe this could be done, but he did not know what additions to the fortress had been made by the new occupants. They might have chiseled out handholds at some point on the wall.

But even so, it would take time to climb from the floor to the rim, so Laramie wormed his way back to a point where he could look down at the blocked entrance. It seemed to be intact; no one had as yet broken through, though he could hear a great deal of pounding and prying going on inside, mingled with torrid profanity, no less sincere because muffled. He crawled back to his sheltering rock in time to see a figure sneaking toward the canyon wall, evidently with ideas of attempting a climb.

Laramie knew this to be impossible at the spot which the man had selected, unless a ladder of hand-niches had been cut, but that did not alter the intentions of the bullet he sent after the fellow. The man dropped as if one leg had been scythed from under him, and rolled to the shelter of a rock, while his companions lifted a hymn of hate and redoubled the fury of their fire . . .

A quarter of an hour later circumstances had not altered, except that Laramie's rifle ammunition was running low. The men in the tunnel banged and hammered and swore, the men in the canyon laid low and showered the rim with hot lead, and Laramie sniped at every bit of cloth, skin or leather he sighted, hoping devoutly that each minute would bring reinforcements. His nervousness grew, and he found himself tensely waiting for the rattle of hoofs that would herald the coming of Ely Harrison or Mart Rawley, to catch him between two fires. He decided to make another trip to the spot where he could see the tunnel, to make sure his rats were not escaping the trap.

"Six-guns against rifles, if this keeps up much longer," he muttered, working his way over the ledges. "Have to be more economical with my cartridges. Looks like my string's dern near played out. Why the devil don't Joel's men show up? I can't keep these *hombres* hemmed up forever—*damn!*"

His arm thrust his six-gun out as he yelped. Stones and brush had been worked out at one place in the tunnel-mouth, and the head and shoulders of a man appeared. At the crash of Laramie's Colt the fellow howled and vanished. Laramie crouched, glaring; they would try it again, soon. And if he was not there to give them lead argument, the whole gang would be squeezing out of the tunnel in no time. He could not get back to the rim, and leave the tunnel unguarded; yet there was always the possibility of somebody climbing the canyon wall. He was like a man who had trapped a bunch of wildcats and could neither hold them nor let them go.

Had he but known it, his fears were justified. For while he crouched on the ledge, glaring down at the tunnel mouth, down in the canyon a man was wriggling toward a certain point of the cliff, where his keen eyes had discerned something dangling. He had discovered Laramie's rope, hanging from the stunted tree on the rim. Cautiously he lifted himself out of the tall grass, ready to duck back in an instant, then, as no shot came from the canyon rim, he scuttled like a rabbit toward the wall. He heard the muffled bang of a six-gun beyond the cliffs, and the yell of Laramie's victim, and he shrewdly surmised that only one man was pitted against them, and that their enemy was at the moment absorbed with the men in the tunnel.

Kicking off his boots and slinging his rifle on his back, he began swarming, ape-like, up the almost sheer wall. No one man in a dozen could have made that climb, but men with unusual accomplishments are common enough in a gang like Harrison's. This fellow's outstretched arm grasped the lower end of the rope, just as the others in the canyon saw what he was doing, and opened a furious fire on the rim to cover his activities. The outlaw on the rope swore luridly, and went up with amazing swiftness and agility, his flesh crawling with the momentary expectation of a bullet in his back.

The renewed firing had just the effect on Laramie that the climber had feared it would have—it drew him back to his breast-work, for he feared it was meant to mask some aggressive move-ment in the canyon. It was not until he was crouching behind his breastwork that it occurred to him that the volleys might have been intended to draw him away from the tunnel. So he spared only a glance over the rocks, and that glance was limited, because the bullets were winging so close that he dared not lift his head high. His view of the canyon was limited, so he did not see the man on the rope cover the last few feet in a scrambling rush, and haul himself over the rim, unslinging his rifle as he did so.

It all proved the impossibility of one man watching two places at once. Renewed activities in the tunnel beneath seemed to clinch Laramie's suspicions, and he turned and headed back for the ledge whence he could see the opening. And as he did so, he brought himself into full view of the outlaw who was standing upright on the rim, by the stunted tree.

The whiplike crack of his Winchester reached Laramie an instant after he felt a numbing impact in his left shoulder. The shock of the blow knocked him off his feet, and his head hit hard against a rock. Even as he fell he heard the crashing of brush down the trail, and his last, hopeless thought was that Rawley and Harrison were returning. Then the impact of his head against the rock knocked all thought into a stunned blank.

Chapter .8.
War in the Canyon

Down in the tunnel a hat crown appeared in the opening; it moved; none could have told that it was occupied by a gun barrel instead of a human head. It was withdrawn and a man snarled: "Out, quick! He must be back on the cliff!"

An outlaw came scrambling out with desperate haste, followed by another and another. One crouched, rifle in hand, glaring up at the wall, while the others tore away the smaller stones, and aided by those inside, rolled the boulder out of the entrance. Three men ran out of the tunnel and joined them.

"One of you *hombres* chase back and tell the others the way's clear," snarled the man with the rifle. "Tell 'em to foller us and we'll surround this meddlin' galoot and settle his hash, and then git the horses, and—by God, ain't that a man layin' up there amongst them rocks? It is! He's been hit! I'm goin' to climb up there, and—"

"*Look out!*" roared one of the men, throwing his rifle to his shoulder, as five horsemen burst out of the brush, down the trail, firing as they came.

It was this firing that roused Buck Laramie to consciousness. He blinked and glared, then oriented himself; he saw the five riders sweeping toward the tunnel, and the six outlaws falling back into it for shelter; and he recognized the leader of the newcomers as Slim Jones, Joel Waters' foreman. The old man had not failed him.

"Take cover, you fools!" Laramie yelled wildly, unheard in the din.

But the reckless punchers came straight on and ran into a blast of lead poured from the tunnel mouth into which the outlaws had disappeared. One of the waddies saved his life by a leap from the saddle as his horse fell with a bullet through its brain, and another man threw wide his arms and pitched on his head, dead before he hit the pebbles.

Then only did Slim and his wild crew swerve their horses out of line and fall back to cover. Laramie remembered the slug that had felled him, and turned to scan the canyon rim. He saw the man by the stunted tree, then; the fellow was helping one of his companions up the same route he had taken, and evidently thought that his shot had settled Laramie, as he was making no effort at concealment. Laramie lifted his rifle and pulled the trigger—and the hammer fell with an empty click. He had no more rifle cartridges. Below him the punchers were futilely firing at the tunnel entrance, and the outlaws within were wisely holding their fire until they could see something to shoot at.

Laramie crawled along a few feet to put himself out of range of the rifleman on the rim, and shouted: "Slim! Swing wide of that trail and come up here with yore men!"

Profane acquiescence told him he was understood, for presently Slim and the three surviving punchers came crawling over the tangle of rocks, having necessarily abandoned their horses.

"'Bout time you was gettin' here," grunted Laramie. "Gimme some .30-30s."

A handful of cartridges were shoved into his eager fingers.

"We come as soon as we could," said Slim. "Had to ride to the ranch to round up these snake-hunters."

"Where's Waters?"

"I left him in San Leon, cussin' a blue streak because he couldn't get nobody to listen to him. Folks got no more sense'n cattle; just as easy to stampede and as hard to git millin' once they bust loose."

"Reckon he'll be able to persuade any of 'em to come and help us?"

"I dunno; I streaked out of San Leon in one direction whilst they was chasin' you out in another. He will if it's humanly possible."

"What about Bob Anders?"

"Doctor said he was just creased, was just fixin' to go over there when me and Joel come into town and he had to wait and dress Joel's leg. Hadn't come to hisself, last time the doc was there."

Laramie breathed a sigh of relief, at least Bob Anders was going to live, even if he hadn't been able to name the man who shot him. Then Laramie snapped into action.

"You bring white belts, Slim; but unless Waters sends us more men, we're licked. Tunnel's cleared and men climbin' the cliff. If any more gets out, they'll swamp us with numbers, and be all set to ambush anybody else that comes—if anybody does come."

"You're shot!" Jones pointed to Laramie's shirt shoulder, soaked with blood.

"So what?" snapped Laramie. "Well, gimme that bandanna—" and while he knotted it into a crude bandage, he talked rapidly. "Three of you *hombres* stay here and watch that tunnel. Don't let nobody out, d'you hear? Me and Slim are goin' to circle around and argy with the gents climbin' the cliffs. Come on, Slim."

It was rough climbing, and Laramie's shoulder burned like fire, with a dull throbbing that told him the lead was pressing near a bone. But he set his teeth and crawled over the rough rocks, keeping out of sight of the men in the canyon below, until they had reached a point beyond his tiny fort on the rim, and that much closer to the stunted tree. They had kept below the crest and had not been sighted by the outlaws on the rim, who had been engrossed in knotting a second rope, brought up by the second man, to the end of the lariat tied to the tree. This had been dropped down the wall again, and now another outlaw was hanging to the rope and being drawn straight up the cliff like a water bucket by his two friends above—a job that must have been muscle racking.

Slim and Laramie fired almost simultaneously. Slim's bullet burned the fingers of the man clinging to the lariat and he howled and let go the rope and fell fifteen feet to the canyon floor. Laramie winged one of the men on the cliff, but it did not effect his speed as he raced after his companion in a flight for cover. Bullets whizzed up from the canyon as the men below spotted Laramie and his companion, and they ducked back, but relentlessly piled lead after the men fleeing along the rim of the cliff.

These worthies made no attempt to make a stand. They knew the lone defender had received reinforcements and they were not stopping to learn in what force. Laramie and Slim caught fleeting glimpses of the fugitives as they headed out through the hills, and from the speed they were making it was evident that they had only one desire and that was to cover as much distance as possible.

"Let 'em go," grunted Laramie. "Be no more trouble from that quarter, and I bet them rannies won't try to climb that rope no more. Come on; I hear guns talkin' back at the tunnel. Likely we'll be needed."

The volume and rapidity of the firing made the supposition seem logical. Laramie and his companion reached the punchers on the ledge in time to see three horsemen streaking it down the trail, with lead humming after them. Three more figures lay sprawled about the mouth of the tunnel.

"They busted out on horseback," grunted one of the men, kneeling and aiming after the fleeing men. "Come so fast we couldn't stop 'em all—uh!"

His shot punctuated his remarks, and one of the fleeing horsemen swayed in his saddle. One of the others seemed to be wounded, as the three ducked into the trees and out of sight.

"Three more hit the trail," grunted Slim.

"Not them," predicted Laramie. "They was bound to seen us—know they ain't but five of us. They won't go far; they'll be sneakin' back to pot us in the back when their pards start bustin' out again."

"No racket in the tunnel now."

"They're layin' low for a spell. Too damn risky now. They didn't have but six horses in the tunnel. They got to catch more and bring 'em to the tunnel before they can make the rush. We can pot most of 'em from the cliffs before they even get to the tunnel. Man can sneak in, under cover, but not a man with a horse. They'll wait till dark, and then we can't stop 'em from gettin' their cayuses into the tunnel—and we can't stop 'em from tearin' out at this end, neither, unless we got more men. Slim, climb back up on the rim and lay down behind them rocks I stacked up. Watch that rope so nobody climbs it; we got to cut that, soon's it gets dark. And don't let no horses be brought into the tunnel, if you can help it."

Slim crawled away, and a few moments later his rifle began banging, and he yelled wrathfully: "They're already at it!"

"Listen!" ejaculated Laramie suddenly.

Down the trail, out of sight among the trees, sounded a thundering of hoofs, yells and shots.

The shots ceased, then after a pause, the hoofs swept on, and a crowd of men burst into view.

"Yippee!" whooped one of the punchers bounding into the air and swinging his hat. "Reinforcements, b'golly! It's a regular army!"

"Looks like all San Leon was there!" bellowed another. "Hey, boys, don't git in line with that tunnel mouth! Spread out along the trail—who's them three fellers they got tied to their saddles?"

"The three snakes that broke loose from the tunnel!" yelped the third cowboy. "They scooped 'em in as they come! Looks like everybody's there. There's Charlie Ross, and Jim Watkins, the mayor, and Lon Evans, Mart Rawley's bartender—reckon he didn't know his boss was a crook—and by golly, look who's leadin' 'em!"

"*Bob Anders!*" ejaculated Laramie, staring at the pale faced, but erect figure who, with bandaged head, rode ahead of the thirty or forty men who came clattering up the trail and swung wide through the brush to avoid the grim tunnel mouth. Anders saw him and waved his hand, and a deep yell of approbation rose from the men behind the sheriff. Laramie sighed deeply. A few hours ago these same men wanted to hang him. It looked like justice, as far as he was concerned, was triumphing at last, after taking an awful licking.

Rifles were spitting from the tunnel, and the riders swung from their horses and began to take up positions on each side of the trail, as Anders took in the situation at a glance and snapped his orders. Rifles began to speak in answer to the shots of the outlaws. Laramie came clambering down the cliff to grasp Anders' outstretched hand.

"I came to just about the time you hit town today, Laramie," he said. "Was just tellin' Judy it couldn't been you that shot me, when all that hell busted loose and Judy run to help you out if she could. Time I could get my clothes on, and out-argy the doctor, and get on the streets, you was gone with these addle-heads chasin' you. We had to wait till they give up the chase and come back, and then me and Judy and Joel Waters lit into 'em. Time we got through talkin' they was plumb whipped down and achin' to take a hand in yore game."

"We're with you to the finish, Laramie!" bawled one of the men from the rocks where he lay—a fellow Buck recognized as one who had yelled "String him up!" loudest of any. "We admits we've been follerin' a blind lead, and we plays yore string!"

"Where's Rawley?" demanded Laramie.

"We thought he was with us when we lit out after you," shouted the San Leon man. "But when we started back we missed him, and ain't seen him since. Reckon he skipped."

"Sorry I didn't come to in time to save you a lot of trouble, Laramie," said the sheriff apologetically.

"Yore sister saved me plenty trouble," Laramie grinned. He knew he was a strange figure, with bandaged shoulder, bloodstained shirt and the skin of face and hands blackened with powder smoke. "But we'll have to hold our powwow later, the war ain't over—" he ducked involuntarily as guns began to thunder in the tunnel—"in fact," he threw over his shoulder as he legged it for a vantage point, "the ball's openin' again."

"Look out!" yelled Slim on the rim above them, pumping lead frantically. "They're rushin' for the tunnel on horses! Blame it, why ain't somebody up here with me? I can't stop 'em all—"

Evidently the gang inside the canyon had been whipped to desperation by the arrival of the reinforcements, for they came thundering through the tunnel laying down a barrage of lead as they came. It was sheer madness. They ran full into a blast of lead that piled screaming horses and writhing men in a red shambles.

The survivors staggered back into the tunnel, and some of the posse, maddened by excitement, would have charged in after them, had not Bob Anders cursed them back to cover.

"Wanta pull the same fool trick they just pulled? Le's don't throw away no more lives on them coyotes than we got to. We got 'em bottled."

"But when it gets dark—which ain't goin' to be long now—" said Laramie, "they're goin' to spill outa that bowl like rats, and some'll climb the cliffs in the dark. I hate for any of that gang to get away."

"How many's in there?"

"Was twenty-five to start with. A couple climbed out on a rope and got away. Three got plugged rushin' the tunnel before you came, and you snared the other three. They lost four men in that last rush. At least four or five of them inside are more or less shot up. Figure it for yoreself. They's enough left to spoil our deal if we ain't careful."

Struck by a sudden thought, he groped among the bushes and hauled out the guard, Braxton, still bound and gagged. The fellow was conscious and glared balefully at his captor. Laramie tore the gag off, and demanded: "Where's Harrison and Rawley?"

"Rawley rode for San Leon after you got away from us this mornin'," growled Braxton sullenly. "Harrison's gone, got scared and pulled out. I dunno where he went."

"Yo're lyin'," accused Laramie.

"What'd you ast me for, if you know so much?" sneered Braxton, and lapsed into stubborn, hill-country silence, which Laramie knew nothing would break, so long as the man chose to hold his tongue.

"They won't none of 'em talk, Buck," said Anders.

"Take him and put him with the other prisoners," growled Laramie. "He may be tellin' the truth, at that. I ain't seen neither

Harrison nor Rawley since I got here. Be just like them rats to double-cross their own men, and run off with the loot they've already got.

"But we still got this nest to clean out, and here's my idea. Them that's still alive in the canyon are denned up in or near the tunnel. Nobody nigh the cabin. If four or five of us can hole up in there, we'll have 'em from both sides. We'll tie some lariats together, and some of us will go down the wall and get in the cabin. We'll scatter men along the rim to see none of 'em climb out, and we'll leave plenty men here to hold the tunnel if they try that again—which they will, as soon as it begins to get dark, if we don't scuttle 'em first."

"You oughta been a general, cowboy. Me and Slim and a couple of my Bar X boys'll go for the cabin. You better stay here; yore shoulder ain't fit for tightrope work and such."

"She's my hand," growled Laramie. "I started dealin' her and I aim to set in till the last pot's raked in."

"Yo're the dealer," acquiesced Anders. "Let's go."

Ten minutes later found the party of five clustered on the canyon rim. The sun had not yet set beyond the peaks, but the canyon below was in shadow. Darkness would settle in the bowl some time before it cloaked the upper slopes. The spot Laramie had chosen for descent was some distance beyond the stunted tree. The rim there was higher, the wall even more precipitous, but it had the advantage of an outjut of rock that would partially serve to mask the descent of a man on a rope from the view of the men lurking about the head of the canyon. Their whole plan depended upon the secrecy of their movements.

The cabin stood in the midst of the canyon, apparently deserted. Up at the head of the canyon white puffs of smoke floated from the rocks as the men fired desperately at their besiegers on the rim. More muffled reports indicated that the men in the tunnel were waging unceasing war with those outside. These latter poured a continual stream of lead into the tunnel mouth, to keep the attention of the besieged.

If anyone saw the descent of the five invaders, there was no sign to show they had been discovered. Man after man they slid down the dangling rope and crouched at the foot, Winchesters ready. Laramie came last, clinging with one hand and gritting his teeth against the pain of his wounded shoulder. Then began the advance on the cabin.

That slow, tortuous crawl across the canyon floor seemed endless. Laramie counted the seconds, fearful that they would be seen, fearful that night would shut down before they were forted. The western rim of the canyon seemed crested with golden fire, contrasting with the blue shadows floating beneath it. He sighed gustily as they reached their goal, with still enough light for their purpose.

The cabin doors were shut, the windows closely shuttered. There was no sign of occupancy.

"Let's go!" Anders had one hand on the door, drawn Colt in the other.

"Wait," grunted Laramie. "I stuck my head into a loop here once already today. You all stay here while I take a *pasear* around to the back and look things over from that side. Don't go in till you hear me holler."

Then Laramie was sneaking around the cabin, Indian-fashion, gun in hand. He was little more than half the distance to the back when he heard a voice inside the cabin call out: "All clear!"

Before he could move or shout a warning, he heard Anders answer: "Comin', Buck!" Then the front door slammed, and there was the sound of a sliding bolt, a yell of dismay from the Bar X men. With sick fury Laramie realized that somebody lurking inside the cabin had heard him giving his instructions and imitated his voice to trick the sheriff into entering. Confirmation came instantly, in a familiar voice—the voice of Ely Harrison!

"Now we can make terms, gentlemen!" shouted the banker, his voice rasping with ferocious exultation. "We've got your sheriff in a wolf trap with hot lead teeth! You can give us road-belts to Mexico, or he'll be deader than hell in three minutes by the clock!"

Chapter .9.
Killer Rawlins

Laramie was charging for the rear of the house before the triumphant shout ended. Anders would never agree to buying freedom for that gang to save his own life; and Laramie knew that whatever truce might be agreed upon, Harrison would never let the sheriff live. All five of them were doomed, Anders among them, unless they hit hard and sudden.

The same thought motivated the savage attack of Slim Jones and the Bar X men on the front door; but that door happened to be of unusual strength. Nothing short of a log battering ram could smash it. But the rear door was of ordinary thin paneling. The Laramies had never thought it necessary to make a fortress of their cabin, secure as they were behind the walls of the canyon. The massiveness of the other door was merely a circumstance of chance.

Bracing his good right shoulder to the shock, Laramie rammed his full charging weight against the rear door—it crashed inward and he catapulted into the room gun first.

He had a fleeting glimpse of a swarthy Mexican wheeling from the doorway that led into the main room, and then he ducked and jerked the trigger as a knife sang past his head. The roar of the .45 shook the narrow room and the knife thrower hit the planks and lay twitching.

With a lunging stride Laramie was through the door, into the main room. He caught a glimpse of men standing momentarily frozen, glaring up from their work of tying Bob Anders to a chair— Ely Harrison, another Mexican, and Mart Rawley.

For an infinitesimal tick of time the scene held—then blurred with gun-smoke as the .45s roared death across the narrow confines. Hot lead was a coal of hell burning its way through the flesh of Laramie's already wounded shoulder. Bob Anders lurched out of the chair, rolling clumsily toward the wall. The room was a mad welter of sound and smoke. The last light of gathering dusk struck through cracks in the window shutters, into waves of drifting smoke, lanced by red spurts of flame, blurring the shapes of half-formed bodies.

Laramie half-rolled behind the partial cover of a cast iron stove, drawing his second gun. The Mexican fled to the bunkroom, howling, his broken left arm flopping, and Mart Rawley backed after him at a stumbling run, shooting as he went; crouched inside the door, he glared, awaiting his chance. But Harrison, already badly wounded, had gone berserk. Disdaining cover, or touched with madness, he came storming across the room, shooting as he came, spattering blood at every step. His eyes flamed through the drifting fog of smoke like those of a rabid wolf.

Laramie raised himself to his full height and faced him. Searing lead whined past his ear, jerked at his shirt, stung his thigh; but his own gun was burning red and Harrison was swaying in his stride like a bull which feels the matador's steel—his last shot flamed almost in Laramie's face, and then at close range a bullet split the cold heart of the devil of San Leon, and the greed and ambitions of Ely Harrison were lost in oblivion.

Laramie, with one loaded cartridge left in his last gun, leaned back against the wall, out of range of the bunkroom.

"Come on, Rawley," he called. "Harrison's dead. Yore game's played out."

The hidden gunman spat like an infuriated cat.

"No, my game ain't played out!" he yelled in a voice edged with bloodmadness. "Not till I've wiped you out, you mangy stray. But before I kill you, I want you to know that you ain't the first Laramie I've sent to hell! I'd of thought you'd knowed me, in spite of these whiskers! I'm Rawlins, you fool! Killer Rawlins, that plugged yore horse-thief brother Luke in Santa Maria!"

"Rawlins!" snarled Laramie, suddenly white. "No wonder you knowed me!"

"Yes, Rawlins!" howled the gunman. "I'm the one that made friends with Luke Laramie and got him drunk till he told me all about this hideout and the trails across the desert. Then I picked a fight with Luke when he was too drunk to stand, and killed him to keep his mouth shut! And what you goin' to do about it?"

"I'm going to kill you, you hell-buzzard!" gritted Laramie, lurching away from the wall as Rawlins came frothing through the door, with both guns blazing. Inspired by a certitude strong as a decree of Fate, Laramie fired once from the hip. And his last bullet ripped through Killer Rawlins' warped brain, and Laramie looked down on him as he died, with his spurred heels drumming a death march on the floor.

Frantic feet behind him brought him around to see a livid, swarthy face convulsed with fear and hate, a brown arm lifting a razor-edged knife. He had forgotten the Mexican. He threw up his empty pistol to guard the downward sweep of the sharp blade—and once more the blast of a six-gun shook the room. And Jose Martinez of Chihuahua lifted one scream of invocation and blasphemy at some forgotten Aztec god, as his soul went speeding its way to hell.

Laramie turned and stared stupidly through the smoke-blurred dusk at a tall, slim figure holding a smoking gun. Others were pouring in through the kitchen. So brief had been the desperate fight that the men who had raced around the house at the first bellow of the guns, had just reached the scene. Laramie shook his head dazedly. It seemed incredible that all that action, revelation and destruction had been packed into such a brief space.

"Slim!" he muttered. "See if Bob's hurt!"

"Not me!" The sheriff answered for himself, struggling up to a sitting posture by the wall. "I fell outa the chair and rolled outa line when the lead started singin'. Cut me loose, somebody."

"Cut him loose, Slim," mumbled Laramie. "I'm kinda dizzy."

Stark silence followed the roar of the six-guns, silence that hurt Buck Laramie's eardrums. Like a man in a daze he staggered to a chair and sank down heavily upon it. Scarcely knowing what he did he found himself muttering the words of a song he hated:

"When the folks heard that Brady was dead,
They all turned out, all dressed in red;

Marched down the street a-singin' a song:
'Brady's gone to hell with his Stetson on!'"

He was hardly aware when Bob Anders came and cut his blood-soaked shirt away and washed his wounds, dressing them as best he could with strips torn from his own shirt, and whisky from a jug found on the table. The bite of the alcohol roused Laramie from the daze that enveloped him, and a deep swig of the same medicine cleared his dizzy head.

Anders was alone with him in the cabin, now lighted by an oil lamp the sheriff had found. Rifles were cracking flatly outside as Slim Jones and the others, crawling through the tall grass, fired at the flame-flashes up the canyon.

"Feel all right, Laramie?" there was sincere solicitude in the sheriff's voice.

Laramie rose stiffly; he glanced about at the dead men staring glassily in the lamplight, shuddered, and retched suddenly at the reek of the blood that blackened the planks.

"For God's sake, le's get out in the open!"

As they emerged into the cool dusk, they were aware that the shooting had ceased. A voice was bawling loudly at the head of the canyon, though the distance made the words unintelligible.

"They're yellin' for quarters," predicted Laramie. "They got enough. They know we got 'em on each side, and they don't know how many there is of us. They bound to figgered out that we've killed Harrison and the rest. Here comes Slim!"

The lanky puncher came running back through the dusk.

"They're makin' a parley, Bob!" quoth he. "They want to know if they'll be given a fair trial if they surrender. They're afeard they'll be mobbed. They want yore word on it."

"I'll talk to 'em. Rest of you all keep under cover."

The sheriff worked toward the head of the canyon until he was within earshot of the men in and about the tunnel, and shouted: "Are you *hombres* ready to give in?"

"What's yore terms?" bawled back the spokesman, recognizing the sheriff's voice.

"I ain't makin' terms. You'll all get a fair trial in an honest court. You better make up yore minds. I know they ain't a lot of you left. Harrison's dead and so is Rawley. I got forty men outside this canyon and enough inside, behind you, to wipe you out. Throw yore guns out here where I can see 'em, and come out with yore hands high. I'll give you till I count ten."

And as he began to count, rifles and pistols began clattering on the bare earth, and haggard, bloodstained, powder-blackened men rose from behind rocks with their hands in the air, and came out of the tunnel in the same manner.

"We quits," announced the spokesman. "Four of the boys are layin' back amongst the rocks too shot up to move under their own power. One's got a broke laig where his horse fell on him. Some of the rest of us need to have wounds dressed."

Laramie and Slim and the punchers came out of cover, with guns trained on the weary outlaws, and at a shout from Anders, the men outside came streaming through the tunnel, whooping vengefully.

"No mob-stuff," warned Anders, as the men grabbed the prisoners and bound their hands, none too gently. "Get those four wounded men out of the rocks, and we'll see what we can do for them."

So presently, a curious parade came filing through the tunnel into the outer valley where twilight still lingered. And as Laramie emerged from that dark tunnel, he felt as if his dark and sinister past had fallen from him like a worn-out coat.

Glancing at the clustered prisoners, he met the sullen glare of the man Braxton.

"You seemed right fond of spillin' this mornin', when you all and me cinched," mused Laramie. "If you wanted to talk some more, you could answer some questions I'd be proud to ask."

Braxton's jaw set grimly; true to his own warped code to the last, he made no reply.

But if Braxton was averse to talking, this disposition was not shared by all the prisoners. One of the four wounded men who had been brought through the tunnel on crude stretchers rigged out of rifles and coats was in a talkative mood. Fear and the pain of his wound had broken his nerve entirely and he was overflowing with information.

"I'll tell you anything you want to know! Put in a good word for me at my trial, and I'll spill the works!" he declaimed, ignoring the sullen glares of his hardier companions.

"How did Harrison get mixed up in this deal?" demanded the sheriff.

"Mixed, hell! He planned the whole thing. He was cashier in the bank when the Laramies robbed it; the real ones, I mean. If it hadn't been for that robbery, old Brown would soon found out that Harrison was stealin' from him. But the Laramies killed Brown and give Harrison a chance to cover his tracks. They got blamed for the dough he'd stole, as well as the money they'd actually taken.

"That give Harrison an idee how to be king of San Leon. The Laramies had acted as scapegoats for him once, and he aimed to use 'em again. But he had to wait till he could get to be president of the bank, and it taken time to round up a gang he could trust."

"So he'd ruin the ranchers, give mortgages and finally get their outfits, and then send his coyotes outa the country and be king of San Leon," broke in Laramie. "We know that part of it. Where'd Rawlins come in?"

"Harrison knowed him years ago, on the Rio Grande. When Harrison aimed to raise his gang, he went to Mexico and found Rawlins. Harrison knowed the real Laramies had a secret hideout, so Rawlins made friends with Luke Laramie, and—"

"We know all about that," interrupted Anders with a quick glance at Buck.

"Yeah? Well, everything was *bueno* till word come from Mexico that Buck Laramie was ridin' up from there. We had spies down there, watchin' for a move like that. Harrison got skittish. He thought Laramie was comin' to take toll for his brother, and was scared that Laramie knew all about *him*. So he sent Rawlins to waylay Laramie. Rawlins missed, but later went on to San Leon to try again. He shot you instead, Anders. Word was out to get you, anyway. You'd been prowlin' too close to our hideout to suit Harrison. Rawlins seen a good chance to put you out of the way and get Laramie killed by the folks of San Leon. But he didn't succeed, and he failed to git Laramie again in San Leon today. Seemed like he never had no luck after Laramie hit the country.

"Harrison seemed to kinda go locoed when first he heard Laramie was headin' this way. He made us pull that fool stunt of a fake bank hold-up to pull wool over folks's eyes more'n ever. Hell, nobody suspected him anyway. Then he risked comin' out here. But he was panicky and wanted us to git ready to make a clean sweep tonight and pull out. When Laramie got away from us this mornin', Harrison decided he'd ride to Mexico with us."

"But how come him and Rawley stayed in the cabin all durin' the fight?" demanded Laramie.

"Rawley dusted it back to the hideout as soon as he'd started them San Leon gents chasin' you. He told Harrison that they'd shore kill you before you could talk; that he'd talked to Joel Waters and others, and didn't believe you'd told anybody that Harrison was the leader of the gang. So he planned it this way: Harrison was to stay hid, with Rawley and the Mexicans for a bodyguard in case you come back while we was gone, and we was goin' to burn a bunch of ranch houses and steal all the cattle we could find, and head for the Border. We'd be bound to capture enough men to find out whether Laramie had told anybody about Harrison or not—we specially meant to grab Joel Waters. Then, if he'd found out, we'd send a fast rider after Harrison. If we found that it was known he was the headman, then Harrison was aimin' to ride to Mexico with us. But if we found out that Laramie hadn't told, Harrison was aimin' to go back to San Leon and resume his pose of a upright citizen. He had plenty of gold—you'll find most of it cached back in that cabin.

"Well, when the fightin' started, Harrison and Rawley stayed outa sight. Nothin' they could do, and they hoped we'd be able to break out of the canyon. They didn't want to be seen and recognized."

"And their derned modesty fooled us plenty," muttered Laramie.

Preparations were being made to start back to San Leon with the prisoners, when a sheepish looking delegation headed by Mayor Jim Watkins approached Laramie. Watkins hemmed and hawed with embarrassment, and finally blurted out, with typical Western bluntness: "Waters told us about that fifty thousand you aimed to give us. We want you to know we're mighty grateful to you for offerin' in, but we feel that today you've earned the right to keep it for yourself. You've wiped out any debt you may feel you owe us on account of them—er, uh, on account of your brothers."

Laramie's wounds stung him; he felt fretful and tired and not at all like a hero.

"I ain't," he responded impatiently. "I come up here aimin' to give that money back to the men it belonged to, and I still aim to do it. That dough is what I got from sellin' the outfit down in Mexico, but the money that bought that outfit was stole here in San Leon. I don't wanta hear no more about it."

"Well, look here, Laramie," said Watkins hesitantly, "we owe you somethin' now, and we're just as hot to pay our debts as you are to pay yours. You're the kind of man we want for a citizen, anyway. Harrison had a small ranch out a ways from town, which he ain't needin' no more, and he ain't got no heirs, so we can get it easy enough. We thought if you was aimin', maybe, to stay around San Leon, we'd like powerful well to make you a present of that ranch, and kinda help you get a start in the cow business."

A curious moroseness had settled over Laramie, a futile feeling of anti-climax, and a bitter yearning he did not understand. He felt old and weary, a desire to be alone, and an urge to ride away over the rim of the world and forget—he did not even realize what it was he wanted to forget.

"Thanks," he muttered. "But I'll be movin' on tomorrow."

"Where to?"

He made a helpless, uncertain gesture.

"You think it over," urged Watkins, turning away. Men were already mounting, moving down the trail. Anders touched Laramie's sleeve.

"Let's go, Buck. You need some attention on them wounds."

"Go ahead, Bob. I'll be along. I wanta kind set here and rest."

Anders glanced sharply at him and then made a hidden gesture to Slim Jones, and turned away. The cavalcade moved down the trail in the growing darkness, armed men riding toward a new era of peace and prosperity; gaunt, haggard bound men riding toward the penitentiary and the gallows. The crack of leather and soft jingle of spurs faded down the trail. Clink of steel-shod hoof on stone drifted back. Stars blinked in the blue velvet of the night. Over the peaks stole a golden glow to betray the rising of the moon.

Laramie sat motionless, his empty hands hanging limp on his knees. A vital chapter in his life had closed, leaving him without a goal. He had kept his vow, discharged the obligation which had motivated him for six long years. He had no plan or purpose to take its place. A deep emptiness and aloneness engulfed him.

Slim Jones, standing nearby, not understanding Laramie's mood, but not intruding on it, started to speak. Then both men lifted their heads at the unexpected rumble of wheels.

"A buckboard!" ejaculated Slim.

"No buckboard ever come up that trail," snorted Laramie.

"One's comin' now, and who d'you think? Old Joel, by golly! And look who's drivin'!"

Laramie's heart gave a convulsive leap and then started pounding as he saw the slim supple figure beside the old rancher. She pulled up near them and handed the lines to Slim, who sprang to help her down. Laramie would have come forward, but he discovered an unexpected stiffness in his limbs as he struggled to rise.

"Biggest fight ever fit in San Leon County!" roared Waters, "and I didn't git to fire a shot! Cuss a busted laig, anyway!"

"You done a man's part, anyway, Joel," assured Laramie; and then he forgot Joel Waters entirely, in the miracle of seeing Judy Anders standing before him, smiling gently, her hand outstretched and the rising moon melting her soft hair to golden witch-fire.

"I'm sorry for the way I spoke to you today," she said softly. "I've been bitter—about things that were none of your fault."

"D-don't apologize, please," he stuttered, inwardly cursing himself because of his confusion. The touch of her slim, firm hand sent shivers through his frame and he knew all at once what that empty, gnawing yearning was, the more poignant now, because so unattainable.

"You saved my neck. Nobody that does that needs to apologize. You was probably right, anyhow. Er—uh—Bob went down the trail with the others. You must have missed him."

"I saw him and talked to him," she said softly. "He said you were behind them. I came on, expecting to meet you."

He was momentarily startled. "You came on to meet *me*? Oh, of course. Joel would want to see how bad shot up I was." He achieved a ghastly excuse for a laugh.

"Mr. Waters wanted to see you, of course. But I—Buck, I wanted to see you too!"

She was leaning close to him, looking up at him, and he was dizzy with the fragrance and beauty of her; and in his dizziness said the most inane and idiotic thing he could possibly have said.

"To see me?" he gurgled wildly. "What—what you want to see *me* for?"

She seemed to draw away from him and her voice was a bit too precise.

"I wanted to apologize for my rudeness this morning," she said, a little distantly.

"I said don't apologize to me," he gasped. "You saved my life—and I—I—I—Judy, dang it, I love you!"

It was out—the amazing statement, blurted out involuntarily. He was frozen by his own audacity, stunned and paralyzed. But she did not seem to mind. Somehow he found she was in his arms, and numbly he heard her saying: "I love you too, Buck. I've loved you ever since I was a little girl, and we went to school together. Only I've tried to force myself not to think of you for the past six years. But I've loved the memory of you—that's why it hurt me so to think that you'd gone bad—as I thought you had. That horse I brought you—it wasn't altogether because you'd helped Bob that I brought it to you. It—it was partly because of my own feeling. Oh, Buck, to learn you're straight and honorable is like having a black shadow lifted from between us. You'll never leave me, Buck?"

"Leave you?" Laramie gasped. "Just long enough to find Watkins and tell him I'm takin' him up on a proposition he made me, and then I'm aimin' on spendin' the rest of my life makin' you happy!" The rest was lost in a perfectly natural sound.

"Kissin'!" beamed Joel Waters, sitting in his buckboard and gently manipulating his wounded leg. "Reckon they'll be a marryin' in these parts purty soon, Slim."

"Don't tell me yo're figgerin' on gittin' hitched?" inquired Slim, pretending to misunderstand.

"You go light on that sarcastic tone. I'm liable to git married any day now. It's just a matter of time till I decide what type of woman would make me the best wife."

The Vultures of Wahpeton

Chapter .1.
Guns in the Dark

The bare plank walls of the Golden Eagle Saloon seemed still to vibrate with the crashing echoes of the guns which had split the sudden darkness with spurts of red. But only a nervous shuffling of booted feet sounded in the tense silence that followed the shots. Then somewhere a match rasped on leather and a yellow flicker sprang up, etching a shaky hand and a pallid face. An instant later an oil lamp with a broken chimney illuminated the saloon, throwing tense bearded faces into bold relief. The big lamp that hung from the ceiling was a smashed ruin; kerosene dripped from it to the floor, making an oily puddle beside a grimmer, darker pool.

Two figures held the center of the room, under the broken lamp. One lay face-down, motionless arms outstretching empty hands. The other was crawling to his feet, blinking and gaping stupidly, like a man whose wits are still muddled by drink. His right arm hung limply by his side, a long-barreled pistol sagging from his fingers.

The rigid line of figures along the bar melted into movement. Men came forward, stooping to stare down at the limp shape. A confused babble of conversation rose. Hurried steps sounded outside, and the crowd divided as a man pushed his way abruptly through. Instantly he dominated the scene. His broad-shouldered, trim-hipped figure was above medium height, and his broad-brimmed white hat, neat boots and cravat contrasted with the rough garb of the others, just as his keen, dark face with its narrow black mustache contrasted with the bearded countenances about him. He held an ivory-butted gun in his right hand, muzzle tilted upward, and men gave back from him hurriedly.

"What devil's work is this?" he harshly demanded; and then his gaze fell on the man on the floor. His eyes widened.

"Grimes!" he ejaculated. "Jim Grimes, my deputy! Who did this?" There was something tigerish about him as he wheeled toward the uneasy crowd. "Who did this?" he demanded, half-crouching, his gun still lifted, but seeming to hover like a live thing ready to swoop.

Feet shuffled as men backed away, but one man spoke up: "We don't know, Middleton. Jackson there was havin' a little fun, shootin' at the ceilin', and the rest of us was at the bar, watchin' him, when Grimes come in and started to arrest him—"

"So Jackson shot him!" snarled Middleton, his gun covering the befuddled one in a baffling blur of motion. Jackson yelped in fear and threw up his hands, and the man who had first spoken interposed.

"No, Sheriff, it couldn't have been Jackson. His gun was empty when the lights went out. I know he slung six bullets into the ceilin' while he was playin' the fool, and I heard him snap the gun three times afterwards, so I know it was empty. But when Grimes went up to him, somebody shot the light out, and a gun banged in the dark, and when we got a light on again, there Grimes was on the floor, and Jackson was just gettin' up."

"I didn't shoot him," muttered Jackson. "I was just havin' a little fun. I was drunk, but I ain't now. I wouldn't have resisted arrest. When the light went out I didn't know what had happened. I heard the gun bang, and Grimes dragged me down with him as he fell. I didn't shoot him. I dunno who did."

"None of us knows," added a bearded miner. "Somebody shot in the dark—"

"More'n one," muttered another. "I heard at least three or four guns speakin'."

Silence followed, in which each man looked sidewise at his neighbor. The men had drawn back to the bar, leaving the middle of the big room clear, where the sheriff stood. Suspicion and fear galvanized the crowd, leaping like an electric spark from man to man. Each man knew that a murderer stood near him, possibly at his elbow. Men refused to look directly into the eyes of their neighbor, fearing to surprise guilty knowledge there—and die for the discovery. They stared at the sheriff who stood facing them, as if expecting to see him fall suddenly before a blast from the same unknown guns that had mowed down his deputy.

Middleton's steely eyes ranged along the silent line of men. Their eyes avoided or gave back his stare. In some he read fear; some were inscrutable; in others flickered a sinister mockery.

"The men who killed Jim Grimes are in this saloon," he said finally. "Some of you are the murderers." He was careful not to let his eyes single out anyone when he spoke; they swept the whole assemblage.

"I've been expecting this. Things have been getting a little too hot for the robbers and murderers who have been terrorizing this camp, so they've started shooting my deputies in the back. I suppose you'll try to kill me, next. Well, I want to tell you sneaking rats, whoever you are, that I'm ready for you, any time."

He fell silent, his rangy frame tense, his eyes burning with watchful alertness. None moved. The men along the bar might have been figures cut from stone.

He relaxed and shoved his gun into its scabbard; the shadow of a sneer twisted his lips.

"I know your breed. You won't shoot a man unless his back is toward you. Forty men have been murdered in the vicinity of this camp within the last year, and not one had a chance to defend himself.

"Maybe this killing is an ultimatum to me. All right; I've got an answer ready: I've got a new deputy, and you won't find him so easy as Grimes. I'm fighting fire with fire from here on. I'm riding out of the Gulch early in the morning, and when I come back, I'll have a man with me. A gunfighter from Texas!"

He paused to let this information sink in, and laughed grimly at the furtive glances that darted from man to man.

"You'll find him no lamb," he predicted vindictively. "He was too wild for the country where gun-throwing was invented. What he did down there is none of my business. What he'll do here is what counts. And all I ask is that the men who murdered Grimes here, try that same trick on this Texan.

"Another thing, on my own account. I'm meeting this man at Ogalala Spring tomorrow morning. I'll be riding out alone, at dawn. If anybody wants to try to waylay me, let him make his plans now! I'll follow the open trail, and anyone who has any business with me will find me ready."

And turning his trimly-tailored back scornfully on the throng at the bar, the sheriff of Wahpeton strode from the saloon.

Ten miles east of Wahpeton a man squatted on his heels, frying strips of deer meat over a tiny fire. The sun was just coming up. A short distance away a rangy mustang nibbled at the wiry grass that grew sparsely between broken rocks. The man had camped there that night, but his saddle and blanket were hidden back in the bushes. That fact showed him to be a man of wary nature. No one following the trail that led past Ogalala Spring could have seen him as he slept among the bushes. Now, in full daylight, he was making no attempt to conceal his presence.

The man was tall, broad-shouldered, deep-chested, lean-hipped, like one who had spent his life in the saddle. His unruly black hair matched a face burned dark by the sun, but his eyes were a burning blue. Low on either hip the black butt of a heavy Colt jutted from a worn black leather scabbard. These guns seemed as much part of the man as his eyes or his hands. He had worn them so constantly and so long that their association was as natural as the use of his limbs.

As he fried his meat and watched his coffee boiling in a battered old pot, his gaze darted continually eastward where the trail crossed a wide-open space before it vanished among the thickets of a broken hill country. Westward the trail mounted a gentle slope and quickly disappeared among trees and bushes that crowded up within a few yards of the spring. But it was always eastward that the man looked.

When a rider emerged from the thickets to the east, the man at the spring set aside the skillet with its sizzling meat strips, and picked up his rifle—a long range Sharp's .50. His eyes narrowed with satisfaction. He did not rise, but remained on one knee, the rifle resting negligently in his hands, the muzzle tilted upward, not aimed.

The rider came straight on, and the man at the spring watched him from under the brim of his hat. Only when the stranger pulled up a few yards away did the first man lift his head and give the other a full view of his face.

The horseman was a supple youth of medium height, and his hat did not conceal the fact that his hair was yellow and curly. His wide eyes were ingenious, and an infectious smile curved his lips. There was no rifle under his knee, but an ivory-butted .45 hung low at his right hip.

His expression, as he saw the other man's face, gave no hint to his reaction, except for a slight, momentary contraction of the muscles that control the eyes—a movement involuntary and all but uncontrollable. Then he grinned broadly, and hailed:

"That meat smells prime, stranger!"

"Light and help me with it," invited the other instantly. "Coffee, too, if you don't mind drinkin' out of the pot."

He laid aside the rifle as the other swung from his saddle. The blond youngster threw his reins over the horse's head, fumbled in his blanket roll, and drew out a battered tin cup. Holding this in his right hand he approached the fire with the rolling gait of a man born to the backbone of a horse.

"I ain't et my breakfast," he admitted. "Camped down the trail a piece last night, and come on up here early to meet a man. Thought you was the *hombre* till you looked up. Kinda startled me," he added frankly. He sat down opposite the taller man, who shoved the skillet and coffee pot toward him. The tall man moved both these utensils with his left hand. His right rested lightly and apparently casually on his right thigh.

The youth filled his tin cup, drank the black, unsweetened coffee with evident enjoyment, and filled the cup again. He picked out pieces of the cooling meat with his fingers—and he was careful to use only his left hand for that part of the breakfast that would leave grease on his fingers. But he used his right hand for pouring coffee and holding the cup to his lips. He did not seem to notice the position of the other's right hand.

"Name's Glanton," he confided. "Billy Glanton. Texas. Guadalupe country. Went up the trail with a herd of mossy horns, went broke buckin' faro in Hayes City, and headed west lookin' for gold. Hell of a prospector I turned out to be! Now I'm lookin' for a job, and the man I was goin' to meet here said he had one for me. If I read your marks right, you're a Texan, too?"

The last sentence was more a statement than a question.

"That's my brand," grunted the other. "Name's O'Donnell. Pecos River country, originally."

His statement, like that of Glanton's, was indefinite. Both the Pecos and the Guadalupe cover considerable areas of territory. But Glanton grinned boyishly and stuck out his hand.

"Shake!" he cried. "I'm glad to meet an *hombre* from my home state, even if our stampin' grounds down there are a right smart piece apart!"

Their hands met and locked briefly—brown, sinewy hands that had never worn gloves, and that gripped with the abrupt tension of steel springs.

The handshake seemed to relax O'Donnell. When he poured out another cup of coffee he held the cup in one hand and the pot in the other, instead of setting the cup on the ground beside him and pouring with his left hand.

"I've been in California," he volunteered. "Drifted back on this side of the mountains a month ago. Been in Wahpeton for the last few weeks, but gold huntin' ain't my style. I'm a *vaquero*. Never should have tried to be anything else. I'm headin' back for Texas."

"Why don't you try Kansas?" asked Glanton. "It's fillin' up with Texas men, bringin' cattle up the trail to stock the ranges. Within a year they'll be drivin' 'em into Wyoming and Montana."

"Maybe I might." O'Donnell lifted the coffee cup absently. He held it in his left hand, and his right lay in his lap, almost touching the big black pistol butt. But the tension was gone out of his frame. He seemed relaxed, absorbed in what Glanton was saying. The use of his left hand and the position of his right seemed mechanical, merely an unconscious habit.

"It's a great country," declared Glanton, lowering his head to conceal the momentary and uncontrollable flicker of triumph in his eyes. "Fine ranges. Towns springin' up wherever the railroad touches.

"Everybody gettin' rich on Texas beef. Talkin' about 'cattle kings'! Wish I could have knowed this beef boom was comin' when I was a kid! I'd have rounded up about fifty thousand of them maverick steers that was roamin' loose all over lower Texas, and put me a brand on 'em, and saved 'em for the market!" He laughed at his own conceit.

"They wasn't worth six-bits a head then," he added, as men in making small talk will state a fact well known to everyone. "Now twenty dollars a head ain't the top price."

He emptied his cup and set it on the ground near his right hip. His easy flow of speech flowed on—but the natural movement of his hand away from the cup turned into a blur of speed that flicked the heavy gun from its scabbard.

Two shots roared like one long stuttering detonation.

Glanton slumped sidewise, his smoking gun falling from his fingers, a widening spot of crimson suddenly dyeing his shirt, his wide eyes fixed in sardonic self-mockery on the gun in O'Donnell's right hand.

"Corcoran!" he muttered. "I thought I had you fooled—you—"

Self-mocking laughter bubbled to his lips, cynical to the last; he was laughing as he died.

The man whose real name was Corcoran rose and looked down at his victim unemotionally. There was a hole in the side of his shirt, and a seared spot on the skin of his ribs burned like fire. Even with his aim spoiled by ripping lead, Glanton's bullet had passed close.

Reloading the empty chamber of his Colt, Corcoran started toward the horse the dead man had ridden up to the spring. He had taken but one step when a sound brought him around, the heavy Colt jumping back into his hand.

He scowled at the man who stood before him: a tall man, trimly built, and clad in frontier elegance.

"Don't shoot," this man said imperturbably. "I'm John Middleton, sheriff of Wahpeton Gulch."

The warning attitude of the other did not relax.

"This was a private matter," he said briefly.

"I guessed as much. Anyway, it's none of my business. I saw two men at the spring as I rode over a rise in the trail some distance back. I was only expecting one. I can't afford to take any chances. I left my horse a short distance back and came on afoot. I was watching from the bushes and saw the whole thing. He reached for his gun first, but you already had your hand almost on your gun. Your shot was first by a flicker. He fooled me. His move came as an absolute surprize to me."

"He thought it would to me," said Corcoran. "Billy Glanton always wanted the drop on his man. He always tried to get some advantage before he pulled his gun. He knew me as soon as he saw me; knew that I knew him. But thought that I didn't know he knew I knew him. He thought he was making me think that he didn't know me. I made him think that. He could take chances because he knew I wouldn't shoot him down without warnin'—which is just what he figured on doin' to me. Finally he thought he had me off my guard, and went for his gun. I was foolin' him all along."

Middleton looked at Corcoran with much interest. He was familiar with the two opposite breeds of gunmen. One kind was like Glanton: utterly cynical, courageous enough when courage was necessary, but always preferring to gain an advantage by treachery whenever possible. Corcoran typified the opposite breed: men too direct by nature, or too proud of their skill to resort to trickery when it was possible to meet their enemies in the open and rely on sheer speed and nerve and accuracy. But that Corcoran was a strategist was proved by his tricking Glanton into drawing when the odds were not on the blond killer as he believed.

Middleton looked down at Glanton; in death the yellow curls and boyish features gave the youthful gunman an appearance of innocence. But Middleton knew that that mask had covered the heart of a merciless grey wolf.

"A bad man!" he muttered, staring at the rows of niches on the ivory stock of Glanton's Colt.

"Plenty bad," agreed Corcoran. "My folks and his had a feud between 'em down in Texas. He came back from Kansas and killed an uncle of mine—shot him down in cold blood. I was in California when it happened. Got a letter a year after the feud was over. I was headin' for Kansas, where I figured he'd gone back to, when I met a man who told me he was in this part of the country, and was ridin' towards Wahpeton. I cut his trail and camped here last night waitin' for him.

"It'd been years since we'd seen each other, but he knew me—didn't know I knew he knew me, though. That gave me the edge. You're the man he was goin' to meet here?"

"Yes. I need a gun-fighting deputy bad. I'd heard of him. Sent him word."

Middleton's gaze wandered over Corcoran's hard frame, lingering on the guns at his hips.

"You pack two irons," remarked the sheriff. "I know what you can do with your right. But what about the left? I've seen plenty of men who wore two guns, but those who could use both I can count on my fingers."

"Well?"

"Well," smiled the sheriff, "I thought maybe you'd like to show what you can do with your left."

"Why do you think it makes any difference to me whether you believe I can handle both guns or not?" retorted Corcoran without heat.

Middleton seemed to like the reply.

"A tinhorn would be anxious to make me believe he could. You don't have to prove anything to me. I've seen enough to show me that you're the man I need. Corcoran, I came out here to hire Glanton as my deputy. I'll make the same proposition to you. What you were down in Texas, or out in California, makes no difference to me. I know your breed, and I know that you'll shoot square with a man who trusts you, regardless of what you may have been in other parts, or will be again, somewhere else.

"I'm up against a situation in Wahpeton that I can't cope with alone, or with the forces I have.

"For a year the town and the camps up and down the gulch have been terrorized by a gang of outlaws who call themselves the Vultures. That describes them perfectly. No man's life or property is safe. Forty or fifty men have been murdered, hundreds robbed. It's next to impossible for a man to pack out any dust, or for a big shipment of gold to get through on the stage. So many men have been shot trying to protect shipments that the stage company has trouble hiring guards anymore.

"Nobody knows who are the leaders of the gang. There are a number of ruffians who are suspected of being members of the Vultures, but we have no proof that would stand up, even in a miners' court. Nobody dares give evidence against any of them. When a man recognizes the men who rob him he doesn't dare reveal his knowledge. I can't get anyone to identify a criminal, though I know that robbers and murderers are walking the streets, and rubbing elbows with me along the bars. It's maddening! And yet I can't blame the poor devils. Any man who dared testify against one of them would be murdered.

"People blame me some, but I can't give adequate protection to the camp with the resources allowed me. You know how a gold camp is; everybody so greedy blind they don't want to do anything but grab for the yellow dust. My deputies are brave men, but they can't be everywhere, and they're not gunfighters. If I arrest a man there are a dozen to stand up in a miners' court and swear enough lies to acquit him. Only last night they murdered one of my deputies, Jim Grimes, in cold blood.

"I sent for Billy Glanton, when I heard he was in this country, because I need a man of more than usual skill. I need a man who can handle a gun like a streak of forked lightning, and knows all the tricks of trapping and killing a man. I'm tired of arresting criminals to be turned loose! Wild Bill Hickok has the right idea—kill the badmen and save the jails for the petty offenders!"

The Texan scowled slightly at the mention of Hickok, who was not loved by the riders who came up the cattle trails, but he nodded agreement with the sentiment expressed. The fact that he, himself, would fall into Hickok's category of those to be exterminated did not prejudice his viewpoint.

"You're a better man than Glanton," said Middleton abruptly. "The proof is that Glanton lies there dead, and here you stand very much alive. I'll offer you the same terms I meant to offer him."

He named a monthly salary considerably larger than that drawn by the average Eastern city marshal. Gold was the most plentiful commodity in Wahpeton.

"And a monthly bonus," added Middleton. "When I hire talent I expect to pay for it; so do the merchants and miners who look to me for protection."

Corcoran meditated a moment.

"No use in me goin' on to Kansas now," he said finally. "None of my folks in Texas are havin' any feud that I know of. I'd like to see this Wahpeton. I'll take you up."

"Good!" Middleton extended his hand and as Corcoran took it he noticed that it was much browner than the left. No glove had covered that hand for many years.

"Let's get started right away! But first we'll have to dispose of Glanton's body."

"I'll take along his gun and horse and send 'em to Texas to his folks," said Corcoran.

"But the body?"

"Hell, the buzzards'll 'tend to it."

"No, no!" protested Middleton. "Let's cover it with bushes and rocks, at least."

Corcoran shrugged his shoulders. It was not vindictiveness which prompted his seeming callousness. His hatred of the blond youth did not extend to the lifeless body of the man. It was simply that he saw no use in going to what seemed to him an unnecessary task. He had hated Glanton with the merciless hate of his race, which is more enduring and more relentless than the hate of an Indian or a Spaniard. But toward the body that was no longer animated by the personality he had hated, he was simply indifferent. He expected some day to leave his own corpse stretched on the ground, and the thought of buzzards tearing at his dead flesh moved him no more than the sight of his dead enemy. His creed was pagan and nakedly elemental. A man's body, once life had left it, was no more than any other carcass, moldering back into the soil which once produced it.

But he helped Middleton drag the body into an opening among the bushes, and build a rude cairn above it. And he waited patiently while Middleton carved the dead youth's name on a rude cross fashioned from broken branches, and thrust upright among the stones.

Then they rode for Wahpeton, Corcoran leading the riderless roan; over the horn of the empty saddle hung the belt supporting the dead man's gun, the ivory stock of which bore eleven notches, each of which represented a man's life.

Chapter .2.
Golden Madness

The mining town of Wahpeton sprawled in a wide gulch that wandered between sheer rock walls and steep hillsides. Cabins, saloons and dancehalls backed against the cliffs on the south side of the gulch. The houses facing them were almost on the bank of Wahpeton Creek, which wandered down the gulch, keeping mostly to the center. On both sides of the creek cabins and tents straggled for a mile and a half each way from the main body of the town. Men were washing gold dust out of the creek, and out of its smaller tributaries which meandered into the canyon along tortuous ravines. Some of these ravines opened into the gulch between the houses built against the wall, and the cabins and tents which straggled up them gave the impression that the town had overflowed the main gulch and spilled into its tributaries.

Buildings were of logs, or of bare planks laboriously freighted over the mountains. Squalor and draggled or gaudy elegance rubbed elbows. An intense virility surged through the scene. What other qualities it might have lacked, it overflowed with a superabundance of vitality. Color, action, movement—growth and power! The atmosphere was alive with these elements, stinging and tingling. Here there were no delicate shadings or subtle contrasts. Life painted here in broad, raw colors, in bold, vivid strokes. Men who came here left behind them the delicate nuances, the cultured tranquilities of life. An empire was being built on muscle and guts and audacity, and men dreamed gigantically and wrought terrifically. No dream was too mad, no enterprise too tremendous to be accomplished.

Passions ran raw and turbulent. Boot heels stamped on bare plank floors, in the eddying dust of the street. Voices boomed, tempers exploded in sudden outbursts of primitive violence. Shrill voices of painted harpies mingled with the clank of gold on gambling tables, gusty mirth and vociferous altercation along the bars where raw liquor hissed in a steady stream down hairy, dust-caked throats. It was one of a thousand similar panoramas of the day, when a giant empire was bellowing in lusty infancy.

But a sinister undercurrent was apparent. Corcoran, riding by the sheriff, was aware of this, his senses and intuitions whetted to razor keenness by the life he led. The instincts of a gunfighter were developed to an abnormal alertness, else he had never lived out his first year of gunmanship. But it took no abnormally developed instinct to tell Corcoran that hidden currents ran here, darkly and strongly.

As they threaded their way among trains of pack mules, rumbling wagons and swarms of men on foot which thronged the straggling street, Corcoran was aware of many eyes following them. Talk ceased suddenly among gesticulating groups as they recognized the sheriff, then the eyes swung to Corcoran, searching and appraising. He did not seem to be aware of their scrutiny.

Middleton murmured: "They know I'm bringing back a gun-fighting deputy. Some of those fellows are Vultures, though I can't prove it. Look out for yourself."

Corcoran considered this advice too unnecessary to merit a reply. They were riding past the King of Diamonds gambling hall at the moment, and a group of men clustered in the doorway turned to stare at them. One lifted a hand in greeting to the sheriff.

"Ace Brent, the biggest gambler in the gulch," murmured Middleton as he returned the salute. Corcoran got a glimpse of a slim figure in elegant broadcloth, a keen, inscrutable countenance, and a pair of piercing black eyes.

Middleton did not enlarge upon his description of the man, but rode on in silence, a slight frown shadowing his brow, as if the meeting had suggested associations which were not entirely pleasant.

They traversed the body of the town—the clusters of stores and saloons—and passed on, halting at a cabin apart from the rest. Between it and the town the creek swung out in a wide loop that carried it some distance from the south wall of the gulch, and the cabins and tents straggled after the creek. That left this particular cabin isolated, for it was built with its back wall squarely against the sheer cliff. There was a corral on one side, a clump of trees on the other. Beyond the trees a narrow ravine opened into the gulch, dry and unoccupied.

"This is my cabin," said Middleton. "That cabin back there—" he pointed to one which they had passed, a few hundred yards back up the road, "—I use for a sheriff's office. I need only one room. You can bunk in the back room. You can keep your horse in my corral, if you want to. I always keep several there for my deputies. It pays to have a fresh supply of horseflesh always on hand."

As Corcoran dismounted he glanced back at the cabin he was to occupy. It stood close to a clump of trees, perhaps a hundred yards from the steep wall of the gulch.

There were four men at the sheriff's cabin, one of which Middleton introduced to Corcoran as Colonel Hopkins, formerly of Tennessee. He was a tall, portly man with an iron grey mustache and goatee, as well dressed as Middleton himself.

"Colonel Hopkins owns the rich Elinor A claim, in partnership with Dick Bisley," said Middleton, "in addition to being one of the most prominent merchants in the Gulch."

"A great deal of good either occupation does me, when I can't get my money out of town," retorted the Colonel. "Three times my partner and I have lost big shipments of gold on the stage. Once we sent out a load concealed in wagons loaded with supplies supposed to be intended for the miners at Teton Gulch. Once clear of Wahpeton the drivers were to swing back east through the mountains. But somehow the Vultures learned of our plan; they caught the wagons fifteen miles south of Wahpeton, looted them and murdered the guards and drivers."

"The town's honeycombed with their spies," muttered Middleton.

"Of course. One doesn't know who to trust. It was being whispered in the streets that my men had been killed and robbed before their bodies had been found. We know that the Vultures knew all about our plan, that they rode straight out from Wahpeton, committed that crime and rode straight back with the gold dust. But we could do nothing. We can't prove anything, or convict anybody."

Middleton introduced Corcoran to the three deputies, Bill McNab, Richardson, and Stark. McNab was as tall as Corcoran and more heavily built, hairy and muscular, with restless eyes that reflected a violent temper. Richardson was more slender, with cold, unblinking eyes, and Corcoran instantly classified him as the most dangerous of the three. Stark was a burly, bearded fellow, not differing in type from hundreds of miners. Corcoran found the appearances of these men incongruous with their protestations of helplessness in the face of the odds against them. They looked like hard men, well able to take care of themselves in any situation.

Middleton, as if sensing his thoughts, said: "These men are not afraid of the devil, and they can throw a gun as quick as the average man, or quicker. But it's hard for a stranger to appreciate just what we're up against here in Wahpeton. If it was a matter of an open fight, it would be different. I wouldn't need any more help. But it's blind going, working in the dark, not knowing who to trust. I don't dare to deputize a man unless I'm sure of his honesty. And who can be sure of who? We know the town is full of spies. We don't know who they are; we don't know who the leader of the Vultures is."

Hopkins' bearded chin jutted stubbornly as he said: "I still believe that gambler, Ace Brent, is mixed up with the gang. Gamblers have been murdered and robbed, but Brent's never been molested. What becomes of all the dust he wins? Many of the miners, despairing of ever getting out of the gulch with their gold, blow it all in the saloons and gambling halls. Brent's won thousands of dollars in dust and nuggets. So have several others. What becomes of it? It doesn't all go back into circulation. I believe they get it out, over the mountains. And if they do, when no one else can, that proves to my mind that they're members of the Vultures."

"Maybe they cache it, like you and the other merchants are doing," suggested Middleton. "I don't know. Brent's intelligent enough to be the chief of the Vultures. But I've never been able to get anything on him."

"You've never been able to get anything definite on anybody, except petty offenders," said Colonel Hopkins bluntly, as he took up his hat. "No offense intended, John. We know what you're up against, and we can't blame you. But it looks like, for the good of the camp, we're going to have to take direct action."

Middleton stared after the broadcloth-clad back as it receded from the cabin.

"'We,'" he murmured. "That means the vigilantes—or rather the men who have been agitating a vigilante movement. I can understand their feelings, but I consider it an unwise move. In the first place, such an organization is itself outside the law, and would be playing into the hands of the lawless element. Then, what's to prevent outlaws from joining the vigilantes, and diverting it to suit their own ends?"

"Not a damned thing!" broke in McNab heatedly. "Colonel Hopkins and his friends are hotheaded. They expect too much from us. Hell, we're just ordinary workin' men. We do the best we can, but we ain't gunslingers like Corcoran here."

Corcoran found himself mentally questioning the whole truth of this statement; Richardson had all the earmarks of a gunman, if he had ever seen one, and the Texan's experience in such matters ranged from the Pacific to the Gulf.

Middleton picked up his hat. "You boys scatter out through the camp. I'm going to take Corcoran around, when I've sworn him in and given him his badge, and introduce him to the leading men of the camp. I don't want any mistake, or any chance of mistake, about his standing. I've put you in a tight spot, Corcoran, I'll admit—boasting about the gunfighting deputy I was going to get. But I'm confident that you can take care of yourself."

The eyes that had followed their ride down the street focused on the sheriff and his companion as they made their way on foot along the straggling street with its teeming saloons and gambling halls. Gamblers and bartenders were swamped with business, and merchants were getting rich with all commodities selling at unheard-of prices. Wages for day labor matched prices for groceries, for few men could be found to toil for a prosaic, set salary when their eyes were dazzled by visions of creeks fat with yellow dust and gorges crammed with nuggets. Some of those dreams were not disappointed; millions of dollars in virgin gold were being taken out of the claims up and down the gulch. But the finders frequently found it a golden weight hung to their necks to drag them down to a bloody death. Unseen, unknown, on furtive feet the human wolves stole among them, unerringly marking their prey and striking in the dark.

From saloon to saloon, dance hall to dance hall, where weary girls in tawdry finery allowed themselves to be tussled and hauled about by bearlike males who emptied sacks of gold dust down the low necks of their dresses, Middleton piloted Corcoran, talking rapidly and incessantly, pointing out men in the crowd and giving their names and status in the community, and introducing the Texan to the more important citizens of the camp.

All eyes followed Corcoran curiously. The day was still in the future when the northern ranges would be flooded by Texas cattle, driven by wiry Texas riders; but Texans were not unknown, even then, in the mining camps of the Northwest. In the first days of the gold rushes they had drifted in from the camps of California, to which, at a still earlier date, the Southwest had sent some of her staunchest and some of her most turbulent sons. And of late others had drifted in from the Kansas cattle towns along whose streets the lean riders were swaggering and fighting out feuds brought up from the far south country. Many in Wahpeton were familiar with the characteristics of the Texas breed, and all had heard tales of the fighting men bred among the live oaks and mesquites of that hot, turbulent country where racial traits met and clashed, and the traditions of the Old South mingled with those of the untamed West.

Here, then, was a lean grey wolf from that southern pack; some of the men looked their scowling animosity; but most merely looked, in the role of spectators, eager to witness the drama all felt imminent.

"You're, primarily, to fight the Vultures, of course," Middleton told Corcoran as they walked together down the street. "But that doesn't mean you're to overlook petty offenders. A lot of small-time crooks and bullies are so emboldened by the success of the big robbers that they think they can get away with things, too. If you see a man shooting up a saloon, take his gun away and throw him into jail to sober up. That's the jail, up yonder at the other end of town. Don't let men fight on the street or in saloons. Innocent bystanders get hurt."

"All right." Corcoran saw no harm in shooting up saloons or fighting in public places. In Texas few innocent bystanders were ever hurt, for there men sent their bullets straight to the mark intended. But he was ready to follow instructions.

"So much for the smaller fry. You know what to do with the really bad men. We're not bringing any more murderers into court to be acquitted through their friends' lies!"

Chapter .3.
Gunman's Trap

Night had fallen over the roaring madness that was Wahpeton Gulch. Light streamed from the open doors of saloons and honkytonks, and the gusts of noise that rushed out into the street smote the passersby like the impact of a physical blow.

Corcoran traversed the street with the smooth, easy stride of perfectly poised muscles. He seemed to be looking straight ahead, but his eyes missed nothing on either side of him. As he passed each building in turn he analyzed the sounds that issued from the open door, and knew just how much was rough merriment and horseplay, recognized the elements of anger and menace when they edged some of the voices, and accurately appraised the extent and intensity of those emotions. A real gunfighter was not merely a man whose eye was truer, whose muscles were quicker than other men; he was a practical psychologist, a student of human nature, whose life depended on the correctness of his conclusions.

It was the Golden Garter dance hall that gave him his first job as a defender of law and order.

As he passed a startling clamor burst forth inside—strident feminine shrieks piercing a din of coarse masculine hilarity. Instantly he was through the door and elbowing a way through the crowd which was clustered about the center of the room. Men cursed and turned bellicosely as they felt his elbows in their ribs, twisted their heads to threaten him, and then gave back suddenly as they recognized the new deputy.

Corcoran broke through into the open space the crowd ringed, and saw two women fighting like furies. One, a tall, fine blond girl, had bent a shrieking, biting, clawing Mexican girl back over a billiard table, and the crowd was yelling joyful encouragement to one or the other: "Give it to her, Glory!" "Slug her, gal!" "Hell, Conchita, bite her!"

The brown girl heeded this last bit of advice and followed it so energetically that Glory cried out sharply and jerked away her wrist, which dripped blood. In the grip of the hysterical frenzy which seizes women in such moments, she caught up a billiard ball and lifted it to crash it down on the head of her screaming captive.

Corcoran caught that uplifted wrist, and deftly flicked the ivory sphere from her fingers. Instantly she whirled on him like a tigress, her yellow hair falling in disorder over her shoulders, bared by the violence of the struggle, her eyes blazing. She lifted her hands toward his face, her fingers working spasmodically, at which some drunk bawled, with a shout of laughter: "Scratch his eyes out, Glory!"

Corcoran made no move to defend his features; he did not seem to see the white fingers twitching so near his face. He was staring into her furious face, and the candid admiration of his gaze seemed to confuse her, even in her anger. She dropped her hands but fell back on woman's traditional weapon—her tongue.

"You're Middleton's new deputy! I might have expected you to butt in! Where are McNab and the rest? Drunk in some gutter? Is this the way you catch murderers? You laws are all alike—better at bullying girls than you are at catching outlaws!"

Corcoran stepped past her and picked up the hysterical Mexican girl, seeing that she was more frightened than hurt; she scurried toward the back rooms, sobbing in rage and humiliation, and clutching about her the shreds of garments her enemy's tigerish attack had left her.

Corcoran looked again at Glory, who stood clenching and unclenching her white fists, while her magnificent breast heaved stormily. She was still fermenting with anger, and furious at his intervention. No one in the crowd about them spoke; no one laughed, but all seemed to hold their breaths as she launched into another tirade. They knew Corcoran was a dangerous man, but they did not know the code by which he had been reared; did not know that

Glory, or any other woman, was safe from violence at his hands, whatever her offense.

"Why don't you call McNab?" she sneered. "Judging from the way Middleton's deputies have been working, it will probably take three or four of you to drag one helpless girl to jail!"

"Who said anything about takin' you to jail?" Corcoran's gaze dwelt in fascination on her ruddy cheeks, the crimson of her full lips in startling contrast against the whiteness of her teeth. She shook her yellow hair back impatiently, as a spirited young animal might shake back its flowing mane.

"You're not arresting me?" She seemed startled, thrown into confusion by this unexpected statement.

"No. I just kept you from killin' that girl. If you'd brained her with that billiard ball I'd have had to arrest you."

"She lied about me!" Her wide eyes flashed, and her breast heaved again.

"That wasn't no excuse for makin' a public show of yourself," he answered without heat. "If ladies have got to fight, they ought to do it in private."

And so saying he turned away. A gusty exhalation of breath seemed to escape the crowd, and the tension vanished, as they turned to the bar. The incident was forgotten, merely a trifling episode in an existence crowded with violent incidents. Jovial masculine voices mingled with the shriller laughter of women, as glasses began to clink along the bar.

Glory hesitated, drawing her torn dress together over her bosom, then darted after Corcoran, who was moving toward the door. When she touched his arm he whipped about as quick as a cat, a hand flashing to a gun. She glimpsed a momentary gleam in his eyes as menacing and predatory as the threat that leaps in a panther's eyes. Then it was gone as he saw whose hand had touched him.

"She lied about me," Glory said, as if defending herself from a charge of misconduct. "She's a dirty little cat."

Corcoran looked her over, from head to foot, as if he had not heard her; his blue eyes burned her like a physical fire.

She stammered in confusion. Direct and unveiled admiration was commonplace, but there was an elemental candor about the Texan such as she had never before encountered.

He broke in on her stammerings in a way that showed he had paid no attention to what she was saying.

"Let me buy you a drink. There's a table over there where we can sit down."

"No. I must go and put on another dress. I just wanted to say that I'm glad you kept me from killing Conchita. She's a slut, but I don't want her blood on my hands."

"All right."

She found it hard to make conversation with him, and could not have said why she wished to make conversation.

"McNab arrested me once," she said, irrelevantly, her eyes dilating as if at the memory of an injustice. "I slapped him for something he said. He was going to put me in jail for resisting an officer of the law! Middleton made him turn me loose."

"McNab must be a fool," said Corcoran slowly.

"He's mean; he's got a nasty temper, and he—what's that?"

Down the street sounded a fusillade of shots, a blurry voice yelling gleefully.

"Some fool shooting up a saloon," she murmured, and darted a strange glance at her companion, as if a drunk shooting into the air was an unusual occurrence in that wild mining camp. He did not miss the implication.

"Middleton said that's against the law," he grunted, turning away.

"Wait!" she cried sharply, catching at him. But he was already moving through the door, and Glory stopped short as a hand fell lightly on her shoulder from behind. Turning her head she paled to see the keenly-chiseled face of Ace Brent. His hand lay gently on her shoulder, but there was a command and a blood-chilling threat in its touch. She shivered and stood still as a statue, as Corcoran, unaware of the drama being played behind him, disappeared into the street.

The racket was coming from the Blackfoot Chief Saloon, a few doors down, and on the same side of the street as the Golden Garter.

With a few long strides Corcoran reached the door. But he did not rush in. He halted and swept his cool gaze deliberately over the interior. In the center of the saloon a roughly dressed man was reeling about, whooping and discharging a pistol into the ceiling, perilously close to the big oil lamp which hung there. The bar was lined with men, all bearded and uncouthly garbed, so it was impossible to tell which were ruffians and which were honest miners. All the men in the room were at the bar, with the exception of the drunken man.

Corcoran paid little heed to him as he came through the door, though he moved straight toward him, and to the tense watchers it seemed the Texan was looking at no one else. In reality, from the corner of his eye he was watching the men at the bar; and as he moved deliberately from the door, across the room, he distinguished the pose of honest curiosity from the tension of intended murder. He saw the three hands that gripped gun butts.

And as he, apparently ignorant of what was going on at the bar, stepped toward the man reeling in the center of the room, a gun jumped from its scabbard and pointed toward the lamp. And even as it moved, Corcoran moved quicker. His turn was a blur of motion too quick for the eye to follow and even as he turned his gun was burning red.

The man who had drawn died on his feet with his gun still pointed toward the ceiling, unfired. Another stood gaping, stunned, a pistol dangling in his fingers, for that fleeting tick of time; then as he woke and whipped the gun up, hot lead ripped through his brain. A third gun spoke once as the owner fired wildly, and then he went to his knees under the blast of ripping lead, slumped over on the floor and lay twitching.

It was over in a flash, action so blurred with speed that not one of the watchers could ever tell just exactly what had happened. One instant Corcoran had been moving toward the man in the center of the room, the next both guns were blazing and three men were falling from the bar, crashing dead on the floor.

For an instant the scene held, Corcoran half-crouching, guns held at his hips, facing the men who stood stunned along the bar.

Wisps of blue smoke drifted from the muzzles of his guns, forming a misty veil through which his grim face looked, implacable and passionless as that of an image carved from granite. But his eyes blazed.

Shakily, moving like puppets on a string, the men at the bar lifted their hands clear of their waistlines. Death hung on the crook of a finger for a shuddering tick of time. Then with a choking rush the man who had played drunk made a stumbling rush toward the door. With a catlike wheel and stroke Corcoran crashed a gun barrel over his head and stretched him stunned and bleeding on the floor.

The Texan was facing the men at the bar again before any of them could have moved. He had not looked at the men on the floor since they had fallen.

"Well, *amigos?*" His voice was soft, the Southern accent more apparent than it commonly was, but it was thick with killing lust. "Why don't you-all keep the *baile* goin'? Ain't these *hombres* got no friends?"

Apparently they had not. No one made a move, pale faces and empty hands only confronted him.

Realizing that the crisis had passed, that there was no more killing to be done just then, Corcoran straightened, shoving his guns back in his scabbards.

"Purty crude," he criticized. "I don't see how anybody could fall for a trick that stale. Man plays drunk and starts shootin' at the roof. Officer comes in to arrest him. When the officer's back's turned, somebody shoots out the light, and the drunk falls on the floor to get out of the line of fire. Three or four men planted along the bar start blazin' away in the dark at the place where they know the law's standin', and out of eighteen or twenty-four shots, some's bound to connect."

With a harsh laugh he stooped, grabbed the "drunk" by the collar and hauled him upright. The man staggered and stared wildly about him, blood dripping from the gash in his scalp.

"You got to come along to jail," said Corcoran unemotionally. "Sheriff says it's against the law to shoot up saloons. I ought to shoot you, but I ain't in the habit of pluggin' men with empty guns. Reckon you'll be more value to the sheriff alive than dead, anyway."

And propelling his dizzy charge, he strode out into the street. A crowd had gathered about the door, and they gave back suddenly. He saw a supple, feminine figure dart into the circle of light, which illumined the white face and golden hair of the girl Glory.

"Oh!" she exclaimed sharply. "Oh!" Her exclamation was almost drowned in a sudden clamor of voices as the men in the street realized what had happened in the Blackfoot Chief.

Corcoran felt her pluck at his sleeve as he passed her, heard her tense whisper.

"I was afraid—I tried to warn you—I'm glad they didn't—"

A shadow of a smile touched his hard lips as he glanced down at her. Then he was gone, striding down the street toward the jail, half-pushing, half-dragging his bewildered prisoner.

Chapter .4.
The Madness That Blinds Men

Corcoran locked the door on the man who seemed utterly unable to realize just what had happened, and turned away, heading for the sheriff's office at the other end of town. He kicked on the door of the jailer's shack, a few yards from the jail, and roused that individual out of a slumber he believed was alcoholic, and informed him he had a prisoner in his care. The jailer seemed as surprised as the victim was.

No one had followed Corcoran to the jail, and the street was almost deserted, as the people jammed morbidly into the Blackfoot Chief to stare at the bodies and listen to conflicting stories as to just what had happened.

Colonel Hopkins came running up, breathlessly, to grab Corcoran's hand and pump it vigorously.

"By gad, sir, you have the real spirit! Guts! Speed! They tell me the loafers at the bar didn't even have time to dive for cover before it was over! I'll admit I'd ceased to expect much of John's deputies, but you've shown your metal! These fellows were undoubtedly Vultures. That Tom Deal, you've got in jail, I've suspected him for some time. We'll question him—make him tell us who the rest are, and who their leader is. Come in and have a drink, sir!"

"Thanks, but not just now. I'm goin' to find Middleton and report this business. His office ought to be closer to the jail. I don't think much of his jailer. When I get through reportin' I'm goin' back and guard that fellow myself."

Hopkins emitted more laudations, and then clapped the Texan on the back and darted away to take part in whatever informal inquest was being made, and Corcoran strode on through the emptying street. The fact that so much uproar was being made over the killing of three would-be murderers showed him how rare was a successful resistance to the Vultures. He shrugged his shoulders as he remembered feuds and range wars in his native Southwest: men falling like flies under the unerring drive of bullets on the open range and in the streets of Texas towns. But there all men were frontiersmen, sons and grandsons of frontiersmen; here, in the mining camps, the frontier element was only one of several elements, many drawn from sections where men had forgotten how to defend themselves through generations of law and order.

He saw a light spring up in the sheriff's cabin just before he reached it, and, with his mind on possible gunmen lurking in ambush—for they must have known he would go directly to the cabin from the jail—he swung about and approached the building by a route that would not take him across the bar of light pouring from the window. So it was that the man who came running noisily down the road passed him without seeing the Texan as he kept in the shadows of the cliff. The man was McNab; Corcoran knew him by his powerful build, his slouching carriage. And as he burst through the door, his face was illuminated and Corcoran was amazed to see it contorted in a grimace of passion.

Voices rose inside the cabin, McNab's bull-like roar, thick with fury, and the calmer tones of Middleton. Corcoran hurried forward, and as he approached he heard McNab roar: "Damn you, Middleton, you've got a lot of explainin' to do! Why didn't you warn the boys he was a killer?"

At that moment Corcoran stepped into the cabin and demanded: "What's the trouble, McNab?"

The big deputy whirled with a feline snarl of rage, his eyes glaring with murderous madness as they recognized Corcoran.

"You damned—" A string of filthy expletives gushed from his thick lips as he ripped out his gun. Its muzzle had scarcely cleared leather when a Colt banged in Corcoran's right hand. McNab's gun clattered to the floor and he staggered back, grasping his right arm with his left hand, and cursing like a madman.

"What's the matter with you, you fool?" demanded Corcoran harshly. "Shut up! I did you a favor by not killin' you. If you wasn't a deputy I'd have drilled you through the head. But I will anyway, if you don't shut your dirty trap."

"You killed Breckman, Red Bill and Curly!" raved McNab; he looked like a wounded grizzly as he swayed there, blood trickling down his wrist and dripping off his fingers.

"Was that their names? Well, what about it?"

"Bill's drunk, Corcoran," interposed Middleton. "He goes crazy when he's full of liquor."

McNab's roar of fury shook the cabin. His eyes turned red and he swayed on his feet as if about to plunge at Middleton's throat.

"Drunk?" he bellowed. "You lie, Middleton! Damn you, what's your game? You sent your own men to death! Without warnin'!"

"His own men?" Corcoran's eyes were suddenly glittering slits. He stepped back and made a half-turn so that he was facing both men; his hands became claws hovering over his gun-butts.

"Yes, his men!" snarled McNab. "You fool, *he's* the chief of the Vultures!"

An electric silence gripped the cabin. Middleton stood rigid, his empty hands hanging limp, knowing that his life hung on a thread no more substantial than a filament of morning dew. If he moved, if, when he spoke, his tone jarred on Corcoran's suspicious ears, guns would be roaring before a man could snap his fingers.

"Is that so?" Corcoran shot at him.

"Yes," Middleton said calmly, with no inflection in his voice that could be taken as a threat. "I'm chief of the Vultures."

Corcoran glared at him puzzled. "What's your game?" he demanded, his tone thick with the deadly instinct of his breed.

"That's what I want to know!" bawled McNab, in a frenzy from rage and the pain of his wound. "We killed Grimes for you, because he was catchin' on to things. And we set the same trap for this devil. He knew! He must have known! You warned him—told him all about it!"

"He told me nothin'," grated Corcoran. "He didn't have to. Nobody but a fool would have been caught in a trap like that. Middleton, before I blow you to hell, I want to know one thing: what good was it goin' to do you to bring me into Wahpeton, and have me killed the first night I was here?"

"I didn't bring you here for that," answered Middleton.

"Then what'd you bring him here for?" yelled McNab. "You told us—"

"I told you I was bringing a new deputy here, that was a gun-slinging fool," broke in Middleton. "That was the truth. That should have been warning enough."

"But we thought that was just talk, to fool the people," protested McNab bewilderedly. He sensed that he was beginning to be wound in a web he could not break.

"Did I tell you it was just talk?"

"No, but we thought—"

"I gave you no reason to think anything. The night when Grimes was killed I told everyone in the Golden Eagle that I was bringing in a Texas gunfighter as my deputy. I spoke the truth."

"But you wanted him killed, and—"

"I didn't. I didn't say a word about having him killed."

"But—"

"Did I?" Middleton pursued relentlessly. "Did I give you a definite order to kill Corcoran, to molest him in any way?"

Corcoran's eyes were molten steel, burning into McNab's soul. The befuddled giant scowled and floundered, vaguely realizing that he was being put in the wrong, but not understanding how, or why.

"No, you didn't tell us to kill him in so many words; but you didn't tell us to let him alone."

"Do I have to tell you to let people alone to keep you from killing them? There are about three thousand people in this camp I've never given any definite orders about. Are you going to go out and kill them, and say you thought I meant you to do it, because I didn't tell you not to?"

"Well, I—" McNab began apologetically, then burst out in righteous though bewildered wrath: "Damn it, it was the understandin' that we'd get rid of deputies like that, who wasn't on the inside. We thought you were bringin' in an honest deputy to fool the folks, just like you hired Jim Grimes to fool 'em. We thought you was just makin' a talk to the fools in the Golden Eagle. We thought you'd want him out of the way as quick as possible—"

"You drew your own conclusions and acted without my orders," snapped Middleton. "That's all that it amounts to. Naturally Corcoran defended himself. If I'd had any idea that you fools would try to murder him, I'd have passed the word to let him alone. I thought you understood my motives. I brought Corcoran in here to fool the people; yes. But he's not a man like Jim Grimes. Corcoran is with us. He'll clean out the thieves that are working outside our gang, and we'll accomplish two things with one stroke: get rid of competition and make the miners think we're on the level."

McNab stood glaring at Middleton; three times he opened his mouth, and each time he shut it without speaking. He knew that an injustice had been done him, that a responsibility that was not rightfully his had been dumped on his brawny shoulders. But the subtle play of Middleton's wits was beyond him; he did not know how to defend himself or make a countercharge.

"All right," he snarled. "We'll forget it. But the boys ain't goin' to forget how Corcoran shot down their pards. I'll talk to 'em, though. Tom Deal's got to be out of that jail before daylight. Hopkins is aimin' to question him about the gang. I'll stage a fake jailbreak for him. But first I've got to get this arm dressed." And he slouched out of the cabin and away through the darkness, a baffled giant, burning with murderous rage, but too tangled in a net of subtlety to know where or how or who to smite.

Back in the cabin Middleton faced Corcoran who still stood with his thumbs hooked in his belt, his fingers near his gun butts. A whimsical smile played on Middleton's thin lips, and Corcoran smiled back, but it was the mirthless grin of a crouching panther.

"You can't tangle me up with words like you did that big ox," Corcoran said. "You let me walk into that trap. You knew your men were ribbin' it up. You let 'em go ahead, when a word from you would have stopped it. You knew they'd think you wanted me killed, like Grimes, if you didn't say nothin'. You let 'em think that, but you played safe by not givin' any definite orders, so if anything went wrong, you could step out from under and shift the blame onto McNab."

Middleton smiled appreciatively, and nodded coolly.

"That's right. All of it. You're no fool, Corcoran."

Corcoran ripped out an oath, and this glimpse of the passionate nature that lurked under his inscrutable exterior was like a momentary glimpse of an enraged cougar, eyes blazing, spitting and snarling.

"Why?" he exclaimed. "Why did you plot all this for me? If you had a grudge against Glanton, I can understand why you'd rib up a trap for him, though you wouldn't have had no more luck with him than you have with me. But you ain't got no feud against me. I never saw you before this mornin'!"

"I have no feud with you; I had none with Glanton. But if Fate hadn't thrown you into my path, it would have been Glanton who would have been ambushed in the Blackfoot Chief. Don't you see, Corcoran? It was a test. I had to be sure you were the man I wanted."

Corcoran scowled, puzzled himself now.

"What do you mean?"

"Sit down!" Middleton himself sat down on a nearby chair, unbuckled his gun-belt and threw it, with the heavy, holstered gun, onto a table, out of easy reach. Corcoran seated himself, but his vigilance did not relax, and his gaze rested on Middleton's left armpit, where a second gun might be hidden.

"In the first place," said Middleton, his voice flowing tranquilly, but pitched too low to be heard outside the cabin, "I'm chief of the Vultures, as that fool said. I organized them, even before I was made sheriff. Killing a robber and murderer, who was working outside my gang, made the people of Wahpeton think I'd make a good sheriff. When they gave me the office, I saw what an advantage it would be to me and my gang.

"Our organization is airtight. There are about fifty men in the gang. They are scattered throughout these mountains. Some pose as miners; some are gamblers—Ace Brent, for instance. He's my right-hand man. Some work in saloons, some clerk in stores. One of the regular drivers of the stage-line company is a Vulture, and so is a clerk of the company, and one of the men who works in the company's stables, tending the horses.

"With spies scattered all over the camp, I know who's trying to take out gold, and when. It's a cinch. We can't lose."

"I don't see how the camp stands for it," grunted Corcoran.

"Men are too crazy after gold to think about anything else. As long as a man isn't molested himself, he doesn't care much what happens to his neighbors. We are organized; they are not. We know who to trust; they don't. It can't last forever. Sooner or later the more intelligent citizens will organize themselves into a vigilante committee and sweep the gulch clean. But when that happens, I intend to be far away—with one man I can trust."

Corcoran nodded, comprehension beginning to gleam in his eyes.

"Already some men are talking vigilante. Colonel Hopkins, for instance. I encourage him as subtly as I can."

"Why, in the name of Satan?"

"To avert suspicion; and for another reason. The vigilantes will serve my purpose at the end."

"And your purpose is to skip out and leave the gang holdin' the sack!"

"Exactly! Look here!"

Taking the candle from the table, he led the way through a back room, where heavy shutters covered the one window. Shutting the door, he turned to the back wall and drew aside some skins which were hung over it. Setting the candle on a roughly hewed table, he fumbled at the logs, and a section swung outward, revealing a heavy plank door set in the solid rock against which the back wall of the cabin was built. It was braced with iron and showed a ponderous lock. Middleton produced a key, and turned it in the lock, and pushed the door inward. He lifted the candle and revealed a small cave, lined and heaped with canvas and buckskin sacks. One of these sacks had burst open, and a golden stream caught the glints of the candle.

"Gold! Sacks and sacks of it!"

Corcoran caught his breath, and his eyes glittered like a wolf's in the candlelight. No man could visualize the contents of those bags unmoved. And the gold madness had long ago entered Corcoran's veins, more powerfully than he had dreamed, even though he had followed the lure to California and back over the mountains again. The sight of that glittering heap, of those bulging sacks, sent his pulses pounding in his temples. Sweat stood out on his forehead, and his hand unconsciously locked on the butt of a gun.

"There must be a million there!"

"Enough to require a good-sized mule-train to pack it out," answered Middleton. "You see why I have to have a man to help me the night I pull out. And I need a man like you. You're an outdoor man, hardened by wilderness travel. You're a frontiersman, a *vaquero*, a trail driver. These men I lead are mostly rats that grew up in border towns—gamblers, thieves, barroom gladiators, saloonbred gunmen, a few miners gone wrong. You can stand things that would kill any of them.

"The flight we'll have to make will be hard traveling. We'll have to leave the beaten trails and strike out through the mountains. They'll be sure to follow us, and we'll probably have to fight them off. Then there are Indians—Blackfeet and Crows; we may run into a war party of them. I knew I had to have a fighting man of the keenest type; not only a fighting man, but a man bred on the frontier. That's why I sent for Glanton. But you're a better man than he was."

Corcoran frowned his suspicion.

"Why didn't you tell me all this at first?"

"Because I wanted to try you out. I wanted to be sure you were the right man. I had to be sure. If you were stupid enough, and slow enough to be caught in such a trap as McNab and the rest would set for you, you weren't the man I wanted."

"You're takin' a lot for granted," snapped Corcoran. "How do you know I'll fall in with you and help you loot the camp and then double-cross your gang? What's to prevent me from blowin' your head off for the trick you played on me? Or spillin' the beans to Hopkins, or to McNab?"

"Half a million in gold!" answered Middleton. "If you do any of those things, you'll miss your chance to share that cache with me."

He shut the door, locked it, pushed the other door to and hung the skins over it. Taking the candle he led the way back into the outer room.

He seated himself at the table and poured whisky from a jug into two glasses.

"Well, what about it?"

Corcoran did not at once reply. His brain was still filled with blinding golden visions. His countenance darkened, became sinister as he meditated, staring into his whisky glass.

The men of the West lived by their own code. The line between the outlaw and the honest cattleman or *vaquero* was sometimes a hair line, too vague to always be traced with accuracy. Men's personal codes were frequently inconsistent, but rigid as iron. Corcoran would not have stolen one cow, or three cows from a squatter, but he had swept across the border to loot Mexican *rancherios* of hundreds of head. He would not hold up a man and take his money, nor would he murder a man in cold blood; but he felt no compunctions about killing a thief and taking the money that thief had stolen. The gold in that cache was bloodstained, the fruit of crimes to which he would have scorned to stoop. But his code of honesty did not prevent him from looting it from the thieves who had looted it in turn from honest men. And he did not see the blood that stained it; he was too dazzled by its tawny blaze.

A keen sense of drama was inherent in all intelligent frontiersmen; sometimes distorted, in the case of gunfighters, into sheer melodrama, acted out in bloody reality. Corcoran was not a melodramatic swaggerer, but he had his share of dramatic instincts. It whetted those instincts to think of the Vultures being looted of their loot at last; and a sort of extension of this plot was growing in his mind, a devilish purpose whose very deviltry fascinated him.

"What's my part in the game?" he asked abruptly.

Middleton grinned zestfully.

"Good! I thought you'd see it my way. No man could look at that gold and refuse a share of it! They trust me more than they do any other member of the gang. That's why I keep it here. They know—or think they know—that I couldn't slip out with it. But that's where we'll fool them.

"Your job will be just what I told McNab: you'll uphold law and order. I'll tell the boys not to pull any more holdups inside the town itself, and that'll give you a reputation. People will think you've got the gang too scared to work in close. You'll enforce laws like those against shooting up saloons, fighting on the street, and the like. And you'll catch the thieves that are still working alone. When you kill one we'll make it appear that he was a Vulture. You've put yourself solid with the people tonight, by killing those fools in the Blackfoot Chief. We'll keep up the deception.

"I don't trust Ace Brent. I believe he's secretly trying to usurp my place as chief of the gang. He's too damned smart. But I don't want you to kill him. He has too many friends in the gang. Even if they didn't suspect I put you up to it, even if it looked like a private quarrel, they'd want your scalp. I'll frame him—get somebody outside the gang to kill him, when the time comes.

"When we get ready to skip, I'll set the vigilantes and the Vultures to battling each other—how, I don't know, but I'll find a way—and we'll sneak while they're at it. Then for California—South America and the sharing of the gold!"

"The sharin' of the gold!" echoed Corcoran, his eyes lit with grim laughter.

Their hard hands met across the rough table, and the same enigmatic smile played on the lips of both men.

Chapter .5.
The Wheel Begins to Turn

Corcoran stalked through the milling crowd that swarmed in the street, and headed toward the Golden Garter Dance Hall and Saloon. A man lurching through the door with the wide swing of hilarious intoxication stumbled into him and clutched at him to keep from falling.

Corcoran righted him, smiling faintly into the bearded, rubicund countenance that peered into his.

"Steve Corcoran, by thunder!" whooped the inebriated one gleefully. "Besh damn' deputy in the Territory! 'S a honor to get picked up by Steve Corcoran! Come in and have a drink."

"You've had too many now," returned Corcoran.

"Right!" agreed the other. "I'm goin' home now, 'f I can get there. Lasht time I was a little full, I didn't make it, by a quarter of a mile! I went to sleep in a ditch across from your shack. I'd 'a come in and slept on the floor, only I was 'fraid you'd shoot me for one of them derned Vultures!"

Men about them laughed. The intoxicated man was Joe Willoughby, a prominent merchant in Wahpeton, and extremely popular for his free-hearted and open-handed ways.

"Just knock on the door next time and tell me who it is," grinned Corcoran. "You're welcome to a blanket in the sheriff's office, or a bunk in my room, any time you need it."

"Soul of gener-generoshity!" proclaimed Willoughby bois-
terously. "Goin' home now before the licker gets down in my legs.
S'long, old pard!"

He weaved away down the street, amidst the jovial joshings of
the miners, to which he retorted with bibulous good nature.

Corcoran turned again into the dance hall and brushed against
another man, at whom he glanced sharply, noting the set jaw, the
haggard countenance and the bloodshot eyes. This man, a young
miner well known to Corcoran, pushed his way through the crowd
and hurried up the street with the manner of a man who goes with
a definite purpose. Corcoran hesitated, as though to follow him,
then decided against it and entered the dance hall. Half the reason
for a gunfighter's continued existence lay in his ability to read and
analyze the expressions men wore, to correctly interpret the jut of
jaw, the glitter of eye. He knew this young miner was determined
on some course of action that might result in violence. But the man
was not a criminal, and Corcoran never interfered in private quarrels
so long as they did not threaten the public safety.

A girl was singing, in a clear, melodious voice, to the accompaniment of a jangling, banging piano. As Corcoran seated himself at
a table, with his back to the wall and a clear view of the whole hall
before him, she concluded her number amid a boisterous clamor of
applause, and her face lit as she saw him. Coming lightly across the
hall, she sat down at his table. She rested her elbows on the table,
cupped her chin in her hands, and fixed her wide clear gaze on his
brown face.

"Shot any Vultures today, Steve?"

He made no answer to her badinage as he lifted the glass of
beer brought him by a waiter.

"They must be scared of you," she continued, and something
of youthful hero-worship glowed in her eyes. "There hasn't been a
murder or holdup in the town for the past month, since you've been
here. Of course, you can't be everywhere. They still kill men and
rob them in the camps up the ravines, but they keep out of town.

"And that time you took the stage through to Yankton! It wasn't your fault that they held it up and got the gold on the other side of Yankton. You weren't in it, then. I wish I'd been there and seen the fight, when you fought off the men who tried to hold you up, halfway between here and Yankton."

"There wasn't any fight to it," he said impatiently, restless under praise he knew he did not deserve.

"I know; they were afraid of you. You shot at them and they ran."

Very true; it had been Middleton's idea for Corcoran to take the stage through to the next town east, and beat off a fake attempt at holdup. Corcoran had never relished the memory; whatever his faults, he had the pride of his profession; a fake gunfight was as repugnant to him as a business hoax to an honest business man.

"Everybody knows that the stage company tried to hire you away from Middleton, as a regular shotgun-guard. But you told them that your business was to protect life and property here in Wahpeton."

She meditated a moment and then laughed reminiscently.

"You know, when you pulled me off of Conchita that night, I thought you were just another blustering bully like McNab. I was beginning to believe that Middleton was taking pay from the Vultures, and that his deputies were crooked. I know things that some people don't." Her eyes became shadowed as if by an unpleasant memory in which, though her companion could not know it, was limned the handsome, sinister face of Ace Brent. "Or maybe people do. Maybe they guess things, but are afraid to say anything.

"But I was mistaken about you, and since you're square, then Middleton must be, too. I guess it was just too big a job for him and his other deputies. None of them could have wiped out that gang in the Blackfoot Chief that night like you did. It wasn't your fault that Tom Deal got away that night, before he could be questioned. If he hadn't though, maybe you could have made him tell who the other Vultures were."

"I met Jack McBride comin' out of here," said Corcoran abruptly. "He looked like he was about ready to start gunnin' for somebody. Did he drink much in here?"

"Not much. I know what's the matter with him. He's been gambling too much down at the King of Diamonds. Ace Brent has been winning his money for a week. McBride's nearly broke, and I believe he thinks Brent is crooked. He came in here, drank some whisky, and let fall a remark about having a showdown with Brent."

Corcoran rose abruptly. "Reckon I better drift down towards the King of Diamonds. Somethin' may bust loose there. McBride's quick with a gun, and high tempered. Brent's deadly. Their private business is none of my affair. But if they want to fight it out, they'll have to get out where innocent people won't get hit by stray slugs."

Glory Bland watched him as his tall, erect figure swung out of the door, and there was a glow in her eyes that had never been awakened there by any other man.

Corcoran had almost reached the King of Diamonds gambling hall, when the ordinary noises of the street were split by the crash of a heavy gun. Simultaneously men came headlong out of the doors, shouting, shoving, plunging in their haste.

"McBride's killed!" bawled a hairy miner.

"No, it's Brent!" yelped another. The crowd surged and milled, craning their necks to see through the windows, yet crowding back from the door in fear of stray bullets. As Corcoran made for the door he heard a man bawl in answer to an eager question: "McBride accused Brent of usin' marked cards, and offered to prove it to the crowd. Brent said he'd kill him and pulled his gun to do it. But it snapped. I heard the hammer click. Then McBride drilled him before he could try again."

Men gave way as Corcoran pushed through the crowd. Somebody yelped: "Look out, Steve! McBride's on the warpath!"

Corcoran stepped into the gambling hall, which was deserted except for the gambler who lay dead on the floor, with a bullet hole over his heart, and the killer who half-crouched with his back to the bar, and a smoking gun lifted in his hand.

McBride's lips were twisted hard in a snarl, and he looked like a wolf at bay.

"Get back, Corcoran," he warned. "I ain't got nothin' against you, but I ain't goin' to be murdered like a sheep."

"Who said anything about murderin' you?" demanded Corcoran impatiently.

"Oh, I know you wouldn't. But Brent's got friends. They'll never let me get away with killin' him. I believe he was a Vulture. I believe the Vultures will be after me for this. But if they get me, they've got to get me fightin'."

"Nobody's goin' to hurt you," said Corcoran tranquilly. "You better give me your gun and come along. I'll have to arrest you, but it won't amount to nothin', and you ought to know it. As soon as a miners' court can be got together, you'll be tried and acquitted. It was a plain case of self-defense. I reckon no honest folks will do any grievin' for Ace Brent."

"But if I give up my gun and go to jail," objected McBride, wavering, "I'm afraid the toughs will take me out and lynch me."

"I'm givin' you my word you won't be harmed while you're under arrest," answered Corcoran.

"That's enough for me," said McBride promptly, extending his pistol.

Corcoran took it and thrust it into his waistband. "It's damned foolishness, takin' an honest man's gun," he grunted. "But accordin' to Middleton that's the law. Give me your word that you won't skip, till you've been properly acquitted, and I won't lock you up."

"I'd rather go to jail," said McBride. "I wouldn't skip. But I'll be safer in jail, with you guardin' me, than I would be walkin' around loose for some of Brent's friends to shoot me in the back. After I've been cleared by due process of law, they won't dare to lynch me, and I ain't afraid of 'em when it comes to gunfightin', in the open."

"All right." Corcoran stooped and picked up the dead gambler's gun, and thrust it into his belt. The crowd surging about the door gave way as he led his prisoner out.

"There the skunk is!" bawled a rough voice. "He murdered Ace Brent!"

McBride turned pale with anger and glared into the crowd, but Corcoran urged him along, and the miner grinned as other voices rose: "A damned good thing, too!" "Brent was crooked!" "He was a Vulture!" bawled somebody, and for a space a tense silence held. That charge was too sinister to bring openly against even a dead man. Frightened by his own indiscretion the man who had shouted slunk away, hoping none had identified his voice.

"I've been gamblin' too much," growled McBride, as he strode along beside Corcoran. "Afraid to try to take my gold out, though, and didn't know what else to do with it. Brent won thousands of dollars' worth of dust from me; poker, mostly.

"This mornin' I was talkin' to Middleton, and he showed a card he said a gambler dropped in his cabin last night. He showed me it was marked, in a way I'd never have suspected. I recognized it as one of the same brand Brent always uses, though Middleton wouldn't tell me who the gambler was. But later I learned that Brent slept off a drunk in Middleton's cabin. Damned poor business for a gambler to get drunk.

"I went to the King of Diamonds awhile ago, and started playin' poker with Brent and a couple of miners. As soon as he raked in the first pot, I called him—flashed the card I got from Middleton and started to show the boys where it was marked. Then Brent pulled his gun; it snapped, and I killed him before he could cock it again. He knew I had the goods on him. He didn't even give me time to tell where I'd gotten the card."

Corcoran made no reply. He locked McBride in the jail, called the jailer from his nearby shack and told him to furnish the prisoner with food, liquor and anything else he needed, and then hurried to his own cabin. Sitting on his bunk in the room behind the sheriff's office, he ejected the cartridge on which Brent's pistol had snapped. The cap was dented, but had not detonated the powder. Looking closely he saw faint abrasions on both the bullet and brass case. They were such as might have been made by the jaws of iron pinchers and a vise.

Securing a wire cutter with pincher jaws, he began to work at the bullet. It slipped out with unusual ease, and the contents of the case spilled into his hand. He did not need to use a match to prove that it was not powder. He knew what the stuff was at first glance—iron filings, to give the proper weight to the cartridge from which the powder had been removed.

At that moment he heard someone enter the outer room, and recognized the firm, easy tread of Sheriff Middleton. Corcoran went into the office and Middleton turned, in the act of hanging his white hat on a nail.

"McNab tells me McBride killed Ace Brent!"

"You ought to know!" Corcoran grinned hardly. He tossed the bullet and empty case on the table, dumped the tiny pile of iron dust beside them.

"Brent spent the night with you. You got him drunk, and stole one of his cards to show to McBride. You knew how his cards were marked. You took a cartridge out of Brent's gun and put that one in place. One would be enough. You knew there'd be gunplay between him and McBride, when you showed McBride that marked card, and you wanted to be sure it was Brent who stopped lead."

"That's right," agreed Middleton. "I haven't seen you since early yesterday morning. I was going to tell you about the frame I'd ribbed, as soon as I saw you. I didn't know McBride would go after Brent as quickly as he did.

"Brent got too ambitious. He acted as if he were suspicious of us both, lately. Maybe, though, it was just jealousy as far as you were concerned. He liked Glory Bland, and she could never see him. It gouged him to see her falling for you.

"And he wanted my place as leader of the Vultures. If there was one man in the gang that could have kept us from skipping with the loot at last, it was Ace Brent.

"But I think I've worked it neatly. No one can accuse me of having him murdered, because McBride isn't in the gang. I have no control over him. But Brent's friends will want revenge."

"A miners' court will acquit McBride on the first ballot."

"That's true. Maybe we'd better let him get shot, trying to escape!"

"We will like hell!" rapped Corcoran. "I swore he wouldn't be harmed while he was under arrest. His part of the deal was on the level. He didn't know Brent had a blank in his gun, any more than Brent did. If Brent's friends want his scalp, let 'em go after McBride, like white men ought to, when he's in a position to defend himself."

"But after he's acquitted," argued Middleton, "they won't dare gang up on him in the street, and he'll be too sharp to give them a chance at him in the hills."

"What the hell do I care?" snarled Corcoran. "What difference does it make to me whether Brent's friends get even or not? Far as I'm concerned, he got what was comin' to him. If they ain't got the guts to give McBride an even break, I sure ain't goin' to fix it so they can murder him without riskin' their own hides. If I catch 'cm sneakin' around the jail for a shot at him, I'll fill 'em full of hot lead.

"If I'd thought the miners would be crazy enough to do any-thing to him for killin' Brent, I'd never arrested him. They won't. They'll acquit him. Until they do, I'm responsible for him, and I've given my word. And anybody that tries to lynch him while he's in my charge better be damned sure they're quicker with a gun than I am."

"There's nobody of that nature in Wahpeton," admitted Middleton with a wry smile. "All right, if you feel your personal honor is involved. But I'll have to find a way to placate Brent's friends, or they'll be accusing me of being indifferent about what happened to him."

Chapter .6.
Vultures' Court

Next morning Corcoran was awakened by a wild shouting in the street. He had slept in the jail that night, not trusting Brent's friends, but there had been no attempt at violence. He jerked on his boots, and went out into the street, followed by McBride, to learn what the shouting was about.

Men milled about in the street, even at that early hour—for the sun was not yet up—surging about a man in the garb of a miner. This man was astride a horse whose coat was dark with sweat; the man was wild eyed, bareheaded, and he held his hat in his hands, holding it down for the shouting, cursing throng to see.

"Look at 'em!" he yelled. "Nuggets as big as hen eggs! I took 'em out in an hour, with a pick, diggin' in the wet sand by the creek! And there's plenty more! It's the richest strike these hills ever seen!"

"Where?" roared a hundred voices.

"Well, I got my claim staked out, all I need," said the man, "so I don't mind tellin' you. It ain't twenty miles from here, in a little canyon everybody's overlooked and passed over—Jackrabbit Gorge! The creek's buttered with dust, and the banks are crammed with pockets of nuggets!"

An exuberant whoop greeted this information, and the crowd broke up suddenly as men raced for their shacks.

"New strike," sighed McBride enviously. "The whole town will be surgin' down Jackrabbit Gorge. Wish I could go."

"Gimme your word you'll come back and stand trial, and you can go," promptly offered Corcoran. McBride stubbornly shook his head.

"No, not till I've been cleared legally. Anyway, only a handful of men will get anything. The rest will be pullin' back into their claims in Wahpeton Gulch tomorrow. Hell, I've been in plenty of them rushes. Only a few ever get anything."

Colonel Hopkins and his partner Dick Bisley hurried past. Hopkins shouted: "We'll have to postpone your trial until this rush is over, Jack! We were going to hold it today, but in an hour there won't be enough men in Wahpeton to impanel a jury! Sorry you can't make the rush. If we can, Dick and I will stake out a claim for you!"

"Thanks, Colonel!"

"No thanks! The camp owes you something for ridding it of that scoundrel Brent. Corcoran, we'll do the same for you, if you like."

"No thanks," drawled Corcoran. "Minin's too hard work. I've got a gold mine right here in Wahpeton that don't take so much labor!"

The men burst into laughter at this conceit, and Bisley shouted back as they hurried on: "That's right! Your salary looks like an assay from the Comstock lode! But you earn it, all right!"

Joe Willoughby came rolling by, leading a seedy-looking burro on which illy-hung pick and shovel banged against skillet and kettle. Willoughby grasped a jug in one hand, and that he had already been sampling it was proved by his wide-legged gait.

"H'ray for the new diggin's!" he whooped, brandishing the jug at Corcoran and McBride. "Git along, jackass! I'll be scoopin' out nuggets bigger'n this jug before night—if the licker don't git in my legs before I git there!"

"And if it does, he'll fall into a ravine and wake up in the mornin' with a fifty pound nugget in each hand," said McBride. "He's the luckiest son of a gun in the camp; and the best natured."

"I'm goin' and get some ham-and-eggs," said Corcoran. "You want to come and eat with me, or let Pete Daley fix your breakfast here?"

"I'll eat in the jail," decided McBride. "I want to stay in jail till I'm acquitted. Then nobody can accuse me of tryin' to beat the law in any way."

"All right." With a shout to the jailer, Corcoran swung across the road and headed for the camp's most pretentious restaurant, whose proprietor was growing rich, in spite of the terrific prices he had to pay for vegetables and food of all kinds—prices he passed on to his customers.

While Corcoran was eating, Middleton entered hurriedly, and bending over him, with a hand on his shoulder, spoke softly in his ear.

"I've just got wind that that old miner, Joe Brockman, is trying to sneak his gold out on a pack mule, under the pretense of making this rush. I don't know whether it's so or not, but some of the boys up in the hills think it is, and are planning to waylay him and kill him. If he intends getting away, he'll leave the trail to Jackrabbit Gorge a few miles out of town, and swing back toward Yankton, taking the trail over Grizzly Ridge—you know where the thickets are so dense. The boys will be laying for him either on the ridge or just beyond.

"He hasn't enough dust to make it worth our while to take it. If they hold him up they'll have to kill him, and we want as few murders as possible. Vigilante sentiment is growing, in spite of the people's trust in you and me. Get on your horse and ride to Grizzly Ridge and see that the old man gets away safe. Tell the boys Middleton said to lay off. If they won't listen—but they will. They wouldn't buck you, even without my word to back you. I'll follow the old man, and try to catch up with him before he leaves the Jackrabbit Gorge road.

"I've sent McNab up to watch the jail, just as a formality. I know McBride won't try to escape, but we mustn't be accused of carelessness."

"Let McNab be mighty careful with his shootin' irons," warned Corcoran. "No 'shot while attemptin' to escape', Middleton. I don't trust McNab. If he lays a hand on McBride, I'll kill him as sure as I'm sittin' here."

"Don't worry. McNab hated Brent. Better get going. Take the short cut through the hills to Grizzly Ridge."

"Sure." Corcoran rose and hurried out in the street which was all but deserted. Far down toward the other end of the gulch rose the dust of the rearguard of the army which was surging toward the new strike. Wahpeton looked almost like a deserted town in the early morning light, foreshadowing its ultimate destiny.

Corcoran went to the corral beside the sheriff's cabin and saddled a fast horse, glancing cryptically at the powerful pack mules whose numbers were steadily increasing. He smiled grimly as he remembered Middleton telling Colonel Hopkins that pack mules were a good investment. As he led his horse out of the corral his gaze fell on a man sprawling under the trees across the road, lazily whittling. Day and night, in one way or another, the gang kept an eye on the cabin which hid the cache of their gold. Corcoran doubted if they actually suspected Middleton's intentions. But they wanted to be sure that no stranger did any snooping about.

Corcoran rode into a ravine that straggled away from the gulch, and a few minutes later he followed a narrow path to its rim, and headed through the mountains toward the spot, miles away, where a trail crossed Grizzly Ridge, a long, steep backbone, thickly timbered.

He had not left the ravine far behind him when a quick rattle of hoofs brought him around, in time to see a horse slide recklessly down a low bluff amid a shower of shale. He swore at the sight of its rider.

"Glory! What the hell?"

"Steve!" She reined up breathlessly beside him. "Go back! It's a trick! I heard Buck Gorman talking to Conchita; he's sweet on her. He's a friend of Brent's—a Vulture! She twists all his secrets out of him. Her room is next to mine; she thought I was out. I overheard them talking. Gorman said a trick had been played on you to get you out of town. He didn't say how. Said you'd go to Grizzly Ridge on a wild goose chase. While you're gone they're going to assemble a 'miners' court,' out of the riff-raff left in town. They're going to appoint a 'judge' and 'jury,' take McBride out of jail, try him for killing Ace Brent—and hang him!"

A lurid oath ripped through Steve Corcoran's lips, and for an instant the tiger flashed into view, eyes blazing, fangs bared. Then his dark face was an inscrutable mask again. He wrenched his horse around.

"Much obliged, Glory. I'll be dustin' back into town. You circle around and come in another way. I don't want folks to know you told me."

"Neither do I!" she shuddered. "I knew Ace Brent was a Vulture. He boasted of it to me, once when he was drunk. But I never dared tell anyone. He told me what he'd do to me if I did. I'm glad he's dead. I didn't know Gorman was a Vulture, but I might have guessed it. He was Brent's closest friend. If they ever find out I told you—"

"They won't," Corcoran assured her. It was natural for a girl to fear such black-hearted rogues as the Vultures, but the thought of them actually harming her never entered his mind. He came from a country where even the worst of scoundrels never dreamed of hurting a woman.

He drove his horse at a reckless gallop back the way he had come, but not all the way. Before he reached the Gulch he swung wide of the ravine he had followed out, and plunged into another, steeper gulley that would bring him into the Gulch at the end of town where the jail stood. As he rode down it he heard a deep, awesome roar he recognized—the roar of the man-pack, hunting its own kind.

A band of men surged up the dusty street, roaring, cursing. One man waved a rope. Pale faces of bartenders, store-clerks and dance hall girls peered timidly out of doorways as the unsavory mob roared past. Corcoran knew them, by sight or reputation: plug-uglies, barroom loafers, skulkers—many were Vultures, as he knew; others were riffraff, ready for any sort of deviltry that required neither courage nor intelligence—the scum that gathers in any mining camp.

Dismounting, Corcoran glided through the straggling trees that grew behind the jail, and heard McNab challenge the mob.

"What do you want?"

"We aim to try your prisoner!" shouted the leader. "We come in the due process of law. We've app'inted a jedge and paneled a jury, and we demands that you hand over the prisoner to be tried in miners' court, accordin' to established legal precedent!"

"How do I know you're representative of the camp?" parried McNab.

"'Cause we're the only body of men in camp right now!" yelled someone, and this was greeted by a roar of laughter.

"We come empowered with the proper authority—" began the leader, and broke off suddenly: "Grab him, boys!"

There was the sound of a brief scuffle, McNab swore vigorously, and the leader's voice rose triumphantly: "Let go of him, boys, but don't give him his gun. McNab, you ought to know better'n to try to oppose legal procedure, and you a upholder of law and order!"

Again a roar of sardonic laughter, and McNab growled: "All right; go ahead with the trial. But you do it over my protests. I don't believe this is a representative assembly."

"Yes, it is," averred the leader, and then his voice thickened with bloodlust. "Now, Daley, gimme that key and bring out the prisoner."

The mob surged toward the door of the jail, and at that instant Corcoran stepped around the corner of the cabin and leaped up on the low porch it boasted. There was a hissing intake of breath and men halted suddenly, digging their heels against the pressure behind them. The surging line wavered backward, leaving two figures isolated—McNab, scowling, disarmed, and a hairy giant whose huge belly was girt with a broad belt bristling with gun butts and knife hilts. He held a noose in one hand, and his bearded lips gaped as he glared at the unexpected apparition.

For a breathless instant Corcoran did not speak. He did not look at McBride's pallid countenance peering through the barred door behind him. He stood facing the mob, his head slightly bent, a somber, immobile figure, sinister with menace.

"Well," he said finally, softly, "what's holdin' up the *baile?*"

The leader blustered feebly.

"We come here to try a murderer!"

Corcoran lifted his head and the man involuntarily recoiled at the lethal glitter of his eyes.

"Who's your judge?" the Texan inquired softly.

"We appointed Jake Bissett, there," spoke up a man, pointing at the uncomfortable giant on the porch.

"So you're goin' to hold a miners' court," murmured Corcoran. "With a judge and jury picked out of the dives and honkytonks— scum and dirt of the gutter!" And suddenly uncontrollable fury flamed in his eyes. Bissett, sensing his intention, bellowed in oxlike alarm and grabbed frantically at a gun. His fingers had scarcely touched the checkered butt when smoke and flame roared from Corcoran's right hip. Bissett pitched backward off the porch as if he had been struck by a hammer; the rope tangled about his limbs as he fell, and he lay in the dust that slowly turned crimson, his hairy fingers twitching spasmodically.

Corcoran faced the mob, livid under his sun-burnt bronze. His eyes were coals of blue hell's-fire. There was a gun in each hand, and from the right-hand muzzle a wisp of blue smoke drifted lazily upward.

"I declare this court adjourned!" he roared. "The judge is done impeached, and the jury's discharged! I'll give you thirty seconds to clear the courtroom!"

He was one man against nearly a hundred, but he was a grey wolf facing a pack of yapping jackals. Each man knew that if the mob surged on him, they would drag him down at last; but each man knew what an awful toll would first be paid, and each man feared that he himself would be one of those to pay that toll.

They hesitated, stumbled back—gave way suddenly and scattered in all directions. Some backed away, some shamelessly turned their backs and fled. With a snarl Corcoran thrust his guns back in their scabbards and turned toward the door where McBride stood, grasping the bars.

"I thought I was a goner that time, Corcoran," he gasped. The Texan pulled the door open, and pushed McBride's pistol into his hand.

"There's a horse tied behind the jail," said Corcoran. "Get on it and dust out of here. I'll take the full responsibility. If you stay here they'll burn down the jail, or shoot you through the window. You can make it out of town while they're scattered. I'll explain to Middleton and Hopkins. In a month or so, if you want to, come back and stand trial, as a matter of formality. Things will be cleaned up around here by then."

McBride needed no urging. The grisly fate he had just escaped had shaken his nerve. Shaking Corcoran's hand passionately, he ran stumblingly through the trees to the horse Corcoran had left there. A few moments later he was fogging it out of the Gulch.

McNab came up, scowling and grumbling.

"You had no authority to let him go. I tried to stop the mob—"

Corcoran wheeled and faced him, making no attempt to conceal his hatred.

"You did like hell! Don't pull that stuff with me, McNab. You was in on this, and so was Middleton. You put up a bluff of talk, so afterwards you could tell Colonel Hopkins and the others that you tried to stop the lynchin' and was overpowered. I saw the scrap you put up when they grabbed you! Hell! You're a rotten actor."

"You can't talk to me like that!" roared McNab.

The old tigerish light flickered in the blue eyes. Corcoran did not exactly move, yet he seemed to sink into a half-crouch, as a cougar does for the killing spring.

"If you don't like my style, McNab," he said softly, thickly, "you're more'n welcome to open the *baile* whenever you get ready!"

For an instant they faced each other, McNab black browed and scowling, Corcoran's thin lips almost smiling, but blue fire lighting his eyes. Then with a grunt McNab turned and slouched away, his shaggy head swaying from side to side like that of a surly bull.

Chapter .7.
A Vulture's Wings Are Clipped

Middleton pulled up his horse suddenly as Corcoran reined out of the bushes. One glance showed the sheriff that Corcoran's mood was far from placid. They were amidst a grove of alders, perhaps a mile from the Gulch.

"Why, hello, Corcoran," began Middleton, concealing his surprise. "I caught up with Brockman. That was just a wild rumor. He didn't have any gold. That—"

"Oh, drop that!" snapped Corcoran. "I know why you sent me off on that wild goose chase—same reason you pulled out of town. To give Brent's friends a chance to get even with McBride. If I hadn't turned around and dusted back into Wahpeton, McBride would be kickin' his life out at the end of a rope, right now."

"You came back—?"

"Yeah! And now Jake Bissett's in hell instead of Jack McBride, and McBride's dusted out—on a horse I gave him. I told you I gave him my word he wouldn't be lynched."

"You killed Bissett?"

"Deader'n hell!"

"He was a Vulture," muttered Middleton, but he did not seem displeased. "Brent, Bissett—the more Vultures die, the easier it will be for us to get away when we go. That's one reason I had Brent killed. But you should have let them hang McBride. Of course I framed this affair; I had to do something to satisfy Brent's friends. Otherwise they might have gotten suspicious.

"If they suspicioned I had anything to do with having him killed, or thought I wasn't anxious to punish the man who killed him, they'd make trouble for me. I can't have a split in the gang now. And even I can't protect you from Brent's friends, after this."

"Have I ever asked you, or any man, for protection?" The quick jealous pride of the gunfighter vibrated in his voice.

"Breckman, Red Bill, Curly, and now Bissett. You've killed too many Vultures. I made them think the killing of the first three was a mistake, all around. Bissett wasn't very popular. But they won't forgive you for stopping them from hanging the man who killed Ace Brent. They won't attack you openly, of course. But you'll have to watch every step you make. They'll kill you if they can, and I won't be able to prevent them."

"If I'd tell 'em just how Ace Brent died, you'd be in the same boat," said Corcoran bitingly. "Of course, I won't. Our final getaway depends on you keepin' their confidence—as well as the confidence of the honest folks. This last killin' ought to put me, and therefore you, ace-high with Hopkins and his crowd."

"They're still talking vigilante. I encourage it. It's coming anyway. Murders in the outlying camps are driving men to a frenzy of fear and rage, even though such crimes have ceased in Wahpeton. Better to fall in line with the inevitable and twist it to a man's own ends, than to try to oppose it. If you can keep Brent's friends from killing you for a few more weeks, we'll be ready to jump. Look out for Buck Gorman. He's the most dangerous man in the gang. He was Brent's friend, and he has his own friends—all dangerous men. Don't kill him unless you have to."

"I'll take care of myself," answered Corcoran somberly. "I looked for Gorman in the mob, but he wasn't there. Too smart. But he's the man behind the mob. Bissett was just a stupid ox; Gorman planned it—or rather, I reckon he helped you plan it."

"I'm wondering how you found out about it," said Middleton. "You wouldn't have come back unless somebody told you. Who was it?"

"None of your business," growled Corcoran. It did not occur to him that Glory Bland would be in any danger from Middleton, even if the sheriff knew about her part in the affair, but he did not relish being questioned, and did not feel obliged to answer anybody's queries.

"That new gold strike sure came in mighty handy for you and Gorman," he said. "Did you frame that, too?"

Middleton nodded.

"Of course. That was one of my men who poses as a miner. He had a hatful of nuggets from the cache. He served his purpose and joined the men who hide up in the hills. The mob of miners will be back tomorrow, tired and mad and disgusted, and when they hear about what happened, they'll recognize the handiwork of the Vultures; at least some of them will. But they won't connect me with it in any way. Now we'll ride back to town. Things are breaking our way, in spite of your foolish interference with the mob. But let Gorman alone. You can't afford to make any more enemies in the gang."

Buck Gorman leaned on the bar in the Golden Eagle and expressed his opinion of Steve Corcoran in no uncertain terms. The crowd listened sympathetically, for, almost to a man, they were the ruffians and riffraff of the camp.

"The dog pretends to be a deputy!" roared Gorman, whose bloodshot eyes and damp tangled hair attested to the amount of liquor he had drunk. "But he kills an appointed judge, breaks up a court and drives away the jury—yes, and releases the prisoner, a man charged with murder!"

It was the day after the fake gold strike, and the disillusioned miners were drowning their chagrin in the saloons. But few honest miners were in the Golden Eagle.

"Colonel Hopkins and other prominent citizens held an investigation," said some one. "They declared that evidence showed Corcoran to have been justified—denounced the court as a mob, acquitted Corcoran of killing Bissett, and then went ahead and acquitted McBride for killing Brent, even though he wasn't there."

Gorman snarled like a cat, and reached for his whisky glass. His hand did not twitch or quiver, his movements were more catlike than ever. The whisky had inflamed his mind, illumined his brain with a white-hot certainty that was akin to insanity, but it had not affected his nerves or any part of his muscular system. He was more deadly drunk than sober.

"I was Brent's best friend!" he roared. "I was Bissett's friend."

"They say Bissett was a Vulture," whispered a voice. Gorman lifted his tawny head and glared about the room as a lion might glare.

"Who says he was a Vulture? Why don't these slanderers accuse a living man? It's always a dead man they accuse! Well, what if he was? He was my friend! Maybe that makes *me* a Vulture!"

No one laughed or spoke as his flaming gaze swept the room, but each man, as those blazing eyes rested on him in turn, felt the chill breath of Death blowing upon him.

"Bissett a Vulture!" he said, wild enough with drink and fury to commit any folly, as well as any atrocity. He did not heed the eyes fixed on him, some in fear, a few in intense interest. "Who knows who the Vultures are? Who knows who, or what anybody really is? Who really knows anything about this man Corcoran, for instance? I could tell—"

A light step on the threshold brought him about as Corcoran loomed in the door. Gorman froze, snarling, lips writhed back, a tawny-maned incarnation of hate and menace.

"I heard you was makin' a talk about me down here, Gorman," said Corcoran. His face was bleak and emotionless as that of a stone image, but his eyes burned with murderous purpose.

Gorman snarled wordlessly.

"I looked for you in the mob," said Corcoran, tonelessly, his voice as soft and without emphasis as the even strokes of a feather. It seemed almost as if his voice were a thing apart from him; his lips murmuring while all the rest of his being was tense with concentration on the man before him, and instinct with lurking menace.

"You wasn't there. You sent your coyotes, but you didn't have the guts to come yourself, and—"

The dart of Gorman's hand to his gun was like the blurring stroke of a snake's head, but no eye could follow Corcoran's hand. His gun smashed before anyone knew he had reached for it. Like an echo came the roar of Gorman's shot. But the bullet ploughed splinteringly into the floor, from a hand that was already death stricken and falling. Gorman pitched over and lay still, the swinging lamp glinting on his upturned spurs and the blue steel of the smoking gun which lay by his twitching hand.

Chapter .8.
The Coming of the Vigilantes

Colonel Hopkins looked absently at the liquor in his glass, stirred restlessly, and said abruptly: "Middleton, I might as well come to the point. My friends and I have organized a vigilante committee, just as we should have done months ago. Now, wait a minute. Don't take this as a criticism of your methods. You've done wonders in the last month, ever since you brought Steve Corcoran in here. Not a holdup in the town, not a killing—that is, not a murder, and only a few shootings among the honest citizens.

"Added to that the ridding of the camp of such scoundrels as Jake Bissett and Buck Gorman. They were both undoubtedly members of the Vultures. I wish Corcoran hadn't killed Gorman just when he did, though. The man was drunk, and about to make some reckless disclosures about the gang. At least that's what a friend of mine thinks, who was in the Golden Eagle that night. But anyway it couldn't be helped.

"No, we're not criticizing you at all. But obviously you can't stop the murders and robberies that are going on up and down the Gulch, all the time. And you can't stop the outlaws from holding up the stage regularly.

"So that's where we come in. We have sifted the camp, carefully, over a period of months, until we have fifty men we can trust absolutely. It's taken a long time, because we've had to be sure of our men. We didn't want to take in a man who might be a spy for the Vultures. But at last we know where we stand. We're not sure just who *is* a Vulture, but we know who *isn't*, in as far as our organization is concerned.

"We can work together, John. We have no intention of interfering within your jurisdiction, or trying to take the law out of your hands. We demand a free hand outside the camp; inside the limits of Wahpeton we are willing to act under your orders, or at least according to your advice. Of course we will work in absolute secrecy until we have proof enough to strike in the open."

"You must remember, Colonel," reminded Middleton, "that all along I've admitted the impossibility of my breaking up the Vultures with the limited means at my disposal. I've never opposed a vigilante committee. All I've demanded was that when it was formed, it should be composed of honest men, and be free of any element which might seek to twist its purpose into the wrong channels."

"That's true. I didn't expect any opposition from you, and I can assure you that we'll always work hand-in-hand with you and your deputies." He hesitated, as if over something unpleasant, and then said: "John, are you sure of *all* your deputies?"

Middleton's head jerked up and he shot a startled glance at the Colonel, as if the latter had surprized him by putting into words a thought that had already occurred to him.

"Why do you ask?" he parried.

"Well," Hopkins was embarrassed. "I don't know—maybe I'm prejudiced—but—well, damn it, to put it bluntly, I've sometimes wondered about Bill McNab!"

Middleton filled the glasses again before he answered.

"Colonel, I never accuse a man without iron-clad evidence. I'm not always satisfied with McNab's actions, but it may merely be the man's nature. He's a surly brute. But he has his virtues. I'll tell you frankly, the reason I haven't discharged him is that I'm not sure of him. That probably sounds ambiguous."

"Not at all. I appreciate your position. You have as much as said you suspect him of double-dealing, and are keeping him on your force so you can watch him. Your wits are not dull, John. Frankly—and this will probably surprise you—until a month ago some of the men were beginning to whisper some queer things about you—queer suspicions, that is. But your bringing Corcoran in showed us that you were on the level. You'd have never brought him in if you'd been taking pay from the Vultures!"

Middleton halted with his glass at his lips.

"Great heavens!" he ejaculated. "Did they suspect me of *that?*"

"Just a fool idea some of the men had," Hopkins assured him. "Of course I never gave it a thought. The men who thought it are ashamed now. The killing of Bissett, of Gorman, of the men in the Blackfoot Chief, show that Corcoran's on the level. And of course, he's merely taking his orders from you. All those men were Vultures, of course. It's a pity Tom Deal got away before we could question him." He rose to go.

"McNab was guarding Deal," said Middleton, and his tone implied more than his words said.

Hopkins shot him a startled glance.

"By heaven, so he was! But he was really wounded—I saw the bullet hole in his arm, where Deal shot him in making his getaway."

"That's true." Middleton rose and reached for his hat. "I'll walk along with you. I want to find Corcoran and tell him what you've just told me."

"It's been a week since he killed Gorman," mused Hopkins. "I've been expecting Gorman's Vulture friends to try to get him, any time."

"So have I!" answered Middleton, with a grimness in his tone which his companion missed.

Chapter .9.
The Vultures Swoop

Down the gulch lights blazed; the windows of cabins were yellow squares in the night, and beyond them the velvet sky reflected the lurid heart of the camp. The intermittent breeze brought faint strains of music and the other noises of hilarity. But up the gulch, where a clump of trees straggled near an unlighted cabin, the darkness of the moonless night was a mask that the faint stars did not illuminate.

Figures moved in the deep shadows of the trees, voices whispered, their furtive tones mingling with the rustling of the wind through the leaves.

"We ain't close enough. We ought to lay alongside his cabin and blast him as he goes in."

A second voice joined the first, muttering like a bodiless voice in a conclave of ghosts.

"We've gone all over that. I tell you this is the best way. Get him off guard. You're sure Middleton was playin' cards at the King of Diamonds?"

Another voice answered: "He'll be there till daylight, likely."

"He'll be awful mad," whispered the first speaker.

"Let him. He can't afford to do anything about it. *Listen!* Somebody's comin' up the road!"

They crouched down in the bushes, merging with the blacker shadows. They were so far from the cabin, and it was so dark, that the approaching figure was only a dim blur in the gloom.

"It's him!" a voice hissed fiercely, as the blur merged with the bulkier shadow that was the cabin.

In the stillness a door rasped across a sill. A yellow light sprang up, streaming through the door, blocking out a small window high up in the wall. The man inside did not cross the lighted doorway, and the window was too high to see through into the cabin.

The light went out after a few minutes.

"Come on!" The three men rose and went stealthily toward the cabin. Their bare feet made no sound, for they had discarded their boots. Coats too had been discarded, any garment that might swing loosely and rustle, or catch on projections. Cocked guns were in their hands, they could have been no more wary had they been approaching the lair of a lion. And each man's heart pounded suffocatingly, for the prey they stalked was far more dangerous than any lion.

When one spoke it was so low that his companions hardly heard him with their ears a matter of inches from his bearded lips.

"We'll take our places like we planned, Joel. You'll go to the door and call him, like we told you. He knows Middleton trusts you. He don't know you'd be helpin' Gorman's friends. He'll recognize your voice, and he won't suspect nothin'. When he comes to the door and opens it, step back into the shadows and fall flat. We'll do the rest from where we'll be layin'."

His voice shook slightly as he spoke, and the other man shuddered; his face was a pallid oval in the darkness.

"I'll do it, but I bet he kills some of us. I bet he kills me, anyway. I must have been crazy when I said I'd help you fellows."

"You can't back out now!" hissed the other. They stole forward, their guns advanced, their hearts in their mouths. Then the foremost man caught at the arms of his companions.

"Wait! Look there! He's left the door open!"

The open doorway was a blacker shadow in the shadow of the wall.

"He knows we're after him!" There was a catch of hysteria in the babbling whisper. "It's a trap!"

"Don't be a fool! How could he know? He's asleep. I hear him snorin'. We won't wake him. We'll step into the cabin and let him have it! We'll have enough light from the window to locate the bunk, and we'll rake it with lead before he can move. He'll wake up in hell. Come on, and for God's sake, don't make no noise!"

The last advice was unnecessary. Each man, as he set his bare foot down, felt as if he were setting it into the lair of a diamond-backed rattler.

As they glided, one after another, across the threshold, they made less noise than the wind blowing through the black branches. They crouched by the door, straining their eyes across the room, whence came the rhythmic snoring. Enough light sifted through the small window to show them a vague outline that was a bunk, with a shapeless mass upon it.

A man caught his breath in a short, uncontrollable gasp. Then the cabin was shaken by a thunderous volley, three guns roaring together. Lead swept the bunk in a devastating storm, thudding into flesh and bone, smacking into wood. A wild cry broke in a gagging gasp. Limbs thrashed wildly and a heavy body tumbled to the floor. From the darkness on the floor beside the bunk welled up hideous sounds, choking gurgles and a convulsive flopping and thumping. The men crouching near the door poured lead blindly at the sounds. There was fear and panic in the haste and number of their shots. They did not cease jerking their triggers until their guns were empty, and the noises on the floor had ceased.

"Out of here, quick!" gasped one.

"No! Here's the table, and a candle on it. I felt it in the dark. I've got to *know* that he's dead before I leave this cabin. I've got to see him lyin' dead if I'm goin' to sleep easy. We've got plenty of time to get away. Folks down the gulch must have heard the shots, but it'll take time for them to get here. No danger. I'm goin' to light the candle—"

There was a rasping sound, and a yellow light sprang up, etching three staring, bearded faces. Wisps of blue smoke blurred the light as the candlewick ignited from the fumbling match, but the men saw a huddled shape crumpled near the bunk, from which streams of dark crimson radiated in every direction.

"*Ahhh!*"

They whirled at the sound of running footsteps.

"Oh, God!" shrieked one of the men, falling to his knees, his hands lifted to shut out a terrible sight. The other ruffians staggered with the shock of what they saw. They stood gaping, livid, helpless, empty guns sagging in their hands.

For there in the door, glaring in dangerous amazement, with a gun in each hand, stood the man whose lifeless body they thought lay over there by the splintered bunk!

"Drop them guns!" Corcoran rasped. They clattered on the floor as the hands of their owners mechanically reached skyward. The man on the floor staggered up, his hands empty; he retched, shaken by the nausea of fear.

"Joel Miller!" said Corcoran evenly; his surprise was passed, as he realized what had happened. "Didn't know you run with Gorman's crowd. Reckon Middleton'll be some surprized, too."

"You're a devil!" gasped Miller. "You can't be killed! We killed you—heard you roll off your bunk and die on the floor, in the dark. We kept shooting after we knew you were dead. But you're alive!"

"You didn't shoot me," grunted Corcoran. "You shot a man you thought was me. I was comin' up the road when I heard the shots. You killed Joe Willoughby! He was drunk and I reckon he staggered in here and fell in my bunk, like he's done before."

The men went whiter yet under their bushy beards, with rage and chagrin and fear.

"Willoughby!" babbled Miller. "The camp will never stand for this! Let us go, Corcoran! Hopkins and his crowd will hang us! It'll mean the end of the Vultures! Your end, too, Corcoran! If they hang us, we'll talk first! They'll find out that you're one of us!"

"In that case," muttered Corcoran, his eyes narrowing, "I'd better kill the three of you. That's the sensible solution. You killed Willoughby, tryin' to get me; I kill you, in self-defense."

"Don't do it, Corcoran!" screamed Miller, frantic with terror.

"Shut up, you dog," growled one of the other men, glaring balefully at their captor. "Corcoran wouldn't shoot down unarmed men."

"No, I wouldn't," said Corcoran. "Not unless you made some kind of a break. I'm peculiar that way, which I see is a handicap in this country. But it's the way I was raised, and I can't get over it. No, I ain't goin' to beef you cold, though you've just tried to get me that way.

"But I'll be damned if I'm goin' to let you sneak off, to come back here and try it again the minute you get your nerve bucked up. I'd about as soon be hanged by the vigilantes as shot in the back by a passle of rats like you-all. Vultures, hell! You ain't even got the guts to be good buzzards.

"I'm goin' to take you down the gulch and throw you in jail. It'll be up to Middleton to decide what to do with you. He'll probably work out some scheme that'll swindle everybody except himself; but I warn you—one yap about the Vultures to anybody, and I'll forget my raisin' and send you to hell with your belts empty and your boots on."

The noise in the King of Diamonds was hushed suddenly as a man rushed in and bawled: "The Vultures have murdered Joe Willoughby! Steve Corcoran caught three of 'em, and has just locked 'em up! This time we've got some live Vultures to work on!"

A roar answered him and the gambling hall emptied itself as men rushed yelling into the street. John Middleton laid down his hand of cards, donned his white hat with a hand that was steady as a rock, and strode after them.

Already a crowd was surging and roaring around the jail. The miners were lashed into a murderous frenzy and were restrained from shattering the door and dragging forth the cowering prisoners only by the presence of Corcoran, who faced them on the jail-porch. McNab, Richardson and Stark were there, also. McNab was pale under his whiskers, and Stark seemed nervous and ill at ease, but Richardson, as always, was cold as ice.

"Hang 'em!" roared the mob. "Let us have 'em, Steve! You've done your part! This camp's put up with enough! Let us have 'em!"

Middleton climbed up on the porch, and was greeted by loud cheers, but his efforts to quiet the throng proved futile. Somebody brandished a rope with a noose in it. Resentment, long smoldering, was bursting into flame, fanned by hysterical fear and hate. The mob had no wish to harm either Corcoran or Middleton—did not intend to harm them. But they were determined to drag out the prisoners and string them up.

Colonel Hopkins forced his way through the crowd, mounted the step, and waved his hands until he obtained a certain amount of silence.

"Listen, men!" he roared. "This is the beginning of a new era for Wahpeton! This camp has been terrorized long enough. We're beginning a rule of law and order, right now! But don't spoil it at the very beginning! These men shall hang—I swear it! But let's do it legally, and with the sanction of law. Another thing: if you hang them out of hand, we'll never learn who their companions and leaders are.

"Tomorrow, I promise you, a court of inquiry will sit on their case. They'll be questioned and forced to reveal the men above and behind them. This camp is going to be cleaned up! Let's clean it up lawfully and in order!"

"Colonel's right!" bawled a bearded giant. "Ain't no use to hang the little rats till we find out who's the big 'uns!"

A roar of approbation rose as the temper of the mob changed. It began to break up, as the men scattered to hasten back to the bars and indulge in their passion to discuss the new development.

Hopkins shook Corcoran's hand heartily.

"Congratulations, sir! I've seen poor Joe's body. A terrible sight. The fiends fairly shot the poor fellow to ribbons. Middleton, I told you the vigilantes wouldn't usurp your authority in Wahpeton. I keep my word. We'll leave these murderers in your jail, guarded by your deputies. Tomorrow the vigilante court will sit in session, and I hope we'll come to the bottom of this filthy mess."

And so saying he strode off, followed by a dozen or so steely-eyed men whom Middleton knew formed the nucleus of the Colonel's organization.

When they were out of hearing, Middleton stepped to the door and spoke quickly to the prisoners: "Keep your mouths shut. You fools have gotten us all in a jam, but I'll snake you out of it, somehow." To McNab he spoke: "Watch the jail. Don't let anybody come near it. Corcoran and I have got to talk this over." Lowering his voice so the prisoners could not hear, he added: "If anybody does come, that you can't order off, and these fools start shooting off their heads, close their mouths with lead."

Corcoran followed Middleton into the shadow of the gulch-wall. Out of earshot of the nearest cabin, Middleton turned. "Just what happened?"

"Gorman's friends tried to get me. They killed Joe Willoughby by mistake. I hauled them in. That's all."

"That's not all," muttered Middleton. "There'll be hell to pay if they come to trial. Miller's yellow. He'll talk, sure. I've been afraid Gorman's friends would try to kill you—wondering how it would work out. It's worked out just about the worst way it possibly could. You should either have killed them or let them go. Yet I appreciate your attitude. You have scruples against cold-blooded murder; and if you'd turned them loose, they'd have been back potting at you the next night."

"I couldn't have turned them loose if I'd wanted to. Men had heard the shots; they came runnin', found me there holdin' a gun on those devils, and Joe Willoughby's body layin' on the floor, shot to pieces."

"I know. But we can't keep members of our own gang in jail, and we can't hand them over to the vigilantes. I've got to delay that trial, somehow. If I were ready, we'd jump tonight, and to hell with it. But I'm not ready. After all, perhaps it's as well this happened. It may give us our chance to skip. We're one jump ahead of the vigilantes and the gang, too. We know the vigilantes have formed and are ready to strike, and the rest of the gang don't. I've told no one but you what Hopkins told me early in the evening.

"Listen, Corcoran, we've got to move tomorrow night! I wanted to pull one last job, the biggest of all—the looting of Hopkins' and Bisley's private cache. I believe I could have done it, in spite of all their guards and precautions. But we'll have to let that slide. I'll persuade Hopkins to put off the trial another day. I think I know how. Tomorrow night I'll have the vigilantes and the Vultures at each others' throats! We'll load the mules and pull out while they're fighting. Once let us get a good start, and they're welcome to chase us if they want to. Hunting us in those mountains will be like trying to find a grain of sand on the beach.

"I'm going to find Hopkins now. You get back to the jail. If McNab talks to Miller or the others, be sure you listen to what's said."

Middleton found Hopkins in the Golden Eagle Saloon.

"I've come to ask a favor of you, Colonel," he began directly. "I want you, if it's possible, to put off the investigating trial until day after tomorrow. I've been talking to Joel Miller. He's cracking. If I can get him away from Barlow and Letcher, and talk to him, I believe he'll tell me everything I want to know. It'll be better to get his confession, signed and sworn to, before we bring the matter into court. Before a judge, with all eyes on him, and his friends in the crowd, he might stiffen and refuse to incriminate anyone. I don't believe the others will talk. But talking to me, alone, I believe Miller will spill the whole works. But it's going to take time to wear him down. I believe that by tomorrow night I'll have a full confession from him."

"That would make our work a great deal easier," admitted Hopkins.

"And another thing: these men ought to be represented by proper counsel. You'll prosecute them, of course; and the only other lawyer within reach is Judge Bixby, at Yankton. We're doing this thing in as close accordance to regular legal procedure as possible. Therefore we can't refuse the prisoner the right to be defended by an attorney. I've sent a man after Bixby. It will be late tomorrow evening before he can get back with the Judge, even if he has no trouble in locating him.

"Considering all these things, I feel it would be better to postpone the trial until we can get Bixby here, and until I can get Miller's confession."

"What will the camp think?"

"Most of them are men of reason. The few hotheads who might want to take matters into their own hands can't do any harm."

"All right," agreed Hopkins. "After all, they're your prisoners, since your deputy captured them, and the attempted murder of an officer of the law is one of the charges for which they'll have to stand trial. We'll set the trial for day after tomorrow. Meanwhile, work on Joel Miller. If we have his signed confession, naming the leaders of the gang, it will expedite matters a great deal at the trial."

Chapter .10.
The Blood on the Gold

Wahpeton learned of the postponement of the trial and reacted in various ways. The air was surcharged with tension. Little work was done that day. Men gathering in heated, gesticulating groups, crowded in at the bars. Voices rose in hot altercation, fists pounded on the bars. Unfamiliar faces were observed, men who were seldom seen in the gulch—miners from claims in distant canyons, or more sinister figures from the hills, whose business was less obvious.

Lines of cleavage were noticed. Here and there clumps of men gathered, keeping to themselves and talking in low tones. In certain dives the ruffian element of the camp gathered, and these saloons were shunned by honest men. But still the great mass of the people milled about, suspicious and uncertain. The status of too many men was still in doubt. Certain men were known to be above suspicion, certain others were known to be ruffians and criminals; but between these two extremes there were possibilities for all shades of distrust and suspicion.

So most men wandered aimlessly to and fro, with their weapons ready to their hands, glancing at their fellows out of the corners of their eyes.

To the surprize of all, Steve Corcoran was noticed at several bars, drinking heavily, though the liquor did not seem to effect him in any way.

The men in the jail were suffering from nerves. Somehow the word had gotten out that the vigilante organization was a reality, and that they were to be tried before a vigilante court. Joel Miller, hysterical, accused Middleton of double-crossing his men.

"Shut up, you fool!" snarled the sheriff, showing the strain under which he was laboring merely by the irascible edge on his voice. "Haven't you seen your friends drifting by the jail? I've gathered the men in from the hills. They're all here. Forty-odd men, every Vulture in the gang, is here in Wahpeton.

"Now, get this—and McNab, listen closely: we'll stage the break just before daylight, when everybody is asleep. Just before dawn is the best time, because that's about the only time in the whole twenty-four hours that the camp isn't going full blast.

"Some of the boys, with masks on, will swoop down and overpower you deputies. There'll be no shots fired until they've gotten the prisoners and started off. Then start yelling and shooting after them—in the air, of course. That'll bring everybody on the run to hear how you were overpowered by a gang of masked riders.

"Miller, you and Letcher and Barlow will put up a fight—"

"Why?"

"Why, you fool, to make it look like it's a mob that's capturing you, instead of friends rescuing you. That'll explain why none of the deputies are hurt. Men wanting to lynch you wouldn't want to hurt the officers. You'll yell and scream blue murder, and the men in the masks will drag you out, tie you and throw you across horses and ride off. Somebody is bound to see them riding away. It'll look like a capture, not a rescue."

Bearded lips gaped in admiring grins at the strategy.

"All right. Don't make a botch of it. There'll be hell to pay, but I'll convince Hopkins that it was the work of a mob, and we'll search the hills to find your bodies hanging from trees. We won't find any bodies, naturally, but maybe we'll contrive to find a mass of ashes where a log hut had been burned to the ground, and a few hats and belt buckles easy to identify."

Miller shivered at the implication and stared at Middleton with painful intensity.

"Middleton, you ain't planning to have us put out of the way? These men in masks are our friends, not vigilantes you've put up to this?"

"Don't be a fool!" flared Middleton disgustedly. "Do you think the gang would stand for anything like that, even if I was imbecile enough to try it? You'll recognize your friends when they come.

"Miller, I want your name at the foot of a confession I've drawn up, implicating somebody as the leader of the Vultures. There's no use trying to deny you and the others are members of the gang. Hopkins knows you are; instead of trying to play innocent, you'll divert suspicion to someone outside the gang. I haven't filled in the name of the leader, but Dick Lennox is as good as anybody. He's a gambler, has few friends, and never would work with us. I'll write his name in your 'confession' as chief of the Vultures, and Corcoran will kill him 'for resisting arrest,' before he has time to prove that it's a lie. Then, before anybody has time to get suspicious, we'll make our last big haul—the raid on the Hopkins and Bisley cache!—and blow! Be ready to jump, when the gang swoops in just before daylight.

"Miller, put your signature to this paper. Read it first if you want to. I'll fill in the blanks I left for the 'chief's' name later. Where's Corcoran?"

"I saw him in the Golden Eagle an hour ago," growled McNab. "He's drinkin' like a fish."

"Damnation!" Middleton's mask slipped a bit despite himself, then he regained his easy control. "Well, it doesn't matter. We won't need him tonight. Better for him not to be here when the jailbreak's made. Folks would think it was funny if he didn't kill somebody. I'll drop back later in the night."

Even a man of steel nerves feels the strain of waiting for a crisis. Corcoran was in this case no exception. Middleton's mind was so occupied in planning, scheming and conniving that he had little time for the strain to corrode his willpower. But Corcoran had nothing to occupy his attention until the moment came for the jump.

He began to drink, almost without realizing it. His veins seemed on fire, his external senses abnormally alert. Like most men of his breed he was high-strung, his nervous system poised on a hair-trigger balance, in spite of his mask of unemotional coolness. He lived on, and for, violent action. Action kept his mind from turning inward; it kept his brain clear and his hand steady; failing action, he fell back on whisky. Liquor artificially stimulated him to that pitch which his temperament required. It was not fear that made his nerves thrum so intolerably. It was the strain of waiting inertly, the realization of the stakes for which they played. Inaction maddened him. Thought of the gold cached in the cave behind John Middleton's cabin made Corcoran's lips dry, set a nerve to pounding maddeningly in his temples.

So he drank, and drank, and drank again, as the long day wore on.

The noise from the bar was a blurred medley in the back room of the Golden Garter. Glory Bland stared uneasily across the table at her companion. Corcoran's blue eyes seemed lit by dancing fires. Tiny beads of perspiration shone on his dark face. His tongue was not thick; he spoke lucidly and without exaggeration; he had not stumbled when he entered. Nevertheless he was drunk, though to what extent the girl did not guess.

"I never saw you this way before, Steve," she said reproachfully.

"I've never had a hand in a game like this before," he answered, the wild flame flickering bluely in his eyes. He reached across the table and caught her white wrist with an unconscious strength that made her wince. "Glory, I'm pullin' out of here tonight. I want you to go with me!"

"You're leaving Wahpeton? *Tonight?*"

"Yes. For good. Go with me! This joint ain't fit for you. I don't know how you got into this game, and I don't give a damn. But you're different from these other dance hall girls. I'm takin' you with me. I'll make a queen out of you! I'll cover you with diamonds!"

She laughed nervously.

"You're drunker than I thought. I know you've been getting a big salary, but—"

"Salary?" His laugh of contempt startled her. "I'll throw my salary into the street for the beggars to fight over. Once I told that fool Hopkins that I had a gold mine right here in Wahpeton. I told him no lie. I'm *rich!*"

"What do you mean?" She was slightly pale, frightened by his vehemence.

His fingers unconsciously tightened on her wrist and his eyes gleamed with the hard arrogance of possession and desire.

"You're mine, anyway," he muttered. "I'll kill any man that looks at you. But you're in love with me. I know it. Any fool could see it. I can trust you. You wouldn't betray me. I'll tell you. I wouldn't take you along without tellin' you the truth. Tonight Middleton and I are goin' over the mountains with a million dollars' worth of gold tied on pack mules!"

He did not see the growing light of incredulous horror in her eyes.

"A million in gold! It'd make a devil out of a saint! Middleton thinks he'll kill me when we get away safe, and grab the whole load. He's a fool. It'll be him that dies, when the time comes. I've planned while he planned. I didn't ever intend to split the loot with him. I wouldn't be a thief for less than a million."

"Middleton—" she choked.

"Yeah! He's chief of the Vultures, and I'm his right-hand man. If it hadn't been for me, the camp would have caught on long ago."

"But you upheld the law," she panted, as if clutching at straws. "You killed murderers—saved McBride from the mob."

"I killed men who tried to kill me. I shot as square with the camp as I could, without goin' against my own interests. That business of McBride has nothin' to do with it. I'd given him my word. That's all behind us now. Tonight, while the vigilantes and the Vultures kill each other, we'll *vamose!* And you'll go with me!"

With a cry of loathing she wrenched her hand away, and sprang up, her eyes blazing.

"Oh!" It was a cry of bitter disillusionment. "I thought you were straight—honest! I worshiped you because I thought you were honorable. So many men were dishonest and bestial—I idolized you! And you've just been pretending—playing a part! Betraying the people who trusted you!" The poignant anguish of her enlightenment choked her, then galvanized her with another possibility.

"I suppose you've been pretending with me, too!" she cried wildly. "If you haven't been straight with the camp, you couldn't have been straight with me, either! You've made a fool of me! Laughed at me and shamed me! And now you boast of it in my teeth!"

"Glory!" He was on his feet, groping for her, stunned and bewildered by her grief and rage. She sprang back from him.

"Don't touch me! Don't look at me! Oh, I hate the very sight of you!"

And turning, with an hysterical sob, she ran from the room. He stood swaying slightly, staring stupidly after her. Then fumbling with his hat, he stalked out, moving like an automaton. His thoughts were a confused maelstrom, whirling until he was giddy. All at once the liquor seethed madly in his brain, dulling his perceptions, even his recollections of what had just passed. He had drunk more than he realized.

Not long after dark had settled over Wahpeton, a low call from the darkness brought Colonel Hopkins to the door of his cabin, gun in hand.

"Who is it?" he demanded suspiciously.

"It's Middleton. Let me in, quick!"

The sheriff entered, and Hopkins, shutting the door, stared at him in surprise. Middleton showed more agitation than the Colonel had ever seen him display. His face was pale and drawn. A great actor was lost to the world when John Middleton took the dark road of outlawry.

"Colonel, I don't know what to say. I've been a blind fool. I feel that the lives of murdered men are hung about my neck for all Eternity! All through my blindness and stupidity!"

"What do you mean, John?" ejaculated Colonel Hopkins.

"Colonel, Miller talked at last. He just finished telling me the whole dirty business. I have his confession, written as he dictated."

"He named the chief of the Vultures?" exclaimed Hopkins eagerly.

"He did!" answered Middleton grimly, producing a paper and unfolding it. Joel Miller's unmistakable signature sprawled at the bottom. "Here is the name of the leader, dictated by Miller to me!"

"Good God!" whispered Hopkins. "Bill McNab!"

"Yes! My deputy! The man I trusted next to Corcoran. What a fool—what a blind fool I've been. Even when his actions seemed peculiar, even when you voiced your suspicions of him, I could not bring myself to believe it. But it's all clear now. No wonder the gang always knew my plans as soon as I knew them myself! No wonder my deputies—before Corcoran came—were never able to kill or capture any Vultures. No wonder, for instance, that Tom Deal 'escaped,' before we could question him. That bullet hole in McNab's arm, supposedly made by Deal—Miller told me McNab got that in a quarrel with one of his own gang. It came in handy to help pull the wool over my eyes.

"Colonel Hopkins, I'll turn in my resignation tomorrow. I recommend Corcoran as my successor. I shall be glad to serve as deputy under him."

"Nonsense, John!" Hopkins laid his hand sympathetically on Middleton's shoulder. "It's not your fault. You've played a man's part all the way through. Forget that talk about resigning. Wahpeton doesn't need a new sheriff; you just need some new deputies. Just now we've got some planning to do. Where is McNab?"

"At the jail, guarding the prisoners. I couldn't remove him without exciting his suspicion. Of course he doesn't dream that Miller has talked. And I learned something else. They plan a jailbreak shortly after midnight."

"We might have expected that!"

"Yes. A band of masked men will approach the jail, pretend to overpower the guards—yes, Stark and Richardson are Vultures, too—and release the prisoners. Now this is my plan. Take fifty men and conceal them in the trees near the jail. You can plant some on one side, some on the other. Corcoran and I will be with you, of course. When the bandits come, we can kill or capture them all at one swoop. We have the advantage of knowing their plans, without their knowing we know them."

"That's a good plan, John!" warmly endorsed Hopkins. "You should have been a general. I'll gather the men at once. Of course, we must use the utmost secrecy."

"Of course. If we work it right, we'll bag prisoners, deputies and rescuers with one stroke. We'll break the back of the Vultures!"

"John, don't ever talk resignation to me again!" exclaimed Hopkins, grabbing his hat and buckling on his gun belt. "A man like you ought to be in the Senate. Go get Corcoran. I'll gather my men and we'll be in our places by midnight. McNab and the others in the jail won't hear a sound."

"Good! Corcoran and I will join you before the Vultures reach the jail."

Leaving Hopkins' cabin, Middleton hurried to the bar of the King of Diamonds. As he drank, a rough-looking individual moved casually up beside him. Middleton bent his head over his whisky glass and spoke, hardly moving his lips. None could have heard him a yard away.

"I've just talked to Hopkins. The vigilantes are afraid of a jail break. They're going to take the prisoners out just before daylight and hang them out of hand. That talk about legal proceedings was just a bluff. Get all the boys, go to the jail and get the prisoners out within a half hour after midnight. Wear your masks, but let there be no shooting or yelling. I'll tell McNab our plan's been changed. Go silently. Leave your horses at least a quarter of a mile down the gulch and sneak up to the jail on foot, so you won't make so much noise. Corcoran and I will be hiding in the brush to give you a hand in case anything goes wrong."

The other man had not looked toward Middleton; he did not look now. Emptying his glass, he strolled deliberately toward the door. No casual onlooker could have known that any words had passed between them.

When Glory Bland ran from the backroom of the Golden Garter, her soul was in an emotional turmoil that almost amounted to insanity.

The shock of her brutal disillusionment vied with passionate shame of her own gullibility and an unreasoning anger. Out of this seething cauldron grew a blind desire to hurt the man who had unwittingly hurt her. Smarting vanity had its part, too, for with characteristic and illogical feminine conceit, she believed that he had practiced an elaborate deception in order to fool her into falling in love with him—or rather with the man she thought he was. If he was false with men, he must be false with women, too. That thought sent her into hysterical fury, blind to all except a desire for revenge. She was a primitive, elemental young animal, like most of her profession of that age and place; her emotions were powerful and easily stirred, her passions stormy. Love could change quickly to hate, and hate was as violent and unreasoning as love.

She reached an instant decision. She would find Hopkins and tell him everything Corcoran had told her! In that instant she desired nothing so much as the ruin of the man she had loved.

She ran down the crowded street, ignoring men who pawed at her and called after her. She hardly saw the people who stared after her. She supposed that Hopkins would be at the jail, helping guard the prisoners, and she directed her steps thither. As she ran up on the porch Bill McNab confronted her with a leer, and laid a hand on her arm, laughing when she jerked away.

"Come to see me, Glory? Or are you lookin' for Corcoran?"

She struck his hand away. His words, and the insinuating guffaws of his companions, were sparks enough to touch off the explosives seething in her.

"You fool! You're being sold out, and don't know it!"

The leer vanished.

"What do you mean?" he snarled.

"I mean that your boss is fixing to skip out with all the gold you thieves have grabbed!" she blurted, heedless of consequences, in her emotional storm, indeed scarcely aware of what she was saying. "He and Corcoran are going to leave you holding the sack, tonight!"

And not seeing the man she was looking for, she eluded McNab's grasp, jumped down from the porch and darted away in the darkness.

The deputies stared at each other, and the prisoners, having heard everything, began to clamor to be turned out.

"Shut up!" snarled McNab. "She may be lyin'. Might have had a quarrel with Corcoran and took this fool way to get even with him. We can't afford to take no chances. We've got to be sure we know what we're doin' before we move either way. We can't afford to let you out now, on the chance that she might be lyin'. But we'll give you weapons to defend yourselves.

"Here, take these rifles and hide 'em under the bunks. Pete Daley, you stay here and keep folks shooed away from the jail till we get back. Richardson, you and Stark come with me! We'll have a showdown with Middleton right now!"

When Glory left the jail she headed for Hopkins' cabin. But she had not gone far when a reaction shook her. She was like one waking from a nightmare, or a dope jag. She was still sickened by the discovery of Corcoran's duplicity in regard to the people of the camp, but she began to apply reason to her suspicions of his motives in regard to herself. She began to realize that she had acted illogically. If Corcoran's attitude toward her was not sincere, he certainly would not have asked her to leave the camp with him. At the expense of her vanity she was forced to admit that his attentions to her had not been necessary in his game of duping the camp. That was something apart; his own private business; it must be so. She had suspected him of trifling with her affections, but she had to admit that she had no proof that he had ever paid the slightest attention to any other woman in Wahpeton. No; whatever his motives or actions in general, his feeling toward her must be sincere and real.

With a shock she remembered her present errand, her reckless words to McNab. Despair seized her, in which she realized that she loved Steve Corcoran in spite of all he might be. Chill fear seized her that McNab and his friends would kill her lover. Her unreasoning fury died out, gave way to frantic terror.

Turning, she ran swiftly down the gulch toward Corcoran's cabin. She was hardly aware of it when she passed through the blazing heart of the camp. Lights and bearded faces were like a nightmarish blur, in which nothing was real but the icy terror in her heart.

She did not realize it when the clusters of cabins fell behind her. The patter of her slippered feet in the road terrified her, and the black shadows under the trees seemed pregnant with menace. Ahead of her she saw Corcoran's cabin at last, a light streaming through the open door. She burst in to the office-room, panting—and was confronted by Middleton who wheeled with a gun in his hand.

"What the devil are you doing here?" He spoke without friendliness, though he returned the gun to its scabbard.

"Where's Corcoran?" she panted. Fear took hold of her as she faced the man she now knew was the monster behind the grisly crimes that had made a reign of terror over Wahpeton Gulch. But fear for Corcoran overshadowed her own terror.

"I don't know. I looked for him through the bars a short time ago, and didn't find him. I'm expecting him here any minute. What do you want with him?"

"That's none of your business," she flared.

"It might be." He came toward her, and the mask had fallen from his dark, handsome face. It looked wolfish.

"You were a fool to come here. You pry into things that don't concern you. You know too much. You talk too much. Don't think I'm not wise to you! I know more about you than you suspect."

A chill fear froze her. Her heart seemed to be turning to ice. Middleton was like a stranger to her, a terrible stranger. The mask was off, and the evil spirit of the man was reflected in his dark, sinister face. His eyes burned her like actual coals.

"I didn't pry into secrets," she whispered with dry lips. "I didn't ask any questions. I never before suspected you were the chief of the Vultures—"

The expression of his face told her she had made an awful mistake.

"So you know that!" His voice was soft, almost a whisper, but murder stood stark and naked in his flaming eyes. "I didn't know that. I was talking about something else. Conchita told me it was you who told Corcoran about the plan to lynch McBride. I wouldn't have killed you for that, though it interfered with my plans. But you know too much. After tonight it wouldn't matter. But tonight's not over yet—"

"Oh!" she whispered moaningly, staring with dilated eyes as the big pistol slid from its scabbard in a dull gleam of blue steel. She could not move, she could not cry out. She could only cower dumbly until the crash of the shot knocked her to the floor.

As Middleton stood above her, the smoking gun in his hand, he heard a stirring in the room behind him. He quickly upset the long table, so it could hide the body of the girl, and turned, just as the door opened. Corcoran came from the back room, blinking, a gun in his hand. It was evident that he had just awakened from a drunken sleep, but his hands did not shake, his pantherish tread was sure as ever, and his eyes were neither dull nor bloodshot.

Nevertheless Middleton swore.

"Corcoran, are you crazy?"

"You shot?"

"I shot at a snake that crawled across the floor. You must have been mad, to soak up liquor today, of all days!"

"I'm all right," muttered Corcoran, shoving his gun back in its scabbard.

"Well, come on. I've got the mules in the clump of trees next to my cabin. Nobody will see us load them. Nobody will see us go. We'll go up the ravine beyond my cabin, as we planned. There's nobody watching my cabin tonight. All the Vultures are down in the camp, waiting for the signal to move. I'm hoping none will escape the vigilantes, and that most of the vigilantes themselves are killed in the fight that's sure to come. Come on! We've got thirty mules to load, and that job will take us from now until midnight, at least. We won't pull out until we hear the guns on the other side of the camp."

"Listen!"

It was footsteps, approaching the cabin almost at a run. Both men wheeled and stood motionless as McNab loomed in the door. He lurched into the room, followed by Richardson and Stark. Instantly the air was supercharged with suspicion, hate, tension. Silence held for a tick of time.

"You fools!" snarled Middleton. "What are you doing away from the jail?"

"We came to talk to you," said McNab. "We've heard that you and Corcoran planned to skip with the gold."

Never was Middleton's superb self-control more evident. Though the shock of that blunt thunderbolt must have been terrific, he showed no emotion that might not have been showed by any honest man, falsely accused.

"Are you utterly mad?" he ejaculated, not in a rage, but as if amazement had submerged whatever anger he might have felt at the charge.

McNab shifted his great bulk uneasily, not sure of his ground. Corcoran was not looking at him, but at Richardson, in whose cold eyes a lethal glitter was growing. More quickly than Middleton, Corcoran sensed the inevitable struggle in which this situation must culminate.

"I'm just sayin' what we heard. Maybe it's so, maybe it ain't. If it ain't, there's no harm done," said McNab slowly. "On the chance that it was so, I sent word for the boys not to wait till midnight. They're goin' to the jail within the next half hour and take Miller and the rest out."

Another breathless silence followed that statement. Middleton did not bother to reply. His eyes began to smolder. Without moving, he yet seemed to crouch, to gather himself for a spring. He had realized what Corcoran had already sensed, that this situation was not to be passed over by words, that a climax of violence was inevitable.

Richardson knew this; Stark seemed merely puzzled. McNab, if he had any thoughts, concealed the fact.

"Say you *was* intendin' to skip," he said, "this might be a good chance, while the boys was takin' Miller and them off up into the hills. I don't know. I ain't accusin' you. I'm just askin' you to clear yourself. You can do it easy. Just come back to the jail with us and help get the boys out."

Middleton's answer was what Richardson, instinctive mankiller, had sensed it would be. He whipped out a gun in a blur of speed. And even as it cleared leather, Richardson's gun was out. But Corcoran had not taken his eyes off the cold-eyed gunman, and his draw was the quicker by a lightning-flicker. Quick as was Middleton, both the other guns spoke before his, like a double detonation. Corcoran's slug blasted Richardson's brains just in time to spoil his shot at Middleton. But the bullet grazed Middleton so close that it caused him to miss McNab with his first shot, which came so close on the heels of the other two that it was like one stuttering volley.

McNab's gun was out and Stark was a split second behind him. Middleton's second shot and McNab's first crashed almost together, but already Corcoran's guns had sent lead ripping through the giant's flesh. His ball merely flicked Middleton's hair in passing, and the chief's slug smashed full into his brawny breast. Middleton fired again and yet again as the giant was falling. Stark was down, dying on the floor, having pulled trigger blindly as he fell, until the gun was empty.

Middleton stared wildly about him, through the floating blue fog of smoke that veiled the room. In that fleeting instant, as he glimpsed Corcoran's image-like face, he felt that only in such a setting as this did the Texan appear fitted. Like a somber figure of Fate he moved implacably against a background of blood and slaughter.

"God!" gasped Middleton. "That was the quickest, bloodiest fight I was ever in!" Even as he talked he was jamming cartridges into his empty gun chambers.

"We've got no time to lose now! I don't know how much McNab told the gang of his suspicions. He must not have told them much, or some of them would have come with him. Anyway, their first move will be to liberate the prisoners. I have an idea they'll go through with that just as we planned, even when McNab doesn't return to lead them. They won't come looking for him, or come after us, until they turn Miller and the others loose.

"It just means the fight will come within the half hour instead of at midnight. The vigilantes will be there by that time. They're probably lying in ambush already. Come on! We've got to sling gold on those mules like devils. We may have to leave some of it; we'll know when the fight's started, by the sound of the guns! One thing, nobody will come up here to investigate the shooting. All attention is focused on the jail!"

Corcoran followed him out of the cabin, then turned back with a muttered: "Left a bottle of whisky in that back room."

"Well, hurry and get it and come on!" Middleton broke into a run toward his cabin, and Corcoran re-entered the smoke-veiled room. He did not glance at the crumpled bodies which lay on the crimson-stained floor, staring glassily up at him. With a stride he reached the back room, groped in his bunk until he found what he wanted, and then strode again toward the outer door, the bottle in his hand.

The sound of a low moan brought him whirling about, a gun in his left hand. Startled, he stared at the figures on the floor. He knew none of them had moaned; all three were past moaning. Yet his ears had not deceived him.

His narrowed eyes swept the cabin suspiciously, and focused on a thin trickle of crimson that stole from under the upset table as it lay on its side near the wall. None of the corpses lay near it.

He pulled aside the table and halted as if shot through the heart, his breath catching in a convulsive gasp. An instant later he was kneeling beside Glory Bland, cradling her golden head in his arm. His hand, as he brought the whisky bottle to her lips, shook queerly.

Her magnificent eyes lifted toward him, glazed with pain. But by some miracle the delirium faded, and she knew him in her last few moments of life.

"Who did this?" he choked. Her white throat was laced by a tiny trickle of crimson from her lips.

"Middleton—" she whispered. "Steve, oh, Steve—I tried—" And with the whisper uncompleted she went limp in his arms. Her golden head lolled back; she seemed strangely like a child, a child just fallen asleep. Dazedly he eased her to the floor.

Corcoran's brain was clear of liquor as he left the cabin, but he staggered like a drunken man. The monstrous, incredible thing that had happened left him stunned, hardly able to credit his own senses. It had never occurred to him that Middleton would kill a woman, that any white man would. Corcoran lived by his own code, and it was wild and rough and hard, violent and incongruous, but it included the conviction that womankind was sacred, immune from the violence that attended the lives of men. This code was as much a vital, living element of the life of the Southwestern frontier as was personal honor, and the resentment of insult. Without pompousness, without pretentiousness, without any of the tawdry glitter and sham of a false chivalry, the people of Corcoran's breed practiced this code in their daily lives. To Corcoran, as to his people, a woman's life and body were inviolate. It had never occurred to him that that code would, or could, be violated, or that there could be any other kind.

Cold rage swept the daze from his mind and left him crammed to the brim with murder. His feelings toward Glory Bland had approached the normal love experienced by the average man as closely as was possible for one of his iron nature. But if she had been a stranger, or even a person he had disliked, he would have killed Middleton for outraging a code he had considered absolute.

He entered Middleton's cabin with the soft stride of a stalking panther. Middleton was bringing bulging buckskin sacks from the cave, heaping them on a table in the main room. He staggered with their weight. Already the table was almost covered.

"Get busy!" he exclaimed. Then he halted short, at the blaze in Corcoran's eyes. The fat sacks spilled from his arms, thudding on the floor.

"You killed Glory Bland!" It was almost a whisper from the Texan's livid lips.

"Yes." Middleton's voice was even. He did not ask how Corcoran knew, he did not seek to justify himself. He knew the time for argument was past. He did not think of his plans, or of the gold on the table, or that still back there in the cave. A man standing face to face with Eternity sees only the naked elements of life and death.

"Draw!" A catamount might have spat the challenge, eyes flaming, teeth flashing.

Middleton's hand was a streak to his gun butt. Even in that flash he knew he was beaten—heard Corcoran's gun roar just as he pulled trigger. He swayed back, falling, and in a blind gust of passion Corcoran emptied both guns into him as he crumpled.

For a long moment that seemed ticking into Eternity the killer stood over his victim, a somber, brooding figure that might have been carved from the iron night of the Fates. Off toward the other end of the camp other guns burst forth suddenly, in salvo after thundering salvo. The fight that was plotted to mask the flight of the Vulture chief had begun. But the figure which stood above the dead man in the lonely cabin did not seem to hear.

Corcoran looked down at his victim, vaguely finding it strange, after all, that all those bloody schemes and terrible ambitions should end like that, in a puddle of oozing blood on a cabin floor. He lifted his head to stare somberly at the bulging sacks on the table. Revulsion gagged him.

A sack had split, spilling a golden stream that glittered evilly in the candlelight. His eyes were no longer blinded by the yellow sheen. For the first time he saw the blood on that gold; it was black with blood, the blood of innocent men, the blood of a woman. The mere thought of touching it nauseated him, made him feel as if the slime that had covered John Middleton's soul would befoul him. Sickly he realized that some of Middleton's guilt was on his own head. He had not pulled the trigger that ripped a woman's life from her body, but he had worked hand-in-glove with the man destined to be her murderer—Corcoran shuddered and a clammy sweat broke out upon his flesh.

Down the gulch the firing had ceased, faint yells came to him, freighted with victory and triumph. Many men must be shouting at once, for the sound to carry so far. He knew what it portended; the Vultures had walked into the trap laid for them by the man they trusted as a leader. Since the firing had ceased, it meant the whole band were either dead or captives. Wahpeton's reign of terror had ended.

But he must stir. There would be prisoners, eager to talk. Their speech would weave a noose about his neck.

He did not glance again at the gold, gleaming there where the honest people of Wahpeton would find it. Striding from the cabin he swung on one of the horses that stood saddled and ready among the trees. The lights of the camp, the roar of the distant voices fell away behind him, and before him lay what wild destiny he could not guess. But the night was full of haunting shadows, and within him grew a strange pain that was like a revelation; perhaps it was his soul, at last awakening.

Alternate Ending

But he must stir. There would be prisoners, eager to talk. Their speech would weave a noose about his neck. The men of Wahpeton must not find him here when they came.

But before he turned his back forever upon Wahpeton Gulch, he had a task to perform. He did not glance again at the gold, gleaming there where the honest people of the camp would find it. Two horses waited, bridled and saddled, among the restless mules tethered under the trees. One was the animal which had borne him into Wahpeton. He mounted it and rode slowly toward the cabin where a woman lay beside dead men. He felt vaguely that it was not right to leave her lying there among those shot-torn rogues.

He braced himself against the sight as he entered the cabin of death. Then he started and went livid under his sun-burnt hue.

Glory was not lying as he had left her! With a low cry he reached her, lifted her in his arms. He felt life, pulsing strongly under his hands.

"Glory! For God's sake!" Her eyes were open, not so glazed now, though shadowed by pain and bewilderment. Her arms groped toward him. He lifted and carried her into the back room, laid her on the bunk where Joe Willoughby had received his death wounds. His mind was a whirling turmoil, as he felt with practiced fingers of the darkly-clotted wound at the edge of her golden hair. She whimpered faintly, but submitted herself to his hands. A joy that was almost an agony in its intensity surged through him. The bullet that had struck her down had only grazed her head, tearing the skin. The skull beneath was not fractured. The blow, shock and pain had overcome her. He had mistaken her unconsciousness for death. The shock of finding her shot had disrupted his mental faculties so that he had not made an investigation. He had thought that she was dead, without proving or disproving the supposition.

"Steve," she whimpered. "I'm afraid! Middleton—"

"He won't hurt you anymore. Don't talk. I'm going to wash that wound and dress it."

Working fast and skillfully, he washed the blood away with a rag torn from her petticoat—as being the cleanest material he could find—and soaked in water and whiskey. She flinched at the bite of the alcohol, but did not whimper. As she recovered from the shock, strength and intelligence returned to her in surges. Corcoran had just ceased bandaging her head when she struggled upright, despite his profane objections, and caught at his arm.

"Steve!" Her eyes were wide with fear. "You must go—go quick! I was crazy—I told McNab what you told me—told Middleton, too, that's why he shot me. They'll kill you."

"Not them," he muttered. "Do you feel better now?"

"Oh, don't mind me! Go! Please go! Oh, Steve, I must have been mad! I betrayed you! I was coming here to tell you that I had, to warn you to get away, when I met Middleton. Where is he?"

"In hell, where he ought to been years ago," grunted Corcoran. "Never mind. But the vigilantes will be headin' this way soon as some of the rats they've caught get to talkin'. I've got to dust out. But I'll take you back to the Golden Garter first."

"Steve, you're mad! You'd run your head into a noose! Get on your horse and ride!"

"Will you go with me?" His hands closed on her, hurting her with their unconscious strength.

"You still want me, after—after what I did?" she gasped.

"I've always wanted you, since I first saw you. I always will. Forgive you? There's nothin' to forgive. Nothin' you could have ever done could be anywhere near as black as what I've been for the past month. I've been like a mad dog; the gold blinded me. I'm awake now. And I want you."

For answer her arms groped about his neck, clung convulsively; he felt the moisture of her passionate tears on his throat. Lifting her, he carried her out of the cabin, pressing her face against his breast that she might not see the stark figures lying there in their splashes of crimson.

An instant later he was settled in the saddle, holding her before him, cradled like a child in his muscular arms. He had wrapped his coat about her, and the pale oval of her face stared up at his like a white blossom in the night. Her arms still clung to him, as if she feared he might be torn from her.

"How the lights blaze over the camp!" she murmured irrelevantly, as they climbed toward the ravine.

"Take a good look," he said, his voice rough with suppressed and unfamiliar emotions. "It's our old life we're leavin' behind, and I hope we're headin' for a better one. And as a beginnin', we're goin' to get married the first town we hit."

An incoherent murmur was her only reply as she snuggled closer in his arms; behind them the lights of the camp, the distant roar of voices fell away and grew blurred in the distance. But it seemed to Corcoran that they rode in a blaze of glory, that emanated not from moon nor stars, but from his own breast. And perhaps it was his soul, at last awakened.

Vultures' Sanctuary

A vagrant wind stirred tiny dust-eddies where the road to California became, for a few hundred yards, the main street of Capitan town. A few mongrel dogs lazed in the shade of the false-fronted frame buildings. Horses at the hitching rack stamped and switched flies. A child loitered along the warped boardwalk; except for these signs of life, Capitan might have been a ghost town, deserted to sun and wind. A covered wagon creaked slowly along the road from the east. The horses, gaunt and old, leaned forward with each lurching step. The girl on the seat peered under a shading hand and spoke to the old man beside her.

"There's a town ahead, father."

He nodded. "Capitan. We won't waste time there. A bad town. I've heard of it ever since we crossed the Pecos. No law there. A haunt of renegades and refugees. But we must stop there long enough to buy bacon and coffee."

His tired old voice encouraged the laboring horses; dust of the long, long trail sifted greyly from the wagon bed as they creaked into Capitan.

Capitan, baking under the sun that drew a curtain of shimmering heat waves between it and the bare Guadalupes, rising from the rolling wastelands to the south. Capitan, haunt of the hunted, yet not the last haunt, not the ultimate, irrevocable refuge for the desperate and damned.

But not all who came to Capitan were scarred with the wolf-trail brand. One was standing even then at the bar of the Four Aces Saloon, frowning at the man before him. Big Mac, cowpuncher from Texas, broad shouldered, deep chested, with thews hardened to the toughness of woven steel by years on the cattle trails that stretch from the live oaks of the Gulf marshes to the prairies of Canada. A familiar figure wherever cowmen gathered, with his broad brown face, volcanic blue eyes, and unruly thatch of curly black hair. There were no notches in the butt of the big Colt .45 which jutted from the scabbard at his right hip, but that butt was worn smooth from much usage. Big Mac did not notch his gun, but it had blazed in range wars and cowtown feuds from the Sabine to Milk River.

"You're Bill McClanahan, ain't you?" the other man asked with a strange eagerness his casual manner could not conceal. "You remember me?"

"Yeah." A man with many enemies must have a keen memory for faces. "You're the Checotah Kid. I saw you in Hayes City, three years ago."

"Let's drink!" At the Kid's gesture, the bartender sent glasses and a bottle sliding down the wet bar. The Kid was Mac's opposite in type. Slender, though hard as steel, smooth-faced, blond, his wide grey eyes seemed guileless at first glance. But a man wise in the ways of men could see cruelty and murderous treachery lurking in their depths.

But something else burned there now, something fearful and hunted. There was a nervous tension underlying the Kid's manner that puzzled Big Mac, who remembered him as a suave, self-possessed young scoundrel of the Kansas trail-towns. Doubtless he was on the dodge; yet that did not explain his nervousness, for there was no law in Capitan, and the Border was less than a hundred miles to the south.

Now the Kid leaned toward him and lowered his voice, though only the bartender and a loafer at a table shared the saloon with them.

"Mac, I need a partner! I've found color in the Guadalupes! Gold, as sure as hell!"

"Never knew you were a prospector," grunted Big Mac.

"A man gets to be lots of things!" the Kid's laugh was mirthless. "But I mean it!"

"Why'n't you stay and work it, then?" demanded the other.

"El Bravo's gang ran me out. Thought I was a sheriff or something!" Again the Kid laughed harshly, almost hysterically. "You've heard of El Bravo, maybe? Heads a gang of outlaws that hang out in the Guadalupes. But with a man to watch and another to work, we could take out plenty! The pocket's in a canyon just in the edge of the hills. What do you say?"

Again that flaming intentness. His eyes burned on Big Mac like the eyes of a condemned man, seeking reprieve.

The Texan emptied his glass and shook his head.

"I'm no prospector," he rumbled. "I'm sick of work, anyway. I ain't never had a vacation all my life, except a few days in town at the end of the drive, or before roundup. I quit my job at the Lazy K three weeks ago, and I'm headin' for San Francisco to enjoy life for a spell. I'm tired of cowtowns. I want to see what a real city looks like."

"But it's a fortune!" urged the Kid passionately, his grey eyes blazing with a weird light. "You'd be a fool to pass it up!"

Big Mac bristled. He'd never liked Checotah anyway. But he merely replied: "Well, mebbyso, but that's how she stands."

"You won't do it?" It was almost a whisper. Sweat beaded the Kid's forehead.

"No! Looks like to me you could find some other partner easy enough."

Mac turned away, reaching for the bottle.

It was a glimpse of the big mirror behind the bar, caught from the tail of his eye, that saved his life. In that fleeting reflection he saw the Checotah Kid, his face a livid mask of desperation, draw his pistol. Big Mac whirled, knocking the gun aside with the bottle in his hand. The smash of breaking glass mingled with the bang of the shot. The bullet ripped through the slack of the Texan's shirt and thudded into the wall. Almost simultaneously Mac crashed his left fist full into the Kid's face.

The killer staggered backward, the smoking pistol escaping his numbed fingers. Mac was after him like a big catamount. There could be no quarter in such a fight. Mac did not spare his strength, for he knew the Kid was deadly—knew he had killed half a dozen men already, some treacherously. He might have another gun hidden on him somewhere.

But it was a knife he was groping for, as he reeled backward under the sledgehammer impact of the Texan's fists. He found it, just as a thundering clout on the jaw knocked him headlong backward through the door to fall sprawling in the dusty street. He lay still, stunned, blood trickling from his mouth. Big Mac strode swiftly toward him to learn whether or not he was possuming.

But he never reached him. There was a quick patter of light feet, a swish of skirts, and even as Mac saw the girl spring in front of him, he received a resounding slap on his startled face.

He recoiled, glaring in amazement at the slender figure which confronted him, vibrant with anger.

"Don't you dare touch him again, you big bully!" she panted, her dark eyes blazing. "You coward! You brute! Attacking a boy half your size!"

He found no words to reply. He did not fully realize how savage and formidable he looked, with his fierce eyes and dark, scarred face as he stood there with his mallet-like fists clenched, glaring down at the man he had knocked down. He looked like a giant beside the slender Kid. Checotah looked boyish, innocent; to the girl, ignorant of men's ways, it looked like the brutal attack of a ruffian on an inoffensive boy. Mac realized this vaguely, but he could not find words to defend himself. She had not seen the bowie knife, which had fallen in the dust.

A small crowd was gathering, silent and inscrutable. The loafer who had been in the saloon was among them. An old man, his hands gnarled and his bony shoulders stooped, came from the store that stood next to the saloon, with bundles in his hands. He started toward a dust-stained wagon standing beside a board fence just beyond the store, then saw the crowd and hurried toward it, concern shadowing his eyes.

The girl turned lithely and knelt beside the Kid, who was struggling to a sitting position. He saw the pity in her wet, dark eyes, and understood. Checotah could play his cards as they fell.

"Don't let him kill me, Miss," he groaned. "I wasn't doing anything!"

"He shan't touch you," she assured him, flashing a look of defiance at Big Mac. She wiped the blood from the Kid's mouth, and looked angrily at the taciturn, leather-faced men who stood about.

"You should be ashamed of yourselves!" she stormed, with the ignorant courage of the very young. "Letting a bully like *him* abuse a boy!"

They made no response; only their lips twisted a little, in grim, sardonic humor she could not understand. Big Mac, his face dark, muttered under his breath and, turning on his heel, he re-entered the saloon. In there the voices reached him only as an incoherent murmur—the faltering, hypocritical voice of the Kid followed quickly by the soothing, sympathetic tones of the girl.

"Hell's fire!" Big Mac grabbed the whisky bottle.

"Wimmen are shore funny critters," remarked the bartender, scouring the bar. Mac's snarl discouraged conversation. The Texan took the bottle to a table at the back of the saloon. He was smarting mentally. The slap the girl had given him was no more than the tap of a feather. But a deeper sting persisted. He was angry and humiliated. A slip of a girl had abused him, like, as he would have put it, an egg-suckin' dog. Like most men of the wild trails, he was extremely sensitive where women were concerned. Indifferent to the opinions of men, a woman's scorn or anger could hurt him deeply. Like all men of his breed, he held women in high esteem, and desired their good opinion. But this girl had condemned him on the appearance of things. His sense of justice was outraged; his soul harbored a sting not to be soothed by the thought of the thousand-odd dollars in greenbacks in his pocket, nor the anticipation of spending them in that faraway city which he had never seen.

He drank, and drank again. His face grew darker, his blue eyes burned more savagely. As he sat there, huge, dark and brooding, he looked capable of any wild, ferocious deed.

So thought the man who after awhile entered furtively and slipped into a chair opposite him. Big Mac scowled at him. He knew him as Slip Ratner, one of the many shady characters which haunted Capitan.

"I was in here when the Kid drawed on you," said Ratner, a faint, evil smile twisting his thin lips. "That girl sure hauled *you* over the coals, didn't she?"

"Shut up!" snarled Big Mac, grabbing the bottle again.

"Sure, sure!" soothed Ratner. "No offense. Sassy snip she was—you ought to of smacked her face for her. Listen!" He hunched forward and lowered his voice: "How'd you like to get even with that fresh dame?"

Big Mac merely grunted. He was paying little attention to what Ratner was saying. Get even with a woman? The thought had never entered his mind. His code, the rigid, iron-bound code of the Texas frontier, did not permit of retaliation against a woman, whatever the provocation. But Ratner was speaking again, hurriedly.

"I don't know why the Kid tried to drill you, but that gold talk of his was a lie. He's been in the Guadalupes, yes, but not after gold. He was trying to join up with El Bravo. I have ways of knowing things—

"Checotah hit Capitan just a few days ago. He's just a few jumps ahead of the Federal marshals. Besides that, there's reward notices for him stuck up all over Mexico. He's killed and robbed on both sides of the Line till there ain't but one place left for him—El Bravo's hideout in the Guadalupes. That's where men go when both the United States and Mexico are barred to them.

"But El Bravo don't take in no man free. They have to buy into the gang. You remember Stark Campbell, that robbed the bank at Nogales? He got ten thousand dollars and he had to give every cent of it to El Bravo to join the gang. Tough, but it was that or his life. They say El Bravo's got a regular treasure-trove hid away somewhere up in the Guadalupes.

"But Checotah didn't have nothing, and El Bravo wouldn't take him. The Kid's desperate. If he stayed here the law would get him in a few days, and there wasn't no place else for him to go. When I seen him playing up to that fool girl, I figgered he had something up his sleeve. And he did! He begged them to take him out of town with them—said he was afraid you'd murder him if he stayed in Capitan. And you know what they done? Invited him to go on to California with them! They laid him in the wagon, him pretending to be crippled, and pulled out, the girl washing the blood off his face, and his saddlehorse tied to the tailboard.

"Well, when they took him to the wagon, I sneaked up behind that board fence and listened to them talk. The girl told Checotah everything. Their names is Ellis; she's Judith Ellis. The old man's got a thousand dollars he saved up, working on a farm back in Illinois or somewhere, and he aims to use it making first payment on a piece of irrigated land in California.

"Now, I know the Kid. He ain't goin' to California. Why, he don't even dare show himself in the next town, out beyond Scalping Knife. Somewhere along the trail he'll kill old Ellis and head for the Guadalupes with the money *and* the girl. He'll pay his way into the Bravo gang with them! El Bravo likes women, and she's purty enough for any man.

"Here's where we come in. I don't figure the Kid'll strike till after they've passed Seven Mule Pass. That's nine miles from here. If we get on our horses and ride through the sagebrush, we can get past them and waylay them in the pass. Or we can wait till the Kid kills the old man, and then crack down on him. We kill the Kid, and that evens you up with him. Then we split the loot. I take the money. You take the girl. Nobody'll ever know. Plenty of places in the mountains you can take her, and—"

For an instant Big Mac sat silent, glaring incredulously at the leering face before him, while the monstrous proposal soaked in. Ratner could not properly interpret his stunned silence; Ratner credited all men with his own buzzard instincts.

"What do you say?" he urged.

"Why, you damned—!" Big Mac's eyes flared red as he heaved up. The table crashed sidewise, bottles smashing on the floor. Ratner, almost pinned beneath it, yelped in fright and fury as he jumped clear. He snatched at a pistol as the berserk cowman towered over him. Mac did not waste lead on him. His movement was like the swipe of a bear's paw as his hand locked on Ratner's wrist. The renegade screamed, and a bone snapped. The pistol flew into the corner, and Big Mac hurled the snarling wretch after it, to lie in a stunned, crumpled heap. Men scattered as Big Mac stormed out of the saloon and made for the hitching rack where stood his big bay gelding.

A few moments later the giant Texan thundered out of town in a whirlwind of dust, and took the road that ran west.

East of Capitan, the road stretched across a dusty level and was visible for miles, which was an advantage to the citizens, for it was from the east that sheriffs and Federal marshals were most likely to come riding. But westward the terrain changed to a broken country in which the road disappeared from view of the town within a mile. Miles away to the southwest rose the grim outlines of the Guadalupes, shimmering under a sky tinted steel-white by the morning sun. Haunt of fierce desert killers they had always been—painted red men once, and later sombreroed *banditos*—but never had they sheltered more deadly slayers than the gang of the mysterious El Bravo. Big Mac had heard of him, had heard, too, that few knew his real identity, save that he was a white man.

The town disappeared behind him, and after that the Texan passed only one habitation—the adobe hut of a Mexican sheepherder, some five miles west of Capitan. A mile further on the trail dipped down into the broad deep canyon cut by Scalping Knife River, in its southerly course—now only a trickle of water in its shallow bed. Three miles beyond the canyon lay a chain of hills, a spur of the Guadalupes, through which the road threaded by Seven Mule Pass. There it was that Ratner expected to lay ambush. Big Mac expected to overhaul the slow-moving wagon long before it reached the Pass.

But as he rode down the eastern slope of the canyon, he grunted and stiffened at the sight of the form lying limply on the canyon floor. The Kid had not waited to get beyond the Pass. Mac bent over old man Ellis. He had been shot through the left shoulder and was unconscious. He had lost a great deal of blood, but the thrum of his old heart was strong. The wagon was nowhere in sight. Wheel tracks wandered away up the canyon; the tracks of a single horse went down the canyon. Big Mac read the sign easily. Ratner had prophesied unerringly, with the wisdom of a wolf concerning the ways of wolves. Checotah had shot the old man—probably without warning. The team, frightened, had run away with the wagon. The Kid had ridden down the canyon with the girl, and, without doubt, the old man's pitiful savings.

Mac stanched the flow of blood with his bandanna. He lifted the senseless man across the saddle and turned back on his trail, leading the big bay, and cursing as the rocks of the flinty trail turned under his high-heeled boots. Back at the sheepherder's hut, a mile from the canyon, he lifted the wounded man down and carried him in, laid him on a bunk. The old Mexican watched inscrutably.

Mac tore a ten dollar bill in two, and handed one half to the *peon*.

"If he's alive when I get back, you get the other half. If he ain't, I'll make you hard to catch. There's a wagon and team up the canyon. Send a boy to find 'em and bring 'em back here."

"*Si, señor.*" The old man gave his attention to the wounded man; more than half Indian, his knowledge of primitive surgery was aboriginal, but effective.

Mac headed back for the canyon. The Kid had not bothered to hide his sign. There was no law in Capitan. There were men there who would not have allowed him to kidnap a girl if they could have prevented it, but they would not attempt to follow him into the outlaw-haunted Guadalupes.

The trail was plain down the canyon. He followed it for three miles, the walls growing steeper and higher as the canyon wound deeper and deeper into the hills. The trail turned aside up a narrow ravine, and Mac, following it, came out upon a benchland, dry and sandy, hemmed in by the slopes of the mountains. At the south edge of the flat buzzards rose and flapped heavily away. They had not feasted; they had been waiting, with grisly patience, for a feast. A few moments later Big Mac looked down on the sprawling form of the Checotah Kid. He had been shot in the open, and a smear of blood on the sand showed how he had wriggled an agonized way to the shade of a big rock.

He had been shot through the body, near the heart. His eyes were glazed, and at each choking gasp bloody bubbles burst on his blue lips.

Big Mac looked down on him with hard, merciless eyes.

"You dirty skunk! I'm sorry somebody beat me to it! Where's the girl?"

"El Bravo took her," panted the Kid. "They saw me riding— with the flag. Came to meet me. I gave him the girl—to pay my way into the gang. Tried to hold out the thousand—I took off the old man. They grabbed me—searched me—El Bravo shot me—for trying to hold out."

"Where'd they take her to?"

"The hideout. I don't know where. Nobody knows but them." The Kid's voice was growing weaker and thicker. "They watch the trails—all the time. Nobody can get—in the Guadalupes—without them knowing it. I carried the signal flag—only reason I got this far." He gestured vaguely toward a cottonwood limb with a shred of white cloth tied to it, which lay near him.

Curiosity prompted Big Mac's next question.

"Why'd you try to shoot me? We never had no trouble in Kansas."

"You were to be my price," gasped the Kid. "That's why I tried to lure you into the hills. El Bravo had rather have you alive. But when you wouldn't come, I thought if I brought him proof I'd downed you, maybe he'd take me in anyway. He's Garth Bissett!"

Garth Bissett! That explained many things. There were reasons why Bissett should hate Big Mac. They had first met in a Kansas cowtown, at the end of a cattle trail from Texas. Bissett was marshal of that town. A hard man, wary as a wolf, quick as summer lightning with the ivory-butted pistols that hung at his hips—and withal as rotten souled a scoundrel as ever ruled a buzzard-roost trail town. It was Big Mac who broke his dominion. Going to the aid of a young cowboy, framed by one of Bissett's gunfighting deputies, the big herd-boss had left the deputy dead on a dancehall floor after a blur of gun-smoke, and in the dead man's pockets were found letters revealing the extent of Bissett's crookedness—proof of theft and murder. A Federal marshal stepped into the game. Bissett might have escaped, but he paused at the cowcamp at the edge of town to even scores with the big trail-driver.

Big Mac came out of the gunplay that followed with a bullet in his breast muscles, while Bissett, his leg broken by a slug from Mac's .45, was taken by the Federal man. He was tried and sentenced to life imprisonment, but on the way to the penitentiary escaped, and dropped out of sight. Rumor said he had fled to Mexico, and become involved in a revolution.

Big Mac absently noted that the Kid was dead. Without another glance he mounted and rode deeper into the hills, following the faint trail the slayers had left. His face was darker and grimmer, but the shadow of a sardonic smile played about the corners of his hard mouth, and in one hand he carried the makeshift flag the Kid had borne. He had made his plan, a desperate, reckless plan, with one chance in a thousand of success. But it was the only one. He knew that he could not go into the Guadalupes shooting. If he tried to force his way to the bandit hangout, even if he should find it, he would be shot from ambush long before he got there. There was but one way to reach the heart of El Bravo's stronghold. He was taking that way.

He did not ask himself why he followed the trail of a girl who meant nothing to him. It was part of him that he should do so—part of the code of the Texas Border, born of half a century of merciless warfare with red men and brown men, to whom the women of the whites were fair prey. A white man went to the aid of a woman in distress, regardless of who she might be. That was all there was to it. And so Big Mac was going to the aid of the girl who had despised him, instead of riding on his way to the far-off city where he expected to squander the wad of greenbacks he carried in his pocket. Only he knew how much hard work and self-denial they represented.

He had left the flat a few miles behind him and was riding through a rugged defile when a harsh voice bawled an order to halt. Instantly he pulled up and elevated his hands. The command came from a cluster of boulders to the right.

"Who're you and what's you want?" came the crisp question.

"I'm Big Mac," answered the Texan tranquilly. "I'm lookin' for El Bravo."

"What you got for him?" was the next demand—a stock question, evidently.

Big Mac laughed. "Myself!"

"Are you crazy?" There was a snarl in the voice.

"No. Take me to Bissett. If he don't thank you, he'll be crazy."

"Well, he ain't!" growled the bushwhacker. "Get off yore horse! Now unbuckle yore gun belt and let 'er drop. Now step back away from it—further back, blast you! Keep yore hands up. I got a .45-70 trained on yore heart all the time."

Big Mac did exactly as he was told. He was standing there, unarmed, his hands in the air, when the man came from behind the rocks, a tall man, who walked with the springy tread of a cougar. Mac knew him instantly.

"Stark Campbell!" he said softly. "So this is why they never got you!"

"And they never will, neither!" retorted the outlaw with an oath. "They can't git to us, up here in the Guadalupes. But a man has to pay high to git in." Bitter anger vibrated in his voice as he said that. "What you done, that you want in?"

"Never mind that. You just lead me to Bissett."

"I'll have to take you to the hangout, if you see him," said Campbell. "He just taken a girl there. He don't let nobody see the hangout and live, unless they're in his gang. If he don't let you join us, he'll kill you. You can go back, though, if you want to, now. I won't stop you. You ain't no law."

"I want to see Bissett," replied the Texan. Campbell shrugged his shoulders and drew a pistol, laying aside the rifle. He ordered Big Mac to turn around and put his hands behind him, and the outlaw then bound his wrists—awkwardly, with one hand, for he kept the pistol muzzle jammed in Mac's back with the other, but when the Texan's hands were partly confined, he completed the job with both hands. Then Campbell led his own horse, a rangy roan, from behind the rocks, and hung Mac's gun belt over the roan's saddle horn.

"Git on yore horse," he growled. "I'll help you up."

They started on, Campbell leading the big bay. For three or four miles they threaded a precarious path through as wild and broken a country as Big Mac had ever seen, until they entered a steep-walled canyon which, apparently, came to a blind end ahead of them, as the walls pinched together. But as they neared it Big Mac saw a cleft in the angle, fifty feet above the canyon floor, and reached by a narrow, winding trail. A man hailed them from above.

"It's me, Campbell!" shouted his captor, and a growling voice bade them advance. "This is the only way into our hangout," said Campbell. "You see how much chance a posse'd have of gittin' in, even if they found it. One man with plenty of shells could hold that cleft agen a army."

They went up the trail, single file. The horses crowded against the wall, fearful of the narrow footing. Mac knew that Campbell spoke the truth when he said no posse could charge up that trail, raked by fire from above.

As they entered the cleft a black-whiskered man rose from behind a ledge of rock and glared suspiciously at them.

"All right, Wilson. I'm takin' this fellow to Bissett."

"Ain't that Big Mac?" asked Wilson, in whom Mac recognized another "lost outlaw." "What's he got for Bissett? You searched him?"

"You know damn' well I ain't, only for guns," snarled Campbell. "You know the rule, well as me. Nobody takes money off 'em except Bissett." He spat. "Come on, Mac. If you got somethin' Bissett'll accept, I'll take yore ropes off. If you ain't, you won't be carin' anyway, not with a bullet through yore head."

The cleft was like a tunnel in the rock. It ran for forty feet and then widened out into a space that was like a continuation of the canyon they had left. It formed a bowl, its floor higher than the floor of the canyon outside by fifty feet, walled by unbroken cliffs three hundred feet high, and apparently unscalable. Campbell confirmed this.

"Can't nobody git at us from them cliffs," he snarled. "They're steep outside as inside. It's jest like somebody scooped a holler in the middle of a rock mesa. The holler's this bowl. G'wan. Git down."

Big Mac managed it, with his hands bound, and Campbell left the horses standing in the shade of the wall, reins hanging. He drove Big Mac before him toward the adobe hut that stood in the middle of the bowl, surrounded by a square rock wall, breast-high to a tall man.

"Last line of defense, Bissett says," growled Campbell. "Even if a posse was to git into the bowl—which ain't possible—we could fight 'em off indefinite behind that wall. There's a spring inside the stockade, and we got provisions and ca'tridges enough for a year."

The renegade marshal was always a master of strategy. Big Mac did not believe the outlaw hangout would ever fall by a direct attack, regardless of the numbers assailing it—if it were ever discovered by the lawmen.

A man Campbell addressed as Garrison came from the corral, adjoining the wall, where a dozen horses grazed, and another met them at the heavy plank gate, built to turn bullets.

"Why, hell!" ejaculated the latter. "That's Big Mac! Where'd you catch him?"

"He rode in with a flag of truce, Emmett," answered Campbell. "Bissett in the shack?"

"Yeah; with the girl," grunted Emmett. "By God, I dunno what to make of *this!*"

Evidently Emmett knew something of Bissett's former life. The three men followed Mac as he strode across the yard toward the hut. Stark Campbell, John Garrison, Red Emmett; Wolf Wilson, back there at the tunnel. He had indeed come into the last haunt of the hunted, last retreat of these, the most desperate of all the Border renegades, to whom all other doors were barred, against whom the hands of all men were raised. Only in this lost canyon of the Guadalupes could they find sanctuary—the refuge of the wolf's lair, for which they had forfeited all their blood-tinged gains.

Theirs could be only a wolf-pack alliance. Bissett dominated them by virtue of keener wits and swifter gun-hand. They hated him for the brutal avarice that stripped from them their last shred of plunder, in return for a chance of bare life; but they feared him too, and recognized his superiority, knew that without his leadership the pack must perish, despite all natural advantages.

Campbell pushed the door open. As Big Mac loomed in the doorway, the man in the room turned with the blurring speed of a wolf, his hand streaking to an ivory-handled gun even in the instant it took him to see the stranger was a captive, with his hands bound behind him.

"You!" It was the ripping snarl of a timber wolf. Bissett was as tall as Big Mac, but not so heavy. He was wiry, rangy; yellow mustaches drooped below a mouth thin as a knife gash. His pale eyes glittered with an icy, blood-chilling fire.

"What the hell!" He seemed stunned with surprise. Big Mac looked past him to the girl who cringed in the corner, her eyes wide with terror. There was no hope in them when they met his. To her he was but another beast of prey.

Big Mac grinned at Bissett, without mirth.

"Come to join your gang, Garth," he said calmly. "Heard you had to have a gift. Well, I'm it! I've heard you'd bid high for my hide!"

He was gambling on his knowledge of Bissett's nature—on the chance that the outlaw would not instantly shoot him down. They faced each other, the big dark Texan smiling, a trifle grimly, but calm; Bissett snarling, tense, suspicious as a wolf.

"Where'd you get him, Campbell?" he snapped.

"He come in under a flag of truce," growled Campbell. "Same as any man that wants to join up with us. Said you'd be glad to see him."

Bissett turned on Mac, his eyes shining like a wolf's that scents a trap. "Why did you come here?" he ripped out. "You're no fool. You wouldn't put yourself in my power unless you had a damned good reason—some edge—" He whirled on his men, in a frenzy of suspicion.

"Get out to the wall, damn you! Watch the cliffs! Watch everything! This devil wouldn't come in here alone unless he had something up his sleeve—"

"Well, I—" began Campbell, but Bissett's voice cut his sullen drawl like the slash of a whip.

"Shut up, damn you! Get out there! I do the thinking for the gang!"

Mac saw the unveiled hate in Campbell's eyes as he slouched silently out after the others, saw Bissett's eyes dwell burningly on the man. Bad blood there. Campbell feared Bissett less than the others, and was therefore the focus of the wolfish chief's suspicion.

As the men left the building, Bissett picked up a double-barreled shotgun, and cocked it.

"I don't know what your game is," he said between his teeth. "You must have a gang following you, or something. But whatever happens, I aim to get *you!*"

Mac appeared helpless, unarmed, his hands bound; but a wolflike suspicion of appearances was at once Bissett's strength and his weakness.

"You're no outlaw," he snarled. "You didn't come here to join my gang. You knew I'd skin you alive, or stake you out on an ant bed. What are you up to?"

Big Mac laughed in his face. A man who followed the herds up the long trail year after year learned to judge men as well as animals. Bissett was reacting exactly as Mac had expected him to. The Texan was playing that knowledge blindly, waiting for some kind of a break. A desperate game, but he was used to games where the Devil dealt for deadly stakes.

"You ain't got a very big gang, Bissett," he said.

"They're not all here," rapped the outlaw. "Some are out on a raid, toward the Border. Never mind. What's your game? If you talk, your finish will be easier."

Mac glanced again at Judith Ellis, cowering in a corner. The stark terror in her wide eyes hurt him. To this girl, unused to violence, her experience was like a nightmare.

"My game, Bissett?" asked Big Mac coolly. "What could it be? Nobody could get past Wilson in the tunnel, could they? Nobody could climb the cliffs, could they? What good would it do if I did have a gang followin' me, like you think?"

"You wouldn't come here without an ace in the hole," Bissett all but whispered.

"What about your own men?" Big Mac played his ace.

Bissett blanched. His suspicions crystallized, for the moment—suspicions of Big Mac's coming, suspicions of his own men, which forever gnawed at his brain. His eyes, glaring at Mac over the shotgun's black muzzles, were tinged with madness.

"You're trapped, Bissett!" jeered Big Mac, playing his hand from minute to minute, for whatever it might be worth. "Your own men have sold you out! For the loot you took from them and hid—"

And at that moment the break came. Outside Campbell had turned back toward the adobe, and Mac saw him and yelled: *"Campbell! Help!"* Bissett whirled like a flash, shifting the shotgun to cover his amazed follower. It was an instinctive movement. Even so he would not have pulled the triggers—would have seen through Mac's flimsy scheme, had he had time to think.

But Mac saw and took his desperate chance. He hurled himself headlong against Bissett, and at the impact the shotgun hammers, hung on hair triggers, fell to the involuntary, convulsive jerk of Bissett's fingers. Both barrels exploded as Bissett went down under Mac's hurtling body, and buckshot blasted Stark Campbell's skull. He died on his feet, without knowing why. That was chance; Mac did not, could not have planned his death.

As they went down together, Mac drove his knee savagely into Bissett's belly and rolled clear as the outlaw doubled in gasping agony. Mac heaved up on his feet somehow, roaring: "His knife, quick! Cut these cords!"

The impact of his voice jolted the terrified girl into action. She sprang blindly forward, snatched the knife from Bissett's boot, and sawed at cords that held Mac's wrists, slicing skin as well as hemp. It had all happened in a stunning instant. Outside, Garrison and Emmett were running toward the house with guns in their hands. Some of the strands parted under the blade, and Mac snapped the others. He stooped and dragged Bissett to his feet. The half-senseless outlaw was clawing dazedly at his pistols. Mac jerked them from him and swung the limp frame around before him.

"Tell your men to get back!" he snarled, jamming a muzzle hard in Bissett's back. "They'll obey you! Tell 'em, quick!"

But the order was never given. The men outside did not know what had happened in the hut. They had only seen Campbell blasted down by a shot through the doorway, and they thought their leader was turning against them. Emmett caught a glimpse of Bissett through the door and fired. Mac felt Bissett's body jerk convulsively in his hands. The bullet had drilled through the outlaw's head.

Mac threw the corpse aside, and fired from the hip. Emmett, struck in the mouth, went down heavily on his back. Garrison, as he saw Emmett fall and Mac loom in the doorway, began to fall back, firing as he went. He was making for the protection of the corral. Once there, he might make a long fight of it. Wilson would be coming up from the tunnel. If it came to a siege, the girl would be endangered by the raking lead.

Mac sprang recklessly into the open, shooting two-handed. He felt hot lead rip through his shirt, burn the skin on his ribs. Garrison snarled, whirled, sprang for the wall. In mid-stride he staggered drunkenly, hard hit. He wheeled and started shooting again, even as he crumpled, holding his six-shooter in both hands. Hit again and yet again, he kept on pulling the trigger, his bullets knocking up the dirt in front of Big Mac's boots. His pistol snapped on an empty chamber before he lurched to the ground and lay still, in a spreading red puddle.

Mac heard Judith scream, and simultaneously came a report behind him and the impact of a blow that knocked him staggering. He came about in a drunken semicircle, glimpsing Wilson's black-bearded face. The outlaw was straddling the wall, preparing to leap down inside before he fired again. Mac's last bullet broke his neck and dropped him at the foot of the wall, flopping for a dozen seconds like a beheaded chicken.

In the deafening silence that followed the roar of the guns, Mac turned back toward the hut, blood streaming down his shirt. The pale girl cowered in the door, still uncertain as to her fate. His first words reassured her.

"Don't be scairt, Miss. I come to take you back to your dad."

Then she was clinging to him, weeping in hysterical relief.

"Oh, you're hurt! You're bleeding!"

"Just a slug in my shoulder," he grunted, self-conscious. "Ain't nothin'."

"Let me dress it," she begged, and he followed her into the hut. She avoided looking at Bissett, sprawling in a red pool, as she bound up Mac's shoulder with strips torn from her dress, fumbling and clumsily.

"I—I misjudged you," she faltered. "I'm sorry. The Kid—he was a beast—my father—" She choked on the words.

"Your dad's all right," he assured her. "Just drilled through the shoulder, like me. Some rotten shootin' in these parts. Couple of horses saddled at the mouth of the tunnel. Go on out there and wait for me."

After she had gone, he began a hasty search. And presently he desisted, swearing. Neither the pockets of the dead chief nor a hasty ransacking of the rooms rewarded him with what he sought. The money taken from Ellis had gone to join the rest of Bissett's loot, in whatever crypt he had hidden it. Surely he had planned, some day, a flight to some other continent with his plunder. But wherever it was, it was well hidden; a man might hunt it for years, in vain. And Big Mac had not time for hunting. Bissett might have been lying when he said he had other men, out on a raid, but with the girl, Mac could not take the chance of being caught by returning outlaws. He hurried from the hut.

The girl had already mounted Campbell's roan. A few minutes later they were riding together down the outer canyon.

"I found that thousand Checotah took off your dad," he announced, handing her a wad of dingy greenbacks. "Next time don't tell nobody about it."

"You're a guardian angel," she said faintly. "It was all we had—we'd have starved without it—I don't know how I can ever thank you—"

"Aw, shucks, don't try!"

His shoulder hurt, but another, deeper sting was gone, and Big Mac grinned contentedly, even as he slapped his flat pocket, and reflected on the dusty miles back to the Lazy K in Texas where the job he had quit still awaited him; after all, he reckoned he could get along another year without a vacation.

Ace High

Slim white fingers
Cutting the pack,
Never they linger
Upon a stack.
Hands of a singer's,
An artist's, a bard's,
Slim white fingers
Dealing the cards.

The Ballad of Buckshot Roberts

(Killed on the Tularosa River, New Mexico,
1878, in the bloody Lincoln County War.)

Buckshot Roberts was a Texas man;
(Blue smoke drifting from the piñons on the hill.)
Exiled from the plains where his rugged life began.
(Buzzards circling low over old Blazer Mill.)

On the floor of 'dobe, dying, he lay,
Holding thirteen men at bay.
Thirteen men of the desert's best,
True born sons of the stark Southwest,
Men from granite and iron hewed —
Riding the trail of the Lincoln feud.
Fighters of steely nerve and will —
But they saw John Middleton lying still
In the thick dust clotted dark and brown,
Where Roberts' bullet cut him down.
So they crouched in cover, on belly or knee,
Warily firing from bush and tree.
Even Billy the Kid held hard his hate,
Waiting his chance as a wolf might wait,
His cold gaze fixed on the brooding Mill,
Where the black muzzle gleamed on the window sill.
There on the floor Bill Roberts lay,
His life in a red stream ebbing away.
Weather-beaten and gnarled and scarred,
Grown old in a land where life was hard.
Soldier, ranger and pioneer,
Rawhide son of the Last Frontier.
Indian forays and border wars

Had left their mark in his many scars.
He had coursed with Death — and the pace was fast!
But he knew he had reached the end at last.
Shot through and through and nearly done —
Close he huddled his buffalo gun,
Propped the barrel on the window sill —
The firing ceased and the land was still.
They knew he had taken his mortal wound,
And they waited like silent wolves around.
All but Dick Brewer who led the band:
His fury burned him like a brand.
Reckless he rose in his savage ire,
Stood in the open to aim and fire.
Roberts laughed in a ghastly croak,
His finger crooked and the old gun spoke.
Blue smoke spat and the whistling lead
Tore off the top of Brewer's head.
Roberts laughed and the red tide welled
Up to his lips — the echoes belled
Clear and far — then faint and far,
Like a haunting call from a twilight star.
The gnarled hands slid from the worn old gun;
A lark flashed up in the golden sun;
A mountain breeze went quivering past —
So he came to the long trail's end at last.

Buckshot Roberts was a Texas man,
(Nightwinds sighing over Ruidosa-way.)
Heart and blood and marrow of a fighting clan!
(As the Tularosa whispers in the dawning of the day.)

The End of the Glory Trail

One man fought for a creed, and one
For freedom to speak, to think, to feel.
On the brow of a cliff that the shadows shun
They closed and the wild goats watched them reel.

　　One for a creed
　　And one to be freed.
　　On the edge of a ledge
　　Where the high winds dreed.

　　And below on the stones
　　Where the river drones
　　'Mid the rocks feasts a fox
　　On a heap of bones.

The Alamo

For days they ringed us with their flame,
For days their swarming soldiers came,
    The battle wrack was gory.
We perished in the smoke and flame,
To give the world their traitor shame
    And our undying glory.

San Jacinto (1)

Flowers bloom on San Jacinto,
Red and white and blue.
Long ago o'er San Jacinto
Wheeling vultures flew.
Long ago on San Jacinto
Soared the battle-smoke;
Long ago on San Jacinto
Wild ranks smote and broke.
Crimson clouds o'er San Jacinto,
Scarlet was the haze —
Peaceful o'er calm San Jacinto
Glide the drowsy days.

San Jacinto (2)

Red field of glory
Ye knew the wild story;
Blazing and gory
Were ye on that day!
Silence before them,
(Warriors; winds bore them!)
Red silence o'er them
Followed the fray!

Horror was dawning!
Furies were spawning!
Hell's maw was yawning,
Fate rode astride!
Skies rent asunder!
Plains a-reel under
Feet beating thunder!
Death raced beside!

Doom-trumps were pealing!
Armies were reeling!
Satan was dealing
The cards in that game!
War-clouds unfurling!
Hell-fires were swirling,
Valkyries whirling
Fanned them to flame!

Redly arrayed there
Glittered the blade there!
Many a shade there
Fled to the deeps!
Wild was the glory!
Down the years hoary
Still the red story
Surges and leaps!

Ghost Dancers

Night has come over ridge and hill
    Where the Badlands starkly lie
Like the tortured fane of a god insane
    That mocks the brooding sky.
The last faint rose of the twilight goes
    And magic's abroad tonight;
There's an eery sheen in the lean ravine
    And witch-fire on the height.
For bleak stars blink in the dusky sky
    And glitter on shield and lance;
In bands o'er the sands of the Shadowlands
    The phantoms come to dance.
They glide, they ride, through the dim night tide,
    Warrior and chief and brave,
Whose bones are strown from the Yellowstone
    To the lake of the Little Slave.
They ride where the mesas dimly lift
    And a wind that shrills and thrills
Drones o'er the stones and the gleaming bones
    That litter the shadowed hills.
Strange and vague through the pale starlight
    Glimmers each painted face
As they creep and leap where the shadows sleep
    In the Ghost Dance of their race.
Row upon row bent low they go
    Then whirl with a sudden bound,
With a rhythmic beat of their fleet lean feet,
    To a drum that makes no sound.

And the bleak stars wave their silver brands
    In the night-sky's dusky blue,
And silence reigns o'er the barren lands
    And the ghosts of the dancing Sioux.

Intro to the Mexico Set of Poems
(editor comment)

The next poem, along with the three that follow it, all feature people going to Mexico at the end of each respective poem. Perhaps this was meant to be the lead up to a story.

The Bandit

Out of the Texas desert, over the Rio Grande,
A young, cold-eyed cowpuncher
Rode into the Mexican land.
With a posse just behind him,
And the desert just before,
He had his horse, his guns and grub,
Think you he wished for more?
He took his life as he found it,
Nor cared where he might go.
So with a shrug of his shoulders,
He rode into Mexico.
He worked on a Mexican rancho,
He roved in a bandit band,
He fought in a Mexican army,
He hunted gold in the river's sand.
He fought the Mexican rurales,
And shot their leader down,
He robbed a Mexican gambling-hall,
He looted a Mexican town.
In the land of his race's foemen,
He did about as he willed,
When they submitted he robbed them
And when they resisted he killed.
The Mexicans would gladly have slain him,
But they dared not meet face to face,
For his was the speed of the gunman,
And his was the pride of race.
So he drifted all over the country,

And he travelled ahead of the news
Of his coming, so finally he landed
In old Vera Cruz.

Farewell, Proud Munster

Night in the county of Donegal,
A castle on the moor,
The sound of music and dancing
Came through the open door;

Sounds of merry revelry
Came from the splendid hall,
Where the prosperous English landlord
Was giving a courtly ball.

A flash of fire from the thicket bog,
The crash of a slamming door,
A yell of fright from the castle,
A low voiced curse from the moor.

A shadowy form in the thicket
With a musket in its hand,
"Bad cess to me aim, I've missed him,
"And now I must l'ave the land.
"Farewell for a whoile, proud Munster,
"Make merry whoile yez may,
"For be the saints, Michael Leary
"Will return to Erin some day!"

He struck the nearest seaport,
He gave the officers the slip,
He gained the pier and stowed away
In the most convenient ship.

The ship sailed in an hour
And, though that he did not know,
It was a trading vessel
And was bound for Mexico.

Over the Old Rio Grandey

Over the old Rio Grandey,
Fifty-odd years ago,
Me and Bill Garfield and Hawkins,
Rode into Mexico.
Bill Garfield and Happy Hawkins,
Down from a Wyoming ranch;
The posse was just behind us
And so we took a chance.
We had to get out of the U.S. quick,
We couldn't pick where to go.
Anyway, there was little to pick from,
So we slid into Mexico.

The Trail of Gold

Come with me to the Land of Sunrise,
The land in the days of old,
And with the Five Free Comrades,
We'll follow the trail of gold.
Over the sands of the deserts,
And through the jungles old,
Over the ancient mountains,
Yes, the trail of gold.

The Weird West

The Horror from the Mound

Steve Brill did not believe in ghosts or demons. Juan Lopez did. But neither the caution of the one nor the sturdy skepticism of the other was shield against the horror that fell upon them—the horror forgotten by men for more than three hundred years—a screaming fear monstrously resurrected from the black lost ages.

Yet as Steve Brill sat on his sagging stoop that last evening, his thoughts were as far from uncanny menaces as the thoughts of man can be. His ruminations were bitter but materialistic. He surveyed his farmland and he swore. Brill was tall, rangy and tough as boot leather—true son of the iron-bodied pioneers who wrenched West Texas from the wilderness. He was browned by the sun and strong as a longhorn steer. His lean legs and the boots on them reflected his cowboy habits and instincts, and now he cursed himself that he had ever climbed off the hurricane deck of his crank-eyed mustang and turned to farming. He was no farmer, the young puncher admitted profanely.

Yet his failure had not all been his fault. Plentiful rain in the winter—rare enough in West Texas—had given promise of good crops. But as usual, things had happened. A late blizzard had destroyed all the budding fruit. The grain which had looked so promising was ripped to shreds and battered into the ground by terrific hailstorms just as it was turning yellow. A period of intense dryness, followed by another hailstorm, finished the corn.

Then the cotton, which had somehow struggled through, fell before a swarm of grasshoppers which stripped Brill's field almost overnight. So Brill sat and swore that he would not renew his lease— he gave fervent thanks that he did not own the land on which he had wasted his sweat, and that there were still broad rolling ranges to the west where a strong young man could make his living riding and roping.

Now as Brill sat glumly, he was aware of the approaching form of his nearest neighbor, Juan Lopez, a taciturn old Mexican who lived in a hut just out of sight over the hill across the creek, and grubbed for a living. At present he was clearing a strip of land on an adjoining farm, and in returning to his hut he crossed a corner of Brill's pasture.

Brill idly watched him climb through the barbed-wire fence and trudge along the path he had worn in the short dry grass. He had been working at his present job for over a month now, chopping down tough gnarly mesquite trees and digging up their incredibly long roots, and Brill knew that he always followed the same path home. And watching, Brill noted him swerving far aside, seemingly to avoid a low rounded hillock which jutted above the level of the pasture. Lopez went far around this knoll and Brill remembered that the old Mexican always circled it at a distance. And another thing came into Brill's idle mind—Lopez always increased his gait when he was passing the knoll, and he always managed to get by it before sundown—yet Mexican laborers generally worked from the first light of dawn to the last glint of twilight, especially at these grubbing jobs, when they were paid by the acre and not by the day. Brill's curiosity was aroused.

He rose, and sauntering down the slight slope on the crown of which his shack sat, hailed the plodding Mexican.

"Hey, Lopez, wait a minute."

Lopez halted, looked about, and remained motionless but unenthusiastic as the white man approached.

"Lopez," said Brill lazily, "it ain't none of my business, but I just wanted to ask you—how come you always go so far around that old Indian mound?"

"No sabe," grunted Lopez shortly.

"You're a liar," responded Brill genially. "You savvy all right; you speak English as good as me. What's the matter—you think that mound's ha'nted or somethin'?"

Brill could speak Spanish himself, and read it, too, but like most Anglo-Saxons he much preferred to speak his own language.

Lopez shrugged his shoulders.

"It is not a good place, *no bueno,*" he muttered, avoiding Brill's eye. "Let hidden things rest."

"I reckon you're scared of ghosts," Brill bantered. "Shucks, if that is an Indian mound, them Indians been dead so long their ghosts 'ud be wore plumb out by now."

Brill knew that the illiterate Mexicans looked with superstitious aversion on the mounds that are found here and there through the Southwest—relics of a past and forgotten age, containing the moldering bones of chiefs and warriors of a lost race.

"Best not to disturb what is hidden in the earth," grunted Lopez.

"Bosh," said Brill. "Me and some boys busted into one of them mounds over in the Palo Pinto country and dug up pieces of a skeleton with some heads and flint arrowheads and the like. I kept some of the teeth a long time till I lost 'em, and I ain't never been ha'nted."

"Indians?" snorted Lopez unexpectedly. "Who spoke of Indians? There have been more than Indians in this country. In the old times strange things happened here. I have heard the tales of my people, handed down from generation to generation. And my people were here long before yours, *Señor* Brill."

"Yeah, you're right," admitted Steve. "First white men in this country was Spaniards, of course. Coronado passed along not very far from here, I hear-tell, and Hernando de Estrada's expedition came through here—away back yonder—I dunno how long ago."

"In 1545," said Lopez. "They pitched camp yonder where your corral now stands."

Brill turned to glance at his rail-fenced corral, inhabited now by his saddle pony, a pair of work horses and a scrawny cow.

"How come you know so much about it?" he asked curiously.

"One of my ancestors marched with de Estrada," answered Lopez. "A soldier, Porfirio Lopez; he told his son of that expedition, and he told *his* son, and so down the family line to me, who have no son to whom I can tell the tale."

"I didn't know you were so well connected," said Brill. "Maybe you know somethin' about the gold de Estrada was supposed to have hid around here somewhere."

"There was no gold," growled Lopez. "De Estrada's soldiers bore only their arms, and they fought their way through hostile country—many left their bones along the trail. Later—many years later—a mule train from Santa Fe was attacked not many miles from here by Comanches and they hid their gold and escaped; so the legends got mixed up. But even their gold is not there now, because Gringo buffalo-hunters found it and dug it up."

Brill nodded abstractedly, hardly heeding. Of all the continent of North America there is no section so haunted by tales of lost or hidden treasure as is the Southwest. Uncounted wealth passed back and forth over the hills and plains of Texas and New Mexico in the old days when Spain owned the gold and silver mines of the New World and controlled the rich fur trade of the West, and echoes of that wealth linger on in tales of golden caches. Some such vagrant dream, born of failure and pressing poverty, rose in Brill's mind.

Aloud he spoke: "Well, anyway, I got nothin' else to do, and I believe I'll dig into that old mound and see what I can find."

The effect of that simple statement on Lopez was nothing short of shocking. He recoiled and his swarthy brown face went ashy; his black eyes flared and he threw up his arms in a gesture of intense expostulation.

"*Dios, no!*" he cried. "Don't do that, *Señor* Brill! There is a curse—my grandfather told me—"

"Told you what?" asked Brill, as Lopez halted suddenly.

Lopez lapsed into sullen silence.

"I can not speak," he muttered. "I am sworn to silence. Only to an eldest son could I open my heart. But believe me when I say better had you cut your throat than to break into that accursed mound."

"Well," said Brill, impatient of Mexican superstitions, "if it's so bad, why don't you gimme a logical reason for not bustin' into it?"

"I can not speak!" cried the Mexican desperately. "I *know*—but I swore to silence on the Holy Crucifix, just as every man of my family has sworn. It is a thing so dark, it is to risk damnation even to speak of it! Were I to tell you, I would blast the soul from your body. But I have sworn—and I have no son, so my lips are sealed forever."

"Aw, well," said Brill sarcastically, "why don't you write it out?"

Lopez started, stared, and to Steve's surprize, caught at the suggestion.

"I will! *Dios* be thanked the good priest taught me to write when I was a child. My oath said nothing of writing. I only swore not to speak. I will write out the whole thing for you, if you will swear not to speak of it afterward, and to destroy the paper as soon as you have read it."

"Sure," said Brill, to humor him, and the old Mexican seemed much relieved.

"*Bueno!* I will go at once and write. Tomorrow as I go to work I will bring you the writing and you will understand why no one must open that accursed mound!"

And Lopez hurried along his homeward path, his stooped shoulders swaying with the effort of his unwonted haste. Steve grinned after him, shrugged his shoulders and turned back toward his own shack. Then he halted, gazing back at the low rounded mound with its grass-grown sides. It must be an Indian tomb, he decided, what of its symmetry and its similarity to other Indian mounds he had seen. He scowled as he tried to figure out the seeming connection between the mysterious knoll and the martial ancestor of Juan Lopez.

Brill gazed after the receding figure of the old Mexican. A shallow valley, cut by a half-dry creek, bordered with trees and underbrush, lay between Brill's pasture and the low sloping hill beyond which lay Lopez's shack. Among the trees along the creek bank the old Mexican was disappearing. And Brill came to a sudden decision.

Hurrying up the slight slope, he took a pick and a shovel from the tool shed built onto the back of his shack. The sun had not yet set and Brill believed he could open the mound deep enough to determine its nature by lantern light. Steve, like most of his breed, lived mostly by impulse, and his present urge was to tear into that mysterious hillock and find what, if anything, was concealed therein. The thought of treasure came again to his mind, piqued by the evasive attitude of Lopez.

What if, after all, that grassy heap of brown earth hid riches— virgin ore from forgotten mines, or the minted coinage of old Spain? Was it not possible that the musketeers of de Estrada had themselves reared that pile above a treasure they could not bear away, molding it in the likeness of an Indian mound to fool seekers? Did old Lopez know that? It would not be strange if, knowing of treasure there, the old Mexican refrained from disturbing it. Ridden with grisly superstitious fears, he might well live out a life of barren toil rather than risk the wrath of lurking ghosts or devils—for the Mexicans say that hidden gold is always accursed, and surely there was supposed to be some especial doom resting on this mound. Well, Brill meditated, Latin-Indian devils had no terrors for the Anglo-Saxon, tormented by the demons of drought and storm and crop failure.

Steve set to work with the savage energy characteristic of his breed. The task was no light one; the soil, baked by the fierce sun, was iron hard, and mixed with rocks and pebbles. Brill sweated profusely and grunted with his efforts, but the fire of the treasure hunter was on him. He shook the sweat out of his eyes and drove in the pick with mighty strokes that ripped and crumbled the close-packed dirt.

The sun went down, and in the long dreamy summer twilight he worked on, oblivious to time or space. He began to be convinced that the mound was a genuine Indian tomb, as he found traces of charcoal in the soil. The ancient people which reared these sepulchers had kept fire burning upon them for days, at some point in the building. All the mounds Steve had ever opened had contained a solid stratum of charcoal a short distance below the surface. But the charcoal traces he found now were scattered about through the soil.

His idea of a Spanish-built treasure-trove faded, but he persisted. Who knows? Perhaps that strange folk men now call Mound Builders had treasure of their own which they laid away with the dead.

Then Steve yelped in exultation as his pick rang on a bit of metal. He snatched it up and held it close to his eyes, straining in the waning light. It was caked and corroded with rust, worn almost paper thin, but he knew it for what it was—a spur rowel, unmistakably Spanish with its long cruel points. And he halted, completely bewildered. No Spaniard ever reared this mound, with its undeniable marks of aboriginal workmanship. Yet how came that relic of Spanish caballeros hidden deep in the packed soil?

Brill shook his head and set to work again. He knew that in the center of the mound, if it were indeed an aboriginal tomb, he would find a narrow chamber built of heavy stones, containing the bones of the chief for which the mound had been reared and the victims sacrificed above it. And in the gathering darkness he felt his pick strike heavily against something granite-like and unyielding. Examination, by sense of feel as well as by sight, proved it to be a solid block of stone, roughly hewn. Doubtless it formed one of the ends of the death-chamber. Useless to try to shatter it. Brill chipped and pecked about it, scraping the dirt and pebbles away from the corners until he felt that wrenching it out would be but a matter of sinking the pick point underneath and levering it out.

But now he was suddenly aware that darkness had come on. In the young moon objects were dim and shadowy. His mustang nickered in the corral whence came the comfortable crunch of tired beasts' jaws on corn. A whippoorwill called eerily from the dark shadows of the narrow winding creek. Brill straightened reluctantly. Better get a lantern before continuing his explorations.

He felt in his pocket with some idea of wrenching out the stone and exploring the cavity with the aid of matches. Then he stiffened. Was it imagination that he heard a faint sinister rustling, which seemed to come from behind the blocking stone? Snakes! Doubtless they had holes somewhere about the base of the mound and there might be a dozen big diamond-backed rattlers coiled up in that cave-like interior waiting for him to put his hand among them. He shivered slightly at the thought and backed away out of the excavation he had made.

It wouldn't do to go poking about blindly into holes. And for the past few minutes, he realized, he had been aware of a faint foul odor exuding from interstices about the blocking stone—though he admitted that the smell suggested reptiles no more than it did any other menacing scent. It had a charnel-house reek about it— gases formed in the chamber of death, no doubt, and dangerous to the living.

Steve laid down his pick and returned to the house, impatient of the necessary delay. Entering the dark building, he struck a match and located his kerosene lantern hanging on its nail on the wall. Shaking it, he satisfied himself that it was nearly full of coal oil, and lighted it. Then he fared forth again, for his eagerness would not allow him to pause long enough for a bite of food. The mere opening of the mound intrigued him, as it must always intrigue a man of imagination, and the discovery of the Spanish spur had whetted his curiosity.

He hurried from his shack, the swinging lantern casting long distorted shadows ahead of him and behind. He chuckled as he visualized Lopez's actions when he learned, on the morrow, that the forbidden mound had been pried into. A good thing he had opened it that evening, Brill reflected; Lopez might even have tried to prevent him meddling with it, had he known.

In the dreamy hush of the summer night, Brill reached the mound—lifted his lantern—swore bewilderedly. The lantern revealed his excavations, his tools lying carelessly where he had dropped them—and a black gaping aperture! The great blocking stone lay in the bottom of the excavation, as if thrust carelessly aside. Warily he thrust the lantern forward and peered into the small cave-like chamber, expecting to see he knew not what. Nothing met his eyes except the bare rock sides of a long narrow cell, large enough to receive a man's body, which had apparently been built up of roughly hewn square-cut stones, cunningly joined together.

"Lopez!" exclaimed Steve furiously. "The dirty coyote! He's been watchin' me work—and when I went after the lantern, he snuck up and pried the rock out—and grabbed whatever was in there, I reckon. Blast his greasy hide, I'll fix him!"

Savagely he extinguished the lantern and glared across the shallow, brush-grown valley. And as he looked he stiffened. Over the corner of the hill, on the other side of which stood the shack of Lopez, a shadow moved. The slender moon was setting, the light dim and the play of the shadows baffling. But Steve's eyes were sharpened by the sun and winds of the wastelands, and he knew that it was some two-legged creature that was disappearing over the low shoulder of the mesquite-grown hill.

"Beatin' it to his shack," snarled Brill. "He's shore got somethin' or he wouldn't be travelin' at that speed."

Brill swallowed, wondering why a peculiar trembling had suddenly taken hold of him. What was there unusual about a thieving old Greaser running home with his loot? Brill tried to drown the feeling that there was something peculiar about the gait of the dim shadow, which had seemed to move at a sort of slinking lope. There must have been need for swiftness when stocky old Juan Lopez elected to travel at such a strange pace.

"Whatever he found is as much mine as his," swore Brill, trying to get his mind off the abnormal aspect of the figure's flight. "I got this land leased, and I done all the work diggin'. A curse, hell! No wonder he told me that stuff. Wanted me to leave it alone so he could get it hisself. It's a wonder he ain't dug it up long before this. But you can't never tell about them Spigs."

Brill, as he meditated thus, was striding down the gentle slope of the pasture which led down to the creek bed. He passed into the shadows of the trees and dense underbrush and walked across the dry creek-bed, noting absently that neither whippoorwill nor hoot owl called in the darkness. There was a waiting, listening tenseness in the night that he did not like. The shadows in the creek bed seemed too thick, too breathless. He wished he had not blown out the lantern, which he still carried, and was glad he had brought the pick, gripped like a battle-ax in his right hand. He had an impulse to whistle, just to break the silence, then swore and dismissed the thought. Yet he was glad when he clambered up the low opposite bank and emerged into the starlight.

He walked up the slope and onto the hill, and looked down on the mesquite flat wherein stood Lopez's squalid hut. A light showed at the one window.

"Packin' his things for a getaway, I reckon," grunted Steve. "Ow, what the—"

He staggered as from a physical impact as a frightful scream knifed the stillness. He wanted to clap his hands over his ears to shut out the horror of that cry, which rose unbearably and then broke in an abhorrent gurgle.

"Good God!" Cold sweat sprung out on Steve. "Lopez—or somebody—"

Even as he gasped the words he was running down the hill as fast as his long legs could carry him. Some unspeakable horror was taking place in that lonely hut, but he was going to investigate if it meant facing the Devil himself. He gripped his pick handle as he ran. Wandering prowlers, murdering old Lopez for the loot he had taken from the mound, Steve thought, and forgot his wrath. It would go hard for anyone he caught molesting the old scoundrel, thief though he might be.

He hit the flat, running hard. And then the light in the hut went out and Steve staggered in full flight, bringing up against a mesquite tree with an impact that jolted a grunt out of him and tore his hands on the thorns. Rebounding with a sobbed curse, he rushed for the shack, nerving himself for what he might see—his hair still standing on end at what he had already seen.

Brill tried the one door of the hut and found it bolted within. He shouted to Lopez and received no answer. Yet utter silence did not reign. From within came a curious muffled worrying sound, that ceased as Brill swung his pick crashing against the door. The flimsy portal splintered and Brill leaped into the dark hut, eyes blazing, pick swung high for a desperate onslaught. But no sound ruffled the grisly silence, and in the darkness nothing stirred, though Brill's chaotic imagination peopled the shadowed corners of the hut with shapes of horror.

With a hand damp with perspiration he found a match and struck it. Besides himself only Lopez occupied the hut—old Lopez, stark dead on the dirt floor, arms spread wide like a crucifix, mouth sagging open in a semblance of idiocy, eyes wide and staring with a horror Brill found intolerable. The one window gaped open, showing the method of the slayer's exit—possibly his entrance as well. Brill went to that window and gazed out warily. He saw only the sloping hillside on one hand and the mesquite flat on the other. He started—was that a hint of movement among the stunted shadows of the mesquites and chaparral—or had he but imagined he glimpsed a dim loping figure among the trees?

He turned back, as the match burned down to his fingers. He lit the old coal oil lamp on the rude table, cursing as he burned his hand. The globe of the lamp was very hot, as if it had been burning for hours.

Reluctantly he turned to the corpse on the floor. Whatever sort of death had come to Lopez, it had been horrible, but Brill, gingerly examining the dead man, found no wound—no mark of knife or bludgeon on him. Wait! There was a thin smear of blood on Brill's questing fingers. Searching, he found the source—three or four tiny punctures in Lopez's throat, from which blood had oozed sluggishly. At first he thought they had been inflicted with a stiletto—a thin round edgeless dagger. He had seen stiletto wounds—he had the scar of one on his own body. These wounds more resembled the bite of some animal—they looked like the marks of pointed fangs.

Yet Brill did not believe they were deep enough to have caused death, nor had much blood flowed from them. A belief, abhorrent with grisly potentialities, rose up in the dark corners of his mind—that Lopez had died of fright, and that the wounds had been inflicted either simultaneously with his death, or an instant afterward.

And Steve noticed something else; scattered about on the floor lay a number of dingy leaves of paper, scrawled in the old Mexican's crude hand—he would write of the curse on the mound, he had said. There were the sheets on which he had written, there was the stump of a pencil on the floor, there was the hot lamp globe, all mute witnesses that the old Mexican had been seated at the rough-hewn table writing for hours. Then it was not he who opened the mound chamber and stole the contents—but who was it, in God's name? And who or what was it that Brill had glimpsed loping over the shoulder of the hill?

Well, there was but one thing to do—saddle his mustang and ride the ten miles to Coyote Wells, the nearest town, and inform the sheriff of the murder.

Brill gathered up the papers. The last was crumpled in the old man's clutching hand and Brill secured it with some difficulty. Then as he turned to extinguish the light, he hesitated, and cursed himself for the crawling fear that lurked at the back of his mind—fear of the shadowy thing he had seen cross the window just before the light went out in the hut. The long arm of the murderer, he thought, reaching to extinguish the lamp, no doubt. What had there been abnormal or inhuman about the vision, distorted though it must have been in the dim lamplight and shadow? As a man strives to remember the details of a nightmare dream, Steve tried to define in his mind some clear reason that would explain why that flying glimpse had unnerved him to the extent of blundering headlong into a tree, and why the mere vague remembrance of it now caused cold sweat to break out on him.

Cursing himself to keep up his courage, he lighted his lantern, blew out the lamp on the rough table, and resolutely set forth, grasping his pick like a weapon. After all, why should certain seemingly abnormal aspects about a sordid murder upset him? Such crimes were revolting, but common enough, especially among Mexicans, who cherished unguessed feuds.

Then as he stepped into the silent star-flecked night he brought up short. From across the creek sounded the sudden soul-shaking scream of a horse in deadly terror—then a mad drumming of hoofs that receded in the distance. Brill swore in rage and dismay. Was it a panther lurking in the hills—had a monstrous cat slain old Lopez?

Then why was not the victim marked with the scars of fierce hooked talons? *And who extinguished the light in the hut?*

As he wondered, Brill was running swiftly toward the dark creek. Not lightly does a cowpuncher regard the stampeding of his stock. As he passed into the darkness of the brush along the dry creek, Brill found his tongue strangely dry. He kept swallowing, and he held the lantern high. It made but faint impression in the gloom, but seemed to accentuate the blackness of the crowding shadows. For some strange reason, the thought entered Brill's chaotic mind that though the land was new to the Anglo-Saxon, it was in reality very old. That broken and desecrated tomb was mute evidence that the land was ancient to man, and suddenly the night and the hills and the shadows bore on Brill with a sense of hideous antiquity. Here had long generations of men lived and died before Brill's ancestors ever heard of the land. In the night, in the shadows of this very creek, men had no doubt given up their ghosts in grisly ways. With these reflections Brill hurried through the shadows of the thick trees.

He breathed deeply in relief when he emerged from the thickets on his own side. Hurrying up the gentle slope to the rail corral, he held up his lantern, investigating. The corral was empty; not even the placid cow was in sight. And the bars were down. That pointed to human agency, and the affair took on a newly sinister aspect. Someone did not intend that Brill should ride to Coyote Wells that night. It meant that the murderer intended making his getaway and wanted a good start on the law, or else—Brill grinned wryly. Far away across a mesquite flat he believed he could still catch the faint and faraway noise of running horses. What in God's name had given them such a fright? A cold finger of fear played shudderingly on Brill's spine.

Steve headed for the house. He did not enter boldly. He crept clear around the shack, peering shudderingly into the dark windows, listening with painful intensity for some sound to betray the presence of the lurking killer. At last he ventured to open a door and step in. He threw the door back against the wall to find if anyone were hiding behind it, lifted the lantern high and stepped in, heart pounding, pick gripped fiercely, his feelings a mixture of fear and red rage. But no hidden assassin leaped upon him, and a wary exploration of the shack revealed nothing suspicious.

With a sigh of relief he locked the doors, made fast the windows and lighted his old coal oil lamp. The thought of old Lopez lying, a glassy-eyed corpse alone in the hut across the creek, made him wince and shiver, but he did not intend to start for town on foot in the night.

He drew from its hiding place his reliable old Colt .45, spun the blue steel cylinder and grinned mirthlessly. Maybe the killer did not intend to leave any witnesses to his crime alive. Well, let him come! He—or they—would find a young cowpuncher with a six-shooter less easy prey than an old unarmed Mexican. And that reminded Brill of the papers he had brought from the hut. Taking care that he was not in line with a window through which a sudden bullet might come, he settled himself to read, with one ear alert for stealthy sounds.

And as he read the crude laborious script, a slow cold horror grew in his soul. It was a tale of fear that the old Mexican had scrawled—a tale handed down from generation to generation—a tale of ancient times.

And Brill read of the wanderings of the caballero Hernando de Estrada and his armored pikemen, who dared the deserts of the Southwest when all was strange and unknown. There were some forty-odd soldiers, servants, and masters, at the beginning, the manuscript ran. There was the captain, de Estrada, and the priest, and young Juan Zavilla, and Don Santiago de Valdez—a mysterious nobleman who had been taken off a helplessly floating ship in the Caribbean Sea—all the others of the crew and passengers had died of plague, he had said, and he had cast their bodies overboard. So de Estrada had taken him aboard the ship that was bearing the expedition from Spain, and de Valdez had joined them in their explorations.

Brill read something of their wanderings, told in the crude style of old Lopez, as the old Mexican's ancestors had handed down the tale for over three hundred years. The bare written words dimly reflected the terrific hardships the explorers had encountered—drought, thirst, floods, the desert sandstorms, the spears of hostile redskins. But it was of another peril that old Lopez told—a grisly lurking horror that fell upon the lonely caravan wandering through the immensity of the wild. Man by man they fell and no man knew the slayer. Fear and black suspicion ate at the heart of the expedition like a canker, and their leader knew not where to turn. This they all knew: among them was a fiend in human form.

Men began to draw apart from each other, to scatter along the line of march, and this mutual suspicion, that sought security in solitude, played into the talons of the fiend. The skeleton of the expedition staggered through the wilderness, lost, dazed and helpless, and still the unseen horror hung on their flanks, dragging down the stragglers, preying on drowsing sentries and sleeping men. And on the throat of each was found the wounds of pointed fangs that bled the victim white, so the living knew with what manner of evil they had to deal. Men reeled through the wild, calling on the saints, or blaspheming in their terror, fighting frenziedly against sleep, until they fell with exhaustion and sleep stole on them with horror and death.

Suspicion centered on a great black man, a cannibal slave from Calabar. And they put him in chains. But young Juan Zavilla went the way of the rest, and then the priest was taken. But the priest fought off his fiendish assailant and lived long enough to gasp the demon's name to de Estrada. And Brill read:

". . . And now it was evident to de Estrada that the good priest had spoken the truth, and the slayer was Don Santiago de Valdez, who was a vampire, an undead fiend, subsisting on the blood of the living. And de Estrada called to mind a certain foul nobleman who had lurked in the mountains of Castile since the days of the Moors, feeding off the blood of helpless victims which lent him a ghastly immortality. This nobleman had been driven forth; none knew where he had fled, but it was evident that he and Don Santiago were the same man. He had fled Spain by ship, and de Estrada knew that the people of the ship had died, not by plague as the fiend had represented, but by the fangs of the vampire.

"De Estrada and the black man and the few soldiers who still lived went searching for him and found him stretched in bestial sleep in a clump of chaparral; full-gorged he was with human blood from his last victim. Now it is well known that a vampire, like a great serpent, when well gorged, falls into a deep sleep and may be taken without peril. But de Estrada was at a loss as to how to dispose of the monster, for how may the dead be slain? For a vampire is a man who has died long ago, yet is quick with a certain foul *unlife*.

"The men urged that the Caballero drive a stake through the fiend's heart and cut off his head, uttering the holy words that would crumble the long-dead body into dust, but the priest was dead and de Estrada feared that in the act the monster might awaken.

"So they lifted Don Santiago softly, and bore him to an old Indian mound nearby. This they opened, taking forth the bones they found there, and they placed the vampire within and sealed up the mound—*Dios* grant till Judgment Day.

"It is a place accursed, and I wish I had starved elsewhere before I came into this part of the country seeking work—for I have known of the land and the creek and the mound with its terrible secret, ever since childhood; so you see, *Señor* Brill, why you must not open the mound and wake the fiend—"

There the manuscript ended with an erratic scratch of the pencil that tore the crumpled leaf.

Brill rose, his heart pounding wildly, his face bloodless, his tongue cleaving to his palate. He gagged and found words.

"That's why the spur was in the mound—one of them Spaniards dropped it while they was diggin'—I mighta knowed it'd been dug into before, the way the charcoal was scattered out—but, good God—"

Aghast he shrank from the black visions evoked—an undead monster stirring in the gloom of his tomb, thrusting from within to push aside the stone loosened by the pick of ignorance—a shadowy shape loping over the hill toward a light that betokened a human prey—a frightful long arm that crossed a dim-lighted window . . .

"It's madness!" he gasped. "Lopez was plumb loco! They ain't no such things as vampires! If they is, why didn't he get me first, instead of Lopez—unless he was scoutin' around, makin' sure of everything before he pounced? Aw, hell! It's all a pipe-dream—"

The words froze in his throat. At the window a face glared and gibbered soundlessly at him. Two icy eyes pierced his very soul. A shriek burst from his throat and that ghastly visage vanished. But the very air was permeated by the foul scent that had hung about the ancient mound. And now the door creaked—bent slowly inward. Brill backed up against the wall, his gun shaking in his hand. It did not occur to him to fire through the door; in his chaotic brain he had but one thought—that only that thin portal of wood separated him from some horror born out of the womb of night and gloom and the black past. His eyes were distended as he saw the door give, as he heard the staples of the bolt groan.

The door burst inward. Brill did not scream. His tongue was frozen to the roof of his mouth. His fear-glazed eyes took in the tall, vulture-like form—the icy eyes, the long black fingernails—the moldering garb, hideously ancient—the long-spurred boots—the slouch hat with its crumbling feather—the flowing cloak that was falling to slow shreds. Framed in the black doorway crouched that abhorrent shape out of the past, and Brill's brain reeled. A savage coldness radiated from the figure—the scent of moldering clay and charnel-house refuse. And then the undead came at the living like a swooping vulture.

Brill fired pointblank and saw a shred of rotten cloth fly from the Thing's breast. The vampire reeled beneath the impact of the heavy ball, then righted itself and came on with frightful speed. Brill reeled back against the wall with a choking cry, the gun falling from his nerveless hand. The black legends were true, then—human weapons were powerless—for may a man kill one already dead for long centuries, as mortals die?

Then the clawlike hands at his throat roused the young cow-puncher to a frenzy of madness. As his pioneer ancestors fought hand to hand against brain-shattering odds, Steve Brill fought the cold dead crawling thing that sought his life and his soul.

Of that ghastly battle Brill never remembered much. It was a blind chaos in which he screamed beastlike, tore and slugged and hammered, where long black nails like the talons of a panther tore at him, and pointed teeth snapped again and again at his throat. Rolling and tumbling about the room, both half-enveloped by the musty folds of that ancient rotting cloak, they battered and rended one another among the ruins of the shattered furniture, and the fury of the vampire was not more terrible than the fear-crazed desperation of its victim.

They crashed headlong into the table, knocking it over upon its side, and the coal oil lamp splintered on the floor, spraying the walls with sudden flame. Brill felt the bite of the burning oil that splattered him, but in the red frenzy of the fight he gave no heed. The black talons were tearing at him, the inhuman eyes burning icily into his soul; between his frantic fingers the withered flesh of the monster was hard as dry wood. And wave after wave of blind madness swept over Steve Brill. Like a man battling a nightmare he screamed and smote, while all about them the fire leaped up and caught at the walls and roof.

Through darting jets and licking tongues of flame they reeled and rolled like a demon and a mortal warring on the fire-lanced floors of hell. And in the growing tumult of the flames, Brill gathered himself for one volcanic burst of effort. Breaking away and staggering up, gasping and bloody, he lunged blindly at the foul shape and caught it in a grip not even the vampire could break. And whirling his fiendish assailant on high, he dashed it down across the uptilted edge of the fallen table as a man might break a stick of wood across his knee. Something cracked like a snapping branch and the vampire fell from Brill's grasp to writhe in a strange broken posture on the burning floor. Yet it was not dead, for its flaming eyes still burned on Brill with a ghastly hunger, and it strove to crawl toward him with its broken spine, as a dying snake crawls.

Brill, reeling and gasping, shook the blood from his eyes, and staggered blindly through the broken door. And as a man runs from the portals of hell, he ran stumblingly through the mesquite and chaparral until he fell from utter exhaustion. Looking back he saw the flames of the burning house cutting the night, and thanked God that it would burn until the very bones of Don Santiago de Valdez were utterly consumed and destroyed from the knowledge of men.

The Valley of the Lost

As a wolf spies upon its hunters, John Reynolds watched his pursuers. He lay close in a thicket on the slope, an inferno of hate seething in his heart. He had ridden hard; up the slope behind him, where the dim path wound up out of Lost Valley, his crank-eyed mustang stood, head drooping, trembling, after the long run. Below him, not more than eighty yards away, stood his enemies, fresh come from the slaughter of his kinsmen.

In the clearing fronting Ghost Cave they had dismounted and were arguing among themselves. John Reynolds knew them all with an old, bitter hate. The black shadow of feud lay between them and himself.

The feuds of early Texas have been neglected by chroniclers who have sung the feuds of the Kentucky mountains, yet the men who first settled the Southwest were of the same breed as those mountaineers. But there was a difference; in the mountain country feuds dragged on for generations; on the Texas frontier they were short, fierce and appallingly bloody.

The Reynolds-McCrill feud was long, as Texas feuds went: fifteen years had passed since old Esau Reynolds stabbed young Braxton McCrill to death with his bowie knife in the saloon at Antelope Wells, in a quarrel over range rights. For fifteen years the Reynoldses and their kin—the Brills, Allisons and Donnellys—had been at open war with the McCrills and their kin—the Killihers, the Fletchers and the Ords. There had been ambushes in the hills, murders on the open range, and gun fights on the streets of the little cowtowns. Each clan had rustled the other's cattle wholesale. Gunmen and outlaws, called in by both sides to participate for pay, had spread a reign of terror and lawlessness throughout the vicinity.

Settlers shunned the war-torn range; the feud became a red obstacle in the way of progress and development, a savage retrogression which was demoralizing the whole countryside.

Little John Reynolds cared. He had grown up in the atmosphere of the feud, and it had become a burning obsession with him. The war had taken fearful toll on both clans, but the Reynoldses had suffered most. John was the last of the fighting Reynoldses, for old Esau, the grim old patriarch who ruled the clan, would never again walk or sit in a saddle, with his legs paralyzed by McCrill bullets. John had seen his brothers shot down, from ambush or in pitched battles.

Now the last stroke had nearly wiped out the waning clan. John Reynolds cursed as he thought of the trap into which they had walked in the saloon at Antelope Wells, where without warning their hidden foes had opened their murderous fire. There had fallen his cousin, Bill Donnelly; his sister's son, young Jonathon Brill; his brother-in-law, Job Allison; and Steve Kerney, the hired gunman. How he himself had shot his way through and gained the hitching rack, untouched by that blasting hail of lead, John Reynolds hardly knew. They had pressed him so closely he had not had time to mount his long limbed rangy bay, but had been forced to take the first horse he came to—the crank eyed, speedy but short-winded mustang of the dead Jonathon Brill.

He had distanced his pursuers for a while, had gained the uninhabited hills and swung back into mysterious Lost Valley, with its silent thickets and crumbling stone columns, seeking to double back over the hills and gain the country of the Reynoldses. But the mustang had failed him. He had tied it up the slope, out of sight of the valley floor, and crept back to see his enemies ride into the valley. There were five of them: old Jonas McCrill, with the perpetual snarl twisting his wolfish lips; Saul Fletcher, with his black beard and the limping, dragging gait that a fall in his youth from a wild mustang had left him; Bill Ord and Peter Ord, brothers; and the outlaw Jack Solomon.

Jonas McCrill's voice came up to the silent watcher: "And I tell yuh he's a hidin' somewhere in this valley. He was a ridin' that mustang and it didn't never have no guts. I'm bettin' it give plumb out on him time he got this far."

"Well," it was the hated voice of Saul Fletcher, "what're we a standin' 'round pow-wowin' for? Why don't we start huntin' him?"

"Not so fast," growled old Jonas. "Remember it's John Reynolds we're a chasin'. We got plenty time."

John Reynolds' fingers hardened on the stock of his single action .45. There were two cartridges unfired in the cylinder. He pushed the muzzle through the stems of the thicket in front of him, his thumb drawing back the wicked fanged hammer. His grey eyes narrowed and became opaque as ice as he sighted down the long blue barrel. An instant he weighed his hatred, and chose Saul Fletcher. All the hate in his soul centered for an instant on that brutal, black-bearded face, and the limping tread he had heard that night he lay wounded in a besieged corral, with his brother's riddled corpse beside him, and fought off Saul and his brothers.

John Reynolds' finger crooked and the crash of the shot broke the echoes in the sleeping hills. Saul Fletcher swayed back, flinging his black beard drunkenly upward, and crashed face down and headlong. The others, with the quickness of men accustomed to frontier warfare, dropped behind rocks, and their answering shots roared back as they combed the slope blindly. The bullets tore through the thickets, whistling over the unseen killer's head. High up on the slope the mustang, out of sight of the men in the valley but frightened by the noise, screamed shrilly, and, rearing, snapped the reins that held him and fled away up the hill path. The drum of his hoofs on the stones dwindled in the distance.

Silence reigned for an instant, then came Jonas McCrill's wrathful voice: "I told yuh he was a ridin' here! Come outa there; he's got clean away."

The old fighter's rangy frame rose up from behind the rock where he had taken refuge. Reynolds, grinning fiercely, took steady aim; then some instinct of self-preservation held his hand. The others came out into the open.

"What are we a waitin' on?" yelled young Bill Ord, tears of rage in his eyes. "Here that coyote's done shot Saul and's ridin' hell for leather away from here, and we're a standin' 'round jawin'. I'm a goin' to—" he started for his horse.

"Yuh're a goin' to listen to me!" roared old Jonas. "I warned yuh-all to go slow, but yuh would come lickety split along like a bunch of blind buzzards, and now Saul's layin' there dead. If we ain't careful, John Reynolds'll kill all of us. Didn't I tell yuh all he was here? Likely stopped to rest his horse. He can't go far. This here's a long hunt, like I told yuh at first. Let him git a good start. Long as he's ahead of us, we got to watch out for ambushes. He'll try to git back onto the Reynolds range. Well, we're a goin' after him slow and easy and keep him hazed back all the time. We'll be a ridin' the inside of a big half circle and he can't git by us—not on that short-winded mustang. We'll just foller him and gather him in when his horse can't do no more. And I purty well know where he'll come to bay at—Blind Horse Canyon."

"We'll have to starve him out, then," growled Jack Solomon.

"No, we won't," grinned old Jonas. "Bill, you hightail it back to Antelope and git five or six sticks of dynamite. Then you git a fresh horse and follow our trail. If we catch him before he gits to the canyon, all right. If he beats us there and holes up, we'll wait for yuh, and then blast him out."

"What about Saul?" growled Peter Ord.

"He's dead," grunted Jonas. "Nothin' we can do for him now. No time to take him back." He glanced up at the sky, where already black dots wheeled against the blue. His gaze drifted to the walled-up mouth of the cavern in the steep cliff which rose at right angles to the slope up which the path wandered.

"We'll break open that cave and put him in it," he said. "We'll pile up the rocks again and the wolves and buzzards can't git to him. May be several days before we git back."

"That cave's ha'nted," uneasily muttered Bill Ord. "The Injuns always said if yuh put a dead man in there, he'd come walkin' out at midnight."

"Shet up and help pick up pore Saul," snapped Jonas. "Here's your own kin a layin' dead, and his murderer a ridin' further away every second, and you talk about ha'nts."

As they lifted the corpse, Jonas drew the longbarreled six-shooter from the holster and shoved the weapon into his own waistband.

"Pore Saul," he grunted. "He's shore dead. Shot plumb through the heart. Dead before he hit the ground, I reckon. Well, we'll make that damned Reynolds pay for it."

They carried the dead man to the cave, and, laying him down, attacked the rocks which blocked the entrance. These were soon torn aside, and Reynolds saw the men carry the body inside. They emerged almost immediately, minus their burden, and mounted their horses. Young Bill Ord swung away down the valley and vanished among the trees, and the rest cantered up the winding trail that led up into the hills. They passed within a hundred feet of his refuge and John Reynolds hugged the earth, fearing discovery. But they did not glance in his direction. He heard the dwindling of their hoofs over the rocky path; then silence settled again over the ancient valley.

John Reynolds rose cautiously, looked about him as a hunted wolf looks, then made his way quickly down the slope. He had a very definite purpose in mind. A single unfired cartridge was all his ammunition; but about the dead body of Saul Fletcher was a belt well filled with .45 caliber cartridges.

As he attacked the rocks heaped in the cave's mouth, there hovered in his mind the curious dim speculations which the cave and the valley itself always roused in him. Why had the Indians named it the Valley of the Lost, which white men shortened to Lost Valley? Why had the red men shunned it? Once in the memory of white men, a band of Kiowas, fleeing the vengeance of Bigfoot Wallace and his rangers, had taken up their abode there and fallen on evil times. The survivors of the tribe had fled, telling wild tales in which murder, fratricide, insanity, vampirism, slaughter and cannibalism had played grim parts. Then six white men, brothers—Stark by name—had settled in Lost Valley. They had reopened the cave which the Kiowas had blocked up. Horror had fallen on them and in one night five died by one another's hands. The survivor had walled up the cave mouth again and departed, where none knew, though word had drifted through the settlements of a man named Stark who had come among the remnants of those Kiowas who had once lived in Lost Valley, and, after long talk with them, had cut his own throat with his bowie knife.

What was the mystery of Lost Valley, if not a web of lies and legends? What the meaning of those crumbling stones, which, scattered all over the valley, half hidden in the climbing growth, bore a curious symmetry, especially in the moonlight, so that some people believed when the Indians swore they were the half-destroyed columns of a prehistoric city which once stood in Lost Valley? Reynolds himself had seen it, before it crumbled into a heap of grey dust, a skull unearthed at the base of a cliff by a wandering prospector, and which seemed neither Caucasian nor Indian—a curious, peaked skull, which but for the formation of the jawbones might have been that of some unknown antediluvian animal.

Such thoughts flitted vaguely and momentarily through John Reynolds' mind as he dislodged the boulders, which the McCrills had put back loosely, just firmly enough to keep a wolf or buzzard from squeezing through. In the main his thoughts were engrossed with the cartridges in dead Saul Fletcher's belt. A fighting chance! A lease on life! He would fight his way out of the hills yet; would gather the remnants of his clan and strike back. He would bring in more gunmen and cutthroats to reinforce the thinning ranks. He would flood the whole range with blood, and bring the countryside to ruin, if by those means he might be avenged. For years he had been the moving factor in the feud. When even old Esau had weakened and wished for peace, John Reynolds had kept the flame of hate blazing. The feud had become his one driving motive, his one interest in life and reason for existence. The last boulders fell aside.

John Reynolds stepped into the semi gloom of the cavern. It was not large, but the shadows seemed to cluster there in almost tangible substance. Slowly his eyes accustomed themselves; an involuntary exclamation broke from his lips—the cave was empty! He swore in bewilderment. He had seen men carry Saul Fletcher's corpse into the cave and come out again, empty-handed. Yet no corpse lay on the dusty cavern floor. He went to the back of the cave, glanced at the straight, even wall, bent and examined the smooth rock floor. His keen eyes, straining in the gloom, made out a dull smear of blood on the stone. It ended abruptly at the back wall, and there was no stain on the wall.

Reynolds leaned closer, supporting himself by a hand propped against the stone wall. And suddenly and shockingly the sensation of solidity and stability vanished. The wall gave way beneath his propping hand, a section swung inward, precipitating him headlong through a black gaping opening. His catlike quickness could not save him. It was as if the yawning shadows reached tenuous and invisible hands to jerk him headlong into the darkness.

He did not fall far. His out-flung hands struck what seemed to be steps carved in the stone, and on them he scrambled and floundered for an instant. Then he righted himself and turned back to the opening through which he had fallen. But the secret door had closed, and only a smooth stone wall met his groping fingers. He fought down a rising panic. How the McCrills had come to know of this secret chamber he could not say, but quite evidently they had placed Saul Fletcher's body in it. And there, trapped like a rat, they would find John Reynolds when they returned. Then in the darkness a grim smile curled Reynolds' thin lips. When they opened the secret door, he would be hidden in the darkness, while they would be etched against the dim light of the outer cave. Where could he find a more perfect ambush? But first he must find the body and secure the cartridges.

He turned to grope his way down the steps and his first stride brought him to a level floor. It was a sort of narrow tunnel, he decided, for though he could not touch the roof, a stride to the right or the left and his outstretched hand encountered a wall, seemingly too even and symmetrical to have been the work of nature. He went slowly, groping in the darkness, keeping in touch with the walls and momentarily expecting to stumble on Saul Fletcher's body. And as he did not, a dim horror began to grow in his soul. The McCrills had not been in the cavern long enough to carry the body so far back into the darkness. A feeling was rising in John Reynolds that the McCrills had not entered the tunnel at all—that they were not aware of its existence. Then where in the name of sanity was Saul Fletcher's corpse?

He stopped short, jerking out his six-shooter. Something was coming up the dark tunnel—something that walked upright and lumberingly.

John Reynolds knew it was a man, wearing high-heeled riding boots. No other footwear makes the same stilted sound. He caught the jingle of the spurs. And a dark tide of nameless horror moved sluggishly in John Reynolds' mind as he heard that halting tread approach, and remembered the night when he had lain at bay in the old corral, with the younger brother dying beside him, and heard a limping, dragging footstep endlessly circle his refuge, out in the night where Saul Fletcher led his wolves and sought for a way to come upon his back.

Had the man only been wounded? These steps sounded stiff and blundering, such as a wounded man might make. No—John Reynolds had seen too many men die; he knew that his bullet had gone straight through Saul Fletcher's heart, possibly tearing the heart out, certainly killing him instantly. Besides, he had heard old Jonas McCrill declare the man was dead. No—Saul Fletcher lay lifeless somewhere in this black cavern. It was some other lame man who was coming up that silent tunnel.

Now the tread ceased. The man was fronting him, separated only by a few feet of utter blackness. What was there in that to quicken the iron pulse of John Reynolds, who had unflinchingly faced death times without number?—what to make his flesh crawl and his tongue freeze to his palate?—to awake sleeping instincts of fear as a man senses the presence of an unseen serpent, and make him feel that somehow the other was aware of his presence with eyes that pierced the darkness?

In the silence John Reynolds heard the staccato pounding of his own heart. And with shocking suddenness the man lunged. Reynolds' straining ears caught the first movement of that lunge and he fired pointblank. And he screamed—a terrible, animal-like scream. Heavy arms locked upon him and unseen teeth worried at his flesh; but in the frothing frenzy of his fear, his own strength was superhuman. For in the flash of the shot he had seen a bearded face with slack-hanging mouth and staring dead eyes. *Saul Fletcher!* The dead, come back from Hell!

As in a nightmare, Reynolds knew that fiendish battle in the dark, where the dead sought to drag down the living. He felt himself hurled to and fro in the grip of clammy hands. He was flung with bone shattering force against the stone walls. Dashed to the floor, the silent horror squatted ghoul like upon him, its horrid fingers sinking deep into his throat.

In that nightmare, John Reynolds had no time to doubt his own sanity. He knew that he was battling a dead man. The flesh of his foe was cold with a charnel-house clamminess. Under the torn shirt he had felt the round bullet-hole, caked with clotted blood. No single sound came from the loose lips.

Choking and gasping, John Reynolds tore the strangling hands aside and flung the thing off, feeling for an instant the darkness again separated them; then the horror came hurtling toward him again. As the thing lunged, Reynolds caught blindly and gained the wrestling hold he wished; and hurling all his power behind the attack, he dashed the horror headlong, falling upon it with his full weight. Saul Fletcher's spine snapped like a rotten branch and the tearing hands went limp, the straining limbs relaxed. Something flowed from the lax body and whispered away through the darkness like a ghostly wind, and John Reynolds instinctively knew that at last Saul Fletcher was truly dead.

Panting and shaken, Reynolds rose. The tunnel remained in utter darkness. But down it, in the direction from which the walking corpse had come stalking, there whispered a faint throbbing that was hardly sound at all, yet had in its pulsing a dark weird music.

Reynolds shuddered and the sweat froze on his body. The dead man lay at his feet in the thick darkness, and faintly to his ears came that unbearably sweet, unbearably evil echo, like devil drums beating faint and far in the dim caverns of Hell.

Reason urged him to turn back—to fight against that blind door until he burst its stone, if human power could burst it. But he realized that reason and sanity had been left behind him. A single step had plunged him from a normal world of material realities into a realm of nightmare and lunacy. He decided that he was mad, or else dead and in Hell. Those dim tom-toms drew him; they tugged at his heart strings eerily. They repelled him and filled his soul with shadowy and monstrous conjectures, yet their call was irresistible. He fought the mad impulse to shriek and fling his arms wildly aloft, and run down the black tunnel as a rabbit runs down the prairie dog's burrow into the jaws of the waiting rattler.

Fumbling in the dark, he found his revolver, and still fumbling he loaded it with cartridges from Saul Fletcher's belt. He felt no more aversion now, at touching the body, than he would have felt at handling any dead flesh. Whatever unholy power had animated the corpse, it had left it when the snapping of the spine had unraveled the nerve centers and disrupted the roots of the muscular system.

Then, revolver in hand, John Reynolds went down the tunnel, drawn by a power he could not fathom, toward a doom he could not guess.

The throb of the tom-toms grew only slightly in volume as he advanced. How far below the hills he was, he could not know, but the tunnel slanted downward and he had gone a long way. Often his groping hands encountered doorways—corridors leading off the main tunnel, he believed. At last he was aware that he had left the tunnel and had come out into a vast open space. He could see nothing, but he somehow felt the vastness of the place. And in the darkness a faint light began. It throbbed as the drums throbbed, waning and waxing in time to their pulsing, but it grew slowly, casting a weird glow that was more like green than any color Reynolds had ever seen, but was not really green, nor any other sane or earthly color.

Reynolds approached it. It widened. It cast a shimmering radiance over the smooth stone floor, illuminating fantastic mosaics. It cast its sheen high in the hovering shadows, but he could see no roof. Now he stood bathed in its weird glow, so that his flesh looked like a dead man's. Now he saw the roof, high and vaulted, brooding far above him like a dusky midnight sky, and towering walls, gleaming and dark, sweeping up to tremendous heights, their bases fringed with squat shadows from which glittered other lights, small and scintillant.

He saw the source of the illumination, a strange carved stone altar on which burned what appeared to be a giant jewel of an unearthly hue, like the light it emitted. Greenish flame jetted from it; it burned as a bit of coal might burn, but it was not consumed. just behind it a feathered serpent reared from its coils, a fantasy carven of some clear crystalline substance, the tints of which in the weird light were never the same, but which pulsed and shimmered and changed as the drums—now on all sides of him—pulsed and throbbed.

Abruptly something alive moved beside the altar and John Reynolds, though he was expecting anything, recoiled. At first he thought it a huge reptile which slithered about the altar, then he saw that it stood upright as a man stands. As he met the menacing glitter of its eyes, he fired pointblank and the thing went down like a slaughtered ox, its skull shattered. Reynolds wheeled as a sinister rustling rose on his ears—at least these beings could be killed—then checked the lifted muzzle. The drums had never ceased. The fringing shadows had moved out from the darkness at the base of the walls, and drawn about him in a wide ring. And though at first glance they possessed the semblance of men, he knew they were not human.

The weird light flickered and danced over them, and back in the deeper darkness the soft, evil drums whispered their accompanying undertone everlastingly. John Reynolds stood aghast at what he saw.

It was not their dwarfish figures which caused his shudder, nor even the unnaturally made hands and feet—it was their heads. He knew, now, of what race was the skull found by the prospector. Like it, these heads were peaked and malformed, curiously flattened at the sides. There was no sign of ears, as if their organs of hearing, like a serpent's, were beneath the skin. The noses were like a python's snout, the mouth and jaws much less human in appearance than his recollection of the skull would have led him to suppose. The eyes were small, glittering, and reptilian. The squamy lips writhed back, showing pointed fangs, and John Reynolds felt that their bite would be as deadly as a rattlesnake's. Garments they wore none, nor did they bear any weapons.

He tensed himself for the death struggle, but no rush came. The snake people sat about him in a great cross-legged circle, and beyond the circle he saw them massed thick. And now he felt a stirring in his consciousness, an almost tangible beating of wills upon his senses. He was distinctly aware of a concentrated invasion of his innermost mind, and realized that these fantastic beings were seeking to convey their commands or wishes to him by medium of thought. On what common plane could he meet these inhuman creatures? Yet in some dim, strange, telepathic way they made him understand some of their meaning; and he realized with a grisly shock that, whatever these things were now, they had once been at least partly human, else they had never been able to so bridge the gulf between the completely human and the completely bestial.

He understood that he was the first living man to come into their innermost realm, the first to look on the shining serpent, the Terrible Nameless One who was older than the world; that before he died, he was to know all which had been denied to the sons of men concerning the mysterious valley, that he might take this knowledge into Eternity with him, and discuss these matters with those who had gone before him.

The drums rustled, the strange light leaped and shimmered, and before the altar came one who seemed in authority—an ancient monstrosity whose skin was like the whitish hide of an old serpent, and who wore on his peaked skull a golden circlet, set with weird gems. He bent and made suppliance to the feathered snake. Then with a sharp implement of some sort which left a phosphorescent mark, he drew a cryptic triangular figure on the floor before the altar, and in the figure he strewed some sort of glimmering dust. From it reared up a thin spiral which grew to a gigantic shadowy serpent, feathered and horrific, and then changed and faded and became a cloud of greenish smoke. This smoke billowed out before John Reynolds' eyes and hid the serpent-eyed ring, and the altar, and the cavern itself. All the universe dissolved into the green smoke, in which titanic scenes and alien landscapes rose and shifted and faded, and monstrous shapes lumbered and leered.

Abruptly the chaos crystallized. He was looking into a valley which he did not recognize. Somehow he knew it was Lost Valley, but in it towered a gigantic city of dully gleaming stone. John Reynolds was a man of the outlands and the waste places. He had never seen the great cities of the world. But he knew that nowhere in the world today such a city reared up to the sky.

Its towers and battlements were those of an alien age. Its outline baffled his gaze with its unnatural aspects; it was a city of lunacy to the normal human eye, with its hints of alien dimensions and abnormal principles of architecture. Through it moved strange figures—human, yet of a humanity definitely different from his own. They were clad in robes, their hands and feet were less abnormal, their ears and mouths more like those of normal humans; yet there was an undoubted kinship between them and the monsters of the cavern. It showed in the curious peaked skull, though this was less pronounced and bestial in the people of the city.

He saw them in the twisting streets, and in their colossal buildings, and he shuddered at the inhumanness of their lives. Much they did was beyond his ken; he could understand their actions and motives no more than a Zulu savage might understand the events of modern London. But he did understand that these people were very ancient and very evil. He saw them enact rituals that froze his blood with horror, obscenities and blasphemies beyond his understanding. He grew sick with a sensation of pollution, of contamination. Somehow he knew that this city was the remnant of an outworn age—that this people represented the survival of an epoch lost and forgotten.

Then a new people came upon the scene. Over the hills came wild men clad in hides and feathers, armed with bows and flint-tipped weapons. They were, Reynolds knew, Indians, and yet not Indians as he knew them. They were slant eyed, and their skins were yellowish rather than copper colored. Somehow he knew that these were the nomadic ancestors of the Toltecs, wandering and conquering on their long trek before they settled in upland valleys far to the south and evolved their own special type and civilization. These were still close to the primal Mongolian rootstock, and he gasped at the gigantic vistas of time this realization evoked.

Reynolds saw the warriors move like a giant wave on the towering walls. He saw the defenders man the towers and deal death in strange and grisly forms to them. He saw the invaders reel back again and again, then come on once more with the blind ferocity of the primitive. This strange evil city, filled with mysterious people of a different order, was in their path, and they could not pass until they had stamped it out.

Reynolds marveled at the fury of the invaders, who wasted their lives like water, matching the cruel and terrible science of an unknown civilization with sheer courage and the might of manpower. Their bodies littered the plateau, but not all the forces of hell could keep them back. They rolled like a wave to the foot of the towers. They scaled the walls in the teeth of sword and arrow and death in ghastly forms. They gained the parapets. They met their enemies hand to hand. Bludgeons and axes beat down the lunging spears, the thrusting swords. The tall figures of the barbarians towered over the smaller forms of the defenders.

Red hell raged in the city. The siege became a street battle, the battle a rout, the rout a slaughter. Smoke rose and hung in clouds over the doomed city.

The scene changed. Reynolds looked on charred and ruined walls from which smoke still rose. The conquerors had passed on; the survivors gathered in the red stained temple before their curious god—a crystalline serpent on a fantastic stone altar. Their age had ended; their world crumbled suddenly. They were the remnants of an otherwise extinct race. They could not rebuild their marvelous city and they feared to remain within its broken walls, a prey to every passing tribe. Reynolds saw them take up their altar and its god and follow an ancient man clad in a mantle of feathers and wearing on his head a gem set circlet of gold. He led them across the valley to a hidden cave. They entered, and, squeezing through a narrow rift in the back wall, came into a vast network of caverns honeycombing the hills. Reynolds saw them at work, exploring these labyrinths, excavating and enlarging, hewing the walls and floors smooth, enlarging the rift that let into the outer cavern and setting therein a cunningly hung door, so that it seemed part of the solid wall.

Then an ever-shifting panorama denoted the passing of many centuries. The people lived in the caverns, and as time passed they adapted themselves more and more to their surroundings, each generation going less frequently into the outer sunlight. They learned to obtain their food in shuddersome ways from the earth. Their ears grew smaller, their bodies more dwarfish, their eyes more cat-like. John Reynolds stood aghast as he watched the race changing through the ages.

Outside in the valley the deserted city crumbled and fell into ruins, becoming prey to lichen and weed and tree. Men came and briefly meditated among these ruins—tall Mongolian warriors, and dark inscrutable little people men call the Mound Builders. And as the centuries passed, the visitors conformed more and more to the type of Indian as he knew it, until at last the only men who came were painted red men with stealthy feet and feathered scalp locks. None ever tarried long in that haunted place with its cryptic ruins.

Meanwhile, in the caverns, the Old People abode and grew strange and terrible. They fell lower and lower in the scale of humanity, forgetting first their written language, and gradually their human speech. But in other ways they extended the boundaries of life. In their nighted kingdom they discovered other, older caverns, which led them into the very bowels of the earth. They learned lost secrets, long forgotten or never known by men, sleeping in the blackness far below the hills. Darkness is conducive to silence, so they gradually lost the power of speech, a sort of telepathy taking its place. And with each grisly gain they lost more of their human attributes. Their ears vanished; their noses grew snout-like; their eyes became unable to bear the light of the sun, and even of the stars. They had long abandoned the use of fire, and the only light they used was the weird gleams evoked from their gigantic jewel on the altar, and even this they did not need. They changed in other ways. John Reynolds, watching, felt the cold sweat bead his body. For the slow transmutation of the Old People was horrible to behold, and many and hideous were the shapes which moved among them before their ultimate mold and nature were evolved.

Yet they remembered the sorcery of their ancestors and added to this their own black wizardry developed far below the hills. And at last they attained the peak of that necromancy. John Reynolds had had horrific inklings of it in fragmentary glimpses of the olden times, when the wizards of the Old People had sent forth their spirits from their sleeping bodies to whisper evil things in the ears of their enemies.

A tribe of tall, painted warriors came into the valley, bearing the body of a great chief, slain in tribal warfare.

Long eons had passed. Of the ancient city only scattered columns stood among the trees. A landslide had laid bare the entrance of the outer cavern. This the Indians found and therein they placed the body of their chief with his weapons broken beside him. Then they blocked up the cave mouth with stones, and took up their journey, but night caught them in the valley.

Through all the ages, the Old People had found no other entrance or exit to or from the pits, save the small outer cave. It was the one doorway between their grim realm and the world they had so long abandoned. Now they came through the secret door into the outer cavern, whose dim light they could endure, and John Reynolds' hair stood up at what he saw. For they took the corpse and laid it before the altar of the feathered serpent, and an ancient wizard lay upon it, his mouth against the mouth of the dead, and above them tom-toms pulsed and strange fires flickered, and the voiceless votaries with soundless chants invoked gods forgotten before the birth of Egypt, until unhuman voices bellowed in the outer darkness and the sweep of monstrous wings filled the shadows. And slowly life ebbed from the sorcerer and stirred the limbs of the dead chief. The body of the wizard rolled limply aside and the corpse of the chief stood up stiffly; and with puppet-like steps and glassy staring eyes it went up the dark tunnel and through the secret door into the outer cave. Its dead hands tore aside the stones, and into the starlight stalked the Horror.

Reynolds saw it walk stiffly under the shuddering trees while the night things fled gibbering. He saw it come into the camp of the warriors. The rest was horror and madness, as the dead thing pursued its former companions and tore them limb from limb. The valley became a shambles before one of the braves, conquering his terror, turned on his pursuer and hewed through its spine with a stone ax.

And even as the twice slain corpse crumpled, Reynolds saw, on the floor of the cavern before the carven serpent, the form of the wizard quicken and live as his spirit returned to him from the corpse he had caused it to animate.

The soundless glee of incarnate demons shook the crawling blackness of the pits, and Reynolds shrank before the verminous fiends gloating over their newfound power to deal horror and death to the sons of men, their ancient enemies.

But the word spread from clan to clan, and men came not to the Valley of the Lost. For many a century it lay dreaming and deserted beneath the sky. Then came mounted braves with trailing war bonnets, painted with the colors of the Kiowas, warriors of the north who knew nothing of the mysterious valley. They pitched their camps in the very shadows of those sinister monoliths which were now no more than shapeless stones.

They placed their dead in the cavern. And Reynolds saw the horrors that took place when the dead came ravening by night among the living to slay and *devour*—and to drag screaming victims into the nighted caverns and the demoniac doom that awaited them. The legions of hell were loosed in the Valley of the Lost, where chaos reigned and nightmare and madness stalked. Those who were left alive and sane walled up the cavern and rode out of the hills like men riding from hell.

Once more Lost Valley lay gaunt and naked to the stars. Then again the coming of men broke the primal solitude, and smoke rose among the trees. And John Reynolds caught his breath with a start of horror as he saw these were white men, clad in the buckskins of an earlier day—six of them, so much alike that he knew they were brothers.

He saw them fell trees and build a cabin in the clearing. He saw them hunt game in the mountains and begin clearing a field for corn. And all the time he saw the vermin of the hills waiting with ghoulish lust in the darkness. They could not look from their caverns with their nighted eyes, but by their godless sorcery they were aware of all that took place in the valley. They could not come forth in their own bodies in the light, but they waited with the patience of night and the still places.

Reynolds saw one of the brothers find the cavern and open it. He entered and the secret door hung open. The man went into the tunnel. He could not see, in the darkness, the shapes of horror that stole slavering about him, but in sudden panic he lifted his muzzle-loading rifle and fired blindly, screaming as the flash showed him the hellish forms that ringed him in. In the utter blackness following the vain shot they rushed, overthrowing him by the power of their numbers, sinking their snaky fangs into his flesh. As he died, he slashed half a dozen of them to pieces with his bowie knife, but the poison did its work quickly.

Reynolds saw them drag the corpse before the altar; he saw again the horrible transmutation of the dead, which rose grinning vacantly and stalked forth. The sun had set in a welter of dull crimson. Night had fallen. To the cabin where his brothers slept, wrapped in their blankets, stalked the dead. Silently the groping hands swung open the door. The Horror crouched in the gloom, its bared teeth shining, its dead eyes gleaming glassily in the starlight. One of the brothers stirred and mumbled, then sat up and stared at the motionless shape in the doorway. He called the dead man's name—then he shrieked hideously—the Horror sprang.

From John Reynolds' throat burst a cry of intolerable horror. Abruptly the pictures vanished, with the smoke. He stood in the weird glow before the altar, the tom-toms throbbing softly and evilly, the fiendish faces hemming him in. And now from among them crept, on his belly like the serpent he was, the one which wore the gemmed circlet, venom dripping from his bared fangs. Loathsomely he slithered toward John Reynolds, who fought the temptation to leap upon the foul thing and stamp out its life. There was no escape; he could send his bullets crashing through the swarm and mow down all in front of the muzzle, but those would be as nothing beside the hundreds which hemmed him in. He would die there in the waning light, and they would send his corpse blundering forth, lent a travesty of life by the spirit of the wizard, just as they had sent Saul Fletcher. John Reynolds grew tense as steel as his wolflike instinct to live rose above the maze of horror into which he had fallen.

And suddenly his human mind rose above the vermin who threatened him, as he was electrified by a swift thought that was like an inspiration. With a fierce inarticulate cry of triumph, he bounded sideways just as the crawling monstrosity lunged. It missed him, sprawling headlong, and Reynolds snatched from the altar the carven serpent, and holding it on high, thrust against it the muzzle of his cocked pistol. He did not need to speak. In the dying light his eyes blazed madly. The Old People wavered back. Before them lay he whose peaked skull Reynolds' pistol had shattered. They knew a crook of his trigger finger would splinter their fantastic god into shining bits.

For a tense space the tableau held. Then Reynolds felt their silent surrender. Freedom in exchange for their god. It was again borne on him that these beings were not truly bestial, since true beasts know no gods. And this knowledge was the more terrible, for it meant that these creatures had evolved into a type neither bestial nor human, a type outside of nature and sanity.

The snakish figures gave back on each side, and the waning light sprang up again. As he went up the tunnel they were close at his heels, and in the dancing uncertain glow he could not be sure whether they walked as a man walks or crawled as a snake crawls. He had a vague impression that their gait was hideously compounded of both. He swerved far aside to avoid the sprawling bulk that had been Saul Fletcher, and so, with his gun muzzle pressed hard against the shining brittle image borne in his left hand, he came to the short flight of steps which led up to the secret door. There they came to a standstill. He turned to face them. They ringed him in a close half-circle, and he understood that they feared to open the secret door lest he dash out, with their image, through the cavern into the sunlight, where they could not follow. Nor would he set down the god until the door was opened.

At last they withdrew several yards, and he cautiously set the image on the floor at his feet where he could snatch it up in an instant. How they opened the door he never knew, but it swung wide, and he backed slowly up the steps, his gun trained on the glittering god. He had almost reached the door—one back-thrown hand gripped the edge—when the light went out suddenly and the rush came. A volcanic burst of effort shot him backward through the door, which was already rushing shut. As he leaped he emptied his gun full into the fiendish faces that suddenly filled the dark opening. They dissolved in red ruin, and as he raced madly from the outer cavern he heard the soft closing of the secret door, shutting that realm of horror from the human world.

In the glow of the westering sun John Reynolds staggered drunkenly, clutching at stones and trees as a madman clutches at realities. The keen tenseness that had held him when he fought for his life fell from him and left him a quivering shell of disrupted nerves. An insane titter drooled involuntarily through his lips, and he rocked to and fro in ghastly laughter he could not check.

Then the clink of hoofs on stone sent him leaping behind a cluster of boulders. It was some hidden instinct which led him to take refuge; his conscious mind was too dazed and chaotic for thought or action.

Into the clearing rode Jonas McCrill and his followers, and a sob tore through Reynolds' throat. At first he did not recognize them—did not realize that he had ever seen them before. The feud, with all other sane and normal things, lay lost and forgotten far back in dim vistas beyond the black tunnels of madness.

Two figures rode from the other side of the clearing— Bill Ord and one of the outlaw followers of the McCrills. Strapped to Ord's saddle were several sticks of dynamite, done into a compact package.

"Well, gee whiz," hailed young Ord. "I shore didn't expect to meet yuh all here. Did yuh git him?"

"Naw," snapped old Jonas, "he's done fooled us again. We come up with his horse, but he wasn't on it. The rein was snapped like he'd had it tied and it'd broke away. I dunno where he is, but we'll git him I'm a goin' on to Antelope to git some more of the boys. Yuh all git Saul's body outa that cave and foller me as fast as yuh can."

He reined away and vanished through the trees, and Reynolds, his heart in his mouth, saw the other four approach the cavern.

"Well, by God!" exclaimed Jack Solomon fiercely, "somebody's done been here! Look! Them rocks are torn down!"

John Reynolds watched as one paralyzed. If he sprang up and called to them they would shoot him down before he could voice his warning. Yet it was not that which held him as in a vise; it was sheer horror which robbed him of thought and action, and froze his tongue to the roof of his mouth. His lips parted but no sound came forth. As in a nightmare he saw his enemies disappear into the cavern. Their voices, muffled, came back to him.

"By golly, Saul's gone!"

"Look here, boys, here's a door in the back wall!"

"By thunder, it's open!"

"Let's take a look!"

Suddenly from within the bowels of the hills crashed a fusillade of shots—a burst of hideous screams. Then silence closed like a clammy fog over the Valley of the Lost.

John Reynolds, finding voice at last, cried out as a wounded beast cries, and beat his temples with his clenched fists, which he brandished to the heavens, shrieking wordless blasphemies.

Then he ran staggeringly to Bill Ord's horse which grazed tranquilly with the others beneath the trees. With clammy hands he tore away the package of dynamite, and without separating the sticks he punched a hole in the end of the middle stick with a twig. Then he cut a short—a very short—piece of fuse, and slipped a cap over one end which he inserted into the hole in the dynamite. In a pocket of the rolled-up slicker bound behind the saddle he found a match, and, lighting the fuse, he hurled the bundle into the cavern. Hardly had it struck the back wall when with an earthquake roar it exploded.

The concussion nearly hurled him off his feet. The whole mountain rocked, and with a thunderous crash the cave roof fell. Tons and tons of shattered rock crashed down to obliterate all marks of Ghost Cave, and to shut the door to the pits forever.

John Reynolds walked slowly away; and suddenly the whole horror swept upon him. The earth seemed hideously alive under his feet, the sun foul and blasphemous over his head. The light was sickly, yellowish and evil, and all things were polluted by the unholy knowledge locked in his skull, like hidden drums beating ceaselessly in the blackness beneath the hills.

He had closed one Door forever, but what other nightmare shapes might lurk in hidden places and the dark pits of the earth, gloating over the souls of men? His knowledge was a reeking blasphemy which would never let him rest; forever in his soul would whisper the drums that throbbed in those dark pits where lurked demons that had once been men. He had looked on ultimate foulness, and his knowledge was a taint because of which he could never stand clean before men again, or touch the flesh of any living thing without a shudder. If man, molded of divinity, could sink to such verminous obscenities, who could contemplate his eventual destiny unshaken?

And if such beings as the Old People existed, what other horrors might not lurk beneath the visible surface of the universe? He was suddenly aware that he had glimpsed the grinning skull beneath the mask of life, and that that glimpse made life intolerable. All certainty and stability had been swept away, leaving a mad welter of lunacy, nightmare, and stalking horror.

John Reynolds drew his gun and his horny thumb drew back the heavy hammer. Thrusting the muzzle against his temple, he pulled the trigger. The shot crashed echoing through the hills, and the last of the fighting Reynoldses pitched headlong.

Old Jonas McCrill, galloping back at the sound of the blast, found him where he lay, and wondered that his face should be that of an old, old man, his hair white as hoar frost.

The Man on the Ground

Cal Reynolds shifted his tobacco quid to the other side of his mouth as he squinted down the dull blue barrel of his Winchester. His jaws worked methodically, their movement ceasing as he found his bead. He froze into rigid immobility; then his finger hooked on the trigger. The crack of the shot sent the echoes rattling among the hills, and like a louder echo came an answering shot. Reynolds flinched down, flattening his rangy body against the earth, swearing softly. A gray flake jumped from one of the rocks near his head, the ricocheting bullet whining off into space. Reynolds involuntarily shivered. The sound was as deadly as the singing of an unseen rattler.

He raised himself gingerly high enough to peer out between the rocks in front of him. Separated from his refuge by a broad level grown with mesquite-grass and prickly-pear, rose a tangle of boulders similar to that behind which he crouched. From among these boulders floated a thin wisp of whitish smoke. Reynolds' keen eyes, trained to sun-scorched distances, detected a small circle of dully gleaming blue steel among the rocks. That ring was the muzzle of a rifle, and Reynolds well knew who lay behind that muzzle.

The feud between Cal Reynolds and Esau Brill had been long, for a Texas feud. Up in the Kentucky mountains family wars may straggle on for generations, but the geographical conditions and human temperament of the Southwest were not conducive to long-drawn-out hostilities. There feuds were generally concluded with appalling suddenness and finality. The stage was a saloon, the streets of a little cow town, or the open range. Sniping from the laurel was exchanged for the close-range thundering of six-shooters and sawed-off shotguns which decided matters quickly, one way or the other.

The case of Cal Reynolds and Esau Brill was somewhat out of the ordinary. In the first place, the feud concerned only themselves. Neither friends nor relatives were drawn into it. No one, including the participants, knew just how it started. Cal Reynolds merely knew that he had hated Esau Brill most of his life, and that Brill reciprocated. Once as youths they had clashed with the violence and intensity of rival young catamounts. From that encounter Reynolds carried away a knife scar across the edge of his ribs, and Brill a permanently impaired eye. It had decided nothing. They had fought to a bloody gasping deadlock, and neither had felt any desire to "shake hands and make up." That is a hypocrisy developed in civilization, where men have no stomach for fighting to the death. After a man has felt his adversary's knife grate against his bones, his adversary's thumb gouging at his eyes, his adversary's boot-heels stamped into his mouth, he is scarcely inclined to forgive and forget, regardless of the original merits of the argument.

So Reynolds and Brill carried their mutual hatred into manhood, and as cowpunchers riding for rival ranches, it followed that they found opportunities to carry on their private war. Reynolds rustled cattle from Brill's boss, and Brill returned the compliment. Each raged at the other's tactics, and considered himself justified in eliminating his enemy in any way that he could. Brill caught Reynolds without his gun one night in a saloon at Cow Wells, and only an ignominious flight out the back way, with bullets barking at his heels, saved the Reynolds' scalp.

Again Reynolds, lying in the chaparral, neatly knocked his enemy out of his saddle at five hundred yards with a .30-30 slug, and, but for the inopportune appearance of a line-rider, the feud would have ended there. Reynolds deciding, in the face of this witness, to forego his original intention of leaving his covert and hammering out the wounded man's brains with his rifle butt.

Brill recovered from his wound, having the vitality of a longhorn bull, in common with all his sun-leathered iron-thewed breed, and as soon as he was on his feet, he came gunning for the man who had waylaid him.

Now after these onsets and skirmishes, the enemies faced each other at good rifle range, among the lonely hills where interruption was unlikely.

For more than an hour they had lain among the rocks, shooting at each hint of movement. Neither had scored a hit, though the .30-30s whistled perilously close.

In each of Reynolds' temples a tiny pulse hammered maddeningly. The sun beat down on him and his shirt was soaked with sweat. Gnats swarmed about his head, getting into his eyes, and he cursed venomously. His wet hair was plastered to his scalp; his eyes burned with the glare of the sun, and the rifle barrel was hot to his calloused hand. His right leg was growing numb and he shifted it cautiously, cursing at the jingle of the spur, though he knew Brill could not hear. All his discomfort added fuel to the fire of his wrath. Without process of conscious reasoning, he attributed all his suffering to his enemy. The sun beat dazingly on his sombrero, and his thoughts were slightly addled. It was hotter than the hearthstone of hell among those bare rocks. His dry tongue caressed his baked lips.

Through the muddle of his brain burned his hatred of Esau Brill. It had become more than an emotion: it was an obsession, a monstrous incubus. When he flinched from the whip-crack of Brill's rifle, it was not from fear of death, but because the thought of dying at the hands of his foe was an intolerable horror that made his brain rock with red frenzy. He would have thrown his life away recklessly, if by so doing he could have sent Brill into eternity just three seconds ahead of himself.

He did not analyze these feelings. Men who live by their hands have little time for self-analysis. He was no more aware of the quality of his hate for Esau Brill than he was consciously aware of his hands and feet. It was part of him, and more than part: it enveloped him, engulfed him; his mind and body were no more than its material manifestations. He *was* the hate; it was the whole soul and spirit of him. Unhampered by the stagnant and enervating shackles of sophistication and intellectuality, his instincts rose sheer from the naked primitive. And from them crystallized an almost tangible abstraction—a hate too strong for even death to destroy; a hate powerful enough to embody itself in itself, without the aid or the necessity of material substance.

For perhaps a quarter of an hour neither rifle had spoken. Instinct with death as rattlesnakes coiled among the rocks soaking up poison from the sun's rays, the feudists lay each waiting his chance, playing the game of endurance until the taut nerves of one or the other should snap.

It was Esau Brill who broke. Not that his collapse took the form of any wild madness or nervous explosion. The wary instincts of the wild were too strong in him for that. But suddenly, with a screamed curse, he hitched up on his elbow and fired blindly at the tangle of stones which concealed his enemy. Only the upper part of his arm and the corner of his blue-shirted shoulder were for an instant visible. That was enough. In that flash-second Cal Reynolds jerked the trigger, and a frightful yell told him his bullet had found its mark. And at the animal pain in that yell, reason and lifelong instincts were swept away by an insane flood of terrible joy. He did not whoop exultantly and spring to his feet; but his teeth bared in a wolfish grin and he involuntarily raised his head. Waking instinct jerked him down again. It was chance that undid him. Even as he ducked back, Brill's answering shot cracked.

Cal Reynolds did not hear it, because, simultaneously with the sound, something exploded in his skull, plunging him into utter blackness, shot briefly with red sparks.

The blackness was only momentary. Cal Reynolds glared wildly around, realizing with a frenzied shock that he was lying in the open. The impact of the shot had sent him rolling from among the rocks, and in that quick instant he realized that it had not been a direct hit. Chance had sent the bullet glancing from a stone, apparently to flick his scalp in passing. That was not so important. What was important was that he was lying out in full view, where Esau Brill could fill him full of lead. A wild glance showed his rifle lying close by. It had fallen across a stone and lay with the stock against the ground, the barrel slanting upward. Another glance showed his enemy standing upright among the stones that had concealed him.

In that one glance Cal Reynolds took in the details of the tall, rangy figure: the stained trousers sagging with the weight of the holstered six-shooter, the legs tucked into the worn leather boots; the streak of crimson on the shoulder of the blue shirt, which was plastered to the wearer's body with sweat; the tousled black hair, from which perspiration was pouring down the unshaven face. He caught the glint of yellow tobacco-stained teeth shining in a savage grin. Smoke still drifted from the rifle in Brill's hands.

These familiar and hated details stood out in startling clarity during the fleeting instant while Reynolds struggled madly against the unseen chains which seemed to hold him to the earth. Even as he thought of the paralysis a glancing blow on the head might induce, something seemed to snap and he rolled free. Rolled is hardly the word: he seemed almost to dart to the rifle that lay across the rock, so light his limbs felt.

Dropping behind the stone he seized the weapon. He did not even have to lift it. As it lay it bore directly on the man who was now approaching.

His hand was momentarily halted by Esau Brill's strange behavior. Instead of firing or leaping back into cover the man came straight on, his rifle in the crook of his arm, that damnable leer still on his unshaven lips. Was he mad? Could he not see that his enemy was up again, raging with life, and with a cocked rifle aimed at his heart? Brill seemed not to be looking at him, but to one side, at the spot where Reynolds had just been lying.

Without seeking further for the explanation of his foe's actions, Cal Reynolds pulled the trigger. With the vicious spang of the report a blue shred leaped from Brill's broad breast. He staggered back, his mouth flying open. And the look on his face froze Reynolds again. Esau Brill came of a breed which fights to its last gasp. Nothing was more certain than that he would go down pulling the trigger blindly until the last red vestige of life left him. Yet the ferocious triumph was wiped from his face with the crack of the shot, to be replaced by an awful expression of dazed surprize. He made no move to lift his rifle, which slipped from his grasp, nor did he clutch at his wound. Throwing out his hands in a strange, stunned, helpless way, he reeled backward on slowly buckling legs, his features frozen into a mask of stupid amazement that made his watcher shiver with its cosmic horror.

Through the opened lips gushed a tide of blood, dyeing the damp shirt. And like a tree that sways and rushes suddenly earthward, Esau Brill crashed down among the mesquite-grass and lay motionless.

Cal Reynolds rose, leaving the rifle where it lay. The rolling grass-grown hills swam misty and indistinct to his gaze. Even the sky and the blazing sun had a hazy unreal aspect. But a savage content was in his soul. The long feud was over at last, and whether he had taken his death wound or not, he had sent Esau Brill to blaze the trail to hell ahead of him.

Then he started violently as his gaze wandered to the spot where he had rolled after being hit. He glared; were his eyes playing him tricks? Yonder in the grass Esau Brill lay dead—yet only a few feet away stretched another body.

Rigid with surprize, Reynolds glared at the rangy figure, slumped grotesquely beside the rocks. It lay partly on its side, as if flung there by some blind convulsion, the arms outstretched, the fingers crooked as if blindly clutching. The short-cropped sandy hair was splashed with blood, and from a ghastly hole in the temple the brains were oozing. From a corner of the mouth seeped a thin trickle of tobacco juice to stain the dusty neckcloth.

And as he gazed, an awful familiarity made itself evident. He knew the feel of those shiny leather wristbands; he knew with fearful certainty whose hands had buckled that gun belt; the tang of that tobacco juice was still on his palate.

In one brief destroying instant he knew he was looking down at his own lifeless body. And with the knowledge came true oblivion.

Old Garfield's Heart

I was sitting on the porch when my grandfather hobbled out and sank down on his favorite chair with the cushioned seat, and began to stuff tobacco in his old corncob pipe.

"I thought you'd be goin' to the dance," he said.

"I'm waiting for Doc Blaine," I answered. "I'm going over to old man Garfield's with him."

My grandfather sucked at his pipe awhile before he spoke again.

"Old Jim purty bad off?"

"Doc says he hasn't a chance."

"Who's takin' care of him?"

"Joe Braxton—against Garfield's wishes. But somebody had to stay with him."

My grandfather sucked his pipe noisily, and watched the heat lightning playing away off up in the hills; then he said: "You think old Jim's the biggest liar in this county, don't you?"

"He tells some pretty tall tales," I admitted. "Some of the things he claimed he took part in, must have happened before he was born."

"I came from Tennessee to Texas in 1870," my grandfather said abruptly. "I saw this town of Lost Knob grow up from nothin'. There wasn't even a log-hut store here when I came. But old Jim Garfield was here, livin' in the same place he lives now, only then it was a log cabin. He don't look a day older now than he did the first time I saw him."

"You never mentioned that before," I said in some surprize.

"I knew you'd put it down to an old man's maunderin's," he answered. "Old Jim was the first white man to settle in this country. He built his cabin a good fifty miles west of the frontier. God knows how he done it, for these hills swarmed with Comanches then.

"I remember the first time I ever saw him. Even then everybody called him 'old Jim.'

"I remember him tellin' me the same tales he's told you—how he was at the battle of San Jacinto when he was a youngster, and how he'd rode with Ewen Cameron and Jack Hayes. Only I believed him, and you don't."

"That was so long ago—" I protested.

"The last Indian raid through this country was in 1874," said my grandfather, engrossed in his own reminiscences. "I was in on that fight, and so was old Jim. I saw him knock old Yellow Tail off his mustang at seven hundred yards with a buffalo rifle.

"But before that I was with him in a fight up near the head of Locust Creek. A band of Comanches came down Mesquital, lootin' and burnin', rode through the hills and started back up Locust Creek, and a scout of us were hot on their heels. We ran on to them just at sundown in a mesquite flat. We killed seven of them, and the rest skinned out through the brush on foot. But three of our boys were killed, and Jim Garfield got a thrust in the breast with a lance.

"It was an awful wound. He lay like a dead man, and it seemed sure nobody could live after a wound like that. But an old Indian came out of the brush, and when we aimed our guns at him, he made the peace sign and spoke to us in Spanish. I don't know why the boys didn't shoot him in his tracks, because our blood was heated with the fightin' and killin', but somethin' about him made us hold our fire. He said he wasn't a Comanche, but was an old friend of Garfield's, and wanted to help him. He asked us to carry Jim into a clump of mesquite, and leave him alone with him, and to this day I don't know why we did, but we did. It was an awful time—the wounded moanin' and callin' for water, the starin' corpses strewn about the camp, night comin' on, and no way of knowin' that the Indians wouldn't return when dark fell.

"We made camp right there, because the horses were fagged out, and we watched all night, but the Comanches didn't come back. I don't know what went on out in the mesquite where Jim Garfield's body lay, because I never saw that strange Indian again; but durin' the night I kept hearin' a weird moanin' that wasn't made by the dyin' men, and an owl hooted from midnight till dawn.

"And at sunrise Jim Garfield came walkin' out of the mesquite, pale and haggard, but alive, and already the wound in his breast had closed and begun to heal. And since then he's never mentioned that wound, nor that fight, nor the strange Indian who came and went so mysteriously. And he hasn't aged a bit; he looks now just like he did then—a man of about fifty."

In the silence that followed, a car began to purr down the road, and twin shafts of light cut through the dusk.

"That's Doc Blaine," I said. "When I come back I'll tell you how Garfield is."

Doc Blaine was prompt with his predictions as we drove the three miles of post-oak-covered hills that lay between Lost Knob and the Garfield farm.

"I'll be surprized to find him alive," he said, "smashed up like he is. A man his age ought to have more sense than to try to break a young horse."

"He doesn't look so old," I remarked.

"I'll be fifty, my next birthday," answered Doc Blaine. "I've known him all my life, and he must have been at least fifty the first time I ever saw him. His looks are deceiving."

Old Garfield's dwelling place was reminiscent of the past. The boards of the low squat house had never known paint. Orchard fence and corrals were built of rails.

Old Jim lay on his rude bed, tended crudely but efficiently by the man Doc Blaine had hired over the old man's protests. As I looked at him, I was impressed anew by his evident vitality. His frame was stooped but unwithered, his limbs rounded out with springy muscles. In his corded neck and in his face, drawn though it was with suffering, was apparent an innate virility. His eyes, though partly glazed with pain, burned with the same unquenchable element.

"He's been ravin'," said Joe Braxton stolidly.

"First white man in this country," muttered old Jim, becoming intelligible. "Hills no white man ever set foot in before. Gettin' too old. Have to settle down. Can't move on like I used to. Settle down here. Good country before it filled up with cowmen and squatters. Wish Ewen Cameron could see this country. The Mexicans shot him. Damn 'em!"

Doc Blaine shook his head. "He's all smashed up inside. He won't live till daylight."

Garfield unexpectedly lifted his head and looked at us with clear eyes.

"Wrong, Doc," he wheezed, his breath whistling with pain. "I'll live. What's broken bones and twisted guts? Nothin'! It's the heart that counts. Long as the heart keeps pumpin', a man can't die. My heart's sound. Listen to it! Feel of it!"

He groped painfully for Doc Blaine's wrist, dragged his hand to his bosom and held it there, staring up into the doctor's face with avid intensity.

"Regular dynamo, ain't it?" he gasped. "Stronger'n a gasoline engine!"

Blaine beckoned me. "Lay your hand here," he said, placing my hand on the old man's bare breast. "He does have a remarkable heart action."

I noted, in the light of the coal-oil lamp, a great livid scar in the gaunt arching breast—such a scar as might be made by a flint-headed spear. I laid my hand directly on this scar, and an exclamation escaped my lips.

Under my hand old Jim Garfield's heart pulsed, but its throb was like no other heart action I have ever observed. Its power was astounding; his ribs vibrated to its steady throb. It felt more like the vibrating of a dynamo than the action of a human organ. I could feel its amazing vitality radiating from his breast, stealing up into my hand and up my arm, until my own heart seemed to speed up in response.

"I can't die," old Jim gasped. "Not so long as my heart's in my breast. Only a bullet through the brain can kill me. And even then

I wouldn't be rightly dead, as long as my heart beats in my breast. Yet it ain't rightly mine, either. It belongs to Ghost Man, the Lipan chief. It was the heart of a god the Lipans worshipped before the Comanches drove 'em out of their native hills.

"I knew Ghost Man down on the Rio Grande, when I was with Ewen Cameron. I saved his life from the Mexicans once. He tied the string of ghost wampum between him and me—the wampum no man but me and him can see or feel. He came when he knowed I needed him, in that fight up on the headwaters of Locust Creek, when I got this scar.

"I was dead as a man can be. My heart was sliced in two, like the heart of a butchered beef steer.

"All night Ghost Man did magic, callin' my ghost back from spirit-land. I remember that flight, a little. It was dark, and gray-like, and I drifted through gray mists and heard the dead wailin' past me in the mist. But Ghost Man brought me back.

"He took out what was left of my mortal heart, and put the heart of the god in my bosom. But it's his, and when I'm through with it, he'll come for it. It's kept me alive and strong for the lifetime of a man. Age can't touch me. What do I care if these fools around here call me an old liar? What I know, I know. But hark'ee!"

His fingers became claws, clamping fiercely on Doc Blaine's wrist. His old eyes, old yet strangely young, burned fierce as those of an eagle under his bushy brows.

"If by some mischance I *should* die, now or later, promise me this! Cut into my bosom and take out the heart Ghost Man lent me so long ago! It's his. And as long as it beats in my body, my spirit'll be tied to that body, though my head be crushed like an egg underfoot! A livin' thing in a rottin' body! Promise!"

"All right, I promise," replied Doc Blaine, to humor him, and old Jim Garfield sank back with a whistling sigh of relief.

He did not die that night, nor the next, nor the next. I well remember the next day, because it was that day that I had the fight with Jack Kirby.

People will take a good deal from a bully, rather than to spill blood. Because nobody had gone to the trouble of killing him, Kirby thought the whole countryside was afraid of him.

He had bought a steer from my father, and when my father went to collect for it, Kirby told him that he had paid the money to me—which was a lie. I went looking for Kirby, and came upon him in a bootleg joint, boasting of his toughness, and telling the crowd that he was going to beat me up and make me say that he had paid me the money, and that I had stuck it into my own pocket. When I heard him say that, I saw red, and ran in on him with a stockman's knife, and cut him across the face, and in the neck, side, breast and belly, and the only thing that saved his life was the fact that the crowd pulled me off.

There was a preliminary hearing, and I was indicted on a charge of assault, and my trial was set for the following term of court. Kirby was as tough fibered as a post oak country bully ought to be, and he recovered, swearing vengeance, for he was vain of his looks, though God knows why, and I had permanently impaired them.

And while Jack Kirby was recovering, old man Garfield recovered too, to the amazement of everybody, especially Doc Blaine.

I well remember the night Doc Blaine took me again out to old Jim Garfield's farm. I was in Shifty Corlan's joint, trying to drink enough of the slop he called beer to get a kick out of it, when Doc Blaine came in and persuaded me to go with him.

As we drove along the winding old road in Doc's car, I asked: "Why are you insistent that I go with you this particular night? This isn't a professional call, is it?"

"No," he said. "You couldn't kill old Jim with a post-oak maul. He's completely recovered from injuries that ought to have killed an ox. To tell the truth, Jack Kirby is in Lost Knob, swearing he'll shoot you on sight."

"Well, for God's sake!" I exclaimed angrily. "Now everybody'll think I left town because I was afraid of him. Turn around and take me back, damn it!"

"Be reasonable," said Doc. "Everybody knows you're not afraid of Kirby. Nobody's afraid of him now. His bluff's broken, and that's why he's so wild against you. But you can't afford to have any more trouble with him now, and your trial only a short time off."

I laughed and said: "Well, if he's looking for me hard enough, he can find me as easily at old Garfield's as in town, because Shifty Corlan heard you say where we were going. And Shifty's hated me ever since I skinned him in that horse swap last fall. He'll tell Kirby where I went."

"I never thought of that," said Doc Blaine, worried.

"Hell, forget it," I advised. "Kirby hasn't got guts enough to do anything but blow."

But I was mistaken. Puncture a bully's vanity and you touch his one vital spot.

Old Jim had not gone to bed when we got there. He was sitting in the room opening on to his sagging porch, the room which was at once living room and bedroom, smoking his old cob pipe and trying to read a newspaper by the light of his coal-oil lamp. All the windows and doors were wide open for the coolness, and the insects which swarmed in and fluttered around the lamp didn't seem to bother him.

We sat down and discussed the weather—which isn't so inane as one might suppose, in a country where men's livelihood depends on sun and rain, and is at the mercy of wind and drought. The talk drifted into other kindred channels, and after some time, Doc Blaine bluntly spoke of something that hung in his mind.

"Jim," he said, "that night I thought you were dying, you babbled a lot of stuff about your heart, and an Indian who lent you his. How much of that was delirium?"

"None, Doc," said Garfield, pulling at his pipe. "It was gospel truth. Ghost Man, the Lipan priest of the Gods of Night, replaced my dead, torn heart with one from somethin' he worshipped. I ain't sure myself just what that somethin' is—somethin' from away back and a long way off, he said. But bein' a god, it can do without its heart for awhile. But when I die—if I ever get my head smashed so my consciousness is destroyed—the heart must be given back to Ghost Man."

"You mean you were in earnest about cutting out your heart?" demanded Doc Blaine.

"It has to be," answered old Garfield. "A livin' thing in a dead thing is opposed to nat'er. That's what Ghost Man said."

"Who the devil *was* Ghost Man?"

"I told you. A witch doctor of the Lipans, who dwelt in this country before the Comanches came down from the Staked Plains and drove 'em south across the Rio Grande. I was a friend to 'em. I reckon Ghost Man is the only one left alive."

"Alive? Now?"

"I dunno," confessed old Jim. "I dunno whether he's alive or dead. I dunno whether he was alive when he came to me after the fight on Locust Creek, or even if he was alive when I knowed him in the southern country. Alive as we understand life, I mean."

"What balderdash is this?" demanded Doc Blaine uneasily, and I felt a slight stirring in my hair. Outside was stillness, and the stars, and the black shadows of the post oak woods. The lamp cast old Garfield's shadow grotesquely on the wall, so that it did not at all resemble that of a human, and his words were strange as words heard in a nightmare.

"I knowed you wouldn't understand," said old Jim. "I don't understand myself, and I ain't got the words to explain them things I feel and know without understandin'. The Lipans were kin to the Apaches, and the Apaches learnt curious things from the Pueblos. Ghost Man *was*—that's all I can say—alive or dead, I don't know, but he *was*. What's more, he *is*."

"Is it you or me that's crazy?" asked Doc Blaine.

"Well," said old Jim, "I'll tell you this much—Ghost Man knew Coronado."

"Crazy as a loon!" murmured Doc Blaine. Then he lifted his head. "What's that?"

"Horse turning in from the road," I said. "Sounds like it stopped."

I stepped to the door, like a fool, and stood etched in the light behind me. I got a glimpse of a shadowy bulk I knew to be a man on a horse; then Doc Blaine yelled: "Look out!" and threw himself against me, knocking us both sprawling. At the same instant I heard the smashing report of a rifle, and old Garfield grunted and fell heavily.

"Jack Kirby!" screamed Doc Blaine. "He's killed Jim!"

I scrambled up, hearing the clatter of retreating hoofs, snatched old Jim's shotgun from the wall, rushed recklessly out onto the sagging porch and let go both barrels at the fleeing shape, dim in the starlight. The charge was too light to kill at that range, but the birdshot stung the horse and maddened him. He swerved, crashed headlong through a rail fence and charged across the orchard, and a peach tree limb knocked his rider out of the saddle. He never moved after he hit the ground. I ran out there and looked down at him. It was Jack Kirby, right enough, and his neck was broken like a rotten branch.

I let him lie, and ran back to the house. Doc Blaine had stretched old Garfield out on a bench he'd dragged in from the porch, and Doc's face was whiter than I'd ever seen it. Old Jim was a ghastly sight; he had been shot with an old-fashioned .45-70, and at that range the heavy ball had literally torn off the top of his head. His features were masked with blood and brains. He had been directly behind me, poor old devil, and he had stopped the slug meant for me.

Doc Blaine was trembling, though he was anything but a stranger to such sights.

"Would you pronounce him dead?" he asked.

"That's for you to say." I answered. "But even a fool could tell that he's dead."

"He *is* dead," said Doc Blaine in a strained unnatural voice. "Rigor mortis is already setting in. But feel his heart!"

I did, and cried out. The flesh was already cold and clammy; but beneath it that mysterious heart still hammered steadily away, like a dynamo in a deserted house. No blood coursed through those veins; yet the heart pounded, pounded, pounded, like the pulse of Eternity.

"A living thing in a dead thing," whispered Doc Blaine, cold sweat on his face. "This is opposed to nature. I am going to keep the promise I made him. I'll assume full responsibility. This is too monstrous to ignore."

Our implements were a butcher knife and a hacksaw. Outside only the still stars looked down on the black post oak shadows and the dead man that lay in the orchard. Inside, the old lamp flickered, making strange shadows move and shiver and cringe in the corners, and glistened on the blood on the floor, and the red-dabbled figure on the bench. The only sound inside was the crunch of the saw edge in bone; outside an owl began to hoot weirdly.

Doc Blaine thrust a red-stained hand into the aperture he had made, and drew out a red, pulsing object that caught the lamplight. With a choked cry he recoiled, and the thing slipped from his fingers and fell on the table. And I too cried out involuntarily. For it did not fall with a soft meaty thud, as a piece of flesh should fall. It *thumped* hard on the table.

Impelled by an irresistible urge, I bent and gingerly picked up old Garfield's heart. The feel of it was brittle, unyielding, like steel or stone, but smoother than either. In size and shape it was the duplicate of a human heart, but it was slick and smooth, and its crimson surface reflected the lamplight like a jewel more lambent than any ruby; and in my hand it still throbbed mightily, sending vibratory radiations of energy up my arm until my own heart seemed swelling and bursting in response. It was cosmic *power*, beyond my comprehension, concentrated into the likeness of a human heart.

The thought came to me that here was a dynamo of life, the nearest approach to immortality that is possible for the destructible human body, the materialization of a cosmic secret more wonderful than the fabulous fountain sought for by Ponce de Leon. My soul was drawn into that unterrestrial gleam, and I suddenly wished passionately that it hammered and thundered in my own bosom in place of my paltry heart of tissue and muscle.

Doc Blaine ejaculated incoherently. I wheeled.

The noise of his coming had been no greater than the whispering of a night wind through the corn. There in the doorway he stood, tall, dark, inscrutable—an Indian warrior, in the paint, war bonnet, breechclout and moccasins of an elder age. His dark eyes burned like fires gleaming deep under fathomless black lakes. Silently he extended his hand, and I dropped Jim Garfield's heart into it. Then without a word he turned and stalked into the night. But when Doc Blaine and I rushed out into the yard an instant later, there was no sign of any human being. He had vanished like a phantom of the night, and only something that looked like an owl was flying, dwindling from sight, into the rising moon.

The Thunder-Rider

Once I was Iron Heart, the Comanche war-hawk.

This is no fantasy that I speak, nor do I suffer from hallucination; I speak with sure knowledge, of the medicine memory, the only heritage left me by the race which conquered my ancestors.

This is no dream. I sit here in my efficiently appointed office fifteen stories above the street that thunders and roars with the traffic of the most highly artificialized civilization the planet has ever known. Looking through the nearest window I see the blue sky only between the pinnacles of the towers that rear above this latest Babylon. If I look down I will see only stripes of concrete, over which pour an incessant stream of jostling humanity and wheeled machines. Here are no oceanlike expanses of naked brown prairie beneath a naked blue sky, here no dry grass waving before the invisible feet of the unseen people of the wastes, here no solitude and vastness and mystery to veil the mind with all-seeing blindness and to build dreams and visions and prophesy. Here all is matter reduced to its most mechanical tangibility—power that can be seen and touched and heard, force and energy that crushes all dreams and turns men and women into whimpering automatons.

Yet, I sit here in the midst of this new wilderness of steel and stone and electricity and repeat the inexplicable: I was Iron Heart, the Scalp-Taker, the Avenger, the Thunder-Rider.

I am no darker than many of my customers and patrons. I wear the clothes of civilization with as great ease as any of them. Why should I not? My father wore blanket, warbonnet and breechclout in his youth, but I never wore any garments except those of the white men. I speak English—and French, Spanish, and German, too—without an accent, save for a slight Southwestern idiom such as you will find in any white Oklahoman or Texan. Behind me lie years of college life—Carlisle, the University of Texas, Princeton. I am reasonably successful in my profession. I am accepted without question in my chosen social circle—a society made of men and women of pure Anglo-Saxon descent. My associates scarcely think of me as an Indian. Apparently I have become a white man, and yet—

One heritage remains. A memory. There is nothing vague or hazy or illusive about it. As I remember my yesterdays as John Garfield, so I remember as more distant yesterdays the life and deeds of Iron Heart. As I sit here and stare out upon the new wasteland of steel and concrete and wheels, it all seems suddenly as tenuous and unreal as the fog that rises from the shores of Red River in the early morning. I see through it and beyond, back to the drab brown Wichita Mountains where I was born; I see the dry grass waving under the southwest wind, and the tall white house of Quanah Parker looming against the steel-blue sky. I see the cabin where I was born, and the lean horses and scrubby cows grazing in the sun-scorched pasture, the dry, straggling rows of corn in the little field nearby—but I see beyond that, too. I see a sweep of prairie, brown and dry and breathtakingly vast, where there is no tall white house, or cabin, or cornfield, only the brown grass waving, and buffalo-hide *tipis*, and a bronzed, naked warrior with plumes trailing like the train of a blazing meteor riding like the wind in the mad gladness of savage exultation.

I was born in a white-man cabin. I never wore warpaint, nor rode the warpath, nor danced the scalp dance. I cannot wield a lance or drive a flint-headed arrow through the bulk of a snorting buffalo. Any Oklahoma farm-boy can surpass me in horsemanship. I am, in short, a civilized man, and yet—

Early in my youth I was aware of a gnawing restlessness, an uneasy and sullen dissatisfaction with my existence. I read the books, I studied, I applied myself to the things the white men valued with a zeal which gratified my white teachers. They pointed me out with pride. They told me, and thought they were complimenting me when they did it, that I was a white man in mind as well as habit.

But the unrest grew, though none suspected it, for I hid it behind the mask of an Indian's face, as my ancestors, bound to an Apache stake, hid their agony from the gaze of their gloating enemies.

But it was there. It lurked at the back of my mind in the classroom when I listened, hiding my innate scorn for the learning I sought in order to advance my material prosperity. It colored my dreams. And these dreams, dim in my childhood, grew more vivid and distinct as I grew older—always a bronzed, naked warrior against a background of storm and cloud and fire and thunder, riding like a centaur, with warbonnet streaming and the lurid light flashing on the point of a lifted lance.

Racial instincts and superstitions began to stir in me at this repeated visitation. My dreams began to color my waking life, for dreams always played a great part in the lives of the Indians. My mind began turning red. I began to lose my grasp on the white man's existence I had chosen for myself. The shadow of a dripping tomahawk began to take shape, to hover over me. There was a need in my mind, a lawless, untamed urge towards violent action, a restlessness I began to fear only blood would quench. I tossed on my bed at night, fearing to go to sleep, fearing that I would be engulfed by this inexorable tide from the murky, fathomless reservoirs of racial subconsciousness. If this happened I knew I would kill, suddenly, savagely, and, according to the white man's understanding, reasonlessly.

I did not wish to kill men who had never harmed me, and to hang thereafter. Though I despised—as I still despise—the white man's philosophy and code, I find—and found—the material things of his civilization desirable, since the life of my ancestors is denied to me.

I tried to work off this primitive, murderous urge in sports. But I found that football, boxing, and wrestling only increased the feeling. The more fiercely I hurled my hard-muscled body into conflict, the less satisfaction I derived from this artificial conflict, the more I yearned for something I knew not what.

At last I sought aid. I did not go to a white physician or psychologist. I went back to the region of my birth, and sought out old

Eagle Feather, a medicine man who dwelt alone among the hills, scorning the white man's ways with a bitter scorn. In my white man's garments I sat cross-legged in his *tipi* of ancient buffalo hides, and as I talked I dipped my hand into the pot of stewed beef that sat between us. He was old—how old I do not know. His moccasins were frayed and worn, his blanket dingy and patched. He was with that band whom General MacKenzie caught in the Palo Duro, and when the general shot all their horses he beggared old Eagle Feather, for the medicine man's wealth lay in horseflesh, like that of all the tribe.

He heard me through without speaking and for a long time thereafter he sat unmoving, his head bent on his breast, his withered chin almost touching his bracelet of Pawnee teeth. In the silence I heard the night wind sighing through the lodge-poles, and an owl hooted ghostily deep in the woods. At last he lifted his head and spoke:

"There is a medicine memory which troubles you. This warrior you see is the man you once were. He does not come to urge you to strike an axe into the heads of the white men. He comes in answer to a wildness in your own soul. You come of a long line of warriors. Your grandfather rode with Lone Wolf, and with Peta Nocona. He took many scalps. The white men's books cannot content you. Unless you find an outlet, your mind will turn red and the spirits of your ancestors will sing in your ears. Then you will slay, like a man in a dream, without knowing why, and the white men will hang you. It is not well for a Comanche to be choked to death in a noose. He can not sing his death song and his soul cannot leave his body, and must dwell forever underground with his rotting bones.

"You can not be a fighting man. That day is past. But there *is* a way to escape the bad workings of your medicine. If you could remember—a Comanche, when he dies, goes for a space to the Happy Hunting Ground to rest and hunt the white buffalo. Then, a hundred years later, he is reborn into a tribe—unless his spirit has been destroyed by the loss of his scalp. He does not remember—or, if at all, but a little, like figures moving in a mist. But there is a medicine to make him remember—a mighty medicine, and a terrible one, which no weakling can survive. *I* remember. I remember the men whose bodies my soul inhabited in past ages. I can wander in the mist and speak with great ones whose spirits have not yet been reborn—with Quanah Parker, and with Peta Nocona, his father, and with Iron Shirt, *his* father—with Satanta, the Kiowa, and Sitting Bull, the Ogalalla, and many another great one.

"If you are brave, you may remember, and live over your ancient lives, and be content, knowing your valor and prowess in the past."

He was offering me a solution—a substitute for a violent life in my present existence—a safety valve for the innate ferocity that lurks at the bottom of my soul.

Shall I tell you of the medicine ritual by which I gained full memory of my yesterdays? Alone in the hills, with only old Eagle Feather to see, I fought out my lone fight against such agony as white men only dream of in nightmares. It is an ancient, ancient medicine, a secret medicine, not even guessed by the omniscient anthropologists. It was always Comanche; from it the Sioux borrowed the rituals of their Sun Dance, and from the Sioux the Arikaras appropriated part of it for their Rain Dance. But it was always a secret rite, with only a medicine man to look on—no dancing, cheering throngs of women and braves to inspire a man, to stiffen his resolution by listening to his war songs and his boastings—only the stark, silent strength of his endurance, there in the windy darkness under the ancient stars.

Eagle Feather cut deep slits in the muscles of my back. The scars are there to this day; a man can put his clenched fists in the hollows. He cut deep into the muscles and, drawing rawhide thongs through the slits, bound them fast. Then he threw the thongs over an oak limb and, with a strength that only a medicine man could explain, he drew me up until my feet hung high above the grassy earth. He made the thongs fast and left me hanging there. He squatted before me and began beating a drum whose head was the skin from the belly of a Lipan chief. Slowly and incessantly he smote it, so that its soft, sinister rumbling played an incessant undertone throughout my agony, mingling with the night wind in the trees.

The night dragged on, the stars changed, the wind died and sprang up and died again. On and on droned the drum until the sound became changed strangely at times, and was a drum no longer but the thunder of unshod horses' hoofs beating the drum of the prairie. The hoot of the owl was a hoot no longer, but the death yell of forgotten warriors. And the flame of agony before my misted eyes was a roaring fire around which black figures leaped and chanted. No longer I swung on bloody thongs from an oak limb, but I stood upright against a stake, with flames lapping my feet, and sang my death song in defiance of my enemies. Past and present merged and blended fantastically and terribly, and a hundred personalities struggled within me, until time was not, nor space, nor form nor shape, only a writhing, twisting, whirling chaos of men and things and events and spirits, until all were dashed triumphantly into nothingness by a bronzed, painted, exultant rider on a painted horse whose hoofs struck fire from the prairie. Across a lurid sunset curtain of dusky flame they swept, in barbaric exultation, horse and rider, black against the glow, and with their passing my tormented brain gave way and I knew no more.

In the grey dawn, as I hung limp and senseless, Eagle Feather bound long-treasured buffalo skulls to my feet and their weight tore away flesh and sinew, so that I fell to the grass at the foot of the ancient oak. The sting of that fresh hurt revived me, but the nameless agony of mangled and lacerated flesh was nothing beside the great realization of power that swept over me. In that dark hour before dawn when the drum merged past and present and the material consciousness that always fights the more obscure senses had succumbed, the knowledge I sought had been made mine. Pain was necessary—great pain, to conquer the conscious part of the spirit that rules the material body. There had been an awakening, a joining together of senses and sensibilities, and memory remained; call it psychology, magic, what you will. No more would I be tormented by a lack of something, an urge to violence, which was but implanted instinct created by a thousand years of roaming, hunting and fighting. In my memories I could find relief by living over again the wild days of my yesterdays. So—

I remember many past lives, lives that stretch back and back into an antiquity that would amaze the historians. This I found—that no hundred years separated the lives of a Comanche. Sometimes rebirth was almost instantaneous—sometimes a stretch of years lay between, for what inscrutable reason I do not know.

I do know that the ego now inhabiting the body of the American citizen now called John Garfield, animated many a wild, painted figure in the past—and not so distant past, either. For instance, in my last appearance as a warrior on the stage of the great Southwest I was one Esatema, who rode with Quanah Parker and Satanta the Kiowa, and was killed at the battle of Adobe Walls, in the summer of 1874. There was an interlude between Esatema and John Garfield, in the shape of a weakly, deformed infant who was born during the flight of the tribe from the reservation in 1878 and, being unfit, was left to die somewhere on the Staked Plains. I was—but why seek to enumerate all the lives and bodies that have been mine in the past? It is an endless chain of painted, feathered, naked figures stretching back and back into an immemorial past—a past so distant and unthinkable that I myself hesitate before its threshold. Certainly, my white reader, I shall not seek to carry you with me. For my race is a very old race; it was old when we dwelt in the mountains north of the Yellowstone and travelled on foot, with our scanty goods loaded on the backs of dogs. The researches of the white men stop there, and well for their peace of mind and their beautifully ordered theories of mankind's past that they do; but I could tell you things that would shock you out of the amused tolerance with which you are reading this narrative of a race your ancestors crushed. I could tell you of long wanderings over a continent still teeming with pre-human terrors—but enough.

I will tell you of Iron Heart, the Scalp-Taker. Of all the bodies that have been mine, that of Iron Heart seems somehow more closely linked with that of John Garfield of the Twentieth Century. It was Iron Heart whom I saw in my dreams; it was the memories of Iron

Heart, dim and uninterpreted, which haunted me in my childhood and youth. Yet as I speak to you of Iron Heart, I must speak as, and through, the lips of John Garfield, else the telling will be but an incoherent raving, meaning nothing to you. I, John Garfield, am a man of two worlds, with a mind that is neither wholly red nor wholly white, yet with a muddled grasp on each. Let me interpret to you the tale of Iron Heart—not as Iron Heart himself would have told it, but as John Garfield must tell it, so that you may understand it.

Remember, there is much I will not tell. There are cruelties and savageries which I, John Garfield, understand as natural products of the life Iron Heart lived, but which you would not, could not understand, and from which you would turn in horror. There are other things I will slur in the telling. Barbarism has its vices, its sophistries, no less than civilization. Your cynicisms and sophistications are weak and childish beside the elemental cynicism, the vital sophistication of what you call savagery. If our virtues were unspoiled as a newborn panther cub, our sins were older than Nineveh. If—but enough. I will tell you of Iron Heart and the Horror he met, a Horror out of a Time older than the forgotten ruins that lie hidden in the jungles of Yucatan.

Iron Heart lived in the latter part of the Sixteenth Century. The events I shall describe must have taken place somewhere about 1575. Already we were a horse-riding tribe. More than a century before we had drifted down out of the Shoshone Mountains to become plainsmen and buffalo hunters, following the herds on foot, from the Great Slave Lake to the Gulf, bickering eternally with the Crows, the Kiowas, and the Pawnees and Apaches. It was a long, wearisome trek. But the coming of the horse changed all that—changed us, within a short span of years, from a poverty-stricken race of shiftless wanderers to a nation of invincible warriors, sweeping a red trail of conquest from the Blackfoot villages on the Bighorn to the Spanish settlements of Chihuahua.

Historians say the Comanches were mounted by 1714. By that time we had been riding horses for more than a century. When Coronado came in 1541, seeking the fabled Cities of Cibolo, we were already a race of horsemen. Children were taught to ride before they were taught to walk. When I, Iron Heart, was four years old, I was riding my own pony and watching a herd of horses.

Iron Heart was a powerful man, of medium height, stocky and muscular, like most of his race. I will tell you how I got the name. I had a brother a little older than myself, whose name was Red Knife. Affection between brothers is not very common among the Indians, but I felt for him the keen and ardent admiration and worship of a youth for an older brother.

It was an age of racial drift. We had not yet settled upon the great Palo Duro Canyon as the cradleland of our race. Our northern range still extended north of the Platte, though more and more we were encroaching upon the Staked Plains of the South, driving the Apaches before us in a series of whirlwind battles. A hundred and twenty-five years later we broke their power forever in a seven-day battle on the Wichita River and hurled them broken and beaten westward into the mountains of New Mexico. But in Iron Heart's day they still claimed the South Plains as their domain, and more of our wars were with the Sioux than with the Apaches.

It was the Sioux who killed Red Knife.

They caught us near the shore of the Platte, about a mile from a steep knob crowned with stunted growth. For that knob we raced, with one thought between us. For this was no ordinary raid; it was an attack in force; three thousand warriors rode there, Tetons, Brules and Yanktons. They meant to sweep on to the Comanche encampment, miles to the south. Unless the tribe was warned it would be caught and crushed by the Sioux. I reached the knob, but Red Knife's horse fell with him and the Sioux took him. They brought him to the foot of the knob, on the crest of which, hidden from their arrows, I was already making ready to send up a signal smoke. The Sioux did not try to climb the knob in the teeth of my lance and arrows, where only one man could come at a time. But they shouted up to me that if I would refrain from sending the signal, they would give Red Knife a quick death and ride on without molesting me.

Red Knife shouted to me: "Light the fire! Warn our people! Death to the Sioux!"

And so they fell to torturing him—but I gave no heed, though the prairie swam in a sea of red about me. They cut him to pieces slowly, member by member, while he laughed at them and sang his death song until his own blood choked him. He lived much longer than it would seem possible for a man to live, sliced as he was sliced. But I gave no heed and the smoke rolling up to the sky warned our people far away.

Then the Sioux knew they had lost and they mounted and rode away, even before the first cloud of dust to the south marked the coming of my brother warriors. With my brother's life I had bought the life of the tribe, and thereafter I had a new name, and it was Iron Heart. And the purpose of my life thereafter was to pay the Sioux the debt I owed them, and again and again I paid it, in singing arrows, and thrusting lance, aye, and in fire, and little, slicing knives—I was Iron Heart, the Scalp-Taker, the Vengeance-Maker, the Thunder-Rider. For when the rolling of the thunder across the echoing prairies made the bravest chiefs hide their heads, then I was wont to ride at a gallop, shaking my lance and chanting of my deeds, heedless of gods or men. For fear died in my heart, there on the knoll when I watched my brother die under the Teton knives, and only once again in all my life did it awaken for a space. And it is of that awakening that I would tell you.

In the autumn, that year of 1575—as I now calculate it—forty of us rode southward to strike the Spanish settlements. It was September, later to be called the Mexican Moon, when the warriors rode southward for horses, scalps and women. Aye, it was an ancient trail in Esatema's day, and many a time have I ridden it, in one body or another, but in Iron Heart's day it was less than forty years old.

We were after horses, but this particular raid never reached the Rio Grande. We turned aside to strike the Lipans on the river now called the San Saba, and that was unwise. But we were young warriors, eager to count coupes on our ancient enemies, and we had not yet learned that horses were more important than women, and women more important than scalps. We caught the Lipans off-guard and made a magnificent butchery among them, but we did not know that there was truce between them and the cannibal Tonkewas, always implacable foes of the Comanches, until we settled that score once and for all in the winter of 1864 when we wiped them out on their reservation on the Clear Fork of the Brazos. Esatema was in that fight, and he—I!—dipped his hands in blood with an ardor that had its roots in a dim and forgotten past.

But that autumn of 1575 was a long, long time removed from the butchery on the Brazos. Following the broken, headlong-fleeing Lipans, we ran full into a horde of Tonkewas and their Wichita allies.

With the Lipans, there were about five hundred warriors confronting us—too great of odds even for Comanches. Besides, we were fighting in a comparatively wooded country, and there we were at a disadvantage, because we were plains-born and bred, and preferred to do our fighting in the open where there was room for our primitive cavalry manoeuvres.

When we broke free of the thickets and fled northward, there were only fifteen of us left to flee, and the Tonkewas hounded us for nearly a hundred miles, even after the Lipans had given up the chase. How they hated us! And then, each was eager to fill his belly with the flesh of a Comanche, properly roasted, for they believed that transferred the fighting spirit of the Comanche to that of his devourer; we believed that too, and that is why, in addition to our natural loathing of cannibalism, we hated the Tonkewas as viciously as they hated us.

It was near the Double Mountain Fork of the Brazos that we met the Apaches. We had struck them on our road south and sent them howling to lick their wounds in the chaparral, and they were eager for revenge. They got it. It was a running fight on tired horses, and of the forty braves who rode south so proudly, only five of us lived to cross the Caprock—that ragged irregular rampart that lies like a giant stairstep across the plains, mounting to a higher level.

I could tell you how the Plains Indians fought. No such fighting was ever seen on this planet before, or ever will be again, for the conditions which produced it have passed forever. From Milk River to the Gulf we fought alike—on horseback, wheeling, darting like hornets with deadly stings, raining showers of flint-headed dogwood arrows, charging, circling, retreating, illusive as wasps and dangerous as cobras. But this meeting below the Caprock was no fight in such a sense. We were fifteen Comanches against a hundred Apaches and we fled, turning to drive arrow or thrust with lance only when we could no longer elude them. It was nearly sundown when they started us, otherwise the saga of Iron Heart had ended there, and his scalp gone to smoke in an Apache *tipi* with the other ten the Tigers of the Prairie took that day.

But somehow, when night fell we scattered and eluded them, and came together again above the Caprock—weary, hungry, with empty quivers, on exhausted horses. Sometimes we walked and led them, which shows in what state they were, for a Comanche never walked unless the need was most desperate. But we stumbled on, feeling that we were doomed already, groping our way northward, swinging further to the west than any of us had ever gone before, in the hopes of avoiding our implacable enemies. We were in the heart of the Apache country and none of us had any hope of ever reaching our camp on the Cimarron alive. But we struggled on, through a vast and waterless waste, where not even cacti grew, and on which not even the unshod hoof of a horse left any impression on the iron-hard soil.

It must have been towards dawn that we crossed the Line. More I cannot say. There was no actual line there, and yet at one stride we all felt—we *knew*—that we had come into a different country. There was a sort of vague shock, felt by both horses and men. We were all walking and leading the horses and we all fell to our knees, as if thrown by an earthquake shock. The horses snorted, reared, and would have torn free and bolted if they had not been too weak.

Without comment—we were too far gone to care for anything—we rose and struggled on, noting that apparently clouds had formed in the sky, for the stars were dim, almost obscured. Moreover the wind, which blows almost incessantly across that vast plateau, had subsided suddenly, so it was in a strange silence that we staggered across the plain, stumbling ever northward, until dawn came slowly, sullenly and dimly, and we halted and stared haggardly at each other, like ghosts in the morn after the destruction of the world.

We knew now that we were in a haunted country. Somehow, sometime in the night we had crossed a line that separated this strange, haunted, forgotten region from the rest of the natural world. Like the rest of the plain, it stretched drearily, flat and monotonous from horizon to horizon. But a strange dimness hung over it, a sort of dusky mist that was less mist than a lessening of the light of the sun. When it rose it looked pale and watery, more like the moon than the sun. Truly, we had come into the Darkening Land, the dread country still whispered of in Cherokee mythology, though how they came to know of it, I do not know.

We could not see beyond its confines, but we could see, ahead of us, a cluster of conical *tipis* on the plain. We mounted our tired horses and rode slowly toward them. We knew instinctively there was no life in them. We looked upon an encampment of the dead. We sat our horses in silence, under the leaden sky, with the drab, darkened waste stretching away from us. It was like looking through a smoked glass. Away to the west of us loomed a more solid mass of mist our sight could not penetrate.

Cotopah shuddered and averted his eyes, covering his mouth with his hand. "This is a medicine place," said he. "It is not good to be here." And he made an involuntary movement to pull about his shoulders the blanket lost in the long flight before the Tonkewas.

But I was Iron Heart, and fear was dead in me. I reined my terrified horse to the nearest *tipi*—and all were of the skins of *white* buffalo—and drew aside the flap. Then, though I was not afraid, my flesh crawled curiously, for I saw the inmate of that tent.

There was an old, old legend, which has been forgotten for more than a hundred years. In Iron Heart's life it was already dim and vague and distorted. But it told how long, long ago, before the tribes had taken shape as men know them now, a strange and terrible people came out of the North which then was populated by many wild and fearful tribes. They passed southward, slaying and destroying all in their path, until they vanished on the great high plains to the south. The old men said they walked into a mist and vanished. And that was long ago, so long ago, even before the ancestors of the Comanches came into the Valley of the Yellowstone. Yet here before my eyes lay one of the Terrible People. He was a giant, he who sprawled on the bearskin within the *tipi*; erect he must have stood fully seven feet in height, and his mighty shoulders and huge limbs were knotted with great muscles. His face was that of a brute, thin lipped, jutting jawed, sloping brow, with a tangled mop of shaggy hair. Beside him lay an axe, a keen-edged blade of what I now know to be green jade, set in the cleft of a shaft of a strange, hard wood which once grew in the far north, and which took a polish like mahogany. At the sight I desired to possess it, though it was too long hafted and heavy for easy use on horseback.

I thrust my lance through the door of the lodge and drew the thing out, laughing at the protests of my companions.

"I commit no sacrilege!" I maintained. "This is no death lodge, where warriors laid the corpse of a great chief. This man died in his sleep, as they all died. Why he has lain here so many ages without being devoured by wolves or buzzards, or his flesh rotting, I do not know, but this whole land is a medicine land. But I will take this axe."

It was just as I was about to dismount and secure it, having drawn it outside the lodge, that a sudden cry brought us wheeling about—to face a dozen Pawnees in full war-paint! And one was a woman! She bestrode her horse like a warrior, and waved a flint-headed war-axe.

Warrior women were rare among the plains tribes, but they did occur now and then. We knew her, instantly—Conchita, the warrior girl of the southern Pawnees. She was a warbird, in truth, leading a band of picked fighting men in reckless forays all over the Southwest. Vividly burns in my memory even now the picture she presented as I whirled and saw her—a slim, supple, arrogant figure, vibrant with life and menace, barbarically magnificent as she sat her rearing charger, with the fierce painted faces of her braves crowding close behind her. She was naked save for a short beaded skirt that lacked something of reaching mid-thigh. Her girdle was likewise beaded and supported a knife in a beaded sheath. Moccasins were on her slender feet, and her black hair, done up in two thick glossy braids, hung down her supple back. Her dark eyes flashed, her red lips parted in a cry of mockery as she brandished her axe at us, managing her bridleless, saddleless steed with a horsemanship that was breathtaking in its negligent grace. And she was a full-blooded Spanish woman, daughter of a captain of Cortez, stolen from below the Rio Grande by the Apaches when a baby and from them stolen in turn by the southern Pawnees, and raised as an Indian.

All this I saw and knew in the brief glance as I turned, for with a shrill cry she hurled herself at us and her braves swept in behind her. I say hurled, for that is the word. Horse and rider seemed to lunge at us rather than gallop, so swiftly did she come to the attack.

The fight was short. How could it be otherwise? They were twelve men, on comparatively fresh horses. We were five weary Comanches on foundered steeds. The tall chief with the scarred face came at me with a rush. In the fog they had not seen us, nor we them, until we were almost together. Seeing our empty quivers they came in to finish us with their lances and war clubs. The tall chief thrust at me, and I wheeled my horse who responded to the nudge of my knee with his last strength. No Pawnee could ever equal a Comanche in open battle, not even a southern Pawnee. The lance swished past my breast, and as the horse and rider plunged past me, carried by their own momentum, I drove my own lance through the Pawnee's back, so the point came out from his breast.

Even as I did so I was aware of another brave charging down on me from the left, and I sought to wheel my steed again, as I dragged the lance free. But the horse was foredone. He rolled like a foundered canoe in the swift tide of the Missouri, and the club in the Pawnee's hand smashed down. I threw myself sidewise and saved my skull from crushing like an egg, but the club fell stunningly on my shoulder, knocking me from my horse. Catlike, I hit on my feet, drawing my knife, but then the shoulder of a horse hit me and knocked me sprawling. It was Conchita who had ridden me down and now, as I struggled slowly to my knees, half-stunned, she leaped lightly down and swung up her flint-headed axe above my head.

I saw the dull glint of the edge, knew in a slow, stunned way that I could not avoid the downward swing—and then she froze, axe lifted, staring wide-eyed over my head toward something beyond me. Impelled beyond my will, I turned my dizzy head and looked.

The other Comanches were down, and five of the Pawnees. All the living froze, just as Conchita had frozen. One who knelt on dead Cotopah's back, wrenching at the scalp, his knife between his teeth, crouched there like one suddenly petrified, staring in the direction toward which all heads were turned.

For the fog to the west was lifting, and into view floated the walls and flat roofs of a strange structure. It was like, yet strangely unlike, the pueblos of the corn-raising Indians far to the west. Like them it was made of adobe, and the architecture was something similar, and yet there was a strange unlikeness. And from it came a train of strange figures—short brown men, clad in garments of brightly-dyed feathers, men who looked somewhat like the pueblo Indians. They were weaponless and carried only ropes of rawhide and whips in their hands. Only the foremost, a taller, gaunter Indian, bore a strange shield-shaped disk of gleaming metal in his left hand and a copper mallet in his right.

The curious parade halted before us, and we stared—the warrior-girl, with her axe still poised; the Pawnees, afoot or a-horse, wounded or whole; I, crouching on one knee and shaking my fast-clearing head. Then Conchita, sensing sudden peril, cried out a shrill, desperate command and sprang, lifting her axe—and as the warriors tensed for the onslaught, the man with the vulture feathers in his hair smote the gong with the mallet, and a terrible crash of sound leaped at us like an invisible panther. It was like the impact of a thunderbolt, that awful crash of sound, a thing so terrible it was almost tangible. Conchita and the Pawnees went down as if struck by lightning, and the horses reared in agony and bolted. Conchita rolled on the ground, crying out in agony, and clutching her ears. But I was Iron Heart, the Comanche, and fear slept in me.

I came up from the ground in a leap, knife in hand, though my skull seemed bursting from that awful blast of sound, and straight at the throat of Vulture-Crest I sprang. But my knife never sheathed itself in that brown flesh. Again the awful gong clanged and yet again, smiting me in mid-leap like a tangible force, hurling me back and back. And again and yet again the mallet crashed against the gong, so that earth and sky seemed split asunder by its deafening reverberation, and down I went like a man beaten to the ground by a war club.

When I could see, hear and think again, I found my hands were bound behind me, a rawhide thong about my neck. I was dragged to my feet and our captors began marching us toward the city. I call it that, though it was more like a castle. Conchita and her Pawnees were served in like manner, except one who was badly wounded. Him they slew, cutting his throat with his own knife, and left him lying among the others. One took up the axe I had dragged from the *tipi*, looked at it curiously, and then swung it over his shoulder. He must take both hands to manage it.

So we stumbled on toward the castle, half-strangled by the thongs about our necks, and occasionally encouraged by the bite of a rawhide lash across our shoulders. Only Conchita was not so treated, though her captor jerked brutally on her rope when she lagged. Her warriors looked haggard. They were the most warlike of the Pawnee nation—a branch which lived on the headwaters of the Cimarron, and which differed in many ways and customs from their northern brothers. They were more typical of a plains culture than the others, and never came in contact with the English-speaking invaders, for smallpox exterminated them about 1641. They wore their hair in long braids that swept the ground, like the Crows and Minnetarees, and loaded the braids with silver ornaments.

The castle—I call it that in the language of John Garfield and in your own language; Iron Heart would have spoken of it as a lodge—the castle stood on the crest of a low rise, not worthy of the name of hill, which broke the flat monotony of the plain. There was a wall around it and a gate in the wall. On one of the flat stages of the roof we saw a tall figure standing, wrapped in a shining mantle of feathers that glistened even in the subdued light. A lifted arm made an imperious gesture and the figure moved majestically through a doorway and vanished.

The gateposts were of bronze, carved with the feathered serpent, and at the sight the Pawnees shuddered and averted their eyes for, like all the plains Indians, they remembered that abomination from the days of old, when the great and terrible kingdoms of the far South warred with those of the far North.

They led us across a courtyard, up a short flight of bronze steps, and into a corridor, and once within all resemblance to the pueblos ceased. But we knew that once houses like this had risen in mighty cities far in the serpent-haunted jungles of the dim South, for in our souls stirred the echoes of ancient legends.

We came into a broad circular room through which the dim light streamed from an open dome. A black stone altar rose in the center of the room, with darkly stained channels along the rims, and facing it, on a raised dais, on an ivory throne heaped with sea-otter furs, there lounged the figure we had seen on the roof.

He was a tall man, slender and wiry, with a high forehead and a narrow, keen, hawklike face. There was no mercy in that face, only a cruel arrogance, a mocking cynicism. It was the face of a man who felt himself above the human passions of anger or mercy or love.

With a cruel amusement he swept his eyes over us, and the Pawnees lowered their gaze. Even Conchita, after boldly meeting his stare for a moment, winced and dropped her eyes. But I was Iron Heart, the Comanche, and fear slept in me. I met that piercing stare with my black eyes unwinking. He looked long at me, and presently spoke in the language of the pueblo Indians, which in those days was the commercial language of the prairies and understood by most of the horse-riding Indians.

"You are like a wild beast. There is the fire of killing in your eyes. Are you not afraid?"

"Iron Heart is a Comanche," I answered scornfully. "Ask the Sioux if there is anything he fears! His axe is still sticking in their heads. Ask the Apaches, the Kiowas, the Cheyennes, the Lipans, the Crows, the Pawnees! If he were flayed alive and his skin cut into pieces no larger than a man's palm, and each piece used to cover a dead warrior he has slain, the dead uncovered would still be more than the covered ones!"

Even in their fear the eyes of the Pawnees smoldered murderously at this boasting. The man on the throne laughed without mirth.

"He is tough, he is strong, he is nerved by his vanity," he said to the gaunt man with the gong. "He will endure much, Xototl. Place him in the last cell."

"And the woman, lord Tezcatlipoca?" quoth Xototl, bowing low, and Conchita started and stared wide-eyed at the fantastic figure on the throne. She knew the Aztec legends, and the name was the name of one of the sun's incarnations—taken, no doubt, in a spirit of blasphemy by the ruler of this evil castle.

"Place her in the Golden Room," said Tezcatlipoca, and as our captors, bending low before him, gathered up the thongs that bound us, he glanced curiously at the jade axe which had been brought into the room and laid on the altar.

"Why, it is the axe of Guar, chief of the Northerners!" quoth he. "The axe he swore would some day split my skull! But Guar and all his tribe have been dead in their caribou-hide tents for more centuries than even I like to remember, and my skull still holds the magic of the ancients! Leave the axe here and take them away! I will talk to the girl presently, and then there shall be sport, as it was in the days of the Golden Kings!"

They led us out of the circular chamber and across a series of broad rooms, where cat-footed brown women, beautiful with a sinister beauty, and naked but for their golden ornaments, crowded close to stare at the prisoners, and especially the warrior girl of the Pawnees. And they laughed at her, sweet, soft, evil laughter, venomous as poisoned honey.

"Giver her to us," they begged mockingly, clustering around Xototl. "She is a wild young thing—let us tame her! She shall be our sister! Let us take her into the Chamber of Maidens and play with her!"

"Make room, sluts," ordered Xototl harshly, cuffing them out of his path. "Are you mad, to demand, even in jest, one already chosen by our master, the Lord of the Mist?"

"Then give us our privilege!" they clamored, their eyes burning avidly with a brooding gleam. "The youngest and the most handsome of the captives! It is the law, laid down by Tezcatlipoca himself! Give us our share!"

"It is the law," grunted Xototl, halting the train of captives. "Choose!"

They swarmed about us with joyous, eager cries, their eyes sparkling, their lips curled in mysterious smiles. They bent close to stare in our faces with greedy eagerness, they snatched and grabbed at the younger men like women who fight over a desired object. The older men they did not heed and after one glance at my scarred, dark, formidable face they avoided me as they might have shunned a wild beast. Only one came too close, a bold-eyed hussy who looked at me searchingly, was not pleased at what she saw, and bent to spit in my face. My hands were tied but not my legs. I drove my knee into her belly with a force that knocked her sprawling and left her doubled up and gasping in agony on the floor. The others shrieked and scattered like frightened birds, but in an instant were back, shrieking with laughter and mocking the victim's anguish as she writhed on the floor.

Even Xototl's grim lips twitched in a cruel shadow of a smile, but he only said: "Have done with this play. Choose, and be gone!"

They dragged from among us the youngest of the Pawnees, a supple, handsome youth, little more than a boy. First they stripped him naked as the day he was born and cut off his long braids. They fastened gold chains on his wrists and ankles, and one about his neck, and then they removed the rawhide thongs. They placed on his head a chaplet of strange, purple flowers which gave forth a poisonously sweet odor and made even our heads swim. He quickly seemed like a man drunken with the perfume. Then they led him away, down another corridor, clustering close about him, laughing, singing, caressing him, calling tender words to him—but there was mockery in their tenderness, and their laughter was crueler than the laughter of the squaws who mock the captive writhing at the smoking stake.

As they vanished through a golden door at the end of the corridor, he glanced back at us once, despair and terror in his dilated eyes. Conchita cried out fiercely and sharply and for the first time struggled against her bonds. But a brutal jerk on the rope about her neck threw her to her knees, and another dragged her to her feet again, half-strangled. So they led us on down the corridor and the muffled laughter behind the golden door dwindled in the distance behind us.

We came into a long, broad corridor, with heavy doors opening into it on either side, and a broad stair at the further end that led up to the next story. As we passed these doors they were thrown open, revealing small cell-like rooms, devoid of furniture, with each a small, barred window. Into each of these cells one of the Pawnees was thrust, until only I and Conchita were left. Xototl turned aside and led her up the stair, while I was thrust into the last cell in the row. As I was dragged inside I saw terror flare in Conchita's lovely eyes as she was dragged up the steps. Within the cell I was tripped suddenly and thrown on my face, and before I could roll on my back, four men were crouching on me, binding my legs with rawhide. And there they left me tormented by hunger and thirst, and by a growing rage that almost strangled me.

After awhile the door opened and the Lord of the Mist entered and looked down at me. I glared up at him, not at all awed, though he seemed inhumanly tall and strange in the dim light, and the feathers that sheathed him from neck to ankle glinted and shone with a thousand dull and changing sheens.

"Poor fool!" he murmured. "I could almost pity you! Bloodthirsty beast of the prairies, with your swaggerings and boastings, your tally of scalps and slayings. How your eyes glare in the dimness!

So burn the eyes of a trapped panther when he looks on his slayer. Fool! Soon you will howl for death!"

"A Comanche does not cry out at the stake," I snarled, my eyes red with the murder-lust. My thews swelled and knotted until the rawhide cut into the flesh, but the thongs held. He laughed.

"Stake? Poor fool! Crude as the beasts you hunt! Crude as the grasp of your savage race on the elemental truth recognized so long ago by my ancestors. Pain! It is part of life. To inflict, to grow drunken on! There is no music so sweet as the screams of a tortured human being. It revives youth, nerves the brain and muscle, stirs hidden depths in the soul. This your paltry tribes realize, and strive to accomplish with your foolish stakes and fires and skinning knives— vengeance? What little meaning! The cries of my own brother or sister would intoxicate me as much as the shrieks of an enemy!"

I grunted disgustedly. Blood ties were strong among the Comanche.

He laughed at me. "Fool! What do you know of the needs and pleasures of the Old Race? As little as the beasts know! If I told you how old I am, your brain would burst. But know this: when I came up alone from the South, long ago, Tenochtitlan was not yet even a dream in the brains of the savages who were the fathers of the Aztecs!"

Again he laughed, scornfully; the feathers of his mantle rustled; the door closed and outside a bolt clashed into place. I lay alone in the dim-lit cell. I heard him ascending the stair with the soft tread of his sandal-shod feet. What happened next, beyond that stair, I did not see, nor did I learn till long afterward. But this came to pass:

When Xototl took Conchita up the stair alone, he led her along a broad hallway and into a chamber where the walls, ceiling, and floor were of that yellow metal which the Lipans traded for or stole from the Yaquis and traded in turn to the Plains tribes to use as ornaments. She knew it was gold; her memories of her life as a baby in Mexico were too dim to remember, for she had been stolen when her baby lips could scarcely lisp her own name. But she had seen it, beaten into ornaments and worn by the Yaquis and the Lipans, and the Plains tribes to which they traded them. She had had no idea it existed in such quantities. The doors were of gold and there were gold bars on the windows. There was a golden couch heaped with sea-otter furs.

Xototl unbound her and like a wild thing she sprang to the windows, wrenching at the bars. But they held, and Xototl stood between her and the door. She was unarmed and there was a gold-hilted dagger in Xototl's girdle. He stood there gazing at her, with a strange look in his eyes, then sullenly, grudgingly, he turned away and left the chamber, locking the door behind him.

How long she remained alone in the chamber she never knew, but suddenly the opening of the door brought her around and she whirled to see the Lord of the Mist before her, tall as a god, with his mantle of rich-hued feathers about him and his black mane bound about his temples with a band in form of a golden serpent with head upreared above his forehead.

Untamed as she was, she recoiled until the backs of her legs pressed hard against the golden couch.

"Are you afraid?"

"No!" She tossed her head. But she lied, and he knew it.

"Do you know who I am?" he asked her curiously.

"I have guessed," she answered sullenly. "The Apaches have legends of your race. Your people dwelt long ago in great kingdoms far to the South, in the hot, jungle lands. They perished long ago. I had not guessed that any lived today."

"They were accursed of the gods," he answered. "Long before the barbarian ancestors of the Toltecs wandered down from the North, the race was declining, from civil war, from pestilence, and from other reasons."

She did not ask him what the other reasons were. She knew the ancient legends of Apacheland too well.

"I was a great magician," he said.

For his own reasons he had come far to the north and established his kingdom on that bleak plain, casting about it a mist of enchantment. He had found a tribe of pueblo Indians besieged by the invaders from the North, and they had appealed to him for aid, giving themselves fully into his hands. He had made magic and brought death to the Northerners. But he left them in their tents, and told the pueblo people that he could bring them to life whenever he wished. Beneath his cruel hands the people dwindled away until now not more than a hundred lived to do his bidding. He had come from the south more than a thousand years before. He was not immortal, but almost so.

Then he left her; and as he went the great serpent which did his bidding slithered silently and evilly through the corridors after him; this serpent had devoured many of the subjects of the Lord of the Mist.

Meanwhile, I lay in my cell and heard them drag forth a Pawnee and haul him along the corridor. After a long while I heard a fearful, animal-like scream of agony, and wondered what torment could wring a cry from the throat of a southern Pawnee. I had heard them laugh under the knives of the flayers. Then for the first time fear awoke in me—not physical fear so much as the fear that under the unknown torment I would cry out and so bring shame to the Comanche nation. I lay there and listened to the end of the Pawnees, and each of them cried out once.

Meanwhile Xototl had glided into Conchita's chamber, his eyes red with lust.

"You are soft, you are white," he mumbled. "I am weary of brown women."

He seized her in his arms, forced her back on the golden couch. She did not resist until she had the dagger in his girdle. Then she sank it in his back, swift and sudden and deadly. Before he could voice the cry that welled to his lips, she choked it in his throat and, falling with him to the floor, stabbed at him again and again until he lay still. Then rising, she hurried through the door and down the stair, snatching a bow, knife and a handful of arrows as she went.

In an instant she was in my cell, bending over me, her wide eyes blazing.

"Swift!" she hissed. "*He* is slaying the last of the warriors! Prove you are a man!"

The knife was keen, but the blade was slender, the rawhide tough. She worked hard, sawing through. Then I was on my feet, knife in my girdle, bow and arrows in my hand.

We stole from the cell and came face to face with a brown-skinned guard. Dropping my weapons I had him by the throat before he could cry out, and bearing him to the floor, I broke his neck with my bare hands before he could let go his spear and bring his knife into play.

Rising, we stole down the corridor until we came to the domed room, then we met the great serpent, and he fell before my arrows.

We came into the room and saw the last Pawnee die strangely and hideously, and I drove my last arrow straight at the Lord of the Mist. It struck him full in the breast, but glanced away. I was paralyzed with surprize, then leaped at him with my knife. Over and over we tumbled about the chamber, for he had sent his slaves into another part of the castle as Xototl had told Conchita. My knife would not bite through the strange, close-fitting garment he wore beneath his feather-mantle and, try as I would, I could not reach his throat or face. He cast me aside, and leaped to try his magic when Conchita cried: "The dead men rise from the tents of the Northerners and march toward the pueblo!"

"A lie!" he cried, going ashy. "They are dead! They cannot rise!"

"Nevertheless, they come!" she cried with a wild laugh.

He faltered, turned toward a window, then wheeled back, realizing the trick. But in that instant I had leaped and seized the great axe, and swung it high. As he turned toward me, fear leaped in his eyes and then the axe crashed through his skull, spilling his brains on the floor.

Then thunder crashed and rolled and balls of fire swept over the plains, and the pueblo rocked. Conchita and I raced to safety, hearing the screams of the people trapped there. Dawn rose on the plains, showing no mist, only a bare, sun-drenched expanse, on which a few bones lay moldering.

"Now we will go to my people," I said, taking her wrist. "There are some horses which did not run away."

But she tried to wrench away from me, and cried disdainfully: "Comanche dog! You live only because of my aid! Go your way! You are fit only to be the slave of a Pawnee!"

Rarely a Comanche struck a woman; not because of any particular chivalry, but because we felt a woman was too low in the scale by which we judged mankind for a warrior to demean himself by striking. But I saw this was a special case, and there was no degradation in connection with coercing this spitfire. So I took her by her glossy braids and flung her face down to the ground, and then I set a foot between her writhing shoulders and, without anger and without mercy, belabored her naked hips and thighs with my bow until she screamed for mercy and sobbingly acquiesced to whatever I might desire. Then I yanked her to her feet and bade her follow me to catch the horses, which she did, weeping and rubbing various smarting bruises. So then we were presently riding northward, toward the camp on the Canadian, and my beauty seemed quite content, now that she was on horseback. And I knew that I had found a woman worthy even of Iron Heart, the Thunder-Rider.

The Dead Remember

Dodge City, Kansas,
November 1, 1877.
Mr. William L. Gordon,
Antioch, Texas.

Dear Bill:
I am writing you because I have got a feeling I am not long for this world. This may surprize you because you know I was in good health when I left with the herd and I am not sick now as far as that goes, but just the same I believe I am as good as a dead man.

Before I tell you why I think so, I will tell you the rest of what I have to say, which is that we got to Dodge City all right with the herd, which tallied 3,400 head and the trail boss John Elston got twenty dollars a head from Mr. R. J. Blaine, but Joe Richards, one of the boys, was killed by a steer near the crossing of the Canadian. His sister, Mrs. Dick Westfall, lives near Seguin, and I wish you'd ride over and tell her about her brother. John Elston is sending her his saddle and bridle and gun and money.

Now, Bill, I will try to tell you why I know I'm a goner. You remember last August just before I left for Kansas with the herd, they found that old nigger and his woman dead that lived in that live oak thicket down by Zavalla Creek. You know his name was old Joel, and they called his woman Jezebel and folks said she was a witch. She was a yellow nigger and a lot younger than Joel. She told fortunes and the niggers were all afraid of her, some of the white folks too.

Well, when we was rounding up the cattle for the trail drive I found myself near Zavalla Creek along towards sundown, and my horse was tired and I was hungry and I decided I'd stop in at Joel's and make his woman cook me something to eat. So I rode up to his hut in the middle of the live oak grove, and Joel was cutting some wood to cook some beef which Jezebel had stewing over an open fire. I remember she had on a red and green checked dress. I am not likely to forget that.

They told me to light and I done so, and set down and ate a hearty supper, then Joel brought out a bottle of tequila and we had a drink, and I said I could beat him shooting craps. He asked me if I had any dice and I said no, and he said he had some dice and would roll me for a five-cent piece.

So we got to shooting craps, and drinking tequila, and I got pretty full and raring to go, but Joel won all my money which was about five dollars and seventy-five cents. This made me mad, and I told him I'd take another drink and get on my horse and ride. But he said the bottle was empty, and I told him to get some more. He said he didn't have no more, and I got madder and begun to swear and abuse him, because I was pretty drunk. Jezebel come to the door of the hut and tried to get me to ride on, but I told her I was free, white and twenty-one, and for her to look out, because I didn't have no use for smart niggers.

Then Joel got mad and said, yes, he had some more tequila in the hut, but he wouldn't give me a drink if I was dying of thirst. So I said: "Why, damn you, you get me drunk and take my money with crooked dice, and now you insult me. I've seen niggers hung for less than that."

He said: "You can't eat my beef and drink my licker and then call my dice crooked. No white man can do that. I'm just as tough as you are."

I said: "Damn your black soul, I'll kick you all over this flat."

He said: "White man, you won't kick nobody." Then he grabbed up the knife he'd been cutting beef with, and ran at me, and I pulled my pistol and shot him twice through the belly. He fell down almost in the fire, and I shot him again, through the head. Then Jezebel come running out screaming and cursing, with an old muzzle-loading musket. She pointed it at me and pulled the trigger, but the cap burst without firing the piece, and I yelled for her to get back or I'd kill her. But she run in on me and swung the musket like a club. I dodged and it hit me a glancing lick, tearing the hide on the side of my head, and I clapped my pistol between her breasts and jerked the trigger. The shot knocked her staggering back several foot, and she reeled and fell down on the ground, with her hand to her bosom and blood running out between her fingers.

I went over to her and stood looking down with the pistol in my hand, swearing and cursing her, and she looked up and said: "You've killed Joel and you've killed me, but by God, you won't live to brag about it. I curse you by the big snake and the black swamp and the white cock. Before this day rolls around again you'll be branding the devil's cows in Hell. You'll see, I'll come to you when the time's ripe and ready."

Then the blood gushed out of her mouth and she fell back and I knew she was dead. Then I got scared and sobered up and got on my horse and rode. Nobody seen me, and I told the boys next day I got that bruise on the side of my head from a tree branch my horse had run me against. Nobody never knew it was me that killed them niggers, and I wouldn't be telling you now, only I know I have not got long to live.

That curse has been dogging me, and there is no use trying to dodge it. All the way up the trail I could feel something following me. Before we got to Red River I found a rattlesnake coiled up in my boot one morning, and after that I slept with my boots on all the time. Then when we was crossing the Canadian it was up a little, and I was riding point, and the herd got to milling for no reason at all, and caught me in the mill. My horse drownded and I would have too, if Steve Kirby hadn't roped me and dragged me out from amongst them crazy cows. Then one of the hands was cleaning a buffalo rifle one night and it went off in his hands and blowed a hole in my hat. By this time the boys was joking and saying I was a hoodoo.

But after we crossed the Canadian, the cattle stampeded on the clearest, quietest night I ever seen. I was riding night-herd and didn't see nor hear nothing that might have started it, but one of the boys said just before the break, he heard a low wailing sound down amongst a grove of trees, and saw a strange blue light glimmering there. Anyway, the steers broke so sudden and unexpected they nearly caught me, and I had to ride for all I was worth. There was steers behind me and on both sides of me, and if I hadn't been riding the fastest horse in South Texas, they'd have trampled me to a pulp.

Well, I finally pulled out of the fringe of them, and we spent all next day rounding them up out of the breaks. That was when Joe Richards got killed. We was out in the breaks, driving in a bunch of steers, and all at once, without any reason I could see, my horse gave an awful scream and rared and fell backward with me. I jumped off just in time to keep from getting mashed, and a big mossy horn give a bellow and come for me. There wasn't a tree bigger than a bush anywhere near, so I tried to pull my pistol, and some way the hammer got jammed under my belt, and I couldn't get it loose. That wild steer was not more than ten jumps from me when Joe Richards roped it, and the horse, a green one, was jerked down and sideways. As it fell, Joe tried to swing clear, but his spur caught in the back cinch, and the next instant that steer had drove both horns clean through him. It was an awful sight.

By that time I had my pistol out, and I shot the steer, but Joe was dead. He was tore up something terrible. We covered him up where he fell, and put up a wood cross, and John Elston carved on the name and date with his bowie knife.

After that the boys didn't joke any more about me being a hoodoo. They didn't say much of anything to me and I kept to myself, though God knows, it wasn't any fault of mine as I can see.

Well, we got to Dodge City and sold the steers. And last night I drempt I saw Jezebel, just as plain as I see the pistol on my hip. She smiled like the devil himself and said something I couldn't understand, but she pointed at me, and I think I know what that means.

Bill, you'll never see me again. I'm a dead man. I don't know how I'll go out, but I feel I'll never live to see another sunrise. So I'm writing you this letter to let you know about this business and I reckon I've been a fool but it looks like a man just kind of has to go it blind and there is not any blazed trail to follow. Anyway, whatever takes me will find me on my feet with my pistol drawed. I never knuckled down to anything alive, and I won't even to the dead. I am going out fighting, whatever comes. I keep my scabbard-end tied down, and I clean and oil my pistol every day. And Bill, sometimes I think I am going crazy, but I reckon it is just thinking and dreaming so much about Jezebel; because I am using an old shirt of yours for cleaning rags, you know that black and white checked shirt you got at San Antonio last Christmas, but sometimes when I am cleaning my pistol with them rags, they don't look black and white anymore. They turn to red and green, just the color of the dress Jezebel was wearing when I killed her.

Your brother,

Jim.

Statement of John Elston. November 4, 1877.

My name is John Elston. I am the foreman of Mr. J. J. Connolly's ranch in Gonzales County, Texas. I was trail boss of the herd that Jim Gordon was employed on. I was sharing his hotel room with him. The morning of the third of November he seemed moody and wouldn't talk much. He would not go out with me, but said he was going to write a letter. I did not see him again until that night. I came into the room to get something and he was cleaning his Colt's .45. I laughed and jokingly asked him if he was afraid of Bat Masterson, and he said: "John, what I'm afraid of ain't human, but I'm going out shooting if I can." I laughed and asked him what he was afraid of, and he said: "A nigger woman that's been dead four months." I thought he was drunk, and went on out. I don't know what time that was, but it was after dark.

I didn't see him again alive. About midnight I was passing the Big Chief Saloon and I heard a shot, and a lot of people ran into the saloon. I heard somebody say a man was shot. I went in with the rest, and went on back into the back room. A man was lying in the doorway, with his legs out in the alley and his body in the door. He was covered with blood, but by his build and clothes I recognized Jim Gordon. He was dead. I did not see him killed, and know nothing beyond what I have already said.

Statement of Mike O'Donnell.

My name is Michael Joseph O'Donnell. I am the bartender in the Big Chief Saloon on the nightshift. A few minutes before midnight I noticed a cowboy talking to Sam Grimes just outside the saloon. They seemed to be arguing. After awhile the cowboy came on in and took a drink of whiskey at the bar. I noticed him because he wore a pistol, whereas the others had theirs out of sight, and because he looked so wild and pale. He looked like he was drunk, but I don't believe he was. I never saw a man who looked just like him. I did not pay much attention to him because I was very busy tending bar. I suppose he must have gone on into the back room. At about midnight I heard a shot in the back room and Tom Allison ran out saying that a man was shot. I was the first one to reach him. He was lying partly in the door and partly in the alley. I saw he wore a gun-belt and a Mexican carved holster and believed it to be the same man I had noticed earlier. His right hand was torn practically off, being just a mass of bloody tatters. His head was shattered in a way I had never seen caused by a gun shot. He was dead by the time I got there and it is my opinion he was killed instantly. While we were standing around him a man I knew to be John Elston came through the crowd and said: "My God, it's Jim Gordon!"

Statement of Deputy Grimes.

My name is Sam Grimes. I am a deputy sheriff of Ford County, Kansas. I met the deceased, Jim Gordon, before the Big Chief Saloon, at about twenty minutes until twelve, November 3rd. I saw he had his pistol buckled on, so I stopped him and asked him why he was carrying his pistol, and if he did not know it was against the law. He said he was packing it for protection. I told him if he was in danger it was my business to protect him, and he had better take his gun back to his hotel and leave it there till he was ready to leave town, because I saw by his clothes that he was a cowboy from Texas. He laughed and said: "Deputy, not even Wyatt Earp could protect me from my fate!" He then turned and went into the saloon. I believed he was sick and out of his head, so I did not arrest him. I thought maybe he would take a drink and then go and leave his gun at his hotel as I had requested. I kept watching him to see that he did not make any play toward anybody in the saloon, but he noticed no one, took a drink at the bar, and went on into the back room. A few minutes later a man ran out, shouting that somebody was killed. I hastily went to the back room, arriving there just as Mike O'Donnell was bending over the man, who I believed to be the one I had accosted in the street. He had been killed by the bursting of the pistol in his hand. I don't know who he was shooting at, if anybody. I found nobody in the alley, nor anybody who had seen the killing except Tom Allison. I did find pieces of the pistol that had exploded, together with the end of the barrel, which I turned over to the coroner.

Statement of Tom Allison.

My name is Thomas Allison. I am a teamster, employed by McFarlane & Company. On the night of November 3rd, I was in the Big Chief Saloon. I did not notice the deceased when he came in. There was a lot of men in the saloon. I had had several drinks but was not drunk. I saw "Grizzly" Gullins, a buffalo hunter, approaching the entrance of the saloon. I had had trouble with him, and knew he was a bad man. He was drunk and I did not want any trouble. I knew if we met there would be a fight. I decided to go out the back way. I went through the back room and saw a man sitting at a table with his head in his hands. I took no notice of him, but went on to the back door, which was bolted on the inside. I lifted the bolt and opened the door and started to step out in the alley. Then I saw a woman standing in front of me. The light was dim that streamed out into the alley through the open door, but I saw her plain enough to tell she was a negro woman. I don't know how she was dressed. She was not pure black but a light brown or yellow. I could tell that in the dim light. I was so surprised I stopped short, and she spoke to me and said: "Go tell Jim Gordon I've come for him."

I said: "Who the devil are you and who is Jim Gordon?" She said: "The man in the back room sitting at the table; tell him I've come!" Something made me turn cold all over, I can't say why. I turned around and went back into the room, and said: "Are you Jim Gordon?" The man at the table looked up and I saw his face was pale and haggard. I said: "Somebody wants to see you." He said: "Who wants to see me, stranger?" I said: "A yellow nigger woman there at the back door."

With that he heaved up from the chair, knocking it over along with the table. I thought he was crazy and fell back from him. His eyes were wild. He gave a kind of strangled cry and rushed to the open door. I saw him glare out into the alley, and thought I heard a laugh from the darkness. Then he screamed again and jerked out his pistol and threw it down on somebody I couldn't see. I don't know whether it was the negro woman or not. But the gun seemed to explode in his hand. There was a flash that blinded me and a terrible report, and when the smoke cleared a little, I saw the man lying in the door with his head and body covered with blood. His brains were oozing out, and there was blood all over his right hand. I ran to the front of the saloon, shouting for the bartender. I don't know whether he was shooting at the woman or not, or if anybody shot back. I never heard but the one shot, when his pistol burst.

Coroner's Report.

We, the coroner's jury, having held inquest over the remains of James A. Gordon, of Antioch, Texas, have reached a verdict of death by accidental gunshot wounds, caused by the bursting of the deceased's pistol, he having apparently failed to remove a cleaning rag from the barrel after cleaning it. Portions of the burnt rag were found in the barrel. They had evidently been a piece of a woman's red and green checked dress.

Signed:

J. S. Ordley, Coroner,	Richard Donovan,
Ezra Blaine,	Joseph T. Decker,
Jack Wiltshaw,	Alexander V. Williams.

Essays

The Strange Case of Josiah Wilbarger

Even amid the stark realities of frontier life, the fantastic and unex-plainable had its place. There was no event stranger than the case of the man whose scalped and bloody head came thrice to a woman in a dream.

One early morning in autumn, 1833, five men were cooking their breakfast of venison over a campfire on the banks of a stream some miles south of what is now the city of Austin. They were Josiah Wilbarger, Christian, Maynie, Strother and Standifer. They had been out on a land prospecting trip and were returning to the settlements. Wilbarger's cabin was on the Colorado River, near the present site of Bastrop, and only one family—the Hornsbys—lived above him.

As the party busied themselves over their meal, there came a sudden interruption—common enough in those perilous days. From the surrounding thickets and trees crashed a volley of shots, a whistling flight of arrows. Unseen, the red-skinned, painted warriors had stolen up and trapped their prey. Three of the men dropped, riddled. The other two, springing to their horses, miraculously untouched by the missiles whistling about them, broke through the ambush and outran their attackers. Looking back as they rode, they saw the three bodies of their companions lying motionless in pools of blood; one of these was Wilbarger, and they plainly saw the feathered end of an arrow standing up from his body. They drove in the spurs and raced madly through the thickets, striving to shut out from their horrified ears the triumphant and fiendish yells of their barbarian attackers.

These had not pursued the survivors far. They returned to the bodies which lay by the small fire, which still burned cheerfully, lighting that scene of horror. They gathered about, tall, lean, naked men, hideously painted, with shaven heads and tomahawks in their beaded girdles. They stripped the bodies and then, as a hunter might strip the pelt from a trapped animal, they took the symbols of their victory—the scalps of their victims.

This horrible practice, which the English settlers first taught the red man, and which did not originate with him, varied with different tribes. Some only took a small part of the scalp. Some ripped off the entire scalp. Such were the braves who had surprized the land prospectors.

Josiah Wilbarger, struck once by an arrow and twice by bullets, was not dead, though he lay like a lifeless corpse. He was only semi-conscious, dimly aware of what was going on about him. He felt rude hands ripping the clothing from his body, saw, as in a dream, the gory scalps ripped from the heads of his dead companions. Then he felt a lean muscular hand locked in his own hair, pulling back his head at an agonizing angle. It is doubtless that he could have so feigned death as to fool the keen hunters in whose hands he lay.

He realized the horror of his position, but he lay like a man struck dumb and paralyzed. He felt the keen edge of the scalping knife slice through his skin; perhaps he would have cried out, but he could not. He felt the knife circle his head above the ears, though he felt only a vague stinging. Then his head was almost wrenched from his body as his tormentor ripped the scalp away with ferocious force. Still no unusual agony was felt, numbed as he was by his desperate wounds, but the noise of the scalp leaving his head sounded in his ears like a clap of thunder. And his remaining shred of consciousness left him.

Had he been capable of any distinct thought, as he sank into senselessness, it must have been that this, at last, was death. Yet again he opened his eyes upon the bloody scene and the naked, scalped corpses about the dead ashes of the fire. Now all was silent and deserted; the red slayers had gone as silently and swiftly as they had come.

And in Wilbarger woke dimly the instinct to live, always so powerful in the iron men who manned the Southwestern frontier.

He began to crawl slowly, painfully, toward the direction of the settlements. To seek to depict the agonies of that ghastly journey would be but to display the frailty of the mere written word. Flies hung in clouds over his bloody head and he left red smears on the ground and the rocks. A quarter of a mile he dragged himself, then even the steely frame of a pioneer could do no more and he sank down beneath a giant post oak tree.

Now the occult element enters into the tale. The survivors of the massacre had ridden through the wide-flung settlements, bearing the tale of the crime. They had passed the cabin of the Hornsbys, which was the only cabin on the river above that of Josiah Wilbarger.

The following night, Mrs. Hornsby lay sleeping and she dreamed. The tale of the massacre was in her mind, and it is not strange that she dreamed of her neighbor, Josiah Wilbarger. Not strange, even, that in her dream she saw him naked and scalped, since the survivors had told her he had been killed, and she was familiar with Indian customs. But what was strange is that, in her dream, she saw him, not at the camping place, but beneath a great post oak tree, some distance from where he was struck down—and living. Wakened by the terror of the nightmare, she told her husband, who soothed her and told her to go back to sleep.

Again she slept, again she dreamed, and again she saw Wilbarger, naked, wounded and scalped, but living, under the oak tree. Again she awakened, and again her husband persuaded her to forget the vision and go back to sleep.

But with her third dreaming, she refused longer to doubt. She rose and began assembling such things as might be needed to bandage the wounds of a wounded man, and her vehemence convinced her husband, who gathered a party and set out. First they went to the place where the attack had occurred; they saw the dead men, and the track Wilbarger had made in dragging his wounded body. And beneath the great post oak tree, they found Wilbarger—alive.

Josiah Wilbarger lived twelve years thereafter, but his wounds never fully healed, and at last he met his death—by a dream. In a nightmare, he again experienced the horror of his scalping, and leaping up, struck his head with terrific force against the bedpost, which blow, coupled with his other wounds, soon caused his death.

The chronicles of the Middle Ages can offer no stranger a tale, yet its truth is well substantiated, and perhaps the most unexplainable event in Texas history.

Editor's Note: *The following paragraphs appeared with this essay, just before the final paragraph above, when it was first published in 1972; Howard's final paragraph was moved to the end.*

Marking the spot where Josiah Pugh Wilbarger of Austin's Colony was stabbed and scalped by the Indians, is a marker placed there by the State of Texas, in 1936, which explains that while Wilbarger was attacked and scalped in 1833, he died on April 11, 1845.

A footnote to the story has it that Wilbarger told his rescuers that he had seen, in a vision, his sister Margaret, at the time when he was sure he would bleed to death without help. She urged him not to give up, that help was on the way, and that he would be found—friends would find him. Three months later, it was learned that about the time Wilbarger had this 'visitation,' and as nearly as they could figure out at the same hour—Margaret died in her home in Missouri.

The Ghost of Camp Colorado

"The muffled drum's sad roll has beat
The soldiers' last tattoo;
No more on life's parade shall meet
That brave and fallen few."
—*The Bivouac of the Dead*

On the banks of the Jim Ned River in Coleman County, central West Texas, stands a ghost. It is a substantial ghost, built of square cut stone and sturdy timber, but just the same it is a phantom, rising on the ruins of a forgotten past. It is all that is left of the army post known as Camp Colorado in the pioneer days of Texas. This camp, one of a line of posts built in the 1850s to protect the settlers from Indian raids, had a career as brief as it was stirring. When Henry Sackett, whose name is well known in frontier annals, came to Camp Colorado in 1870, he found the post long deserted and the adobe buildings already falling into ruins. From these ruins he built a home and it is to his home and to the community school house on the site of the old post, that the term of Camp Colorado is today applied.

Today the house he built in 1870 is as strong as if erected yesterday, a splendid type of pioneer Texas ranch-house. It stands upon the foundations of the old army commissary and many of its doors and much of its flooring came from the old government buildings, the lumber for which was freighted across the plains three-quarters of a century ago. The doors, strong as iron, show plainly, beneath their paint, the scars of bullets and arrows, mute evidence of the days when the Comanches swept down like a red cloud of war and the waves of slaughter washed about the adobe walls where blue-clad iron men held the frontier.

This post was first begun on the Colorado River in 1856, but was shifted to the Jim Ned River, although it retained the original name. Built in 1857, in the stirring times of westward drift and Indian raid, the old post in its heyday sheltered notable men—Major Van Dorn, Captain Theodore O'Hara, whose poem, "The Bivouac of the Dead," has thrilled the hearts of generations, General James B. Hood, General James P. Major, General Kirby Smith, and the famous General Fitzhugh Lee, nephew of General Robert E. Lee. From Camp Colorado went Major Van Dorn, first commander of the post, to Utah, in the days of the Mormon trouble. And from Camp Colorado went General James P. Major with the force under Van Dorn, and Captain Sol Ross, later Governor of Texas, on the expedition which resulted in the death of Peta Nocona, the last great Comanche war chief, and the capture of his white wife, Cynthia Ann Parker, whose life-long captivity among the Indians forms one of the classics of the Southwest.

When the clouds of Civil War loomed in the East and the boys in blue marched away from the post in 1861, their going did not end Camp Colorado's connection with redskin history. For from the ranch house and store built on the site of the post, Henry Sackett rode with Captain Maltby's Frontier Battalion Rangers in 1874, on the path of Big Foot and Jape the Comanche, who were leaving a trail of fire and blood across western Texas. On Dove Creek, in Runnels County, which adjoins Coleman County on the west, the Rangers came up with the marauders and it was Henry Sackett's rifle which, with that of Captain Maltby, put an end forever to the careers of Big Foot and Jape the Comanche, and brought to a swift conclusion the last Indian raid in central West Texas.

Of the original buildings of the post, only one remains—the guard house, a small stone room with a slanting roof now connected with the ranch house. It was the only post building made of stone; the others, adobe built, have long since crumbled away and vanished. Of the barracks, the officers' quarters, the blacksmith shop, the bakery and the other adjuncts of an army camp, only tumbled heaps of foundation stones remain, in which can be occasionally traced the plan of the buildings. Some of the old corral still stands, built of heavy stones and strengthened with adobe, but it too is crumbling and falling down.

The old guard house, which, with its single window, now walled up, forms a storeroom on the back of the Sackett house, has a vivid history all its own, apart from the military occupancy of the post. After the camp was deserted by the soldiers, it served as a saloon wherein the civilian settlers of the vicinity quenched their thirst, argued political questions and conceivably converted it into a blockhouse in event of Indian menace. One scene of bloodshed at least, it witnessed, for at its crude bar two men quarreled and just outside its door they shot it out, as was the custom of the frontier, and the loser of that desperate game fell dead there.

Today there remains a deep crevice in one of the walls where two military prisoners, confined there when the building was still serving as a dungeon, made a vain attempt to dig their way to liberty through the thick, solid stone of the wall. Who they were, what their crime was, and what implements they used are forgotten; only the scratches they made remain, mute evidence of their desperation and their failure.

In early days there was another saloon at the post, but of that building no trace today remains. Yet it was in use at least up to the time that Coleman County was created, for it was here that the first sheriff of the county, celebrating the gorgeous occasion of his election, emerged from the saloon, fired his six-shooter into the air and yelled: "Coleman Country, by God, and I'm sheriff of every damn' foot of her! I got the world by the tail on a downhill pull! Yippee!"

A word in regard to the builder of the house that now represents Camp Colorado might not be amiss. The Honorable Henry Sackett was born in Orsett, Essexshire, England, in 1851 and came to America while a youth. Building the house, largely with his own labor, in 1870, he lived there until his death a few years ago, acting as postmaster under seven Presidents, and as storekeeper for the settlers. The south side of the stone house, built into a single, great room, was used as post office and general store. Henry Sackett was a pioneer in the truest sense of the word, an upright and universally respected gentleman, a member of the Frontier Battalion of Rangers, and later Representative in the Legislature of Texas, from Brown and Coleman Counties. He married Miss Mary MacNamara, daughter of Captain Michael MacNamara of the United States Army. Mrs. Sackett still lives at Camp Colorado.

The countryside is unusually picturesque—broad, rolling hills, thick with mesquite and scrub oaks, with the river winding its serpentine course through its narrow valley. On the slopes cattle and sheep graze and over all broods a drowsy quiet. But it is easy to resurrect the past in day dreams—to see the adobe walls rise out of dusty oblivion and stand up like ghosts, to hear again the faint and spectral bugle call and see the old corral thronged with lean, wicked-eyed mustangs, the buildings and the drill grounds with blue-clad figures—bronzed, hard-bitten men, with the sun and the wind of the open lands in their eyes—the old Dragoons! Nor is it hard to imagine that yonder chaparral shakes, not to the breeze, but to crawling, stealthy shapes, and that a painted, coppery face glares from the brush, and the sun glints from a tomahawk in a red hand.

But they have long faded into the night—the reckless, roistering cavalry men, the painted Comanches, the settlers in their homespun and buckskins; only the night wind whispers old tales of Camp Colorado.

A half mile perhaps from the Sackett house stands another remnant of the past—a sort of milestone, definitely marking the close of one age and the opening of another. It stands on a hillside in a corner of the great Dibrell ranch—a marble monument on which is the inscription:

BREEZE 21ST 31984
HEREFORD COW
BORN 1887 DIED 1903
MOTHER OF THE DIBRELL HERD
DIBRELL

This monument marks the resting place of one of the first registered, short-horn cows of central West Texas. When Breeze was born, West Texas swarmed with half-wild longhorns, descendants of those cattle the Spaniards brought from Andalusia; now one might look far before finding one of those picturesque denizens of the old ranges. Fat, white-faced, short-horned Herefords of Breeze's breed and kind have replaced them, and in the vast pageant of the West, the longhorn follows buffalo and Indian into oblivion.

The Ghost of Camp Colorado - photographs

The following photographs appeared in the article written by Howard. He took some of the photographs himself, and some are stock photos that were used.

The Sackett home built in the former Camp's grounds

Camp Colorado's Original Guardhouse

Photo was identified as "A Few Relics of the Old Post"

Monument of the grave of one of the first shorthorn cattle in
Central West Texas.
The gentleman in the photo is Howard's good friend, Dave Lee

A group of Longhorns

Miscellanea

Six-Gun Interview

(unfinished)

"I'm tellin' yuh, Jim Lamark," I snarls, "if'n you ruins old Yucca Mullarney like you aims, I'm shore gonna come gunnin' for you!"

Lamark grinned cold and hard like a wolf snarling.

"I takes my chances," he answers. "Any time you comes lookin' for me, I'm ready and ra'rin' to go, *sabe?* I don't see why you're so blame hostile, though. You ain't no kin to old Mullarney."

"I been his deputy for a long time," I growls, "and I ain't aimin' to see him get no raw deal if I can help it."

"You talks like I'm rustlin' his cows or somethin'," he snaps. "All I'm askin' him is to pay them notes he owes. I guess I got a right to demand that."

I merely snarled. Everybody in south Arizona knowed that the reason Jim Lamark bought up Yucca's notes and was pressing him so hard was because he was mad on account of Yucca beating him out for Sheriff in the last election. Lamark was a mean man, and nasty with a gun. Meeting him in Tijuana has just about spoilt my vacation.

"Well," I tells him, "I know you hates old Yucca, which is the best blame sheriff in Arizona. You knows that if you gives him a little more time on them notes he'll be able to pay, whereas if you presses him, he'll lose that little ranch he's payin' out to retire on when he gits too old to chase bandits."

"G'wan and trail yore loop," sneers Lamark. "I got no time to fool away with muttonhead deputies. I got beat in the election, but they's folks in the world which appreciates my ability. I'm here on important guver'ment business. On yore way."

"Remember what I tells you," I threatens and stalks away, using remarkable control to keep from socking him on the nose. I was good and mad; here was old Yucca, back in Lazy Horse, Arizona, slaving to pay out a little ranch so he wouldn't be plumb on the county when he got too old to work, and here was this coyote squeezing him on them blame notes, just for spite.

Thinking a little beer might cool me off some, I stalked into a bar and, glancing around, seen a maverick which looked plumb familiar to me. He was setting at a table in the back part of the bar, with his back towards me, sipping at a beer stein. He had on city clothes and I knowed him—it was Joey Manson, a reporter on the *Los Angeles Tribune*.

I walked over and slapped him on the back and yelled: "Howdy, Joey!"

He lept three foot into the air and threwed up his hands and squawked: "Don't shoot!"

"Dog bite me," says I profanely. "Whatever ails you, pard?"

He sank trembling into the chair and wiped his forehead with a bandanner.

"Oh, it's you, Bill Kirby," said he. "Boy, you gave me a start! I sort of forgot where I was—I was sitting there thinking over things, and you sure startled me. It's been a long time since I saw you, Bill—what you doing? Still playing deputy to old Yucca Mullarney back in Lazy Horse? And what are you doing here?"

"Aw, I just took me a vacation," says I. "Times is slow on the Arizona border lately and I thinks I'll catch me a little rest. What you doin'?"

His face growed long and mournful.

"I'm facing the doggondest proposition I was ever up against," said he. "My paper sent me down here on a job—if I don't go through with it, I lose my job; and if I do go through with it, likely I'll lose my life."

"Golly," I says. "Spill the beans, old timer."

"Well," he says, "my editor sent me down here to find and interview Juan Zapojos, the bandit. You've heard of him?"

"Plenty," says I. "Why, ain't he the mutt that bumps off that reporter from San Francisco awhile back?"

"Boy, you said!" says Joey, busting out into a sweat. "I didn't find that out till I got here—at least, I hadn't known the details. I thought Zapojos thought the reporter was a spy or something, but I find out that he had him shot because of something his paper had said about Zapojos. The bandit keeps up with the news—and now he'll be madder'n a wet hen, because all the American papers have been roasting him something fierce because of his raids on the American side—calling him a murderer and a horse thief, and urging the Mexican government to take some definite action against him. Just between me and you, I got it on good authority that the California Cattlemen's Association has promised to furnish a man that will get Zapojos, dead or alive, and the Mexican government has agreed to give him full hand. A sweet time for a hard-working newspaper man to be dumped down in the middle of the brawl—" Here Joey stops suddenly, fixing his eyes on me.

"By golly, Bill," says he, "you ain't doing nothing—how would you like to earn a hundred dollars?"

"Whatcha mean?" says I.

"Why listen," he urges. "You're born and bred to the Border and can speak Spanish like a native—you're not doing anything now. Do this for me! You'd have ten times the chance of getting out alive that I would. Anybody can tell you're not a newspaper man, but those bandits would fill me full of lead before I could even speak to 'em. Come on, pardner!"

"But how'll I find this Zapojos?" said I. "And what'll I say to him if I does find him?"

"Finding him would be a cinch," says Joey. "Just ride south and ask the *peons* where he hangs out—they're all in league with him. As for the other, I'll write you out a list of questions to ask him. Wait a minute."

Joey grabbed out a writing pad and a pencil and scribbled some questions on it.

"Just write the answers opposite the questions," says he, "and don't make Zapojos mad."

"Well, hey," I said, "I ain't said I'd do it have I—aw, well, I reckon I ain't got nothin' else to do."

So an hour later I was trotting south into the open country on my buckskin mustang, Cap'n Kidd. It was about the middle of the morning and I was heading for a little village called La Paz, which lay about three hours' ride to the south. It wasn't much of a place—just a scattering of 'dobe huts and one general store and saloon. I tied my bronc to the hitching rail and went in, slapping the dust offa my breeches with my Stetson. I drunk me a bottle of cold beer and was about to ask the Mex barkeep about Zapojos when a very smooth-rigged Mexican come in. He was tall and slim and right handsome, with a costly sombrero, a brocaded silk jacket, flaring-bottomed pants with silver dollars on 'em and worn outside high heeled boots that musta cost plenty. He wore big Spanish spurs, chased with silver, and the ivory handle of a pistol jutted from his hip.

I decided I'd ask him instead, so I walked over to him, saying very polite, *"Buenos días, amigo,"* and then I says: "I'm lookin' for Juan Zapojos—"

Zowie! Quick as a flash his eyes blazed and he went for his gun like a streak. It was so unexpected he caught me plumb off guard; I didn't had time to think of drawing myself, and instinctively hit him on the jaw. He stretched out on the 'dobe floor and he didn't even quiver. At that moment a frightened Mexican face looked in at the doorway, and then vanished, and I heard the drum of hoofs heading south.

"Doggawn it," says I peevishly, blowing on my skinned knuckles. "What kinda racket is this?"

Well, the Mexes in the bar was jabbering like a bunch of guineas and not wishful to engage in any more scraps, being on a peaceful mission, I didn't wait for the Mex to come to, but left 'em pouring water on him and mounted Cap'n Kidd and rode. The only other village anywheres near was a little place called Autlan, a few miles to the west of La Paz, and I thought maybe I could get some information there. I just didn't like the idee of striking out blind amongst them hills. I thought I could stumble on to some spig which was secretly one of Zapojos' gang, and let him know I just wanted to ask the big boy some harmless questions. If I rode into the hills without letting nobody know why, I'd likely get shot from ambush. I couldn't figger why the Mexican at La Paz drawed on me. He didn't know me and I had my deputy badge hid.

I didn't hurry none, but it wasn't long before I rode into Autlan—or up to it, I oughta say. It wasn't as big as La Paz—just a 'dobe store and bar combined. Well, it being past noon I bought me a can of peaches and some sardines and crackers and et my dinner, and when I'd got through and drunk me a bottle of beer, I decided to try the Mex barkeep.

"Hey, *amigo*," says I, "answer me a question, will ya?"

"*Quién sabe?*" says he.

"Can the evasions," I growls. "I wanta know where I can find Juan Zapojos—"

Once again I got sudden and unexpected action.

"Spy! Dog!" howls the Mex, plumb oary eyed, and come charging around the bar with a butcher knife in his hand and murder in his eye. I was so plumb disgusted by this time that I shot the knife outa his hand and kicked him heartily in the pants.

"By golly," I snarls, "I've heered tell that every *peon* in this part uh the country was Zapojos' man, but I hadn't no idee they was so hostile about it. Now you spill the beans about Zapojos before I bends this gun barrel over yore dome."

"*No sabe,*" says he, sullen-like, and I was about to repeat my request in Spanish when a shadow falls across the door. I wheeled, ready to shoot it out with whoever it was, but the man that stood there had his sombrero in his hand and a smile on his dark handsome face. He was dressed a lot like the Mexican I knocked out in La Paz, only even more slick. His spurs had gold on 'em instead of silver and he wore two big ivory handled Colts, swinging low on his hips. Right off I knowed he, as well as the other one, was Zapojos' men. They dressed too expensive for ordinary *vaqueros*.

"You wish to meet Zapojos?" he said, very friendly-like. "You are a friend, no?"

"I just wanta ask him some questions," I said. "I won't take up more'n an hour of his time."

"*Bueno,*" says the Mex. "I am Jose Lopez; it is my honor to escort you."

Well, we got on our broncs and rode nearly due south, toward the big, bare wild looking hills which was the haunt of outlaws and renegades—the wildest, toughest hombres in the world, I reckon.

Lopez was a very companionable sorta fellow, talking and laughing and telling jokes, and singing Spanish songs. We rode for maybe two hours and then, swinging far to the southwest, we entered the foothills of the Diablo Range. After an hour of rough going, we come out into a sorta level plateau and Lopez pointed ahead of us towards the mouth of a narrow canyon.

"There is the doorway to Zapojos' lair," said he, and he politely reined aside for me to precede him. But one thing I've learned as a deputy sheriff, and that is to never go first into anything with a stranger at yore back.

"I don't know the way," says I, "so I reckon you better go first."

We looked each other eye to eye for a minute, and then he bowed and made a gesture of agreeing, and rode ahead of me. I rode right behind him and I found the canyon even more narrow then I'd thought; they really wasn't room for two horses to go abreast. The floor was smooth and level, the sheer walls rose on each side for a hundred feet. It was really less like a real canyon than a cleft in the hill. A few hundred yards ahead it narrowed a little more and beyond the narrowest part I believed it widened into a respectable sized canyon, judging from what I could see through the cleft.

Now Lopez began to sing, and he sung so loud that his voice fairly boomed along the cliffs. I spoke to him about something but he paid no attention but kept right on singing, which was unusual for a polite Mexican. And I noticed he seemed to be pulling slowly away from me, leaving several yards between us. I got an idee he didn't want to be very close to me when we rode through the cleft into the wider canyon. Now we was close to the cleft and, as he stopped to catch his breath a second, I heard a noise beyond that made me all alert; it was a sound that you couldn't mistake—a pebble bouncing and rattling down the side of the cliff and falling on the canyon floor. It mighta been dislodged from above by some small varmint—and it mighta been knocked off by a rifle barrel being pushed over the edge of the canyon wall. In a flash I had reined up behind Lopez and had my .44 against his spine. His dark face paled and he quit singing pronto.

"Easy all," I said in a low voice, slipping his ivory-handled guns outa the holsters. "Rein yore cayuse around and drift back down the canyon. If yuh make any false move or yell, yuh'll trade yore saddle for a harp."

Well, it wasn't very easy to get both broncs turned in that narrow cleft, but we done it and cantered back down the canyon and out into the open again, Lopez saying nothing, but riding with his hands well up.

Outside the canyon I reined in behind a clump of chaparral and, still keeping my gun on Lopez, I says: "I'm on to you, hombre; you got some gunmen planted on the cliffs, in that canyon beyond the cleft in the rock, and was leadin' me into a ambush. You thought maybe you'd herd me in ahead, and when I made you go first, you started singing so that your coyotes wouldn't shoot you as you rode through the cleft, thinking it was me."

He shrugged his shoulders: "You are mad, *señor.*"

"Well," says I, "me and you is goin' to change clothes and horses, get me? Then I'm goin' to gag you so's you can't sing and I'm goin' to herd you ahead of me through that cleft."

His swarthy face turned ashy: *"Por amor Dios!* Don't do that, *señor!* Would you murder me? They'll think it's you and riddle me with bullets!"

"Just as I thought!" I snorted. "Now you spill the beans or I'll shore do it!"

"Will you spare my life if I tell all?" said he.

"I ain't no murderer," I growls. "I ain't here to kill nobody, only just to defend myself. All I wanta do is interview Zapojos, get me?"

"Listen, *señor,*" says Lopez. "As I love my life, I swear I speak the truth; we have had the tip for some time that you were coming—for a week or more—"

"Hold yore horses," I interrupts. "That's lie Number One—I didn't know I was comin' myself till this mornin'."

His eyes widened: "But *señor*, I swear, Zapojos had word that the Cattlemen's Association was sending a man to get him—"

"Oh, I see," I grunted. "Well, they's been misunderstandin' all around. I ain't the man the Association sent. I'm just doin' reportin' work for a friend."

I could see Lopez didn't believe me, but he made like he did.

"Well," said he, "when you asked Restajus, this morning in La Paz, where Zapojos was, he at once thought it was the detective who asked. That was why he drew his gun—"

"And that's why that barkeep maverick tries for to carve me," I mutters.

"Exactly, *señor*; he too is one of Zapojos' men secretly. Well, Diego was at La Paz and when you knocked Restajus senseless, he mounted swiftly and rode like the wind to warn Zapojos. But when he came to the lair, Zapojos was gone on business of his own. But I was there; I felt that you would ride on to Autlan, so with Diego and Gomez I rode swiftly to the Caballero Canyon, and leaving them in ambush on the cliffs beyond the cleft, I rode on to meet you. Had I known you were not the detective, I would not have sought to harm you."

"Hokum," I growls, and making him dismount, I tied him hand and foot with his own lariat, but didn't gag him. Then I fired a shot into the air and told him: "You yell for Diego and Gomez, and don't you say nothin' that might make 'em suspicious. I'll be right behind this here chaparral and if you say anything but what I tell you, I'll shore drill you."

I slid behind the chaparral and he yelled as instructed; it wasn't so far away but what they could hear; I knowed they'd begin to wonder what was happening and why he hadn't rode on through the cleft when they heered him singing. He yelled, according to my instructions, till we heered a faint answer from up the canyon; and I told him to shout for them to come down, because he'd killed the Gringo hisself. He done so and I gagged him, to make sure. Purty soon two Mexicans come in sight, riding; they'd had their horses hid in the wide canyon. They couldn't see Lopez, because I had him behind the chaparral; they give a yell and he answered, and they rode on, though they looked puzzled.

Purty soon they come to the chaparral and dismounted, and I slide around to the other side. They come stalking around the brush and give exclamations as they seen Lopez all tied up, and at that instant I stepped up behind 'em with a gun in each hand. I had the drop on them alright, and in a few minutes they joined Lopez.

"Now," says I, "how do I reach Zapojos?"

"He is not in the camp," sullenly says Lopez. "He has ridden away for his own reasons."

"Well, how do I git to the camp?" I asks, emphasizing my question by flicking his nose with my gun muzzle.

"Ride back to the point where we swung westward," said he, "and there take the other direction; ride east past the jutting end of Yellow Mountain; there within a mile's ride is a wide canyon running due south. Ride down this canyon for five miles; other smaller canyons open into it on both sides, but pay no heed until you come to what appears to be but a cleft in the canyon wall, with a tiny spring bubbling up and running into it. That is the entrance into the valley where Zapojos' camp lies; doubtless it will be guarded. But what of us?"

"You got to stay here awhile," I says. "I don't trust you none, though I believe yore tellin' the truth just now."

Well, they kicked and cussed, but I dragged 'em into the shade of the scanty brush, give 'em each a drink outa my canteen, in case they was thirsty, and rode off on Cap'n Kidd, telling 'em I would send some of Zapojos' men back to release them.

The sun was slanting westward when I rounded the shoulder of Yellow Mountain and seen the canyon mouth ahead of me. I rode into it and found it was a wide, sheer-walled canyon with a flat sandy floor and it didn't seem to run very straight. I rode down it for maybe a mile and a half and, just after I passed a narrow gulch which debauched into the main canyon from the east, I heered the clink of a hoof on the stones. Instantly I reined back and in a minute or so out of the gulch rode a big Mexican on a fine black stallion; he was dressed in black silk jacket and trousers and the sunlight glinted on his pistols.

He seen me as quick as I seen him and went for his guns with a yell. I seen they wasn't no time to explain nothing, and they wasn't so much as a rock I could take cover behind, so I struck in the spurs and we come charging together through the canyon, our guns blazing. The echoes of the shots thundered from the cliffs. Maybe you think it's a treat to ride into the teeth of two roaring guns thataway! The Mexican was guiding his horse with his knees and was firing two-handed. The whole blamed air seemed like it was full of bullets. My hat skipped offa my head, a slug zipped through my sleeve, a lock of Cap'n Kidd's flying mane flew away, something like a red-hot bee nipped my ear, and then, with not more'n forty feet between us, my third shot caught my enemy square and knocked him outa his saddle.

The black stallion thundered past me, eyes wild, foam flying, and I pulled up Cap'n Kidd and swung off where the Mexican was kicking and floundering and cussing fit to curl your hair. He tried to reach his guns with his left hand, but I kicked 'em outa the way. He was shot through the right shoulder, near the arm joint—not a fatal wound, but he was bleeding plenty.

"Well, Zapojos," says I, "I didn't come out here to plug you—I just wanted to ask you some questions."

"Fool!" he roars. "I am not Zapojos! I am his lieutenant, Hernando Mentez. Soon Zapojos himself will come and when he comes, he will skin you, Gringo, and hang your hide to a cactus!"

"Well, lie still while I stop yore wound from bleedin'," I snaps, and though he raved and cussed, I bandaged him as well as I could and stanched the blood flow.

"Is Zapojos comin' down that gulch?" I asked, but all Hernando did was to cuss me. Well, I figgered Zapojos was coming, and that now that he'd bound to of heered the shots, and would be coming on the run; I hadn't took more'n five minutes bandaging Hernando, so I left him laying in the shade of the canyon wall and got on Cap'n Kidd and cantered up the gulch, going swift but cautious. Sure enough, in a minute or so I heard the rattle of hoofs ahead of me, so I reined in behind a jutting rock and waited, with my gun drawed. I'd done concluded that I wouldn't be able to peaceably and in order interview Zapojos. Purty soon a horseman come in view. He was kind of a short, fat Mexican and very gaudily dressed. He was riding a good-looking bay which seemed to have gone far that day, and he had big saddlebags which bulged with something or other. He was holding a long-barreled Colt in his right hand, and another was at his hip. He was almost abreast of me when I rode and ordered, "Hands up!"

He give a howl and wheeled, throwing down on me, but I had the drop on him. My old .44 barked and his gun flew outa his hand. He raised his arms, working his numbed right fingers, and cussing something fierce. I reined alongside of him, reaching for the gun on his left hip and still keeping him covered, when he took a desperate chance. He drove in both spurs viciously and his bay screamed and lunged, striking Cap'n Kidd a terrific smash in the flank with his shoulder. Cap'n Kidd reared wildly to keep from going down, and it all happened in a flash. I was sitting my saddle very loose and careless, reaching away over, and the unexpectedness of the move unseated me.

I pitched headlong out the saddle, hitting the ground with a jolt that made me see stars and knocked the gun outa my hand. But as I fell I grabbed Zapojos' cartridge belt and dragged him with me. And there we was, both on the ground. He was up quicker'n me and handed me a most stunning kick on the ear. Another kick like that would of stretched me out, but he grabbed for his other gun instead, and I swung my legs around and kicked his feet out from under him as he drew. He pulled the trigger as he fell but the bullet went wild and I had him in a grizzly grip before he could shoot again. He was a lot stronger and more active than he looked, and we had a merry time.

I finally twisted his wrist till he yelled like a coyote and dropped the gun, and then I hauled him to his feet and pushed him away so's I could get a clean swing at him. But quick as a flash he whipped a knife outa his boot and sunk it into my chest muscles. This so enraged me that I socked him under the jaw with all my beef behind it and he kind of soared off the earth and lighted on the back of his neck. Following up I kicked the knife outa his hand and getting astride of him, pinned him down helpless with his arms under my knees.

"Dog! Pig! Donkey of a gringo!" he yelled. "For this I will hang your vile hide to a cactus!"

"Aw, shut up!" I growled, irritated by the sting of my knife stab, which was bleeding considerable. "I didn't come here lookin' for trouble, but I been hounded like a criminal and I mean business. All I wanta do is ask you some questions, and I better get a civil reply, by golly.

[. . .]

"I met him first at the Paradise Saloon . . ."
(untitled and unfinished)

I met him first in the Paradise saloon. A fairly tall, well-built young man, with fine, keen grey eyes and a somewhat handsome face. He had quiet manners and moved with the lithe grace of a panther. On each hip hung a big black gun, low down, and the holster ends tied down.

And—but I can make you more acquainted with him by telling what happened. There were four of us sitting in a poker game when he came in: Ratty Ganson, Mike Cassidy, Shorty McKeever and me. Just as this young fellow came in, Shorty quit the game and he took Shorty's place.

Well, the cards were with him, for in no time he had over half the chips on the table. And he kept on winning.

He had just scooped in a big pot, when Ganson jumped up, slammed his cards down on the table and said, "I'm through. This game is crooked!"

[. . .]

The Killer's Debt

(untitled and unfinished fragment)

[. . .] fabulous amount stated in the exaggerated legend, but a fortune unattainable by the average man in a whole lifetime of drudgery.

Brill kept glancing back at the bulging packsacks as they rode down the canyon, as if to assure himself that the whole affair was not some fantastic dream.

"We're goin' to make a break through the wild country," said Texas abruptly. "I got a feelin' that Beldon is on our trail. We must have a long start on him, but if he's hit our spoor, he'll kill his horses to catch us. I know a way through here that I don't think he knows anything about. I prospected this country some myself, once. There's a spring along it—the only spring in these here hills so far as I know. Are you game to take the chance?"

"Looks like our only shot," answered Brill shortly. "Lead on."

They drove onward, through a labyrinth of slopes and gorges, at a steady pace that ate up the long miles. Silence reigned on that furnace of desolation. Their ears were alert for some sound behind them—the creak of a stirrup leather, the clink of a hoof on a stone— to tell them of their pursuers. But they heard only the monotonous sounds of their own flight. And so the day wore on.

The sun was setting in a wallow of red behind the canyon wall. The cliffs seemed banded with bloody fire and the deepening sky above was a great copper bowl. Texas drew rein.

"There's the spring, behind that big boulder. It's a freak. I bet there ain't three men livin' knows about it. We got to rest the horses. At midnight we'll push on again."

They dismounted, unsaddled, fed and watered the horses, ate sparingly themselves and set down cross-legged, backs to the canyon wall to smoke.

"I don't believe Beldon's followin' us," said Brill. "All day we've seen nothin' of him."

Texas shook his head gloomily. "That ain't like him. He's worse'n a bloodhound on the trail. I got a feelin' he's ridin' on our tracks. That's why we ain't stayin' here no longer'n it'll take the hosses to rest up some."

[. . .]

"Wait!" snapped Texas. "I'll go. I tell you, it's a trick; but if you're sot on rescuin' somebody, why, I'll go. I know this country better'n you; you stay here. Watch up the canyon, the way we come; that's where Beldon would come from."

And oblivious to Brill's protests, Texas snatched the canteen and, gliding into the shadow cast by the canyon wall, vanished from Brill's sight. The Montanan strained his eyes after him. Again he heard that wild cry, rising from the outer darkness. The thin moon was setting; the mountains were cloaked in dense shadows. He glanced at the horses, cropping the scanty vegetation close to the tiny spring; at the packsacks with their precious load, piled among the saddles at the foot of the cliff wall. Silence followed the last wild wail, which was not repeated. Had Texas reached the unknown sufferer? Surely he had not had time—Brill stepped from the mouth of the cleft, straining his eyes up the canyon.

A boot-heel crunched in the shale and Brill wheeled, cursing his carelessness. In one fleeting glance he saw, in the dim uncertain light, the figures of four men—one of them a giant in stature—*Beldon!* With frantic haste Brill whipped out his gun and fired full at the murderer. But Beldon had stepped quickly behind his men. A stocky fellow in front of him dropped and before Brill could fire again, another pistol spat. Brill felt a terrible blow on the side of his head and the stars went out in a blinding blaze of light.

Slowly Jim Brill drifted back to life. His head throbbed fiercely and, when he sought to lift his hands to his wound, he realized that he was bound hand and foot, so closely that the circulation of his blood was almost cut off, and his limbs felt numb. There was a great deal of dried blood on his head and face, but the wound seemed to have ceased bleeding.

In front of him a fire flickered and in its light he saw three men: he recognized the huge bulk of Beldon, the lean rangy figure of Yaqui Kane, the saturnine countenance of La Costa. These two companions of Beldon, Brill knew, were accounted the deadliest gunfighters on the Border, since that king of bad men, Mike O'Meara, had gone to his last accounting. Taken like a blind fool, he thought bitterly, yet how could he have known they would come?

"Well, well," rumbled Beldon. "Durned if our friend ain't conscious again."

[. . .]

Gunman's Debt

(four synopses)

(1)

The story opens with John Kirby, a gun-fighting trail-driver from South Texas, riding into San Juan, a Kansas prairie-town, built in expectation of the railroad, which had not yet reached it. Kirby was coming to San Juan, because of a message sent him by an old friend, Billy Lynch, who was tending bar in San Juan. The message had reached Kirby at Ellsworth, and merely asked him to [. . .]

(2)

The story opens with John Kirby, a gun-fighting trail-driver from South Texas riding into San Juan, a Kansas prairie-town which was expecting a railroad, and whose inhabitants hoped to grab the trail-herds. He came there because he wished to learn whether Jim Garfield were really dead. The Garfields and Kirbys were feudists down in Texas. Garfield had drifted up the trail and word had come down that he had been killed in Kansas. Billy Donnelly, Kirby had heard, was tending bar in San Juan. Donnelly was an old friend of Kirby's, and would know if it were true. Kirby had been driving a herd to Ellsworth, and had turned aside to see Donnelly. On riding into the town, he thought he saw a man he recognized duck behind a stable, but could not be sure. He went into the stable and left his horse, and was accosted by the marshal, who said there was a law against carrying guns in San Juan and took his pistol. Kirby went on to the Big Chief saloon, and entered in time to hear the tag-end of an argument between a dancehall girl and a young gambler; the man slapped the girl, told her all was over between them, and reeled out drunkenly, and Kirby noticed he was wearing a gun openly. While drinking at the bar, Kirby suddenly turned to be confronted by Jim Garfield and a gang of gunmen. Garfield told him that he, Garfield, had sent word down the trail that he was dead, but in reality he had come to San Juan to gather a gang of gunmen to go south and exterminate the Kirbys. He was going to start by killing Kirby. The marshal was in on the deal and had disarmed Kirby according to Garfield's orders. At that moment the girl extinguished the lamp and Kirby got away in the dark. She guided him to her shack on the edge of a ravine that ran along the edge of town. There she told him she wanted him to kill Jack Corlan, the gambler who had thrown her down. He refused, and in a fury she shot him. The bullet knocked him cold, and when he came to, she was gone. He staggered out of the shack and tumbled into the ravine, just as he heard some men coming. She had brought Jim Garfield, his sidekick Red Donaldson, and Captain Blanton, the real ruler of the town. She thought she had killed Kirby and told a lie to the effect that he had sneaked in her shack and attacked her, and she had shot him in self defense. When they found that Kirby was not there, they sent her back to the Silver Boot with Donaldson, who was in love with her, and presently Corlan appeared, drunk and quarrelsome. He demanded money from Blanton, reminded him that he had just gone on a dangerous mission for him. Blanton had established the town. Corlan threatened to spill the beans to a buffalo-hunter named Elkins, and in an argument he drew his gun, and Garfield killed him. They left the body there, and returned to the Silver Boot and told Joan Laree that Kirby had shot Corlan through the window. Meantime Kirby had returned to the jail, taken his gun away from the deputy and locked him in a cell, and went to his stable to get his horse and ride away from San Juan. There he found three men waiting for that very move, and listening to their conversation, overheard that he had been accused of killing Corlan. In the meantime Elkins, the buffalo hunter had ridden in on a staggering horse, telling a tale of his camp being wiped out by the Comanches. Kirby was accosted by Joan Laree who pretended to think that he had killed Corlan because of her. She inveigled him into a log cabin and locking him in, summoned Blanton, Elkins, Garfield and their mob. Firing through the door, Kirby mortally wounded one McVey, who, angered by Blanton's callousness, told Joan that either Garfield or Blanton killed Corlan. She attacked Blanton, who shot her. While dying, she told Elkins that Blanton had set the Indians on him—had sent Corlan, who had been raised by the Comanches, to tell Yellow Tail where the hunter's camp lay. Blanton planned to steal all Elkins' hides. This turned Red Donaldson, Garfield's pal, against Blanton, and when Blanton killed Donaldson, Garfield turned on him. A savage three cornered fight ensued, between Elkins and Kirby on the one side, Garfield on another, and Blanton and his men on another, and the town of San Juan was practically destroyed.

(3)

John Kirby, gunman and cowboy from South Texas, came into San Juan, a new town on the Kansas prairie. The railroad had not extended that far yet; Kirby had been riding with a trail herd bound for Ellsworth, but, wearying of the drive, had turned aside and ridden into San Juan. As he rode into town he saw a man who looked familiar duck back into an alley. He stabled his horse and went into a saloon, where he was accosted by the marshal, Bill Rogers, who demanded his gun. Kirby gave up his gun, left the saloon, and as he went down the street, be noticed to his surprize that every man he saw was wearing weapons. He turned into a saloon, just after dark, and was drinking at the bar, when he wheeled to see Jim Garfield enter the saloon. Garfield was an old enemy, leader of the Garfield faction in South Texas, in the Kirby-Garfield feud. With him was Red Donaldson, a Texas gunman, whom Kirby had seen duck into the alley, and half a dozen hard-looking strangers—cowtown gunmen. All were armed, and Bill Rogers was nowhere in sight. Garfield announced his intention of shooting Kirby down in cold blood; all drew their guns, and Garfield took deliberate aim at Kirby. The loafers in the saloon shrank back, and a girl on the gallery above, leaned over to watch. She was within arm's reach of the great swinging lamp which lighted the place. Just as Rogers was about to pull the trigger, the lamp was smashed, and Kirby escaped in the darkness. As he emerged from the saloon, the girl ran out of the back door and told him she had broken the lamp. She led him to a shack at the edge of the town, on the edge of a ravine which ran around the town and passed close behind the jail and marshal's office. She told him her name was Joan Laree, and she tried to persuade him to shoot a former lover of hers. She did not tell him his name. Kirby refused, and started to leave the shack, and in a screaming fury, she caught up a pistol and shot him. The bullet grazed his head, knocking him senseless. When he regained his senses, a short time later, he found the oil lamp still burning on the table, but the shack was empty. Sick and weak from the wound, he hauled himself up, staggered out of the shack, and tumbled into the ravine. Lying there, he heard voices. Joan had brought Garfield to the shack. Joan had told Kirby that Garfield had come to San Juan to recruit gunmen to wipe out the Kirbys. A man they called Captain Blanton was the boss of the town; he owned the saloons, gambling houses and dance halls, and levied tribute from all who came there. Garfield had recognized him as a former outlaw, and member of Cullen Baker's desperadoes, and Blanton had agreed to furnish Garfield with enough gunmen to carry out his purpose of destroying the Kirbys. They planned nothing less than a huge system of outlawry, extending from the Rio Grande to Ellsworth. They intended looting trail herds, buffalo hunters and horse dealers. While lying in the ravine, Kirby heard them discussing some of their plans, and one of the men, drunk, renewed a discussion interrupted by their visit to the shack. Joan had returned to the dance hall, at an order from Blanton. He demanded more money for something he did not mention, and threatened to tell something to a man he called Grizzly Elkins. The fellow was a half-breed. Blanton threatened him, the man drew a gun, and Garfield shot him. Leaving the body to lie, the outlaws left the shack. Kirby crawled along the ravine until he came behind the jail, which was empty. A deputy was in the marshal's office, reading a dime novel. Kirby entered disheveled, bloody, and said he had been attacked in the dark and robbed. The deputy did not recognize him, and Kirby suddenly snatched his gun from the wall where it hung, disarmed the deputy, locked him into a cell, and slipped forth, intending to go to the stable and get his horse. As he entered the street, a man came galloping into town on a reeling mount. He slid off and staggered into a saloon, surrounded by a throng of men; he was a big man, hairy, clad in buckskins. He gasped out a tale of Indian attack. He was a buffalo hunter, and his outfit had been set upon by the Comanches and wiped out. He alone had escaped. They had sent in the wagons of skins, driven by Blanton's men, and had gone into camp, to await supplies the wagons were to bring back, when the Indians swarmed down on them without warning. Only by hard fighting and hard riding had the survivor escaped. Somebody called him Grizzly Elkins. Kirby went on to his stable, but found men there with guns, guarding his horse. From their conversation he was amazed to learn that he had been accused of murdering Jack Gorlan, the handsome mixed-breed Garfield had killed in Joan Laree's shack. They said that Kirby had sneaked back and shot Gorlan through the window. Kirby, turning away, was accosted by Joan Laree, who had come to the stables and lurked in hiding, expecting Kirby to come there. She refused to believe that he had not killed Gorlan, and said she was sorry she shot him. Gorlan was the man she wanted killed. She led him into a trap but he shot his way out and escaped into a log cabin, where he turned at bay, realizing that Joan now wished to kill him because, woman-like, she had loved the man she had once urged him to kill. He was crouched in a room, which had only one door and one small high window. The logs were too thick for a bullet to penetrate. Matters were at a temporary deadlock. His enemies were in the outer room, out of range. They could not reach him without breaking down the door; neither could he escape. He could hear them talking. One of the men he had shot was dying and begging Blanton to fetch him some water. Blanton refused brutally, and in his dying agonies, the man gasped out the truth of the killing of Jack Gorlan. Instantly Joan went into hysterics of fury, and cried out to Grizzly Elkins, who was present, that he had been tricked by Blanton. Blanton had sent Gorlan to the Comanches to stir them up to attack Elkins camp, and wipe out the hunters, so that Blanton would have the whole load of skins for himself. Blanton shot Joan and ran from the cabin. Elkins went into roaring fury, knifed one of the gunmen, was wounded by Garfield, and then Kirby went into action, leaping through the door with his gun blazing. He killed one of Garfield's men and wounded Garfield, and the latter ran out of the cabin and across the street into a saloon. Kirby and Elkins joined forces, ducked out of the cabin the back way and into a rooming house where they procured rifles and began to bombard the saloon. Blanton had taken refuge in a saloon, Garfield and his men in a dance hall. Red Donaldson rode into town, ran into the cabin, found Joan's body and shrieked to know who killed her. A girl stuck her head out of the dance hall window and shrilled that Blanton did it, ducking back as the man shot at her. Donaldson charged screaming across the street, and was met by a blast of buckshot; he fell before the saloon. Enraged, Garfield began shooting at Blanton, and was shot in the back by his men—Blanton's gunmen. These fell before the fire of Kirby and Elkins, and the buffalo hunter began to fire the houses. Men emerged from the houses and fought hand to hand on the street. Blanton, running from the burning saloon with his guns blazing, was knifed by Elkins, after being shot by the dying Donaldson. Then Elkins and Kirby mounted and rode out of the blazing town taking the trail southward.

(4)

In the Silver Boot saloon and dance hall Kirby overheard a violent quarrel between Jack Corlan, a young gambler, and a dance hall girl, Joan Laree. While drinking at the bar, Kirby was confronted by Jim Garfield, an old enemy from Texas. Their families had been fighting each other for years, and Garfield told him boastingly that he had gathered a gang of cowtown gunmen for the purpose of going south and wiping out the entire Kirby family. Garfield was wearing his gun, and so were his men, and Kirby realized that the marshal had disarmed him simply so that Garfield could kill him. But the girl, Joan Laree, extinguished the lamp, and Kirby escaped from the saloon in the darkness.

Joan Laree guided Kirby to a shack on the edge of a gully outside the town, and there told him that she had saved his life because she wanted him to kill a man for her. The man being the gambler, Jack Corlan, who had thrown her over. Kirby refused, not being a cold-blooded murderer, and in a gust of rage, she caught up a pistol and shot him. The bullet creased his scalp and knocked him out.

When he recovered consciousness she had left, thinking him dead, and staggering from the shack he lay in the ravine and hid, as she returned with Garfield, his gunman Red Donaldson, and Captain Blanton. She had told them that she had killed Kirby, but when they found him gone, they thought she was lying, and sent her back to the Silver Boot with Red Donaldson who was in love with her.

Listening outside the shack, while Garfield and Blanton quarreled, Kirby learned that Garfield had a hold over the boss of San Juan. Garfield knew that Blanton had been one of Cullen Baker's outlaw gang, and that the Federal Government still had a price on his head.

[missing page 2]

Garfield was using Blanton's money, power and men for his own ends, in the Kirby-Garfield feud, or intended to so use them. Corlan came to the shack, drunk, and demanding money from Blanton. As is developed later in the story, Blanton planned a business of wholesale thievery of many phases. One of these phases included the theft of a great quantity of buffalo hides recently freighted into San Juan from Grizzly Elkins' camp down in the wild country. Blanton had sent Corlan, who had been raised by the Indians, to betray to the reds the location of Elkins' camp. Corlan had just returned from this mission, and threatened to expose Blanton's duplicity unless he was paid more. Garfield killed Corlan, and later they told Joan Laree, who had recovered from her anger at her lover, that John Kirby had killed him, firing through the window.

In the meantime, Kirby had stolen away in the darkness to get his horse and escape from San Juan, but found Garfield's men ambushed about the stable awaiting his return. About this time Grizzly Elkins, who had escaped the massacre of his men when the Indians swooped down on his camp, rode into San Juan, ignorant of Blanton's treachery.

Kirby, despairing of escaping with his life, determined to kill Jim Garfield before they got him, and was making his way toward the Silver Boot, when he was met by Joan Laree who tricked him into entering a cabin, where she locked him in. To avenge the death of Jack Corlan, of which she thought Kirby was guilty, she summoned Garfield, Elkins, Blanton, and his gang. (On the surface it seems paradoxical, perhaps, that Joan Laree should first shoot Kirby for *not* killing Corlan, and later betray him to his enemies because she thought he *did* kill Corlan; but in the working out of her primitive, wayward character, the matter is not only logical, but inevitable.)

Firing through the door, Kirby mortally wounded McVey, one of Blanton's men. Outraged by Blanton's callousness, McVey told Joan that Blanton, not Kirby, had caused Corlan to be killed. In a fury Joan told Elkins that Blanton had betrayed him and his men to the Indians, disclosed the fact that Blanton planned to steal the buffalo hides, and was the real head of the gang of cattle-thieves and bandits, and incidentally that Billy Lynch had been murdered by Garfield because he was a friend of the Kirby's. Blanton killed the girl, which caused Red Donaldson to turn on Blanton, and, on Donaldson's being murdered, Garfield broke with Blanton.

A savage three-sided fight ensued, with Elkins and Kirby allied on one side, Garfield on another, and Blanton and his mob on the third. Garfield was killed by Blanton's men, and Blanton himself was stabbed to death by Elkins, who then rode south with Kirby, leaving San Juan in flames behind them.

Wild Water Timing

Bisley was on Locust Creek, in Locust Valley. Jim Reynolds drove in from Lost Knob at 9 o'clock, and killed Saul Hopkins. That took perhaps ten minutes. At ten past nine, he drove out of Bisley. In twenty minutes he drew up at Joel Jackson's house. It was then 9:30, and already raining up on the head waters of Locust Creek and Mesquital. It took Reynolds and Jackson about half an hour to get the car hidden and get back to the house, which made it 10 o'clock. Half an hour passed in eating and in conversation. It was about 10:45 when Jackson called the police in Bisley. They came in a hurry, and it was a few minutes past 11 when Reynolds ambushed them on the side of the hill. A few minutes later it began raining; it took him until daylight to get to Bisley Lake.

The Devil's Joker

(alternate version)

A crash of shots ripped through the smoke-hazed atmosphere of the Gila Monster gambling hall. Cactus Lemark, rustler and killer, swayed like a tall tree in a high wind. He crumpled at the waist and fell slowly, crumpling upon his rangy length like a dying snake. The pistol dropped from his nerveless fingers and he was dead before he hit the floor.

Steve Allison, alias The Sonora Kid, backed against the opposite wall, glaring at his handiwork through the drifting smoke. The Kid's face was white with passion, his thin lips writhed in a snarl, his narrow eyes blazing. A moment he stood so, both smoking guns still raised. Then he spat a curse at the men who were still scrambling wildly for safety or peering at him fearfully over the tops of the bar, and whirling, sprang for the door.

As he vanished through it, pandemonium broke out behind him. Encouraged by his flight, men ran from their coverts howling threats and curses. They jammed the doorway, and over each others' shoulders, saw the Kid swing into the saddle and pull his bronc's head toward the desert. A lean evil-eyed renegade in the doorway fired at random and Allison heard the vicious hiss of the bullet by his ear. As his horse reared and veered away in a half-circle, he shot left-handed over his right arm and the man in the doorway howled, dropped his gun and, pressing back desperately into the crowd, clutched at his left ear, which had been half-torn from his head.

Like an echo of this amazing snapshot came a short snarl of mocking laughter, and then a swift drum of hoofs told the milling crowd that their foe was leaving the town of Del Diablo.

Some miles out on the desert, Steve Allison looked back. His gallop had become a swift cantor and the cantor an easy trot, as he had seen no signs of pursuit. But he was suspicious. However, that was Steve's normal condition. A hard life on the Border had rendered him as alert and dangerous as a wolf. At an age when most young men were thrilling at football games and writing languishing letters to beautiful co-eds, Steve had the doubtful distinction of being known as one of the most deadly gunfighters from the Panhandle to Durango.

The craft of the wolf there was in his keen brain and the strength and speed of a wolf in his slim, lithe form. Moreover, he was the possessor of a most devilish temper, the heritage perhaps of innumerable Scotch-Irish ancestors, and he was one of those rare persons whom violent rage only makes more quick and accurate.

Now the sun beat hard on Steve Allison's sombrero and he cursed fervently.

"I'm oppressed and down trod," he said to his indifferent mustang. "Why can't folks learn to leave me alone? All I crave is peace and quiet. But no sooner do I hit town anywhere than up swaggers some gent with corn licker in his belly and a chip on his shoulder. Dash blank triple blank semi-colon!" he finished profanely.

He pulled up. "Bronc, where are we headin'? South and east she's desert with nothin' to drink but mirages and nothin' to eat but dry bones of jackasses and prospectors. North they's a posse and a noose waitin' for me. West—"

He hesitated. His eyes took in the gaunt stark outline of the Muertos—the great grim crests and defiles, dark and barren, which lay miles away across the heat-shimmering sands. The Mountains of Death, the Mexicans called them, and they told fearful tales of broken, white-haired wanderers who had won back across the deserts from their grip—only to die, babbling strange, hideous things of the Mountains of Death. In the blazing sunlight Steve Allison shuddered slightly.

"Bronc," said he, gathering up the reins, "I might's well take the barrel in my teeth and jerk the trigger as to go back to Del Diablo. The only man in the village that wasn't a close friend of Cactus Lemark's was me. I shore hate it that I got *you* in such a jamb—but—well, I hear tell they's water, anyhow, in the mountains and it's our only shot."

As he jogged on Steve reflected somberly. To this pass had his temper brought him. Though openly a gunfighter, and one never very fastidious about what he did south of the Border, he had never, until lately, committed any indiscretion north of it to bring him into the serious notice of the law. He had killed in Texas, it is true, and in Arizona and New Mexico also, for that matter, but it had in every case, with one exception, been an even break, and his victims had been men of evil reputation. The one exception was his last escapade and the one from the consequences of which he was fleeing.

The details of this were these: there was in the little cowtown just north of the Rio Grande which Steve frequented, a large and self-important personage named Sam Herd. Unfortunately, he was a county sheriff. Herd was not a bad man, but he was blatant and loudmouthed. He had a bullying manner and he loved a practical joke. The Sonora Kid was soft spoken except when angry, and Herd made the mistake of misjudging him. His friends tried to make him understand that Steve was really a devil incarnate under a mask of Southern courtesy but, like all his type, Herd was bullheaded.

He started in to ride the Kid, and Steve took more off him than was his wont, simply because he did not think there was anything in it. When it was suddenly borne in on him that Herd was deliberately hazing him, he saw red. It was Herd's misfortune to conceive, that very day, what he thought a brilliant practical joke. Allison was of a breed which sees little humor in jests of that sort. The joke Herd played on him, Steve would not have forgiven in a close friend—and he considered Herd in the light of a deadly enemy. Even then, he would not have taken the course he did, had he not been betrayed into it by his uncontrollable temper. When he saw Herd's round red fool's face leering at him, and heard the man's empty guffaws at his discomfort, something snapped in his brain. To the shocked amazement of all concerned, including himself, he drew and shot Herd down in cold blood. This time there were no mitigating circumstances. Even his best friends had to admit that the provocation was not equal to the vengeance. It was simply a cold-blooded murder; Herd had no time to make a motion toward his gun—he was in the midst of a loud laugh when Steve's bullet struck him down. Steve realized this quicker than anyone and the smoke was still curling from his gun muzzle when his mustang was burning the trail for the border. Remorse filled him, but not to the extent of desiring to atone for his mistake on the gallows.

"I'm a plumb fool," he said now, viciously, as the grim mountains loomed up forebodingly ahead of him. "I oughta slapped his face and kicked him loose from his pants—or else bent a pistol barrel over the blank-blank fool's head. They wasn't no need to kill him. But heck, I just went offa muh nut for a second. That's the way with us gun-throwers; we get so our hands think for us, instead of our brains. Aw, hell."

He rode on, broodingly. He really was in a desperate plight. Now that the village of Del Diablo was barred from him, he knew not where to turn. That foul village, perched like a vulture on the fringe of the desert, peopled only by the scum of two nations, nameless men, half-breeds, outlaws and renegades, had at least proved a sanctuary for him. If the company repelled him, still there had been shelter, food and drink. But now, as in his own land, Del Diablo was tabooed for him and he had good reasons for not wishing to wend his way toward the nearest legitimate Mexican town, some forty miles away. He felt extremely lonely—an outcast by the lowest of his kind, he thought moodily. Remained now for him only the solitary life of a desert wolf. Eventually he might be able to make his way to some isolated village where the name of the Sonora Kid was unknown, and so to the far interior or to the seacoast where he could take ship for South America and start life all over again. But it was not an alluring prospect. And just now his needs were urgent: a refuge from the avengers of Lemark, who he felt would be on his trail sooner or later, and a plentiful supply of water for himself and his horse.

The sun had set; he pushed on, taking advantage of the coolness of the night. After awhile he dismounted, poured more than half of the water in his canteen into his hat and shoved the hat under his horse's nose.

"Ain't scarcely enough to wet yore muzzle, bronc," he apologized, "but if we get any luck at all we oughta hit water before daylight."

Against the stars the mountains, which meant life or death to him, loomed blacker, gaunter, more forbidding. A faint breeze which blew from them ruffled Steve's hair, and to his imaginative mind seemed to whisper grisly secrets into his ears. It was after midnight before he reached the first of the slopes. A sinister crimson moon rose and made the lurking shadows blacker. Above the solitary rider menaced the grim outline of the Mountains of Death—the mountains into which many had gone—out of which few had returned.

The slopes gave way to broken terrain. Stark cliffs rose sullenly as if to bar the fleeing gunfighter's progress. Through a maze of defiles and deep ravines he made his way slowly, watching the stars and keeping his sense of direction with the instinct of the desert man. Here no vegetation grew. Only once he saw a sign of life—a shimmer of scales in the moonlight, a glitter of two beady evil eyes, the rustle of a crawling thing. Steve's flesh crept and he winced and swore. Afraid of nothing on four legs or two, his aversion to snakes amounted to an obsession almost.

He found himself riding down a deep canyon which widened at the other end. There at the base of towering cliffs he came upon the first of the mysteries of the Death Mountains. A tiny spring bubbled up in a faint circle of tiny green things which strove bitterly for life.

Steve drank deep and filled his canteen, and his thirsty horse satisfied himself and began to nip eagerly at the scant vegetation. As Steve rose from his knees, he froze suddenly, hand at his belt. From somewhere up among the black jumble of cliffs and canyons above him there sounded a strange wild call. A thin quavering cry, it mounted higher and higher to a penetrating crescendo, then ceased at the highest note. The horse snorted and trembled. Steve Allison licked dry lips and twitched his shoulders to rid himself of the icy chills which trickled up and down his spine.

"Bobcat up in the hills," he said aloud, in a voice which rang hollow to his own ears. "Maybe a mountain lion." In his heart he knew he was lying.

"We camp here, bronc."

In the shadow of an overhanging cliff, in the cleft of two huge boulders, Steve took his stand to wait for morning. His horse he tethered near; he dared not take a chance of its wandering away from him. But it showed a disposition to remain close to him—as horses will do in a mountain lion country until the near scent of the beast throws them into a wild panic and they break their picket ropes and charge away desperately into the darkness.

Mountain lion, man or devil, Steve Allison had no intention of being left afoot in that place. Back against the cliff wall, gun across his knees, chewing an unlighted cigarette, he sat stolidly waiting the dawn. What action he would take then, he did not know. He did know that he was not going to keep riding through unknown hills at night, where he was likely to come unexpectedly on the owner of the ghastly voice he had heard. Steve was confident in his pistol ability against mortal foes—but a superstitious whispering at the back of his Celtic mind would not be stilled.

He sat waiting for anything, but in spite of his alertness, sleep began to steal over him. He fought it off, but the sensation returned and he found himself waking with a start again and again. Time dragged interminably. At last, despite his efforts, he drifted imperceptibly into dreamland and rioted through a horror country of nightmare, peopled by monstrous ghoulish things neither man nor beast.

He awoke suddenly and leaped to his feet, feeling both chagrin and relief. He had slept against his wishes, but he was still alive. No terror of the night or the black hills had stolen down upon him. The sun had just risen.

Steve was aware of a raging hunger. Up in the hills, perhaps, was game on which he could breakfast. A ground squirrel, a chaparral bird, anything.

"I could enjoy a steak uh mountain lion meat, right now," he soliloquised. But first he had other employment. Selecting a weather-worn slope in the wall of the canyon, he climbed up and eventually, after much effort and perspiring, gained a point in the cliff from which he could look some distance back over the way he had come. He saw the defiles through which he had made his way, the glimmer of the desert beyond—then he stiffened. His quick eyes had caught a glimpse of a man just entering the first defiles that led from the lower slopes.

"Man riding into the mountains," he muttered. "Now who you reckon that'd be? Friends uh Lemark? Then where's the rest of 'em? Was that one man all? Shore I didn't see but just that 'un."

He strained his eyes trying to pick out the lone rider among the ravines but failed.

"Couldn't see him no way from here, but in just a place or two between here and there, and likely he's huggin' the walls close. Maybe just a bird like me runnin' from everybody. Maybe he's friendly—likely he ain't. Blame few friends in this desert. Anyway, this ain't no place to meet him."

A short time later, Steve was riding out of the canyon and up a long narrow gorge which led into another shorter canyon. At the further end, this canyon narrowed so that two horses could not have ridden abreast between its walls. As Steve reached this place, a man stepped out into the open.

Steve swore to himself at having been thus surprised. He had been too intent on watching the way behind him. His hand had instinctively flashed to his gun, but halted as he saw the man had the drop on him. The rifle in the fellow's hands lay negligently across his left arm, but its muzzle was trained full on the Kid and a grimy finger was crooked about the trigger.

For a moment the two eyed each other, recognition coming into the eyes of both.

"The Sonora Kid," grunted the other, a lanky, hard-eyed man whose unshaven face was almost black from sunburn. "What you doin' here?"

"Thought I knowed you, Wells," said Steve, relaxing. "Never thought to meet you here, though. Thought your lay was along in Durango."

"We range plenty," answered the other enigmatically. "What you doin' up here? Nobody comes into these here mountains 'less'n they have to—and we heard you was hidin' out in Del Diablo."

"I was," admitted Steve, "but I had trouble with Cactus Lemark over a poker game."

"And he run yuh outa town?"

"His friends did. Cactus ain't runnin' nothin'."

A touch of admiration entered the lanky one's gaze. He understood Steve's implication. He lowered the muzzle of his rifle.

"Well, come on to camp. Me and a coupla boys is restin' up a bit. Maybe yuh'd like some grub. Looks to me like yuh lit out travelin' light."

"I could use some sourdough and beans," Steve admitted. "And my bronc wouldn't kick you if you'd offer him some rations. But listen, I seen a feller ridin' into the hills a while ago."

Wells rapped out an oath. "Just one? Who was he?"

"Search me. One was all I saw."

A frown of worriment puckered Well's narrow brow. "Well, come on. We got time to make preparations for 'im. Let's git back to camp."

Steve dismounted and followed his guide, leading his horse. Wells led the way through the narrow gorge and across a sort of plateau. This was thickly scattered with huge boulders and rounding one of these they came upon a rude camp. Several horses browsed close to a spring and two men sat playing cards. They gaped up at Steve who greeted them easily. He knew them both and knew that he could not have chosen three more shady characters for his companions in all the Southwest. All three were fighters of wide repute. Wells, the Kid knew, was a rustler, a crooked gambler and a smuggler. Of the other two, Larson, a broad-built man of medium height with a square sullen face, was a straight-out gunman—a hired killer, who should have swung long ago. The third man was even more sinister than his comrades. Yucca La Costa, men called him, and he was a lean snaky fellow whose dark skin, straight black hair and beady eyes betrayed his Indian blood. Part Indian, part Spanish, part American and all devil he was. Though Wells seemed to be in command, his record, as well as Larson's, faded in comparison to the whispered hints of La Costa's deeds. Whispers linked the half-breed's name to grim unmentionable crimes—secret murders—kidnappings—torture.

"You birds know the Sonora Kid," said Wells. "He smoked up Cactus Lemark at Del Diablo yesterday and took it on the lam. He's on the up and up."

The other two gazed at the youth with renewed interest. They knew Steve by reputation if not by sight, and the name of Cactus Lemark rated high, even with such desperate characters as they.

Steve fed his horse with what they doled him from their small store, and turned the bronc loose to graze. Then he sat down to a breakfast of bacon and beans.

"Musta figured on a long hard ride through bare country, packin' all the grub, an' the hoss fodder too," he commented casually. Wells frowned absently and kept on talking to the others. He was telling them about the man Steve had seen. They nodded presently and La Costa rose negligently and sauntered away in the direction of the narrow gap through which Steve and Wells had come. Steve said nothing, but continued his breakfast.

Wells rolled a cigarette and said suddenly: "Kid, yuh better throw in with us. Yuh got no choice, to tell yuh the truth. Yuh can't go back; yuh can't live in these mountains 'thout us helpin' yuh. If I hadn't a knowed yuh, yuh wouldn't be alive this minute. We knowed when yuh come into the hills last night, an' we knowed where yuh slept. We coulda had yuh picked off any time—"

"How'd you all know so much?"

"—Only," continued Wells as if Steve had not spoken, "we kinda wanted to know who it was—couldn't tell in the moonlight so good. This mornin' I went back to stop yuh. I figured on pluggin' yuh as yuh come through the narrow gap, if yuh didn't look good.

"Now then, lissen. I'm goin' to make yuh a good proposition—better'n I ever made anybody. It's a cinch you need us, an' we can use you fine. We've heard tell of you plenty; more'n that, I seen you plug that Mex *rurale* in the arm down Sonora way a few months ago, and I know you're about the slickest hand with a gun ever come down the pike.

"What I can't understand is, how come you ain't gone in the business right? Why, with the influence you got as a gun-thrower, you could lead a gang that'd drag down a million dollars worth of loot inside of a year."

"I just ain't never felt drawn towards that racket, Wells," answered Steve. "Rustlin' an' hijackin' just ain't been in my line."

Larson laughed gratingly. Steve shot a sudden glance at the swart gunman. The Sonora Kid's eyes had grown suddenly cold and hard as ice, his face immobile as an Indian's. The leer faded from Larson's unshaven face to be replaced by a sullen scowl. But his eyes dropped before the icy stare of the Kid.

"Shut up, Larson," broke in Wells. "Kid, you got a bad name all along the Border. Most folks don't understand how a man can be a gambler and a gun-thrower and still make his livin' honest. Nine men outa ten would swear you was runnin' a secret racket uh some kind. Now lissen: see them saddlebags? Well, they's fifteen thousand dollars in American greenbacks in 'em. We stuck up the Bueno Santa bank a week ago and the fools are combin' all the north part uh Chihuahua. We're safe. And yore safe as long as yore with us."

Steve sensed a sinister meaning in the man's words.

"Whata you mean?"

"Well, we got grub and water. We planned this proper and made arrangements for a long ride, even to bringin' feed for the hosses, loaded on pack-hosses. It's a hard ride from Bueno Santa to here. We couldn't a done it if it wasn't for La Costa. He's got friends in these mountains."

"Friends?"

"Yeah; fact is, he was born here. They're a hard lot. They don't like strangers. They kill whoever they catch here and sometimes they do it kind of slow. We couldn't stay here if it wasn't for LaCosta. They seen yuh come into the hills and warned us. They watched yuh all last night and would a kilt yuh, but I told La Costa to tell 'em to lay off till we could see who you was. I kinda had a hunch it might be a feller we could use.

"Now to come to the pint: join up with us and you git a share uh this loot which yuh ain't done nothin' to git. If that ain't handsome, I'm a liar. And uh course you cut in heavy, equal parts, on what else we git. This here's just a beginnin'. With Death Mountains to run to an' hide in, right here close to the line uh Sonora, we can raid into Sonora and Chihuahua and scoot back here. Even if the *rurales* find out where our hangout is, they'll have a sweet time getting' in here, long uh La Costa's relatives. What say, Kid? Join us and you're sittin' purty; refuse an' it's the same as blowin' yore own head off."

Steve sat silent for a moment, but his eyes narrowed slightly.

"I know what yore thinkin'," broke in Wells. "Yore thinkin' yuh could maybe hold me and Larson up, take part of our grub and scoot. Well, forget it. Yuh got to kill us to do it, and Larson's just about as fast on the draw as you are. Anyway, La Costa and his folks would pick yuh off before yuh got a mile. What say?"

There was no alternative. Steve did not wish to die of starvation in these hills or be shot from behind by some renegade.

"I don't want none of your money," he said shortly. "None uh this, I mean. But I'm with you for the rest."

Truth to tell, Steve felt he had reached the end of his tether. He was desperate. The reckless rebellion of youth spoke to him to drown his conscience: you're an outlaw anyway, it said to him; you hang if they catch you—don't be a weakling! Go the limit!

"That's good," grunted Wells. "Now lissen, our next job is goin' ta be that train that carries the payroll for the El Lobo mines—"

A sudden shot cracked venomously in the direction from which Steve had come. The Kid started, hand flashing to his right-hand gun.

"Guess La Costa's met the man who was trailin' yuh," grunted Wells, his evil eyes lighting. A tense silence reigned for a space while all three men watched the narrow cleft that marked the entrance of the plateau. Presently, through this came a strange procession. La Costa was leading a horse across whose saddle a limp form was bound. But it was not this which riveted Steve's attention. On each side of the loaded horse walked men of a strange race. Stocky men of medium height they were, with the deep chests of mountaineers, and faces like wrinkled leather. They were clad only in loincloths, sandals and turban-like head gear. But each bore a rifle in the crook of his arm, and wore a wicked knife at his girdle.

"Indians!" exclaimed Steve. "Desert Indians! No wonder these mountains has been sure death to white men and greasers. But say, them ain't Yaquis!"

"Not by a long shot," grunted Wells. "See them turbans? Them fellers is Apaches. A gang that broke off from the main tribe when old Geronimo was rampagin' down here, they say, an' have lived in these mountains ever since. I dunno. But I do know that they never leave these hills, and few white men ever see 'em—an' live to tell about it. La Costa's old man was one that did—Yucca's mother was a full-blooded Indian."

Steve shrugged his shoulders as he looked at the beady-eyed countenances of the warriors. He saw there all the brute ferocity and blind savagery of the desert and the barren mountains which mothered that lost tribe. Then his gaze was drawn to the man on the horse who was being lifted off onto the ground. He gave a quick exclamation.

"MacFarlane! What in the dickens—"

La Costa smiled thinly. "*Si, si, Señor Allison*. MacFarlane, the brave ranger! He follow you, maybeso?"

"Well, gee whiz," said Steve in bewilderment. "Maybe he got extradition papers or somethin', but I always thought Mack was a friend of mine. Is he dead?"

"Naw," Wells was examining the furrow in the ranger's scalp. "La Costa, you musta nearly missed entirely. You just creased him."

The half-breed shook his head. "I aim to mees nearly. I weesh to crease him. I want not to keel him."

"Good for you, La Costa," exclaimed Steve impulsively. "Mack's a regular fellow, if he is a ranger. Guess he thinks it's his duty to drag me back to get hung."

"Well, he won't," said Wells.

"Naw, but they ain't no use in mistreatin' him while he's helpless," answered Steve. "Hey, gimme some water an' I'll dress this bullet wound."

"No, *señor*," said La Costa. "My friends, they will feex it. They weel treat Señor MacFarlane well." He smiled gently as he spoke, but his eyes held a sinister gleam. Larson chuckled under his breath and Wells scowled. Steve sensed an undertone of mockery in it all. Only the faces of the fierce little desert men were immobile as they gathered about, and one with a feather in his turban whose face was as old and weather-beaten as a granite boulder, cleansed, dressed and bandaged MacFarlane's wounded head. Then the Apaches, without a word, turned and filed away, silently, all except the old man who squatted without a word and stared unwinkingly at the unconscious ranger. Steve watched them go in perplexity, but even his keen eyes could hardly tell when they faded from sight among the cliffs. One moment they were there, another moment they had vanished without a trace. Steve stirred uneasily. He was unused to the ways of the red man and their stealth and craft seemed uncanny to him.

MacFarlane opened his eyes and gasped for water. His gaze was clouded and there was no recognition in it when Steve held a cup of water to his lips. He drank deep and after awhile his eyes cleared, and he groaned and cursed, holding his head.

"Judas, what a headache!" His roving eye fell upon the silent and motionless chief, and he started. "Say, what kind of a nightmare is this? What happened? What's all this about, anyhow?"

"Get yoreself together, Mac," said Steve. "You're all right."

The ranger eyed the Kid. "Ah—umhum—I remember now. I was trailin' you through a canyon when a cliff fell on me." His eyes wandered over the others. "Well, well, some line up. Yucca La Costa—I ain't never seen you face to face before, but the pictures they paste up about you is strikin'ly similar. And Snake Wells—I seen you in Texas—just before you robbed the Juarez bank an' skipped. Don't believe I know the other gent."

"That's Bill Larson," said Steve.

"Once of Yuma? Yeah, I recollect the name—can't seem to recall anything good connected with it. Well, Kid, you shore ain't particular who you gang up with."

"Cut it, MacFarlane," broke in Wells, harshly. "You got no papers for the Kid, an' if you had, it wouldn't do you no good. Even if you was on yore feet with yore guns on, yore authority don't cut no ice in Mexico—an' it never did with us, anyhow."

"I can't see," said the Kid rather petulantly, "what you wanta come bullin' down here for anyhow. You knowed you couldn't take me back legal, and I wouldn't come anyhow. Anyway, what I done was in New Mexico, where you don't have no authority anyhow. Now lissen, you done got yourself in a jam, but it's your own fault you got a headache, Mac. I don't wish you no harm and I'm mighty glad La Costa didn't kill you. But we're goin' to give you some rations and water, and as soon as your head feels better, you got to hit the trail for the Border."

"You're takin' a mighty high hand, here, considerin' you just joined the gang, Allison," growled Larson menacingly.

Steve felt the old red anger rising in him but he fought it down.

"Well, whada you want to do—let him die in the hills?"

"My friends weel attend to that," said La Costa suddenly. Something in his voice made Steve wheel. In the half-breed's reptilian eyes he saw mirrored the same gleam that lit the eyes of the old chief.

"Whata you mean?"

"My people have gone in the heels to prepare for Señor Mac-Farlane. Eet is their right. Lissen!" From far up among the crags there came a regular throb of sound.

"A tom-tom!" exclaimed Steve. "But say, from what the old timers say, they never beat the drum like that only when they're goin' to torture a man!"

"*Si, señor,*" purred La Costa.

A sudden sickening wave swept over Steve. Good God, this was incredible. He saw as through a mist of horror, MacFarlane's face whiten, though he grinned gamely. Steve whirled to the other two.

"Wells! Larson!" he cried sharply. "You won't—you can't do this! You won't stand by and see a white man tortured to death by these red devils!"

We can't do nothin', Allison," answered Wells shortly. "MacFarlane had no business comin' here. Them Indians is gatherin' wood right now—an' if we stand in their way, we'll go to the stake too."

"But my God, we can't let 'em burn him!"

Larson's jaws snapped viciously, "Damn' right, we'll let him burn! Whata we care? He'd see us burn in the chair, wouldn't he? Let the Injuns have him! I'll watch him sizzle and enjoy it. And Allison, you ain't goin' to do nothin'. If you start anything with the Injuns, you'll have 'em down on us. Rather'n have that, I'll plug yuh m'self."

Steve whirled to La Costa, looking to face all. "La Costa," he cried, "you can stop this!"

The half-breed grinned wolfishly. "Why should I? Señor Mac is no frien' of me. It weel not be the first white man I have watch' roast."

For a moment white man and half-breed stood eye to eye, unspeaking. La Costa's lips were smiling, but his eyes were fiendish. Steve was white and shaking in his horror and passion. Men who live by their hands understand each other; they have a code that needs no written speech. And suddenly, in the blazing eyes of the Sonora Kid, La Costa read that the white man had reached a lightning decision. His hand flashed to his gun—and even as the muzzle cleared the holster he spun to the impact of the Kid's bullets, spun and crumpled in a heap. Even as he fell and the Kid whirled, he felt a bullet cut his cheek, and his hat flew from his head. Both guns blazing, he faced the other two; in the haze of the powder smoke and the crashing of the volleys Steve Allison was himself again—the old Sonora Kid, swift and deadly as a trapped wolf. Wells was down, writhing on the ground like a crippled snake, biting at the earth as he died. Larson's smoking gun had fallen from his bleeding hand and with his left he was clawing at a second gun in the shoulder holster under his shirt.

And so he died, on his feet, true to the tradition of his breed, with a snarl of undying fury on his thin lips. A racking silence followed the sudden crash of battle; far up in the hills the drum had ceased as though the beater had been struck dead.

Steve Allison stood erect above the still bodies of his victims and looked about him. MacFarlane was limping toward him, a heavy stone in his hand. Beyond him Steve saw the prostrate form of the old chief.

"Well, Kid," said the ranger with a grin, "that was plenty fast and furious work. I've seen some slick gunplay in my time, but that was—"

Steve caressed his bleeding cheek and swore. "What I don't understand," said he, "is how come Larson to miss me so close. Wells wasn't never much of a shot, but looks like Larson was."

MacFarlane laughed. "Well, I was layin' tolerably close to him, so when he drew I just naturally kicked him on the ankle. That kinda throwed him off balance an' 'steada blowin' off yore worthless head as you turned, he just grazed yore cheek. His next bullet took yore hat off, him havin' already some uh yore lead in him, and Wells missed clean the only shot he had time to take. Larson also missed his third shot, account of bein' practically dyin' when he made it. Meanwhile, seein' old Geronimo what's-his-name here, sneakin' toward a rifle, I just naturally up with a rock and beaned him. What next?"

"Gettin' outa here to a safer part uh the country," answered Steve. "This sort of life ain't to my taste no ways."

The Vultures of Whapeton

(untitled synopsis)

The story opens in a saloon in a mining camp. A deputy sheriff had just been shot; he came in to arrest a man who was drunk and shooting at the ceiling. The drunk had just shot out the light, and when it came on again, the deputy lay on the floor full of lead. The drunk had only an empty gun and was exonerated from the charge. John Middleton, the sheriff of the town, told the people that a gunfighter from Texas was on his way to take the job of deputy, and that in the morning he was going to go meet this man and hire him.

The scene of the story then shifts in time and place to the next morning, at the point where Middleton was to meet the Texan. A man was camped by the spring, and another rode up to the spring. Both were Texans. One was Billy Glanton, a medium-sized youngster, blond, smiling, a gunman on the Billy the Kid order, always merry and affable, and utterly ruthless, and soulless. Like the Kid, he seldom made a gunplay unless he had the advantage; not lacking in courage, but preferring to rely on his crooked wits, and cynically averse to taking risks that could be avoided by treachery. The other was Steve Corcoran, tall, dark, and a gunfighter on the style of John Wesley Hardin—keen witted and a strategist, but one who ordinarily preferred to meet his man openly and relied upon his quickness of draw and accuracy to win for him.

They came of warring clans down in Texas; but after a display of trickery on each side, Corcoran tricked Glanton into thinking he had the edge, and drilled him. Hints and conversation revealed that Glanton was the man Middleton was expecting, though Glanton did not reveal this to Corcoran. Corcoran, hearing that Glanton was in that country, had cut his trail intentionally.

Middleton had seen the killing from the bushes, as he came to talk with Glanton, and he now accosted Corcoran and made him the same proposition he had made Glanton. Middleton was sheriff of the mining town, and he frankly admitted that he was helpless against a well-organized gang of robbers and murderers. He said that his deputies, McNab, Richardson and Stark, were brave men, but helpless against the criminals arrayed against them. He needed a gunfighter like Corcoran for another deputy.

Corcoran agreed to take the job, and they rode into the town, where Middleton introduced him to his deputies, hard-looking men who seemed well able to take care of themselves, in spite of their protests that they were unable to prevent the many crimes which took place. It was all but impossible for a man to leave the town with any gold dust, and the stage was held up almost every trip. Men lost their money on the gambling tables, and sometimes gamblers were robbed and murdered, but most of the money vanished mysteriously. Corcoran instantly suspected that many of the gamblers were members of the gang. This had occurred to other men, miners and citizens, and suspicion centered on a gambler named Ace Brent. It was well known that the gang had spies throughout the camp. A vigilante committee had never been organized simply because the men were too busy taking out gold to care so long as they were not molested, and because no man knew who to trust.

Corcoran's first job was settling a dispute in a dance hall where a fine big blond girl named Glory Bland was beating up a Mexican girl for lying about her. Corcoran stopped the fight, and Glory jeered at him, saying he and his brother deputies were better at bullying dance hall girls than they were at catching criminals.

Corcoran was much taken with her, but shortly afterwards he heard the sound of shots, as a drunk shot holes in the ceiling of a saloon. Approaching warily, he saw a man staggering around firing at the ceiling, while a bunch of men leaned on the bar and watched. He noticed that everyone in the place—besides the pseudo-drunk—was lined up at the bar. He saw three men with hands on their guns, and knew that a trap had been set for him. When he went to arrest the drunk, the lights would be shot out; the drunk would fall flat on the floor, and the men at the bar, aiming at the spot where they knew the deputy would be, would riddle him, shooting in the dark.

Walking into the saloon, he suddenly wheeled and dropped the three men at the bar, knocked the pseudo-drunk in the head with the barrel, and dragged him off to jail. This caused much uproar in town, the honest citizens rejoicing, since they believed those three had been members of the gang, and the toughs swearing vengeance. One of the men had been a friend of Bill McNab, the deputy, and McNab came for Corcoran, but finding him gone, rushed over to the office of the sheriff.

Corcoran entered, and McNab burst into vituperation and drew his gun, whereupon Corcoran wounded him in the arm. McNab then turned on Middleton and cursed him for a double-crossing rat who sent his own men to their deaths—revealing in his tirade that Middleton himself was the head of the gang, and had had the other deputy killed because the man was really honest and endeavoring to do his duty. Middleton replied that he had not told the gang to try to frame Corcoran, and forced McNab to admit the truth of that statement. McNab answered that no definite orders had been given, and he supposed Middleton intended doing away with Corcoran as he had the others. Middleton said that he had told one of the men Corcoran had killed to lay off the new deputy. McNab finally stumbled forth, furious, vindictive but bewildered and baffled by Middleton's superior mind.

Corcoran then accused Middleton of having double-crossed him. He told Middleton that he had inveigled his men into trying to kill Corcoran without actually giving the order. Middleton calmly admitted that it was so, and then told Corcoran that he did it merely in order to test him, to see if Corcoran were the man he wanted. Middleton was the chief of the gang, and his deputies were his right-hand men; his chief spy and partner was Ace Brent, the gambler. Middleton was planning to double-cross his own men and ride out of the town with the gold they had looted, and which was concealed in a cave behind his cabin. The town was built in a gulch, and the buildings backed up against the cliffs. Middleton suggested that Corcoran throw in with him, allay the suspicions of the citizens by pretending to uphold law and order, capture such criminals as were not affiliated with the gang, and at last, when they had all the loot they wanted, Middleton and Corcoran would skip out, carrying the gold on pack mules. Corcoran was just such a man as Middleton needed, for the venture would entail fighting and hard journeying through mountains and deserts. Corcoran was an outdoor man, a pioneer and a cowboy, just as the rest of Middleton's men were rats bred in the border towns and unfit for the hardships of such a flight.

Corcoran agreed to all this, privately planning to double-cross Middleton at the last and take all the loot for himself. He kept order in the town as well as could be expected for that time and place, and soon learned that the people were agitating a vigilante organization. He saw much of Glory Bland, and she became convinced that he was what he seemed to be—an honest upholder of law and order. A young miner, Jack McBride, shot and killed Ace Brent, the gambler, in an affair engineered by Middleton, who was determined to destroy as many of his gang as he could before he broke with them. It was Middleton who was secretly instigating the vigilantes; he intended slipping out with the loot while the gang and the vigilantes were fighting.

Corcoran arrested McBride, merely as a matter of form, since he knew that the youth would be acquitted in a miner's court. But it was in line with Middleton's plans to have McBride killed, since it would seem to the gang that Middleton was avenging the death of their friend. A false rumor of a rich strike up in the hills drew most of the miners out of town, and a gang of men—made up of the robbers—pretended to overpower Middleton, appointed one of their number as a judge, and rushed up to the jail to take McBride out and hang him. They would claim it had been done by regular process of law.

Glory Bland, hearing of this, informed Corcoran, who had been sent on a wild goose chase out of town by Middleton. He had given his word that no harm should come to McBride, while he was under arrest. He rode back into the town, halted the mob before the jail, ruthlessly shot down the robber who was to play the part of the judge, and drove the others away. He then gave McBride his liberty and told him to dust it out of town, which McBride did. This affair cinched Glory's belief that Corcoran was an honest man. Middleton was angered at Corcoran's interference, and tried to find out who had told him about the proposed lynching, but Corcoran refused to give any information, not because he had any idea that Middleton would harm Glory, but simply because he did not consider that he was obliged to answer Middleton's questions.

Three of the gang committed a peculiarly brutal murder, and Corcoran captured them, and, at Middleton's instructions, turned them over to McNab and the deputies. Middleton told them that in order to continue his deception, they must be captured. That night, he swore, McNab and the others would let them escape. And he gave the instructions to McNab to let them escape just before daylight. But Middleton sent for the leader of the vigilantes and pretended that he had just learned that McNab was the real leader of the gang. He very plausibly laid all the crimes at McNab's door, and told the vigilantes that the deputies would let the criminals escape just before daylight, and advised them to surround the jail and capture both prisoners and deputies around midnight. He promised to be there with Corcoran. And he convinced the vigilantes of his honesty, and made them believe he had been victimized by his deputies. He then sent word to the other members of the gang that the vigilantes were coming after their comrades at midnight, and told them to get ready for a counterattack, which he and Corcoran would lead. He planned to make his getaway with Corcoran while the vigilantes and outlaws were fighting each other.

But Corcoran had gotten drunk and spilled the works to Glory Bland, who was maddened by the realization that the man she thought honest and honorable, was in reality an outlaw himself. Following her feminine instincts she ran to look for the vigilantes to tell them everything, but ran into McNab and blurted out Middleton's treachery; then regretted her action and ran after him, fearing that he would kill Corcoran as well as Middleton, which was his intention. McNab took Richardson and Stark, leaving other outlaws to guard the prisoners, and went after Middleton. Glory, looking for Corcoran, encountered Middleton, who had learned that she was the one who told Corcoran about the proposed lynching of McBride. He accused her of it, and she, not understanding what he was talking about, betrayed the fact that she knew of his full treachery. He shot her down, and just then Richardson, McNab and Stark entered from one side, while Corcoran, roused from his sleep by the shot, entered from the other. He did not see Glory, who had fallen behind a table. In the fight that followed McNab, Richardson and Stark were killed by Corcoran and Middleton, and Middleton hurried to his cabin to begin loading the pack mules. Corcoran discovered Glory, and learned what had happened. Shocked and maddened, he killed Middleton, and in a revulsion of feeling, sickened by the mess of lies and intrigue through which he had passed, left the looted gold where it was, and rode away in the night.

Vultures' Sanctuary

(untitled synopsis)

The action began in the little village of Capitan, set where the desert runs up to the Guadalupe Mountains. Dogs lazed in the shade of the stores, clean-cut patches of shade against the dazzling white glare. A covered wagon creaked slowly along the road that was at once the main street of the village and the road to California.

Big Mac, Texas cowpuncher, trail driver, drifter, stood in the Four Aces saloon, a big man, broad shouldered, deep chested, strong as a bull, supple as a cougar, with thews hardened to the toughness of woven steel by years on the long cattle trails that stretch from the moss-hung

live oaks of the Gulf marshes to the sweeping prairies of Canada. Big Mac, with a broad, brown face, marked by scars of knives and bullets, volcanic blue eyes, an unruly thatch of curly black hair. There were no notches on the black butt of the big Colts which hung at his thighs, but those butts were worn smooth by long use and they jutted from scabbards with wide open mouths, from which all leather that might in the slightest obstruct their swift removal had been cut away.

Big Mac faced the Checotah Kid—a drifter, the Kid, bad all the way through, the smooth-faced type of killer; slender, though hard as steel, beardless, blonde, with an almost babyish face and wide grey eyes that seemed frank and guileless at first glance. But a wise man could see cruelty and murderous treachery lurking in their depths, like the reflection of hidden fires.

Big Mac was puzzled and annoyed. The Kid had approached him, and introduced himself, asked him if he were not McClanahan. There was a strange eagerness in the Kid's manner; a gaunt, desperate light burned in his eyes. He wanted Big Mac to ride with him into the desert, telling him he had found sign of gold. Mac was a cattleman, not a prospector; he said so with emphatic oaths. Then as he turned back to the bar, he caught a glimpse in the mirror of the Kid, his face ghastly with desperation, drawing a gun. Wheeling he knocked the gun from his hand with a bottle, smashed the Kid down and out of the saloon with thundering blows of his heavy fists. He did not spare his strength, for he knew the Kid was dangerous as a rattlesnake.

As he knocked the Kid into the street, a girl sprang down from a wagon stopped in front of the general store which stood next to the saloon—a dark-haired girl with blazing eyes, to whom Mac was but a ruffian and bully, battering a defenseless youth. Big Mac fell back, abashed. She made much of the Kid, and so did her father, a gaunt, kindly old man who came from the store, stoop-shouldered, with a side of bacon and a can of coffee in his hands.

The Kid told them he had no friends in the town and dared not remain for fear of his life. They took him in with them. They were on their way to California. They trailed out of town, the Kid lying in the bed of the wagon, his horse plodding along behind it.

Big Mac sat in the saloon, brooding, half-drunk, raging from what the girl had said to him. Her name was Judith Ellis. To him, as he sat, came one Slip Ratner, a furtive, shifty-eyed creature of the shady ways of the desert towns. He asked Mac if he wished to get even with Judith for what she had said to him, and Mac answered that he would. He was aware of only a vague resentment. Real retaliation never occurred to him; it was outside his code. Like a boy he wished vaguely to show off in front of her.

Ratner told his plan, judging all men by himself. Old man Ellis was going to California with a thousand dollars he had saved on some little homestead back in Kansas, or someplace. Enough to make a first payment on a piece of irrigated land in California. The Kid, Ratner said, was desperate. Law-riders were on his track. Capitan was the jumping-off place for such as he. He was too far from the Border. His only chance was to join up with Bissett, the outlaw of the Guadalupes. But Bissett was strange in his customs, hard and avaricious. His stronghold was impregnable. He refused to allow "any range tramp that came along" to join his hard-bitten gang, who were aristocrats in their line. No man could join him free, but must pay his way with a gift. Many a hard-pressed robber he had looted of his plunder, offering in return only safety from the law.

The Kid had nearly run his course; his last refuge was the hideout in the Guadalupes. But he could not go empty-handed. He planned, Ratner knew, to betray the girl Judith into the hands of the outlaws. It would be his price. Ratner suggested that he and Mac forestall him, ambush the slow-moving wagon (the Kid, he believed, would strike at a certain point along the trail) slay the Kid and Ellis; Ratner's share would be the thousand dollars. Mac could have the girl.

Mac, outraged, rose and struck him down, got on his horse and rode out of town. He followed the wagon trail. He found the wagon, the horses wandering aimlessly over the desert, Ellis lying inside, shot through the shoulder. The Kid had struck before Ratner suspected. He had taken the girl into the hills. Mac carried the old man to a Mexican sheepherder's shack, left him there, telling the Mexican if Ellis lived he would pay him fifty dollars; if he died, the Mexican's life would pay.

Mac rode into the hills on the Kid's trail, and presently found the Kid, by the low-circling buzzards. The Kid had been shot three times through the body, but he was not yet dead. He gasped out the tale of his treachery in return for a sip of water. He had met Bissett's men, had given them the girl, but tried to hold out the thousand dollars. They had shot him and ridden away. He died as he finished the telling. But he told Mac who Bissett was, and why he had tried to bring him to Bissett, as price for his entry into the Buzzard gang. Bissett was an old enemy of Mac's, a former sheriff of a Kansas cowtown who had gone bad. Bissett would give much to get Mac into his power.

Mac, knowing he could not fight his way into the stronghold, hid his pistols, went forward and surrendered voluntarily. He was brought into the stronghold, his hands bound, but the strands weakening under the pressure of his powerful muscles. Bisset confronted him in the 'dobe house surrounded by the stone wall. He was wary as a wolf, believing Mac would not thus confront him unless he held some hidden advantage. He sent his four men to the wall. Then Mac played on his suspicions of his own men. Fate played into Mac's hands when one of them started toward the hut without orders. Bissett turned with a shotgun cocked and Mac, hurling against him, caused the gun to be discharged and killed the man. They went to the floor together and Mac, breaking the cords that held him, snatched Bissett's gun and ordered the man to tell his men to disarm. But before the order could be given, one of them shot through the open door and killed Bissett. In the fight that followed Mae killed the other three men. Then he carried the girl to safety.

Bissett had hid his loot where none would ever find it. Mac gave the girl the thousand dollars he had, pretending that was hers; he had intended spending the winter in San Francisco; he turned back toward the cattle trail, broke, but singing with lusty relish.

Juvenilia

A Faithful Servant

(written February 9, 1921; received a grade of "A")

Beneath the hot, burning rays of the sun lay the great Arizona desert. As far as eye could reach the desert stretched, a vast expanse of dust and sand and alkali, shimmering with heat waves. A buzzard flapped by overhead. Far away over the rim of the desert a coyote was loping in his long, tireless stride. A horned toad basked in the heat of the sun. Besides these, who seemed a part of the desert, there was no sign of life. The sun rays began to slant. A solitary horseman rode into sight. He came at a steady, swinging trot that showed that the horse he rode was a tough, range pony. Close behind the pony trotted a dog. This was a somewhat unfamiliar sight for there are few dogs in the desert.

This dog was long, tall, and lean. He was evidently a mongrel. He was lank and long of body, lean but muscular of leg, and his jaws looked as powerful as a steel trap. His face and body were gashed with scars. He was neither white nor black nor spotted, but of a strange brindle, mottled hue. He was not a dog of any special kind, but a mixture of many dogs. He had the blood of collie, hound, bulldog, Great Dane and bloodhound and his eyes gave token that one of his ancestors had been a coyote. He gave the appearance of great endurance, but now he was panting and seemed to be in distress from fatigue and thirst.

The man stopped his horse, looked at the dog, and dismounted. "Skagen, old man, you ought to have minded me and stayed at home," he remarked, patting the dog's head. He took his canteen from his saddle and examined it. It was half full. He drank a sip or two himself and poured half of the rest into the dog's mouth. The balance he used to quench the horse's thirst, pouring the water into his mouth just as he had done with the dog. This done, he glanced around over the prairie. Then he spoke to his dumb companions.

"Well, boys, I guess we might as well mosey along the home trail. There don't seem much chance of us finding that plagued old cayuse today. We've covered at least thirty miles and maybe more since we started out this morning and we haven't seen a sign of that runaway pinto."

He mounted, and turning his horse's head, he started on the back track.

He had gone only about one hundred feet when the vicious whir of a rattlesnake sounded. The mustang snorted in fright, swerved wildly, caught his foot in a prairie dog hole, and fell heavily, throwing his rider over his head.

The horse was up in an instant, snorting and trembling in every limb. The man attempted to rise but sank back with a groan. His face was white with pain.

"Broken leg as sure as my name's Landon," he exclaimed in dismay.

He saw that it would be impossible for him to get into his saddle. He made up his mind quickly.

Rising on his elbow he took up a pebble and threw it at the horse, commanding him to "go home!"

The mustang started obediently, holding his head to one side to avoid stepping on the bridle reins.

Skagen did not follow the horse. He came and lay down beside his master, licking his hand.

Landon was thinking hard. On a straight course his ranch was twenty miles away. His horse would arrive there about midnight. The cowboys at the ranch would start on their search for him as soon as the horse with its empty saddle arrived. They would follow his tracks, but he could not hope for them to arrive before the middle of the following morning.

After an hour's time the sun went down and the stars came out. The moon rose presently, making the desert as light as day. It began to get uncomfortably cold. Then suddenly Landon heard

Skagen growl, for out on the desert had sounded the wild, lonely howl of the lobo wolf.

Landon felt a vague uneasiness. He was unarmed, and he felt sure that in his helpless condition a lobo would not hesitate to attack him.

An hour passed. Suddenly Skagen started to his feet, bristling and snarling. Landon turned his head and a cold chill of fear shot through him. There, not twenty yards away, stood a great lobo or lone wolf.

The beast approached, not with the slinking gait of the coyote, but with the bold step of the monarch of the desert. Skagen advanced to meet him. The dog was silent now. He met the wolf perhaps ten yards away. They began to circle each other with bared fangs in silence. Then quick as a flash the wolf leaped in. The dog avoided his rush and slashed his side as he went by. Like lightning the lobo wheeled. Their fangs clashed, both fought with quick sideways slashes of their fangs. The wolf was larger and heavier than the dog, but Skagen made up the lack by his cunning and swiftness. But the wolf was cunning too, a seasoned, hardened old desert fighter, and in a few moments the dog was bleeding from a dozen wounds. He was fast weakening. He knew this, and casting caution to the winds, he rushed madly in, striking low. His jaws closed with a snap of breaking bone on the wolf's left foreleg. He bounded away. The lobo faced him on three legs. Skagen rushed him. The lobo fought with the mad ferocity of desperation, but he fought with a handicap. He went down after a few moments and Skagen's jaws closed on his throat.

Bleeding, torn, scarcely able to stand, Skagen staggered back to the master he had saved and slumped down beside him.

And when the cowboys arrived at ten o'clock the next morning, Skagen's wounds were dressed and he was placed in the wagon they had brought in case Landon was not able to ride.

For as Landon said, "That dog saved my life and he's going to be treated like a human the rest of his life."

"Golden Hope" Christmas

(from The Tattler, December 22, 1922)

Chapter 1

Red Ghallinan was a gunman. Not a trade to be proud of, perhaps, but Red was proud of it. Proud of his skill with a gun, proud of the notches on the long blue barrel of his heavy .45s. Red was a wiry, medium-sized man with a cruel, thin-lipped mouth and close-set, shifty eyes. He was bowlegged from much riding, and, with his slouching walk and hard face he was, indeed, an unprepossessing figure. Red's mind and soul were as warped as his exterior. His sinister reputation caused men to strive to avoid offending him but at the same time to cut him off from the fellowship of people. No man, good or bad, cares to chum with a killer. Even the outlaws hated him and feared him too much to admit him to their gang, so he was a lone wolf. But a lone wolf may sometimes be more feared than the whole pack.

Let us not blame Red too much. He was born and reared in an environment of evil. His father and his father's father had been rustlers and gunfighters. Until he was a grown man, Red knew nothing but crime as a legitimate way of making a living and by the time he learned that a man may earn a sufficient livelihood and still remain within the law he was too set in his ways to change. So it was not altogether his fault that he was a gunfighter. Rather, it was the fault of those unscrupulous politicians and mine owners who hired him to kill their enemies. For that was the way Red lived. He was born a gunfighter. The killer instinct burned strongly in him—the heritage of Cain. He had never seen the man who surpassed him or even equaled him in the speed of the draw or in swift, straight shooting. These qualities together with the cold nerve and reckless bravery that goes with red hair, made him much in demand with rich men who had enemies. So he did a large business.

But the fore-van of the law began to come into Idaho and Red saw with hate the first sign of that organization which had driven him out of Texas a few years before—the vigilantes. Red's jobs became fewer and fewer for he feared to kill unless he could make it appear self-defense.

At last it reached a point where Red was faced with the alternative of moving on or going to work. So he rode over to a miner's cabin and announced his intention of buying the miner's claim. The miner, after one skittish glance at Red's guns, sold his claim for fifty dollars, signed the deed and left the country precipitately.

Red worked the claim for a few days and then quit in disgust. He had not gotten one ounce of gold dust. This was due partly to his distaste for work, partly to his ignorance of placer mining and mostly to the poorness of the claim.

He was standing in the front door of the saloon of the little mining town, when the stagecoach drove in and a passenger alit.

He was a well-built, frank-appearing young fellow and Red hated him instinctively. Hated him for his cleanness, for his open, honest, pleasant face, because he was everything that Red was not.

The newcomer was very friendly and very soon the whole town knew his antecedents. His name was Hal Sharon, a tenderfoot from the east, who had come to Idaho with high hopes of striking a bonanza and going home wealthy. Of course there was a girl in the case, though Hal said little on that point. He had a few hundred dollars and wanted to buy a good claim. At this Red took a new interest in the young man.

Red bought drinks and lauded his claim. Sharon proved singularly trustful. He did not ask to see the claim but took Red's word for it. A trustfulness that would have touched a less hardened man than Red.

One or two men, angered at the deliberate swindle, tried to warn Hal but a cold glance from Red caused them to change their minds. Hal bought Red's claim for five hundred dollars.

He toiled unceasingly all fall and early winter, barely making enough to keep him in food and clothes, while Red lived in the little town and sneered at his uncomplaining efforts.

Christmas in the air. Everywhere the miners stopped work and came to town to live there until the snow should have melted and the ground thawed out in the spring. Only Hal Sharon stayed at his claim, working on in the cold and snow, spurred on by the thought of riches—and a girl.

It was a little over three weeks until Christmas when, one cold night Red Ghallinan sat by the stove in the saloon and listened to the blizzard outside. He thought of Sharon, doubtless shivering in his cabin up on the slopes, and he sneered. He listened idly to the talk of the miners and cowpunchers who were discussing the coming festivals, a dance and so on.

Christmas meant nothing to Red. Though the one bright spot in his life had been one Christmas years ago when Red was a ragged waif, shivering on the snow-covered streets of Kansas City. He had passed a great church and, attracted by the warmth, had entered timidly. The people had sung, "Hark, the Herald Angels Sing!" and when the congregation passed out, an old, white-haired woman had seen the boy and had taken him home and fed him and clothed him. Red had lived in her home as one of the family until spring, but when the wild geese began to fly north and the trees began to bud, the wanderlust got into the boy's blood and he ran away and came back to his native Texas prairies. But that was years ago and Red never thought of it now.

The door flew open and a furred and muffled figure strode in. It was Sharon—his hands shoved deep in his coat pockets.

Instantly Red was on his feet, hand twisting just above a gun. But Hal took no notice of him. He pushed his way to the bar. "Boys," he said; "I named my claim the Golden Hope, and it was a true name! Boys, I've struck it rich!"

And he threw a double handful of nuggets and gold dust on the bar.

Christmas Eve Red stood in the door of an eating house and watched Sharon coming down the slope, whistling merrily. He had a right to be merry. He was already worth twelve thousand dollars and had not exhausted his claim by half. Red watched with hate in his eyes. Ever since the night that Sharon had thrown his first gold on the bar, his hatred of the man had grown. Hal's fortune seemed a personal injury to Red. Had he not worked like a slave on that claim without getting a pound of gold? And here this stranger had come and gotten rich off that same claim! Thousands to him, a measly five hundred to Red. To Red's warped mind this assumed monstrous proportions—an outrage. He hated Sharon as he had never hated a man before. And, since with him to hate was to kill, he determined to kill Hal Sharon. With a curse he reached for a gun when a thought stayed his hand. The Vigilantes! They would get him sure if he killed Sharon openly. A cunning light came to his eyes and he turned and strode away toward the unpretentious boarding house where he stayed.

Hal Sharon walked into the saloon. "Seen Ghallinan lately?" he asked. The bartender shook his head.

Hal tossed a bulging buckskin sack on the bar.

"Give that to him when you see him. It's got about a thousand dollars' worth of gold dust in it."

The bartender gasped. "What! You giving Red a thousand bucks after he tried to swindle you? Yes, it is safe here. Ain't a galoot in camp touch anything belonging to that gunfighter. But say—"

"Well," answered Hal, "I don't think he got enough for his claim; he practically gave it to me. And anyway," he laughed over his shoulder, "It's Christmas!"

Chapter 2

Morning in the mountains. The highest peaks touched with a delicate pink. The stars paling as the darkness grew grey. Light on the peaks, shadow still in the valleys, as if the paint brush of the Master had but passed lightly over the land, coloring only the highest places, the places nearest to Him. Now the light-legions began to invade the valleys, driving before them the darkness; the light on the peaks grew stronger, the snow beginning to cast back the light. But as yet no sun. The king had sent his couriers before him but he himself had not appeared.

In a certain valley, smoke curled from the chimney of a rude log cabin. High on the hillside, a man gave a grunt of satisfaction. The man lay in a hollow, from which he had scraped the drifted snow. Ever since the first hint of dawn, he had lain there, watching the cabin. A heavy rifle lay beneath his arm.

Down in the valley, the cabin door swung wide and a man stepped out. The watcher on the hill saw that it was the man he had come to kill.

Hal Sharon threw his arms wide and laughed aloud in the sheer joy of living. Up on the hill, Red Ghallinan watched the man over the sights of a Sharps .50 rifle. For the first time he noticed what a magnificent figure the young man was. Tall, strong, handsome, with the glow of health on his cheek.

For some reason Red was not getting the enjoyment he thought he would. He shook his shoulders impatiently. His finger tightened on the trigger—suddenly Hal broke into song; the words floated clearly to Red.

"Hark, the Herald Angels Sing!"

Where had he heard that song before? Then suddenly a mist floated across Red Ghallinan's eyes; the rifle slipped unnoticed from his hands. He drew his hand across his eyes and looked toward the east. There, alone hung one great star and as he looked, over the shoulder of a great mountain came the great sun.

"Gawd!" gulped Red. "Why—it is Christmas!"

The Sonora Kid—Cowhand

Ogallala Brent, foreman of the Double Z-U Ranch was rather irritable. It was hot and some unspeakable person had discovered his private store of liquor and used it as it should be used.

Therefore, he was in no mood for pleasantries when a young, lithe-built youth rode up, dismounted and strode up to the ranch house porch where Ogallala sat, in the absence of the owners.

"Greetings, fair one," spoke the youth airily.

The foreman gave a noncommittal grunt, eyeing him with suspicion. The young man returned his gaze innocently.

"Do you want to hire a good man?" he asked.

"Yeah," replied the foreman. "Bring him 'round."

The young man ignored the ponderous sarcasm. "We ought to get along well, then," he remarked sprightly. "You got a job, I want a job; you need a good man, hey?"

"Well?" glared Ogallala.

"I'm him!" announced the amazing youth, taking off his sombrero and sitting down on the veranda.

"Well, of all the unmitigated nerve!" the foreman swore. "Look-a-here, young feller, what do yuh want, where you from, what's your name and what can you do?"

The young man got up and faced Ogallala, hooking his thumbs into a belt from which swung a big gun.

"My name's Steve Allison," he announced. "It's none o' your business where I'm from, but I was born in the state of Texas; I want a job; I can lick any man on this ranch, ride anything on four hoofs, drink any man I ever saw off his feet and commit wholesale robbery at poker."

The foreman grinned. "I can see yore a man of some few accomplishments. Ain't they some other virtue you forgot to mention?"

"Yeah, they is, now you remind me of it," agreed Mr. Allison. "There's two: modesty and mindin' muh own business."

The foreman looked him over. "I'm goin' to take yuh at yore word." he announced. "Hey, Gunboat!" This last in a shout.

A bellow answered him and presently a small crowd of cowpunchers came around the house. In the lead was a burly, ugly-looking individual, so heavily built as to appear short. Yet he was above the average height. His jaw was prognathous and his eyes were small and piglike.

"Wotcher want?" inquired this interesting individual, in a deep, rumbling voice.

"This young feller is laboring under the illusion that he can lick any man on the ranch," explained Ogallala, indicating Allison.

"That runt!" gasped Gunboat. "Haw! Haw!"

"Haw! Haw!" echoed the cowpunchers.

"I done told him he could have a job if he could lick you and ride 'Cyclone,' and he's done accepted," went on the foreman smoothly.

"Him?" The astonishment was rather justified. Gunboat was some ten years older, eight inches taller and seventy-five pounds heavier. In fact, when Mr. Allison looked his opponent over, he wished he had not been so specific in stating his accomplishments and the job began to lose its attractions. But there was no backing out now.

"Name your weapons," Allison suggested. "Fists, knife or gun?"

"I ain't no gunfighter," Gunboat answered, "ner yet no Mex knifer. Fists is a gentleman's weepons."

Steve shrugged his shoulders. That was the answer he had expected.

"Let's adjourn to the back of the corral," suggested one of the cowboys, known as Skinny. "Yuh'd trample Miss Gladys's flowerbeds here and out there they's shade and th' spectators can sit on the corral."

At the back of the corral Gunboat removed his shirt with great deliberation and Allison did likewise, first taking off his gun-belt and handing it to Ogallala.

"Boy, what I'm goin' to do to you," opined Gunboat, knotting an enormous fist, "is a plumb shame."

"Gwan, yuh big boob," Steve retorted, fervently hoping no one would notice how profusely he was sweating. "I hate to demean muhself by killin' yuh with my bare hands, but yuh got yoreself to blame."

"The rules of this here combat," announced the foreman, from his vantage point on the corral fence, "is plumb rough-and-tumble. Yuh can hit, kick, gouge or whatever yuh want to do. Let's go!"

At the word, Gunboat lunged forward and launched a blow that would have demolished Mr. Allison had it landed. Owing to Mr. Allison's earnest efforts, it did not land, although it came so close that its breeze fanned the young man's face.

Followed a battle which, for pure, innocent primitive actions and cheerful ignoring of the Marquis of Queensberry rules, was a masterpiece.

A boxing enthusiast would have cursed soulfully and left in disgust, but ordinary mortals, like the cowboys on the fence, would have yelled as loud and felt as uplifted as they did.

Allison was about fifty times as quick on his feet as Gunboat and that was all that saved him from defeat. But it seemed he was unable to hurt Gunboat. Time and again, he got in a blow that would have laid out an ordinary man but which seemed to make no impression on Gunboat. It was like a bear and a wolf fighting; a big, surly, grizzly bear, at that.

Finally Gunboat's fist caught Allison on the shoulder and the very force of the blow knocked him down. Gunboat leaped into the air with the intention of coming down feetfirst on Allison's face. Allison rolled out of the way and kicked Gunboat's feet out from under him. Gunboat came down on his back, rolled over and grabbed Allison before the youth could get away. He dragged Steve to him and staggered to his feet, and with arms around him attempted to crush him against his chest.

Steve kicked him on the knee and then, getting his fingers at his eyes, made an earnest attempt to gouge. Gunboat had either to release Steve or lose an eye. He hurled Steve away from him and rushed after him. Allison made another effort to knock out his opponent and only succeeded in bruising his knuckles against Gunboat's unshaven jaw.

Then to the infinite astonishment and disgust of the watching cowpunchers, Steve turned and fled fleetly!

There was a tree close-by and Steve seemed to be running for it. Gunboat pursued as fleetly as possible for one of his bulk.

"He's goin' to climb the tree!" Skinny yelled excitedly. "Th' yellow coward!"

Indeed, it seemed that Skinny was right, for as Steve neared the tree he leaped high in the air and caught a low limb with both hands. The momentum of the leap caused him to swing far out, and to elude Gunboat's grasping hands.

Then, as the cowboys gasped in amazement, Steve swung back, with a heave of his lithe body and put terrific force to the kick he launched out.

Both heels hit Gunboat's jaw with a force that knocked the heel from one shoe and knocked Gunboat to the ground as if the man had been hit with a pile driver.

Allison dropped to the ground beside Gunboat and examined him. "His jaw ain't broke," he announced to the cowpunchers. "He'll be all right if you'll pour some water on him. He's just knocked out."

"My gosh!" Ogallala marveled. "Yore a fightin' wonder, boy!"

"Gimme my shirt," requested Steve.

Having donned it, he said, "Now lead me to yore wild cayuse."

"Cayuse nothin'," answered a puncher. "He's throwed every man on this ranch."

Cyclone was a weary looking steed of indifferent hue.

He slumbered while being saddled. However, Steve knew that the appearance was deceiving.

Mr. Allison mounted with care. The cowpunchers fled to the corral fence.

The noble steed still slumbered.

"Let's go," Mr. Allison requested.

The horse made no move to comply.

Steve tickled him gently with a spur.

The horse turned his head and gave Steve a long look of shocked surprize, but stood still.

"Well, of all the no-good nags!" Steve exclaimed disgustedly. "I'm goin' to get off if—"

He stopped suddenly. The horse turned his head again and gave Steve such a diabolical stare that he felt his hair rise.

And then abruptly the show started. The bronc bounded high in the air and changed ends repeatedly and with dizzy speed.

Mr. Allison lost his hat but he did not pull leather.

Then the horse tried straight bucking. Leaping high in the air and coming down stiff legged. Mr. Allison rocked with the jolts but he stayed.

The cowpunchers on the fence yelled delightedly.

Having tried all the regular pitching stunts without avail, the horse launched into a series of his own invention.

He appeared to turn himself from a horse to a whirlwind.

He danced. He pranced. He tangoed. He pirouetted gracefully on one leg. With a whoop of enjoyment he tried his favorite trick and then paused to see where Mr. Allison had landed. To his surprize and disgust, Mr. Allison was still in the saddle.

With a curse, the bronc hurled himself backward, but he landed only on an empty saddle, for Steve leaped off just in time.

He still held the reins, however, and when Cyclone regained his feet he was enraged to find his rider back in the saddle.

Cyclone felt sulky. After a few more lunges and an attempt to scrape his rider off against the corral fence—an attempt which was foiled by Mr. Allison's swinging half-out of the saddle on the opposite side—the horse walked out into the center of the corral and stood, sulking.

Steve dismounted and walked, somewhat unsteadily, to the corral fence.

"Do I get the job?" he asked the foreman.

"You do!" replied Ogallala, gazing at him with wonder.

The Sonora Kid's Winning Hand

Dusk was gathering over the cattle town of _____. A horseman rode down the street, humming a cowboy song. As he neared the outskirts of the town he heard someone call his name. He turned toward a small house on one side of the street. A slim, girlish form was standing on the porch.

"Evening, Miss Marion," said the horseman, raising his hat.

"Do you know where Steve is?" the girl asked.

"He was at the Mountain Rose when I saw him," he answered, then, rather thoughtlessly, "He sure was stacking up the spondoolicks, too. Just before I left he scooped in two hundred dollars on a straight flush."

"Thank you, Billy," she answered, turning back into the house.

An elderly woman was preparing supper and Marion said to her, "I wish Steve would stay away from those awful saloons and gambling houses. He's there now, gambling."

"Is he winning?" asked her aunt.

"Billy Buckner said he had just won two hundred dollars."

"Well, goodness sakes!" exclaimed her aunt. "What are you grumbling about? If he was losing it would be different."

"But I don't want him to be with those gamblers and saloonmen. They are so rough."

Her aunt laughed. "That's silly. Steve is no angel himself. Besides, you shouldn't nag him about gambling; when he wins he spends most of the money on you."

The girl did not answer. She went to the door and looked down the street. Her eyes lighted as she saw a man coming down the street, his spurs jingling as he walked on the board sidewalk.

He was little more than a boy, a slim youth of medium height with clean-cut features, dressed in the ordinary attire of the cow-puncher, a heavy gun swinging low on his hip. He stepped up on the porch and greeted the girl cheerfully.

"Chow ready, sis?"

"Yes," she answered. "Where have you been?"

"Down at the Mountain Rose, relieving the honest gamblers of their hard-earned mazuma," he chuckled. "How about a new silk dress, kid?" and he slipped a banknote into her hand.

She hesitated, then pushed it back. "I can't take it, Steve."

"Why not?" he demanded.

"Oh, I just can't. It isn't honest, it isn't right. I wish you would stop gambling, Steve."

[. . .]

Red Curls and Bobbed Hair

The Allison family was at dinner. That is, all the family except the eldest son Frank, and the youngest daughter, Mildred.

Frank was in Arizona and as for Mildred—

She entered and sat down without remark—rather unusual for her. Presently she looked about her with more timidity than was usual for her. Some of the family noted this.

"Edith Burton had her hair bobbed," she returned casually.

The family received that startling information without enthusiasm.

"I wonder—" Mildred mused, avoiding the eyes of the family.

"You wonder what?" inquired her older sister Helen.

"If—if—if I had *my* hair bobbed—"

The family rose and fell on her, with one exception. She was surrounded, stormed and captured, verbally. Her feeble attempts at defense were smothered under by the words.

"Don't you dare to think of such a thing—" that was Mrs. Allison.

"You leave your hair alone, you little idiot—" that was Helen.

"You have such beautiful hair, Milly—" that was gentle Marion.

"Aw, you make me tired," cried the harassed girl. "Darn it, all the other girls are having their hair bobbed. Whose hair is it anyhow? What right have you to tell me whether to bob my hair or not?"

"You try it and see," warned Helen.

The exception was Steve, her brother. Throughout the argument he had remained calm, not speaking a word but eating industriously.

The feminine part of the family now turned to him.

"Don't you think it's perfectly awful for Mildred to want her hair bobbed?"

"Why?" he asked coolly. "It's her hair. Let the kid have it bobbed if she wants to. All the other girls of her set are doing it."

Mildred sent him a grateful glance.

But Steve was in the minority. Even Mr. Allison, who nearly always let his girls have their way, forbade Mildred bobbing her hair.

After dinner, Steve was taking his ease in an easy chair when a soft arm was slipped around his neck and a soft voice whispered, "Good old Steve." Mildred slipped into his lap; she nestled in his arms and kissed him. It was a perfect picture of sisterly love.

But Steve knew his sisters. He eyed Mildred suspiciously.

"What have you done now?" he demanded.

"I haven't done anything—"

"Well, what do you want then? I'm broke—"

"I don't want anything." She pouted; her lip quivered and there was a suggestion of tears in her dark violet eyes.

"I think it's horrid of you to suggest that I 'want something' when I only try to be nice," and she made as if to slip off his lap. He slipped an arm around her slim waist and held her.

"There, there, child," he soothed, caressing her gently. "Don't cry, little girl, I didn't mean to offend you."

"Well, you have," she responded indignantly.

"Don't be angry," he begged contritely.

"I'm not," she relented, nestling her face against his shoulder to hide the smile on her lips. Mildred was a wise little lady.

Presently she said, "Steve, do you think it would be a sin for me to bob my hair?"

There was a wistfulness in her voice that made Steve glance pityingly at her.

"Of course not."

"It makes me so furious," she sat up and her eyes flashed. "All the family pounces on me like a bunch of hawks after a poor little dove every time I mention bobbing my hair."

Steve gently pulled her back against his shoulder. He caressed her hair, running his fingers through the tresses. Her hair was black and glossy and curly and wavy. It was very beautiful.

"Your hair is beautiful," he said. "It does seem a shame."

"And now you—" she jerked away and glared.

"But of course it's your hair and might look better bobbed," he added hastily.

"I wish all the rest of the family were as sensible as you. They're tyrants and they treat me shamefully," said Mildred. "I've been to each in turn and they all *forbid* me to bob my own hair. And Helen said she'd spank me if I did," she added resentfully.

"She's quite capable of it," Steve chuckled.

"You all treat me as if I were a kid," Mildred exclaimed indignantly.

Steve discreetly hid a smile. "What do you want me to do?"

"You could persuade the family to let me," she informed him.

"I could not," he denied flatly.

"How do you know?"

"Because I've already tried it."

She was silent for a few moments and her eyes glittered. Finally she slipped out of her brother's lap and stood up. "My family had better beware," she said ominously. "I am a desperate woman when driven too far." And she turned and climbed the stairs in a dignified manner. Steve watched her in mirthful silence.

"Poor kid," he mused. "It's a shame she can't be in style.'"

Mildred did not reappear until nearly bedtime, when she came downstairs in her little nightie and went to Steve, carefully ignoring the rest of the family. She kissed him drowsily, and sleepily begged to be carried upstairs to bed. Steve objected.

"Please," she murmured, "you're the only one who is kind to me. Please."

Touched by this childish appeal, Steve lifted the slim, girlish form in his arms and carried her to her room. She was asleep when he reached it, so he tucked her into her bed as tenderly as a woman could have done. A moment he stood looking down at her as she lay with one white arm thrown back, a few curls resting on her rosy cheek. Then he kissed her gently and left the room.

If Mildred could have read his thoughts as he went downstairs she would have been shocked, for he was thinking, "What is the little devil up to now?"

The family was discussing Mildred as Steve reentered the drawing room. "The poor child thinks we are treating her shamefully, not letting her bob her hair," Mrs. Allison was saying. "And I hate to refuse her anything, too; she is so pretty and innocent."

"Oh, yes, very," agreed Steve, strolling from the room.

Some minutes later Mildred slid down a rope made of sheets tied together, from her window—into Steve's waiting arms.

Her startled shriek was muffled by his hand, her frantic struggles were promptly overpowered and a familiar voice hissed, "For goodness sake, be still, you little idiot; this isn't an abduction."

"Set me down," she ordered. "How could I know it was you?"

"Where were you going?" he demanded, as he complied with her request.

"None of your business," she answered sulkily.

"Don't get fresh," he reproved. "I suppose you were going to the Van Dorn ball?"

"Yes."

"Nice way for a girl of your age to act. Who were you going with?"

She stamped her little foot with vexation. "Will you lay off the subject of my age?" she cried angrily. "I'm going with Jack."

"You mean you were going with Jack," he corrected.

"How did you know I was going anywhere?" she asked resentfully.

"You're not in the habit of coming downstairs to kiss brother Steve goodnight," he answered. "You wanted an alibi. You wanted the family to know you went to bed. You're a quick worker, all right. I know you didn't have your clothes on under your nightie, but I reckon you had the sheet-ladder already prepared."

She was silent.

"That's a nice way to treat a fellow, isn't it?" his voice held an unaccustomed note of slight resentment. "Making me carry you upstairs and put you to bed so you could get the laugh on me. I feel like turning you over my knee."

"Go ahead," she said listlessly. "I'm never allowed to do things like other girls."

He smiled. "I just did this to let you know you can't put anything over on brother Steve. How were you going to get back in the house? You couldn't climb that ladder."

"I don't know," she confessed.

"You can come in through my room," he offered. "I'll leave the window open. But you stay with Jack and don't you dare let any boy kiss you, and if you're not back by twelve I'll wear out the butter paddle on you. Now run along and have a good time."

At about midnight a small, girlish form clambered through the window of Steve's bedroom.

"Take off your slippers," Steve said softly, "so you won't wake any of the family."

Steve always rose earlier than the rest of the Allison family, and next morning he mused as he dressed, "I guess I better wake Mildred up or she'll sleep late and the family may find out she was out late. I hope the little imp didn't kiss more than a dozen boys."

He went upstairs to Mildred's room. Evidently she was still asleep. He entered her room and stopped, astounded. On the pillow of the bed rested a mass of dark red hair! A quick step took him to the bed. He rubbed his eyes. What magic was this? Under that outlandish hair was his sister's face, but what was such hair doing there?

Just then Mildred opened her eyes and yawned. "Good morning, Steve," she said.

Sudden suspicion fell upon him. He caught a lock of hair and jerked. It came away! A wig! And underneath was Mildred's real hair—bobbed!

"So!" he exclaimed. "That was where you went! But why on earth didn't you get a black wig?"

Mildred was staring wildly at the wig. "Oh, goodness!" she wailed. "It's red!"

"Of course it is, what do you expect?"

"I didn't go to the ball," she said. "I went to the beauty shop and had my hair bobbed and—and I bought that wig."

"But why—"

"It looked black in the electric light," she wailed. "And Mrs. Dupaise said it was black. And it was pretty and wavy like mine! I was going to wear it at home. And now what am I going to do?" she asked piteously.

Steve sat down and laughed. "I don't know," he replied. "You've sure let yourself in for a row."

"And Helen will spank me, too, like she said," wailed Mildred. "But don't you think my hair looks nice?"

"I suppose it does," Steve commented dubiously, "but—"

"But what?"

"But the family may not think so," he added dexterously.

"But what will I do?" she wailed. "The family will delight in this opportunity. And I'll be lectured and scolded and spanked and shaken—I'm going to leave."

"If I had time I could run over to the beauty shop and get another wig, but as it is—"

"It's all your fault," she said resentfully. "If you hadn't let me go, I wouldn't have had my hair bobbed."

"Well, talk about gratitude," he gasped. He eyed the wig a moment and then grinned. "Let me have that wig," he ordered, "and you lock the door from the inside and don't let anyone in until I come back." He picked up the wig and left the room.

Somewhat later he entered, carrying a bundle. Mildred eyed it suspiciously, until he drew forth a wig. It was the same wig, but how different! Now it was a deep black, glossy and curly as before.

"How did you do it?" she wondered.

"My own invention," he answered proudly. "I've been experimenting with dyes in my laboratory and I dyed the wig and dried it, too, by a special process. Be still, now." He placed the wig over her real locks.

"Now you look natural and pretty," he complimented. She had dressed during his absence and now went to the mirror. She gazed dubiously.

"It's damp," she remarked.

"Of course. I couldn't dry it completely."

"It's too black, somehow."

"Well, for goodness sake," he exclaimed somewhat impatiently. "Quit finding fault with that wig and come downstairs. I hear mother calling you."

"All right."

As Steve turned toward the door, certain not-too-distant childhood memories caused her to say, "Steve!"

"Well?"

"While you are in the kitchen, hide the butter paddle, will you?"

Some moments later Mildred came downstairs, looking unusually demure. She breakfasted in silence—another unusual thing for her.

Helen remarked, "Your hair looks damp, Milly. What have you been putting on it?"

"If you won't let me bob my hair, it does look like you would let me put tonics on it without scolding me," Mildred replied reproachfully.

She looked so subdued that Helen felt pity for her and said in a gentle voice, "I'm not scolding you, child."

Mildred merely gave her a reproachful glance and continued her meal in silence. She seemed so quiet and subdued that the whole family wished that they had not scolded her the day before and wished to make amends. All of their approaches Mildred received in subdued silence, only casting reproachful glances that seemed to say, "So, you repent of your tyrannical treatment of me, do you? No matter, I am accustomed to such treatment." Which made the family wince and decide that Mildred was indeed a very badly used girl.

Suddenly Marion gave a gasp. All eyes were centered on her. She was leaning back in her chair, her soft gray eyes staring wildly, her finger pointing—at Mildred's hair!

ROBERT E. HOWARD

"For heaven's sake!" exclaimed Mrs. Allison wildly. "What have you been doing to your hair, Mildred?"

Mildred turned pale and raised her hands to her curls. Steve leaned back in his chair and laughed hysterically. Mildred's hair was changing in color with incredible rapidity. It changed before the family's wildly glaring eyes, from black to sandy-color and then to auburn—and it didn't stop there, but changed to red, bright red, flaming red!

"She's on fire!" shrieked Mrs. Allison, snatching wildly at her daughter's hair. She nearly fainted when it came away in her hand. Then for a lone moment utter silence reigned. All eyes were turned toward the shrinking girl who sat in the same attitude, her hands clutching her locks, her cheeks white.

"So!" said Helen deliberately. Then the storm of words rose and descended on the small shoulders of the shrinking culprit. Mildred tried bravely to defend herself but it was futile. All the scoldings she had ever received were nothing to the one she received then. When talk of physical violence began to be cast about, she literally threw up her hands and fled to Steve for protection. She threw herself in his arms and clung to him like a terrified wild thing.

"It's all your fault," she hissed in his ear. "Now you've got to protect me."

Steve laughed and held the slender form close to his. The verbal storm raged about them. Mildred hid her face against his shoulder and refused to speak, trusting to him to defend her from the family's wrath. Which he did.

"But, Steve," Mrs. Allison was almost in tears, "to cut off her beautiful hair that way—"

"And after we had all expressly forbid her, too," Helen was toying with a switch. "Really, Steve, you ought to let us whip her for discipline's sake."

Mildred turned her head to make an angry retort, saw the switch, winced and hid her face again.

"I'm surprized," remarked Steve. "I sure am. You talk about spanking Milly like she was a kid of ten instead of a young lady. Just because she's the youngest of the family is no reason to treat her like a baby. It would be indecent, whipping a girl of her age. And you've scolded the kid enough. So stop it."

"But—" Helen began.

"You hush," Steve ordered. Helen bit her lip and was silent.

"As I said before, it's Milly's hair and she has a right to do with it what she wants to. She won't always be young, so let her have her fun. I took her to the beauty shop myself. So you let the child alone."

It seemed the family was ashamed of itself. It turned and went its way, except Mrs. Allison.

"I suppose you're right, Steve," she said rather wistfully. "But she had such beautiful hair." She gazed for a moment at the slight form in Steve's arms and then smiled and left the room.

Mildred raised her head and looked about. "Are they all gone?" she asked.

Steve laughed. "Yes."

"Thank goodness," she stood erect. "Steve, you're a good sport and I'm going to kiss you." And she did. "But what on earth made that silly old wig change color?"

Steve began to laugh. He laughed and laughed and laughed.

Mildred stood, her hands on her hips, and glared at him.

"Imperfect dyes," he gasped at last. "I dried it too quick. The dyes faded as they dried and made the hair redder than before. Oh, my! The expression on Marion's face when she saw your hair changing! Ha! ha! ha! 'She's on fire!' Haw! haw! And how funny you looked when you saw your wig!"

"Laugh if you want to," she replied haughtily, "but I think your mirth is very provoking. My hand fairly tingles to slap you, Steve."

"You better not," he chuckled. "If it hadn't been for me, you might be tingling somewhere else, just now."

She blushed. "Thank you for protecting me, Steve."

"You are welcome, Mildred."

"Madge Meraldson"
(untitled and unfinished)

Madge Meraldson sat her travelling bag on the station platform and glanced about for the buckboard that was to take her out to the Allison ranch.

A cowpuncher approached her, lifting his sombrero. He was a black-haired youth of medium height, lean and wiry of build.

"If yore Miss Meraldson," he said, flushing beneath his tan, "I'm to take yuh and the buckboard, I mean, I got the buckboard—aw." In evident confusion he picked up her travelling bag and led the way to the two-seated hack that stood close to the station, but far enough away to prevent the possible bolting of the wiry, half-wild range ponies that were hitched to it.

He tossed the bag into the back seat, helped the girl in the front, untied the horses, and got in.

"I suppose yuh had supper on the train?" he asked.

She answered that she had, and stole a glance at him. He seemed extremely capable and able to take care of himself, yet he flushed and stammered each time he spoke to her.

"You haven't introduced yourself," she reminded, smiling.

"Me? I'm Billy Buckner. 'Drag,' most folks call me."

"Drag? What does that mean?"

"Oh, nuthin' much," he squirmed. "Just foolishness."

"Where is Steve?" asked the girl.

"Roundin' up some mavericks," he answered.

[. . .]

"The Hades Saloon"
(untitled and unfinished)

The Hades Saloon and gambling hall, Buffalotown, Arizona, was in full swing when two sun-bronzed and dust-covered riders swung down in front of the saloon and strode through the doors.

They had hardly entered when they were recognized. And from the events which followed, it would seem that they did not crave recognition. Red McGaren, gunman of note, walked toward the two, something sinister in his catlike stride, his hands swinging lightly near the heavy guns that hung at either thigh.

He stopped directly in front of the two.

"In from a long ride?" he said in his sneering, menacing voice.

"Maybe," was the noncommittal reply.

"I figure the sheriff might be interested in you two birds," McGaren said cooly, half-crouching, his hands hovering close above his gun-butts, a sinister figure.

Silence fell over the saloon, the gamblers paused, the bartenders made ready for a swift duck behind the bar. Dancing girls and cowboys drew back against the wall. A few hard-looking individuals edged forward.

McGaren spoke, "There's a big reward out for the Sonora Kid and Drag Buckner, and I figure on collectin' it."

McGaren went down, riddled by the bullets of the Sonora Kid, his only shot striking the saloon wall. Then the Kid and Buckner proceeded to shoot up the saloon, which deed speaks for their nerve, for the Hades Saloon was well-named and was the rendezvous for the outcasts and ruffians of three states. The two outlaws escaped in the confusion, leaving behind them a raging mob.

Helen Channon came to the West on the invitation of a ranchgirl friend, and she came with little idea of the country or the people. She had always been skeptical in regard to the stories she had heard of the West.

[. . .]

"A blazing sun"

(untitled and unfinished)

A blazing sun in a blazing sky reflected from a blazing desert. Two horsemen riding slowly over the desert; no other sign of life except a Gila monster basking in the sun. Blazing heat, furious heat, desert heat.

The horses of the two men were tough, wiry cayuses, well adapted for desert travel. The riders were young, boys in fact. They dressed alike in wide-brimmed hats, plain, serviceable clothes, boots and spurs. Except for one thing they were no different from any of the other cowboys that rode the Arizona ranges. Low on the hip of each hung a heavy black Colt in a stiff black leather holster; and one of the youths wore two. Moreover, the end of each holster was tied to the leg of the wearer. The guns were big, single-action Colts and their stocks were polished from much use.

The riders themselves were both of a type: clean-built, wiry youths of medium height with black hair and gray eyes. They might have been mistaken for brothers, but in reality there was little real resemblance between them. The one with the two guns was slightly taller than his companion and of a somewhat slimmer build. His eyes, too, were different, being long and narrow and of a steely glint.

In the features of both could be read determination and courage, with a liberal amount of humor; one could see at a glance that here were two young men who lived clean and thought clean.

He with the two guns shifted in his saddle and gazed ahead at the mountains which flung up their jagged crests against the skyline.

"We'll be there presently," he remarked.

"Oh, yeah," replied his companion. "A few hundred more miles of this—desert and we'll have the privilege of climbin' those confounded mountains. This was a fool idea of yours, Steve."

"The urge of exploration, Buck," explained Steve Allison whimsically. "That everlastingly driveth the weary wayfarer onward to discover new worlds to conquer. The what-do-you-call-it of, well, you know what I mean."

"Oh, yeah!" Buckner answered sarcastically. "Quite so; very clear."

Steve grinned. "You know that yuh want to explore those old pueblos as much as I do."

Billy Buckner merely grunted. Ever since Steve had told him of the lost pueblos up in the mountains of the _____ range, Bill had looked forward eagerly to the rediscovering and exploring of them.

For a while they rode in silence, broken only by the creak of saddles or the clink of a hoof striking a stone.

"I betcha Miguel Gonzales is hidin' out in those mountains," opined Drag. "And furthermore, I betcha he sees us before we see him and ambushes us."

"He can try, if he wants to," Steve answered.

"He's some gun-fanner, for a Mex," mused Buckner. "Those two gamblers he drilled were pretty slick with a gun, themselves."

"They had no business framin' on him to roll him for his money," said Steve. "Cheap crooks, I call 'em."

"Yeah, that's right," agreed Drag.

Less than an hour's ride brought the two to the mountains. The range was wild, steep and rugged. They rode on, going higher and farther into the mountains, until they were forced to dismount and go on foot, after hobbling the horses and leaving them close to a mountain spring where there was water and mountain grass in abundance.

"Just right for Gonzales to grab a horse and make a slick getaway," Drag remarked.

"They wouldn't let a stranger come near them," Steve answered. Which was true, for Steve was always careful to train his horses in certain ways.

After something like an hour's climbing, they came to a ledge overlooking a wide valley. On all sides of the valley, high, steep cliffs stood. The valley seemed a barren waste; the soil was dry and appeared alkaline and was bare except for a scattering of mesquite and sagebrush.

"What's the idea of comin' here?" Buckner asked. "I don't see any place where the pueblos could be."

"The pueblos are in that valley," Steve stated.

"Huh? In that valley? Nix, Steve. There's nothing in that valley."

"Have you explored it?" Steve demanded.

"No."

"Has anybody ever explored it?"

"No, why should they? It's nothing but a desert, nothing growing, no springs, and besides there's no way of getting down into the valley. The cliff's at least a hundred and fifty feet high at this ledge and on the other sides the cliffs are higher. And they are straight up and down."

"Anyway," Steve said, "we're going into that valley."

"But say, Steve," Buckner protested, "we can see most of the valley from the ledge and if there were any pueblos we'd see them."

"They're there, all right," Steve replied imperturbably. "And I'm going into the valley, myself."

Buckner shrugged his shoulders. "All right, let's get started."

Steve chuckled. He turned to a rope that lay on the rocks and picked it up.

"Good hundred feet of hair-rope here," he announced. "That lariat I had you bring along is about forty feet long. Extra long lariat. We'll have to drop about ten feet, maybe not so far."

"I bet we get our hands burned goin' down," remarked Buckner. "And how are we going to get back up the cliff?"

"We can climb up easy, with knots in the rope," Allison replied. He tied the two ropes together carefully and made one end fast to a stunted oak several feet back from the edge of the cliff.

"I'll go first," Steve said, and wrapping the rope loosely about his waist he started down the cliff. The trip was none too easily accomplished, for though Steve was as active as an acrobat or a mountain-cat and the rope was knotted at intervals, at places the cliff bulged outward and the rope, not being fastened at the lower end, had a tendency to swing back and forth. Steve stopped frequently to rest and even then he was tired when he dropped the few feet from the rope to the floor of the valley.

Buckner, who had watched Steve's progress closely, and experienced much relief when he landed, then drew up the rope again. He tied the two rifles and the canteens to the rope and lowered them to Steve, who managed to reach them by standing on a boulder.

Then Buckner started down the rope with Steve bracing himself against the lower end to steady it.

He came down successfully and picked up his rifle and canteen.

"Now show me your pueblos," he demanded.

Steve looked up the cliff swiftly.

"Quick, duck into the sage!" he exclaimed, springing back into the scanty bushes. Buckner did likewise and as they did so the report of a high-powered rifle rang out and a bullet buzzed through the sagebrush close to Steve. Steve's own rifle spoke as he fired at a movement of the bushes at the top of the cliff.

Then the rope came sliding down the cliff.

"Adios, señors!" came a mocking voice from the cliff.

"Gonzales, _____ him!" swore Buckner, firing in the direction of the voice.

Allison swore softly. Then he rose cautiously.

"Hey!" exclaimed Buckner. "You boob! You wanta get drilled?"

"Gonzales has gone," Steve answered. He stood erect and walked to the foot of the cliff.

Buckner rose and came forward. Steve picked up the rope.

"He didn't even cut the rope," Steve remarked. "See, he untied it. I'm glad he did. It's a good hair rope."

"I'm glad he didn't cut the rope while I was coming down it," Buckner said.

"And now for the Indian pueblos," said Steve.

[. . .]

"The way it came about"

(untitled and unfinished)

The way it came about that Steve Allison, Timoleon Lycurgus Casanova de Quin and me came to be in the mountains of Thibet, was like this.

Steve and me went up there just for the fun of it and because Steve read where some scientist said that accordin' to his calculations and researches, the missing link was somewhere in the Himalaya Mountains, in Thibet. I didn't take much stock in that; I have seen lots of guys which easy pass for the missing link, but Steve said we'd make up an expedition and invade Thibet.

As for Timmy, which is Timoleon etc., he went along partly because he was studying botany and partly because Steve allowed the trip would make a man of him. Anyhow, Tim is wealthy and stood a lot of the expense.

So we rambled up the Himalayas, through northern India and Nepal and up into Thibet.

No use in describing the whole trip. I'll just start at the place where the guides scooted with most of the luggage and left us sitting on a mountain in central Thibet.

"This," remarked Steve, kicking over a camp chair, he was that peeved, "is some how-de-do. Why should those unmentionable coolies light out and leave us here?"

I'd been wondering about that myself.

"Maybe a hostile tribe of cannibals or somethin' is lurkin' about," I suggested. "Maybe the coolies got wind of it and blew."

"Cannibals? In Thibet?" Steve says. "But it may be something like that." He drew his gun and looked it over careful. Then he picked up his rifle and examined it.

"Anyhow," says he, "here we are, stranded in Thibet, and we gotta find our way out of these mountains, which is all Thibet is, anyway."

He looked all around at the high, snow-covered peaks.

"Some country, Thibet."

It is, too. It isn't all mountains, of course. It's more like a high, wide plateau, with tall peaks here and there. Mostly just desert-land. A bleak, barren country, but we were there in the summer, and it wasn't so bad. Cold enough, though.

Our camp was located on the top of a big, round mountain, as bare as the desert.

Our idea of camping so high up was so we could see anybody if they tried to raid the camp or anything, though Steve says the Thibetans were friendly and peaceable as a rule. He said the same thing, oncet, about some Sioux Indians that later tried to scalp him.

"Lookit here," says Steve, gettin' down on his hands and knees and drawin' a map on the ground with a stick. "Here's Thibet. We ain't far north enough to be anywhere near the Kuenlun or any of those other mountains. Moreover, we ain't nowheres near the borders of East Turkestan because there's not enough mountains and we haven't seen any Taghliks. East and south I know the country better. The way I figure it, we're in the nomad plateau of Thibet, somewhere north of Bogtsang-tsangpo."

"And havin' deducted that," says I, "what are you goin' to do?"

"Well," says he, "we had to have a startin' place, didn't we?"

"Why?" I want to know. "We're here, ain't we? And what does it matter what the name of the place is, so long as we're lost in it?"

"Well, you sap," says Steve, "how'd we know which way to start if we didn't know where we was?"

There's somethin' in that, come to think about it.

Just then we noticed Timoleon Casanova was missin'. He usually was when we was busy.

We looked around and saw him fussing around on the mountain slope with his fool magnifyin' glass and botanist outfit. We yelled at him and he came up to the camp.

"Lycurgus," says Steve plumb stern, "you gotta stick closer to camp and to us. This is a strange country and they is no tellin' what is lurkin' in the offing."

"Ah, yes," says Timoleon, blinking like a mild mannered mud-turtle. "I have been examining a specimen of the genus—" and he went off into a lot of botany names and words and such that maybe Steve understood, but not me.

"Well," says Steve, "try not to roam no further away from camp than you think is your bounden duty." Well knowin' Timoleon would be chasin' off the next minute, like as not. Butterflies was Timoleon's specialty. He knew more about them than Steve Allison did about guns, which is goin' some.

"Oh, yes," says Timoleon, "I nearly forgot. I found this." And he handed Steve what looked like a yellow pebble.

Steve took it and then gave a kind of a snort.

"Drag," says he, "look here!"

I looked. That "pebble" was as big as a goose-egg and it was solid gold!

"Gosh!" says I.

Steve pounced on Timoleon. "Where'd you find this?"

"Why, down the slope there, somewhere. I really do not remember exactly. I stumbled on it while pursuing the genus—"

Me and Steve was breakin' speed records down that mountain.

"Half an' half," says Steve, "or rather thirds."

Well, we searched that slope up and down but we didn't find any more gold.

Finally we sat down and rested.

"Funny about that nugget," I said. "You reckon somebody dropped it?"

"If they did and I can find 'em they'll drop some more," says Steve. "That gold is the real stuff. But there's gold somewhere in Thibet."

And just then we heard a noise and looked around to see ten big tribesmen covering us with rifles. Just like that.

That's the way. When a man gets after gold he can't see, feel or think of anything else. Ordinarily an Indian couldn't sneak up on Steve and me, but we were so busy gold-huntin' we hadn't noticed.

"Shall we put up a fight, Steve?" I asked, not putting my hand on my gun but getting ready to.

"No," said he, "these Thibetans are a peaceful people."

[. . .]

"The hot Arizona sun"

(untitled and unfinished)

The hot Arizona sun had not risen high enough to heat the clear, chill air of the morning. The shadows still lingered among the cliffs and the desert had just begun to shimmer in the sunlight. Along the cliffside a trail ran, skirted on one side by a sheer precipice and on the other by the cliff wall that grew lower and lower as the trail ascended, until at last it emerged upon a kind of high-flung plateau. This was the highest point of the trail; beyond, it dipped down into the lower levels.

Along this trail two horsemen rode. One of the riders was not what you would expect in a scene like this. It was a girl. She was a slim, lithe young thing, her rosy, untanned complexion proving her to be a newcomer, yet she rode with the ease that comes only with much riding and with a grace that proved her to be a Westerner. She possessed a fresh, vivacious beauty such as is seldom met with.

Her companion was a young man of medium size and a light, wiry build. He was dressed in ordinary cowboy outfit: Stetson hat, chaps, boots, and so on; a very commonplace figure except for two things. The first was his eyes; they drew the glance of one as a magnet draws metal. They were long, narrow eyes, of a grey that glinted like steel. Ordinarily they were perfectly inscrutable, but on occasion they blazed like flame or leaped like daggers. The other thing that drew the attention was the fact that, low on each hip, swung a heavy Colt in a black leather holster.

The girl and boy, (for he was little more) showed plainly some marks of kinship. There was a certain resemblance about the nose and the girl, too, had grey eyes, but there the resemblance ceased. There was no likeness between the lean, rather long jaw and thin lips of the youth and the soft, ruby lips and delicately molded, dimpled chin of the girl. Even the eyes differed, for hers were large and soft and gentle. But the main difference was in the hair, for while his was black and straight, hers was a silky, wavy, gold which cast back the beams of the sun most beautifully.

The pair rode up the trail until they were upon the summit of the plateau. There they stopped.

"Well, here you are," said the boy, casting his arm around in a gesture that embraced the whole landscape. "You wanted scenery so here it is; lots of it." The girl drew in her breath and clasped her hands ecstatically. To south and west the desert stretched away until it vanished in the blue haze of the horizon. To the north and the east, crags, cliffs and peaks were piled in magnificent chaos, as if hurled together by the hands of the Titans and then torn apart again in giant play. Man seemed to have no part in that colossal stage, yet the hand of man was there; high up on the cliffs, close under jutting rocks, on high flung crags, were the dwellings of prehistoric man, the Cliff Dwellers. There were the caves and pueblos that were deserted ruins countless ages before ever the man of Genoa dreamed his dream or the first mail-clad Conquistador turned his face to the West.

The boy had seen it all a score of times before, but it was all new and wonderful to the girl.

As she sat her horse, her soft eyes alight with wonder and joy and her silken hair, blown loose and whipping the air in the morning breeze, she made a picture that is but seldom equaled.

"Oh! I love it all!" she cried. "The mountains, the desert, everything! It's so big and grand and I've been shut in by city walls and people so long!"

The boy smiled at her enthusiasm and pointed with his quirt toward where a ribbon of silver wound its way among a scanty fringe of trees.

"The Rio Grande," he said.

"It looks near," she remarked.

"Twenty miles," he answered absently. He was gazing at the river with a faraway look in his gray eyes.

"Looks like a kriss blade," he murmured, half to himself. That was bringing up a train of thought. He forgot the girl at his side. He was hearing again the fanatical shriek, "Ai, hai, Allah il Allah! Allaho akbar!" and was seeing again the fleeing people, and the glittering blade flashing amid the press.

He shrugged his shoulders and turned to the girl. "When you're through admirin' the scenery, Helen," he remarked, "we'll start back for the ranch before it gets hot enough to ruin your complexion."

"I could look all day, and still not see enough," she responded, turning her horse toward the trail.

As they rode down it, there came the clip-clip of horse hoofs. Helen looked toward the turn of the trail and did not notice her companion lean forward in his saddle and drop a hand to a gun. A moment later he drew it away as a rider swept around the bend; a tall, broad-shouldered young man riding a magnificent black stallion. As he passed the two, his bold eyes sought the girl's face and he swept off his sombrero with a courtly gesture. Scarcely realizing what she did, Helen turned in her saddle and watched him until he vanished around a shoulder of the cliff. She was still gazing after him, a pleased smile on her lips, when her brother laid his hand on her shoulder and shook her gently.

"Tut, tut," he chided whimsically. "Is this the kind of manners they taught you in that Eastern college, gazing after strange gentlemen?"

She blushed and answered demurely, "What a splendid horse he was riding."

"Yes, wasn't it?" he asked, mildly sarcastic. "I'll bring him back and introduce you, if you like."

"Who, the horse?"

"No, the man."

"Why, who would think of such a thing!" she exclaimed, half-indignantly. "I do think you're the limit, Steve Allison."

[. . .]

"Steve Allison"

(untitled and unfinished)

Steve Allison settled himself down comfortably in a great armchair in the library of the Allisons' New York home. He drew towards him a massive, leather-bound volume entitled *Early Assyrian Art*, and settled himself for a quiet evening.

Thereafter the body of Steve Allison was sitting in the library in New York, but his mind was wandering among the temples and avenues of ancient Nineveh.

Presently he was aroused by the entrance of his young sister. She came over to where he was sitting, with the intention, apparently, of conversing with him.

With something of an effort, Steve brought himself out of his silent contemplation of the art of the ancient Assyrians, and gazed at the girl before him.

She made quite a pretty picture, he reflected, standing there, with her slim, graceful figure, her lips and cheeks rosy with a natural glow, her dark hair disarranged prettily.

Her skirt was a trifle too short, he decided, her clothing too prone to cling to her soft form; and her hair was not at its best advantage bobbed.

But if his sister wished to be a flapper, and it gave her any pleasure, Steve Allison was not one to stand in her way.

Nay, he took her part against the other members of the household and always shielded her if any of her escapades got her into any trouble.

Steve knew the girl was honest and virtuous and that whatever she did was either the passionate protest of a rebellious spirit against staid convention, or the mere expression of a joyful and jubilant child.

She sat upon the chair-arm and gave a sniff of disapproval.

"Fie on you, Steve," she scolded. "Why must you seclude yourself among old, dusty books, when there's all the great outdoors?"

Steve chuckled. "Your idea of outdoors is the riding park and suburban streets, where the scenery consists of signboards."

"It isn't," she defended, "but even that's outdoors and I can't stand to stay in, especially now in the summer."

"And you shouldn't," he answered promptly. "You are much like some wild bird, anyway; a mockingbird. Develop your body, child, and let your mind develop itself. A girl as pretty as you doesn't need any especial intellectual powers, anyway."

"Why, Steve!" exclaimed the girl, "I think you're just horrid and I'm not going to talk to you."

But when she would have slipped from the chair arm, Steve slipped his arm about her slim waist and held her.

"Don't fly away, little mockingbird," he said and drew her into his lap.

"Let me go," she ordered.

"Not until I wish," he answered, and the girl, seeing that he meant it, leaned her head against his shoulder and rested in his arms, quite contented.

Steve ran his fingers lightly through her soft, dark hair. He smiled as he remembered what a row there had been in the Allison family when Mildred bobbed her hair.

"Steve," Mildred said, "do you know a dark-complexioned woman with black eyes and black hair, oh, much blacker than mine, blacker than yours, even?"

"I couldn't say," Steve answered. "I've met so many people, in my travels. Why do you ask?"

"A woman like that was inquiring for you," Mildred said. "I was riding through the park to meet some friends, when a big limousine rolled up and stopped and a woman called to me from it. I rode back and she asked me if I was Steve Allison's sister and I said yes, and she invited me to take a ride in the limousine, but of course I had no one to leave the horse with. She asked if you were in New York, Steve, and said she was a friend of yours."

"What sort of looking woman was she?" Steve asked.

"She was dark, as I said," replied Mildred, "with very bold, black eyes and she had a way of looking at one with her eyes slanting. She was slender, but had a full, curvy figure and was rather beautiful in a bold way. But there was something rather coarse about her face, in spite of her beauty."

Steve was silent. His face betrayed none of his thoughts.

Mildred drew his arms from about her and sat up very straight upon his knee. "Steve," she said accusingly, "have you been mixed up with that woman somewhere?"

Where other men would have made vehement denial, Steve merely shook his head. That seemed to satisfy the girl.

"Did the woman strike you as being a foreigner?" Steve asked.

"Yes, she did," was the prompt reply. "She had a slight accent, different from any I ever heard before. And she looked foreign. She must have come from the Orient."

"Aye, from the Orient," Steve agreed, absently.

For awhile he sat silent. Then with a shrug of his shoulders he seemed to dismiss the woman from his mind.

As if she were a child, he drew his sister to him and kissed her rosy cheek and lifted her off his lap.

"Run along and play now, like a good little girl," he said, and the girl left the room, casting a rather puzzled glance at her brother, as she went.

Steve sat still for a moment and then rose quickly and with quick, silent strides, paced across the room and back. Then he threw himself into the great armchair and engaged in deep thought for some minutes. As usual, even when alone, Steve Allison's features gave no sign of his thoughts. His face was placid and expressionless, but once his eyes roamed to where two Arab scimitars hung on the wall, their blades crossed, and once his hand wandered to his left armpit.

Then he rose and, stepping across the room, scrutinized a large map that hung there. His eyes wandered across it and rested on Asia. Then his gaze centered on a dot in Turkestan, which was marked, "Yarkand."

Steve turned away from the map and paced the room for a few seconds. Then he turned swiftly toward the door and as he turned, from the large window thrown wide open for the hot summer night, a thing came singing through the air, a thing that flashed in the light, and thudded into the opposite wall.

Steve crouched back against the wall, a heavy pistol appearing in his hand, as if by magic.

The light button was close to his hand. With a swift motion he pressed it and stood motionless in the dark, his pistol poised, his thumb pressing down the hammer.

For some moments he stood so, then he switched the light on again, springing aside as he did so. The room was as empty as it had been before. Outside there was no sound except the passing of vehicles and the roar of the traffic in the business part of New York.

Alert and ready, Steve walked deliberately across the room. Nothing occurred. Then with a feeling of relief he turned his attention to the missile that had come through the window.

It was a knife of odd shape, driven inches into the wood. He drew it out and examined it. Hilt, blade and guard, were made of one piece of iron. The blade was long, slightly curved and furnished with double edges of fine steel. The haft and hilt were strangely and skillfully inlaid with gold.

He turned the knife idly in his hand and then seemed to come to a swift decision. Stepping to the telephone on a nearby table, he called a certain number and presently heard a familiar voice.

"Listen, Buck," he said rapidly, "don't ask questions."

He went on, speaking in a low tone and in the Pima Indian dialect. "Buck, meet me at Delmonico's as soon as you can get there."

"Sure," the other replied in the same language.

Steve hung up the receiver and turned toward the door, slipping the knife inside his shirt.

Presently, in an expensive limousine, he was speeding toward the famous cabaret in New York.

[. . .]

Brotherly Advice

(unfinished)

Piretto's Place was in full swing. A Greenwich combination cabaret and gambling house run on the style of _____, Piretto's Place was a new sensation and the "fast livers" flocked there.

The dancing floor was crowded with couples doing the latest and frankest steps; the orchestra blared jazz music. Wine flowed freely, in contemptuous defiance of the Volstead Act.

But in the gambling room above, the excitement was greater, for a party of the "highbrows," dapper young men in dress suits and women in furs and jewels, were gathering around the roulette wheels and faro and poker tables and were squandering money in a way that made even the expressionless gamblers gasp.

At a certain table sat four young men, engaged in a game of poker. One of them was a quiet, rather pale-faced young man, a professional gambler, hired by the establishment. Two of the other three were of the type so common on Broadway, well-dressed, blasé young men, elegant and affected.

It was the fourth man that attracted attention. He seemed somewhat out of place there, yet he was perfectly at ease. His features were clean cut and rather lean, his eyes narrow and gray, his hair black.

There was nothing in common between him and the young men who patronized Piretto's. There was a certain something about him, undefinable, yet suggesting the gamblers of the place more than anyone else.

He was the youngest at the table, little more than a boy, yet the poker chips and money were stacked high in front of him. He accorded the gambler a certain amount of respect, but there seemed to be an amused sneer beneath his courteous manner toward the other two, even as he won their money.

Steve Allison had little liking for the young "highbrows" although at present he was accepted as one of their set.

Occasionally he cast a glance toward a roulette table, his eyes resting on a slim, black-haired little beauty, who was throwing money away by the handfuls. He shrugged his shoulders and set himself to win a sum equivalent to the amount she lost, which was not so difficult as it seems, for Steve had been a professional gambler himself, though his friends did not know that.

The girl was certainly enjoying herself and it was also certain that she was intoxicated by excitement and pleasure—and perhaps by a little champagne, likewise.

It was evident that she was a newcomer into the "fast set." Her cheeks were flushed, her laugh rang clear above the other noise of the gambling room. She was perfectly reckless; she lost money, laughed with pure enjoyment, tossed back her unruly curls and doubled her bet, again and again.

The young women watched her with a certain amount of fascination, and a certain amount of jealousy; the young men clustered about her, applauding her with the most frank admiration, some of them casting glances at her that made Steve curse beneath his breath.

By listening closely he could hear what was said, and he shamelessly proceeded to eavesdrop.

"Come," one of the young men coaxed, "just one spin of the roulette wheel for a wager."

"I'm broke," she laughed. "I'll have to get some money from Steve first."

"But I don't want you to wager money," he answered. "Don't interrupt Steve; he's winning."

"What, then?" she inquired.

"A hundred dollars against a kiss," he answered.

"All right!" she laughed. "Fair enough."

Without a word, Steve laid down his cards and rose. He was no prude; he wanted the girl to have a good time, but he had old-fashioned ideas about kissing and he did not care for his sister to cheapen herself by throwing kisses away. Especially to the man who made the wager. Steve knew him and felt that his very glance soiled the woman he looked on.

The patrons of the place flocked around the roulette table. Such bets were common enough, but it was the first time Mildred Allison had made such a one, and she was the "find" of the season.

"Prepare to be kissed, Milly!" laughed one of the women. "Kurt always gets what he wants."

Kurt Vanner smiled and bowed in acknowledgment of the compliment.

Just then Steve stepped up to the table and swept up the money Vanner had laid down. He placed it in the astonished man's hand.

"Bet's off," he announced.

"Why, what—" Kurt stammered, then flushed. "What do you mean by this?"

Steve stepped forward and gazed into Vanner's face.

"Do you want to argue the question with me?" he asked softly.

Vanner was larger, taller and heavier, than young Allison, but he had no desire to try conclusions with him.

Steve's slim form was deceptive, as Vanner knew, for he had seen him fight the New York light-weight champion to a bloody draw. A panther, that was what Vanner thought of when he looked at Steve Allison.

Kurt stepped back, bowing politely, with an apology that was intended to contrast his manners with Allison's and put the youth in an unfavorable light.

Steve ignored him and turned to his sister.

"Time to go home, Mildred."

Mildred didn't want to go home and she was angry at Steve; but his eyes were glinting and she knew that it wasn't well to argue with her brother when he had such an expression.

She rose and made apologies to the party; Steve escorted her to the street and hailed a taxi.

Mildred's indignation found vent in words, then. She was furious at Steve for breaking up her party. She scolded him and declared her intention of going back to the dancehall.

"You're a perfect tyrant," she declared, stamping her little foot. "I won't go home. I won't, I tell you."

However, she was mistaken. Steve, who could manhandle three men, was not to be resisted by a young girl who stood exactly five feet high and lacked several pounds of weighing a hundred pounds.

The taxi drew up to the curb just then and Steve picked his sister up and deposited her inside.

He gave the driver a certain number and stepped in also.

"Don't act like a baby, Milly," he admonished.

The girl overcame a desire to slap him. She sat in dignified silence until they reached their destination, a rather palatial residence on Riverside Drive.

"Everybody's gone to bed, I reckon," Steve remarked as he let them in at a side door.

"They are not," Mildred answered. "Madge is at a ball. She don't have any silly old brother to drag her away from everything," she added pointedly.

"Well, her brother ought to," Steve retorted.

Mildred's indignation at Steve had been increasing all the way home and now as they mounted the stairs to the floor where they each had a room, she became reckless in a desire to shock him.

"Anyone would think I was awfully bad, the way you haul me around," she began.

"Well, I don't want you kissing Kurt Vanner," he answered, "or anyone else."

"You're a tyrant."

"I'm not. But you don't know what kind of a man he is—and I do."

"Oh, you do?" sarcastically. "I suppose he's a villain."

"He is," was the imperturbable reply. "Also a cradle robber. That's why he selected you."

Mildred winced. Her age was a source of great dissatisfaction to her. She was the youngest of five and this gave the others a right to "boss" her around and "make her mind," or so it seemed to her. Steve's remark served to make her angrier and more reckless.

"He's a gentleman and you're not," she retorted.

"I never pretended to be," was his unruffled reply.

They had entered a large drawing room, elegantly furnished and brightly lighted. Steve noted his sister's flushed cheeks.

He caught her by the shoulders, drew her close to him and sniffed her breath.

"Hades!" he said disgustedly. "Half-drunk, too."

"I'm not!" she protested indignantly, struggling to free herself. "I had only two glasses of champagne."

"One's enough for a kid like you," he answered.

"You needn't be so prudish," she retorted. "I'm just naturally bad."

He laughed. "You? A wild woman? You're nothing but a baby playing make-believe."

"Oh, I am, am I?" she said deliberately, exasperated beyond caution. "What about that bet I had with Jack Doorn?"

"What was that?" he asked.

"On a horse-race. He bet two hundred dollars against my stocking." Steve was eyeing her in a way she did not like, but she plunged on recklessly. "If he won he was to take off the stocking himself."

"You little devil!"

Steve's hair rose. He snatched his sister with one hand and a light riding whip with the other.

"I won!" Mildred fairly shrieked, striving desperately to wriggle off Steve's knee.

He hesitated, then deposited her on the floor, somewhat shaken and slightly pale. All desire to shock Steve had vanished. She had succeeded more than she wished. She didn't believe Steve would really have whipped her but still—

He was still toying with the whip.

"You stop making bets like that," he ordered.

"And what if I don't?" she retorted defiantly, getting back some of her courage.

"Then I'll give you a good whipping and send you back home," he responded promptly.

"You wouldn't dare!"

"Why wouldn't I?"

"You haven't any right to whip me."

"I haven't any legal right," he answered grimly, "but I've got the right of the stronger. Might's not right, but you disobey me and see what happens!"

"You have said you never could strike a woman," she accused.

"I wouldn't be striking a woman," he retorted. "I'd be spanking a naughty child."

"Oh, you—" words failed her in her exasperation.

"I don't want to seem like a tyrant, Milly," he continued in a milder voice, "and I want you to have a good time. But I can't let you cheapen yourself and have your name bandied about over wine cups. You don't know anything about the men you make these foolish bets with and the best men are not to be trusted with an innocent young girl. So you do as I say."

This advice was lost on Mildred who was furious at her brother for his self-imposed authority and she was humiliated in the extreme at the thought of having to submit to being spanked.

Her answer was prompt and unexpected. She slapped him soundly and fled to her room.

Desert Rendezvous

(unfinished)

The Allison family, at least the feminine part, were touring Egypt. The younger son of the family, Steve, who was the only man of the family with them, had left them at Alexandria with the avowed intention of seeing Khartoum. The family's leisurely progress was too slow for him.

Steve was to meet them in a certain time at Assuan.

Some weeks had elapsed since they had left Alexandria when Steve, leaner and tanned darkly by the African sun, rode into Assuan.

The first member of the family he met was his sister Marion.

That gentle person submitted to being kissed and immediately afterwards gave him some news that jolted him out of his habitual calm.

"You wouldn't think Helen was very romantic, would you?" was how she began the news. "But do you know what she has done?"

"What has she done?"

"Well, we met a very handsome man in Cairo; he was part Arab and part French, with some Spanish blood in him, I think, and he's some kind of a prince. He is a very gallant, handsome man, and all the women just flock after him and he's very wealthy, too. And what do you know! Helen fell in love with him! What did you say?"

"Go on," replied Steve between his teeth.

"He spent a lot of his time with her and he's in love with her, too. So yesterday, when I saw Helen talking to two Arabs through her window, she told me that they were the prince's men and that they had come to guide her to an oasis in the desert where he is. They had it all arranged in Cairo! She said he wanted it kept secret until after the marriage, and I promised not to tell, but I know she wouldn't care for you knowing. I wanted to go with her, but she wouldn't let me. So she rode off with the Arabs secretly this morning. Isn't that romantic?"

Steve laughed harshly. "What is this gentleman's name?"

"He is a gentleman," she answered. "If it were anyone else I wouldn't like the idea of Helen riding off to meet him, but he loves her wildly and is a perfect gentleman besides. His name is Sir Ahmed Narrudi. He's a lord."

"Ahmed Narrudi!" Steve turned toward the door.

"Where are you going, Steve?" she asked, surprized.

"After that little fool of a sister," he answered.

She sprang up, startled. "Do you mean—oh, you don't mean that—that Sir Ahmed isn't a good man?"

She was standing, a sudden fear in her eyes.

He laughed, gratingly. "If I am not back in a week you may notify the consul and the government," he answered. "Otherwise say nothing about this to anyone."

- - - - - - - - - -

Helen sat in the shelter of her tent and gazed dreamily out across the desert. The two Arabs were nowhere to be seen. They had taken the camels off to a wadi somewhere. She was alone.

Ahmed had not been there to meet her, but he would soon come and with him would come a priest or a minister. Soon she would be in his arms! She thrilled at the thought. He was an ardent lover, perhaps too ardent. Sometimes she had had difficulty in preventing herself being swept away by the tide of his passions.

He was different from Western suitors. His touch thrilled her. His avowals of love thrilled her. Yet, in spite of his Arab name, there could not be much Arab blood in him. He was too handsome. Then, too, she felt no racial aversion toward him, as surely would have been the case had he been an Arab. For she was a Southern girl and keenly racial-conscious.

She wondered what her people would say to her marriage.

Then she started up. Someone was riding at full speed across the desert. Was it Ahmed? It would be like him to come in that manner.

She shaded her eyes. No, it could not be Narrudi. The rider was coming from the direction she had come, following her trail it seemed, and Ahmed would come from the direction of Siut. Then, the rider was alone and was not large enough for Ahmed.

It was—surely it couldn't be! Yes, it was her brother Steve!

Steve it was who had ridden hard and fast, covering in a day and night what had taken Helen and her escort two days and a night, travelling in easy stages.

He had found out by inquiry what direction she had taken and then had ridden for the oasis, which he knew was her destination, there being no other within two hundred miles.

Born and raised on another desert, Steve Allison, known on the Mexican Border as the "Sonora Kid," found no difficulty in travelling and in marshalling the strength of his mount, a swift footed Bishareen camel.

As he rode he studied the problem of persuading his sister to return with him. That she would not go willingly he was sure and he shrank from the thought of using force with her. His natural chivalry was coupled with a respect and a slight amount of awe for his sister, who was a year older than he. Yet this feeling was not caused by the difference in age.

As he came in sight of the tent he saw that Helen was alone. So Ahmed had not arrived. He felt a mixture of relief and disappointment, relief because of the fact that Ahmed had not harmed Helen and disappointment because the Arab was not there for him to kill. For Allison was in a killing-rage about Narrudi. A dirty Arab trying to run off with a white girl! It had been done before.

Helen smiled as Steve rode up and dismounted. She was fond of Steve, but she was not afraid of him. Quite the contrary. In the few conflicts they had had, she had always come out victor.

She was aware of his awe of her and, woman-like, always took advantage of it. He would beg her to go back with him. She would laugh and invite him to stay to the wedding. She did not even consider the possibility that he might try to compel her to return.

"Hello, Steve," she greeted, as he strode up. "How did you find Khartoum?"

She was really majestic. She was only of medium height, and slender, but there was something queenly about her. She was the prettiest of the Allison girls, a real beauty, with wavy golden hair and large, dark-violet eyes.

"Helen," Steve began abruptly, "you can't intend to marry this Arab?"

"He isn't an Arab," she replied airily. "He took his mother's name. He's more French than anything."

"Will you answer my question?"

His tone annoyed her. "Yes, I will. I am going to marry him."

He laughed gratingly. "You little idiot, do you think he'll bring a priest with him? He's done this trick before."

The color rushed to her cheeks and she turned coldly away. He caught her hand.

"Wait!" he pleaded. "Helen, for heaven's sake, think what you are doing!"

"Let go my hand, please," was all she said.

He released her instantly.

"Helen, please go back with me," he begged.

She smiled. "You must stay to the wedding, Steve."

He felt helpless as he looked at her and the feeling put him in an ugly mood.

"I haven't time to argue with you, Helen," he warned. "You had better do as I say. I don't want to use violence, but you've got to go back with me."

"Violence!" she laughed scornfully; his slim, lithe form, except for the shoulders not much stronger built in proportion than hers, deceived her as it had deceived many men. She had never seen her brother exhibit his strength.

"Violence! You can't make me go. I think I am nearly as strong as you."

She was much mistaken. Steve's gray eyes glittered suddenly.

He stepped forward and caught her in his arms. She tried to resist and he swung her up against him, crushing her to him. She cried out in pain and fright. His arms felt like iron bands around her. She had never felt such strength. Resistance was perfectly futile. The world reeled before her terrified gaze. He was crushing her.

She writhed in his grasp. "Steve!" she screamed, "you're killing me!"

He made no answer. "Have mercy!" she gasped. "Oh, please, please! I'll—obey—you! Please put me down!"

Instantly the arms relaxed and she slipped to the ground. She felt terribly weak; her limbs would not support her. She sank to the sands and lay in a pitiful heap, sobbing from fright and weakness.

Steve bent over her and she shrank away, her arm raised as if to guard off a blow. Steve winced; his face was pale and he was sweating. He had never handled a girl so roughly in his life.

"Will you go back with me?" he asked, hating himself.

"Yes, yes!" she sobbed. "I'll do anything you want me to. Please don't hurt me, Steve."

He gathered her tenderly in his arms, kissed her, smoothed back her hair and arranged her dress.

"I hate to hurt or frighten you, child," he said, repentantly, "but I'd kill you before I'd leave you to that Arab. Now run along and put on your riding-suit, while I go get the camels."

For a moment he held her in his arms, gazing into her tear-wet eyes, then he set her down inside the tent and strode away across the desert.

She watched him. Her eyes widened with fear as she saw the two Arabs coming across the desert. They were coming swiftly, carrying long jezail rifles. Steve was advancing slowly toward them. Now one of the Arabs threw his gun to his shoulder and fired. Steve continued to advance. Now they were within pistol range and Steve stopped. The Arabs were firing wildly. Steve's hand flew to his hip. Two revolver reports rang out above the crackling of the rifle fire. One of the Arabs threw his hands high above his head and pitched forward. The other staggered, fired again, then as Steve's revolver spoke again, spun around and fell.

Helen leaned against the tent pole, white and weak. But she had seen men slain before, on the Border, and she did not faint.

Slowly she changed her costume, gazing wistfully at the pretty dress. She had put it on, hoping to please Ahmed.

She arranged her things for travel and had hardly finished when Steve returned.

He had selected the swiftest camel, the one she had ridden, and divided the load between it and his Bishareen.

While he was working with the loading of the camels, the girl noticed that his shirt on the right shoulder was wet with blood.

"Steve!" she cried, frightened. "You're hurt."

"A mere scratch," he answered. "A jezail bullet cut the skin. Those Arabs are very poor marksmen."

However, she insisted on binding his shoulder up. It was, as he had said, a mere scratch.

When he finished loading he made the camels kneel and turned to Helen.

She gazed at him wistfully.

"Are you going to take me to Assuan," she asked.

"Yes."

Suddenly she dropped to her knees before him. "Steve, please—" she began.

"Helen!" he exclaimed in a horrified voice, lifting her to her feet. She threw both arms about his neck and clung to him, gazing beseechingly into his face.

"Steve, please let me stay," she pleaded piteously. "Please!"

She used all the arts of a woman begging a favor. She kissed him. She clung to him, begging not to be taken away.

Steve only held her in his arms, his face white and haggard. Finally he lifted the weeping girl and placed her on her camel.

He spoke no word, but did all he could to make her comfortable.

[. . .]

The West Tower

(unfinished)

Helen Tranton was pleased and surprized, when, glancing across the lobby of a certain large hotel, she observed two figures whom she recognized.

"Steve Allison and Billy Buckner!" she exclaimed. "Who would have thought of seeing them in Berlin!"

"Ah, friends of yours, perhaps?" asked her companion, a blond young man with an upcurving mustache.

"Of course." She started across the lobby and her companion, raising his blond eyebrows slightly, followed.

"Steve! Billy!" The two young men turned quickly. In fact, they turned with a quickness that was surprising, and their hands darted toward their coats, then fell away as they saw the girl.

"Miss Helen Tranton!" exclaimed Allison, taking the hand she offered him.

"This is indeed a pleasure," said Buckner, flushing to his hair.

"I'm certainly glad to see you," Helen said, introducing her companion, one Captain Ludvig von Schlieder. The captain placed a monocle to his eye and gazed at the two Americans almost superciliously.

"What are you doing in Germany?" asked Helen. "I thought you were going to Mexico."

"We did go to Mexico," answered Allison, "but the climate was too warm to suit us. We came to the land of the Mailed Fist as collectors."

"Collectors?" Helen asked. "Collectors of what?"

"Jewels, mostly," Allison replied. "We're working for a corporation that pays our expenses and gives us a rake-off on the jewels."

"That's nice," declared Helen. "I'd like to see more of you. You're staying in this hotel?"

Allison assented. "I suppose you're here for pleasure?"

"Yes," she laughed, "that's my only reason. I suppose I'm like a butterfly, always flitting from place to place and living for pleasure alone. I'm going to a big house-party soon, and I wish I could give you an invitation."

"Speaking for my friend, Erich Steindorf," spoke the captain, "I take the liberty of inviting you to the house party, mein herrein."

"Oh, that's so nice of you," exclaimed Helen.

"Any friend of Fraulein Tranton is welcome," answered the captain, bowing.

"You must come," said the girl. "We are going to have the house party in an old castle in the Black Forest. Think how thrilling and romantic."

"Certainly," answered Allison. "We'll be clean delighted."

Later on, up in their suite, Buckner looked at Allison with a disapproving eye.

"What's the game, Steve?" he asked. "You got a nerve, talkin' about collectin' jewels and acceptin' bids to house parties. Castle in the Black Forest, huh! We ain't done any scoutin' in Berlin, yet."

Steve Allison sat down and chuckled. "I didn't want to lie to Miss Helen about why we're in Germany. We are collecting jewels, aren't we?"

"Well," said Buckner, "yuh don't need to advertize it. I'm skittish enough, as it is. When Miss Helen yelled at us, I was as sure as —— that Moriarty had us by the collar. Why do you suppose the lager-swigger with the monocle invited us to the house party?"

"Well," answered Steve, "ginks that collect jewels, in the regular way, I mean, are very likely to carry a good deal of coin. When a duke or something sells his sparklers, he usually wants the cash, right there. Did you notice Captain Sckudlefuze's fingers? Long and slim and handy. Never did any work with them, you bet. A gambler, if I ever saw one."

Buckner nodded. Steve Allison, too, had hands of such a type.

"Captain Schooblebooze's idea is to get us into a friendly game and lift all our coin. All right, let him. But I had another idea in accepting. Miss Helen is a nice American girl and I know these lager-swiggers. Anyway, it's a good chance to see if there's anything worth collecting in the castle. We'll have plenty of time for Berlin."

"You was to a house party in England once, wasn't you, as a private detective?" asked Buckner.

A slight expression of distaste crossed Steve's face.

"Yes, I was," he replied. "I came as a private detective and found my sister Marion there, as a guest. One of the men was murdered in his room. I killed the thing that killed him. It was a —— big snake. A python. It had got away from a circus and denned up in a dungeon under the castle."

Buckner rose, walked over to a large window and stood looking out upon the busy streets of Berlin. An officer was swaggering down the street, the civilians scrambling to get out of his way.

"Steve," said Buckner, "there's a representative of a bigger snake than that python, the Prussian army. Some day it'll try to throw its coils around the world."

"Probably," answered Allison. "When it does it'll get cut in a great many pieces. Let's wander down the street and admire the goose-steppers."

The house party accepted the two Americans cordially enough, but to Steve it seemed that there was a rather thinly veiled contempt in the manner of some of them.

There was rather a large party, young men and women of the wealthy and noble houses, a few Britishers and a Russian. Helen Tranton was the only other American.

It was a huge, grim old castle, set amongst great old trees that flung out long, thick branches. It was on level ground; the forest surrounded it and ran close to the high wall that circled the whole castle. Around the wall ran a moat, long unused, but which had been cleared out and was used for a swimming pool. There was a drawbridge and great, iron-clad doors, as there had been in the Middle Ages.

The guests were delighted. The host, Erich Steindorf, was a tall, strongly built young man, with very blond hair and a very blond mustache, curving up in the Prussian officer style. He had a bluff, forceful way which passed for frank good nature. He was wealthy and popular in Berlin society, where, if there was money and forceful character to back it, arrogance and conceit were no objections.

The castle had been remodeled to suit modern tastes. The great hall, where the medieval lords of the castle had feasted and caroused, had been left unchanged except for various modern appliances. The rooms of the castle had been made into smoking rooms, cardrooms, breakfast rooms, bedchambers for the guests, and so on. The architectural lines of the old castle remained unchanged, for the most part. There were still the long corridors, the winding stairs, the towers at each corner of the castle, the dungeons beneath the castle.

"Select your rooms!" shouted Steindorf, flinging out his arms in a grandiloquent manner. "There are plenty of them. Go through the castle and choose your own rooms."

The guests scattered through the rooms and corridors, laughing, shouting and skylarking.

Helen Tranton, finding herself separated for a moment from the rest of the party, felt a slight touch on her arm and turned to see Billy Buckner.

"We've got the upper room of the east tower," he said in a low voice. "You take one near us." Then he was gone, leaving Helen somewhat puzzled.

Presently the guests, having selected their rooms, assembled again in the great hall. A luncheon was served, consisting largely of liquid refreshments, then a game of hide-and-seek was proposed, the great castle with so many nooks and alcoves naturally suggesting it.

The rooms and corridors were filled with merry shouts and laughter, the girls and young men scampering in all directions, hunting and searching and springing out suddenly from some recess to startle each other.

"For the love of mud!" commented Buckner. "Would yuh have thought grownups would cut up so?"

"Get into the game, yuh sap," Allison urged. "Listen," he whispered. Steve was a man who saw opportunities. Buckner joined the merrymakers.

Helen, seeking some good hiding place, opened a door and found herself in a large room that evidently had been left untouched when the workmen had remodeled the castle. Dust lay thick on the floors and, except for a few broken chairs, there was no furniture. There was another door in the opposite wall. She opened it and saw a flight of winding stairs leading up. To one of the towers, she supposed. The dust lay thick upon the stairs as upon the floor of the room. It was dark upon the stairs and she decided that she did not care for it as a hiding place. She shut the door and, turning, crossed the room to the door that opened into the corridor. As she did, she felt an uncanny feeling that someone or something was watching her, through the door of the stairway. Some of the guests, hiding there, she thought. She returned to the door, and called through it. There was no answer. She was about to open the door when a sudden and unaccountable panic assailed her. She turned and fled across the room, and did not stop until she was in the corridor. Then she laughed shamefacedly.

"I'm silly," she thought. "The silence and antiquity of this old castle must be getting on my nerves. I'm glad no one saw me act like a goose."

The guests tired of hide-and-seek and trooped down into the great hall, laughing and telling of their adventures.

Erich was called on to tell the history of the castle, which he did.

"It was originally the home of the Steindorfs," said he. "A long line of barons held it, who were virtually kings of the Black Forest. Their power was absolute and no one questioned them nor opposed them, unless they were very powerful. Some sixty years ago, however, the Steindorfs took up another castle on the Rhine. We retained this old castle, but no one occupied it and it was allowed to fall into disuse. Lately, however, I conceived the idea of making it into a pleasure castle."

He related tale after tale of the old barons who had ruled their domains with a hand of iron. Some of the tales were hardly the thing for ladies' ears, but Steindorf related them with a brutal directness that made nothing of modesty.

"Surely there must be ghosts!" exclaimed one of the guests, a vivacious young Englishwoman, Miss Elinor Winniston. "Such a grim old castle with such a bloody history certainly ought to be haunted."

"I certainly thought it was haunted," said Helen, and she related her adventure in the room of the winding stair.

"That is the stair that leads to the west tower," said Erich. "That tower is deserted and is reputed to be haunted."

"How delightful!" cried some of the guests. "Tell us about it."

"In the early part of the Fifteenth Century," said Erich, "the castle was held by a baron, Sir Otho Steindorf, a man noted for his great strength and dominance. One of his peculiarities was the hair which grew all over his body and limbs; in fact, he must have somewhat resembled an ape in that respect. He was a man who would own no power higher than his own. His soldiers and the other barons feared him, and as for his tenants, they scarcely dared to speak without his permission. There was among his tenants a handsome young maid whom he had his eye upon. He sent his soldiers to bring her before him, but she had fled with a young henchman of his. The couple were captured before they had gone far, and brought before him. What followed took place in the west tower. Otho killed the young man with his own hand and offered the girl her freedom, in return for a certain thing. The girl refused and Otho took by force what she would not give willingly. Then, infuriated by her opposing him, he hurled her from the tower. The next morning the henchmen found the baron Otho sprawled on the floor of the upper room of the west tower, a score of dagger wounds in his hairy breast, his bearded head severed from his shoulders. Who murdered him and how the murderer escaped from the castle, they did not know. Nor did they ever know, but at night it seemed to them that there was a rustling and a sound in the west tower as of a fiendish struggle. A knight who tried to spend a night in the room, leaped screaming from the window, and finally the west tower was closed and a great lock put upon the door. To this day the old legends persist, and one of my servants resigned and left the castle, swearing that a long, hairy arm clutched at him from a dark recess close to the west tower. I tried to get into the tower, but it would have required a charge of dynamite to shatter the great lock, and the hinges of the door are doubtless so rusted that the whole door would have to be demolished. As it is of the hardest material and nearly a foot thick, braced with iron, it would be no easy task. The west tower differs from the others in that it has but one door, that opening into the upper room. The lower room is evidently connected with the upper by a trapdoor and a flight of stairs. Some grim crimes must have been committed there."

"There must have been more murders?" asked one of the girls, eager for horrifying details.

"There were the usual numbers of medieval murders and assassinations," answered Erich, "but most of the crimes were of another sort. The old castle has heard more shrieks of girls than screams of murdered men. My ancestors," he went on, with a meaningful smile, "were ladies-men of a forceful sort. Their methods of courtship were effective, though sometimes rather violent. The women often objected, but it was seldom that they successfully opposed their passionate wooers. When one of the barons looked with favor upon a maiden, her willingness made little difference."

"Caveman stuff," laughed one of the young women.

"Rather rough on the girls, eh?" one of the Englishmen remarked.

"Oh, perhaps," Erich answered. "However, they belonged to their overlord, soul and body, hand and limb. What he chose to do with them was his affair."

"Strong, virile dominant males," said Helen Tranton. "I can't say that I admire the type."

"Yes, you would," laughed Erich. "All young women secretly wish for some man who would carry them off by force and rule them with a hand of iron. That is a girl's nature. They adore a strong, masterful man."

"I've met several of that type," remarked Steve Allison. "There was one, a big, domineering giant of a man, a Boer I met in Rhodesia. After playing the caveman with every black woman he met, he tried the same thing with a young British girl. We disagreed and I left Rhodesia."

"And the Boer?" asked one of the Britishers.

"He's there yet," Steve answered. "If the jackals left anything of him."

One of the British girls said, "Oh!" in a rather shocked voice.

"I take it that is your opinion of that type of men?" Erich asked, rather disagreeably.

Allison shrugged his shoulders.

"Perhaps some of us would find a game of cards agreeable?" broke in Captain von Schlieder. The suggestion was met with approval. Several of the guests went to the cardroom and several games were started.

"Perhaps Herr Allison would prefer American poker?" suggested the captain. "There are some of us who play it."

"Well, I'm partial to poker," Steve admitted. Six of them made up a game: Allison; the captain; the Russian, Zuranoff; two of the Englishmen; and a burly German, von Seigal.

The stakes were not large, and Allison was careful not to play anything but an ordinarily good game.

When he went up to his room in the east tower, Buckner was seated, gazing out over the forest.

Steve sat down and poured himself a glass of champagne.

"I managed to glance through all the rooms," said he, "and I looked into some of the alcoves and such. If Steindorf keeps any jewels or any large amount of money here, it's well hidden. Do you see any place where such stuff might be concealed?"

Buckner shook his head. "I didn't look very closely," he answered. "I went up a winding stair into an upper corridor. Hand me a glass of champagne."

Steve did so, also pouring out another glass of wine for himself.

"I went up into the upper corridor," Buckner continued, "where a lot of the guest rooms are. There were quite a few guests there, skylarking. I came onto another winding stair and went up it and came out into a big room. The room looked like it hadn't been used for a good many years, all dusty. There wasn't anything in it but a few suits of armor, like the knights wore in the medieval ages. The room looked out over the castle yard and there were several windows, pretty good sized, that had iron bars in them. I heard somebody coming up the corridor and I slipped into one of the nooks in the wall. There's lots of them in the castle, small spaces set back in the walls, for the baron to spy on his subjects, I reckon.

"I stepped into the nook and Erich Steindorf and that British girl, Dalia Sinclair, came in.

"Erich was talkin' to her right ardent. He picked up some armor and said, 'When men wore these, they were men indeed. They took what they wished and did not wait on a girl's whim.'

"Dalia laughed and said something I didn't hear.

"Erich said, 'Why should you resist me? I am a man and I am wealthy. What more do you want? Is it some other man? Am I not more of a superman than those simpering fools who are your countrymen? Or those American fools? Faugh! Some day Germany will arise in her might and crush the world. Then no one will oppose a German. The old barons, my ancestors, brooked no opposition and neither will I.'

"'Don't be silly,' said Dalia. They turned and walked toward the door. When they reached it, he stopped and wouldn't let her pass.

"'An old German custom, my dear,' said he. 'A kiss and I will let you through.'

"'Oh, a tollgate, eh?' she laughed. 'Very well, I suppose you are intent upon it.' She held up her pretty, rosy lips and he kissed her, several times.

"'A German custom modified to suit the modesty of the modern girl,' Erich said as they went out the door. 'I will tell you what the custom was in the early ages.'

"I heard her laugh as they went down the corridor."

Buckner paused and poured another glass of champagne. "What then?" asked Allison.

"I wandered around amongst the upper corridors for awhile, but there isn't much there. It's mostly big rooms, bare and dusty. Erich evidently didn't do much remodeling on them. There's a cardroom or two, and two or three rooms that might do for a ladies' boudoir. I suspect that Erich has entertained feminine visitors before now."

"Sure. That was why he remodeled the castle," answered Allison. "In Berlin it's quite the fad to take old castles and make them into pleasure resorts. A lot of wealthy young Germans are doing it. And you know how Germans are about women."

"Well," Buckner said, "I went down a stair and came into a lower corner. There don't seem to be any well-defined stories to the castle. Some of the rooms and the corridors seem to be higher than others on the same floor. I went into a room where there were a lot of paintings on the wall. They showed men in armor and old-style clothing and were well painted, I suppose, but of all the mean looking galoots I ever saw. Arrogant, domineering, cruel, some with Kaiser-ish mustaches and some with long beards. I'd hate to have such fellows for my ancestors, but Erich seems proud of it. Because he's like them, I reckon. Sir Otho's picture wasn't there. I suppose the artists were afraid to come near him. There were several girls and men looking at the paintings, so I eased out of there. And, say, I saw that west tower he was talking about. It's like the other towers, rises from the ground up above the roof of the castle. I suppose there were two rooms, like there is in this tower, lower and upper, with doors opening into the corridors and an outer door in the lower room. But, like Erich said, there wasn't. I looked it over from foundation to roof and there was only that one door, to the upper room, and it fastened with a monster of a lock. There was a winding stair that led up from a corridor to a kind of a landing in front of the door and another stair ran down in another direction. It was rather dark on the other stair and I guessed it led to another part of the castle. Steve, it sure sounded to me like I heard something in that room. It could have been bats, but it sounded more like something big and heavy crossing the floor, walking with hardly any noise."

"Bosh!" snorted Steve. "Buck, those ghost stories the guests have been telling are getting on your nerves."

"No, sir," Buckner insisted. "Ghost yarns don't bother me and anyway that was before Erich and the others got to telling them. Maybe it was bats, but I bet it was something. Say, do you reckon that Steindorf has got maybe a girl shut up in that tower? Or somebody else that he's holding prisoner?"

"It might be," Allison answered, musing. "Or, say, the German government might have some inventor at work on some war machine. They'd want to keep it a secret, if they invented some new weapon."

"Or the inventor might be a prisoner," suggested Buckner.

Allison mused a while. "Well," said he, "we'll see what we can find out. What did you do after you thought you heard the noise?"

"I didn't hear anything else," Buckner answered. "I went down the other flight of stairs. It was rather dark and the stair was twisting and winding. I wouldn't like to try to charge up those stairs. I was nearly at the foot of them when somebody opened a door. I crouched back on the stairs and watched. It was Helen. She looked about but didn't see me, and closed the door. I came on down the stairs. There was a small opening in the door that can hardly be seen from the other side. I looked through it and saw the door opened into a big, bare, dusty room. Helen was just walking to the door. She stopped, came back, and started to open the door; then she got frightened or something and ran out of the room. I didn't like to scare her, but I didn't care to explain why I was prowling around in that part of the castle. I had an idea that Erich didn't want anyone exploring around the west tower. I went on down to the big hall where the other guests soon came."

"We'll scout about," Allison said in an absent way. He was musing about the mystery of the west tower.

He rose. "Let's go down to the hall. Most of the guests are there."

"Helen has her rooms just across the corridor," remarked Buckner.

Steve nodded. "Buck," said he, "you leave the hall early and pretend to go to the tower. Then you scout around. I'll tell some long tale to keep the attention of the guests. Don't let anybody see you."

Buckner did not reply. He was not particularly pleased with the thought of wandering up and down among those dark corridors.

"I can do the scouting," Allison went on.

"I'll do it," said Buckner, "but if anything jumps me, or anybody, I'm going to shoot first."

"All right," Allison said, "but don't harm any of the guests. Any that wouldn't be mixed up in any plot, I mean."

Buckner nodded.

A few card games were going on in the big hall and several couples were dancing.

Erich was playing the part of host-royal, stepping from one group to another, at his bluff gayest.

Presently some of the young women, their minds still on the ghost stories that had been told by members of the party, captured him and drew him away from the others. Others joined them and presently the party was matching tales of haunted castles and ancient crimes.

Allison, who had danced with Helen Tranton, presently strolled toward the storytelling group, glancing casually at Buckner, who was playing pinochle with the Russian, Captain von Schlieder, and one of the Englishmen.

Allison listened to a tale related by one of the German girls, which dwelt upon the naughtiness of a certain countess of medieval times, then he said, "I am an American and America has been the homeland for my race for over three hundred years. But the Allisons came from Scotland and some of the old legends have come down to this day.

"There is a tale of the time of the Border wars and Highland forays, during the rule of the first Scotch kings, when the Picts were still raiding, burning, slaughtering, from the wilds of Galloway.

"Fergus the Black, of the ancient Allison line, was a red-handed outlaw with a price on his head. He was wanted by the English and by the Scotch king and had a dozen feuds on his hands with Border chieftains and Highland clans."

As Allison talked, couples stopped dancing and card games ceased, the players and dancers gathering about the group of which Allison was the center. Allison could tell a tale when he would and the members of the house party listened and it seemed to them that they gazed upon the scenes he pictured. It was a tale of feud and raid and battle he told. There was no romance of the wooing of maidens, but the sheer, fierce struggle of men against men. The clashing of sword on sword ran through his narrative, oppression and rebellion, cruel injustice and savage vengeance and the ambition of a strong man. Bleak, wild mountains, barren heath and men, wild and grim as the land in which they lived. And from some of the scenes of the narrative leaped stark, wild savagery, the savagery of man of the early ages, from which some of the gay pleasure seekers shrank aghast. Allison noted that most of the members of the house party were there listening to him, and he made the narrative as lengthy as possible. He wished Buckner to have plenty of time to prowl through the castle and explore about the west tower.

When Allison ceased speaking, he rose.

"I ask your pardon for boring you with that long, tedious tale," said he. "And I will retire with your permission. I really am not used to late hours."

As he swung across the great hall with his easy, catlike stride, the others watched him.

"A strange chap," declared one of the Englishmen.

The Russian smiled in his beard, watching Allison with eyes that were slightly narrowed.

"I believe that he could be such a man as he pictured his ancient ancestor, Fergus, to be," remarked Dalia Sinclair. "Helen, are all your countrymen killers?"

"Certainly not," Helen laughed.

"Who knows any more good murder tales?" put in one of the young men.

"Not any tales of murderers," shuddered one of the young German women. "Herr Allison's story has me almost afraid to look behind me."

"Tales not dealing with murder then," said Erich. "About some jolly old baron such as bluff old Sir Ludwick Steindorf, whose favorite jest was in having the young women of the village stripped, forcing them to put masks on their faces, and then having the young men of the village to pick out their wives and lovers."

"The bally bounder," commented one of the Englishmen.

Erich laughed uproariously. "Not at all," said he. "The girls were not harmed, though they were probably very much ashamed. You British have false ideas of women's modesty."

Steindorf had been drinking. Zuranoff glanced at him and suggested that the dancing be renewed.

In the east tower Steve Allison rose from his chair with catlike quickness, a gun flashing into his hand, then slipping back into its concealed scabbard as he saw it was Buckner who had flung open the door.

Buckner turned and locked the door before he spoke. He was somewhat pale and his clothing was dusty and disarranged.

He poured himself a glass of wine and seated himself.

"Who saw you?" asked Allison.

"Nobody," answered Buckner, then after a pause, "and what was—strange, I didn't see anybody."

Allison said nothing, waiting for him to speak.

"I started toward the east tower," said Buckner, "then I sneaked around and made straight for the west tower. I went in the room where the winding stair is. I went up the stairs and before I got to the landing, something came plunging down the stairs and slammed into me. I didn't use my gun, because I thought it might be one of the guests or a castle servant. We bumped down the stairs in a clinch. The thing, whatever it was, didn't try to use its fists, just seemed to be trying to tear off my arms and legs. We hit the foot of the stairs with a bump and broke the clinch. I couldn't see where the thing was, but I swung at a guess with all my strength. I must have hit the thing in the face, if it had a face, but it didn't even jolt it. It was coming for me, head-on, and I jumped aside. The thing crashed into the stairs and went right on up them. Maybe it thought I had gone up the stairs. Well, I got out of that room as fast as I could leg it."

"What was it?" asked Steve.

"I don't know," Buckner hesitated, and looked at Allison. "Steve, you know Steindorf said that old Baron Otho was hairy all over? Well, the thing I fought, whether man or beast, was as hairy as a gorilla!"

Steve shrugged his shoulders. "You trying to make me believe it was Otho?"

"I don't know," Buckner answered, "but if it was a man, why didn't it use its fists or a weapon? And if it was an animal, why didn't it use its fangs and talons? It wasn't an animal. It had hands. Four or five, it felt like. And if there ever was a man any stronger, I never saw him."

[. . .]

"Drag"
(unfinished)

Chapter 1.

It was a strange experience and I don't expect anybody to believe just for the simple reason that it don't seem possible. I wouldn't have believed it myself and, therefore, I'm not going to slam anybody that calls me a liar.

There was four of us in that adventure: Gordon, Steve Allison, Lal Singh, and me.

Maybe you've heard of Gordon, he that is quicker than any other man in the world on the draw and is a wonder in lots of other ways.

And Lal Singh, the Sikh, who is a marvel with a sword and knows a lot about Hindu magic.

And Steve Allison, who is something of a wonder himself in some ways.

Me? My name is William Buckner, usually known as "Drag." I was with Steve and Gordon in Afghanistan that time we captured the mullah and stopped a holy war, and before that I have helped Steve pull off some slick stunts down on the Border where Steve is known as "The Sonora Kid."

[. . .]

ROBERT ERVIN HOWARD (1906-1936) grew up in the boomtowns of early twentieth-century Texas, eventually settling in Cross Plains where he lived for the remainder of his short life. Deciding early on a literary career, he spent the bulk of his time crafting stories and poems for the burgeoning pulp fiction markets: *Weird Tales*, *Action Stories*, *Fight Stories*, *Argosy*, etc. Howard's literary reputation was assured with the publication of "The Shadow Kingdom" in 1929, which featured a unique blend of Fantasy and Adventure which has since been termed Heroic Fantasy. The creation of Conan the Cimmerian in the pages of *Weird Tales* has earned him lasting recognition.

ROB ROEHM has edited more than a dozen Howard-related books for the REH Foundation Press as well as a couple with his own Roehm's Room Press. He has won multiple awards for his research and writings in a variety of Howard-themed publications. He has traveled to every location in the United States that Howard mentions visiting—from New Orleans to Santa Fe, and dozens of Texas towns in between—verifying and expanding our knowledge of Howard's biography. His research has also uncovered lost Howard stories, letters, and poems. He writes about these discoveries, infrequently, at howardhistory.com.

PAUL HERMAN, long-time engineer and intellectual property attorney, began publishing REH in 1999 via his own Hermanthis Press and later, Wildside Press; he has edited well over one million words. His etexts have been the starting material for a significant number of REH books published in the last 17 years. His REH bibliography, *The Neverending Hunt* became the new standard when it was first published in 2006, and is the basis for the HowardWorks website. His wife of 38 years, Denna, continues to tolerate his hobbies. Paul currently resides in Weatherford, Texas, a few miles from Robert E. Howard's birthplace.

MARK WHEATLEY holds the Eisner, Inkpot, Golden Lion, Mucker, Gem and Speakeasy Awards and nominations for the Harvey Award and the Ignatz Award. He is also an inductee to the Overstreet Hall of Fame. His work has often been included in the annual Spectrum selection of fantastic art and has appeared in private gallery shows, the Norman Rockwell Museum, Toledo Museum of Art, Huntington Art Museum, Fitchburg Art Museum, James A. Michener Art Museum and the Library of Congress, where several of his originals are in the LoC permanent collection.

JAMES REASONER has been telling tales and spinning yarns as far back as he can remember. He's been doing it professionally for more than 45 years, and during that time, under his name and dozens of pseudonyms, he's written more than 400 novels. His books have appeared on the *New York Times*, *USA Today*, and *Publishers Weekly* bestseller lists. One of the biggest influences on his career is another Texas author, Robert E. Howard, whose work he first encountered in the Sixties. He's been a Howard fan ever since.

STÅLE GISMERVIK has been passionate about REH since discovering Conan in 1990. He established one of the earliest and largest Conan-focused websites, and currently manages the comprehensive REH resource at reh.world. Ståle also administers the Robert E. Howard Foundation website and its Press counterpart, and oversees the curation and editing of Foundation eBooks. Recently, he has taken on the role of preparing the new Ultimate Books for publication. His work contributes to the preservation and promotion of Howard's legacy.